"This anthology is a magnificent homage to the memory of John Oliver Killens, and to the African-American literary tradition."
—Henry Louis Gates, Jr., Du Bois Professor
of Humanities, Harvard University

"How fortunate that before he died John Killens had a dream of compiling a book that would be as good as a big pot of greens. *Black Southern Voices* presents the true spice and richness of African-American literature. It captures the songs of blues people and celebrates the stories of the land; it also pays tribute to all those generations that walked in dignity . . . a book for all readers with an appetite for something American."
—E. Ethelbert Miller,
Director, African American
Resource Center, Howard University

"The South—ancestral home and metaphor—is central to the African-American experience. *Black Southern Voices* is an impressive and timely offering . . . that displays the many facets of a literature made brilliant and durable by the pressure of a people's survival . . . indispensable for a clear vision of the full tradition of American writing."
—Lorenzo Thomas, Writer-in-Residence,
University of Houston-Downtown

"It is clear to me that the central motif of *Black Southern Voices* is affection. It combines deceased artist (Killens) and experienced critic (Ward) in a conjunctive labor of love for this place (the spiritual home of all Black Americans) and the ethos from which the voices of slavery were transposed into the artistry of the written word. . . . This is a remarkable work for its testimony to the scope and range of the geography and the aesthetics of the Black Southern imagination."
—Charles L. James, editor of *From the Roots:*
Short Stories by Black Americans

JOHN OLIVER KILLENS was born in Macon, Georgia, in 1916. A novelist, social critic, screenwriter, and essayist, Killens founded the legendary Harlem Writers Guild. He influenced a generation of writers through workshops he conducted at Fisk University, Howard University, and Medgar Evers College. Among his novels are *Youngblood* (1954), *And Then We Heard the Thunder* (1963), *'Sippi* (1967), and *The Cotillion, or One Good Bull Is Half the Herd* (1971). Killens died in 1987.

JERRY W. WARD, JR., born in Washington, D.C., and raised in Mississippi, is Lawrence Durgin Professor of Literature at Tougaloo College. A teacher, critic, and poet, Ward has published in *New Orleans Review, OBSIDIAN, The Southern Quarterly, Black American Literature Forum,* and *Callaloo.* His work has appeared in several anthologies, and he co-edited *Redefining American Literary History* in 1990 with A. LaVonne Brown Ruoff.

BLACK SOUTHERN VOICES

AN ANTHOLOGY OF FICTION, POETRY, DRAMA, NONFICTION, AND CRITICAL ESSAYS

EDITED BY
John Oliver Killens
and
Jerry W. Ward, Jr.

A MERIDIAN BOOK

MERIDIAN
Published by the Penguin Group
Penguin Books USA Inc., 375 Hudson Street,
New York, New York 10014, U.S.A.
Penguin Books Ltd, 27 Wrights Lane,
London W8 5TZ, England
Penguin Books Australia Ltd, Ringwood,
Victoria, Australia
Penguin Books Canada Ltd, 10 Alcorn Avenue,
Toronto, Ontario, Canada M4V 3B2
Penguin Books (N.Z.) Ltd, 182–190 Wairau Road,
Auckland 10, New Zealand

Penguin Books Ltd, Registered Offices:
Harmondsworth, Middlesex, England

First published by Meridian, an imprint of New American Library,
a division of Penguin Books USA Inc.

First Printing, December, 1992
10 9 8 7 6 5 4 3 2 1

 REGISTERED TRADEMARK—MARCA REGISTRADA

LIBRARY OF CONGRESS CATALOGING IN PUBLICATION DATA:
Black southern voices : an anthology of fiction, poetry, drama, nonfiction, and critical
essays / edited by John Oliver Killens and Jerry W. Ward, Jr.
    p.   cm.
  ISBN 0-452-01096-9
  1. Afro-Americans—Southern States—Literary collections. 2. Afro-Americans—Southern
States—Civilization. 3. American literature—Afro-American authors. 4. Southern
States—Literary collections. 5. American literature—Southern States.
6. Southern States—Civilization. I. Killens, John Oliver, 1916–1987.
II. Ward, Jerry Washington.
  PS509.N4B53 1992
  810.8′0896073075—dc20   92-3700
                                                               CIP

Printed in the United States of America
Set in Times, Helvetica, and Caxton
Designed by Julian Hamer

To the memory of John Oliver Killens

and to Jerry W. Ward, Sr. and Mary Theriot Ward.

—Jerry W. Ward, Jr.

For my dear husband John
and his eternal love for our people.

For John, Barbara, Louis, Abiba, Barra, and Kutisa,
and for all our strong and beautiful folk.

—Grace Killens

I wish to thank Grace Killens, Lawrence Jordan, and Rosemary Ahern for all their help.

—*Jerry W. Ward, Jr.*

CONTENTS

I. FICTION

II. POETRY

Spirituals and Blues: Selections from *The Negro Caravan*

Spirituals

Blues

III. DRAMA

IV. NONFICTION

V. CRITICAL ESSAYS

INTRODUCTION
John Oliver Killens

Numerous volumes, tomes, and dissertations have been written about the great Southern tradition in American literature. When the great Southern literary tradition, the "Southern Voice," the point of view, the very profound and special Southern sensitivity and perspective are alluded to, what comes to the minds of most of the American literary establishment and reading public are men and women like William Faulkner, Robert Penn Warren, Eudora Welty, William Styron, Carson McCullers, Truman Capote, Tennessee Williams, Flannery O'Connor, and so on.

Somehow writers such as Richard Wright, Ernest Gaines, Margaret Walker, John Killens, Arna Bontemps, Maya Angelou, Frank Yerby, Alice Walker, Zora Neale Hurston, and Charles Chesnutt are never considered. Thus, the American literary establishment has relegated the black Southern writer to a state of invisibility and oblivion.

No matter, there is a black Southern literary tradition, a voice that is special, profound, and distinct from any other in the country. It is a voice, more often than not, that is distinguished by the quality of its anger, its righteous indignation, its reality, its truthfulness. It is a voice that speaks eloquently, and artistically, for change. A voice that has the strength and the awesome courage of its convictions, a Robesonian integrity. It speaks of the past in order to impact upon the present and the future. The universal premise of most of its literary endeavors has been influenced by the sentiments of Frederick Douglass, who more than a hundred years ago wrote:

> *If there is no struggle there is no progress. Those who profess to favor freedom and yet deprecate agitation are men who want the crop without plowing the ground; they want the rain without the thunder and the lightning. They want the ocean without the awful roar of its many waters . . . Power conceded nothing without a demand. It never did and it never will. Find out just what any people will quietly submit to and you have found out the exact measure of injustice and wrong which will be imposed upon them. And these will continue until they are resisted with words or with blows or with both. The limits of tyrants are prescribed by the endurance of those whom they oppress.*

Consider also the words of Dean Kelly Miller, late of Howard University, also a product of the Southern clime:

1

It is not the treatment of a people that degrades them, but their acceptance of it.

Much of black Southern literature is about the call to struggle and against the abjectness of acceptance. The white Southern literary voice is, in large measure, a voice of complacency and contentment. The sum total of the Southern literary tradition constitutes an apologia for the status quo, a voice of make-believe and pretext. It is a tradition going back to the days of American slavery, the time of so-called loyal slaves and kindly masters, which to blacks are obviously contradictions in terminology.

We refer to the so-called masterpieces such as *The Clansman*, upon which the "epic" *Birth of a Nation* was based and produced as a filmic "masterpiece," as was Margaret Mitchell's *Gone with the Wind*. On the other hand, Afro-American literary tradition goes back to *David Walker's Appeal* and to that autobiographical epic, *The Life and Times of Frederick Douglass*.

The entire Southern culture—myth, literature, attitudes toward life—is constructed upon and influenced by the impact of American slavery, its nostalgia for the magnolia-scented, honey-suckled status quo. In Summerville, Tennessee, one of the elders of the struggle of black sharecroppers for the right to vote once spoke to me of his philosophy vis-à-vis the black Southern psyche.

"I listen very carefully to the white man as to what I ought to do in a given situation. Sometimes when he's through talking, I say, 'Yessir.' Then I head like a bat out of hell in the opposite direction."

Black Southern literary voices have been, for the most part, unalterably opposed to the status quo, which they recognize as the bane of their existence, as writers, as it is for African-Americans as a whole. Even during the 1960s black writers themselves seemed to relegate the Southern black experience to a state of unimportance and irrelevance, seemed to have thought that the only happenings worth writing about were those occurring in such Northern urban areas as Harlem, Chicago's South Side, and Detroit.

Ironically, those writers of the sixties, who claimed universally that it was "Nation Time!" (and it was indeed "Nation Time") seemed not to understand that with any people the bottom line for "Nationhood" and "Liberation" is land, earth, soil, dirt. Black dirt; our own black dirt to dig black hands into, black Southern dirt to create upon, the good clean sweet black loamy earth, to hold, to smell, to touch, to taste, to cultivate, to watch the good earth grow, harvest and prosper, to forge black and positive images. There certainly was and is no dirt available in the crowded Northern cities except in the filth- and vermin-infested tenements of the Northern ghettos, and the cold earth of the cemeteries.

Ironically also, there seemed to be a lack of understanding that we live in a Southern country. As I stated in *Black Man's Burden*, "Macon, Georgia, where I was born is downSouth, New York City, to which I escaped, is up-South. And the only difference is the sugar-coating." The cosmetology. The slave understood this fundamentally. He understood that American slavery was a continuous war against his humanity, and that he had an obligation to him-

or herself and his posterity to overthrow the system by any means that came to hand, even to killing his master, and that the "kindly slave master" had a commitment to keep the slave in bondage through a reign of terror, with the auction block, the driver's lash, the use of "kindly guile," and Biblical misquotations and interpretation. Oftentimes when a slave escaped via the Underground Railroad, he did not stop running until he crossed over into Canada. Where are the epics of Great Harriet of the Eastern Shore? Sojourner Truth and Frederick Douglass?

So actually to be precise, what we're really talking about are *"Black Down-Southern Voices."*

The black Southern voice, although it has a quality of depth and resonance and anger, contains a soft lilting musical tone that reminds one of great Africa.

The black Southern literary voice is a most important voice. As the South goes, so goes the nation, with all due respect to the rock-bound coast of Maine and all the Hampshires. It is the voice of hard truth and reality. The black Southern tradition, in its uniqueness as an authentic American voice, may be compared with the unique voice of truly indigenous American music, which is Southern, which is black, which is anguished. The spirituals, gospel, blues, jazz: black Southern voices one and all.

There is a black Southern psyche, a point of view that is both unique and distinct. Our outlook is different. We look at life out of dark eyes from the vantage point of the bottom rung of the ladder. Consequently our outlook is from far greater depths. More breadth. More elevating. Our viewpoint is more profound. Yes, we are different, and we are not invisible. We are the most visible folk in these Americas. Our system of values is different. Our emotional chemistry is different from white America's. Its joy is often our anger, and its despair our hope. Its freedom was our slavery.

Our fight is not to be white men or women, in black skins, but to inject some black blood, some black sensibility and intelligence, some black values and humaneness into the pallid mainstream of American life—culturally, socially, psychologically, philosophically, intellectually, literarily. As Richard Wright said in his *Twelve Million Black Voices*, voices America chose not to heed: "Each day when you see us Black folk upon the dusty land of the farms or upon the hard pavement of the city streets, you usually take us for granted and think you know us, but our history is far stranger than you suspect, and we are not what we seem."

The people of the black South are much closer to their African roots, in its culture, its humanity, the beat and rhythms of its music, its concept of family, its dance, and its spirituality. Anybody who has made the *hadj* to Africa and has lived in the American South can testify to the kinship of the songs and rhythms, the shouting that takes place in the church, with the songs and rhythms of great Africa.

I remember being in Tougaloo, Mississippi, once and visiting with an elderly lady on the outskirts of Tougaloo. She could neither read nor write. She was in her seventies with 25 children and 37 grandchildren. She told us a ghost story that had a familiar ring to it, which I was unable to identify in terms of time and place. It was not until I was back home in Brooklyn that, while rereading Amos Tutuola's *Palm? Wine Drinkard*, I came across the identical ghost story! Almost word for word. From a woman who could not have found Africa on any map.

A people cannot transcend its history unless it first faces that history squarely and truthfully, which is the essence of what the *black Southern literary tradition* is all about. In the entire recognition of the American literary tradition there is a woeful vacuum based on the exclusion of the black Southern voice. No wonder. The black Southern literary tradition gives the lie to the American profession of freedom and humaneness and democracy.

Our anthology, *Black Southern Voices*, includes selections of fiction, nonfiction, drama, and poetry from such so-called established writers as Richard Wright, Margaret Walker, John Killens, Lorenz Graham, Frank Yerby, Sterling Brown, Maya Angelou, Addison Gayle, Joyce Ladner, and Alice Childress among others, together with the perceptions and perspectives of such new black Southern writers as Joyce Dukes, Doris Jean Austin, Arthur Flowers, Kalamu ya Salaam, Malaika Adero, and Helen Quigless. The collection contributes substantially and qualitatively toward filling the vacuum. *Black Southern Voices* will necessarily broaden and deepen the literary picture of this nation, promote a deeper understanding of the First World countries and the world at large, and give wider and profounder dimensions to a woefully neglected aspect of the American experience.

FOREWORD

Jerry W. Ward, Jr.

The South, perhaps to a greater extent than is true of other regions of the
United States, is considered a place where myth is both lived and created.
Visitors to Oxford, Mississippi, might expect to be greeted by the characters
who peopled Faulkner's novels; someone exploring southern Georgia is not
overmuch surprised to find weathered farmers who would fit perfectly in Er-
skine Caldwell's sensational stories; the topping for a vacation in New Orleans
is to spy at least one Blanche Dubois in the half-shadows of the French
Quarter. The stereotype is stronger than the real thing. It is easier, less threatening, to be entertained by the myths of the South than to grapple with the living
contradictions, complexities, and tensions that give an authentic shape to the
region.

Failure to confront the real is especially noticeable in discussions of Southern
literature. Until recently, it had been traditional to pretend that the Southern
imagination has been articulated only by white women and men. It was rarely
admitted that black women and men had something to say.

This habit of listening to only one set of the voices that give form to the
thoughts and emotional responses of Southern culture is treacherous. Listening
with half an ear, as it were, one cannot hear the pulsating heart that secures
meaning for Southern myth or drama or poetry. This habit is a matter of
choice; it is not an accident. In a racist society, people choose not to hear,
and thus admit the significance of, the African and then African-American
voices that have given uniqueness to the culture and mind of the South since
the seventeenth century. If one will not hear the black Southern voices, richly
textured and sonorous in the oral traditions and no less eloquent and compelling
in the literate traditions, it is impossible to discern fully the beauty and values
of Southern literature and imagination.

One of the functions of *Black Southern Voices* is to turn up the volume, to
make it possible to hear all the notes—the sorrow songs, the blues and seculars,
the dirges and the martial melodies, the jubilees—the full range of sounds
representing the history and creativity of a people who were and are cocreators
of the South as a literal and figurative realm. The full range of sounds we call
literature.

Moreover, *Black Southern Voices* provides an opportunity to reconsider how
vision or perspective determines what the *voice* might say. Perspective is more
than the angle from which one looks at something, be the something land and
plant life or the people with whom one lives day to day. Perspective concerns

5

the image received by the eye and thoughts the image might evoke. One man looks at a field of cotton, envisions wealth, and sings, as did Henry Timrod in "Ethnogenesis," of King Cotton as

> . . . one among the many ends for which
> God makes us great and rich!

Another man looks at the same field, thinks of the merciless sun and back pains, and sings

> Nobody knows de trouble I see, Lord,
> Nobody knows de trouble I see;
> Nobody knows de trouble I see, Lord,
> Nobody knows like Jesus.

Here the perspectives are radically different. The difference, in part, is the result of how each man understood his place in the history of the South.

We will never know precisely what the earliest slaves in the South thought and felt. We can be certain, however, they were not mute about what they experienced in their new world. Through oral transmission they passed on their perspectives on slavery. Stolen from their homelands, they felt strongly the loss of what was familiar—freedom, family relationships, a community that shared their languages, values, rituals, and traditions. Slavery necessitated either outright revolt or adjustment to unfamiliar climate and geography, people, language, and customs. How the early Southern slaves responded to slavery can be recovered from the oral literature they created, from their folklore. Many songs deal with the desire to return home; tales that seem at first glance to be quaint, entertaining, are subtle lessons in how lack of power can be used to advantage; spirituals, riddles, folk sermons, work songs, and "how come" and "why" tales reveal much about the slave's daily concerns within the "peculiar institution." The absence of written documents is no evidence that early Southern slaves lacked the ability or desire, in the words of Margaret Walker, to make "a creative and humanistic response to the violent and negative philosophy of white racism."

That we must recover much of the slave's worldview from folklore is important, because we are forced to consider how the denial of access to literacy (or training in reading and writing) played a role in the evolving of black creative expression in the South. On one hand, it forced the slaves to depend very much on memory and invention as they enlarged and transformed the body of folklore. On the other hand, the denial created a great hunger for skill in reading and writing; that skill, as the young Frederick Douglass noted, was indeed "the pathway from slavery to freedom." By diverse means, some slaves did acquire literacy and used it to create, among other forms, the remarkable slave narratives. These narratives themselves embody a considerable amount of folklore.

Such post-Civil War writers as Charles Chesnutt, Sutton Griggs, and Booker

T. Washington knew the literary potential of folk materials as did James Weldon Johnson and Zora Neale Hurston and other writers of the New Negro Renaissance. Borrowing from the treasury of folk imagination continues in writing as recent as Brenda Marie Osbey's *Ceremony for Minneconjoux* (1983) and C. Eric Lincoln's *The Avenue, Clayton City* (1988). For black Southern writers, the notion that folk roots are subliterary or wanting in aesthetic integrity is absurd. They have always blended the oral and the written traditions.

Whether we approach them from the angles of history or of literary study, the specialized speech acts of the Southern slave demonstrate their creators, now only nameless presences, were indeed actors rather than objects. Within folklore, as Lawrence Levine discovered in *Black Culture and Black Consciousness: Afro-American Folk Thought from Slavery to Freedom* (1977), lie the contours of the black Southern imagination. From the vantage point of the twentieth century, we can see how the germinal seeds of folklore blossomed into genres. In its many varieties, black Southern literature steadfastly holds to dreams tempered by historical realities. It gives the lie to the idea that the language of literature is divorced from the language of everyday experiences.

The work collected in *Black Southern Voices* focuses mainly on twentieth-century examples of what can be broadly identified as black Southern literature. As has been noted, that literature began with oral creation, evolved from the blending of oral and written traditions, and continues to grow as self-conscious artists adapt or modify their literary heritage to serve contemporary needs. To be sure, there is a dialectic between the spoken and the written within this literature. Richard Wright described these tendencies in "The Literature of the Negro in the United States" (1957) as The Forms of Things Unknown and The Narcissistic Level. Writers who embrace The Forms of Things Unknown (Henry Dumas is a stellar example) seem most concerned with the features of oral creation, speech and song, the folk. Those who work at The Narcissistic Level may be more concerned with traditional literary forms. Yet, as Stephen E. Henderson cautions in *Understanding the New Black Poetry* (1973), "it is fallacious to think of these two levels as discrete entities, although for the most part the influence has been from the folk to the formal during the periods of greatest power and originality." Henderson's caution is to be taken seriously, for we may find the tendencies or levels crisscrossing in the poetry of Margaret Walker or the fiction of Ernest Gaines or the autobiographical writing of Albert Murray.

By their very nature, anthologies are parts not wholes, and *Black Southern Voices* can only provide an abbreviated historical geography of black Southern literature and thought, a small portion of the immense landscape that has yet to be fully explored and mapped. In that sense, this collection invites us to become familiar with the continuity and change, themes, consciousness and sensibilities, the calls and geometric progressions of response, and the contradictions that are distinguishing features of the terrain.

The very concept of black South as place is based on what Lerone Bennett once called "parahistory," the possibility that Euro-Americans and African-Americans in the South occupied the same space but that their perceptions of time and its significance were fundamentally different. Within this conceptual context, the literature collected here is Southern by virtue of its place of origin and its direct or indirect response to historical circumstances that existed or exist only in the South.

There is, of course, great variety in how the writers respond to Southern experience. Arna Bontemps's *Black Thunder*, a portrayal of the slave insurrection led by Gabriel Prosser, gives us a perspective on plantation economy very different from the one found in Margaret Walker's *Jubilee*. The South we behold in Zora Neale Hurston's *Their Eyes Were Watching God* seems diametrically opposed to the South of Richard Wright's *Uncle Tom's Children*. John Oliver Killens's *'Sippi*, Lance Jeffers's *Witherspoon*, and Alice Walker's *Meridian* can be classified as civil rights novels, but the authors' visions have much more to do with their artistic and political sensibilities than with the Civil Rights Movement as a historical phenomenon. Each black Southern writer brings her or his individual voice and vision to a long history of struggle with the land and the matter of color. As for their white Southern counterparts, the South is both a geography and a state of mind.

In addressing the matter of history as central underpinning for a black Southern literature, Addison Gayle, in his essay "Reclaiming the Southern Experience: The Black Aesthetic 10 Years Later," noted

> an excursion into the cultural past can provide images by which we may measure ourselves as a people; it tells us that we are a people whose history and culture exemplify those values by which men throughout the history of the world have lived and died, and that these values found their greatest expression in the Western world in the South in the first home away from home for the African-American. It is there, where men and women, having undergone the racial holocaust and survived, that the best examples of a viable Black literary and cultural tradition exist.

Gayle is hinting that history is more than a narrative of events; it is a continuous negotiating with the past and the present, a particular way of sensing the world and valuing the meaning of human existence. Here Gayle is echoing Richard Wright's insistence that literature enable us to make some sense of our struggle beneath the stars. So too black Southern writers embrace the necessity of creating works of art that are grounded in the lived experience of Southern culture. They may share certain formal and thematic similarities with white Southern writers, but they most surely march to the beat of a different parahistorical drummer. That is the only way to make sense of the intensely felt experience of being black and Southern.

This particular way of making sense of experience involves the art of maintaining some balance between the forces of history and the forces of personal or collective experience. Both the matter and the techniques for mastering that balancing art are contained in the oral black folk culture of the South. Touchstone examples are Ernest Gaines's *The Autobiography of Miss Jane Pittman* and John Oliver Killens's *'Sippi*. The poet Tom Dent has commented that

Gaines's novel works so well because it dips into "a vast pool of on-going oral literature, retaining and making a small part of it permanent. . . . It [the novel] is built over a long established (possibly African) mode of Afro-American storytelling—elders passing down necessary historical knowledge to younger folk, though the younger person must ritually be tested for acceptability by the elder and his or her agents. The novel is shaped by the form of an older, time-tested oral form; its viability is thus enhanced." In *'Sippi*, as the folklorist William Wiggins has established, oral tradition is crucial to the novel's theme and structure; in addition, Killens used the literary strategies of critical realism to comment on such contemporary concerns as gender, race, and class. Although these novels are but two touchstones among many, they are especially revealing syntheses of the autobiographical, dramatic, and poetic currents that mark black Southern literature: the artistic mastery of specific historical contexts with the complex simplicity that informs the best of world literature, mastery of the mythic impulse.

The visions and voices of black Southern speakers and writers, their perspectives, the history and heritage they make accessible to us serve to clarify, to illuminate, and to persuade us creatively of a truth only now beginning to be universally recognized: like jazz, the literary expressions of the black Southerner constitute America's most genuine gift to the humanistic tradition of literature.

PART ONE

FICTION

Arna Bontemps
(1902–1973)

A poet, fiction writer, critic, teacher, librarian, and anthologist, Bontemps is a significant figure in the history of twentieth-century African-American literature. Indeed, one might claim he and his friend Langston Hughes were keepers of the flame between the end of the Harlem Renaissance and the resurgence of black literary activity in the 1960s. Born in Alexandria, Louisiana, Bontemps was raised in California and received his B.A. from Pacific Union College. His early poems appeared in *The Crisis* and *Opportunity*, winning prizes from both magazines. During the 1930s, he studied at the University of Chicago from which he earned a degree in library science. Bontemps was the librarian at Fisk University from 1943 to 1966; in 1966 he joined the faculty of the University of Illinois-Chicago. His novels *God Sends Sunday, Black Thunder,* and *Drums at Dusk* were all published in the 1930s. His single book of poems, *Personals*, was not published until 1963. Although Bontemps wrote a considerable body of prize-winning literature for children, he is best known for his work as an editor. He coedited the anthologies *The Poetry of the Negro* (1949 and 1974) and *The Book of Negro Folklore* with Hughes. The other books he edited include *American Negro Poetry, Great Slave Narratives,* and *The Harlem Renaissance Remembered*. The following excerpt is from Book Two of *Black Thunder*.

---

from Black Thunder

CHAPTER SEVEN

That same blue brightness flickered over the line of stumbling shadows. Gabriel could hear a boisterous plop-plopping behind him, and he could see, when he turned his head, a parade of blurred silhouettes in the rain. Juba was back now, moving at his side on the fretful colt.

"We's got a crowd what can do the work. On'erstand?"

"I reckon so. They'll do the work if you's leading. But the country folks was many again as this. We's obliged to get along without them, and that's a care for sure."

"Too many is a trouble some time. A nigger ain't equal to a grasshopper when he scairt, and a scairt crowd is worser'n a scairt one."

13

The leader's immense shoulders slouched. He tramped in the heavy mud with a melodious swing of loose limbs. He had shed his coachman's frock-tailed coat, but the coachman's tall hat was still on his head; the front of his drenched shirt was open.

"Whoa, suh. Easy now, Araby," the girl said, pulling up the bridle and slapping the colt's face. "Easy, suh."

The rain was whipping him badly, but Araby decided to behave.

"We can do as good 'thout the others. Ditcher's here. It's bad to turn back."

"They's feeling mighty low-down now, I bound you—beingst they's left out."

"I reckon—maybe. The rain's bad and all, but I don't just know."

"You don't know what?"

"I don't know was it the deep water or was it something else that's holding them up."

"You talk funny. What you mean something else?"

Gabriel threw a glance over his shoulder. The line was coming down a rise. Here and there, in the blur and the downpour, a stray glint caught the point of a tall pike. Gabriel led them beneath a clump of willows and discovered an immense bough torn from one of the trees and hurled across the way. He went around it, churning mud up to his knees. Araby had a brief struggle before regaining firm ground.

"You ain't seen nothing, gal? You ain't noticed nothing funny?"

"I don't know what you means, boy."

Again Gabriel refrained from answering promptly. He walked a short way, swinging his arms meditatively, then paused to wipe the water from his face with an open hand.

"The line's getting slimmer and slimmer," he said.

Juba took a sudden quick breath through her open mouth.

"No!"

"It's the God's truth. I can tell by they feet. They ain't as many back there now."

"Hush, boy. I ain't seen none leave."

"Some's left, though. But that ain't nothing. They'll all come back tomorrow, the country crowd too. There won't be nothing else for them to do after we gets in our lick. Nobody's going to want a black face around they place tomorrow. You mind what I say, it's going to be who shall and who sha'n't, do we get in a good lick tonight. Do we fall down, the niggers what's left'll be looking for us too. They going to find out that the safest place is with yo' own crowd, sticking together."

"What make you so sure they's leaving, though? What you think make them go way like that?"

"Afeared," Gabriel said.

"Afeared to fight?"

"No, not afeared to fight. Scairt of the signs. Scairt of the stars, as you

A Heroic Voice. Refigures: Black men As men.
— Pre consciousness; The Ethics of Living Crow, Not Timid; Foot shuffling

BLACK THUNDER   **15**

call it. You heard them talking. 'The stars is against us,' they says. They says, 'All this here rain and storm ain't a nachal thing.' ''

There was a light in a tiny house beyond the thicket to the left. The line didn't pause, however. Gabriel swung along beside the colt, his elbow now and again touching the naked thigh of the girl astride. He glanced at the light, but he knew that no stone had been left unturned. The thing for the present was to keep going. The rain was no lighter; the wind was not letting up, and somewhere ahead a branch could be heard roaring like a river.

A little later Gabriel whispered, "I'm tired of being a devilish slave.''

"Me, too. I'm tired too, boy.''

"There ain't nothing but hard times waiting when a man get to studying about freedom.''

"H'm. Like a gal what love a no-'count man.''

"He just as well to take the air right away. He can't get well.''

"No, not lessen he got a pair of wings. They ain't no peace for him lessen he can fly.''

"H'm. No peace.''

"Didn't you used to loved a yellow woman, boy? A yellow woman hanging her head out the window?''

"Hush, gal. I'm a bird in the air, but it's freedom I been dreaming about. Not no womens.''

"You got good wings, I reckon.''

"Good wings, gal. Us both two got good wings.''

There was still the line of stumbling shadows behind. Suddenly they halted. They were at the crossing of the stream that lay between the plantations and the town. The colt whinnied and shivered, his front feet in the fast water.

"Wide,'' Juba said. "Deep, too.''

Gabriel stood with his feet in it. Rain whipped his back. There was grief in the treetops, a tall wind bearing down. Gabriel could see the flash and sparkle of water through the blackness. He bowed his head, heavy with thoughts, and waited a long moment without speaking.

Meanwhile the storm boomed. The small branch, swollen beyond reason, twisted and curled in its channel, hurled its length like a serpent, spewed water into the air and splashed with its tail.

CHAPTER EIGHT

Meanwhile, too, each in his place, the quaint confederates fought the storm, kept their posts or carried on as occasion demanded.

General John, his strength failing, crept into an abandoned pig sty and gave up the journey. He bent above his lantern, muttering aloud and trying to shield it from the wind.

'Twa'n't no use, nohow. Nothing outdoors this night but wind and water, God helping. Lord a-mercy, what I'm going to do with my old raw-boned self? Here I is halfway 'twixt town and home and as near played out as ever

I been. They ain't no call to turn back, though. After Gabriel and Ditcher and them gets done mopping up, it ain't going to be no place for we-all but right with the crowd. Gabriel said it and he said right. Do they get whupped, us going to have to hit for the mountains anyhow, so there ain't no cause to study about turning back. Yet and still, Richmond ain't for this here black man tonight, much less Petersburg. No, suh, not this night.

He squatted, his hands locked around his knees, and gave himself to meditation. Now and again a humorless grin altered his face, exposed the sparse brown fangs. The general's mood became first sluggish then mellow.

His head fell on his knees. A little later, his lantern gone out, he tumbled over on a heap of damp litter and slept.

The buck wagon came to a standstill midway the creek. The jack fretted and presently got himself at right angles with the cart.

"It's way yonder too deep for driving across," Ben said.

"Well, what I'm going to do now?" Pharoah asked.

"Turn round or stay here—one thing or t'other."

Pharoah moaned softly, sawing the reins back and forth while the animal danced in the fast current.

"These is bad doings," he said passionately. "I ain't never seen no sense in running a thing in the ground."

"Listen," Ben told him curtly. "Come to think about it, you was the nigger kneeling down side of me at old Bundy's burying."

"Maybe I was. What that got to do with all this here fool-headed mess?"

"Nothing. Only I remembers as to how you jugged yo' elbow in my belly that day and says, 'Don't you want to be free, fool?' Seem to me you was a big one on the rising then."

"Anybody gets mad some time. Freedom's all right, I reckon."

"But if you'd kept yo' elbow out of my belly, I'd of like as not been in my bed this very minute."

"You can't put it on me, Ben."

"No. Not trying to. Just getting you told. You making mo' fuss than me."

The jack whimpered and danced. Suddenly Pharoah rose to his feet in the cart, braced himself and put all his strength on the lines. The terrified, half-wild animal threw up his heels, bounded forward with a violent effort that jerked the shafts from the cart and sent the fat, pumpkin-colored Negro hurtling forward into the creek. The jack leaped again, and Pharoah felt the hot lines tear through his hands, heard the broken thills pounding the ground and the terrified animal galloping against the rain, fury against fury.

Ben climbed over the wheel and waded waist deep to the sloppy bank. He heard Pharoah slushing the mud on his hands and knees, heard him calling God feverishly.

"Lord Jesus, help. Lord a-mercy, do."

Ben felt a quick chill. He noticed that his good clothes were near ruined; and as he stood there trembling, he closed his eyes and tried to imagine himself tucked in a dry feather bed at home. But it was no good. He was wet to the bone, and that was a fact.

*   *   *

It was like hog-killing day to Criddle. He knew the feel of warm blood, and he knew his own mind. He knew, as well, that his scythe-sword was ready to drink. He could feel the thing getting stiffer and stiffer in his hand. Well, anyhow, he hadn't told anyone to snatch that door open and come legging it outside without looking where he was going.

Criddle had heard the columns in the road. They were not noisy, but there was something different in the sound they made. It was something like the rumble of the creek, nothing like the swish and whisper of poplars. He heard them go by, and he felt as if he were free already. He could just as well run and catch up with them now. Why not? But for some reason there wasn't much run left in his legs. They were, for the moment, scarcely strong enough to hold him up.

Cheap old white man, poorer'n a nigger. That's you, and it's just like you, hopping around like a devilish frog. You won't hop no mo' soon. Plague take yo' time, I didn't tell you to be so fidgety. You could of stayed in yonder and woke up in the morning. This here ain't no kind of night to be busting outdoors like something crazy.

And that there gal in the long nightgown and the lamp in her hand. Humph! She don't know nothing. Squealing and a-hollering round here like something another on fire. She need a big buck nigger to—no, not that. Gabriel done say too many times don't touch no womens. This here is all business this night. What that they calls it? Freedom? Yes, that's the ticket, and I reckon it feel mighty good too.

Where the nation that gal go to? Don't reckon I ought to leave her running round here in that there nightgown like a three-year filly. Where she go?

Criddle knew what blood was like. He remembered hog-killing day.

CHAPTER NINE

Gabriel heard the murmur that passed down the line as he stood in the water. He turned slowly, put out his hand and touched the nearest shadow.

"You, Blue?"

"Yes, this me."

"Where'bouts Martin and Solomon?"

"Back in the line, I reckon."

"Call them here."

He was gone with the word, and the confused and frightened Negroes began circling like cattle in the soft mud. Now and again one groaned at the point of hysteria. Gabriel didn't doubt that the groaners presently vanished and that the others lapsed directly into their former animal-like desperation. Juba was on the ground now, twitching her wet skirt lasciviously and clinging to the colt's bridle.

"Tired, boy?"

He shook his head.

"Tired ain't the word," he said. "Low."

"Niggers won't do."

"They's still leaving, slipping away—scairt white. How we's going to get them across this high-water branch is mo'n I know."

"We could of been gone from here, was it just me and you. Biggest part of the others ain't got the first notion about freedom."

"Maybe. That wouldn't do me, though. I reckon it's a birthmark. Running away won't do me no good long's the others stays. The littlest I can think about is a thousand at a time when it come to freedom. I reckon it's a conjure or something like that on me. I'm got to do it the big way, do I do it at all. And something been telling me this the night, the onliest night for us."

"It won't be the night if they keeps slipping away, though."

"I reckon it won't, gal. It won't be the night if we can't get them across this high-water branch."

"H'm. It's wasting time staying here if we can't cross. Just as well to be home pleasuring yo'self in a good sleeping place, dry, warm maybe, two together maybe."

"H'm."

They gathered quickly, Martin, Solomon, Blue and Ditcher with Gabriel and Juba. The others kept mulling in a sloppy low thicket beneath boughs that drooped under the relentless punishment.

"The branch is deep," Gabriel said. "And they's two mo' to cross like it further on. Y'-all reckon we can get this crowd in town tonight?"

Blue lost his breath.

"Quit the game now?"

"The weather's bad," Gabriel said. "It ain't too bad, but the niggers is leaving fast. They's scairt white, and they ain't more'n two hundred left, I reckon. We might could get them together again in two-three days."

"They's leaving for true," Ditcher said. "I heard some talk and I seen some go. They's afeared of the water and they's scairt to fight 'thout the whole eleven hundred. But they's most scairt of the signs. It look like bad luck, all this flood."

"It's bad to turn round and go back," Gabriel said. "Something keep telling me this here's the night, but you can't fight with mens what's scairt. What you say, Solomon?"

"You done said it all, Bubber. They ain't no mo'."

Gabriel turned first to one, then to the other, the question still open.

"You said it all," Blue echoed.

"They ain't no mo'," Juba murmured. "No mo' to say, boy."

"Well, then, it's pass the word along. Pass it fast and tell them all to get home soon's they can. On'erstand? If they don't mind out somebody'll catch up with them going back. Send somebody to tell Criddle ne'mind now and somebody to town to head off Ben and Gen'l John and tell Mingo and them that's with him. Somebody got to wade out to tell the country folks, too. We's got to turn round fast. It's bad to quit and go back. It's more dangerouser than going frontwise. These fools don't know it.''

In a few moments the crowd left the low thicket, scurrying across fields by twos and threes. Gabriel walked in the slushy path, his shoulders slouched wistfully, his hand hooked in Araby's bridle. Rain blew in Juba's face. She sat erect, feeling the pure warmth of the colt's fine muscles gnawing back and forth between her naked thighs. There was something sadly pleasant about retreat under these circumstances. Hope was not gone.

"We's got tomorrow," she said.

"Not yet," Gabriel answered. "The sun ain't *obliged* to rise, you know."

"I hope it do."

"H'm."

The storm boomed weakly, flapping the shreds of a torn banner.

CHAPTER TEN

The cabins on the Prosser place were running a foot of water. Negroes sleeping in the haymow opened their eyes stupidly and tottered over to the loft window. A village of corn shocks in the low field was completely inundated. A scrawny red rooster, looking very tall and awkward on a small raft, drifted steadily downstream. He had not lost his strut, but his feathers were wet and he seemed, in his predicament, as dismayed as an old beau. The rain was over; there was a vague promise of sunshine in a sky that was lead-colored.

Mingo's frightened jack was still running, an arm of the broken thills dangling from his harness, sliding over the ground with a bump-bump-bump. Something had snapped in his head. He imagined the devil would pounce on him if he lost a single bound. He was running in circles sometimes and sometimes straightening out for a mile at a stretch. Leaping streams, plowing up flower beds, tearing through thickets and underbrush, it did not occur to him that the storm was over.

Ben and Pharoah stood in mud by the roadside, their heads together. They were still dripping wet and their clothes were mud-spattered from heel to crown. The wagon in the creek near by had been thrown on its side by the current; its wheels were lodged on the underside.

"It was a pure fool's doings, Ben."

"No need to stand here saying that all day. We best get gone."

"I reckon."

"That's all what's left to do. Come on."

Pharoah cried shamelessly.

Ben whispered beneath his breath.

Criddle was bewildered when he met the other two on the road.

"What done come of everybody?"

"Gone home. Ain't you heard?"

Arna Bontemps

"I ain't heard nothing. Gone home for what?"

"Tell him, Pharoah."

The pumpkin-faced Negro tried to explain.

"They couldn't make it on account of the water and all. They's telling everybody to lay low two-three days and wait till the weather clear up. They didn't get across the first branch. Somebody was looking for you directly after the lines broke up."

"They broke up, hunh?"

"They *been* broke up. They been gone since before midnight, I reckon."

Criddle's domino spots got smaller and smaller. Finally they disappeared altogether.

"You ain't fixing to cry about it, is you?" Ben said. "It just going to be two-three mo' days."

"I ain't crying, but I don't see how they going to wait no two-three days with that white gal running loose in her nightgown. She'll let it out befo' you can spit."

"How she know?"

"Gabriel told me what to do, and I done it, me. I don't know what come of the gal?"

"I help you to say she going to tell it."

Ben thought of nothing but the broken wagon in the creek and Mingo's half-wild jack running furiously. He began to pray under his breath again, crying in his mind like a child. Pharoah stood like a wooden man, his mouth hanging open, his swine-like eyes extremely bright. Suddenly he quaked violently. Then he covered his face and cried, cried absurdly loud and long for a grown man. When he recovered again and looked up, his eyes were quite empty. Some strange, inarticulate decision of his blood made a new man of him. It was evident on his face.

The three of them started walking. Ben led the dazed Pharoah by the hand a little way. Criddle followed, his shoulders rounded, his long arms hanging a bit in front of his short body as he walked. It was sloppy weather for a Sunday.

Zora Neale Hurston
(1891–1960)

One of the most important literary figures of the Harlem Renaissance and the 1930s, Hurston was born in the all-black town of Eatonville, Florida. She was a brilliant, multitalented woman who moved through the roles of novelist, anthropologist, folklorist, essayist, and playwright with an inimitable sense of the dramatic. Hurston spent much of her life documenting the speech and culture of the rural black South, and her *Mules & Men* (1935) is a classic study of Southern folklore. A Guggenheim fellowship (1936–1938) enabled her to study Caribbean folklore and to write *Tell My Horse* (1938). She wrote four novels: *Jonah's Gourd Vine* (1934), *Their Eyes Were Watching God* (1937), *Moses, Man of the Mountain* (1939), and *Seraph on the Suwanee* (1948). She published her autobiography, *Dust Tracks on the Road*, in 1942. During the 1950s and 1960s her work was virtually ignored. Robert Hemenway's exemplary critical biography and Alice Walker's editing *I Love Myself When I Am Laughing & Then Again When I Am Looking Mean and Impressive: A Zora Neale Hurston Reader* helped to revive interest; Hurston is now recognized as having established a paradigm wherein subsequent works by black women writers might be examined. Because interest in Hurston continues to grow, most of her works, including the play *Mule Bone: A Comedy of Negro Life*, which she coauthored with Langston Hughes, are now in print. The following excerpt is from *Their Eyes Were Watching God*.

---

from Their Eyes Were Watching God

And then again Him-with-the-square-toes had gone back to his house. He stood once more and again in his high flat house without sides to it and without a roof with his soulless sword standing upright in his hand. His pale white horse had galloped over waters, and thundered over land. The time of dying was over. It was time to bury the dead.

"Janie, us been in dis dirty, slouchy place two days now, and dat's too much. Us got tuh git outa dis house and outa dis man's town. Ah never did lak round heah."

"Where we goin', Tea Cake? Dat we don't know."

"Maybe, we could go back up de state, if yuh want tuh go."

"Ah didn't say dat, but if dat is whut you—"

"Naw, Ah ain't said nothin' uh de kind. Ah wuz tryin' not tuh keep you outa yo' comfortable no longer'n you wanted tuh stay."

"If Ah'm in yo' way—"

"Will you lissen at dis woman? Me 'bout tuh bust mah britches tryin' tuh stay wid her and she heah—she oughta be shot wid tacks!"

"All right then, you name somethin' and we'll do it. We kin give it uh poor man's trial anyhow."

"Anyhow Ah done got rested up and de bed bugs is done got too bold round heah. Ah didn't notice when mah rest wuz broke. Ah'm goin' out and look around and see whut we kin do. Ah'll give *any*thing uh common trial."

"You better stay inside dis house and git some rest. 'Tain't nothin' tuh find out dere nohow."

"But Ah wants tuh look and see, Janie. Maybe it's some kinda work fuh me tuh help do."

"Whut dey want you tuh help do, you ain't gointuh like it. Dey's grabbin' all de menfolks dey kin git dey hands on and makin' 'em help bury de dead. Dey claims dey's after de unemployed, but dey ain't bein' too particular about whether you'se employed or not. You stay in dis house. De Red Cross is doin' all dat kin be done otherwise fuh de sick and de 'fflicted."

"Ah got money on me, Janie. Dey can't bother me. Anyhow Ah wants tuh go see how things is sho nuff. Ah wants tuh see if Ah kin hear anything 'bout de boys from de 'Glades. Maybe dey all come through all right. Maybe not."

Tea Cake went out and wandered around. Saw the hand of horror on everything. Houses without roofs, and roofs without houses. Steel and stone all crushed and crumbled like wood. The mother of malice had trifled with men.

While Tea Cake was standing and looking he saw two men coming towards him with rifles on their shoulders. Two white men, so he thought about what Janie had told him and flexed his knees to run. But in a moment he saw that wouldn't do him any good. They had already seen him and they were too close to miss him if they shot. Maybe they would pass on by. Maybe when they saw he had money they would realize he was not a tramp.

"Hello, there, Jim," the tallest one called out. "We been lookin' fuh you."

"Mah name ain't no Jim," Tea Cake said watchfully. "Whut you been lookin' fuh *me* fuh? Ah ain't done nothin'."

"Dat's whut we want yuh fuh—not doin' nothin'. Come on less go bury some uh dese heah dead folks. Dey ain't gettin' buried fast enough."

Tea Cake hung back defensively. "Whut Ah got tuh do wid dat? Ah'm uh workin' man wid money in mah pocket. Jus' got blowed outa de 'Glades by de storm."

The short man made a quick move with his rifle. "Git on down de road dere, suh! Don't look out somebody'll be buryin' *you!* G'wan in front uh me, suh!"

Tea Cake found that he was part of a small army that had been pressed into service to clear the wreckage in public places and bury the dead. Bodies had to be searched out, carried to certain gathering places and buried. Corpses were not just found in wrecked houses. They were under houses, tangled in shrubbery, floating in water, hanging in trees, drifting under wreckage.

Trucks lined with drag kept rolling in from the 'Glades and other outlying parts, each with its load of twenty-five bodies. Some bodies fully dressed, some naked and some in all degrees of dishevelment. Some bodies with calm faces and satisfied hands. Some dead with fighting faces and eyes flung wide open in wonder. Death had found them watching, trying to see beyond seeing.

Miserable, sullen men, black and white under guard had to keep on searching for bodies and digging graves. A huge ditch was opened across the white cemetery and a big ditch was opened across the black graveyard. Plenty quick-lime on hand to throw over the bodies as soon as they were received. They had already been unburied too long. The men were making every effort to get them covered up as quickly as possible. But the guards stopped them. They had received orders to be carried out.

"Hey, dere, y'all! Don't dump dem bodies in de hole lak dat! Examine every last one of 'em and find out if they's white or black."

"Us got tuh handle 'em slow lak dat? God have mussy! In de condition they's in got tuh examine 'em? What difference do it make 'bout de color? Dey all needs buryin' in uh hurry."

"Got orders from headquarters. They makin' coffins fuh all de white folks. 'Tain't nothin' but cheap pine, but dat's better'n nothin'. Don't dump no white folks in de hole jus' so."

"What tuh do 'bout de colored folks? Got boxes fuh dem too?"

"Nope. They cain't find enough of 'em tuh go 'round. Jus' sprinkle plenty quick-lime over 'em and cover 'em up."

"Shucks! Nobody can't tell nothin' 'bout some uh dese bodies, de shape dey's in. Can't tell whether dey's white or black."

The guards had a long conference over that. After a while they came back and told the men, "look at they hair, when you cain't tell no other way. And don't lemme ketch none uh y'all dumpin' white folks, and don't be wastin' no boxes on colored. They's too hard tuh git holt of right now."

"They's mighty particular how dese dead folks goes tuh judgment," Tea Cake observed to the man working next to him. "Look lak dey think God don't know nothin' 'bout de Jim Crow law."

Tea Cake had been working several hours when the thought of Janie worrying about him made him desperate. So when a truck drove up to be unloaded he bolted and ran. He was ordered to halt on pain of being shot at, but he kept right on and got away. He found Janie sad and crying just as he had thought. They calmed each other about his absence then Tea Cake brought up another matter.

"Janie, us got tuh git outa dis house and outa dis man's town. Ah don't mean tuh work lak dat no mo'."

"Naw, naw, Tea Cake. Less stay right in heah until it's all over. If dey can't see yuh, dey can't bother yuh."

"Aw naw. S'posin' dey come round searchin'? Less git outa heah tuhnight."

"Where us goin', Tea Cake?"

"De quickest place is de 'Glades. Less make it on back down dere. Dis town is full uh trouble and compellment."

"But, Tea Cake, de hurricane wuz down in de 'Glades too. It'll be dead folks tuh be buried down dere too."

"Yeah, Ah know, Janie, but it couldn't never be lak it 'tis heah. In de first place dey been bringin' bodies outa dere all day so it can't be but so many mo' tuh find. And then again it never wuz as many dere as it wuz heah. And then too, Janie, de white folks down dere knows us. It's bad bein' strange niggers wid white folks. Everybody is against yuh."

Explain

"Dat sho is de truth. De ones de white man know is nice colored folks. De ones he don't know is bad niggers." Janie said this and laughed and Tea Cake laughed with her.

"Janie, Ah done watched it time and time again; each and every white man think he know all de GOOD darkies already. He don't need tuh know no mo'. So far as he's concerned, all dem he don't know oughta be tried and sentenced tuh six months behind de United States privy house at hard smellin'."

"How come de United States privy house, Tea Cake?"

"Well, you know Old Uncle Sam always do have de biggest and de best uh everything. So de white man figger dat anything less than de Uncle Sam's consolidated water closet would be too easy. So Ah means tuh go where de white folks know me. Ah feels lak uh motherless chile round heah."

They got things together and stole out of the house and away. The next morning they were back on the muck. They worked hard all day fixing up a house to live in so that Tea Cake could go out looking for something to do the next day. He got out soon next morning more out of curiosity than eagerness to work. Stayed off all day. That night he came in beaming out with light.

"Who you reckon Ah seen, Janie? Bet you can't guess."

"Ah'll betcha uh fat man you seen Sop-de-Bottom."

"Yeah Ah seen him and Stew Beef and Dockery and Lias, and Coodernay and Bootyny. Guess who else!"

"Lawd knows. Is it Sterrett?"

"Naw, he got caught in the rush. Lias help bury him in Palm Beach. Guess who else?"

"Ah g'wan tell me, Tea Cake. Ah don't know. It can't be Motor Boat."

"Dat's jus' who it is. Ole Motor! De son of a gun laid up in dat house and slept and de lake come moved de house way off somewhere and Motor didn't know nothin' 'bout it till de storm wuz 'bout over."

"Naw!"

"Yeah man. Heah we nelly kill our fool selves runnin' way from danger and him lay up dere and sleep and float on off!"

"Well, you know dey say luck is uh fortune."

"Dat's right too. Look, Ah got uh job uh work. Help clearin' up things in general, and then dey goin' build dat dike sho nuff. Dat ground got to be cleared off too. Plenty work. Dey needs mo' men even."

So Tea Cake made three hearty weeks. He bought another rifle and a pistol and he and Janie bucked each other as to who was the best shot with Janie ranking him always with the rifle. She could knock the head off of a chicken-hawk sitting up a pine tree. Tea Cake was a little jealous, but proud of his pupil.

Rabies

About the middle of the fourth week Tea Cake came home early one after-noon complaining of his head. Sick headache that made him lie down for awhile. He woke up hungry. Janie had his supper ready but by the time he walked from the bedroom to the table, he said he didn't b'lieve he wanted a thing.

"Thought you tole me you wuz hongry!" Janie wailed.

"Ah thought so too," Tea Cake said very quietly and dropped his head in his hands.

"But Ah done baked yuh uh pan uh beans."

"Ah knows dey's good all right but Ah don't choose nothin' now, Ah thank yuh, Janie."

He went back to bed. Way in the midnight he woke Janie up in his nightmar-ish struggle with an enemy that was at his throat. Janie struck a light and quieted him.

"Whut's de matter, honey?" She soothed and soothed. "You got tuh tell me so Ah kin feel widja. Lemme bear de pain 'long widja, baby. Where hurt yuh, sugar?"

"Somethin' got after me in mah sleep, Janie." He all but cried. "Tried tuh choke me tuh death. Hadn't been fuh *you* Ah'd be dead."

$\Longleftarrow$

"You sho wuz strainin' wid it. But you'se all right, honey. Ah'm heah."

He went on back to sleep, but there was no getting around it. He was sick in the morning. He tried to make it but Janie wouldn't hear of his going out at all.

"If Ah kin jus' make out de week," Tea Cake said.

"Folks wuz makin' weeks befo' you wuz born and they gointuh be makin' 'em after you'se gone. Lay back down, Tea Cake. Ah'm goin' git de doctor tuh come see 'bout yuh."

"Aw ain't dat bad, Janie. Looka heah! Ah kin walk all over de place."

"But you'se too sick tuh play wid. Plenty fever round heah since de storm."

"Gimme uh drink uh water befo' you leave, then."

Janie dipped up a glass of water and brought it to the bed. Tea Cake took it and filled his mouth then gagged horribly, disgorged that which was in his mouth and threw the glass upon the floor. Janie was frantic with alarm.

"Whut make you ack lak dat wid yo' drinkin' water, Tea Cake? You ast me tuh give it tuh yuh."

"Dat water is somethin' wrong wid it. It nelly choke me tuh death. Ah told yuh somethin' jumped on me heah last night and choked me. You come makin' out Ah wuz dreamin'."

"Maybe it wuz uh witch ridin' yuh, honey. Ah'll see can't Ah find some mustard seed whilst Ah's out. But Ah'm sho tuh fetch de doctor when Ah'm come."

Tea Cake didn't say anything against it and Janie herself hurried off. This sickness to her was worse than the storm. As soon as she was well out of sight, Tea Cake got up and dumped the water bucket and washed it clean. Then he struggled to the irrigation pump and filled it again. He was not accusing Janie of malice and design. He was accusing her of carelessness. She ought to realize that water buckets needed washing like everything else. He'd tell her about it good and proper when she got back. What was she thinking about nohow? He found himself very angry about it. He eased the bucket on the table and sat down to rest before taking a drink.

Rabies ⇒

Finally he dipped up a drink. It was so good and cool! Come to think about it, he hadn't had a drink since yesterday. That was what he needed to give him an appetite for his beans. He found himself wanting it very much, so he threw back his head as he rushed the glass to his lips. But the demon was there before him, strangling, killing him quickly. It was a great relief to expel the water from his mouth. He sprawled on the bed again and lay there shivering until Janie and the doctor arrived. The white doctor who had been around so long that he was part of the muck. Who told the workmen stories with brawny sweaty words in them. He came into the house quickly, hat sitting on the left back corner of his head.

"Hi there, Tea Cake. What de hell's de matter with *you?*"

"Wisht Ah knowed, Doctah Simmons. But Ah sho is sick."

"Ah, naw Tea Cake. 'Tain't a thing wrong that a quart of coon-dick wouldn't cure. You haven't been gettin' yo' right likker lately, eh?" He slapped Tea Cake lustily across his back and Tea Cake tried to smile as he was expected to do. But it was hard. The doctor opened up his bag and went to work.

"You do look a little peaked, Tea Cake. You got a temperature and yo' pulse is kinda off. What you been doin' here lately?"

"Nothin' 'cept workin' and gamin' uh little, doctah. But look lak water done turn't aginst me."

"Water? How do you mean?"

"Can't keep it on mah stomach, at all."

"What else?"

Janie came around the bed full of concern.

"Doctah, Tea Cake ain't tellin' yuh everything lak he oughta. We wuz caught in dat hurricane out heah, and Tea Cake over-strained hissel swimmin' such uh long time and holdin' me up too, and walkin' all dem miles in de storm and then befo' he could git his rest he had tuh come git me out de water agin and fightin' wid dat big old dawg and de dawg bitin' 'im in de face and everything. Ah been spectin' him tuh be sick befo' now."

"Dawg bit 'im, did you say?"

"Aw twudn't nothin' much, doctah. It wuz all healed over in two or three days," Tea Cake said impatiently. "Dat been over uh month ago, nohow. Dis is somethin' new, doctah. Ah figgers de water is yet bad. It's bound tuh be. Too many dead folks been in it fuh it tuh be good tuh drink fuh uh long time. Dat's de way Ah figgers it anyhow."

"All right, Tea Cake. Ah'll send you some medicine and tell Janie how tuh take care of you. Anyhow, I want you in a bed by yo'self until you hear from me. Just you keep Janie out of yo' bed for awhile, hear? Come on out to the car with me, Janie. I want to send Tea Cake some pills to take right away.''

Outside he fumbled in his bag and gave Janie a tiny bottle with a few pellets inside.

"Give him one of these every hour to keep him quiet, Janie, and stay out of his way when he gets in one of his fits of gagging and choking.''

"How you know he's havin' 'em, doctah? Dat's jus' what Ah come out heah tuh tell yuh.''

"Janie, I'm pretty sure that was a mad dawg bit yo' husband. It's too late to get hold of de dawg's head. But de symptoms is all there. It's mighty bad dat it's gone on so long. Some shots right after it happened would have fixed him right up.''

"You mean he's liable tuh die, doctah?''

"Sho is. But de worst thing is he's liable tuh suffer somethin' awful befo' he goes.''

"Doctor, Ah loves him fit tuh kill. Tell me anything tuh do and Ah'll do it.''

" 'Bout de only thing you can do, Janie, is to put him in the County Hospital where they can tie him down and look after him.''

"But he don't like no hospital at all. He'd think Ah wuz tired uh doin' fuh 'im, when God knows Ah ain't. Ah can't stand de idea us tyin' Tea Cake lak he wuz uh mad dawg.''

"It almost amounts to dat, Janie. He's got almost no chance to pull through and he's liable to bite somebody else, specially you, and then you'll be in the same fix he's in. It's mighty bad.''

"Can't nothin' be done fuh his case, doctah? Us got plenty money in de bank in Orlandah, doctah. See can't yuh do somethin' special tuh save him. Anything it cost, doctah. Ah don't keer, but please, doctah.''

"Do what I can. Ah'll phone into Palm Beach right away for the serum which he should have had three weeks ago. I'll do all I can to save him, Janie. But it looks too late. People in his condition can't swallow water, you know, and in other ways it's terrible.''

Janie fooled around outside awhile to try and think it wasn't so. If she didn't see the sickness in his face she could imagine it wasn't really happening. Well, she thought, that big old dawg with the hatred in his eyes had killed her after all. She wished she had slipped off that cow-tail and drowned then and there and been done. But to kill her through Tea Cake was too much to bear. Tea Cake, the son of Evening Sun, had to die for loving her. She looked hard at the sky for a long time. Somewhere up there beyond blue ether's bosom sat He. Was He noticing what was going on around here? He must be because He knew everything. Did He *mean* to do this thing to Tea Cake and her? It wasn't anything she could fight. She could only ache and wait. Maybe it was some big tease and when He saw it had gone far enough He'd give her a sign. She looked hard for something up there to move for a sign. A star in the daytime, maybe, or the sun to shout, or even a mutter of thunder. Her arms went up in a desperate supplication for a minute. It wasn't exactly pleading, it was asking questions. The sky stayed hard looking and quiet so she went inside the house. God would do less than He had in His heart.

Tea Cake was lying with his eyes closed and Janie hoped he was asleep. He wasn't. A great fear had took hold of him. What was this thing that set his brains afire and grabbed at his throat with iron fingers? Where did it come from and why did it hang around him? He hoped it would stop before Janie noticed anything. He wanted to try to drink water again but he didn't want her to see him fail. As soon as she got out of the kitchen he meant to go to the bucket and drink right quick before anything had time to stop him. No need to worry Janie, until he couldn't help it. He heard her cleaning out the stove and saw her go out back to empty the ashes. He leaped at the bucket at once. But this time the sight of the water was enough. He was on the kitchen floor in great agony when she returned. She petted him, soothed him, and got him back to bed. She made up her mind to go see about that medicine from Palm Beach. Maybe she could find somebody to drive over there for it.

"Feel better now, Tea Cake, baby chile?"

"Uh huh, uh little."

"Well, b'lieve Ah'll rake up de front yard. De mens is got cane chewin's and peanut hulls all over de place. Don't want de doctah tuh come back heah and find it still de same."

"Don't take too long, Janie. Don't lak tuh be by mahself when Ah'm sick."

She ran down the road just as fast as she could. Halfway to town she met Sop-de-Bottom and Dockery coming towards her.

"Hello, Janie, how's Tea Cake?"

"Pretty bad off. Ah'm gointuh see 'bout medicine fuh 'im right now."

"Doctor told somebody he wuz sick so us come tuh see. Thought somethin' he never come tuh work."

"Y'all set wid 'im till Ah git back. He need de company right long in heah."

She fanned on down the road to town and found Dr. Simmons. Yes, he had had an answer. They didn't have any serum but they had wired Miami to send it. She needn't worry. It would be there early the next morning if not before. People didn't fool around in a case like that. No, it wouldn't do for her to hire no car to go after it. Just go home and wait. That was all. When she reached home the visitors rose to go.

When they were alone Tea Cake wanted to put his head in Janie's lap and tell her how he felt and let her mama him in her sweet way. But something Sop had told him made his tongue lie cold and heavy like a dead lizard between his jaws. Mrs. Turner's brother was back on the muck and now he had this mysterious sickness. People didn't just take sick like this for nothing.

"Janie, whut is dat Turner woman's brother doin' back on de muck?"

"Ah don't know, Tea Cake. Didn't even knowed he wuz back."

"Accordin' tuh mah notion, you did. Whut you slip off from me just now for?"

"Tea Cake, Ah don't lak you astin' me no sich question. Dat shows how sick you is sho nuff. You'se jealous 'thout me givin' you cause."

"Well, whut didja slip off from de house 'thout tellin' me you wuz goin'. You ain't never done dat befo'."

"Dat wuz 'cause Ah wuz tryin' not tuh let yuh worry 'bout yo' condition. De doctah sent after some mo' medicine and Ah went tuh see if it come."

Tea Cake began to cry and Janie hovered him in her arms like a child. She sat on the side of the bed and sort of rocked him back to peace.

"Tea Cake, 'tain't no use in you bein' jealous uh me. In de first place Ah couldn't love nobody but yuh. And in de second place, Ah jus' uh ole woman dat nobody don't want but you."

"Naw, you ain't neither. You only sound ole when you tell folks when you wuz born, but wid de eye you'se young enough tuh suit most any man. Dat ain't no lie. Ah knows plenty mo' men would take yuh and work hard fuh de privilege. Ah done heard 'em talk."

"Maybe so, Tea Cake, Ah ain't never tried tuh find out. Ah jus' know dat God snatched me out de fire through you. And Ah loves yuh and feel glad."

"Thank yuh, ma'am, but don't say you'se ole. You'se uh lil girl baby all de time. God made it so you spent yo' ole age first wid somebody else, and saved up yo' young girl days to spend wid me."

"Ah feel dat uh way too, Tea Cake, and Ah thank yuh fuh sayin' it."

" 'Tain't no trouble tuh say whut's already so. You'se uh pretty woman outside uh bein' nice."

"Aw, Tea Cake."

"Yeah you is too. Everytime Ah see uh patch uh roses uh somethin' over sportin' they selves makin' out they pretty, Ah tell 'em 'Ah want yuh tuh see mah Janie sometime.' You must let de flowers see yuh sometimes, heah, Janie?"

"You keep dat up, Tea Cake, Ah'll b'lieve yuh after while," Janie said archly and fixed him back in bed. It was then she felt the pistol under the pillow. It gave her a quick ugly throb, but she didn't ask him about it since he didn't say. Never had Tea Cake slept with a pistol under his head before. "Neb' mind 'bout all dat cleanin' round de front yard," he told her as she straightened up from fixing the bed. "You stay where Ah kin see yuh."

"All right, Tea Cake, jus' as you say."

"And if Mis' Turner's lap-legged brother come prowlin' by heah you kin tell 'im Ah got him stopped wid four wheel brakes. 'Tain't no need of him standin' round watchin' de job."

"Ah won't be tellin' 'im nothin' 'cause Ah don't expect tuh see 'im."

Tea Cake had two bad attacks that night. Janie saw a changing look come in his face. Tea Cake was gone. Something else was looking out of his face. She made up her mind to be off after the doctor with the first glow of day. So she was up and dressed when Tea Cake awoke from the fitful sleep that had come to him just before day. He almost snarled when he saw her dressed to go.

"Where are you goin', Janie?"

"After de doctah, Tea Cake. You'se too sick tuh be heah in dis house 'thout de doctah. Maybe we oughta git yuh tuh de hospital."

"Ah ain't goin' tuh no hospital no where. Put dat in yo' pipe and smoke it. Guess you tired uh waitin' on me and doing fuh me. Dat ain't de way Ah been wid *you*. Ah never is been able tuh do enough fuh yuh."

"Tea Cake, you'se sick. You'se takin' everything in de way Ah don't mean it. Ah couldn't never be tired uh waitin' on you. Ah'm just skeered you'se too sick fuh me tuh handle. Ah wants yuh tuh git well, honey. Dat's all."

He gave her a look full of blank ferocity and gurgled in his throat. She saw him sitting up in bed and moving about so that he could watch her every move. And she was beginning to feel fear of this strange thing in Tea Cake's body. So when he went out to the outhouse she rushed to see if the pistol was loaded. It was a six shooter and three of the chambers were full. She started to unload it but she feared he might break it and find out she knew. That might urge his disordered mind to action. If that medicine would only come! She whirled the cylinder so that if he even did draw the gun on her it would snap three times before it would fire. She would at least have warning. She could either run or try to take it away before it was too late. Anyway Tea Cake wouldn't hurt *her*. He was jealous and wanted to scare her. She'd just be in the kitchen as usual and never let on. They'd laugh over it when he got well. She found the box of cartridges, however, and emptied it. Just as well to take the rifle from back of the head of the bed. She broke it and put the shell in her apron pocket and put it in a corner in the kitchen almost behind the stove where it was hard to see. She could outrun his knife if it came to that. Of course she was too fussy, but it did no harm to play safe. She ought not to let poor sick Tea Cake do something that would run him crazy when he found out what he had done.

She saw him coming from the outhouse with a queer loping gait, swinging his head from side to side and his jaws clenched in a funny way. This was too awful! Where was Dr. Simmons with that medicine? She was glad she was here to look after him. Folks would do such mean things to her Tea Cake if they saw him in such a fix. Treat Tea Cake like he was some mad dog when nobody in the world had more kindness about them. All he needed was for the doctor to come on with that medicine. He came back into the house without speaking, in fact, he did not seem to notice she was there and fell heavily into the bed and slept. Janie was standing by the stove washing up the dishes when he spoke to her in a queer cold voice.

"Janie, how come you can't sleep in de same bed wid me no mo'?"

"De doctah told you tuh sleep by yo'self, Tea Cake. Don't yuh remember him tellin' you dat yistiddy?"

"How come you ruther sleep on uh pallet than tuh sleep in de bed with me?" Janie saw then that he had the gun in his hand that was hanging to his side. "Answer me when Ah speak."

"Tea Cake, Tea Cake, honey! Go lay down! Ah'll be too glad tuh be in dere wid yuh de minute de doctor say so. Go lay back down. He'll be heah wid some new medicine right away."

"Janie, Ah done went through everything tuh be good tuh you and it hurt me tuh mah heart tuh be ill treated lak Ah is."

The gun came up unsteadily but quickly and levelled at Janie's breast. She noted that even in his delirium he took good aim. Maybe he would point to scare her, that was all.

The pistol snapped once. Instinctively Janie's hand flew behind her on the rifle and brought it around. Most likely this would scare him off. If only the doctor would come! If anybody at all would come! She broke the rifle deftly and shoved in the shell as the second click told her that Tea Cake's suffering brain was urging him on to kill.

"Tea Cake put down dat gun and go back tuh bed!" Janie yelled at him as the gun wavered weakly in his hand.

He steadied himself against the jamb of the door and Janie thought to run into him and grab his arm, but she saw the quick motion of taking aim and heard the click. Saw the ferocious look in his eyes and went mad with fear as she had done in the water that time. She threw up the barrel of the rifle in frenzied hope and fear. Hope that he'd see it and run, desperate fear for his life. But if Tea Cake could have counted costs he would not have been there with the pistol in his hands. No knowledge of fear nor rifles nor anything else was there. He paid no more attention to the pointing gun than if it were Janie's dog finger. She saw him stiffen himself all over as he levelled and took aim. The fiend in him must kill and Janie was the only thing living he saw.

The pistol and the rifle rang out almost together. The pistol just enough after the rifle to seem its echo. Tea Cake crumpled as his bullet buried itself in the joist over Janie's head. Janie saw the look on his face and leaped forward as he crashed forward in her arms. She was trying to hover him as he closed his teeth in the flesh of her forearm. They came down heavily like that. Janie struggled to a sitting position and pried the dead Tea Cake's teeth from her arm.

It was the meanest moment of eternity. A minute before she was just a scared human being fighting for its life. Now she was her sacrificing self with Tea Cake's head in her lap. She had wanted him to live so much and he was dead. No hour is ever eternity, but it has its right to weep. Janie held his head tightly to her breast and wept and thanked him wordlessly for giving her the chance for loving service. She had to hug him tight for soon he would be gone, and she had to tell him for the last time. Then the grief of outer darkness descended.

So that same day of Janie's great sorrow she was in jail. And when the doctor told the sheriff and the judge how it was, they all said she must be tried that same day. No need to punish her in jail by waiting. Three hours in jail and then they set the court for her case. The time was short and everything, but sufficient people were there. Plenty of white people came to look on this strangeness. And all the Negroes for miles around. Who was it didn't know about the love between Tea Cake and Janie?

The court set and Janie saw the judge who had put on a great robe to listen about her and Tea Cake. And twelve more white men had stopped whatever they were doing to listen and pass on what happened between Janie and Tea Cake Woods, and as to whether things were done right or not. That was funny too. Twelve strange men who didn't know a thing about people like Tea Cake and her were going to sit on the thing. Eight or ten white women had come to look at her too. They wore good clothes and had the pinky color that comes of good food. They were nobody's poor white folks. What need had *they* to leave their richness to come look on Janie in her overalls? But they didn't seem too mad, Janie thought. It would be nice if she could make *them* know how it was instead of those menfolks. Oh, and she hoped that undertaker was fixing Tea Cake up fine. They ought to let her go see about it. Yes, and there was Mr. Prescott that she knew right well and he was going to tell the twelve men to kill her for shooting Tea Cake. And a strange man from Palm Beach who was going to ask them not to kill her, and none of them knew.

Then she saw all of the colored people standing up in the back of the courtroom. Packed tight like a case of celery, only much darker than that. They were all against her, she could see. So many were there against her that a light slap from each one of them would have beat her to death. She felt them pelting her with dirty thoughts. They were there with their tongues cocked and loaded, the only real weapon left to weak folks. The only killing tool they are allowed to use in the presence of white folks.

So it was all ready after a while and they wanted people to talk so that they could know what was right to do about Janie Woods the relic of Tea Cake's Janie. The white part of the room got calmer the more serious it got, but a tongue storm struck the Negroes like wind among palm trees. They talked all of a sudden and all together like a choir and the top parts of their bodies moved on the rhythm of it. They sent word by the bailiff to Mr. Prescott they wanted to testify in the case. Tea Cake was a good boy. He had been good to that woman. No nigger woman ain't never been treated no better. Naw suh! He worked like a dog for her and nearly killed himself saving her in the storm, then soon as he got a little fever from the water, she had took up with another man. Sent for him to come there from way off. Hanging was too good. All they wanted was a chance to testify. The bailiff went up and the sheriff and the judge, and the police chief, and the lawyers all came together to listen for a few minutes, then they parted again and the sheriff took the stand and told how Janie had come to his house with the doctor and how he found things when he drove out to hers.

Then they called Dr. Simmons and he told about Tea Cake's sickness and how dangerous it was to Janie and the whole town, and how he was scared for her and thought to have Tea Cake locked up in the jail, but seeing Janie's care he neglected to do it. And how he found Janie all bit in the arm, sitting on the floor and petting Tea Cake's head when he got there. And the pistol right by his hand on the floor. Then he stepped down.

"Any further evidence to present, Mr. Prescott?" the judge asked.

"No, Your Honor. The State rests."

The palm tree dance began again among the Negroes in the back. They had come to talk. The State couldn't rest until it heard.

"Mistah Prescott, Ah got somethin' tuh say," Sop-de-Bottom spoke out anonymously from the anonymous herd.

The courtroom swung round on itself to look.

"If you know what's good for you, you better shut your mouth up until somebody calls you," Mr. Prescott told him coldly.

"Yassuh, Mr. Prescott."

"We are handling this case. Another word out of *you;* out of any of you niggers back there, and I'll bind you over to the big court."

"Yassuh."

The white women made a little applause and Mr. Prescott glared at the back of the house and stepped down. Then the strange white man that was going to talk for her got up there. He whispered a little with the clerk and then called on Janie to take the stand and talk. After a few little questions he told her to tell just how it happened and to speak the truth, the whole truth and nothing but the truth. So help her God.

They all leaned over to listen while she talked. First thing she had to remember was she was not at home. She was in the courthouse fighting something and it wasn't death. It was worse than that. It was lying thoughts. She had to go way back to let them know how she and Tea Cake had been with one another so they could see she could never shoot Tea Cake out of malice.

She tried to make them see how terrible it was that things were fixed so that Tea Cake couldn't come back to himself until he had got rid of that mad dog that was in him and he couldn't get rid of the dog and live. He had to die to get rid of the dog. But she hadn't wanted to kill him. A man is up against a hard game when he must die to beat it. She made them see how she couldn't ever want to be rid of him. She didn't plead to anybody. She just sat there and told and when she was through she hushed. She had been through for some time before the judge and the lawyer and the rest seemed to know it. But she sat on in that trial chair until the lawyer told her she could come down.

"The defense rests," her lawyer said. Then he and Prescott whispered together and both of them talked to the judge in secret up high there where he sat. Then they both sat down.

"Gentlemen of the jury, it is for you to decide whether the defendant has committed a cold blooded murder or whether she is a poor broken creature, a devoted wife trapped by unfortunate circumstances who really in firing a rifle bullet into the heart of her late husband did a great act of mercy. If you find her a wanton killer you must bring in a verdict of first degree murder. If the evidence does not justify that then you must set her free. There is no middle course."

The jury filed out and the courtroom began to drone with talk, a few people got up and moved about. And Janie sat like a lump and waited. It was not death she feared. It was misunderstanding. If they made a verdict that she didn't want Tea Cake and wanted him dead, then that was a real sin and a shame. It was worse than murder. Then the jury was back again. Out five minutes by the courthouse clock.

"We find the death of Vergible Woods to be entirely accidental and justifiable, and that no blame should rest upon the defendant Janie Woods."

So she was free and the judge and everybody up there smiled with her and shook her hand. And the white women cried and stood around her like a protecting wall and the Negroes, with heads hung down, shuffled out and away. The sun was almost down and Janie had seen the sun rise on her troubled love and then she had shot Tea Cake and had been in jail and had been tried for her life and now she was free. Nothing to do with the little that was left of the day but to visit the kind white friends who had realized her feelings and thank them. So the sun went down.

She took a room at the boarding house for the night and heard the men talking around the front.

"Aw you know dem white mens wuzn't gointuh do nothin' tuh no woman dat look lak her."

"She didn't kill no white man, did she? Well, long as she don't shoot no white man she kin kill jus' as many niggers as she please."

"Yeah, de nigger women kin kill up all de mens dey wants tuh, but you bet' not kill one uh dem. De white folks will sho hang yuh if yuh do."

"Well, you know whut dey say 'uh white man and uh nigger woman is de freest thing on earth.' Dey do as dey please."

Janie buried Tea Cake in Palm Beach. She knew he loved the 'Glades but it was too low for him to lie with water maybe washing over him with every heavy rain. Anyway, the 'Glades and its waters had killed him. She wanted him out of the way of storms, so she had a strong vault built in the cemetery at West Palm Beach. Janie had wired to Orlando for money to put him away. Tea Cake was the son of Evening Sun, and nothing was too good. The undertaker did a handsome job and Tea Cake slept royally on his white silken couch among the roses she had bought. He looked almost ready to grin. Janie bought him a brand new guitar and put it in his hands. He would be thinking up new songs to play to her when she got there.

Sop and his friends had tried to hurt her but she knew it was because they loved Tea Cake and didn't understand. So she sent Sop word and to all the others through him. So the day of the funeral they came with shame and apology in their faces. They wanted her quick forgetfulness. So they filled up and overflowed the ten sedans that Janie had hired and added others to the line. Then the band played, and Tea Cake rode like a Pharaoh to his tomb. No expensive veils and robes for Janie this time. She went on in her overalls. She was too busy feeling grief to dress like grief.

Richard Wright
(1908–1960)

The recent founding of the Richard Wright Circle as an international network of scholars committed to the study of Wright's life and work is yet another signal of the regard for Wright's achievements in American and African-American literary traditions. Wright's first novel, *Native Son* (1940), was a major announcement that black fiction need no longer maintain a deferential posture; it might speak very clearly of a nation's pathologies. Wright had addressed some of these problems in his proletarian poetry of the 1930s and in his first book, *Uncle Tom's Children* (1938), a collection of short stories based on black experiences of oppression in the South, and he would deal with them again in *Twelve Million Black Voices*, a folk history, his autobiography *Black Boy* (1945), and the novel *The Long Dream* (1958). Born near Natchez, Mississippi, Wright left the South as a young man. Yet, whether he was in Chicago, New York, or living as an expatriate in Paris, his need to speak against injustices that prevailed in the South and in colonized lands was always a matter of priority. Wright was a very productive writer in the 1950s, publishing three novels (*The Outsider*, 1953; *Savage Holiday*, 1954; *The Long Dream*), three books based on his travels in Africa, Asia, and Spain (*Black Power*, 1954; *The Color Curtain*, 1956; and *Pagan Spain*, 1957), and a collection of essays *White Man, Listen!* (1957). After his death, a second collection of short fiction, *Eight Men* (1961); the first novel he wrote, *Lawd Today* (1963), and the second half of his "Black Boy" manuscript, *American Hunger* (1977) were published. Although Wright severed his ties with the Communist party at least by 1942, his analytic imagination continued to be receptive to varieties of Marxist social analysis. On the other hand, Wright was a very independent thinker and much interested in philosophies and global problems that were in a sense beyond communism. Wright's life and accomplishments are well documented in biographies by Michel Fabre, Addison Gayle, Jr., and Margaret Walker, and in critical studies by such scholars as Keneth Kinnamon, Joyce Ann Joyce, Donald Gibson, and Edward Margolies. The following short story, one of Wright's earliest, is reprinted from *Eight Men*.

The Man Who Saw the Flood

When the flood waters recede,
the poor folk along the river
start from scratch.

At last the flood waters had receded. A black father, a black mother, and a black child tramped through muddy fields, leading a tired cow by a thin bit of rope. They stopped on a hilltop and shifted the bundles on their shoulders. As far as they could see the ground was covered with flood silt. The little girl lifted a skinny finger and pointed to a mud-caked cabin.

"Look, Pa! Ain tha our home?"

The man, round-shouldered, clad in blue, ragged overalls, looked with bewildered eyes. Without moving a muscle, scarcely moving his lips, he said: "Yeah."

For five minutes they did not speak or move. The flood waters had been more than eight feet high here. Every tree, blade of grass, and stray stick had its flood mark; caky, yellow mud. It clung to the ground, cracking thinly here and there in spider web fashion. Over the stark fields came a gusty spring wind. The sky was high, blue, full of white clouds and sunshine. Over all hung a first-day strangeness.

"The henhouse is gone," sighed the woman.

"N the pigpen," sighed the man.

They spoke without bitterness.

"Ah reckon them chickens is all done drowned."

"Yeah."

"Miz Flora's house is gone, too," said the little girl.

They looked at a clump of trees where their neighbor's house had stood.

"Lawd!"

"Yuh reckon anybody knows where they is?"

"Hard t tell."

The man walked down the slope and stood uncertainly.

"There wuz a road erlong here somewheres," he said.

But there was no road now. Just a wide sweep of yellow, scalloped silt.

"Look, Tom!" called the woman. "Here's a piece of our gate!"

The gatepost was half buried in the ground. A rusty hinge stood stiff, like a lonely finger. Tom pried it loose and caught it firmly in his hand. There was nothing particular he wanted to do with it; he just stood holding it firmly. Finally he dropped it, looked up, and said:

"C mon. Les go down n see whut we kin do."

Because it sat in a slight depression, the ground about the cabin was soft and slimy.

"Gimme the bag o lime, May," he said.

With his shoes sucking in mud, he went slowly around the cabin, spreading the white lime with thick fingers. When he reached the front again he had a little left; he shook the bag out on the porch. The fine grains of floating lime flickered in the sunlight.

"Tha oughta hep some," he said.

"Now, yuh be careful, Sal!" said May. "Don yuh go n fall down in all this mud, yuh hear?"

"Yessum."

The steps were gone. Tom lifted May and Sally to the porch. They stood a moment looking at the half-opened door. He had shut it when he left, but somehow it seemed natural that he should find it open. The planks in the porch floor were swollen and warped. The cabin had two colors; near the bottom it was a solid yellow; at the top it was the familiar gray. It looked weird, as though its ghost were standing beside it.

The cow lowed.

"Tie Pat t the pos on the en of the porch, May."

May tied the rope slowly, listlessly. When they attempted to open the front door, it would not budge. It was not until Tom placed his shoulder against it and gave it a stout shove that it scraped back jerkily. The front room was dark and silent. The damp smell of flood silt came fresh and sharp to their nostrils. Only one-half of the upper window was clear, and through it fell a rectangle of dingy light. The floors swam in ooze. Like a mute warning, a wavering flood mark went high around the walls of the room. A dresser sat cater-cornered, its drawers and sides bulging like a bloated corpse. The bed, with the mattress still on it, was like a giant casket forged of mud. Two smashed chairs lay in a corner, as though huddled together for protection.

"Les see the kitchen," said Tom.

The stovepipe was gone. But the stove stood in the same place.

"The stove's still good. We kin clean it."

"Yeah."

"But where's the table?"

"Lawd knows."

"It must've washed erway wid the rest of the stuff, Ah reckon."

They opened the back door and looked out. They missed the barn, the henhouse, and the pigpen.

"Tom, yuh bettah try tha ol pump n see if eny watah's there."

The pump was stiff. Tom threw his weight on the handle and carried it up and down. No water came. He pumped on. There was a dry, hollow cough. Then yellow water trickled. He caught his breath and kept pumping. The water flowed white.

"Thank Gawd! We's got some watah. Yuh bettah boil it fo yuh use it," he said.

"Yeah. Ah know."

"Look, Pa! Here's yo ax," called Sally.

Tom took the ax from her. "Yeah. Ah'll need this."

"N here's somethin else," called Sally, digging spoons out of the mud.

"Waal, Ahma git a bucket n start cleanin," said May. "Ain no use in waitin, cause we's gotta sleep on them floors tonight."

When she was filling the bucket from the pump, Tom called from around the cabin. "May, look! Ah done foun mah plow!" Proudly he dragged the silt-caked plow to the pump. "Ah'll wash it n it'll be awright."

"Ahm hongry," said Sally.

"Now, yuh jus wait! Yuh et this mawnin," said May. She turned to Tom. "Now, whutcha gonna do, Tom?"

He stood looking at the mud-filled fields.

"Yuh goin back t Burgess?"

"Ah reckon Ah have to."

"Whut else kin yuh do?"

"Nothin," he said. "Lawd, but Ah sho hate t start all over wid tha white man. Ah'd leave here ef Ah could. Ah owes im nigh eight hundred dollahs. N we needs a hoss, grub, seed, n a lot mo other things. Ef we keeps on like this tha white man'll own us body n soul."

"But, Tom, there ain nothin else t do," she said.

"Ef we try t run erway they'll put us in jail."

"It coulda been worse," she said.

Sally came running from the kitchen. "Pa!"

"Hunh?"

"There's a shelf in the kitchen the flood didn git!"

"Where?"

"Right up over the stove."

"But, chile, ain nothin' up there," said May.

"But there's somethin on it," said Sally.

"C mon. Les see."

High and dry, untouched by the flood-water, was a box of matches. And beside it a half-full sack of Bull Durham tobacco. He took a match from the box and scratched it on his overalls. It burned to his fingers before he dropped it.

"May!"

"Hunh?"

"Look! Here's ma bacco n some matches!"

She stared unbelievingly. "Lawd!" she breathed.

Tom rolled a cigarette clumsily.

May washed the stove, gathered some sticks, and after some difficulty, made a fire. The kitchen stove smoked, and their eyes smarted. May put water on to heat and went into the front room. It was getting dark. From the bundles they took a kerosene lamp and lit it. Outside Pat lowed longingly into the thickening gloam and tinkled her cowbell.

"Tha old cow's hongry," said May.

"Ah reckon Ah'll have t be gittin erlong t Burgess."

They stood on the front porch.

"Yuh bettah git on, Tom, fo it gits too dark."

"Yeah."

The wind had stopped blowing. In the east a cluster of stars hung.

"Yuh goin, Tom?"

"Ah reckon Ah have t."

"Ma, Ah'm hongry," said Sally.

"Wait erwhile, honey. Ma knows yuh's hongry."

Tom threw his cigarette away and sighed.

"Look! Here comes somebody!"

"Thas Mistah Burgess now!"

A mud-caked buggy rolled up. The shaggy horse was splattered all over. Burgess leaned his white face out of the buggy and spat.

"Well, I see you're back."

"Yessuh."

"How things look?"

"They don look so good, Mistah."

"What seems to be the trouble?"

"Waal. Ah ain got no hoss, no grub, nothin. The only thing Ah got is tha ol cow there . . ."

"You owe eight hundred dollahs down at the store, Tom."

"Yessuh, Ah know. But, Mistah Burgess, can't yuh knock somethin off of tha, seein as how Ahm down n out now?"

"You ate that grub, and I got to pay for it, Tom."

"Yessuh, Ah know."

"It's goin to be a little tough, Tom. But you got to go through with it. Two of the boys tried to run away this morning and dodge their debts, and I had to have the sheriff pick em up. I wasn't looking for no trouble out of you, Tom . . . The rest of the families are going back."

Leaning out of the buggy, Burgess waited. In the surrounding stillness the cowbell tinkled again. Tom stood with his back against a post.

"Yuh got t go on, Tom. We ain't got nothin here," said May.

Tom looked at Burgess.

"Mistah Burgess, Ah don wanna make no trouble. But this is jus *too* hard. Ahm worse off now than befo. Ah got to start from scratch."

"Get in the buggy and come with me. I'll stake you with grub. We can talk over how you can pay it back." Tom said nothing. He rested his back against the post and looked at the mud-filled fields.

"Well," asked Burgess. "You coming?" Tom said nothing. He got slowly to the ground and pulled himself into the buggy. May watched them drive off.

"Hurry back, Tom!"

"Awright."

"Ma, tell Pa t bring me some 'lasses," begged Sally.

"Oh, Tom!"

Tom's head came out of the side of the buggy.

"Hunh?"

"Bring some 'lasses!"

"Hunh?"

"Bring some 'lasses for Sal!"

"Awright!"

She watched the buggy disappear over the crest of the muddy hill. Then she sighed, caught Sally's hand, and turned back into the cabin.

Jean Toomer
(1894–1967)

Until recently, Toomer's reputation was based mainly on *Cane* (1923), one of the great works of experimental modernist literature to emerge during the Harlem Renaissance period. With the publication of *The Wayward and the Seeking: A Collection of Writings by Jean Toomer*, edited by Darwin T. Turner; Nellie McKay's *Jean Toomer, Artist: A Study of His Literary Life and Work 1894–1936*; and *The Lives of Jean Toomer: A Hunger for Wholeness* by Cynthia E. Kerman and Richard Eldridge, as well as an increasing number of critical essays, there is the promise that Toomer's considerable body of works will gain more prominence in discussion of African-American literary history. Born in Washington, D.C., Toomer was fascinated and confused by his mixed ancestry. By 1918 Toomer's sketches, poems, and reviews began to appear in national magazines. He taught for a brief period in Georgia, and his intense response to blacks in the rural South and to his own ancestry led to the creation of *Cane*. After the publication of this groundbreaking book, Toomer had great difficulty in getting work published. He finally settled into a reclusive existence in Bucks County, Pennsylvania. "Withered Skin of Berries" is reprinted from *The Wayward and the Seeking*.

Withered Skin of Berries

CHAPTER ONE

Men listen to her lispings and murmurs. Black souls steal back to Georgia canefields, soft and misty, underneath a crescent moon. The mystery of their whispered promises seems close to revelation, seems tangibly incarnate in her. Black souls, tropic and fiery, dream of love. Sing joyful codas to forgotten folk-songs. Spin love to the soft weaving of her arms. Men listen to her lispings and murmurs. White souls awake to adolescent fantasies they thought long buried with the dead leaves along the summer streets of mid-western towns. Solvents of melancholy burn through their bitten modes of pioneer aggressiveness to a southern repose. They too spin love to the soft weaving of her arms. White men, black men, only in retrospective kisses, know the looseness of her lips . . . pale withered skin of berries . . .

*   *   *

Departmental buildings are grey gastronomic structures, innocuously coated with bile. They pollute the breath of Washington. Washington's breath is sickish and stale because of them. With the slow, retarded process of dyspeptics, they suck the life of mediocrities. They secrete a strange preservative that keeps flesh and bones intact after the blood is dry . . . Vera is a typist. She is a virgin. A virgin whose notion of purity tape-worms her. Men sense her corporeal virginity. Her slim body, her olive skin, clear as white grapes held to the sun, are pure. Sandalwood odor of her thick brown hair, the supplication of her eyes, her lifeless lips, all pure. Men like to paw pure bodies. They adore them. So Vera came to find out. "They only want to paw me." She blamed the beast in men, black men especially. Pure bodies tease. So the men found out. "Vera is a tease." The thought found its way to her. She set up her creed: Tease the beast . . . Vera is a typist. She is neither more nor less palatable than the other morsels that come in from South Carolina, Illinois, or Oregon. But there is a condiment-like irritability in the process of her digestion. Unquestionably, Vera is white. Routine segregates niggers. Black life seems more soluble in lump. White life, pitiably agitated to superiority, is more palatable. Black life is pepper to the salt of white. Pepper in the nose of white. Sneezes are first-rate aids to digestion. Unquestionably, Vera is white. Her fellow workers sneeze about the niggers. Niggers are all right as janitors, as messengers; in fact, anywhere they keep their place. Niggers, despite their smell and flat feet, aren't so bad. They are good to joke about. Sneezes over colored girls using powder and straightening their kinky hair to look like white. But it is a different thing when niggers try to pass for white. They are slick at it. Youve got to watch out. But there is always a way of telling: finger-nails, and eyes, and odor, and oh, any number of things. Vera listens to them, smiles, jokes, laughs, sometimes with a curious gurgle-like flutter, says goodby to them of evenings outside the office door, and rides uptown to the respite of a Negro home.

Carl. A fellow in the office. From a small town across the lake from Chicago where his father is an independent dealer in oil. Carl got in the government service to earn a little money against the coming of a dream he had. He would be rich some day—when his uncle died. He had plans for the conquest of the Argentine. He had studied agriculture at Wisconsin. He read books, and even took a correspondence course in foreign trade. Spanish he was learning from Cortina. He went out of his way to pick acquaintances with South Americans, Spaniards, and Portuguese. This trait it was that first led him to Vera. She looked Spanish. Casual remarks led to their having lunch together. Carl was sincere. He held roseate and chivalrous notions of womanhood. His enthusiasm bid well to hold out, for a time, against the stale utilitarian atmosphere of governmental Washington. In the office, and during the brief strolls they had after lunch, the inward anemia of Vera fed on it. She liked him. She established a sort of moral equilibrium and dulled a growing sense of deceit by resolving not to tease him. Carl wanted to take her home, to call on her, to take her to the movies, to Penn Gardens, to the dances the office gave. She put him off. Her soft reticence and sly evasions implied purity, evoked an aura of desirability and charm. Carl was buying a car, a Dodge. One afternoon in early spring the departments were given a holiday. It was unexpected. Vera could not possibly have any plans for it, and Carl told her so. He insisted on the falsity of the reasons she gave for refusing to drive with him. Vera was more than usually nervous that day. Carl's stubbornness irritated her. She felt herself getting hot, as if her nerves were heated pins and needles pricking her. That would not do. Carl's friendship made the office tolerable. He took hold of her arm. Vera went with him.

Driving down Seventeenth Street, Carl only spoke to call the names of buildings. That was the Corcoran Gallery of Art, that, the Pan-American building. Negroes were working on the basin of an artificial lake that was to spread its smooth glass surface before Lincoln's Memorial. The shadow of their emancipator stirred them neither to bitterness nor awe. The scene was a photograph on Vera's eye-balls. Carl was concentrated on the road. He squirmed skillfully in the traffic that was getting dense. The exotic fragrance of cherry blossoms reached them, slightly rancid as it mingled with the odor of exploded gasoline. As they passed the crescent line of blossomed trees, a group of Japanese, hats off, were seen reverently lost in race memories of reed lutes, jet black eyebrows, and jeweled palanquins. Consciously, the episode meant nothing to Vera. But an unprecedented nostalgia, a promise of awakening, making her feel faint, clutched her throat almost to stricture, and made her swallow hard. Her face was pallid. Carl noticed it and said he guessed it was the heat from the engine and the motion of the car . . . A word was struggling with her throat . . . They swung into the speedway. Potomac's water was muddy, streaked with sea-weed. A tug, drawing a canal barge from miles in the interior, blew its whistle for the bridge to turn and let it by. Across the river, the green, and white marble splotches of Virginia's hills. Curious for her, lines of a poem came unbidden to her mind:

> far-off trees
> Whose gloom is rounded like the hives of bees
> All humming peace to soldiers who have gone.

She was trying to think where she had heard them. They hadnt impressed her at the time. No poems ever did. She would not let them. A word was struggling with her throat . . . Carl called her attention to the superb grace of a Pierce Arrow that glided by. They had reached the point. A hydroplane was humming high above the War College.—That man, what was his name? Who Arthur Bond introduced to me the other night. Who hardly noticed me, he was so stuck up. Whom Art called a genius, and the poet of Washington. The lines, she felt sure, were his. Yes, Art had recited them.—What was his name? He had irritated her. He was closed up in himself. She had felt she could not tease him.—Well, so much the worse for Art Bond. What was his name? Men were fishing, casting their lines from the river wall. Straight ahead, between low banks of trees, the Potomac rolled its muddy course, and, miles away, emptied into the Chesapeake. Smoke from Alexandria was blown up-stream by the river breeze.

"What do you say we run out the Conduit road to Cabin John's and make a day of it?"

Vera answered automatically.

"Sorry I cant to-day. I have an engagement at eight."

"Youve broken what should have been mine enough to break one date with him."

The almost perfect white of his skin was flushed, and rubbed to glowing by the wind. The hair he brushed so smooth was free and rumpled. His grey eyes were eagerly expectant. Vera's seemed to be glowing with prana. The coils of her hair threatened to uncurl and stream out backward like loose waves of silken bunting. Her skirt, rustling and flapping, was pressed close to her thighs.

"What do you say? We'll have dinner there, and afterwards go on to Great Falls. It would be a crime to waste a day like this."

Bud of a word was bursting in her throat.

"Beautiful!"

"Good. I knew youd go. Come on, lets get on our way."

"It is a word I've never said before."

"You bet it is. But youve said it now—no more holding off like you used to do. 'Yes' is a word that once said can be said again. Oh I knew you would someday, Vera, but what made you wait so long? Look at the good times we have already missed. Come on. Lets make up for lost time."

Carl held her hand and was propelling her. A little startled, she looked at him.

"Where are you pulling me, Carl?"

That was a good move on Vera's part. Carl had never seen her playful. Good. He'd play the game.

"To the sand-dunes of Lake Michigan where two loves build a bungalow."

"Really, Carl, I mean it. Where are you pulling me to?"

A fly-like shadow of doubt lit on Carl. He tossed his head, and drove it off.

"Just where I said: to the sand-dunes, where rippling waves make music all the time."

Vera realized that she must have promised something. Well, why not. She let herself be pulled. She'd cover herself with play. Her hair uncurled.

"Beautiful Michigan's azure waves—"

"Fine! Sweet! O poetess of Benton Harbor!"

"How many rooms will the bungalow be?"

Carl was completely red.

"Three."

Shadows of clouds, lazy-like, were gliding over the canopy-trees of the Potomac palisades. Below, the river, eddying in shallows, churning to a cream foam against mud-colored rocks, was carrying the brown burden of a wasted sediment . . . John Brown's body . . . from Harper's Ferry to the Chesapeake and the sea. Carl and Vera spun along the smooth asphalt of Conduit Road. The country beside the pike was dotted now and then by clustered shanties— poor white homes. Carl was quite happily absorbed in the handling of his car. It was vaguely good to have her there beside him. Vera, since she had come with him, would have been hurt to know her temporary relegation to the position of a pleasant accessory. Silence released her for the uncertain attempt at recapturing a mood which, save as an unreal memory, was new and strange to her. Art Bond . . . What was his name? What dreams she had had, always swerved up from the concrete image of a man. The mood that had struggled to a hesitant and spattered ecstasy, that had forced some unused crevice of her soul to a vocalization of beauty, came from—What was his . . . ? She could not tease him. That hurt her. She had thrust him from her mind. Even his image would not come. The mood lay fallow before the unfound symbol of its evocation.

Carl was chatting over his cigarettes and cheese and coffee.

"You are sympathetic, Vera, and you'll understand. America, now the war is over, don't give a young fellow with push and brains and energy half a chance. Of course you can make money with a million. It makes itself. But what I want is not to loaf around and see it grow, or get tied down to some machine where even if you are a captain of industry youre no more than a petty officer in the army. Thats not what America stands for; but its what it is. And going to be more so in the future. The spirit of the country is one of individual enterprise. But unless it be in the oil-fields—and there the Standard gets you—its dying out, or, rather, its passing on to new lands. Now the Argentine is virginal. Or if not the Argentine, then some of those smaller countries. Theyre now just where this country was when Vanderbilt and Carnegie and Rockefeller first came up. Why a young fellow with go can go down there and clean up. But he's got to be quick about it. Ford and other men are pushing out over the world . . . It sounds hard to say it, but I wish the Uncle would hurry up—and do whatever he's going to do. I'm studying hard—and say, Vera, heres where you can help me if you will. Lets talk Spanish when we're together. I don't know so much yet, but you can help me."

"I'd like to Carl, but I dont know any more Spanish than you do."

"But I thought—"

"If someone has told you that I am of Spanish descent, its true. My great grandfather was a Spaniard, but I was born in America, just like you. English is the only language that I know. Except for the smattering of others that I've picked up in school."

"I didnt think that you acted like a foreigner. Theyre all right, you know. I'm not prejudiced against them like I am against the niggers. A couple of them are friends of mine. Foreigners, I mean. But they do act a little different."

"Why do you hate niggers?"

"Hang if I know. Dont you?"

"Sometimes."

White Male Sexuality

"Of course I dont hate them like these southern fellows do. And not as much as I hate Jews. The kikes are spreading all over the country; you see their names everywhere. There was one I remember at Wisconsin. He went out for football. We tried to break him up. And then there was Bugger—thats what we called the nigger—he was a good sort of fellow, and we had good fun with him. A good linesman—tackle he was—but he didnt make the team. Ever been to Madison, Vera? Swell place. Ideal location for a college town. A few snobs like there are everywhere, but most of the men came from the middle-west—good fellows, Vera. Youd like them. And there was one colored fellow I remember—say, did you ever see Sang Osmond run? Conference quarter miler from Chicago. I ran against him once. Clean cut fellow, good sport—I liked him. Niggers arent so bad, if only they didnt look so."

"All colored people arent disagreeable—"

"No, of course not. Theres Osmond. But you cant judge people by their exceptions. Look what we would have come to if we'd tried to believe that all Germans toed the mark of a man, say, like Beethoven."

"Why judge at all?"

"Good lord, Vera, youve got to have something to go by. Take me, when I go down into South America. I'll feel superior to those greasers—all Americans do. And thats the reason why we're running things. . . . Come on, lets get out of here and run up to the falls before it gets too dark."

"Dont forget that I have an engagement at eight."

"Hang it, Vera, I thought youd broken it."

"That wouldnt be right, Carl. You wouldnt want me to break one with you. I've been with you all day. And there are other times."

She had meant to make this the first and last.

"All right. Its a go. We'll make it Friday. Dance some place, and then take a drive. Thats closed. Come on, lets hurry up."

Carl paid the waiter.

The Dodge was purring along towards Great Falls.

Parked. They crossed a narrow springy toll-bridge into the clump of wood that vibrates like a G-string to the deep bass of the falls. Dusk, subtly scented violet, sprayed through the scant foliage of clustered trees. Carl's skin was of a greenish pallor. Vera's, almost as purple as the dusk. The agitation of the ground, the fall's thunder, conjured the sense of an impending lightning. Vera shivered. Carl drew her close to him. As they walked, she began to fancy she saw things behind the trunks and rocks, hiding in the bushes. A twig cracked. Vera's jumping upset Carl. But only for a moment. The heavy pounding of the falls was getting nearer. Quarter heaven in the west, the evening star. She pressed his arm. He was holding her waist. Slender, supple waist, trembling at unseen tremors in the forest. Carl would walk in many forests. Across great wastes and plains. The pampa grass, great stationary sea. Villages of untamed Indians. Stealthy marauding savages. This little wood near Washington was tame. Vera, for no reason, vaguely thought of Africa. She shivered. Carl stopped in their now winding path, and kissed her. Her lips were cool. Carl

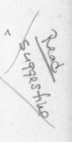

Jews

What the statement does. it say. Politics/ Military Domination.

Read suggestive

To 42

did not think of them as pale withered skin of berries. They reached the high-piled rocks. Footing was insecure. Vera stumbled. Carl lifted her in his arms. Carrying her, he almost fell over lovers hidden in the alcove of a giant boulder. With apologies, he moved on some paces, and set her down. The falls were below them. The foam, the dark suggestion of whirlpools, were weird, wildly arush. One's shouting voice was barely heard above a whisper. Vera leaned against him. Her mind was blank. It was just good to be held in his arms. A flickering light, a torch perhaps, flared up on the other bank. An intangibly phosphorescent glow gave light. Sandalwood odor of hair. Carl's conscious mind had not planned on love. With a million coming, things could wait. It came. Love was a tender joy, protective-like, that gave soft scents of sandalwood above the din of churning waters, beneath the chaste fire of the evening star.

They too had found a boulder. One's voice could be heard. Vera seated Indian fashion, responding, perhaps, to some folk persuasion of the place, rested Carl's head in her lap. Carl had been talking brokenly, trying to tell himself just how he felt. Her holding him made it easier to think. If it was love, it was curiously without passion. Passion was not love; but it was a part of it. One should pretend not to feel too much until one was married. But hiding it, and not feeling it at all, were two different things. "Once at Madison," he said aloud to Vera, "I felt like this." Her mind wanted Vera to listen. She must not tease or play with him.—Tease Art Bond though. Its almost time, it must be time, for my date with him. What was his name? O wont you come to me. Poet. I will not admit that he ever did or ever could hurt me. Oh yes and just you wait, I'll tease him too. Him whom I cannot tease. Who put beauty, a senseless warm thing like a sucking baby, in my mouth.
"I have never said it before."
"Said what, Vera?"
"Oh, nothing."
"As I was saying, he was an odd sort of chap. Peculiar, and most of the fellows resented it. It wasn't that he was stuck up. We couldnt see any reason why he should be. Enough money, but not too much at that. And I dont guess his folks were anything to brag about. He never mentioned them. In fact he never mentioned anything unless you sort of forced him to it. It looked as though he was acting up to mystery, and all that sort of thing. And then he was dark, and that made some difference. I gave him the duck until it came to summer school and myself and two other fellows from the frat moved over to the Y and on the sleeping porch I found myself in the bed next to him. We got to talking, and walking up the hill together. One day he asked me if I'd like to sail with him, him and two girls. He was strong for girls. That started it. And say, you should have seen him with that boat, as neat as I can handle a six-horse plow. We went to dances, and swam around a bit. One night he took me in his canoe. Just him and I. The moon was shining. When we got out in the middle of the lake, he slid down on the bottom, on the cushions, and began to hum. Yodels and singing were coming from canoes all over the water. I didn't notice him at first. And then, something like a

warm finger seemed to touch my heart. I cant just explain it. I looked around and saw him. His eyes, set in that dark face, looked like two stars. 'Put the paddle in,' he said, 'we'll drift.' I did. 'Turn around and slide over the bar, theres a cushion on the bottom for you,' he then said. He saw me try, tip the canoe, and hesitate. 'Come on, dont be afraid, youre with an Indian, pale-face friend.' Saying that, way out in the middle of the lake, surrounded by shores that were once the home of Indians, made me feel strange and queer, you bet. Lights gleaming from the boat-house were far to shore. I made it, and again he started humming. 'Are you an Indian, really?' I asked. He kept on humming. And God if it didnt raise a lump the size of an apple in my throat. 'Whats that?' I asked. 'A negro folk-song,' he stopped long enough to say. 'God, I didnt know niggers could sing like that.' An answer, I guess, wasnt necessary. Abruptly he stopped singing, and I could feel him quiver-like—"

—He does not paw me. His arms embrace the shadow of a dream. I cannot tease him. His dream is a solvent of my resolution. He has taken something from me. It will be hard to face the office. I'd like to hate him for it. Easier to face the office because I share his dream. Will it melt something in me? Why cant I feel? If Art Bond should dream, I could not tease him. Time to go. What was his name? Will no one ever awake a dream in me? Poet. He must be like the fellow Carl is talking about. Him whom I cannot tease. What is his name? Who put beauty, a senseless warm thing like a sucking baby, in my mouth.

"I have never said that before."

"There you go again. Said what, Vera? Youre not listening."

"Oh nothing. Yes I am. Go on, Carl."

"I could feel him quiver-like. 'Carl,' he said, his eyes were gleaming, 'the wonder and mystery of it.' I had a quick foolish notion that he was trying to play up to the role we'd given him. Then I think I began to feel like he did. 'Dead leaves of northern Europe, Carl, have decayed for roots tangled here in America. Roots thrusting up a stark fresh life. Thats you. Multi-colored leaves, tropic, temperate, have decayed for me. We meet here where a race has died for both of us. Only a few years ago, forests and fields, this lake, Mendota, heard the corn and hunting songs of a vanished people. They have resolved their individualism to the common stream. We live on it. We live on them. And we are growing. Life lives on itself and grows . . . The mystery and wonder of it.' He paused. And then, 'Deep River spreads over Mendota. Whirl up and dance above them new world soul!' God if he hadnt stirred me. Songs, and young girls' voices yodeling, criss-crossed on the waters. He turned to me and asked, 'Carl, you are a field man, have you ever felt overpowered by the sum of something, of which plowed fields, blue sky, and sunset were a part, overpowered till you sank choking with wonder and reverence?' I had, almost, once. I told him. He closed his hand over mine. Me, a football man, holding hands with a man on the lake. If that had ever got out it would have done for me. But it never did. I could never tell it. Only to you. You are the first. And thats the point of all I've told you. I feel like that with you, here by the falls, in the shadow of a boulder where some Indian made love.''

Carl's words were strange to him.

Vera shivered.

''Chilly?''

''A little.''

Carl shifted positions and took her in his arms. He kissed her lips . . . pale withered skin of berries, puckered a little tight . . . and drew her to him with a tension that was more muscular than passionate . . .

> John Brown's body, rumbles in the river,
> John Brown's body, thunders down the falls . . .

''What was that Carl?''

''I didnt hear a thing, sweetheart.''

It would be good to fall in love with Carl, really. With anybody. Tease? Her mind said that because no man torrential enough—but there had been men, men with swift brutal passions—they didnt love. They bruised her with their instincts, bruised and frightened and disgusted her . . . she must keep her body pure . . . Carl didnt paw. He loved as she had long wanted men to. Why couldnt she feel? She recalled that she had not had a genuine emotion in the presence of a man . . . at night, when she was alone . . . since her last affair at home. Ugly. Why were men so callous? Brutal in insisting on her sacrifice. Then they wouldnt want her . . . she must keep her body pure. Why couldnt she feel? This was pure love. Why couldnt she feel to return it? Feel for him the emotion that had spattered in ''beautiful.'' Perhaps—Vera, lead in her heart, faced the possibility, that, for some unknown reason, maybe she really couldnt love. Some shameful defect made her incapable of it. She pressed Carl close to her. Held him to her lips. Tensioned thighs. Her heart beat faster. She strained. Carl's strength was tender. Why couldnt she feel? Something in her felt like it was empty. Men poured themselves into her because she was empty . . .

''Its time to go, now, Carl.''

''I had forgotten. Of course, sweetheart.''

Deep bass of the falls seemed coming from a throat that had been turned the other way . . . John Brown's body . . . They crossed the toll-bridge and found their car.

As Carl swung into S Street from Sixteenth, Vera saw Art Bond come out of her gate, and walk their way. The car passed. He did not see them. With a hasty goodby she ran up the steps and waited in the vestibule until Carl had gone. Coming down, Vera called to Art who was standing, undecided, on the corner. He seemed impersonalized, a shadow, beneath the great bulk of the Masonic Temple.

''I had a car, and everything,'' Art was irritably saying.

''I'm sorry Art, I tried to be on time. Is it so very late?''

''How'd you get in anyway? Was that you in that car?''

"I dropped from the stars."

"It was a Dodge. Whose was it? Dave Teyy's?"

"What a simple name!"

Her eyes were sparkling.

"I dont guess its too late yet; that is, if you really want to go."

"And I have been searching. Oh how I have been searching all afternoon."
Vera seemed talking to the apex of the Temple.

"Now whats the use of lying, Vera? You could have found me easy enough
if you wanted to."

"David Teyy."

"Oh hang him, Vera. Youre with me now. That is, if you want to go."

Vera looked down into a dark serious face, mobile and expressive, like
shifting, sun-shot dusk.

"Of course I want to go, Art. Where's the car?"

"Can I use your phone a minute?"

Vera was hard to talk to, hard to touch to-night. It was to lead her into a
mood for loving when they reached the park that Art had hired a car. The
Cadillac had hummed up Sixteenth Street, like a shuttle, between the Castle
and Meridian Hill, past the portentous embassies. Turning, it had followed the
curve of Park Road, across the broad bridge blanketed in a chill vapor. Down
the hill, hemmed in by the quickening life of Rock Creek Park. The driver
had been dismissed and told to return within an hour. During the whole ride
Vera seemed absorbed in herself, and kept to her corner of the car. The wind
whistled on the sharp edge of an invisible partition that was between them.
Now they sat, Vera hugging her knees, on the slope of a knoll within earshot
of the purling of the creek. Great curved massy trees in sharp planes of shadow
and moonlight. Mountain clouds, fleecy silver. Massive undulations, barely
perceptible—earth's respiration, earth breathing to life. Vera felt dwarfed. She
felt that Art could be of no aid to her. Dwarfed by the great heaving blocks of nature.
By the shadow of a man. David Teyy. He should be riding the backs of trees, spur-
ring them to swing up and trumpet. Him whom she could not tease. Who put
beauty, a senseless warm thing like a sucking baby—Suppose I cannot love him?
The thought gave her a sinking feeling, and made her shiver.

"Chilly."

"A little."

Art tucked a robe around her shoulder. He stretched out, lit a cigarette.
Women were like that; you had to wait for them. Vera was thankful for the
glow of Art's cigarette. It was a small point one could look at. Narrowing her
eyes, Art's face looked like a far-off mountain, faintly ruddy, beneath the
supernal glowing of a red star. Black man, white man, lips seeking love, souls
dreaming . . . Man of the multi-colored leaves, dreaming, will your lips seek
love? Vera raised her hand, delicate, tapering olive fingers, and pressed it
against her lips . . . pale withered skin of berries . . . The contact was loose
and cool. Her heart sank. She shivered. Art reached up and pulled her down
beside him.

"Whats the matter, sugar?"

"Nothing, only I dont feel so well to-night."

"Driving all afternoon should have done better for you than that. And with Dave Teyy."

"I wasnt with him, Art."

"Now whats the use of lying, Vera?"

"I tell you I wasnt."

"Oh well, dont lets scrap about it. He's my friend. But I've got to bar him with my girls. He doesnt believe in letting them out."

"What do you mean?"

"You know what I mean."

"Well, he let me out."

"I thought you wasnt with him."

"Art, you are so stupid when you fuss. Why dont you sing, or . . . love me?"

"You irritate me. You wont let me."

"There, there. Thats a good sweet boy."

Vera, softly weaving arms. Sandalwood odor of hair. Murmurs. Lispings. Art's arms tightened around her. Vera averted her lips. He kissed her throat. Caught a soft fold in his teeth and bit it.

"You mustnt Art."

"Mustnt love you?"

"Not that way . . . O cant you see I'm empty . . . Art, Art I'm empty, fill me with dreams."

"With love."

"No, with dreams. Dreams of how life grows, feeding on itself. Dreams of dead leaves, multi-colored leaves. Dreams of leaves decaying for a vernal stalk, phosphorescent in the dusk, flaming in dawn. O Art, in that South from which you come, under its hates and lynchings, have you no lake, no river, no falls to sit beside and dream . . . dream?"

"Red dust roads are our rivers, the swishing of the cane, our falls. I am an inland man."

"Then you have choked with the sum—O tell me, Art, tell me, I know you have."

"Beside the syrup-man?"

"Beside the syrup-man."

"He comes to boil the cane when the harvest is through. He pitches camp in a clearing of the wood. You smell only the pines at first, and saw-dust smoke. Then a mule, circling with a beam, begins to grind. The syrup, toted in a barrel, is poured on the copper boiling stove. Then you begin to smell the cane. It goes to your head like wine. Men are seated round. Some chewing cane-stalk, some with snuff. They tell tales, gossip about the white folks, and about moonshine licker. The syrup-man (his clothes look like a crazy-quilt and smell sweetish) with his ladle is the center of them. His face is lit by the glow. He is the ju-ju man. Sometimes he sings, and then they all commence to singing. But after a while you dont notice them. Your soul rises with the smoke and songs above the pine-trees. Once mine rose up, and, instead of travelling about the heavens, looked down. I saw my body there, seated with the other men. As I looked, it seemed to dissolve, and melt with the others that were dissolving too. They were a stream. They flowed up-stream from Africa and way up to a height where the light was so bright I could hardly see, burst into a multi-colored spraying fountain. My throat got tight. I guess it was that that pulled me back into myself—"

—This black man from the South has choked with beauty. He does not paw me. His arms embrace the shadow of a dream. I cannot tease him. Why cant I feel? David Teyy. Can I love him? Vera shivered. Art drew her closer to him. Her arms tightened like strong slender vines across his back. Lips met. Something was tautening her lip-strings to the firmness of a bow. Their thighs were vines. Her heart beat faster. She strained. Art was a wedge . . . she tried to push loose . . . a black wedge of hot red life, cleaving. Arms strained against his chest. Wedge . . . cleaving . . . Trees whirl! Stab. Stampede. Spinning planes, shadow, silver. Night thrust back before a burning light. They were rolling, over, over, down the hill. Trees stand still, glowering, in a stationary sky. Trees continuing to whirl. Art's lips still clung to her. She clawed his face. Pushed at his eye. Her face was wet and grass streaked. Weeds tangled in her uncurled hair. She clawed his face.

"You are a beast. O let me go."

Wedge trying to cleave her.

"Black nigger beast."

Art swung loose, and as if a lash had cut him, groaned. Whip him lash! Art groaned, choked, groaned. Shrinking on a slave-block black man groan! His head swung loose as if his neck had been wrenched . . . Vera couldnt think what she had done to him. Her eyes were dizzy pendulums of her soul.

"Art . . ."

". . . Go way . . . go way . . . ohhh."

"Art, what have I—"

"Go way . . . go way . . . ohhh . . . Go way . . . O why dont you go way . . ."

"Art, Art, have I hurt you so? O Art have I hurt you so?"

He sprang to his feet. Vera hoped he would hit her. Swung off across the road, crashed through the bushes, going towards the creek. John Brown's body . . . she heard him splashing through the creek . . . thunders down the falls.

Vera buried her teeth in the ground to steady the convulsions of her sobbing.

CHAPTER TWO

Vera was walking down Sixteenth Street to work. Young green leaves looked yellow in the thick flood of sunlight. Morning, clover-sweet and ruddy; melancholy morning. Vera's buoyancy seemed to rest on a nervous and slightly unreal basis. She tried to rid herself of this curious haze by walking. The muscles of her limbs were firm, the skin of her face, flushed and tight. Men passing in sleek expensive cars turned to look at her. Memory of Art was a stinging insect, aflutter, pinned down . . . that it was not dead denied by her will. Carl. Carl had proposed to her. She'd put him off. Vera tried to write to her mother. That she could not bring herself to do it gave her a sense of isolation so swift and intolerable that she had rushed from the house, impotently dreading, as in a bad dream. She hid from herself in desperately trivial details of office work. And then, a vicarious peace was vouchsafed her by the innocent loveliness of external Washington. The well-paved streets, the rows of comfortable, inconspicuous houses, the men and women that walked and lived in them, established a perfect sympathy with her in her attempt to defer a settlement with life. If life would only let her alone—save when she beckoned to it. Vera was too aware of her physical loveliness to desire a complete negation. Walking to work helped her to put off. Moving pictures, dances, men whom she could handle. David Teyy. She feared to see him. As a dream, he could be evoked, a final recourse, in dispelling the evil of a too-insistent nightmare. This morning, Vera had no need of David Teyy. The young green leaves looked yellow. The air was sweet with clover. The Masonic Temple, receding over her left shoulder, was a granite chrysalis that had emerged from the mystery of moonlight and shadow into the solid implications of day. A car, full of young girls in brilliant scarfs and sport shoes, drew up to the curb. Vera heard someone call her name. One or two, she slightly recognized. Just a bunch driving to [the] office. Would she go along? They were happy about nothing. Vera caught their spirit. She reached the office tingling and aglow. Anemic thin odor of stale tobacco. She went from sash to sash, throwing up the windows. A digested fellow came in, changed his street-coat for one that had been worn glossy and thread-bare, grumbled at the draft that was coming in, cancelled Vera's efforts for fresh air with quick successive bangs, went to his desk, opened a drawer from which exuded a musty smell, drew out some papers, sharpened his pencils, and, with an habitual show of infinite diligence, virtue, and purpose, started work. Younger voices greeted her upon their arrival. Carl entered, flushed as if just from a shower-bath. He threw up the windows. He and the digested fellow had a fuss. Ingloriously routed, he whispered something into the dark coil that covered Vera's ear. She laughed. The gong rang. Flutter of those almost late. A few stragglers. Tick, tick, tick, tick, pounding of typewriters, metallic slide of files, rustle of starched paper, and the day began. Young girls who worked all month to imitate leisure class flappers. Young girls from South Carolina, Illinois, Oregon, waiting. Widows of improvident men who had been somebody in their day. Boys who had left school. Men dreaming of marriage and bungalows in Chevy Chase. Old digested fellows. Negro messengers. Something was up. The girls were whispering. A group gathered around Vera. The head-clerk looked up uneasily and scowled at them.

"What do you know about it?" one was saying.

"Shows you how slick they are."

"How'd they find out?"

"Oh she left a note-book in her desk. Somebody was looking for papers and came across it."

"What was in it?"

"Nothing, except a date she had to go to the Howard Theatre. Thats a nigger place, you know. It looked suspicious. So somebody followed her home, and saw her go out with a nigger. The chief was told, and he had her up about it. And they say she stood there brazen as anything, and said yes she was a nigger and proud of it. What do you think of that?"

"You could never have told."

"Oh yes you could. Some of them had been suspicious for a long time. And nigger blood will out. Its like Lincoln said, you can fool some of the people some of the time, but you cant fool all of the people all the time."

"But they are slick at it."

"I don't see what they want to be white for anyway. The way they boast about progress and all that youd think they'd be satisfied with their own race. But theyre not, theyre always trying to push into ours."

"Its because these northern politicians—I dont mean the President of course—coddle them. Theyd never even think of having such notions down South. In the South they know where their place is, and they keep it."

"Well, its good we caught her. It'll be a lesson to others."

"Oh, we always do. Sometimes its long, sometimes its short, but we catch up to them. You cant fool all of the people all of the time. I wonder if they know that saying of Lincoln's? Somebody ought to write it on a slip of paper and put it in their desks."

"Lets do."

"Here, Vera, you make some carbon copies."

"Are there as many as that?"

"Well, you cant tell. We've got our eyes on any number."

"Oh I cant see how anyone can be so deceitful."

Carl had drifted up.

"Whats all the row about?"

"Oh just another nigger we caught passing."

"What is it? A game or something?"

"You wouldnt think it was a game if you had been deceived and imposed upon."

"Serious as all that?"

"They'll think so by the time we get through with them."

Carl winked at Vera. The head-clerk came up, smiling behind his scowl.

"And now what's occupying the governments time?"

"Oh, nothing, just something about that Preston person."

"Yes, well, um, well better settle that at lunch. Run along now."

"Yes, Mr. Darby."

"Just as you say, Mr. Darby."

"Aurwewar, Mr. Darby."

Vera, left to herself plunged into work. Carl took her out to lunch. He insisted that she go out with him that night. Vera knew that he wanted an answer. Pressure was becoming intense, almost to suffocation. Not tonight, Carl, she had managed to say only by promising the next evening. He assured her that if she didnt give an answer to him, he would come after her. The afternoon, hugely unreal, ticked away. Reaching home, she plunged into a hot bath and tried to vaporize herself, one with its fumes. The towel but accentuated life. She had a banal observation: now I see why men drink. She tried to sleep. She exhausted herself with the tangled covers. Tossed out of bed and ran down to the phone. Yes, David Teyy would come around to see her; fortunately, he had no date. Vera, dressed, a trifle drawn, but with eyes brilliant in their searching sparkle, compounded of pain and hope and wistfulness, had the sincere impression that for the first time in her life she was really beautiful.

Something from David Teyy ran down the steering-gear, down the brakes and clutches, and gave flesh and blood life to the car. Vera was curled, as if she was in the dark enclosure of a womb. She could drive on forever. Covered by life that flowed up the blue veins of the city. Up Sixteenth Street. David was a red blood center flowing down. She sucked his blood. Go on forever with David flowing down. He had hardly spoken to her. She wished he would never speak. Life flowed away from her to gestate his words.

"What is that, Vera?"

His face, a bronze plate engrossed in sharp lines and curves, emerged from a blood-shot dusk. His words tasted of blood and copper. Why could he not let her be?

"The Masonic Temple, David."

"I mean to you."

"To me?"

"Who live under the shadow of it."

"I have never thought."

"Who live under the shadow of it. Under life."

"How do you know?"

"I have been told that you tease—"

"Men who are not strong enough—"

"—yourself."

"I am pure."

"You are a living profanation of the procreative principle of Deity."

Smile, which she could not see in the dusk.

"Because black children are repulsive to me?"

"Because you hold a phallus to the eye, and tease yourself."

"I do not understand."

"That is a rite of profanation."

"Your words cannot make me bad."

"My words were not used in your making."

Smile, she feels.

"You give me sarcasm when what I need is love."

"The necessary complement of giving is the capacity to take."

Smile.

"I cannot understand your words. Let me be."

"You wanted me?"

"After a while. O dont talk now. Please. Let me be."

. . . David flowing down. Vera had wanted to pass the cherry trees. And on out to the point. A word might struggle with her throat.

"Look, the cherry trees. I have seen them bloom. I have seen Japanese in reverence beneath them."

—Would it come?

"Lafcadio Hearn—"

" 'Lafcadio,' that is a soft word, David."

"You are sensitive—"

"Oh to so many things if I would only let myself be."

"Lafcadio Hearn tells of how the Japanese visit regions where the trees are blooming, much as we go to the mountains or the sea, drawn by their fragrance. It is hard to think of them succumbing to gaudy show and blare like our Americans at Atlantic City."

"You do not like Americans, David?"

"Do you feel Americans apart from you?"

"Answer my question first."

"One does not dislike when one is living. Life is inconceivable except in relation to its surrounding forms. I love."

"People?"

"The process and mystery of life. Life feeding on itself . . ."

Deep River, Mendota. Vera saw souls drifting to the rhythm of forgotten cadences, whirled up . . . and growing. The inexplicable wonder of it! And our scientists, who can name more strangely minute exceptions than anyone, believing that they have caught it in a formula. Churchmen and scientists contending over formulas, over beliefs! Could anything be more militantly superstitious, more doggedly naive??

. . . David flowing down. David flowing out. David like mass undulations of shadow-silver trees. She wished he would light a cigarette. They were curving into the Potomac Speedway.

—Would it come?

far-off trees
Whose gloom is rounded like the hives of bees
All humming peace to soldiers who have gone

"Echoes."

"They are yours?"

"Mine two years ago. Now, more yours than mine? Where did you hear them?"

Potomac swishes and gurgles in the crevices of the river wall. Cars parked beneath the willows are more frequent. Lovers, swift receding oval faces, float in the gloom of back seats.

"Art Bond. He is a friend of yours?"

Vera, restless.

"One of the best. The best, here, perhaps, except for his habit of fastening on the ghosts of my dead selves. Ghosts, the spiritualists tell us, should be allowed to depart, with a bon voyage for the way. That is a serviceable truth that should be brought from the cheap tappings and illogic of the seance room to the practice of broad day."

Smile; serious.

"You believe in ghosts?"

"Your meaning of the word is beside the question. Things die, transmute. Their memory lingers. A preoccupation with them clogs creative life. People who are forever fastening on them give tangibility to the clogs. They can very easily slip from friends to nuisances."

"But do you believe in the ghosts I mean?"

"In the ghosts of hysterical women, their fortune-tellers, ouija-boards, and cards? Perfectly valid as symptoms."

"I do not understand."

"Apis, steer god, cock your ears and listen to the rite of profanation. Vera, you wanted me?"

"I do not understand your words. Let me be. After a while. Lets stop here and run out to the point.—And plunge in the river. Lord, I want to cross over into camp ground."

Mobile river, scintillant beneath the moon . . . John Brown's Body . . . River flowing from Harper's Ferry to the Chesapeake and the sea. Open ocean for brown sediment of the river. Tide in, send your tang. Resistant ripples. Wave in, send your waves. Wash back. John Brown's body rumbles in the sea. Mobile river, scintillant beneath the moon . . . Lights twinkle on the wharves of Seventh Street. Wash red blood. Search-lights play on Lincoln Memorial and the Monument. Wash red blood. Blue blood clots in the veins of Washington. Wash red blood. John Brown's body . . . Mobile river, carrying brown sediment, scintillant beneath the moon.

They were standing on the point. David's face seemed unreal, and high above her. The line of his nose was a thin rim of silver. You have teased me. Your easy phrases when they turned on me, were teasing. Yours is a sin. Not mine. I cannot help it. You whom I turn to, tease me. Whom I love. Who carry solution within you. Who could, but by a touch, make me feel the world not so utterly dreadful, so sinking, without bottom, so utterly outside, and me alone. You tease me. O you do not know my need. It is not in you to sin callously. You are here . . . why will you not touch me? . . . the dream vanishes, the floor slips, and I dangle, dangle. O you do not know my need. Tease you? You know I cannot, and you play with me. O dreamer of Life why do you tease your dream? Do you not see that I have never wanted to tease? You place my compulsions to your eye, and play with me. What vision is it that lets you be blinded by the eye? You sing of rivers. O cant you see? Beneath the scum I am a river. You who plunge and cause stale drifts to stampede, releasing the river, will you not even touch me? You cannot sin so. O Christ forgive him if he sins. Virgin Mother, you will understand if I drown in the river. Forgive him, Christ. O God, I dangle. Lord God, I want to cross over into the camp ground.

David was humming.

"David, it would be a Godsend for the river to overflow and sweep me under."

. . . David flowing down.—Was that his hand that touched me? Are these his eyes bending over mine? Christ eyes, do not let me cry for loving you.

"Emptiness desires Nirvana. At best, I thought that was what you would want."

—Words, do not take him from his eyes. Glow, Christ eyes.

"Living from herself."

—Christ eyes, do not let me cry for loving you.

Perfect within yourself, incarnate mystery.

"I kneel in reverence before the wonder of it."

David's hand was almost crushing hers. It must have been a tear she felt, so hot it was. Her free hand tingled to the electric of his bent head.

"I am not worthy that you should kneel to me."

Vera shivered. Shook with a strange convulsion.

Roll river!

Something so complete and overpowering came over her that she sank, almost senseless, to her knees on the grass beside him.

"David," she was leaning against him, trembling, "what was it?"

Mobile river, scintillant, flowing to the sea.

"You ask me, who could but kneel before it?"

"I almost sinned, and then God struck me."

They were rolling over the smooth asphalt of Conduit Road, going towards the Falls. Head-lights of approaching cars glared at them. Rushed swiftly by. Across the river, Potomac palisades, great wavy outlined masses, glided leisurely with them. John Brown's body rumbles up the river . . .

"I have nothing to say to him but 'No'."

"People, Vera, unless you insult them, are insistent for reasons of refusal. Now Art—"

"It is unkind of you to remind me of him—after to-night."

"Ghosts of our dead selves—"

"And yet, if I have gained any strength at all, I should be able to face him. That wont be a ghost until it has been faced. I will sometime. But it will be purely selfish. People cant really forgive. Yet in this case there is nothing to forgive. I dont know how I shall meet him."

"Carl, first. He will want reasons."

"That I love you."

"Will that satisfy your own integrity? It was a half-truth up till tonight."

"It Has been a whole truth, always."

"But you see, sweetheart—"

"You do not say that like you would say it if you loved me."

"—your tendency is to make of love a sort of sublimated postponement. Love solves inner complications for a while. It holds little or no solution for the outside world. Perhaps in a better day . . . Especially is this true of the two worlds you dangle over. Love is inoperative here."

"Then what is?"

"A burning integrity of vision."

"You have it, man of the multi-colored leaves . . . O I knew it was you Carl dreamed about. I seemed to love him when the dreams he poured into me were you. I could not feel—"

Vera looked at David, and grew frightened.

"—not with him. I guess I led him on. But it was you who were struggling to birth in a word beneath the cherry trees, you along the river, at the point, above the falls, you. David, David, I love you . . . You have it, man of the multi-colored leaves, but I? . . ."

"When you knelt beside me at the point?"

"I saw only a wonderful glow that I was too afraid to really look at."

"You have never, not once, succeeded in facing yourself?"

"I have run."

"Where?"

"What is it you say? Nirvana. To you."

"Before me?"

"Men's arms, up to a point. And my bed at night."

"Before that?"

"Before my father died, his arms. Before him, mother's."

"And now mine?"

"Now yours . . . if you will let me."

"I seem then, to be in the direct descent of varied and sundry prehensiles—"

"How can you joke?"

"Once learn to laugh at arms and you will find that they will release you. Hasnt your experience taught you that?"

"You are cruel, cruel. Why do you torment me so?"

"Art's spirit working through me, perhaps."

"David."

Tears, by the motion of the car, were shaken from her eyes.

"Seriously, I want you to see this thing through. Answer Carl, and his look will lead you to an answer for the world."

"That I love you."

Clump of wood that vibrates like a G-string to the deep bass of the falls. Night, furtive and shifting where shafts of moonlight stab in quick succession through the veering leaves. Ground trembles to the storm and lightning from clouds of trees. John Brown's body . . . John Brown's body thunders up the falls . . .

"I always feel nervous and unreal in these woods."

"They are under a spell."

"Hold me, David."

David slipped his arm around her, and, bending over, chanted:

> Court-house tower,
> Bell-buoy of the Whites,
> Charting the white-man's channel,
> Bobs on the agitated crests of pines
> And sends its mellow monotone,
> Satirically sweet,
> To guide the drift of barges . . .
> Black barges . . .

> African Guardian of Souls,
> Drunk with rum,
> Feasting on a strange cassava,
> Yielding to new words and a weak palabra
> Of a white-faced sardonic God—

"Oh dont, David."

"You who would mate with me—"

"Not that way, David."

"—quail at such a simple evocation? What would you do, if a whole troupe of souls who love the earth-sphere too well to go away, were to suddenly materialize before you? You who are still neither in nor out yourself."

"You are only trying to frighten me."

"Well, so I am. Here, see the good fairy beckoning to you from my lips? Do you wish her?"

"David."

Lips that but a few moments ago were the pale withered skin of berries, who tautened you with dew? Brushed you with the sweet scent of cane?

"Now—let us hurry to the falls, David."

John Brown's body was below them . . . Lovers let your dreams fly out the moon . . . The golden flare of torches was diluted by the cold white light. Torches flare! It was wonderful to be in his arms.

"Do you know what I say of you, David?"

"I cannot hear you."

"Come, I know a rock."

David smiled at this girl leading him to secret places in his boulders.

"Carl will come to this place."

"How do you know, David? Oh lets not think of him. Tell me, do you know what I say of you? I will tell you. I say that you, man of the multi-colored leaves, put beauty, a senseless warm thing like a sucking baby, in my mouth."

"How did that come to you?"

"It just came, O man, who knows better yet cant help seeking solutions of mysteries. Wouldnt you love, sometimes, to get rid of your mind?"

"Ask me if I would love to postpone."

"Must you ever refer to it?"

"The western world demands of us that we not escape. The implication of fresh life is its use. Monasteries and sepulchres are the habitats of shades."

"Not even in love? O David I love you."

"For yourself; for me?"

"Your questions chill me. Your words. O do not talk to me David. Love."

Lips that but a few moments ago were the pale withered skin of berries, who tautened you with dew? Brushed you with the sweet scent of cane? Sandalwood odor of hair. Murmurs. Lispings. Love spinning to the tight pressure of tensioned arms. David . . . wedge . . . cleaving. Bronze sun, hammered to a sharp wedge . . . cleaving . . . His lips tasted of copper and blood.

"O David, David, not that. Not that, David. How could you—after tonight, your kneeling at the point?"

"Passion?"

"No, David, O no—love."

"Young girl asking for the moon."

"What do you mean? O David, you cannot sin so. Love."

"Young girl asking for the moon."

"David, you are killing something in me. You cannot sin so. Mother of Christ, forgive him."

Hands that tautened with dew, brushed with the sweet scent of cane, you are Indian-givers.

Vera lay, a limp, damp thing, like a young bird fallen from its nest, found in the morning, in David's arms. John Brown's body rumbles in the river . . .

"Cry."

"I cant, David. I want to go home."

A shadowy shape was silhouetted above them.

"Beg pardon," it said.

"Carl."

"Is that you, Vera? I cant see. What are you doing here? Oh, beg pardon."

"Its all right, Carl. Sit with us. He is a friend of yours."

"Hello, Carl."

"I cant quite see—well I'll be damned if it isnt David Teyy. Where did you come from? I didnt know that you were in town. Vera, you didnt tell me you knew Dave Teyy. How long you been here? Working? Well I'll be damned. Pardon, Vera. And out here at the falls. What on earth ever brought you out here? This is a surprise. Damn. Pardon, Vera."

"Sit down, Carl. I have something I want to tell you."

Carl crouched down, Indian fashion. The three of them seemed as though gathered round an improbable fire.

"Dave Teyy. Old man, I havent seen you since that summer at Wisconsin. But I've thought of you. Havent I, Vera? Its good to see you. Recalls old days, and everything. Hows the world using you? Piled up a fortune I bet. But no, as I remember it, that wasnt your line. Man of the multi-colored leaves. What was that you used to get off about faces that chiseled dreams?

From American marble? Or something like that? Like the fellows used to say, you were a queer duck, but they couldn't help liking you. Damn.''

"Carl, this is as good a time as any other. I want to tell you that I cannot marry you.''

"But not here, Vera. You cant mean it. Wait till another time. Hell's bells.''

"But I do mean it, Carl. And I want to get it over with.''

"Cant marry me? Oh this is an h of a time to tell a feller. Pardon, Dave. But it sort of upsets a feller.''

"Deep down in your heart you really don't care, Carl. You think you do. But someday you'll find the right girl. Then you'll see.''

"You dont love me. Thats it. But thats no reason—what is it Vera, tell me. I thought you did—up till to-night. What is it?''

David was trying to whip her with his will.

"I love David Teyy.''

"Oh—well—congratulations, Dave. Hell's bells. Pardon. Guess I'd better be running on.''

Something held him.

"Vera, Carl, both of you will sit as you are.''

Life was thrashing in David. He would stampede these pale ghost people. He gathered wood, built a fire. Its flare disturbed nearby lovers who grumbled at it and moved away. Carl and Vera could not believe themselves. Fingers pulled down their stomachs. They shivered. Drew nearer the flames. David, holding them with his eyes, was crouching.

"Know you, people, that you sit beside the boulder where Tiacomus made love. Made love, do you understand me? Know you, people, that you are above a river, spattered with blood. John Brown's blood. With blood, do you understand me? White red blood. Black red blood. Know you, people, that you are beneath the stars of wonder, of reverence, of mystery. Know you that you are boulders of love, rivers spattered with blood, stars of wonder and mystery. Roll river. Flow river. Roll river. Flow river. River, river, roll, Roll!

> The river was empty, flowing to the sea.
> From Harper's Ferry to the Chesapeake and the sea—
> . . . They hung John Brown . . .
>
> The river was empty, flowing to the sea,
> From Harper's Ferry to the Chesapeake and the sea—
> . . . They hung John Brown . . . Roll river . . .
>
> River was empty, flowing to the sea,
> From Harper's Ferry to the Chesapeake and the sea—
> . . . They hung John Brown . . . Roll river roll!
>
> John Brown's body, rumbles in the river,
> John Brown's body, thunders down the falls—
> . . . Roll river roll!

"Know you, people, that you sit beside the boulder where Tiacomus made love. Made love, you understand me? Know you, people, that you are above a river, spattered with blood. With blood, you understand me? John Brown's blood. Know you, people, that you are beneath the stars of wonder, of reverence, of mystery. Know you that you are boulders of love, rivers spattered with blood, white red blood, black red blood, that you are stars of wonder and mystery. Roll river! Flow river! Roll river! Flow river! River, river, roll, Roll!!

The boulder seemed cleft by a clap of thunder. As if the falls had risen and were thundering its fragments away . . .

Tick, tick, tick, tick, pounding of typewriters, metallic slide of files, rustle of starched paper. Young girls who work all month to imitate leisure-class flappers. Young girls from South Carolina, Illinois, Oregon, waiting. Widows of improvident men who had been somebody in their day. Boys who have left school. Men dreaming of marriage and bungalows in Chevy Chase. Old digested fellows. Negro messengers. Carl but little changed. The slow process of digestion. Black life pepper to the salt of white. Sneezes. Tick, tick, tick, tick. Vera listless, nervous . . .

Men listen to her lispings and murmurs. Black souls steal back to Georgia canefields, soft and misty, underneath a crescent moon. The mystery of their whispered promises seems close to revelation, seems tangibly incarnate in her. Black souls, tropic and fiery, dream of love. Sing joyful codas to forgotten folk-songs. Spin love to the soft weaving of her arms. Men listen to her lispings and murmurs. White souls awake to adolescent fantasies they thought long buried with the dead leaves along the summer streets of mid-western towns. Solvents of melancholy burn through their bitten modes of pioneer aggressiveness to a southern repose. They too spin love to the soft weaving of her arms. White men, black men, only in retrospective kisses, know the looseness of her lips . . . pale withered skin of berries . . .

Margaret Walker
(1915–   )

In Margaret Walker's writing as a poet, novelist, essayist, and critic, one finds a special affirmation of black Southern experiences, history, and humanism. Born in Birmingham, Alabama, Walker spent her formative years in New Orleans. She received the A.B. from Northwestern University and the M.A. and Ph.D. from the University of Iowa. Educating students has been significant in her career, for she has taught at Livingstone College, West Virginia State College, Northwestern, and Jackson State University and has lectured widely. Margaret Walker won the 1942 Yale Younger Poets award for her first book of poetry *For My People* and began to develop a national reputation. Her other collections of poetry are *Prophets for a New Day, October Journey*, and *This Is My Century*. She received a Houghton Mifflin Literary Award for *Jubilee* (1966), a historical novel based on the life of her great-grandmother. Some of her essays have been collected in the book *How I Wrote "Jubilee" and Other Essays on Life and Literature*, and her long-awaited *Richard Wright: Daemonic Genius* was published in 1988. Her work-in-progress includes her autobiography, a sequel to *Jubilee* entitled *Minna and Jim*, and the novel *Mother Broyer*. The following excerpt is Chapter 14 of *Jubilee*.

---

from Jubilee

> *There's a star in the East*
> *on Christmas morn.*
> *Rise up shepherds and foller,*
> *It'll lead to the place*
> *where the Savior's born.*
> *Rise up shepherds and foller.*

14: *"THERE'S A STAR IN THE EAST ON CHRISTMAS MORN"*

Christmas time on the plantation was always the happiest time of the year. Harvest time was over. The molasses had been made. Marster's corn was in his crib and the slaves' new corn meal had been ground. Lye hominy and sauerkraut were packed away in big jars and stone or clay crocks. Elderberry, blackberry, poke weed and dandelion, black cherry and scuppernong, muscatine and wild plum, crab apple and persimmon, all had been picked and made into jars of jelly, jam, preserves, and kegs of wine. There were persimmon beer and home-made corn likker, and a fermented home brew for future use. Despite Big Missy's clever vigilance with her ipecac, some of those jars of jelly and preserves and peach brandy had inevitably gone out of the pantry window into the waiting fingers of black hands. What the slaves could not conveniently steal, they begged and made for themselves. Many of the delicacies that they loved were free for the taking in the woods. Who did not know how to mix the dark brown sugar or black cane molasses or sorghum with various fruits and berries to make the good wine and brew the beer and whiskey from the corn or rye that every clever finger learned early how to snatch and hide? When the frost turned the leaves and the wind blew them from the trees, it was time to go into the woods and gather nuts, hickory nuts and black walnuts, and chinkapinks. There were always more pecans on the place than could be eaten and the hogs rooted out the rotting ones. If Marster had not given them a goober patch, they had patches of goober peas around their cabins anyway. Sometimes there were whole fields of these wonderful peanuts. Like the industrious squirrels around them they scrupulously gathered the wild harvest and wrapped them in rags, laying-by their knick-knacks for the long winter nights. When the autumn haze ended and the chilling winter winds descended upon them it was time to hunt the possum and to catch a coon. No feast during the Christmas holidays would be good without a possum and a coon. Of course, Vyry said, ''You got to know how to cook it, or it ain't no good. You got to boil that wild taste out with red-hot pepper and strong vinegar made out of sour apple peelings and plenty salt. You got to boil it in one water and then take it out and boil it in another water, and you got to soak the blood out first over night and clean it real good so you gits all the blood out and you got to scrape all the hair left from the least bit of hide and then you got to roast it a long, slow time until you poured all that fat grease off and roast sweet potatoes soft and sugary, and if that stuff don't make you hit your mama till she holler and make you slobber all over yourself, they's something wrong with you and the almighty God didn't make you at the right time of the year. Marster, he like foxes, but what good is a fox when you can't eat him? Make sense to catch varmints stealing chickens, foxes and wolves, for that matter, and it's good to catch an old black bear, or a ferocity vicious bobcat, and nasty old varmint like a weasel when he come sneaking around, but when you hunting for meat and you wants fresh meat, kill the rabbit and the coon, kill the squirrel and the possum and I'll sho-nuff be satisfied.''

If the slave did not kill his meat, he wasn't likely to eat fresh meat, although at hog-killing time they were given the tubs of chitterlings, the liver and the lights, and sometimes even the feet. After a very good harvest Marster might let them have a young shoat to barbecue, especially at Christmas time. Marse John was generous to a fault and always gave plenty of cheap rum and gallons of cheap whiskey to wash the special goodies down.

Big Missy had a taste for wild game too, but it was quail and pheasant, wild turkey and wild ducks, and occasionally the big fat bucks that came out of their own woods for wonderful roasts of venison. The Negroes were not allowed to kill these and if they made a mistake and accidentally killed birds or deer they had better not be caught eating it. Vyry had learned from Aunt Sally how to lard quail with salt fat pork and how to cook potted pheasant in cream, to roast and stuff turkey and geese and ducks, but she knew also the penalty for even tasting such morsels if Big Missy found out about it. Sometimes, however, half a turkey or goose was stolen from the springhouse, after some expert had carefully picked the lock. Most of the time, however, they did not worry about Big Missy's game as long as they could get enough of what they could put into their hands while foraging through the woods. By some uncanny and unknown reason real white flour came from somewhere for Christmas, and eggs were hoarded from a stray nest for egg bread instead of plain corn pone, but real butter cake and meat and fruit pies were seldom found in a slave cabin. Sometimes on Christmas they tasted snacks of real goodies such as these as part of their Christmas. On Christmas morning all the field hands stood outside the Big House shouting, "Christmas gift, Christmas gift, Marster." Then, and only then, did they taste fresh citrus fruit. Every slave child on the place received an orange, hard Christmas candy, and sometimes ginger cake. There were snuff and chewing tobacco for the women, whiskey and rum for the men. Sometimes there were new clothes, but generally the shoes were given out in November before Thanksgiving.

On Christmas morning there was always a warm and congenial relationship between the Big House and the slave Quarters. If it was cold, and very often it was not, the slaves huddled in rags and shawls around their heads and shoulders, and Marse John would open his front door and come out on the veranda. His guests and family and poor white kin, who were always welcomed in the house at Christmas time, came out with him and gathered round to hear his annual Christmas speech to the slaves. He thanked them for such a good crop and working so hard and faithfully, said it was good to have them all together, and good to enjoy Christmas together when they all had been so good. He talked about the meaning of Christmas—"When I was a boy on this place at Christmas time, seems only yesterday . . . ." He got sentimental about his father and mother, and he told a "darkey" joke or two, and then he wished them a merry Christmas, ordered whiskey and rum for everyone, handed out their gifts of candy and oranges and snuff and tobacco, and asked them to sing a song, please, for him and his family and all their guests. Then they sang their own moving Christmas carols, "Wasn't that a mighty day when Jesus Christ was born" and "Go tell it on the Mountain that Jesus Christ is born" and the especially haunting melody that everybody loved:

> There's a star in the East on Christmas morn,
> Rise up shepherds and foller,
> It'll lead to the place where the Savior's born,
> Rise up shepherds and foller.

Then Marse John and all his white family and their friends would wipe their weeping eyes and blow their running noses and go inside to the good Christmas breakfast of fried chicken and waffles and steaming black coffee with fresh clotted cream. And the slaves, happy with the rest that came with the season, went back to their cabins, certain that for one day of the year at least they would have enough to eat. They could hardly wait for night and the banjo parties to begin. On Marse John's plantation, Christmas was always an occasion and all during the holidays there were dancing parties and dinners with lots of wonderful food and plenty of the finest liquor. Marse John and Big Missy became celebrated for their fine turkeys and English fruit cakes and puddings, duffs full of sherry and brandy, excellent sillabub and eggnog, all prepared by their well-trained servants, who cooked and served their Marster's fare with a flourish.

But for Vyry, Christmas meant as much hard work as any other time of the year. Of course, she had her chance to get whatever she wanted to eat simply by slipping and hiding grub in her apron and skirt pockets as she had watched Aunt Sally do. But this Christmas she had no appetite for Marster's delicious food, none for the gaiety of the parties in the Big House nor for the banjo singing and dancing in the Quarters, nor for anything the Christmas season meant. Randall Ware could no longer console her. She was already his and she had no freedom either. Now they would have a child in the spring and this child would not be free either. This child would belong to Marster. Desperately she pressed Randall Ware to do something about her freedom. He tried to satisfy her by having Brother Ezekiel "marriage" them in the way the slaves called it, "Jump the broom," but this was not all Vyry wanted. She wanted to be free, and more than that now, she wanted freedom for her unborn child. A number of her fellow slaves were jumping the broom that Christmas. For them it was simple, so she reasoned. They were already slaves on Marster's plantation or on his "other plantation" or from the plantations nearby, and their children were naturally doomed to be slaves. But Vyry sensed, more than Randall Ware seemed to care, that this child of a free father should be free. Randall Ware brought her gifts of food and game, but she was indifferent. He declared that he would buy her at the first opportunity, but that he must buy her through some white man and Marse John would not think of selling her to him. Laws governing slave marriage to free Negroes were very strict in Lee County. Randall Ware contended that he must bide his time. One wrong move now could mean disaster for both of them.

Finally in desperation, Vyry decided to go to Marse John and ask his permission for her to marry Randall Ware. She planned to go when Big Missy was not around to influence his decision. She would go in the midst of this Christmas season while his heart was softened and his generosity at its height, when he would be mellow with brandy and whiskey, and everything seemed to be going right on his plantation, and therefore with his world. She picked a night when the slaves were having a big party and all around one could hear the fiddlers and the banjo picker singing, "Oh, Sally come up, Oh, Sally come down, Oh, Sally come down the middle," while all the others joined in the singing and you could hear one voice louder than the others calling the rounds of the dancing.

"Evening to yall, Marster," Vyry spoke from the doorway, fumbling with her apron in her hands.

Marse John, startled, turned from his desk where he was wrestling with bills for merchandise and accounts with his drivers. He nearly let his book fall when he saw Vyry. This white-looking, thin-lipped girl always managed to make him feel ill at ease. But he spoke in such a condescending tone and his usual patronizing fashion, that she would never have known how much she disconcerted him.

"Why, good evening, Vyry. Why aren't you over at the party dancing and having a good time?"

"Don't feel like it, Marster. I ain't in no shape for dancing."

"Why, what's the trouble?" Her eyes were on the floor before her, and she did not look at him when he spoke. "Are you sick, or is something the matter?"

"Yessuh. They is something the matter. I don't know as you'd call it trouble, but in a way, I's sick and in a way I ain't, and it's sho-nuff trouble for me."

Marse John turned all the way around in his chair now to face Vyry. He looked her over warily, and then he said in an offhand fashion, "Well, if you don't tell me the trouble, I can't help you. What do you want me to do about it?"

She lifted her eyes then, and looked him squarely in the eye. "Marster, I wants your permission for me to get married."

"Oh, is that all," and he seemed relieved, "I thought it was something serious. You mean you're going to have a baby?"

"Yessuh, that's what I means. I'm big all right, and I wants to get married."

"Well, now that's no trouble, lots of gals are getting married around here every day, how do you say, jumping the broom?" And he laughed, but she did not crack a smile and she remained silent. Between them arose a silent question, but Vyry waited for him to speak first.

"By the way, who do you want to marry? Is it one of my boys around here or a boy from a plantation somewhere around here?"

"It ain't needer one."

"Well, if it's none of my nigra boys and none around here, who could it be? You don't mean some of these overseers or guards have been getting fresh with you, do you?"

"No sir." She looked up again and through narrowed eyelids with her face still solemn she said, "It ain't none of your boys around here, and it ain't no white man neither. This here man's black, *but he free*." If she had shot him, he could not have been more deeply shocked. His face turned pale as death and he looked as if he had surely seen a ghost. For a full moment that seemed very long he could not trust himself to speak. Vyry looked at him and waited.

"You mean you're asking me to give you permission to marry a free-issue nigger?"

"Yessuh, I is. He ain't a slave cause he borned free."

"Do you know what that means?"

"I reckon so, Marster, I reckon I does."

"Why don't you ask me for your freedom and be done with it?" Now he spat out the words with such fury that Vyry jumped as if he had hit her.

"Marster, is you mad cause I asked you to let me marriage with my child's own daddy?"

Now, red with anger, he stood up and came close to her, leaving only a step or two between them, and his voice moderated to a low but urgent tone while his hands were raised as if in self-defense:

"You should have thought of this before you got a free-issue nigger to get a child by. Getting a child by you don't make him own you nor own the child. I own you, and I own your unborn child. When you ask me to let you marry a free-issue nigra you ask me by the law of the state of Georgia to set you, a mulatto woman, free, and that's a mighty lot to ask. There's a big difference between asking to get married and asking to be set free. Why, I never heard of such in all my life!"

She drew back from him in fear as if he had hit her, or might decide to do so. Suddenly she burst into tears and looking up at him again with the tears on her face she spoke cuttingly, "Marster, does you think it's a sin for me to want to be free?"

Her words were knifing him like a two-edged sword. He opened his mouth and his lower jaw sagged. A dull red moved again over his face and mottled the blood through his skin. Again the silence between them crackled with tension they could feel. But he was master of his situation, and he knew it. He did not intend to let that mastery get away from him. But now he tried another tactic. He deliberately moved back to his desk, and half sitting upon it, he crossed one leg and folded his arms. Then he looked steadily at her.

"So. That is what you wanted in the first place. And what do you think it would be like for you to be free? And where do you think you would go? Who would take care of you, feed you, and clothe you, and shelter you, and protect you? What do you think it would be like to be free?"

She knew he expected her to say she didn't know. She started to speak the sober thought in her mind—that her husband would do these things for her—but she knew he would consider her impudent so she thought better of it and held her peace. When she did not answer him, he went on, "Do you think you would be better off free than you are working for me? Look all around you at the poor white people who are free. You don't want to be like *them*, now do you? What is it you call them, 'po buckra'? They are free, free and white; but what have they got? Not a pot to piss in. Every blessed thing they get they're knocking on my door for it. Can't feed their pot-bellied younguns; always dying of dysentery and pellagra; eating clay cause they're always hungry; and never got a crop fit for anything; no cotton to sell, and can't get started in the spring unless I help them. Do you think you would be better off if you were like them? And being black and free! Why, my god, that's just like being a hunted animal running all the time! All over the South now they're talking about making free-issue niggers take masters and become slaves.

They're not that much better off now anyway. Suppose that happened to your free-issue nigger and you fell into the hands of a cruel master? Does anybody bother you here? Aren't you free to come and go as you please?''

Again she did not answer. He was watching her as he talked, and seeing the growing bitterness in her face, her tight lips, her jaws working grimly as she occasionally bit her lips and twisted her hands, he tried still another tactic.

''I've often thought about setting you free.''

She looked up now at this, and he thought he caught the faintest gleam of hope in her surprised eyes.

''But here in Georgia it's very hard to manumit a slave, you know what I mean—set you free. I don't have the right to break the law. I would have to have you taken out of this state and carried to a state like Kentucky or Maryland where the law permits a man to set his slave free if he wants to. Here in Georgia manumission is only permitted as a great reward for saving a white person's life and sometimes, in great exceptions when a slave has been very faithful, on the death of his master he may be set free. When I die you will surely be free. It's already in my will.''

Now the scorn in her face was quite apparent to him. He knew she did not believe him, and he was withered before her scorn. He had no additional weapon with which to fight such scorn and he was forced to drop his eyes and hang his head. But when she still said nothing, he quickly brought this painful conference to an end.

''Now that is all, I'll have to ask you to leave. I was working on my accounts and I'm very busy tonight. You'll have to excuse me.''

Dismissed, she turned with drooping shoulders and went out without saying another word. But now her hope was shriveled and dead within her. Her beautiful dream of freedom again seemed forever lost.

Sitting alone in her cabin door with her own bitter thoughts, she heard music. In her mind there was the bitter music of an acid little jingle she had heard the slaves often sing among themselves:

> My old marster clared to me
> That when he died, he'd set me free
> He lived so long and got so bald
> He give out the notion of dying at all.

Over and over the bitter jingle kept recurring to her, but the music she heard floating out on the balmy December air was another Christmas carol also in keeping with the season and her thoughts:

> Oh, Mary, what you going to name your newborn baby?
> What you going to name that pretty little boy?

John Oliver Killens
(1916–1987)

John Oliver Killens, novelist, social critic, screenwriter, and essayist, was a founder of the legendary Harlem Writers Guild, a workshop that strongly influenced such writers as Maya Angelou, Sarah Wright, Lonne Elder, and Paule Marshall. Killens also influenced such younger writers as Malaika Adero, Helen Quigless, and Carol Dixon through the workshops he conducted at Fisk University, Howard University, and Medgar Evers College. Born in Macon, Georgia, Killens was himself influenced by his Southern experiences and reflected them in the themes and critical realism of his fiction, in his historically grounded social analyses. Killens's work with the National Labor Relations Board (1936–1942), his service in the U.S. Army during World War II (1942–1945), and his deep commitment to a variety of civil rights and nationalist causes are important for understanding his artistic choices. His first novel, *Youngblood*, was published in 1954. His other novels are *And Then We Heard the Thunder* (1963), *'Sippi* (1967), *The Cotillion, or One Good Bull Is Half the Herd* (1971), and *Great Black Russian: A Novel of the Life and Times of Alexander Pushkin* (1989). He occasionally wrote for television and the cinema, including the screenplay for *Odds Against Tomorrow* (1959). His interest in heroic acts during the slave period led to the writing of *Great Gittin' Up Morning: A Biography of Denmark Vesey* and of *A Man Ain't Nothin' But a Man: The Adventures of John Henry*, a narrative about the legendary steel driver. Killens published a collection of essays, *Black Man's Burden*, in 1965. As Abraham Chapman noted in *New Black Voices*, Killens's work was "evidence of complex literary development and changes." The breadth of Killens's contribution will become more apparent as literary historians and critics move toward comprehensive treatments of African-American literature. The prologue from *'Sippi* is reprinted here.

---

from 'Sippi

PROLOGUE

It was one of those moments all over the world when time caught up with history. From Johannesburg to Birmingham, from Rangoon to Ouagadougou, from Timbuktu to Lenox Avenue, time and history ran a dead heat down the last lap of the human race. Even a sophisticated disenfranchised city like Washington in the District of Columbia in the United States of North America could no longer maintain with dignity its "objective" posture on the sidelines of the main event. And this race was the main event of the entire twentieth century.

It was on a Monday morning, a day not unlike a thousand other days in Washington in the springtime season. And spring came earlier than usual that year. Cherry blossoms already gleamed and glittered along the famous "speedway," that boulevard of feverish lovers, where Romeos and Juliets oohed and aahed and told eternal truths and lied magnificently and swore love everlasting and necked until ungodly hours. And thought that the whole world loved them, save the Capital police.

On Wilburger Street at the corner of 6½ and T in the little alley next to the Howard Theater, some sucker, black and sentimental, played Dusty Fletcher's record all night long that night before the fateful day.

Open the door, Richard

Already a bright and sparkling greenness lay over the land from Capitol Hill to the Washington Monument to the Lincoln Memorial to Mount Vernon in old Virginia, all the way to Mississippi. The sun had risen that fateful morning from a long night's winter sleep and with a giant paintbrush had splashed the stone and concrete of this pure-white-as-the-driven-snow city with dazzling colors of pink and orange and red and blue. Children went to school as they had always done, or played hookey as they sometimes did. The city was white, virginally immaculate, in the downtown governmental section. The august halls of Congress, as per usual, rang to the rafters with memorable rhetoric, Southern drawl, Northern brogue, Middle West and Western twang, but drawl, brogue, or Western twang, it was more than likely pretty talk for talk's own sake and seldom led to concrete action. Like art for art's own precious sake. Men and women (civil servants) went dutifully to work that morning mostly in the gleamingly white governmental edifices, or they stayed at home on "sick leave" as they sometimes had a way of doing, devilishly. The Capital Transit buses were as crowded that memorable morning as they always were, as Washingtonians went about their daily business, as if nothing out of the ordinary were about to happen. Notwithstanding, it did happen. And nothing, repeat, absolutely nothing, was ever quite the same again. It was, moreover, time and history in a conspiracy of dastardly subversion.

The man on Wilburger Street said:

Open the door, Richard
The man's out here.

He had knocked on the damn door all of his life, but Richard had never answered. Not to mention Mister Charlie.

On that morning of May 17, 1954, nine highly distinguished Americans, noted for their wisdom and broad vision, grimly lit a fuse to a keg of dynamite upon which a mighty nation had reclined sublimely for more than nine decades. It was indeed a devilish prank for men of such high respectability to engage in; notwithstanding, these wise men set off a chain of reactions that caused explosion after explosion all over this peaceful, democratic, best-of-all-possible worlds. Even down in Mississippi.

Legend has it that when old Jesse Chaney got the word that the Supreme Court had spoken, it was all of two weeks later. Somehow, even with television (he didn't own one anyhow), it took all of two weeks for the word to reach him bending deep in the cotton field on Mister Charles James Richard Wakefield's plantation. Jesse didn't stop running till he reached the Big House more than a mile and a half away. He was in his late fifties, and he had been working cotton since he was seven. Jesse was the best cotton-picking cotton chopper in all of Wakefield County.

He was a tall gangling hulk of brownish-black man. He seemed pure Yoruba stock. Mister Charlie had had no fingers in the pie of his ancestry. He'd tell anybody, and proudly. His skin was smooth and tight, burnished-black, and tender as a newborn baby's backside. You'd have thought a razor had never touched his face. But you could see the years of pain and anguish etched forever in the deep set of his eyes; the years had painstakingly sculptured the contours of his face, had sketched a tender firmness in the corners of his mouth. After he had been running for six or seven minutes, his breathing came in heavy, quick, short gasps. He was too old to run so fast so far. But he had waited so long for this moment. He had bowed and scraped and agreed with his close friend, Mr. Wakefield, so long, so Lord-have-mercy-long, he had begun to walk bent over ever since he was twenty-five years old. But at last the day had come. The day he had hoped for, prayed for, watched for, but had sometimes thought would never happen in his lifetime. The Federal Government was on his side now. Hallelujah! Lift every voice and sing! His bowing and scraping days were over. His heart began to silently sing an old song he had almost forgotten.

> King Jesus got his arms all around me.
> No evil can ever harm me,
> For I, thank God, am in His care.

Against his will his legs slowed down almost to a walk. His heart and soul and mind cried out to his body to keep moving. But his legs felt like he was jumping up and down in forest fire. Can't stop now, his soul entreated him. His chest would burst wide open any minute, and he saw white spots before his face. His head was swimming around and around in a white and swirling river. Can't stop now. He stumbled. He thought the earth was coming up to smack him in the face. But he kept his footing. Can't stop now. His mouth was parched, his throat was scratchy. It was as if he had been running up a long steep hill all the days of his life, and now that he saw the summit in sight, it seemed to move further and further away. Closer—further, closer—

further, closer—further. His heart boomed away like thunder. He thought it might leap from his chest. It was frightening, the way he could hear his old heart pounding like the sound of distant drums. Pounding way up in his forehead. But then he got his second wind. He was like an old car going up a mountainside. It reached a high plateau and shifted gears to make the final slope.

Charles James Richard Wakefield (some of his close friends called him "Jimmy Dick," affectionately, as did some of his distant friends and likewise some who were not his friends at all) saw Jesse from his front porch when Jesse was still quite a distance away, still deep, deep in the cotton, chugging like an old freight train, but gaining all the time. Wakefield wondered idly, what in the hell was anybody doing running like that in all this God-forsaken heat? Especially a poor-ass Negro. What in the hell did he have to run for? Wakefield smiled. Must be the Devil chasing him.

Wakefield was an unusual white man for these parts. Ask any black man. "He spoiled the niggers." Any white man would tell you how he spoiled them. A Negro was lucky to work on his plantation. You only had to work sixty hours a week. And Wakefield paid his lowest workers all of fifty cents an hour. Some folk called the Wakefield plantation, "Nigger Heaven." And another thing: He paid his workers wages. He did not believe in cropping shares. He'd tell anybody's body. "Cropping shares is tantamount to slavery."

He was a big, handsome, black-haired man with eyes as blue-green as the ocean's edge. A modernistic Mississippian, a world traveler, a true cosmopolitan. Sometimes he felt more contempt for his white contemporaries than for the Negroes who worked for him. After all, the Negro never had had the opportunity to lift himself. But in this land of the free and home of the courageous, what the hell was the poor-ass peckerwood's excuse?

Yes, Wakefield was the gracious lord of the manor and the manor was a vast sprawling Mississippi plantation, where cotton was still king and he was King Cotton. Fields of white fruit, row after row, rolled for miles to and from the river, flowing like the river itself. Rolling like the river. His plantation was seventy-six miles south by southwest of Oxford, Mississippi, the home and the site of another famous Mississippi plantation owner. Oh yes, he and Willie Faulkner had emptied many a bottle of Scotch and bourbon together in their day, and laughed about the poor-ass peckerwoods and commiserated over the poor downtrodden colored people, especially those of the "noble savage" genre. He liked to think of people like himself and Willie Faulkner as being the last proponents of noblesse oblige. And he would be the first to admit that, these days, they were a rare breed indeed in Mississippi and everywhere else throughout his beloved Southland. Some of the more literate peckerwoods referred to him as the "Duke of Wakefield County," and to his good wife as the "Duchess." The manor house of the duchy was modern like his lordship. Well, it was not exactly modern. It was of another century. Tall and wide and awesome and white against a background and a foreground of green shrubbery and white cotton. But it had all of the modern amenities. For example, Wakefield and the Duchess did not sit on the front porch fanning themselves with funeral-parlor fans as old-fashioned, rich white folk did in Tennessee Williams and Willie Faulkner movies. "The Duke" believed in automation. Manual fanning was self-defeating anyhow.

One of his famous Wakefieldisms was: "If it's hot enough to fan yourself, it's certainly too damn hot to engage in the physical exertion required to do the fanning." And even before the Supreme Court decision, he had had the foresight to know that it was not slavery time anymore, and you could not expect Negroes to pretend it was and stand around and do your fanning for you. So Charles James Richard Wakefield had had four electric fans installed in the ceiling of his porch, and they were going every waking hour of the good old summertime (April through October). Not that he spent that much time on the front porch, but Anne Wakefield did, and he did everything in his power to make things comfortable for her.

"Who in the hell is that running so fast in all that God-forsaken heat?" he wondered aloud. It made him sweat just to watch and contemplate. His wife knew the question was not meant for her, so she kept rocking and humming softly to herself some half-remembered hymn.

It was a hot and suffocating day for the first day of June, a hot day even for Mississippi, where summer had an awful habit of coming early and staying late and always wearing out its welcome. Summer was in love with Mississippi. This was the one hour in the day in a workaday week that he allowed himself a momentary respite from his terribly frenetic schedule. He was the busiest businessman in all the county, maybe even in all the state. Sometimes he did not know which way was up. But for one solid hour after noonday dinner every Tuesday he just sat on the porch and sipped his Scotch and branch water and meditated on the sad state of the race. Upon very rare occasions he even read his Holy Bible to the Duchess, who faithfully fell asleep. "Let the Words of my mouth and the meditations of my heart be acceptable in Thy sight, Oh Lord, my strength and my Redeemer." It was his favorite quotation. He was not a fanatically religious man. But he was an avid reader, when he found the time, and he looked upon the Bible as the most beautiful book in all the world. He had a feeling that everything was worked out right here on this earth and therefore he did not really believe in the Hereafter in which his wife believed with unimaginable devotion. But to be on the safe side, just in case she knew something he did not know, he paid the preacher regularly, much more regularly than he went to church. Indeed he was the church's most substantial benefactor. He was the Good Lord's right hand. Financially speaking.

At first sight, as she sat there rocking back and forth and humming a church song for her own entertainment, one would conclude that the Duchess was the Duke's diametrical opposite. And one would be absolutely right. She was, of course, first of all a woman, but a woman who had begun to waste away early in the game of life, and by now the waste as well as the game was just about complete.

"Damn I reckin! That poor black bastard is hauling ass!" Wakefield wiped imaginary perspiration from his brow, as he empathized with the black, long-distance runner.

Wakefield stared sideways at the Duchess. He was filled with a great compassion for her, and he immediately felt better for it. Sometimes he wondered why she did not go to the cemetery and give herself up. He wondered why she persisted in this meaningless camouflage, which was what he pictured her life to be to her. A pitiful charade. There were times when he felt an overwhelming sorrow for this gentle woman, who looked so much older than her fifty-five years. You could tell that she had been a pretty one in her day, maybe even beautiful. But her day had been of a very brief duration, a billionth of a tick-tock of infinity. She was swarthy, tan almost, and dark and wide of eye. Her nose was thin, turned slightly upward toward the heavens. Once upon a time, her hair had been as black as midnight in the colored quarters. But now it was as white as cotton balls at picking time.

He watched her now, rocking back and forth. Her eyes were deep black canyons of nothingness. His own eyes almost filled, but not quite. As a young girl she had been the gentlest woman he had ever known. She'd been too good to be true. She would not have harmed a mosquito had it been biting her on the top of her nose. And in bed she had been completely passive. So gentle and doll-like, he'd felt like a rapist every time he had gone inside her. He would swear on a stack of Bibles she had never known what it was to have an orgasm, except as she had sneaked and read about it in the modernistic novels. That was one of her few vices, probably her only one. She read all the cheap spicy novels when no one was looking. He knew she read them. But she could never live them, except vicariously. He knew this too. That is why, after awhile, he had felt that he was imposing on her with the sexual act. And he was sexual from head to toe. So he had put his queen, his angelic "Duchess," on the pedestal where she belonged and had gone out in his dukedom and planted his seed all over the place, in black earth as well as white. He'd tell you he did not discriminate. He thought satirically of himself sometimes as "the Last of the Great White Planters." Others called him more vulgarly a "whoremonger." Some called him "Jimmy Dick, the pussy chaser."

Sometimes, when he felt lonesome and sorry for himself, he blamed Anne Barkley Wakefield for the fact that he was the lonesomest man in Wakefield County. At his age, still going from pillar to post, with no place permanently to lay his handsome head. He, the wealthiest, the most intelligent, the most important, the most sophisticated, the most powerful, and the most generous man in that section of the state, was the loneliest man in Mississippi. But deep in him he knew she was not to blame. If there ever were a blameless woman in this satanic world it was his Duchess, Anne Barkley Wakefield.

His mind and eyes went back to the runner now. Ain't that something! He got up and walked to the edge of the porch and stared. He could make him out now. Goddamn! How did that man run like that in all this heat with all those years behind him?

Jesse Chaney was one of the closest friends he had in all this world. But what the hell was he running for? Something must have happened to his boy, Chuck Othello. It was the only thing that could make a man that age run like his house was burning down. Jesse's boy, Chuck Othello, had been born around the same time as Wakefield's daughter, Carrie. Their births came less than a week apart. He had kidded Jesse that they must have gone on the same picnic. And Jesse had named his baby "Charles" after the lord of the manor. In democratic reciprocation and in the spirit of jolly good humor, Charles Wakefield had named his daughter "Carrie" after Jesse Chaney's wife.

Carrie had been a long time coming. Charles and Anne were well into middle age when the blessed miracle occurred. It had been their last clear chance. It had been years since he and Anne had lived together as man and wife. But one evening, after he had come home from the Great War, he had pursued a young, good-looking, buxom, black woman to her shack and she had rebuffed him, the Duke of Wakefield Manor.

"Get the hell outa my house, you old dilapidated peckerwood mother-fucker!" She had to be pulling his leg, so he put his arms around her like a damn fool. She couldn't be serious. She couldn't be rejecting the Duke of Wakefield Manor. "Come on, baby!" Pleading like a little boy for his mother's nipple. And she had to be kidding. He pushed himself up against her. And she backed away from him and spat in his face. He raised his arms to slap her, but his enormous ego would not let him. When he thought about it later, he thought maybe it was his latent democratic chivalry. Because he was a chivalrous man, and he was overly democratic. But Lillie Brown's rejection of him had scared him half to death! Had he actually deteriorated into an old dilapidated peckerwood? It was as if Lillie Brown had sentenced him to hell's fire and eternal castration.

He went home roaring drunk and raped his fragile Duchess and planted the seed of Carrie Louise Mariah Wakefield. It was the last time that he would rape the Duchess. She literally raped him from then on. Sexually, she had been rotting on the vine, dying for want of attention. But now she came suddenly alive and made demands on him. Sexual ones. And she wanted retroactive payment. She wanted all the goodies she had missed before and had never even known she'd missed. And the more pregnant she got, the more sexual and demanding. She took the initiative and wanted to call the shots and lay the ground rules.

In a way, she was pathetic. The fatter she became, the more lipstick and rouge she used. Wakefield was shocked at first. She unnerved him with her greed, with her vulgarity, and vulgarity was one word he had never dreamed of associating with his Duchess. Her lips seemed to grow larger and larger during that season, and she never ever got enough. She even started to flirt with other men. He indulged her and her insatiable appetite at first, but after awhile he fled from her. He had awakened the sleeping animal in her and the animal was out to destroy his manhood, he thought. She started reading books about it. She wanted to experiment. She wanted to be in the saddle and ride astraddle. She wanted to discuss it with him, which was, of course, out of the question as far as a Southern gentleman was concerned. Yet he was never really sure that she had ever had an actual orgasm. With all the screaming and moaning and groaning and swearing she did each time she went for broke, he was never ever sure.

A couple of months after the baby came he turned away from her and went back to his old ways again. After a few futile and pathetic extramarital flirtations on her part, which he knew about and tolerated, she went back to rotting on the vine again, and he to his role of Great White Planter, feeling guiltier than ever before.

Jesse's boy would be close to nine years old now. Time sure did fly. Before you turned around he'd be in high school and out already. Unknown to Jesse, Wakefield generously arranged for the boy's college education the very day the boy was born. He purchased an annuity for him, out of his deep and abiding friendship for the father. Wakefield and Jesse grew up together on Wakefield Farms. Wakefield always said that if other Southerners showed the same attitude toward their Negroes that he showed toward his, there wouldn't be the rigmarole about a Supreme Court decision. He had warned his white colleagues many times everywhere he went, everywhere he spoke, everywhere he drank.

As Jesse came within about a hundred yards of the Big House, Wakefield broke into a great big smile of friendly welcome. Jesse's mere presence always gave him a genuine warm feeling of one human being to another, the kind of feeling that did not come easily these days. It also gave him a feeling of the rightness of his approach to *his* Negroes. But now the smile left his face, unknowingly, as he watched Jesse continue toward the front porch where he stood beneath the electric fan. Instead of his flanking movement to go around to the back door, old Jesse came straight across the yard. In the entire relationship between these lifelong friends, Jesse had never before come straight across the front yard. Never ever. Wakefield did not want to believe what his eyes beheld. But by the time Jesse was ten or fifteen feet away from the porch, it became obvious, even to a friend like Wakefield, that this particular day was different from all the other days in the world. And Jesse was not going to stand on tradition or formality. Wakefield was afflicted with lockjaw, momentarily. As Jesse kept coming toward the porch, he ultimately found his voice again.

He was more flabbergasted than angry with his boyhood friend. "What's the matter with you, Jesse boy? The heat got the best of you?"

"The Supreme Court done spoke!" Jesse shouted, like he had just got that old-time religion and his soul had been converted. "Ain't going around to the back door no more. Coming right up to the front door from now on!"

"What'd you say?" Wakefield asked him, thinking maybe he had not heard properly. It was too hot to get angry with the best friend he had in all this world. Jesse was humility personified. Yet and still—

"And another thing—ain't no more calling you Mister Charlie. You just Charles from here on in. Or Jimmy Dick."

Wakefield's face lost color. The fan blew heat onto his forehead now. "Jesse, you going too damn—"

Jesse turned to saintly Anne Barkley Wakefield who wouldn't harm a mosquito if it were biting the tip of her turned-up nose. "And another thing—no more calling you Missy Anne. You just plain old common Annie from now on."

The sweet angelic woman gasped and put her handkerchief to her mouth. She stopped rocking momentarily. Her world was moving swiftly out from under her. This was too much for Charles Wakefield. Friendship or no friendship. Wakefield was completely out of control, a thing that seldom happened to him. Sweet and painful years of racial understanding and race philosophizing went by the everlasting boards. Even as he told himself, "Keep calm, C. J. R. Wakefield," almost against his will he heard himself shout:

"Nigger, don't you know you're in Mississippi?"

Wakefield immediately wished he could call the words back but they were gone from him forever. He had not meant to call his close friend, "nigger." Yet he felt a kind of cleansing of his heart and soul. He felt whiter, purer, inside. The atmosphere was clearer now. And he was somehow glad he had brought things out in the open, things that had been hidden between them all these many years. Sometimes the "word" had to be used to put things in perspective. Even between the best of friends. It had a therapeutic value for everyone concerned. Jesse would bow his humble head now, ever so slightly, and hide the hurt in his eyes with the noble savage's smile of profound humility. He would put his tail between his legs and go around to the back door, and God would be up in His Heaven again and all would be right with the world. Wakefield would forgive and forget. He was the biggest man in Mississippi. He could afford to be forgiving.

Obviously, Jesse had not read the script. "That's another thing," the noble savage shouted, like he was preaching from a colored Hardshell Baptist pulpit. "Ain' no more Mississippi. Ain' no more Mississippi. It's jes' 'Sippi from now on!"

John Henrik Clarke
(1915–   )

Professor Emeritus of Black and Puerto Rican Studies at Hunter College, Clarke is widely respected as an essayist, social critic, short-story writer, and eminent Pan-African historian. Born in Union Springs, Alabama, Clarke has worked as a feature writer for the *Pittsburgh Courier* and *Ghana Evening News*, as associate editor of *Freedomways*, and as a teacher at the New School for Social Research, Cornell University, and Columbia University. In 1948, he published a collection of poems, *Rebellion in Rhyme*. He has published more than fifty short stories, the best known one being "The Boy Who Painted Christ Black." Given his unfaltering commitment to exploring the lost, stolen, and betrayed aspects of African and African-American cultures, Clarke has written extensively about history and has served as editor for an impressive number of books that project a nationalist perspective. Among them are *Harlem U.S.A.; Harlem: A Community in Transition; American Negro Short Stories; William Styron's* **Nat Turner:** *Ten Black Writers Respond; Malcolm X: The Man and His Times; Marcus Garvey and the Vision of Africa*; and *Harlem* (short stories). The following story is reprinted from *Talk That Talk*.

The Lying Bee

For a long time my uncle Albert held the record as the greatest yarn spinner or the most convincing liar in our town. He was proud of this record in spite of the criticism showered upon him by the church-going branch of our family. Sometimes he used to tell me hair-raising stories of his adventures in foreign lands, and I listened to them with great interest, fully aware that he had never set foot outside the state of Georgia.

One day a stranger came to our town who began to dim the glow of Uncle Albert's lying record. The lies that this stranger told were more farfetched than Uncle Albert's. The stranger told his lies with a unique choice of words that was fascinating to people of a small town. As if this was not enough, his well-tailored clothes and his big-city mannerisms gained him the attention of the crowd and held him aloft from them all at the same time.

All of a sudden Uncle Albert began to lose the enthusiastic flock that formerly gathered around him whenever he sat down to tell a yarn. The invasion by an out-of-town liar so enraged Uncle Albert that his ability as a yarn-spinner was dulled almost to the point of being uninteresting. He spent most of his time moping around the streets of the town, labeling the out-of-town liar as an impostor and reprimanding the people for paying attention to him. Soon he dropped all other activities and devoted all of his time to conceiving a way he could avenge himself upon the other liar and retrieve his former status.

Twice Uncle Albert challenged the stranger to fight, and twice the stranger refused, saying there was nothing to fight about, for he had nothing against Uncle Albert. After this, Uncle Albert was more disturbed than ever. Every avenue for revenge seemed to have been closed, and his reputation as the greatest liar in Columbus, Georgia, had declined pathetically.

Finally one day after Felix Wilkinson, the town's leading grocer, had heard a lengthy discussion about the discord between Uncle Albert and the stranger, he suggested that a "lying bee" should be arranged, to determine once and for all who was the greatest liar.

Some of the church-going people protested, calling the whole affair a sinful outrage. This did not alter anything because most of the people in town were anxious to see the outcome of such a contest.

Three of the town's noted yarn-spinners, Jed Williams, the blacksmith, George Davis, the town's lone milkman, and Wilber Freepoint, the local drunk, who had partially sobered up for the occasion (this event was almost as noteworthy as the contest itself), were selected by Wilkinson to be the judges. Mr. Wilkinson, whose lies merited considerable attention, although they were nothing compared with Uncle Albert's, appointed himself supervisor of the contest, and to give himself more authority, he suggested that the affair be held in his grocery store.

During the three days before the contest a flood of comments and anticipation swept through the town. There were two groups of boosters: one group considered it their civic duty to favor Uncle Albert, and the other was bold enough to favor the stranger. A number of small bets were waged. Two townsmen came to striking blows while boosting the merits of the two liars. This contest was, by far, the most unusual thing that had ever happened in our town. Even some of the church people who had condemned it at first were quietly taking sides.

Finally the evening of the long-awaited lying bee arrived. Long before the time set for the contest an enthusiastic crowd was packed into Mr. Wilkinson's store. Uncle Albert, who had arrived well ahead of the crowd, had gained some attention by saying that the stranger had backed out, but the store was packed before the stranger arrived.

After the impatient crowd had started to whisper among themselves and Mr. Wilkinson had almost chewed up two pencils in near rage, the stranger appeared. He was quite handsome and he carried his tall, erect form in a smooth, effortless manner that always demanded attention. For this occasion he was dressed more stylish than ever. Although he had not said so, everybody took it for granted that he was from a big city. When he was fully inside the door, he removed his hat and fur-collared overcoat. He seated himself before removing his gloves. Everyone had fixed an avid stare upon him.

Gradually the atmosphere became tense. With an air of envy, Mr. Wilkinson observed the stranger's well-tailored outfit and rapped on the glass counter to turn the eyes of the audience in his direction.

"Ladies and gentlemen," he announced, "the much discussed lying bee will now begin. You know as well as I do why this affair has been arranged. For a long time Albert Carrol has held the record as the greatest liar in this town. Since the coming of one Josef Hendrick, there has been some doubt as to Albert's right to claim that title. We have assembled here on this December evening to settle, once and for all, the question of who is the greatest liar in Muskogee County. On my right sit the judges. They are too well-known to be introduced. After the two gentlemen have delivered their lies, the judges will retire to the back room of my store and reach a decision. To add more interest to this contest, I will give the winner a box of my most expensive cigars."

Mr. Wilkinson came from behind the counter and said, "Will the contestants please step forward." The stranger rose promptly and started toward Mr. Wilkinson. Both his expression and his graceful stride mirrored confidence. Albert threw one resentful glance at him, then rose and followed him to the front of the store.

"There is no use introducing you two gentlemen," Mr. Wilkinson said. "I have no doubt you know each other. This contest has been delayed long enough, so without further ado, we will get under way. I will thump a coin. If it lands heads up, the stranger will be the first to tell his lie; if it falls the other way, our Albert Carrol will be first."

Mr. Wilkinson thumped a coin into the air. A slight murmur came from the audience as it fell to the floor. Hesitantly, he bent over and lifted the coin. "It's heads, ladies and gentlemen," he said. "The stranger will tell the first lie."

Mr. Wilkinson climbed upon the high stool in front of the counter. Uncle Albert went back to his seat. The stranger waited until the audience became quiet, then he spoke.

"Friends," he began, "there is a little unfairness attached to my competing in this lying bee . . ." His voice possessed a cultured clearness that fastened the eyes of the audience upon him at once. "You see," he continued, "I am a professional liar. My opponent is an amateur."

An indignant murmur came from the crowd. With surprising swiftness Uncle Albert was on his feet, his face aflame with resentment.

The stranger stretched his hands forward, pleading for attention. "No offense, ladies and gentlemen," he said. "I only meant to convey that I tell lies for a living. You see, I write gags and jokes for stage comedians."

Uncle Albert sat down as if he had won some sort of victory. This put the audience back at ease. All eyes were again turned toward the stranger. At last he said:

"My favorite lie, the one that I shall now tell, is about Hi-John, the Great

Magician. Hi-John stopped off in a small southern town, and he was unnoticed and unheard of until one day two fellows, who were once partners, came to him for advice. The one-time partners had bought a mule together for one hundred dollars. One of the partners had paid twenty-five dollars; the other had paid seventy-five. When they broke up partnership, each wanted a share of the mule. The one who owned the greater interest offered to buy the other one out, but he refused to sell.

"Puzzling as this problem was, the great Hi-John encountered no difficulty in finding a solution. With one wave of his wand, he turned the mule into a mare. The two partners were frightened speechless.

"He paused and observed his accomplishment. Then with one more wave of his mighty wand, he gave the mare a beautiful colt. He instructed the partner who had paid the seventy-five dollars to take the mare, the one who had paid twenty-five dollars to take the colt. The one-time partners were too shocked by this miracle to ask questions or disobey his orders. They thanked him and went away, amazed but satisfied.

"After that the fame of Hi-John, the Great Magician, grew like a potato vine. He performed many more miracles, some of them far greater than the first one.

"One day, in spite of the great throng that flocked around him, the mighty magician found himself getting lonesome. So right then and there he decided to take himself a wife. There wasn't a woman in the town who didn't consider it an honor to be the wife of the great magician. Hi-John exercised his privilege to its fullest extent by choosing the most beautiful woman in the town for his wife. They were married in the finest style.

"For a long time their marriage was the marvel of all the townspeople. Hi-John, who had long been very rich, was now very happy. His happiness lasted until one day he came home from his miracle-performing and found his wife in the arms of another man. On seeing this, the magician flew into an awful rage. His wife and her lover fell at his feet, pleading for mercy. He gave one scornful look and turned away, walking toward the door. He stopped suddenly and spoke in a troubled tone: 'This is a grave situation,' he said. 'The great Hi-John is not accustomed to coping with such problems. I think I'll let the Lord take care of this one.'

"The magician turned his great figure back toward his wife and her lover, scratching his head as if he were expecting to discover a super-thinking machine. He spoke again, the pitch of his voice rising with every word. 'Probably the Lord is too busy with other things,' he said, 'I think I will take over this situation myself.'

"The two betrayers continued to plead for mercy, but Hi-John paid little heed to them. He seemed to be searching for his real self. Then, as if he had suddenly reached a decision, he pulled out his mighty wand and the whole house disappeared. The three of them were now standing in an empty lot. Hi-John's wife fought her way through the veil of astonishment and began to scream. Her lover made an attempt to run. Hi-John spoke just one word; the lover halted in his tracks and stood as if in a trance. The magician paused as if in meditation. When his wife started to plead again, he waved his mighty wand as if guided by a streak of madness and turned both his wife and her lover into mammoth oak trees.

"After this, the great magician walked away, weeping sorrowfully. He loved his wife, and this was one miracle he had hated to perform. Soon he disappeared and since then no one has ever heard any more about Hi-John, the Great Magician."

Josef Hendrick, the stranger, took a slight bow, indicating that he had finished his lie. As he started for his seat, he smiled, reflecting a tinge of victory. The few ladies in the audience gasped in utter amazement. There was some applause from the men. The three judges stared at one another in wonderment. Mr. Wilkinson moved down from his high stool, stroking his chin. At least the stranger had told a good lie. No one seemed to doubt that.

Uncle Albert threw a scornful glance at him as he took his seat. Suddenly a series of whispering debates about the merits and demerits of the stranger's lie spread through the store. Mr. Wilkinson rapped on the counter for silence, and the murmuring died down.

"Ladies and gentlemen," he announced, "we will now hear from our great liar, Albert Carrol." "Hurray for Albert," a local drunk yelled. A slight shower of applause greeted these words, although there were some among the crowd who doubted whether Uncle Albert could tell anything that would surpass the stranger's lie.

Mr. Wilkinson climbed back up on his high stool as Uncle Albert rose and walked to the front of the store. He was the center of attraction now. All eyes were fixed on him, burning with anticipation. He glanced at Mr. Wilkinson and the box of cigars that was to become the property of the winner. He smiled at his audience, then spoke in a thick, uncultured tone, as he always did:

"Folks," he began, "I only know one lie that I haven't tol' roun' this burg, an' that's th' one about Sam Tolbert's jackass. That's th' one I will now tell y' all.

"To begin with, Sam Tolbert's jackass was the kickingest thing that ever put a foot in this worl'. Th' first time Sam took 'im t' town, 'e kicked th' court house two miles outside th' city limit and left the ol' jedge an' all th' members of his court hangin' on midair. On his way back t' th' country th' jackass passed th' court house, an' t' prove that th' first mess of kickin' was no accident, th' durn jackass kicked th' court house all th' way back t' town. After this, Sam had t' keep his jackass in th' country. Hit was against th' law t' let 'im enter a city.

"Very li'l was heard about th' jackass until, finally, one day two beggars came by Sam's farm an' axed fer some food. Sam tol' 'em dat he had no food ready, but dey didn't believe 'im. So dey kept on axin'. Th' jackass was standing nearby, an' after a while 'e became annoyed by th' beggars' pleas. Sam could tell by th' look in th' jackass's eyes that one of his kickin' spells was comin' on. Th' nearest thing t' th' jackass was one of Sam's cows. So, like a streak o' lightnin', th' dern jackass kicked th' cow two miles in th' air.

One minute later th' cow fell at th' beggars' feet on a pure gold platter, in the form of nice, fat, juicy steaks wit' onions an' gravy for good measure. I tell ya, ladies an' gennemun, dem steaks was cooked t' please a king.

"Dis struck th' beggars as bein' very funny, so dey began t' laughin', an' never in dis worl' have any two people laughed so much. Ladies an' gennemun, those two beggars laughed until holes split in dere sides big enuf fer a wagon train t' go through. But dey didn't stop laughin'. No sir, not den. Dey was laughin' an' cryin' all at th' same time, and th' water from dere cryin' eyes was floodin' Sam Tolbert's farm. After a while dere eyes began t' shine like th' sun, but dey went right on laughin', ladies an' gennemun. Dey laughed until their eyes was brighter den th' sun. No, dey didn't stop den.

"In a li'l while th' beggars' eyes an' th' sun began t' fight a little battle fer th' right t' shine all over th' worl'. Soon th' sun threw up its hands, admitting defeat. Now th' beggars' eyes took dat of th' sun . . . an' dey was still laughin'.

"As I've said before, their sides had split open wide enuf fer a wagon train t' go through, an' th' water from dere cryin' eyes was floodin' Sam Tolbert's farm, 'n' dere eyes had outshined th' sun. But in spite of all dis, dey went right on laughin', ladies an' gennemun. . . . Fer all I know, dey could still be laughin'."

Upon finishing his lie Uncle Albert glanced again at Mr. Wilkinson and the box of cigars at his elbow. An expression of complete astonishment was on every face in the store. There was a heavy silence, a silence of tribute and approval. Uncle Albert's lie had so affected the audience that no one would dare speak. The judges thought it useless to retire to the back room of the store for their decision. The decision was written plainly across the face of everyone in the store.

Mr. Wilkinson climbed down from his high stool, scanned the audience, and took a deep breath. Without uttering a word, he went over and placed the box of cigars in Uncle Albert's hands.

Frank Yerby
(1916–1991)

Although Yerby has published more than thirty novels since 1946, it is only his short story "Health Card" (that won the O. Henry Memorial Award in 1944), which has been noted for its literary merits. Born in Augusta, Georgia, Yerby received a B.A. from Paine College and an M.A. from Fisk University. He taught briefly at Florida A. & M. University and Southern University before he became a writer of "costume" novels, many of which exploit readers' fascination with the romance and myths of the plantation South. His short stories appeared in such magazines as *Harper's, Phylon, Common Ground*, and *Tomorrow* before his first novel *The Foxes of Harrow* (1946) became a startling success; it sold more than a million copies in its first year. Yerby moved to Spain in the 1950s. "Health Card" is reprinted from the May 1944 issue of *Harper's* magazine.

Health Card

Johnny stood under one of the street lights on the corner and tried to read the letter. The street lights down in the "Bottom" were so dim that he couldn't make out half the words, but he didn't need to: he knew them all by heart anyway.

"Sugar," he read, "it took a long time but I done it. I got the money to come to see you. I waited and waited for them to give you a furlough, but it look like they don't mean to. Sugar, I can't wait no longer. I got to see you. I got to. Find a nice place for me to stay—where we can be happy together. You know what I mean. With all my love, Lily."

Johnny folded the letter and put it back in his pocket. Then he walked swiftly down the street past all the juke joints with the music blaring out and the GI brogans pounding. He turned down a side street, scuffing up a cloud of dust as he did so. None of the streets down in Black Bottom was paved, and there were four inches of fine white powder over everything. When it rained, the mud would come up over the tops of his Army shoes, but it hadn't rained in nearly three months. There were no juke joints on this street, and the Negro shanties were neatly whitewashed. Johnny kept on walking until he came to the end of the street. On the corner stood the little whitewashed Baptist Church, and next to it was the neat, well-kept home of the pastor.

85

Johnny went up on the porch and hesitated. He thrust his hand in his pocket and the paper crinkled. He took his hand out and knocked on the door.

"Who's that?" a voice called.

"It's me," Johnny answered; "it's a sodjer."

The door opened a crack, and the woman peered out. She was middle-aged and fat. Looking down, Johnny could see that her feet were bare.

"Whatcha want, sodjer?"

Johnny took off his cap.

"Please, Mam, lemme come in. I kin explain it t yuh better settin down." She studied his face for a minute in the darkness.

"Aw right," she said; "you kin come in, son."

Johnny entered the room stiffly and sat down on a corn-shuck-bottomed chair.

"It's this way, Mam," he said. "I got a wife up Nawth. I been tryin and tryin t git a furlough so I could go t see huh. But they always put me off. So now she done worked an saved enuff money t come an see me. I wants t ax you t rent me a room, Mam. I doan know nowheres t ax."

"This ain't no hotel, son."

"I know it ain't. I can't take Lily t no hotel, not lak hotels in this heah town."

"Lily yo wife?"

"Yes'm. She my shonuff, honest t Gawd wife. Married in th Baptist Church in Detroit."

The fat woman sat back, and her thick lips widened into a smile.

"She a good girl, ain't she? An you doan wanta take her to one o these heah hohouses they calls hotels."

"That's it, Mam."

"Sho you kin bring huh heah, son. Be glad t have huh. Reveren be glad t have huh too. What yo name, son?"

"Johnny. Johnny Green. Mam—"

"Yas, son?"

"You understands that I wants t come heah too?"

The fat woman rocked back in her chair and gurgled with laughter.

"Bless yo heart, chile, I ain't always been a ole woman! And I ain't always been th preacher's wife neither!"

"Thank you, Mam. I gotta go now. Time for me t be gittin back t camp."

"When you bring Lily?"

"Be Monday night, Mam. Pays you now if you wants it."

"Monday be awright. Talk it over wit th Reveren, so he make it light fur yuh. Know sodjer boys ain't got much money."

"No Mam, sho Lawd ain't. G night, Mam."

When he turned back into the main street of the Negro section, the doors of the joints were all open and the soldiers were coming out. The girls were clinging onto their arms all the way to the bus stop. Johnny looked at the dresses that stopped halfway between the pelvis and the knee and hugged the backside so that every muscle showed when they walked. He saw the purple lipstick smeared across the wide full lips, and the short hair stiffened with smelly grease so that it covered their heads like a black lacquered cap. They went on down to the bus stop arm in arm, their knotty bare calves bunching with each step as they walked. Johnny thought about Lily. He walked past them very fast without turning his head.

But just as he reached the bus stop he heard the whistles. When he turned around he saw the four MPs and the civilian policemen stopping the crowd. He turned around again and walked back until he was standing just behind the white men.

"Aw right," the MPs were saying, "you gals git your health cards out."

Some of the girls started digging in their handbags. Johnny could see them dragging out small yellow cardboard squares. But the others just stood there with blank expressions on their faces. The soldiers started muttering, a dark, deep-throated sound. The MPs started pushing their way through the crowd, looking at each girl's card as they passed. When they came to a girl who didn't have a card, they called out to the civilian policemen:

"Aw right, Mister, take A'nt Jemima for a little ride."

Then the city policemen would lead the girl away and put her in the Black Maria.

They kept this up until they had examined every girl except one. She hung back beside her soldier, and the first time the MPs didn't see her. When they came back through, one of them caught her by the arm.

"Lemme see your card, Mandy," he said.

The girl looked at him, her little eyes narrowing into slits in her black face.

"Tek yo han offn me, white man," she said.

The MP's face crimsoned, so that Johnny could see it, even in the darkness.

"Listen, black gal," he said, "I told you to lemme see your card."

"An I told you t tek yo han offen me, white man!"

"Gawddammit, you little black bitch, you better do like I tell you!"

Johnny didn't see very clearly what happened after that. There was a sudden explosion of motion, and then the MP was trying to jerk his hand back, but he couldn't, for the little old black girl had it between her teeth and was biting it to the bone. He drew his other hand back, and slapped her across the face so hard that it sounded like a pistol shot. She went over backward and her tight skirt split, so that when she got up Johnny could see that she didn't have anything on under it. She came forward like a cat, her nails bared, straight for the MP's eyes. He slapped her down again, but the soldiers surged forward all at once. The MPs fell back and drew their guns and one of them blew a whistle.

Johnny, who was behind them, decided it was time for him to get out of there and he did; but not before he saw the squads of white MPs hurtling around the corner and going to work on the Negroes with their clubs. He reached the bus stop, and swung on board. The minute after he had pushed his way to the back behind all the white soldiers, he heard the shots. The bus driver put the bus in gear and they roared off toward the camp.

It was after one o'clock when all the soldiers straggled in. Those of them who could still walk. Eight of them came in on the meat wagon, three with gunshot wounds. The Colonel declared the town out of bounds for all Negro soldiers for a month.

"Dammit," Johnny said, "I gotta go meet Lily, I gotta. I cain't stay heah. I cain't!"

"Whatcha gonna do," Little Willie asked, "go AWOL?"

Johnny looked at him, his brow furrowed into a frown.

"Naw," he said, "I'm gonna go see th Colonel!"

"Whut! Man, you crazy! Colonel kick yo black ass out fo you gits yo mouf open."

"I take a chanct on that."

He walked over to the little half-mirror on the wall of the barracks. Carefully he readjusted his cap. He pulled his tie out of his shirt front, and drew the knot tighter around his throat. Then he tucked the ends back in at just the right fraction of an inch between the correct pair of buttons. He bent down and dusted his shoes again, although they were already spotless.

"Man," Little Willie said, "you sho is a fool!"

"Reckon I am," Johnny said; then he went out of the door and down the short wooden steps.

When he got to the road that divided the colored and white sections of the camp, his steps faltered. He stood still a minute, drew in a deep breath, and marched very stiffly and erect across the road. The white soldiers gazed at him curiously, but none of them said anything. If a black soldier came over into their section it was because somebody sent him, so they let him alone.

In front of the Colonel's headquarters he stopped. He knew what he had to say, but his breath was very short in his throat and he was going to have a hard time saying it.

"Whatcha want, soldier?" the sentry demanded.

"I wants t see th Colonel."

"Who sent you?"

Johnny drew his breath in sharply.

"I ain't at liberty t say," he declared, his breath coming out very fast beyond the words.

"You ain't at liberty t say," the sentry mimicked. "Well I'll be damned! If you ain't at liberty t say, then I ain't at liberty t let you see th colonel! Git tha hell outa here, nigger, before I pump some lead in you!"

Johnny didn't move.

The sentry started toward him, lifting his rifle butt, but another soldier, a sergeant, came around the corner of the building.

"Hold on there," he called. "What tha hell is th trouble here?"

"This here nigger says he wants t see tha Colonel and when I ast him who sent him, he says he ain't at liberty t say!"

The Sergeant turned to Johnny.

Johnny came to attention and saluted him. You aren't supposed to salute NCOs, but sometimes it helps.

"What you got t say fur yourself, boy?" the Sergeant said, not unkindly. Johnny's breath evened.

"I got uh message fur th Colonel, suh," he said; "I ain't sposed t give it t nobody else but him. I ain't even sposed t tell who sont it, suh."

The Sergeant peered at him sharply.

"You tellin tha truth, boy?"

"Yassuh!"

"Awright. Wait here a minute."

He went into HQ. After a couple of minutes he came back out.

"Awright, soldier, you kin go on in."

Johnny mounted the steps and went into the Colonel's office. The Colonel was a lean, white-haired soldier with a face tanned to the color of saddle leather. He was reading a letter through a pair of horn-rimmed glasses which had only one ear-hook left, so that he had to hold them up to his eyes with his hand. He put them down and looked up. Johnny saw that his eyes were pale blue, so pale that he felt like he was looking into the eyes of an eagle or some other fierce bird of prey.

"Well?" he said, and Johnny stiffened into a salute. The Colonel half smiled.

"At ease, soldier," he said. Then: "The Sergeant tells me that you have a very important message for me."

Johnny gulped in the air. "Beggin th Sergeant's pardon, suh," he said, "but that ain't so."

"What!"

"Yassuh," Johnny rushed on, "nobody sent me. I come on m own hook. I had t talk t yuh, Colonel, suh! Yu kin sen me t th guard house afterwards, but please suh lissen t me fur jes a minute!"

The Colonel relaxed slowly. Something very like a smile was playing around the corners of his mouth. He looked at his watch.

"All right, soldier," he said, "you've got five minutes."

"Thank yuh, thank yuh, suh!"

"Speak your piece, soldier; you're wasting time!"

"It's about Lily, suh. She my wife. She done worked an slaved fur nigh onto six months t git the money t come an see me. An now you give th order that none o th cullud boys kin go t town. Beggin yo pahdon, suh, I wasn't in none o that trouble. I ain't never been in no trouble. You kin ax my capn, if you wants to. All I wants is permission to go into town fur one week, an I'll stay outa town fur two months if yuh wants me to."

The Colonel picked up the phone.

"Ring Captain Walters for me," he said; then, "What's your name, soldier?"

"It's Green, suh. Private Johnny Green."

"Captain Walters? This is Colonel Milton. Do you have anything in your files concerning Private Johnny Green? Oh yes, go ahead. Take all the time you need."

The Colonel lit a long, black cigar. Johnny waited. The clock on the wall spun its electric arms.

"What's that? Yes. Yes, yes, I see. Thank you, Captain."

He put down the phone and picked up a fountain pen. He wrote swiftly. Finally he straightened up and gave Johnny the slip of paper.

Johnny read it. It said: "Private Johnny Green is given express permission to go into town every evening of the week beginning August seventh and ending August fourteenth. He is further permitted to remain in town overnight every night during said week, so long as he returns to camp for reveille the following morning. By order of the Commanding Officer, Colonel H. H. Milton."

There was a hard knot at the base of Johnny's throat. He couldn't breathe. But he snapped to attention, and saluted smartly.

"Thank you, suh," he said at last, then: "Gawd bless you, suh!"

"Forget it, soldier. I was a young married man once myself. My compliments to Captain Walters."

Johnny saluted again and about-faced, then he marched out of the office and down the stairs. On the way back he saluted everybody—privates, NCOs, and civilian visitors, his white teeth gleaming in a huge smile.

"That's sure one happy darky," one of the white soldiers said.

Johnny stood in the station and watched the train running in. The yellow lights from the windows flickered on and off across his face as the alternating squares of light and darkness flashed past. Then it was slowing and Johnny was running beside it, trying to keep abreast of the Jim Crow coach. He could see her standing up, holding her bags. She came down the steps the first one and they stood there holding each other, Johnny's arms crushing all the breath out of her, holding her so hard against him that his brass buttons hurt through her thin dress. She opened her mouth to speak but he kissed her, bending her head backward on her neck until her little hat fell off. It lay there on the ground, unnoticed.

"Sugah," she said, "sugah. It was awful."

"I know," he said, "I know."

Then he took her bags and they started walking out of the station toward the Negro section of town.

"I missed yuh so much," Johnny said, "I thought I lose m mind."

"Me too," she said. Then: "I brought th marriage license with me like yuh told me. I doan want th preacher's wife t think we bad."

"Enybody kin look at yuh an see yuh uh angel!"

They went very quietly through all the dark streets and the white soldiers turned to look at Johnny and his girl.

Lak a queen, Johnny thought, lak a queen. He looked at the girl beside him, seeing the velvety nightshade skin, the glossy black lacquered curls, the sweet wide hips and the long, clean legs, striding beside him in the darkness. Behold I am black but comely, oh ye daughters of Zion!

They turned into the Bottom where the street lights were dim blobs on the pine poles and the dust rose up in little swirls around their feet. Johnny had his head half turned so that he didn't see the two MPs until he had almost bumped into them. He dropped one bag and caught Lily by the arm. Then he drew her aside quickly and the two men went by them without speaking.

They kept on walking, but every two steps Johnny would jerk his head around and look nervously back over his shoulder. The last time he looked the two MPs had stopped and were looking back at them. Johnny turned out the elbow of the arm next to Lily so that it hooked into hers a little and began to walk faster, pushing her along with him.

"Whas yo hurry, sugah?" she said. "I be heah a whole week!"

But Johnny was looking over his shoulder at the two MPs. They were coming toward them now, walking with long, slow strides, their reddish-white faces set. Johnny started to push Lily along faster, but she shook off his arm and stopped still.

"I do declare, Johnny Green! You th beatiness man! Whut you walk me so fas fur?"

Johnny opened his mouth to answer her, but the military police were just behind them now, and the Sergeant reached out and laid his hand on her arm.

"Cmon gal," he said, "lemme see it."

"Let you see whut? Whut he mean, Johnny?"

"Your card," the Sergeant growled, "lemme see your card."

"My card?" Lily said blankly. "Whut kinda card, Mister?"

Johnny put the bags down. He was fighting for breath.

"Look heah, Sarge," he said; "this girl my wife!"

"Oh yeah? I said lemme see your card, sister!"

"I ain't got no card, Mister. I dunno whut you talkin bout."

"Look, Sarge," the other MP said, "th soldier's got bags. Maybe she's just come t town."

"These your bags, gal?"

"Yessir."

"Awright. You got twenty-four hours to git yourself a health card. If you don't have it by then, we hafta run you in. Git goin, now."

"Listen," Johnny shouted; "this girl my wife! She ain't no ho! I tell you she ain't—"

"What you say, nigger," the MP Sergeant growled, "whatcha say?" He started toward Johnny.

Lily swung on Johnny's arm.

"Cmon, Johnny," she said; "they got guns. Cmon Johnny, please! Please, Johnny!"

Slowly she drew him away.

"Aw, leave em be, Sarge," the MP Corporal said, "maybe she *is* his wife."

The Sergeant spat. The brown tobacco juice splashed in the dirt not an inch from Lily's foot. Then the two of them turned and started away.

Johnny stopped.

"Lemme go, Lily," he said, "lemme go!" He tore her arm loose from his and started back up the street. Lily leaped, her two arms fastening themselves around his neck. He fought silently but she clung to him, doubling her knees so that all her weight was hanging from his neck.

"No, Johnny! Oh Jesus no! You be kilt! Oh, Johnny, listen t me, sugah! You's all I got!"

He put both hands up to break her grip but she swung her weight sidewise and the two of them went down in the dirt. The MPs turned the corner out of sight.

Johnny sat there in the dust staring at her. The dirt had ruined her dress. He sat there a long time looking at her until the hot tears rose up back of his eyelids faster than he could blink them away, so he put his face down in her lap and cried.

"I ain't no man!" he said, "I ain't no man!"

"Hush, sugah," she said. "You's a man awright. You's my man!"

Gently she drew him to his feet. He picked up the bags and the two of them went down the dark street toward the preacher's house.

Lance Jeffers
(1919–1985)

Jeffers was born in Fremont, Nebraska, and spent his formative years in that state and in San Francisco. Nevertheless, his fiction, poetry, and critical articles demonstrate a profound regard for the people and land of the black South. Jeffers gained some acclaim as a writer when "The Dawn Swings In" was published in *The Best American Short Stories, 1948*, but he did not receive widespread attention in black literary circles until Broadside Press published *My Blackness Is the Beauty of This Land*, his first volume of poetry, in 1970. He subsequently published three more volumes, *When I Know the Power of My Black Hand*, *O Africa Where I Baked My Bread*, and *Grandsire*. His poetry is marked by sustained interest in the themes of heroic grandeur, love, and global oppression. In his poetry, the novel *Witherspoon* (1983), and his critical essays, Jeffers was dedicated to a nationalist posture. His work is also informed by an unrelenting sense of morality, articulated quite strongly in "The Death of the Defensive Posture: Toward Grandeur in Afroamerican Literature," an essay he wrote for the anthology *The Black Seventies*. He taught at many colleges, including Morehouse, Tuskegee, Howard University, Duke University, and North Carolina State University. His work appears in the anthologies *Nine Black Poets*, *A Galaxy of Black Writers*, *New Black Voices*, *Vietnam and Black America*, *You Better Believe It*, and *A Broadside Treasury*. The following excerpt is from the novel *Witherspoon*.

---

from Witherspoon

1967

Rev. Lucius Witherspoon stood deep in the shadows of his study, alone in the depths of the semidark.

In his mind, chains clanked, and black slaveflesh walked before him. At first there were nothing but black and ashy ankles, bare, unlacerated, emaciated almost to the bone. Then the ankles were chained, they moved before him up a hill ungrassed and dusty, the ankles were chained and emaciated, they moved slowly and in pain. The vision changed: he saw the bare breasts of African women, full and luscious breasts, the women were rowing a boat, there was anguish on their faces as they rowed.

An ironic half-smile parted his mouth as he watched the vision in his brain, then his face grew grim again as there resounded in his mind the metallic crack of battle axes against shields, and the clang of an enormous cloth-covered hammer against a great round gold disc high enough to hide a man behind. In his vision Witherspoon heard suddenly a black woman's soaring voice great with grief—he could see her: middle-aged huge-bosomed, bending far over in agony to one side as she sang, her voice soaring: "My Lord, what a morning," the poetry of her voice so powerful that it seemed as if it could rip the horizon up from where it lay and send the dusk-colors streaming back down across the sky past earth into the black and mindless heavens whence they came.

"My Lord . . . what a morning," he said. "Oh Lord . . . Lord . . . ."

Sweat cracked from his forehead, rolled in tiny rivers down his roughhewn cavern-cheeked dark brown face, skin rough and graveled where he shaved; there where he shaved, his visage like a crude mask, brown and thickpored. The sweat poured down his face, tears glistened in his great eyes that protruded Africanly from their sockets. In his chest there was a mighty shaking as if great-trunked trees were being uprooted from his torso.

"My Lord, what a morning," he exclaimed bitterly. "My Lord, what a morning." He gritted his teeth and whispered hoarsely, "My Lord, what a morning!"

He saw Willie sit in the electric chair, saw the brutefaced frightened guards fasten him into the chair, saw them adjust the terrible hood about his head, saw him wait in the utter darkness:

Witherspoon glanced at the electric clock on his desk. It was time!

He saw Willie's face as he waited in the darkness for the strike of death.

Witherspoon wanted to fling himself groaning into the over-stuffed chair. He stood upright: this, what little he could do—to stand erect like a man at the moment of Willie's death, as he remembered Willie Armstrong's heavy black-Southern accent, heavy and loving, rough and guttural, basic and uni- verse-defying as Willie stood staring through the bars at Witherspoon:

"Ah wouldn't ask a cracker fo the time uh day."

Love, fear, shame, and wonderment had flooded Witherspoon's heart as he had listened and stared back at the condemned man through the bars: how could a black man talk like this? this was not niggers' street-corner bravado that disappeared (the moment a policeman rounded the corner) into cringing: this was audacity, for there seemed to be no fear in this man: it was as if he were rock inside, rock and lightning, and nothing could crush the rock and nothing could dispel the lightning: how could a black man who had been programmed for fear from the day that he was born, who had sucked fear from his mother's tittie, be fearless? Even Jesus had trembled with fear . . . Willie was—more than Christ?—a black boy who had to scrounge for love and acceptance where he could get it, no one had welcomed him as the Re- deemer, no one had welcomed him into the world as anything more than just another poor black child, wretchedly poor, yet now he was fearless, made of a flesh that was not cruel but a flesh to which fear and weakness were alien: *more* than Christ, Witherspoon thought.

As he had looked through the bars at this black man to whom he had been sent by a white man to ask him, Willie, to betray himself, Witherspoon had shivered with shame; he had looked with awe and reverence at the man who was going to shuffle to the chair his pantleg split and his black head shaved, glance fascinated for one single second at the death seat, then plop himself into it without a moment's further hesitation, with an air as if to say "Let's get it over with, motherfuckers," look fiercely at the dough-faced guards, sit and wait with a dignity, with a calm and offhandedness that would strike fear into the spectators.

When he could have saved his life by pleading to the governor for his life on television, as many a black man had done, "Save my life, guvnor, please sir, if you can. . . ."

Now they were carrying his body like a sack of potatoes from the electric chair, or a corpse-faced doctor was leaning over Willie with a stethoscope to his stilled heart, the doctor's face was hard and cold and unafraid, Witherspoon imagined that he saw Willie come alive, open his eyes and snarl at the doctor like a wolf. The doctor, middle-aged though he was, danced expressionlessly out of range like an inhuman ballet dancer. . . .

"Hell naw ah ain beggin *nothin* from these motherfuckers. . . ."

Shame washed over Witherspoon.

"Lucius," Witherspoon's wife's thin voice reached through the closed door like a tentacle. He started, then looked down at his torso in contempt.

"Lucius," she called again.

"In the study here," he called back in his deep voice of professional sorrow.

Her long very light brown face, unwrinkled but aged somehow at 30, came longly through the doorway like a ghost's visage, half in the dark, half in the light.

"He gone?" she quavered.

"Yes," he said sternly.

Pursilla Witherspoon lowered herself cautiously like an old woman into the maroon-colored leather couch.

"Gone," she echoed. "Gone."

With massive dignity, great-muscled and broad across the chest as a ship-mast, he turned to survey her.

He shook his head savagely, the luscious-breasted African women came to his mind again, black in their blackness, succulent as oranges whose juice tasted like rich milk; while she his wife, sweet crippled spirit, unable, kind and lonely in her bed with him.

"Gone," she repeated hollowly.

"I be damned," he muttered.

"Do you think he was guilty," she said cautiously, a feeble tendon of severity in her voice.

She frightened him: this was the depth in her he did not know.

He would not be harsh, he thought; he waited a moment and tried to flavor his reply with his weight, but his reply was impatient nevertheless:

"He's dead now."

She glanced in her melancholy way up at him. Despite his consciousness that the wrong tone would hurt her, or the wrong word, he had not taken care enough. How she looked up at him like a kicked dog, then lowered her head, hoping that he would not notice!

He shook his head in pity.

"Revand!"

"Yes," he answered.

"Was he guilty?" A trace of hysteria.

He turned to face her directly.

"I don't know," he said, trying to curb his growing anger. "I don't care," he said, his grief suddenly rising.

"Revand . . . Why?"

"Because . . ."

He choked down his grief. He could not understand why in his heart the Willie Armstrongs of his race had always been objects of awe, fear, admiration: the dangerous black men who had love in their hearts: the black men who could quickly kill without compunction who were stern with tenderness for children: the black men who had tears of rock, who were violent who met agony and defeat head on; the black men with the knife in their hands who would plunge it into the heart of the world, mutter imprecations and depart with a quick and evil eye who were yet capable of deeds of great kindness and sacrifice, the wanderers who rarely took families but wandered till the end of their days, then looked death in the eye, sullenly into its bony face: the violent yet secretly sweet-natured gods; such men, legion in his race, were dearer to Witherspoon than his own blood father. He had a last vision of Willie on his death slab, yet more alive dead . . . than he Witherspoon had ever been. He let his head sink upon his chest. He shook his head. More man than I will ever be. . . .

He looked up to find his wife's eyes fixed upon him. Her expression was keen, sly, penetrating, evil, mad. To Witherspoon there was treachery in her face.

"Was he guilty? *Why* don't you care?"

"Shit no, I—" he began passionately, and stopped, astonished.

In the name of sweet Jesus, what is happening to me? To use the language of the gutter, to use it in conversation with this lady, my wife?

She was stunned, began rapidly to sink into herself.

He mastered an impulse to run to her, sink at her knee, and apologize. Upon the heels of this impulse came the vision of his wife in coitus, groaning as he took her but never a groan of rapture or sweet pain, only the groan and heaving of one in slaughterous war with the life inside her. She fought her compulsion to trample herself with a mighty tumult, there was tumultuous within her the nature to be rent and plunged into by maleness; the two—the urge to give herself in love and the urge to destroy herself, each impulse fought the other until at last, exhausted, collapsed, unjoyed, unsweetened, and he bitter to his heart's deep gall, they lay upon their bed of spikes in an evil peace. Always after this struggle with her and with her struggle with herself, he felt as if he had left his phallus cut off within her; as if his scrotum were lying, a bloody sack, beneath him in the bed; as if his whole body were blistered and pierced, mountainous tears unshed behind his eyehollows.

Willie would not have had anything but pity and revulsion for Pursilla. He would never have touched her, would have moved unerringly with assurance past her to a woman who would have worshipped his maleness, his manhood, who would have worshipped his confidence in his manhood and his maleness, a woman who would have doubled him as a man when she made love to him, who would have brought her womanhood to him and humbly pressed it on him, a casual but feeling king: he would never have had anything to do with a woman who was fighting a demon inside her; that was why, Witherspoon thought, Willie could go all the way through with a thing and lay his life on the line: killing a cracker and picking the right woman to go to bed with— these things came from the same place inside a man . . .

Closely he watched her crazed closed face.

"He ain't guilty." The words popped out of his mouth without thought.

She came from within herself and looked up at him with malice.

"He *killed* a man. He killed *two* men. He *ought* to been hanged."

He drew breath in with a hiss.

"Why ain't he guilty?" she demanded.

He looked down at the floor and shook his head.

"I don't know," he said sadly.

"He denied his God!" she accused.

"A man doesn't have to believe in God," he said, not entirely convinced.

"A man doesn't have to believe in God," she echoed tonelessly. "But he refused to take the oath in court, and when the judge ask him, he said, 'Cause I don't believe in it.' " She gathered momentum. "He wouldn't let you pray for him, wouldn't let you come to him the last day and say a prayer over him. He told you he didn't *need* prayers. And he broke the Lord's commandment!"

Gently Witherspoon said to her: "I'm going to the ministerial conference."

He turned and left the room.

Ironically he watched himself walk through the house, through the front door, into the brilliant sunshine of the porch. He considered himself ridiculous. He descended the porch and got into his old blue Plymouth and drove off to the meeting at Whitney's church around the corner. He felt false and apart from himself, he watched himself drive down the street and thought of himself as an aimless fool.

If Willie wouldn't have had anything to do with a woman like Pursilla, then what's wrong with *me*, he thought. Can't pleasure a man, fightin a devil inside herself. I must have my *own* devil. If she's got a demon, I must have my own—otherwise I wouldn't be with her.

Man ain't shit. (He bit his lip.) What come over me—cussing, cussing, like I'm goin crazy or sompm. I never did that before. But it's true—man *ain't* shit—can't get any peace, no happiness, spend all his days fightin ghosts and demons, and where are they? Right inside himself! That's where God is! That's where the devil is! Right inside you! Man doesn't have to believe in God— it's in him or it ain't!

He pulled up in front of the Second Presbyterian Church, got out of the car and closed the door, stood motionless, and viewed with old contempt the modernism of Whitney's church: like some modern Noah's Ark that had run aground and tipped over onto its top. A church should be a cathedral, thought Witherspoon, or it should be a plain whitewashed humble Baptist church like my own, not a showoffy so-called temple like this for dicty nigger women to show their furs off in every Sunday. A church should be for religious ecstasy— the quiet ecstasy of saints or the shouting ecstasy of his congregation in Quiver every Sunday. All one could usually feel in life was the foul feeling he had right now—shame and chagrin, humiliation and weakness, inadequacy and self-contempt. A church was to purge those feelings, that's what religion was for, that's what religious ecstasy was for. Those Presbyterian niggers never had ecstasy. To them, shouting was revolting. Their furs covered coldness, sickness, falseness, despair, impotence, humiliation by the white man; these Presbyterian niggers were too busy hiding these feelings to be true to themselves and shout, like his own black sisters of the church whose spirits he could touch on Sundays. Yet their shouting was unsatisfying too, false even though it was real. He thought of his wife's face in coitus, agonized and conflicted.

Willie wasn't false. Condemned men are the only *men* I've ever known, Witherspoon thought, turning his mouth down in scorn for the false Presbyterian church which stood before him, the only men who have no falseness to them. And Willie was the best of em because he wasn't afraid.

Prisons frightened Witherspoon; he always drove away from a prison with the feeling that he too was in prison: the darkness of his house seemed a prison: living with Pursilla seemed a prison: being a preacher seemed a prison: the South was a prison: walking around in the midst of falseness, false greetings and false handshakes, was a prison. His own skin was a prison, his own mind, and his frustrated longing for a woman, the repressed thoughts and the unexperienced raptures were a prison. . . . Sometimes he thought he might as well exchange places with the condemned prisoners. . . . And he had always felt particularly inadequate in talking to a condemned man, had always gone away feeling small, petty, trivial, sometimes angry with himself, sometimes enraged at white people (who were surely responsible for the execution of black people), but above all, he drove away from the prison feeling false. Always he had felt that the condemned men he had gone to console and say prayers over had towered over him morally. Some were scared, but none of them was on the verge of collapse. All of them held up and accepted death as a reality. There was an undefinable cleanness about them. And when he had gone (as he had done on four occasions) on an errand for Health and Welfare Commissioner Rainey to ask condemned men to appear on television and plead to the governor for their lives—then when he had left with the condemned men's consent—usually given with dignity and restraint, though one man had been obscenely eager, his eagerness making his black skin seem a filth—then, driving away with their consent, Witherspoon had felt cheap and corrupt.

When he had stood before the bars of Willie's cell and greeted the man, Willie had responded with only a stare. He reminded Witherspoon of a trapped wolf: neither friendly nor hostile, simply watchful.

The wolf said nothing, nor did he take his eyes from Witherspoon's; the convict dug his eyes into the other man's like a spade into earth. It was a stare of absolute directness, fearlessness.

A white prison guard sat with his feet on a desk ten feet from Willie's cell, a man big, beefy, reddish-blond, his face reduced to a hard and bloated paste. He barked at Willie, "Say good mornin to the revand. Willie. He come all the way from Palmerton to see you. Don't be so damn mean."

Willie said ominously, "Ain't I teach you to keep yo mouth shut, Blanton."

The white man put his feet down. "You dirty . . . they NEED to kill yo kind. Ain no place on earth for sompm like you!"

Willie gazed at the white man. "If you don quiet down, cracker, I'll stick a pin in you and you'll pop," he said quietly.

The white man leaped to his feet and drew a pistol, raged to the bars and pushed Witherspoon aside, pointed the pistol at Willie. "I'll kill you right on the spot, nigger!"

Willie stared silently and impassively at the guard.

"I'll fix yo ass," the guard shouted. "We'll work you over until they aint nothin left of you but black oatmeal!"

Willie drew a pack of cigarettes from his left breast pocket, dumped one into two fingers of his right hand, returned the pack to the breast pocket of his shirt, lit the cigarette, inhaled, blew out smoke, all the while gazing inflexibly at the harshly breathing white man.

"Ain nothin you can do to me. Now jus go on over there and sit down where you belong." He lifted his left hand and pointed authoritatively to the desk. He continued to hold his hand aloft.

Defeated, outraged, the white man holstered his pistol and retreated to his desk, whence he shot baleful glances at Willie. "You wastin' yo time, Revand," he said. "Only thing can do him any good is that ee-*lec*-tric chair down the hall." He put his feet on the desk, picked up a newspaper, shook it mightily and disappeared behind it.

Willie laughed wisely and lowered his hand stiffly like a man whose orders have been finally followed.

"You too bad fo yo own good," a bass Negro voice tonelessly remonstrated from a cell a few feet down the corridor.

"Jus bad enough to get along," replied Willie inoffensively.

Witherspoon stared with awe at Willie and smiled uncomfortably.

Willie did not return the smile. "Revand," he said sharply, "you come here to soften me up for that chair?"

Witherspoon looked aghast.

"Ah doan want no Bible talk. Ah ain fo that shit. Ah ain gonna let nobody say no prayers over me. You wastin yo time."

There was a great rattling of newspaper from the guard's desk.

Witherspoon was stunned.

Willie went on more kindly. "Ahm not a Bible man, ahm not a God-man. When ahm dead, ahm done—and that won't be long. Ah ain't goan tuh hell and ah ain't goan to heaven—when ah leave that lectric chair, only place ahm goan is a pine box—if they give me that."

Witherspoon managed to gasp, "What do you mean, soften you up?"

"These crackers like to see a man die scared. You din know that?" he asked brutally.

"But I don't want nothing like that!"

"Doan mattuh, one way or other," Willie said, looking sharply at Witherspoon. "Ahm goan die way *ah* wanta die. An ah might not go peaceable."

"May the Lord be my witness, Mr. Armstrong," Witherspoon began emotionally, then stopped.

After a moment, Willie said, "Ah see what you mean." He chuckled shortly. There was a trace of good humor on his grave face. "Why you come here?"

Witherspoon stared into the man's black-marble eyes and knew that his own eyes gave the answer to the question. Yet he had to play out the game:

"Mr. Armstrong, I came here because the state office called my home and said that maybe I could get you to appear before the govnor in public hearing tomorrow and ask for a commutation of your sentence."

Willie turned his back and walked toward his cot. He turned in the middle of the tiny cell and looked at Witherspoon. "They wouldn't commute mah sentence if ah *asked* for it, Revand. Ah killed two white men. An ah wouldn't ask for it." A band of sweat had appeared on his forehead. Willie's face was expressionless.

"Mr. Armstrong, I know the state commissioner, and he wouldn't ask me to come down here if they wouldn't commute your sentence."

There was silence. Then:

"You got a chuch in Quiver, that right?"

"That's right, Mr. Armstrong."

"I live in Quiver. You know that?"

Witherspoon trembled at the irony. "Co'se I do."

"I got kin go to yo chuch."

Witherspoon nodded agreement: Willie meant his sister Nambi Ruth and her husband, Lonnie, who were in his congregation but rarely came to church.

"Witherspoon," Willie went on, "they got mah life, and it ain't theys to take. But they gonna take it. Ah caint hep mahself. But they caint make me crawl. Thass one thing they *caint* make me do." He spat with such scornful force that Witherspoon half-expected smoke to pop up from the cement floor where the spittle landed. Armstrong waited once more, then he said with a bitterness hot and pungent, sharper and more raging because the voice was quiet: "Ah wouldn't ask a cracker fo the time uh day. Ah ain beggin *nothin* from these motherfuckers."

Willie looked significantly at Witherspoon, and Witherspoon felt as if he were a piece of paper being slashed by a razor. "Whattya doin his work fuh?" the convict asked, with open bitterness.

"Why—what do you mean?"

"You come down here for 'im. What he sent you down here for?"

The blood rushed like a flood to Witherspoon's face.

"To—to ask you—to ask you if you want to appear before the guvnor in public hearing, and—"

"On television, right?"

"That's right."

"Thass not why he sent you here."

"Well—"

" 'Well,' hell, Witherspoon. They sent you down here cause they don want a nigger to be a man. They want me to get on television and crawl cause then they can say—'see that nigger, he ain't nothin', look at him, on his belly like a snake, axin a white man for his life. Nigger ain as good as we is. Nigger ain a man; nigger's a snake, crawlin on his belly. Well, lemme think, should we let that nigger live?' "

He paused.

"An you come down here to help him out. That what religion is, Witherspoon? Hep the cracker keep the nigger down?"

Witherspoon dropped his head; shame crawled from his pores.

He made one last effort. He looked pitiably into the man's hard eyes and said, "Mr. Armstrong. . . ." He could get no further. He gasped words incoherently, grasped the bars of the cell as if he were drowning.

How could he get away, how could he walk from this place? Somehow he had to get away from here, there was nothing he could say to this man, he could not even look up at him, he could stay here no longer, yet he could not find the strength to walk away. Willie said nothing; Witherspoon could feel his black-marble eyes on him, waiting and destroying, waiting and destroying.

Finally, intuitively, Witherspoon looked up. On Willie's grave face there was an expression of unspeakable kindness.

The two men stared into each other's eyes.

Witherspoon felt that anything he said would be a hideous violation.

He put out his hand to shake Willie's, not knowing whether he would take it; the condemned man took it and grimly returned the pressure. "Ah hope yuh luck," Willie said gravely. Witherspoon gasped and stared in consternation at the condemned man.

Then, head down, Witherspoon hurried past the guard whose collapsed face brewed with hatred of him.

He felt broken. Sobs kept trying to explode from his throat, he forced them back down.

* * *

He listened to the ministers around him talk, and he felt unmanned, and he felt that they were unmanned.

He was silent.

He was dissatisfied with his physical position; there must, he thought, be something wrong about the way that he was sitting. For a while he sat with his cheek in right palm, legs crossed. Suddenly, reflecting, he sat bolt upright. He felt that he was somehow a child, a castrate, like the Italian singers of a bygone century who were gelded before their voices could change with the onset of puberty. He sat now, ankles crossed, his hands before him separated, palms flat on the table, his head cocked on one side, his total aspect suggesting grave alert consideration of the matter being discussed. But his attention was mechanical. He wanted to touch himself: his scrotum, his penis, his belly, his face, to see whether he was there; he knew he was there, that his scrotum was intact, that his belly was full of his intestines, that his face was covered with flesh—but an intuition suggested that his torso might be empty, that these men sitting around the table were empty, that all their scrotums and penises and intestines lay on the floor in a bloody heap beneath the long mahogany table, that they only pretended to be unaware of the pile of bloody penises and testicles and intestines beneath the table.

I am sick, he thought.

His thoughts dipped deeper, like a hand into ocean water.

These are not men: the words punched up through the ocean water like an underwater human giant come up for air.

These are not men . . . and I ain no man.

The thought frightened him; he shrugged his shoulders violently, violently shifted himself on his buttocks.

Now he was in a forest, the depth of a jungle, so deep within that jungle that he could not even see the sun; dark jungle heavy with a startling and lush green tincted with wickedness, trees so fecund that they vomited growth everywhere and suffocated animal life, and here he was, stranger in this sunless jungle, machete in hand, hacking his way through—only to become more deeply intertwined, but hope was a blazon on his brain, and now suddenly he saw the sun through the limb-black and leaf-green, and the sun was a man's black face: tough, stern, kind—whose?

He gazed with cold curiosity around the table from face to face, finding the faces repulsive, and finding himself, the watcher, repulsive. Only the sun, the black-faced sun, was healthy and attractive and whole.

Of course, he thought: Willie.

That's why we're not men, none of us, cause Willie is a man—and if he's a man, why, all of us sitting around this table are dressed up like men, walking and talking like men, doing men's jobs, having sexual intercourse like men, but we're all unnatural.

He felt relieved.

Now he gave total attention to the discussion; he watched carefully, and listened intently. But over his observe was the tough and delicate patina: we're freaks.

"I think we need to give them a chance. I think we need to give them a chance," Rev. Walton was saying from his strong weathered black face, and the two sentences, identical and repeated, were like incantatory music. His round black middle-aged face glinted beneath the shining baldness of his black head, and Witherspoon thought he detected something sinister in the gleam of his eyes. "The school board is not composed of evil men—weak, yes, but not wicked; and if we press them too hard, they may simply turn recalcitrant and defy the black community." He looked around the table and found acceptance. "We can't press them too hard, too hard," he continued, mellifluous. "These children of ours are well-intentioned, but they're young, have nothing to lose, and they have the buoyancy and recklessness of youth; they lack the maturity, the balance, the *judgment* of their elders." A murmur of agreement circled the great rectangle of the mahogany table. "Amen," called Rev. Spieler, a black shrewd-faced man in his sixties, a gold chain straining across the vest that covered the vast expanse of his belly.

"Thank *God* for them!" emphasized Rev. Walton, "but I think that we, in the wisdom that informs our years, cannot permit ourselves to be pushed into *un*wisdom." He looked pleased with himself. Witherspoon wondered why so often black men with strong faces were Uncle Toms.

"Thank *God* for them!—for without their youthful spirit we might have waited long, too long, for a spirit of justice to sweep this community. But now, now, now that the doors of justice have been cracked—and more than cracked, I hasten to say, we must remember that needless antagonism, not to mention failure and frustration to our cause, may result from hostile pushiness. . . . I think . . . I think that we must urge the meeting to accept the mayor's call . . . call for no . . . no . . . demonstrations while talks continue."

Earnest words of approbation circled the table. Witherspoon noticed that Rev. Spieler, leaning back in his chair at one end of the great table, seemed to smile sardonically, even as he enthusiastically praised Rev. Walton's remarks.

"Well," boomed Rev. Whitney aggressively from a broad brown face, "is it the consensus of the group then that we shall urge the meetin tonight to accept the mayor's call for no demonstrations while talks continue?" He paused and looked out of the corner of his eye at Rev. Corwul, the thin young man who sat silent and glaring like an irascible light brown candle next to Spieler. Whitney turned expansively to Witherspoon and thundered, "Rev. Witherspoon, sir, what about you? You have not given the conference the benefit of *your* thinking this morning."

Lucius Witherspoon sat with his hands spread before him on the table, a slightly comic expression on his face. He had been caught off guard. He rubbed his right hand over his face in a gesture of weariness and despair. He was afraid to speak. A sudden vision of Willie came and went. He was afraid.

He looked into Whitney's eyes. They were dark and hard and mocking, as bereft of feeling as a bear's. The man doesn't even know, Witherspoon thought. Doesn't even know what he is doing. Witherspoon seemed to crack into small pieces and flow like glue.

Freaks, he thought.

He shook his head with great dignity, but the words came spontaneously and controlless from his mouth. He said firmly, "I have nothing to say."

He started, for he was startled at what he had said, and there was a rustling around the table.

Whitney probed with hard eyes and hard words masked in graciousness. He had thought that Witherspoon would be of the same mind as Walton and himself and the rest except Corwul. "But what do you think we ought to *do*, Rev. Witherspoon," Whitney said. "The young people are clamoring for demonstrations, the mayor and the businessmen are demanding no demonstrations. Requesting, that is. All of us here"—he paused and glanced with cunning malevolence at Corwul—"seem to think we should grant the mayor what he wants. What do *you* think?"

Whitney angered Witherspoon. But by this time Witherspoon had regained control, and he moved smoothly in his role of dignified pastor, cautious, firm, circumspect, good-humored.

"I'm not sure *what* I think," he said easily, shifting in his chair and looking good-humoredly at Whitney. For a split-second Witherspoon thought of Whitney as a mass of cancerous flesh in which all human identity had totally disappeared as it does in a body mangled in an airplane crash or burned beyond recognition in a fire.

"I'm not really sure *what* I think, Reverend," he repeated, nodding in subtly ironic deference to Whitney.

Witherspoon drew his eyes slowly around the table. He didn't really care for Whitney's position and Walton's, the majority position, or for what he was sure was Corwul's position, the radical position, the burn-the-town-down position. He didn't care for either position, and he wasn't going to be pushed. As he had too often in the past, he thought grimly. He smiled, assuming the mask of goodwill. He saw in his mind the face of Miss James, black and African as a Nigerian mask, the mouth long and thick, the nose round and blunt, the forehead low and pointing backward, the lower face pointing forward Africanly; everytime he saw Miss James, her face was so radiant with strength and warmth and vitality and intelligence that he thought her beautiful; he saw her striding toward him now on Main Street downtown or in the hallway of the school, smiling her magnificent smile, tall, longlegged, widehipped; yet there was something so forceful and vital about her that she seemed in one isolated sense masculine—it was, he reflected now with surprise, because she was so different from these men here, so much more honest and sincere and forceful; certainly, compared to Willie, she was as feminine as roses. *That*, he thought, is the kind of woman Willie would have liked. A man like Willie would surely make her come, he thought—and he turned with distaste on his thought, and became suddenly aware of his wormy penis resting atop his scrotum between his legs: I'm repulsive, he thought, I ain no man. His face looked startled, and again unintended words flew from his mouth: "Who cares *what* the mayor wants?"

He jumped as Corwul's voice rasped from the other end of the table: "That's what *I* say. All the crackers wanta do is rob our schools of the best teachers and the best students. Hell, anybody can see that! They're tryin to castrate a whole people! They fought integration as long as they could, and now they've got it *forced* on em, they're gonna try to cripple our kids and ruin our schools. I say let's run this town out of business if they don't assign Miss James back to Booker!''

Whitney brought a fat brown palm sharply down on the table. "Rev. Witherspoon has the floor!''

"We don't *want* to run this town out of business," crackled Reverend Sharpe, the bullet-headed old dentist who pastored Mount Lebanon, his face crinkled and strong. "That's damn-fool talk—run this town out of business." He looked around as if the utter senselessness of Corwul's words would be apparent to an idiot. "What damn fool would *want* to run this town out of business cause they assign a black teacher to a white school. This is *our* town, this town is *us*. Where would *we* be, if we *ran* it out of business? Hell, we wanted integration, now we got it. *You* wanta take us back to slavery with your run-the-town-out-of-business talk.''

Corwul poked his head down and forward with a sudden determined movement. He addressed the floor beneath him, and his face was now slightly crazed. "Maybe," he said thoughtfully, "integration was a mistake.''

Sharpe raised his hands high to heaven with a magniloquent "You see?'' gesture. Hostile and indignant murmurs went the round of the table.

Whitney raised his hand imposingly to stop Corwul.

"I have the floor," Corwul cried, his voice highpitched. "Can't old men ever learn? Five years ago integration was the watchword. The biggest thing in the world was to get into a cracker school. What did we get when we got in there? A lot of disturbed kids, first and second and third graders, kids not big enough to fight back, being destroyed by cracker teachers. Kids going to high school and havin soup spilled on em, harassed by cracker kids and teachers alike. I'm not saying integration's wrong, maybe it was necessary for the future of the South, maybe these kids had to suffer. But enough is enough: my boy ain't goin to no cracker school and end up disturbed for the rest of his life with a pain he will never forget and a compulsion to be white. I salute Miss James with every drop of blood in my body for refusing to be transferred: it's *our* kids who need a superior education, in their own schools where they can do their thing free of the white man's hangups: *why* should they take our best teachers, our *very best* teacher—the most brilliant and versatile teacher we've got, the idol of every kid at Booker Washington School, somebody for these kids to worship and look up to and say, '*That's* what a teacher oughta be!' And a model for all the black teachers, for them to say, '*That's* the way we ought to be teaching!' And *this* is the teacher they take and put into a cracker school to teach crackers and threaten to fire if she won't go! Why, a fool could see what they're trying to do to us! The kids can see it; why can't *we*!?''

Leers appeared on lips, and Witherspoon could read the universal thought: Is he going with her?

Corwul perceived it too, and added: "And she's clean. Nobody's been able to say a bad word about her." The smiles were more open now, sympathetic and respectful.

The table was silent, waiting, and Corwul moved into the silence.

"You know those crackers ain't gonna teach our kids about Paul Lawrence Dunbar and Frederick Douglass and Harriet Tubman. What cracker teacher in Palmerton in the Deep South is gonna teach her class about Martin Luther King? Richard Wright? James Baldwin? Malcolm X? The Black Revolution? Hell, use your heads." An ice descended upon the room. "We *need* our schools to learn about our literature and our history, and to talk about black folk. Where can black folk talk frankly about black folk frankly except *among* black folk? We *need* our schools, and we need Miss James."

"The future of the South is not in segregation," intoned Rev. Spieler sagely. "You're wrong, young man."

"Look at those teachers at Booker—would you want to send your kids there?" Corwul shot back. Witherspoon winced.

"That's exactly the point," Spieler came back, "that's the point exactly," he said greedily.

"No, no, no, that's not what I mean; I mean, that's why we need Miss James. We ain't got but a few topnotchers—and we need them. They send them away, what the hell *we* got? Hell, them white teachers at Lee ain't raisin no hell, they mediocrities too, nobody wants to send his kids to those teachers, they ain't never thought nothin', they ain't never had an original thought in they lives—who would want to go to them to sit at *their* feet for wisdom. The point is, we need our own schools to develop our own teachers. We don't want to turn *white*," he burst with sudden passion, "ain't nothin' in the integration doctrine that says we want our brains to be *white*. Hell, the south has never in its life produced a great original thinker, or a great original *nothin'* since the slaves produced the spirituals. Why we want so bad to go among crackers, when we produced the only great art this godforsaken country ever produced? Why shouldn't we want to go to ourselves for wisdom. I say raise Miss James to the highest. And let those kids demonstrate if they want. Do whatever they want, burn the town down if they want: Let em demonstrate for black education! Cary Lee James was educated right in our schools right here in Palmerton and educated at Palmerton College, and the only degree she got from a white school was when she went off to New York to get a master's in education, and says *that* wasn't worth nothin'—she's a black girl educated in black schools, and she's a teacher we can put up against anybody anywhere. Let *us* keep her, and use *her* knowledge and brilliance for *our* children—and let the crackers get one of our third-rate niggers if they want a nigger teacher so bad, and send us one of their first-rate crackers if they believe in integrated education so much! But no, they would never do that—that would be too humiliating for any of *their* teachers except the dregs from the bottom of the barrel to come over to a nigger school and teach *nigger* chil-urn!"

There were some nods and grunts of semi-affirmation, and Rev. Singleton, his pink ascetic flat-nosed face shining, murmured "Amen!"

There was a long silence. Then Sharpe said quietly, "I say we oughta use some common sense." He cocked his bullet head significantly at Rev. Spieler, who laughed exuberantly. "As Rev. Spieler so eloquently and *wisely* said, 'The future of the South is not in segregation.' "

"I'm not denying that—" Corwul began hotly, pathos subtly tingeing his voice.

Whitney raised his hand. Corwul subsided.

"There are many good teachers at Booker," Rev. Walton said shrewdly. "You slander the school."

"I don't slander nothin'!" Corwul protested.

"Just a minute, young man," Walton said condescendingly. "We have *fine* schools. We need not sorrow for the quality of our schools. And as for Miss James, a somewhat proud and arrogant young lady who thinks a very great deal of herself, she should be proud to have an opportunity to teach at Robert E. Lee High School. Cary James came from the cotton patch; her father was a sharecropper. Imagine a woman who once picked cotton, teaching at Robert E. Lee High School!"

"Maybe that's why she's such a good teacher," Corwul said angrily; "she ain't dyin' to be white like some niggers."

"I don't know whether I should take offense to that, young man," Walton said.

"An offensive statement," boomed Whitney.

"Common sense, common sense," Sharpe said sardonically. He glanced sharply at Spieler and they smiled finely at each other.

Corwul looked piercingly for a long moment at Sharpe, then spat out, "I say we ought to get up off our knees and be men—instead of white folks' niggers who'd sell their souls to be white." With one quick and exaggerated movement, he leaned back in his chair and crossed his legs, pronouncing victory. Nervously he swung one crossed leg repeatedly.

Rev. Sharpe's yellow face reddened. He gazed with menace at Corwul. Witherspoon was frightened. Years ago, long before the onset of integration, Sharpe had scared a white grocer (with whom he had been feuding) into selling his store and leaving town by entering the latter's store and threatening him with a gun. How he had gotten away with it, no one knew, but no one doubted that if it had come to a showdown, Sharpe would have killed the white man. Yet Sharpe was a notorious conservative, and everyone suspected him, above all, of being a pipeline to the town's leading whites.

"Say that again," Sharpe said quietly to Corwul.

"Gentlemen, gentlemen," Whitney called in a conciliatory tone.

Corwul leaned forward and whipped out sharply and deliberately, "I say we ought to be men—and not white folks' niggers who'd cut off their very nuts to be able to mix with crackers. Ten years ago you were selling out integration, dragging your feet so hard a team of mules couldn't budge yuh. Hell, not ten years ago, five years ago. Now you're doing exactly the opposite; whatever the white man wants you to do, you'll do!"

Sharpe bellowed so that the room shook: "ARE YOU SAYING I AM A WHITE FOLKS' NIGGER?"

Corwul threw back his head and laughed enthusiastically. Witherspoon was relieved: Sharpe had made himself absurd.

The roundheaded Episcopal minister, Jacob Bishop, his completely round face a brown bland mask, said quietly, quickly, kindly, "I certainly hope that Rev. Corwul does not think that violence would apply in this situation. He has raised viable issues to which we must certainly give thought. But you said, and I have taken it down in my notes—"

"Oh you have?" Corwul said sarcastically.

"Yes I have: let them burn," he enunciated carefully, "let them burn down the town if they want. Now that is a horse—"

"—of another color!"

"Indeed, it is," Bishop said coolly. "Would you respond to that question, Rev. Corwul?"

Corwul's face was a razor of wrinkles and sneer. Witherspoon's stomach heaved in fear for Corwul, but he dared not speak.

Breathing hard, his voice quavering, Corwul said, "Are you implying that I meant that literally?"

"I am asking *you*, sir!" Bishop replied.

"I'm not going to answer that question," Corwul slashed.

"Actually you have answered the question," Bishop said smoothly.

"I don't actually mean 'burn the town down,' " Corwul raged, "I meant that as a figure of speech. I'm for demonstration!"

"Peaceful demonstrations, sir?" Bishop pursued.

"Demonstration!" Corwul blurted, "demonstration! How the hell can you contain a demonstration! How can you tell whether a demonstration will be peaceful or not! The police will determine that—not *us*!"

"But you said," Rev. Walton said, " 'let em burn the town down!' That's not peaceful."

"I advocate that we bring these crackers to their knees by any means necessary!"

"To keep a black teacher from being assigned to a white school?" said light-brown-skinned Rev. Ellicott, thick lips curled in a good-natured smile.

"Yes, to keep a black teacher from being assigned to a white school!" Corwul glared at Ellicott as if he were about to pounce upon him and devour him. Ellicott's lip quivered, but he continued to smile.

"Hell, yes to keep her from being assigned to a white school. She doesn't wanta be transferred, the student council got up a petition of almost 1,000 students and 200 parents against her transfer, nobody in that community wants her to be transferred—then why the hell are we trying to back the mayor and the board of education up? Aren't you tired of white folks telling us what to do? As a matter of fact, what right have they got to tell us what to do? Instead of backing the mayor up, why aren't you proposing that we demand that we get representation on the board of education—they ain't a white face, I mean a black face on there, yet they're tellin us what to do. As a matter of fact, why don't we have our own board of education to rule over black schools? What kinda democracy is this, where an all-white board tells us what to do every time we turn around, and we haven't got even an Uncle Tom''—and his eyes roved the table—''on the board of education. This is what the revolutionaries dumped tea in the Boston harbor for—taxation without representation! Yet here we sit defending taxation without representation! 'Let us follow the mayor's leadership!' I say to hell with Mayor Young, and to hell with the board of education—they don't represent me, and they're against everything I want, which is the way it's always been in the South anyway—whenever have you ever had a white man to represent black interests! Yes, let—'' and he stopped precipitately.

"Burn down the town?'' asked Rev. Bishop smoothly.

"I wasn't gonna say that.''

"Oh, yes you were,'' said Rev. Ellicott, smiling. "I don't think the issue is whether they represent us. The Supreme Court of this country represented us, and they said integration when the NAACP asked for integration.''

"Well, the black community of Quiver says it don't want Miss James integrated. Do *they* count?''

"Of course they count,'' Rev. Bishop assured him. "But that is hardly the issue now. The issue is the position that you are taking, and the position that you are taking, Rev. Corwul, is a *violent* position. You want to assault, attack, smash. It's not so much a matter of whether you mean 'burn the town down' figuratively or literally but rather it is a matter of the violence of your language, your gestures, the spirit in which you advocate your attacks and assaults. Your very rage, Rev. Corwul, is violent. I think that is why you might in your heart advocate violence—and against the precepts of Christ—who urged that we turn the cheek rather than return blow for blow—perhaps in your heart you *do* advocate violence. Do you?''

"I advocate that we bring those crackers to their knees!'' Corwul shouted.

"You see,'' returned Bishop solemnly.

"See *what*? Why *shouldn't* we bring em to their knees? We've been on *our* knees for three hundred years!''

"But do two right—I mean two wrongs—make a right?''

"Is that the *Christian* approach?'' said Rev. Ellicott goodnaturedly. "After all, you *are* a Christian minister!''

"That's precisely it! Is that the *Christian* approach—bringing people to their knees! Violence!'' boomed Whitney. "Sometimes I wonder whether you are really a Christian—or whether you are a revolutionary atheist!''

"Do you really believe in the nonviolent approach?'' purred Bishop.

Corwul panted like a trapped animal seeing the hunter approach. He looked desperately and outraged from face to face. Witherspoon wanted to go to the cornered man's aid, but fear yawned in his torso and trickled out his arms to his fingertips. He wanted to express in his face, his eyes, the sympathy he felt, but he was frightened, and when he tried to express sympathy in his eyes, hoping that when Corwul looked into his eyes he would see fellow-feeling, then instantly thereafter Witherspoon would attempt to neutralize the expression on his face and in his eyes, so that none of Corwul's enemies would be able to suspect that he sympathized with the baited man and his position.

Now Bishop gave Corwul a reprieve, but it was the reprieve of taunting the trapped beast with fire.

"Surely you must know," Bishop said, kind, measured, pedantic, "that it is not the aim of this movement to bring the white folks to their knees. It is not our aim to destroy the white man nor to impose our will upon him. We want to gain our rights, yes, but we want to gain them with love—we want to overcome him with our love, not with hatred, not with violence!"

"Love! Love! That's all you people can talk, love!" shouted Corwul. "You don't want to do anything—that's what's wrong with you!"

"Of course we do," Bishop replied. "At the right time. But this is not the right time. Demonstrations will only muddy the waters, destroy the relationship that has grown between the races in the past five years, antagonize—"

"Who gives a damn if we antagonize him? Who cares? He's been intimidating me for three hundred years! I want my right to control my own community and I want it now! And I'm not going to get on my knees and lick a white man's ass to get a little integration!"

"PLEASE," thundered Whitney. "A little decorum here! You're a minister of the cloth, not a common hoodlum from the streets!"

"Don't tell me how I'm supposed to talk," shouted Corwul. "I know better than you do what I am! I ain't no white folks' nigger sitting behind closed doors selling out my people!" A resentful mutter rose. "You want to make it if I'm an atheist, if I want violence, if I'm a revolutionary, if I'm a Christian who turns the other cheek, if I curse! That ain't it! I ain't gonna talk about that! That ain't the issue! The issue is do we control our community or do the white man control it! The issue is do those kids keep the best teacher they've got or do they send her cross town to teach crackers who will be on her like white on rice if she even *thinks* 'black rights!' The issue is do we back these kids and their parents or do we crawl down to the white man and suck his ass! That's what I said—suck his ass!" He lost his control. "You want to sell out those kids!" He leaped from his seat. "You Toms!" he screamed. "Toms, handkerchief heads—that's all you are—sittin here behind your clerical collars talkin bout do I believe in violence! Yes, I believe in violence! I believe in anything that'll get Charlie off my back!"

He looked frightened. He rose.

He was silent, and the table was silent, the men about the table stared at him with a grim satisfaction in which a grim amusement lurked.

"And you *love* the white man!" he burst out again. "You love the man that sucks the life from your body. That starves your kids and gives em second-rate schools and won't even give em a playground! You love him! You don't want to hurt him! I resign this ministerial conference."

A barely audible snicker from the staring table.

Corwul stood now halfway between the door and the chair he had occupied, breathing hard, wild-faced, scared, defiant, wondering frantically whether to say more.

He's like a boy, Witherspoon thought, but he's magnificent.

Whitney, sounding old and breathy, said, "We accept your resignation. And the community will be informed of all your various Christian sentiments," he concluded heavily.

From the hatrack Corwul raged, "I'll tell my *own* congregation, I don't need no . . ."

"We hope you do," purred Sharpe cordially.

"Well, I will," Corwul shouted.

At the door he stopped again, outraged at his enemies, humiliated at his loss of control, unwilling to break off finally. His wild glance caught Witherspoon's eyes, and Lucius did not drop his grave, his sorrowed compassionate eyes.

Vengefully Corwul opened the door, went through it, and slammed it, and Witherspoon's body shuddered at his own cowardice, and the blood rushed maddened to his face.

There was silence until the front door of the church slammed. Then the men, except for Singleton and Witherspoon, looked at one another and crashed into laughter. But there was a chastened feeling in their faces: Corwul had scalded them.

Witherspoon spoke first. "I don't think we should have let him run off like that. I don't think we should have let him run off like that."

Whitney looked at him querulously. "Nobody run him off. Nobody stopped him from talking and nobody stopped nobody from listening . . . to his crap!"

Hostility lay on the silence like a burning mantle draped across a stone.

"That nigger'll ruin us all," Whitney said, "he'll ruin everything we're trying to do." The black had come out in his speech, the Southern black poor, and he was sullen and bitter.

Witherspoon thought to ask, Well, what *are* we trying to do? But he was intimidated by Whitney's imposing anger, his dominant large-man's sullenness and readiness to strike down.

"Well," Rev. Singleton said tentatively, "he's got a point, you know." The sun's giant scissors slit suddenly through the high windows of the conference room and glinted upon his glasses and obscured his eyes; pink-faced, looking like a grey-haired blinded white man in their midst, this fair-skinned Negro seemed to Witherspoon like an exotic diplomat dropped mysteriously in their midst. "I don't see what *we* gain by her being transferred. I can't see why the board and the mayor's being so adamant about it."

Whitney ignored him. "I think something has to be done about that nigger. He's always like the fly in the pie, always about to make everybody else look like an Uncle Tom. That nigger wants violence," he said viciously. "That nigger wants violence and I think he ought to be stopped before he brings the red rage of hatred down on this town."

"Maybe we ought to simply advise the board not to transfer Miss James," Singleton suggested inoffensively. "That would eliminate any possibility of violence."

Whitney again ignored him. "I don't want to go through what I went through forty years ago, and I don't want my family touched. I don't want my house bombed,'' he proclaimed. He looked at the group as if he were seeing them for the first time, and they gazed back at him with keen interest.

"I'll never forget," Whitney said with a quiet theatrical intensity that caressed the silence as a lover confidently caresses an aroused mistress, "when they came into my father's church and dragged a man out for just *staring* a white man down. That's all he did—stared a white man down that cursed him on Davis Boulevard and walked on home and minded his business. And someone recognized him and they went to his house and didn't find him there and came to *my father's* church," Whitney said passionately, as if there were a profound truth hidden in the fact that it was his father's church—"and dragged this man out, D.C. Odum's father, you know him, and spilled his blood right on the cement steps of my father's church. Now what are they doing, all these bombings? DO WE NEED *THAT* IN PALMERTON? Do we have to face the bombs in Palmerton?" he demanded. "Do I have to fear that my little grandchild," and his voice broke, "my little grandbaby or my . . . my . . . wife . . . will lie dead beneath some maniac's bomb?"

Witherspoon sensed a sealed smile go around the table, for it was no secret that Whitney, a notorious lecher, treated his wife with courteous coldness and had not slept with her for a decade.

Witherspoon wanted to rise and leave the table, but his limbs were concrete pillars.

Discussion resumed. The question was raised and decided—except for Witherspoon and Singleton—who were silent—that Corwul would be notified that he could not speak tonight. Singleton's question—whether the ministerial conference should advise the board not to transfer Miss James—was lost in discussion, and for it was substituted the motion, which passed, that the ministerial conference advise the board of education that a prominent member of the black community, perhaps a member of the ministerial conference, be invited by emergency vote of the board of education, to serve on that board. Then the meeting, thoroughly decided now, was over in a gradual rising-to-feet, loud and jovial Negro talk, head-ducking blasts of laughter, narrow-eyed standing with single hands on chairbacks, and hips jointed out, tall and solemn standing, and vehement oratory in restrained voices to the effect that Corwul was a danger to the black community: shrewd-eyed debate whether it would be wisest to ask him to return so that he might possibly be restrained or whether it would be best to let him hang himself with his own rope of wild advocacy. It was remembered that benediction had not been offered, and then eyes were closed above black suits yoked by white priest-collars, the brown faces tense and closed, faces old somehow even in the men in their thirties and forties, faces strong and thoughtful and determined and corrupt, throwing up into the air their prayer to God like a blind Renaissance nobleman throwing up into the air a wingless falcon.

Witherspoon sneaked a look at the faces, and terror ate at his backbone like wolfteeth.

When the last orotund syllable had climbed the dusty air, Witherspoon, head bowed, left without a word. The men stared after him and then themselves moved toward the door while they chatted restrainedly, soberly, in a hissing prideful way, and dismissed him from mind.

"What a shameful way for a *man* to behave!" Witherspoon exclaimed aloud as he drove from the church. Again, aloud, in self-contempt: "What a shameful way for a *man* to behave!"

Mechanically, he drove.

He had no particular conviction that there should be demonstrations—although he saw no powerful reason that there should not; and certainly the position of the ministers was unwholesome, suspicious, *political*. Nor did he swallow Corwul's raging and tactless advocacy. He saw no certain merit in the position of either side, except that, for certain, it would be evil to fire Miss James if she refused transfer. But the way the ministers had baited that young man: how evilly they had treated him: and it was clear to anyone that whether Corwul believed in violence or not, whether he was indeed, as some suspected, a revolutionary and an atheist: it was clear that he was earnest. That he believed. That he was a religious man, whatever his religion happened to be. And how wickedly, how venomously they had treated him! And how he, Witherspoon, like an un-Willie, had cravenly kept his silence.

Yet Willie had not dropped his eyes even to Death!

Like a swift icy river, shame streamed through his arms, his chest, his belly.

Before his car there ran suddenly a laughing ragged black child.

Witherspoon braked the car, the tires shrieked in anguish.

The girl panicked, stumbled, fell on her back, terror and dismay wizened her face, she threw up her arms and legs to feebly ward off death, revealing all brown nakedness from ankle to waist.

Half-maddened, Witherspoon leaped from the car. He ran to the girl. "Are you hurt, darlin'?" he pleaded, hysterical.

The ten-year-old child looked at him crazed from where she lay. She screamed as if he were a murderer. She jumped up and ran from him; once, as she ran, turning her face blistered with insanity and stupidity and terror. Into the rickety house she frantically ran, screaming, into the house foundationed on wooden props, curtainless, front porch planks awry, half the window panes broken, through whose open door Rev. Witherspoon, standing gaping before his car, saw the rugless floor, the broken furniture, the existence of the incoherent destitute, and at the door as the child ran up the broken plank steps, a black woman of forty appeared, fat, wild, evil, raged, and destructive, to bellow words of Negro-hatred as terrible at that moment as the soulless white men who would stand hipdeep in Negro blood and know no conscience-stirring: out of her destitution and destruction, the total robbery of every human eye-lookupward, the battering-to-death of every hope of cleanliness and sanity, the crushing of every slender fingerhold on order in her life: in despair, the mother shouted her hatred at the insane child, cuffed and violently pulled the screeching girl into the house, and Witherspoon cringed at the sound of the duet of the woman's shouted hatred and the child's staccato screams.

He started up toward the house.

Driven, he walked up the steps. One plankstep had been broken in two, and pointed sharply upward from the ground to welcome the soft groin of anyone who fell between the steps.

On the top step he tottered.

If I were to die at this moment, he thought . . .

He walked to the threshold. He groaned at what he saw: the dirty rags that served for blankets upon the mattress lying on the floor, cotton lumps poking great dead heads out of the mattress like blackened pus; the floor gapped so that he could see the weeds in the earth beneath; no chair unbroken; the smell of feces and urine from a toilet in the kitchen; wallpaper hanging from the wall like strips of rotting flesh; in one corner, rags and newspapers and ancient toys and dollsheads and junk, all of an unspeakable filth heaped together, and from this pile too the smell of urine.

From the back of the house the blows stopped now, but the screams did not lessen in intensity, and the woman's shouted threats and imprecations continued.

Suddenly these stopped too, and the woman appeared from the kitchen, her round black face tortured.

"What *choo* want!" she demanded of him, and the words were like a physical blow.

She stood like a mountain: defiant, challenging, powerful, absolute.

Lucius gulped. "I just come up to see if I—if the little girl was—all right. She—my car almost hit her. It was mah fault."

She gazed at him fiercely and was silent, hands on hips, she was a rhinoceros deciding whether to charge.

He turned quickly and retreated down the ragged stairway, tripping over the bottom step and falling to his hands and knees.

From the doorway at the top of the stairs he heard the woman's contemptuous male grunt.

From hands and knees he glanced quickly and apprehensively back, and saw standing there beside her in the doorway a black boy-child with a smiling goodnatured puckered fourteen-year-old face above a body so thin and tiny that it seemed a five-year-old's.

Sardonically the boy asked, "Whatchoo doin' down there, prayin'?"

In a comment of vigorous and ironic affirmation, the woman grunted again, then began in powerful updrafts an hysterical and musical laughter: it sounded like a mutilated aria.

Slowly Witherspoon pushed himself up and to one knee, and the woman continued to laugh. He felt the boy's eyes on him, kindly yet evil.

Rev. Witherspoon felt like crying: here he, on his knees, and felt like praying for this woman and her idiot child and her quick and brilliant deformed one, and she, her life snapped shut like a grotesque trap upon her and mangled her and all her brood, and she, laughing at him to turn her eyes from her own misery in so deep a trap, so deep a pit, that the sun could not even be seen from trapbottom. What sense, what sense? Tears thrust through and boiled his eyes. He got to his feet and began to walk toward his car.

Then sullen anger took him like a pincers by the temples. When he reached his car, he was sobbing. He couldn't see. He stood there in the street, head on arm against the cartop, his sobbed face mutilated, chest heaving, and it seemed to him as if all his viscera were coming out of his mouth in the sobs. On the porch the woman laughed on, her hysterical musical laugh bereft now of the quality of brutal amusement, now each updraft was a question as if she were asking, "You crying? You crying?" and by her the now-silent boy looked awed, suspicious, amused, and kindly.

Witherspoon could feel the eyes of slowed and stopped passersby upon him, and now the woman's laughter had ceased.

As if that were his signal, he got half-blindly into the car.

He sat there a moment, feeling the wash of humiliation over his body; then hurriedly he started the car and drove lurching off like a drunken man.

The rage pounded in his brain and at the pit of his stomach.

What sense, what sense?

He saw Willie sit in the electric chair, majestic and scornful, a ripple of frigid fear beneath his skin, saw Willie look about him in command so masterful that the sneer in his eyes and mouth was more eminent than derision, the hatred that lay above the heartbreak was like a whip, the hatred, whose thong was as thick as an oaktree, and Willie sat there level-eyed and contemptuous and majestic while the trembling guard pulled the hood down over his face: only then the heartbreak threatened to come through, but he lifted his head in human pride; then, when the hood was ablast his face, the rage burst through like a flood, "GOD *DAMN* YOU MOTHERFUCKERS! GOD *DAMN* YOU MOTHERFUCKERS!" then the electric rage, so littler than his own, curled its own fierce whip about his body, he fought it with his flame-and-anger and was still.

The white faces were blanched and frightened.

No gloating.

No ventured contempt, for they knew that the hollowness and fear of their breath would shake their words as if their words were rotten fruit sent shaken and splashing to the ground.

They were silent and afraid, so grand was his anger, so straight the torrent of hatred, so terrible an indictment of them was his faith in his humanity.

He sprawled there dead and grimacing, and Witherspoon thought he could see them shake to see him, they feared that he would rise and curse them, terrify them with his touch, strike them with his eyes.

Witherspoon sat now in his car before his house, seeing the last wisps of his vision, tears zizzagged down over his thickpored face like tiny rivers down a rockrugged mountainside, while love and pity and self-pity and impotent hatred heaved heavily inside him like giant naked lovers wrestling and cursing and weeping as they sought unsuccessfully to consummate desire.

He smacked the steering wheel violently with a palm: he thought of S.C. Rainey, the State Commissioner, who had sent him to see Willie to arrange the condemned man's appearance on TV in order to beg for his life to the governor . . .

How he had fawned upon S.C. Rainey!

How he had pretended dignity while he was all hollowness inside and a gladness to be fawning, an eagerness to be in terms of seeming familiarity with the conqueror; he, Lucius, all hail-fellow-well-met with the white man, but in reality the white man S.C. Rainey gave commands that he the conquered was not bound to accept but accepted because he felt black and below and glad to have any kind of white man's acceptance. . . .

He got out of his car and in his own mind it was as if he were crawling across the sidewalk and up the steps to his house; again and again he shook his head, and a chill of humiliation ran over his body for the way he had talked to S.C. Rainey . . . Nigger Lucius, he thought, who would do anything the crackers wanted him to do!

Heavily, he opened the front door.

"Hi Dad!"

Witherspoon started back in terror at the sound of his son's voice.

The eager boyish face that had greeted him full with joy and love was now bitten with wonder and hurt:

Witherspoon stood haggard before his son as if the boy were his accuser.

He looked into his son's face and saw Willie's face.

He took his son into his arms and hugged him hard. He put the wondering grateful boy down and looked at him.

Witherspoon's lips parted in a tender smile, his wet eyes warmed and embraced his son.

"Well, son," he drawled lovingly, "how was school today?"

Their eyes fused in affection.

"Fine, Dad," the boy cried joyfully.

"Well, son, that's just fine. Come on in and tell me all about it."

A thought crisped the end of his mind like bacon crisped in a frying pan: My son.

They walked in from the vestibule into the living room, and Witherspoon, sadness handling him with its hundred soft-pressured hands, sat down, strained sad smile on his face, beside his unseeing son.

Witherspoon emptied his whole blooded warmfleshed self into the boy's being so that Witherspoon and the boy were of the same age, and Witherspoon relaxed, and the tension and the anguish that he had felt, slipped behind the door of his mind and waited.

But the anguish peeked from behind the door, and he caught his anguish' eye, and the strain returned.

What is this boy going to be, he asked himself. Is he going to be another Whitney, or Sharpe, or another . . . what word was it that refused to come to his mind's tongue? Would he be another quick and clever nigger doctor or minister, soulless and shallow and sick, a backslapper and pokerplayer and sexual adventurer, wandering through life like a gregarious fool?

Or is he going to be like me, he thought grimly.

He saw himself talking to Rainey. The hideous name: S.C. Rainey. Himself Witherspoon grinning like a pompous latterday slave, confident, lips crinkled, holding the telephone receiver in an eager businesslike way as if he were talking to an equal, Rainey's voice coming over the phone, confidential, ingratiating, intimate—how if Armstrong would ask the governor to save his life in public session just as other condemned prisoners did, then the governor would give him life imprisonment, and it would help remove the unpleasant issues from the minds of our Nigra citizens (Witherspoon stiffened and then immediately told himself not to be oversensitive, to remember the white man's background, to be loving). "It would be better for both the colored *and* the white if this colored man, even if he *is* a killer twice over, was just put aside for life so as to get any irritating factors out of the way so *both* races could quiet down and relax and get all of this bile out of their systems, and if this stubborn guy went in public before the guvnor during the guvnor's regular conference with condemned men and ask for the guvnor's pardon, then the guvnor would give it, and nobody would holler that they're always puttin black men to death but never a white man, don't you agree, Lucius?" S.C. Rainey had asked suddenly, veering toward the black man as if the latter were a target.

"Yassuh," Witherspoon had said unthinkingly—and for the remainder of the conversation Witherspoon thought of himself as a dirty piece of underwear hanging from a clothesline sagging and swaying forlornly in the wind. The ignoble slave words had come from his mouth before he had had time to think—and there was the white man on the other end of the line, chuckling with gentle knowing malice when Lucius stiffly answered yes and no thereafter.

Yassuh.

And what would Willie Armstrong have thought, who refused to say sir to Death?

Witherspoon peered hard before him, trying to create Willie's face in his mind: he saw it before him, darkbrown face, deep and black marble eyes, skin that seemed to Witherspoon as if a knife could not cut it, yet the face, surprisingly full of compassion now in his mind's eye, seemed to be saying something to him, the lips were moving and Willie shook his head mysteriously. Now Witherspoon saw his son sitting a few feet from him, gazing at him in perplexity, and he smiled reassuringly at the boy, who lifted the corners of his lips in polite response as if to smile, and Witherspoon, as he gazed in love into his son's face, saw Willie's face and S.C. Rainey's, and Willie shook his head, S.C. Rainey smirked knowingly; now Witherspoon felt something on the tip of his mind, something he was trying to remember, and he felt that something huge was about to fall away inside him, a mountain was inside him and half of it was about to cave away like an avalanche, and he reached inside him with an unknown hidden hand, trying to feel that mountain.

His chattering boy's voice reached him instead.

Then his wife's feet on the concrete pathway leading to the house; he heard her old-woman's step on the porch. His son smiled and frowned simultaneously, a strange grown-up expression on his seven-year-old face as if he understood his mother and was annoyed by her even as he approved of her kindness. Witherspoon was astonished by this sign of maturity.

His wife's voice, heavy and crooked with the illness of her soul, creaked through the door, "Rev. Witherspoon, could you hep me with the packages?"

Arthenia B. Millican

(1920–   )

Born in Sumter, South Carolina, Millican received her B.A. from Morris College, her M.A. from Atlanta University, and her Ph.D. from Louisiana State University. She has taught at Morris College, Mississippi Valley State University, Norfolk State University, and Southern University from which she retired in 1980. A poet, folklorist, novelist, and short-story writer, Millican focuses her work on the mores and culture of black people in South Carolina and Louisiana. The stories in her first collection *Seeds Beneath the Snow* (1969), the novel *The Deity Nodded* (1973), the tales in *Such Things from the Valley* (1977), the unpublished novella *A Journey to Somewhere*, and her literary sketches in such magazines as *Callaloo*, *OBSIDIAN*, and *Black World*, give evidence of her exceptional ear for speech and her extraordinary sense of oral history and folk humor. Her work is also included in *James Baldwin: A Critical Evaluation* and *Sturdy Black Bridges*. Her work-in-progress includes a second novel *Invisible Woman*. The following story is reprinted from *Seeds Beneath the Snow*.

Return of the Spouse

Tole used the signal when he knocked on Penny Motts' front door. He had reached front-door status before going on the road, so he could think of no reason to do otherwise now, because he had been gone only ninety days.

After repeating the signal five times in a row, he became discouraged and started to walk away. Just before he reached the steps, Penny's voice called out.

"Who knock?"

He could not call his own name.

"Who knock, I say. If you can't speak," she said, "I got me something in here that will."

"Me," he answered.

"Me, who?" She mocked his tone. "If that ain't a fool for you; I don't know who 'me' is."

"This is Tole, Penny." His patience was wearing out.

"Tole who?"

"Tole Kirkman, and you can save your damn bullets for your niggers who don't pay for the week on Saturday night."

Penny cracked the door, sticking only her head out and holding her robe shut with one hand. Little silvery sensations crept down his spine. He moved closer, getting a whiff of an oversweet perfume which made his head swim.

"Oh, that's you, Tole. You got off, didn't you?"

"Don't seem to matter none with you," he snapped.

"To tell you the truth, Buster, I don't like the laws near so well as you. I stay outa trouble, and I don't like folks who's always mixed up with 'm."

"Meaning what?" he asked.

"Meaning you come in here and get your goods 'n check."

"So that's the kind you are?"

"No, that's the way it is. I like my fun." She stepped outside of the door, holding the knob with one hand and the robe with the other. "I love fun well as anybody. And I love this town, but I don't want no trouble with no law. Come on in."

"Who you got in there? I know this old act of poking your head out the door and stalling for time asking who knock."

"Nobody in here to hurt you, if you know how to act and if you know how to check." She started taking a cleaner's bag from behind the door.

"I don't have nothing to put no clothes in tonight, honey. Nothing but my hands, sugar plump."

"Should've brought you a suitcase."

"Penny."

"You just lay off my name and just don't be wasting so much time. These your cover-alls and suits. Here's your pajamas and little things in this paper sack."

"So you had me all packed up before I came?"

"If that's the way you want to put it." She smiled as she opened the door to usher him out.

Once under the sky of the early August night, he felt the impact of Penny's sentence more severely than the judge's order to serve on the road for ninety days.

This was the second big lie that had exploded in his face. The first lie was one which had encouraged him to get away from his father's household of twelve and from Old Man Griffin's seventh-grade class to find happiness.

"Man," everybody had said, "if you get yourself a good job making you a lot of money, you can drop them books, and your old man too. Then you can get yourself a good-looking wife what got enough skin and hair to give the children some looks and be happy. After that, get you a woman. And be sure to get you a good boss to keep you out of trouble."

Tole believed this enough to stop school to become a delivery boy for Mr. Crews. He had a motorbike marked CREWS PHARMACY that could take him anywhere he needed to go in the residential section of Wedgefield. He was

known as a good delivery boy because he didn't stop by to talk to anyone
when he had to make a trip.

Three years later, when he was fifteen, Mr. Crews recommended him as a
good boy to work with his friend who had a grocery store. Now he went out
with the man in a truck to deliver groceries in Wedgefield and as far out as
Dubose Crossing. When they got out of the residential district, the truck driver
started teaching him to drive. By the time he was seventeen, he had gotten
his driver's license. When he was nineteen, he married Elease Stenson, a cute
seventeen-year-old, and rented two rooms of a duplex on South Mary Street.
All his father had said was, "Take a blue hen chicken to get up and scratch
for her biddies every day." And his mother had responded in her tired voice
by saying, "Tole's a smart boy, Titus. You know all my folks work hard.
What's in the blood can't be beat out the bones." Elease's people had said
only, "You not worrying how the children'll come out that don't take skin
and hair atta us."

Youth and the good job saved them from the cares of life for two months.
He was a full-time delivery man for Howell's Wholesale Grocery Company,
and enjoyed taking Elease with him on longer trips to show her off. They
talked and giggled together about a dog fight or any other trivial incident. She
kept the two rooms like a showplace. The bedroom was the living room too,
and the kitchen served as dining room and bathroom. The porch lavatory was
shared by both families, but the other couple was young and competed with
the Kirkmans in keeping their part of the premises tidy.

The washtub baths in the kitchen were a special treat. Elease always had
Tole's water heated when he arrived. He remembered how his father had had
to thunder and threaten his mother in order to get water for his bath. He started
bringing ice cream or a cake or candy to Elease on bath nights as a treat for
being a thoughtful wife.

At the end of their second month of marriage, she knew she was pregnant.
The July sun which set on their side of the house caused their apartment to
feel like an oven for the greater part of the night. She became irritable and
complaining because she had heard that a pregnant woman was a sick woman
and immediately needed extra attention, different food and an exceptional
amount of rest. From the day she received the doctor's statement until the day
her baby became a month old, her mother paid a visit every day or sent one
of her children to check on Elease's condition. If Tole got his bath water only
once in a while during this period, he was uncomplaining. If he got one meal
a day, he was completely satisfied. He made excuses for the slights he received
because of her condition, and felt that things would be different when the baby
got on his own feet.

But Junior was a puny baby who cried and kept him in Mr. Crew's drug-
store. The trouble with the baby and what her mother said she should do were
the only things they talked about. But he loved Elease and the baby, so he
worked hard on the job and at home to make the best of his marriage. They
stayed in the two rooms until after the fifth baby came. They got a four-room
house and three more babies. He could see no end to diapers in the bathroom,

diapers drying on the back of kitchen chairs, and in the oven if the weather was bad. He could see no end to diapers and doctors bills or Elease's suffering through each nine-month period of each pregnancy, with no time to comb her hair, or to clean the house. No time to love him. But then, when they loved, it was the making of another baby.

The lie was a gross one. He had a wife and a family, but he was not happy. He had a good job, but he was not able to save one cent. He had been so anxious to leave his father's house to begin his own family, but now he wished that he had not rushed into adult responsibility. The thought occurred to him that neglecting a duty at home now and then would bring some kind of satisfaction. Other men were enjoying themselves at Joe's Place while he walked the floor with his babies.

Mr. Crews had known him since his teen-age years, so he decided to ask for a credit account there for drugs. That way he could have for his own pleasure the money he pretended to pay for the medicine. His first evening at Joe's Place was disgusting—that is, he provoked the seasoned old scoundrels with his bragging and gluttonous drinking bout. Ed Scott pulled him aside later and told him that the men were sure to mark him as an apron-string boy if he didn't know how to be casual about his escapades. He allied himself with Ed's group after the talk, taking cues from Ed on how to proceed until it was his time to set the house up. After this, the men who frequented Joe's Place considered him a brother. He met them faithfully for bull sessions, drinking rounds, card games, and checkers. He was becoming satisfied, which was just as good to him as being happy.

The choice topic became women, and he had nothing to say because he had been a faithful husband. Ed told him that there wasn't any need for him to play pretty with the gang, because all of them were married but all of them had at least one extra.

Ed laughed as he said, "What's for a colored guy who won't write no book, never cross the ocean unless Uncle Sam send him, never have a real holiday— say nothing 'bout a vacation—never be the president or nothing—I say, a fun loving, sweet-smelling mama is about all you got to sparkle you up."

Tole's mouth fell open as Ed talked.

"Just play it cool," he advised Tole. "Just give your extra enough time to keep her happy and enough money to keep her sweet. Just keep her on the tip of your finger. If you squeeze her in the palm of your hand, you're in for trouble."

How to meet a girl was the next problem. He knew that women considered him "a good-looking black nigger" who was tall enough for his clothes to look right on him. And some girls had said all he had to do was to look at them, because his eyes hypnotized them. But he had taken it all lightly in the old days, because his mother had told him that only forward women said such things, and they would not make him a decent wife because they'd tell other men the same things. He remembered that he had never really given his wife a compliment or said outright, "I love you." And she had never once said,

"I love you, Tole." But they had agreed, without saying too much, that they liked each other and wanted to make each other happy. Still, he wanted some woman, not Elease—some sweet-smelling mama, to spin in a romantic dream with him.

As he stopped to deliver orders for the wholesale company, he found himself looking around for this woman. He wanted something within himself to leap up and say, "That's her!"

About two months after Ed's conference, it happened. He walked into Counts' Grocery Store to find a set of hazy-brown eyes standing still in the roundest sweet Georgia-brown face that he had ever seen. She just stood there behind the counter with her lips pursed and her right fingers stroking her coal-black hair which hit even to her shoulders. Instead of asking for Mr. or Mrs. Counts, he stood there checking her down to the waistline.

"Thought you brought the stuff in, then checked," she said.

"Pardon?" he asked.

"I thought you delivery men brought the stuff in, then checked the ticket." She began stroking her hair with the left hand. "You delivery guys sure don't worry about no time schedule."

"Look, baby," he slapped the hand which smoothed her hair. "You can make time stop for me, if you know what I mean?"

She backed away from the counter.

"I got my work to do in the house, you know. Mr. Counts had to take his wife to Emergency in the hospital's, why I'm here. So you come on and bring the stuff in."

"He likes to check the sheet, because one time they put the wrong name on the order, so we had to reload a big order," Tole explained.

"Whatever you say."

"Tole Kirkman—just Tole to you, sugar plump."

"I'm Penny, Penny Motts, and business is business. I got my work to do in the house. I'm just getting the order in. I'm closing up soon's the order's in, if it ever get in. And they got telephones in this town now, and a telephone book."

"That's telling me off all right." He smiled and pinched her arm.

He left the order, and did his first bit of reckless driving because he was sure that she was watching from the window as he took off.

When he did find her place in Field Quarters, and when she finally consented to be his girl, he held her, cherishing her, forgetting about Elease and the eight children. Penny got him in her clutches the very first time. He had gotten as drunk as a dog, had even wallowed a few times (he was told); but the liquor was not so strong as that of his new love.

Elease seemed more detestable now than ever, and the children too. Elease, sleeping heavily with mangled hair in a faded gown, never inspired him now to seek her love. The tired little demons piled into several beds suited him best when they were sleeping. He could remember each new baby as something desirable, smelling of baby oil and powder, and something nice to touch and to kiss because they smiled. Some even made dimples. But later they became little pests. They cried too much or ate too much or made too much noise. He had helped to people this jungle, but he swore that he wouldn't endure it.

He could picture the old rose-flowered wallpaper in Penny's bedroom, and the array of pretty pictures tucked around the wall of trees, birds, flowers and rustic scenes where beautiful girls and their lovers lay in tall, cool grass. He thought of the ice bucket and the service for two on the night table at Penny's house. He was getting a record player for her birthday, and they would have sweet music to go along with that sweet-smelling perfume while they made sweet love.

His reverie was often broken with, "Tole, go take the baby up; she had the fever all day, and you know this was washday for me." Or, "Tole, if you don't bring some more meal or flour when you come back from work, won't be nothing here to feed the children on in the morning." Or a sigh, "Lord help me to live at this poor dying rate."

The sound of Elease's voice came on with laments, and Penny's with pleas. "Daddy, when you going to be all mine? It takes you too long to get here and you leave too early. I can't hold on to you, when you won't let loose."

To please Penny, Tole started staying until an hour before time to go to work. No matter what time he came home, Elease opened the door and fixed whatever she had to cook, even though she fussed until he left. After a while, he would wait until she fixed it, then empty it in the garbage pail. He hoped that she would cry, but she didn't. It would provoke him that she was not passionate enough to demand a showdown by not letting him in or by not fixing his food. Twice he wrecked the truck, and twice his employer paid for the offenses to keep him from serving on the chain gang when he told him frankly that he was having trouble at home.

"Look, Tole," Mr. Howell told him, "why don't you do like the other boys? Get you a girl. Too many women in the world for you to upset yourself. You the best boy I've got. You don't steal, like some I had, so I want to keep you outta trouble. Wisen yourself, then. You're young and got money in your pocket."

With an ally, Tole got bolder. He moved his Sunday clothes and shoes to Penny's house so that he could spend the whole weekend with her. Then he moved his work clothes and his personal items, going by his house only to leave the rent and money for food and to half-tease the children. Then he came only to leave the money when the children were asleep.

Nothing, nobody, mattered as much as Penny. She made his blood sing and he was happy.

After he had lived with Penny for two months, he decided that he would speed up deliveries so that he could spend an extra hour at home during the noon hour on her day off from work. For one thing, he was hungry—more hungry for food this day than for love. He picked up four pounds of T-bone steaks and planned to have her make some creamed potatoes. He could kick off his shoes and relax, listen to music, eat, then take a nap.

When he came to the house, the blinds were drawn and there was apparently no one stirring. Two glasses on the night stand had been used and a mound of cigarette ashes filled the big tray. There was a platter with particles of food.

"Penny," he called. "Penny."

"For the love of Mike, why you yelling your guts out? I'm right here in the bathroom."

"What are you doing in the bathroom this time of day?" he demanded.

"The hell with you!" she retorted. "If you're not the damndest fool I ever met. What the hell's a bathroom for, any time of day? Want me to tell you? I will if your mama forgot to tell you."

"I brought us some good steak to cook, and I want some of those creamed potatoes you make."

"The burners'll turn on for you just like for me. Never saw such a goddamn helpless-assed bull. I'm not your slave, you know. Say, Buster, what you know I don't know? That's interesting, that I'd like to know."

"I'll cut your living throat, that's what I'll do!" He walked to the bathroom door. Tole tried the door, but she had it locked on the inside.

"Open the door, you two-cent hussy. If you don't, I'll break it down."

"You do that," she said, "and they'll only have to clean up the bathroom."

He left the house storming. He was tempted to go back, but decided to lunch at the shop and go back to work. He drove through the Quarters not seeing and not caring. He turned the corner onto the next street and plunged into the back of the Wedgefield Furniture truck.

Judge Moise sat with his broad shoulders heaved frontwise. He was a new judge in the Ville County courthouse, but he was old in the knowledge of rustic fox play. He had no love for Negroes, but he hated the bosses who indulged their boys more than his preacher grandfather had hated female gospel-mongers. He was for law which bore the stamp of moral integrity. And Tole Kirkman, he had been told, had a boss who paid him out of trouble every time he offended the law.

"Make an example outta him," he told the clerk, "and I'll be in or out and be done with it. If it's anything I can't stand, it's a white man playing papa to a niggrah culprit. And I'll be damned if I don't make an end to it or be found trying."

Working through his help down to the janitor, Judge Moise had a "case history" on Tole Kirkman by the date of his trial. Besides, he had baited the trap in an easy way. He called Tole's employer, talked pleasantly and said that he understood that Negro men had to have an extra woman to keep themselves happy. Somehow the word got to Tole that Mr. Howell had fixed things up with the new judge. He decided to make up with Penny by buying her a new outfit if she promised to come to the trial. She promised, so they were reconciled.

Meanwhile, Judge Moise sent a welfare worker to check on Tole's family. The report strengthened the judge's resolve to execute his plan. He was told that the children were undernourished and ill taken care of because the mother's health was failing and her operating funds were insufficient. The welfare worker requested Elease to appear with the eight children at the trial at Judge Moise's request.

Tole Kirkman came in dressed in his next-best Sunday clothes and with a new summer straw hat in his hand. Penny looked like a cut-out doll in her new outfit. He sat down calmly, crossed his legs and winked at Penny. He felt for the signed, incomplete check which Mr. Howell had given him with orders to be back to work after lunch. She winked back, smiling carefully, her mouth full of gum which she popped on the slightest provocation.

She almost swallowed her gum as she followed Tole's eyes across the courtroom.

Elease came in with the baby in her arms and all of the others straggling behind her. Junior prodded the smaller ones, getting them all seated in a row just before court was called to order.

"That's them?" Penny asked. He nodded. He felt that Elease was trying to provoke him by coming there, straggling along with all their puny, ill-kept children.

Tole was called to the bench and pleaded guilty, as Mr. Howell had told him to do. He then handed the judge the envelope. He took it, put it on the stand and continued.

"Are you married, Kirkman?"

"Yes, sir."

"I assume you have no children; you seem to be a newly wed."

Tole dropped his head. "In a way," he answered.

"What way?"

"I wouldn't like to talk about no way, because my business up here is about hitting that truck."

"You're right," the judge said. "You're right. You hit the truck, when it had a red flag out in the back."

"I said I was guilty." Tole raised his voice.

"Yes, you're a man against the law because you have two wives, so that makes you a bigamist who goes around smashing up things just like you smash up people. I ought to sentence your other wife, your common wife, right along with you."

"Your sentence is ninety days on the road, and suspension of your driver's license for a year. The Welfare Department will take care of Elease and the children. I'll mail this back to your boss." He waved it.

Neither of the women, no doubt for their separate reasons, visited him on the prison farm.

Ten o'clock was not too long after dark, the way time was measured during the summer in Wedgefield. As he walked away from Penny's house in the August night, life was just beginning for the couples who lived for fun and loving. He had been put out, and tried not to care, but the thought of another's taking his place provoked him. A man, a real man, the group would say, would ambush the new guy, or at least shoot him in the foot. A real man would not let another man take his woman without a fight. He wanted Penny's affection, but he did not want to fight for her. He had never really seen another man in her house or leaving it. He wondered if she had devised the trick to test his spunk or to prove her worth by egging him on so that he could divorce his wife, Elease.

The scene with the judge made him think of Elease and the children. That day he was ashamed of her and the children. They had looked the part of the dispossessed that they were, and he hadn't liked it. Elease could have spruced up to keep the other woman from seeming so attractive. She could have styled her hair and put on some lipstick. She had helped to drive him away.

He walked on through the Quarters with his clothes rolled in a tight bundle under his arm. He did not have the money to rent a room for the night, and for the first time in his life he did not know where he would sleep.

"Hell," he said. "I'm going home. That's where I'm going. If that bastard Moise wants to put me in trouble because I took Penny, then damn it to hell, he's not making me work ninety days to wander around in the streets." He thought of saying "Elease, I'm sorry and I want to come back home." Instead he decided to bully her. He'd tell her that he was going to the World's Fair, to Atlantic City, New Jersey, and then on over to the West Coast to visit his brother in Los Angeles. He'd let her know that he was no trash and that he had people in far-away places who stood for something and who cared for him.

He reached 1490 South Mary Street before he had finished mapping out his tour.

He knocked the second time before the light went on.

Elease asked, "Who is it?"

"Me."

"What you want, Tole?" she asked.

"Open the door, woman," he commanded.

She opened the door and stood cautiously in the clearing.

"You're not going to let me in?"

"Why should I let you in?"

"Jesus Christ, a man can't come in his own house?"

"You didn't leave from here, Tole, so you got no right to come stirring me up if she turned you out."

"I just want to talk over something," he said in a casual voice.

"All right, just a minute." She put on a pink-flowered cotton housecoat and a pair of soft pink house-slippers. He noticed that her hair was put up in pink curlers. She had gotten up from a hide-a-way bed that looked clean and comfortable.

"You sick?" he asked. "Nobody slept in here unless they were sick—made it convenient when company called?"

"No, the lady said it was best for the parents not to sleep in the room with the children. I put the girls in the front bedroom and the boys in the back room. If one gets to feeling bad, I take him in here until he feels better."

"I see. Well, I'm going to the World's Fair and to California. Nobody wants to take a wife to California with her hair standing up on the top of her head. And nobody likes baby diapers drying in the stove where you got to cook his bread. It's some things a man won't stand. And he feels like a fool when he wants to disown his own blood. I'm going to California, to Los Angeles, where my brother is, the one who's living like a king.''

"Whatever are you raving about?" she asked. "You're your own man. The Welfare is taking care of us. But I said I didn't want to stay on the Welfare. Bad enough for the children with you on the road, and this Penny business, and now people tease them about 'not to be sold.' But they helped, and I had time to get myself together. I'm studying to be a hairdresser.''

"You didn't even say you loved me, never did. Every little brat around here rated more than me.''

"I can have my shop at home. I'll start in the kitchen, but I'll ask Mr. Jenkins to add two rooms so I can have a bedroom for myself and a room to work in.''

"Here I haven't eaten since this morning, and my own wife hasn't offered me a thing to eat. A man'll have to leave the South to find a woman who knows how to treat people.''

"Junior's not but ten, but he's a little man. He helps my father gather his vegetables and sell them.''

"I used to say we don't talk, but we do. We talk forever. Especially when a man's starving to death in his own home.''

"You stop saying that, you hear me. You stop saying that, Tole Kirkman. You left me. Remember. You left me. Go bully your whore." She stood firmly waited for his reply.

"Well, the sickly little saint has got some mule in her at last," he goaded her.

"Call it what you want to; but at the beauty shop, I learned how people act, good and bad, listening to the customers. Both of us were wrong; you worked hard, and I stayed out the street, and that's about all we called our marriage. We had a real nice time for two months; and after I started the family, everything fell to pieces.''

"I don't know you," he said, looking at Elease. "I married you, but I didn't know you. I don't now, but you make a lot of sense.''

"And I don't know you either. And I didn't know you hated the baby diapers in the oven, because you didn't say so.''

"I guess all that's not's hard as a man laboring hard everyday for nothing. Not even eight babies in ten years.''

"Did Penny Mott put you out, or did you put her down to come back home?''

"I guess, if she put me out, you don't want me either." He kept his eyes away from her.

"Tole." She stood before him. "I'm not saying I'm right. I have to know the truth.''

"She sent me away, Elease. And I'm not going to beg to stay here, either. I need to find myself. I want to be a good father and a good husband, but I'm not sure that I want to scratch everyday.''

"I understand," she said.

"You understand that I don't want to miss out on life because of you and the children; that I, me, myself, want to live?"

"Yes, Tole, I didn't know what it was like for one to feel that he had to keep things moving every day, but I got a taste of it when you left. It's not easy. And I've found out that people work together. They go to church, to picnics, to programs and to visit their people, even though they have more children than we've got; and they're not complaining about it, either."

"Jesus Christ, I can't stay in the street all the time, or up in the air, or wherever I've been."

"Don't use the Lord's name in vain, Tole."

"I guess not," he agreed.

They sat, exhausted from the talk. Several minutes passed in silence. After all of the talk, she noticed that Tole still held the rolled cleaner's bag in his arm; he had his hat on, and the smaller bag at his feet.

"Tole," she got up to leave, "rest your hat and hang the bag behind the door in the other room while I fix some bath water for you."

He took his hat off, then his shoes, and walked quietly into the other room.

Alice Childress

(1920–   )

A native of Charleston, South Carolina, Childress has used her Southern heritage to explore racial issues forthrightly. Indeed, her frankness was unacceptable to certain Southern audiences in the 1960s; the state of Alabama banned the telecast of her drama *Wine in the Wilderness* in 1969. An actress, playwright, and novelist, Childress has created a substantial body of work that critics have only recently begun to evaluate judiciously. Her plays include *Florence* (1949); *Gold Through the Trees* (1952); *Trouble in Mind* (1955), which won a 1956 Obie Award; *Wedding Band* (1966), televised by ABC in 1973; *Mojo: A Black Love Story* (1970); and *Moms: A Praise Play for a Black Comedienne* (1986). Her novel *A Hero Ain't Nothin' but a Sandwich* was named one of the outstanding books of 1973 by the *New York Times*. Among her other works are *Like One of the Family: Conversations from a Domestic's Life* (1956), *A Short Walk* (1979), *Rainbow Jordan* (1981), and *Many Closets* (1987). The excerpt that follows is from *A Short Walk*.

---

from A Short Walk

CHAPTER ONE

One morning, in the middle of the year 1900, in a two-room shack in Charleston, South Carolina, Bill James has a comforting breakfast of mackerel and hominy grits. Jesus looks down from the wall with compassion, down from his frame of pink and blue seashells. Bill is lean, good looking, and keen featured. His skin is dull, velvety, almost blue. Gently puffed lips glow grape-purple against strong white teeth. In one knotted, work-hardened hand he holds a newspaper, in the other a piece of fried fish. He shakes his head slowly, with great authority. "Etta, this world is somethin, first one thing, then another."

His brown wife peeps over his shoulder, pouring another cup of coffee, leaning in close, enjoying the odor of Dr. Alimine's Flower Pomade. She thinks of telling him how good looking he is, but says something else.

"You like to show off, don'tcha? Just cause you can read. You oughta be thinkin' 'bout buyin another paper. All that news happen so long ago till folks done forgot."

B:11

130

On how they have been blessed.

"I'm gonna buy a new one when new things start happenin. No point in buyin the same news every day, a waste a money."

Etta takes off her apron and picks her best black skirt free of lint. Looking in the speckled, cracked mirror hanging under Jesus on the wall, she smooths thick, bushy hair and rolls down her sleeves. "Bill, what kinda eyes I got?"

"Gingerbread eyes and stand-up ninnies."

"Shame, shame, no way to talk on the day of a funeral."

"Yeah, it is. You got pretty little feet and a nice round boonky."

"Stop talkin underneath my clothes. No shame."

"Got dimples in her cheeks, all up behind her knees and everywhere."

Her eyes light with love. They think love thoughts about how good it is to be together, how good it was each time they had it, touching hands beneath the covers even when they weren't having it. How good it is to be black and brown in a morning glory-covered house; to have mackerel and grits on a four-eyed stove; to own plates, cups, spoons and an iron bed with a big, comfortable mattress.

"Billie-boy, ain't it time we 'dopted ourself a baby?"

He lowers his head as if examining the workboots, turning his feet this way and that. "Well, folks oughta have they own chirrun and—"

Adoption

"Look like we ain't gonna have any of our own. Looks like I'da got that way in five years, but no sense in accusin Gawd."

Married 5 yrs.

Bill carefully folds the newspaper and places it in the sideboard drawer. "Folks should be kinda well-off when they think bout taking in a stranger-chile."

"We's well-off. Ain't many people got as much to show as we got. Not a meal goes by that we don't have food left in the pot. There's bedclothes in the drawer and a pump in the kitchen. We got pots, pans and dishes. How much can a baby use?"

"They don't stay little. They grow up."

"Let her grow if she wants to. That's what babies is for, for to grow."

"I gotta go to work. We gonna dig ditches behind the mill road. . . ."

"And I'm bringin Murdell's baby back after the funeral."

Funeral Baby

"But you dern well can't do it less I give the word."

"Give me your word."

"Look like Murdell's mama would keep it."

"Mrs. Johnson's gone so cripple till the next door people have to do for her."

"How come the next door people don't keep the baby?"

"'Cause they got nine of they own. Haven't you been sayin and also silent-wishin for me to have a baby?"

9 children

Bill pops his knuckles and fine beads of sweat appear on his forehead. "I don't know how the baby look."

"You got eyes; come see."

"I can't look at the chile, then say I don't want it. That's rude. Bet they name it somethin I wouldn't like. Did they call her Murdell?"

"No, and you must never speak ill of the dead."

"Not speakin ill, just don't like that name."

"They gonna let me name her."

"You did it already?"

[handwritten: Baby 3wks old] "I thought of a name and they callin her by it, but she's only three weeks old—we can change it."

"What yall callin her?"

[handwritten arrow] "Cora, after your gone-to-glory mother who was born in slavery. Cora is a sound that's short, sweet and easy on your mouth."

He turns away to hide the pleasure in his eyes, having a hard time of giving in, giving up and taking in the stranger-child. . . . "That baby is half white, Etta." *[handwritten: Mulatto (hybrid discursive spre)]*

"But she's so sweetly brown, like coffee and condense milk mix together."

"But even so. . . ."

She cups his face in her hands. "Please, sweet daddy, do it just for me?"

His knees go weak. "Sure, for you and for me, too—but where will she *[handwritten: Resistance]* sleep?"

She pulls his shirtsleeve, leads the way to the tiny bedroom. Squeezing her roundness past the washstand, she reaches under the bed and drags out a wooden box lined with cotton quilting. Bill stamps the floor and the walls tremble. "You ain't fixin to put our Cora to sleep in a Octiggen soap box!"

"What's wrong with that?"

"I wouldn't want nobody to visit and see her in a soap box. She suppose to sleep in a cradle."

"There's no cradle finer than this."

"Baby won't be able to see. She'll be thinkin the world look like the inside of a soap box."

"She won't catch no drafts."

"And no fresh air, either."

"Well, our Cora can sleep in the box till you get a cradle. Bill, we got us a baby."

Her face is so alive with happiness he has to reach out and take her in his arms as she cries out joy and relief. One hot, salty teardrop falls on his throat and trickles over his chest. Desire moves through his body and he is ready to lie down with her. She feels him stir, clings to him, kissing his lips, nostrils and eyes, nuzzling her nose into the hollow of his neck, wetting his face with her crying. He moves the soap box from the bed to the washstand and pulls back the patchwork quilt.

"Ain't this a damn shame . . . and I was all ready to go to work . . . a damn shame."

[handwritten: They make love] Unbleached muslin sheets are cool to warm bodies and this morning is the best of all times, a moment with them tight together in it, and the new baby waiting, and the Octagon soap box ready on the washstand. A sweet twenty minutes, the two of them one within the protection of drawn shades and friendly walls; with the sound of bees humming as they rob morning glories

for honey. Bill rubs purple lips across her throat and whispers down the golden corridor of her ear.

"Ain't this a shame, a damn shame, and I gotta go to work. . . ."

People gather at the Johnson house to take one last look at Murdell Johnson before following her narrow casket out to the colored cemetery. Sad-faced little children stand around the front yard, starchily dressed in their best bits of finery—limp, threadbare hair ribbons, hand-me-down dresses, thrice-patched knickerbockers and overalls. One little girl pulls at a tall, skinny woman's skirt. "Miss Odessa, can we go back in the house and look at the daid again?"

"No, yall have looked several times before. Oh, children, I tell you, this life is for suffering." She waves a black-edged handkerchief, stretches out gaunt but graceful arms and showers boys and girls with clear, silvery, cultivated words. "Be good, live righteous, for we know not the day or the hour. Kojie, lad, you are the tallest, so when we start our march to the graveyard please lead the way for the little ones carrying bouquets."

The long-legged tan boy stands at attention, one hand respectfully held behind his back. A sharp crease is pressed in each pants leg of his denims. "Yes, Ma'am, Miss Odessa. Can I get you some*thing*? Maybe a cool, refresh*ing* dipper of water from the well?"

Odessa rewards him with a sad storybook smile and gracefully flutters her handkerchief. "Kojie, I do declare, you're going to someday be somebody of importance. You prove to us that color is nothing and that the heart is all; as the French say, *'Couleur n'est rien, le coeur est tout.'* I'll have a dipper of water, God bless you. Let us all try to lift our race and remember to put *ing* on the end of our words. Death is indeed hard, children, we know not the day or the hour." She sweeps over to the rickety bench where paper flowers of every description are piled high; some old, some wilted, others heavily waxed, a few bright and new. "Oh, how good and sweet of kind friends to lend their flowers. Let's arrange them in small bunches to be carried by our angels. Yes, we know not the day. . . ."

"Stop all that drat goin on!"

Odessa and the children look up to see Addie scowling down from the porch. Addie—fat, red-brown, with black ribbons braided through her straight Indian hair neatly crisscrossed behind her shoulder blades. Odessa slowly unfolds the petals of a red paper rose.

"We're not making noise, Miss Addie."

"Then how come we can hear you talkin bout nobody knowin the day or the hour? Murdell's mama is quiet now, but if you'da heard her this mornin it woulda chilled the blood in your very veins. When she saw her child laid out she went to screamin and shakin. Her breath drawnin in and out was like death rattles."

Odessa ties a pink streamer around a dusty cluster of waxed sweet peas. "Poor soul, life will test you—will test us all. What is it all about? That's the question, and who's to answer?"

Addie shakes her braids. "Don't let a little schoolin turn you fool. Gawd knows what it's about. He's movin, workin his will and payin no never-mind to what niggas understand.''

The children clutch their flowers and search Odessa's face for answers. She says, ''Handle bouquets with care because we must return them to owners after the procession.'' The children stare, waiting to see if she will dare answer back.

"I'm teaching these children not to use the word *nigger*."

"Well, I ain't no chile."

"But we shouldn't tell them not to say it and . . . and say it ourselves."

"And you shouldn't correct me before chirrun."

"I had to, I'm sorry."

"When white folk call us names I notice that nobody is ever on hand to correct them."

Odessa draws herself up even taller. ''We can't be responsible for what they say but we can set the proper example.''

Addie sucks her teeth, making a popping sound with her lips, picks up a tin pail and heads for the pump. ''Oh my, we gettin so muckty-muck and dicty. Well, whilst yall play with flowers, I'm the one that's cleanin up. Schoolin and learnin ain't worth a poot in a china pot.''

"May we help?"

Addie shoves her away. ''No, go play with your flowers.'' She turns up the front of her black cotton skirt and pins it behind, showing a snowy petticoat patched with a bag from Webster's Rice Mills. ''Fact is,'' she grumbles, ''you right. It ain't nice to say 'nigga', but I don't be sayin it like white folk. I just say it dry-long-so. When they say it, it's to hurt.'' She presses down on the pump with both hands; there's a low, gurgling sound as it gives up a thin stream of water. ''Fact is,'' she goes on, ''I don't expect to hear chirrun sayin that word. First one do is gonna get a fast backhand slap in the mouth. Yall hear?''

The children nod solemnly out of respect for Addie. After winning the battle with the pump, she squares her shoulders and picks up the pail. ''Yes, chirrun, there's many a thing we got to learn cause life will test us. We know not the day or the hour and things like that, so you listen to Miss Odessa, cause she don't have to spend her time on no dumb chirrun. Long ago she could have shook the dust of Carolina off her shoe sole and gone Nawth where streets are pave with gold and sprinkle with diamonds, where all a nigga—a *person*—has to do is bend down and scoop up a bountiful fortune.''

A little girl with wide, flaring nostrils suddenly holds them together and whispers. ''Pewie, pewie, here comes the dog-nanny man.''

Kojie snickers, then righteously scolds her. ''Shouldn't say that. Suppose to respect grown people. Ain't she, Miss Odessa?''

"Yes, children, be very kind."

They watch the old man slowly pull the familiar sack up the street. He stops to sweep up something with a whisk broom and a small shovel, then empties it into his crokersack.

Addie sucks her teeth and spits. "Gawd, that poor man stink. Dog-nanny smell is all through his skin."

Kojie puts on a sorrowful expression and shifts his weight from one foot to the other. "Why he pick*ing* it up like that, Miss Odessa?"

"Mr. July is in the fertilizer business. He gathers—collects—er—dog droppings, then he dries them out in the sun . . ."

Another boy, with long fuzzy hair, leans over to Kojie and says, "You oughta smell his yard."

Miss Odessa pinches the boy's ear and goes on with the explanation. ". . . then he sells them over at the fertilizer mill so they can make fertilizer, which is then put in the earth to make the lovely flowers grow."

Addie shakes her head with grudging admiration. "See there? White folk so smart they can even make money outta dog turds."

Mr. July rests his sack in the middle of the road and, cap in hand, approaches the gate. "Mornin, Miss Addie, Miss Dessa, just stop to pay respeck to the daid. Won't come in, ain't fit to come in, but wanta give this fifty cent piece." He places the coin on the gatepost.

"I hope you don't think we're going to let you leave without looking on Murdell's face!" Odessa protests. "Shame on you, Mr. July!"

He straightens his shirt collar and breaks into a snaggle-toothed smile, eyes glistening with appreciation. "That's kind of you, but makes no sense for me to come in the house while I'm out workin this way."

Addie places her hands on her hips and moves closer to the gate. "Mr. July, go look on Murdell's face."

Odessa flings the gate open. "Mr. July, Murdell had a high regard for you. Go in, present your respects and your money, look on her face."

He enters the yard, easing past the gate with delicate hesitation, three steps forward, a half step back, advancing and retreating, bowing to Odessa, the children, and even to people who aren't there—his walk a mute but grand apology for his station in life.

Miss Addie darts a barbed wire look at the children, threatening to butt heads if they laugh at him. She follows at a less-than-comfortable distance from July.

Murdell's mother, mumbling prayers, is seated to one side, in front of the varnished oak coffin. A few months before, a stroke had lifted and twisted one corner of her mouth, leaving her right arm uselessly dangling by her side. She wears forty-five years like seventy. Wisps of dry, snowy white hair show from under a black cotton headcloth. The good left hand drums out a tattoo on her knee. Odessa leads Mister July to the coffin. The corpse is a picture of regal, peaceful calm, laid out in a lavender voile dress collared with white hand crochet. Her jet black hair is a billowing storm cloud against the lavender lace pillow. Murdell . . . sixteen, darkly beautiful with the near-yet-far-away look of youth in death.

Mister July fears he may disturb her immaculate rest. A knot of pain forms in the pit of his stomach, grows larger and works its way up to his throat;

shoulders shake and scalding tears run down his cheeks. He tries to hold back sound but it pours out in a hoarse torrent. "Ease, Gawd, give us ease!"

He places the half dollar in a glass bowl on the table at the foot of the casket. Murdell's mama holds out her good hand.

"No, Ma'am, I been workin."

"Why you wanta act sometimey?"

He gently shakes her hand. "Gawd move in a mysterious way his wonder to perform. He never forsake the orphan. Most forty years done pass since the last day a bondage, so Murdell's baby gonna someday walk where we now can't go, live to say what we can't, gonna taste the sweet years to come. Her life will live easy."

He leaves the way he came; three steps forward, a half step back, nervously twirling his old, weatherbeaten hat, smiling and bowing to those there and those who are not, begging pardon for his existence. "Thank yuh, thank yuh, yas'm, indeedy, scuse me, beg pardon. . . ."

Odessa says goodbye at the gate. "We are fortunate to have kind friends in the hour of sorrow."

Mr. July whispers a secret. "This work a mine ain't no bed-a-roses, but I gotta be m'own boss cause I don't like workin for white folk in a direck way. They too mean, treated me so bad at the lumber yard, cuttin down my pay. They keep the white and lay me off when work slack. I held my tongue in check so much till it was givin me pains in m'chest."

"We know, Mister July, we know."

"Yas'm, this ain't no bed-a-roses, but I ruther pick up behind dawgs than work for white folk."

More people arrive for the funeral, scrubbed with brown soap, neatly dressed in their darkest clothes. They stream through the gate carrying imitation palm wreaths trimmed with bows of white ribbon, fresh cut garden flowers, bunches of wild purple clover, yellow dandelions and pots of ivy. Women carry agate pans and ironstone jars of food. Men are wearing white cotton gloves and purple satin badges stamped in gold—First Colored Brotherhood Lodge. They walk solemnly, holding the right hand behind the back, their heads respectfully bowed. Some stand on the porch speaking in whispers.

"Where is Murdell's mama's brother? You'da think Sam would come home for buryin his niece."

"He's travelin with Rabbit Ears minstrel show."

"What he doin in a minstrel?"

"Go out in a parade, be buckin and wingin to advertise—in face black."

"His face black enough."

"But that's how they do."

"Yeah, black it and make the mouth white."

"Got a pretty wife name Francine, I hear."

"Rabbit Ears travels through Georgia—Chicago even."

"You think Gawd like that?"

"No. They do better to pray."

Etta James hurries through the gate carrying her best gray agate pot and a

Ritual & Ceremony

newspaper-wrapped bundle. "How's Murdell's mama? I brought mulatto rice and clothes to take home the baby." She has a hard time keeping up with Odessa's long strides as they head for the kitchen.

"She's holding up. Relatives came from Edisto Island to take her back. They'll keep the baby until you're ready."

"I'm takin Cora today. People don't like to give up children after havin 'em awhile."

"If Bill is ready."

"He is ready."

The minister's face looks like dark, crumpled cardboard; a face in perpetual mourning, lit by black diamond eyes staring out on a world just beyond his understanding. In his heart he carries a burden of guilts: once, long years ago, laying with his best friend's wife; once stealing a pair of secondhand shoes; hating his old slave master; looking at a white woman's nakedness as he went about the business of carrying wood to her house; refusing to lend a brother five dollars the day before he lost his life under the wheels of a freight train; the sin of longing for such worldly things as a gold tooth, a horse and buggy, a Prince Albert coat and a gold ring with a cat's-eye stone. Reverend Mills is ever at war with himself to win the battle against sin and desire, against the feelings within, the churning thoughts which keep him wondering how the flock can look to him for guidance. But he is winning the war, and daily turns the other cheek and goes about his humble way, trying to deal with unreasonable colored and white folk, taking low when backed into a corner. Yet there is sin in it too; he feels the acid drops of hatred eating into the core of his heart—a heart which skips and flutters. The inner struggle has etched a pained, resigned and bewildered look in his eyes. People say, "Reverend Mills looks like a picture of a saint—a black saint."

He stands behind the coffin studying his congregation—crowded elbow to elbow in the small room, spilling out to the porch and looking in at the windows. He squares his shoulders and tries to feel like Moses or Daniel as he fights the fear inside and wonders, What is death? He longs for a secret word that, once spoken, could bring peace instantly. He lifts his arms, holds out roughened hands, flexing gnarled fingers that will never wear a gold ring with a cat's-eye stone. "The Lawd giveth, the Lawd taketh away, blessed be the name of the Lawd."

The congregation agrees with light groans and sighs.

"The grim reaper strikes like a thief in the night. Every time you look in the jaws a death, ask yourself: Is my house in order?" The little flock grows fearful, they avoid each other's eyes, look at the walls and the few floral pieces. The men smooth their white gloves and purple badges. They are uncomfortably sorry for the times they have quarreled, fought, lusted after strangeness, sinned against the flesh. They feel defiled, rejected, inferior and stupid from worldly sin. Their misery is cold, stiff, wooden. They lick their lips and swallow saliva to ease dry throats. Each thinks his or her sin is the ugliest or the heaviest to bear, all except Miss Emily. She knows God forgave when she lost her sight. She has paid her sin-debt with blindness. She serves the term in hell now and there's nothing to look forward to but the happy-ever-after of an eternity filled with the blazing promise of everlasting joy.

"Glory! Praise his name!" Reverend Mills folds his arms and eases into preaching. "Gawd is tired a sin. If Gabriel was to blow today, where would you stand?"

Silence except for a few sighs mingling in the air with the smell of dying clover.

Murdell's mama closes her eyes, reliving the memory of her daughter's confession about a day long ago when the girl stood admiring herself in the white folk's looking glass, trying on the woman's clothes while they were all gone off to a wedding party. The son returned home early as she was trying on his mother's cambric and lace wrapper.

"I got no business doin this. They back?"

"No. I left. Why do you always run?"

"We not s'pose to be friends."

"Don't you get lonesome . . . workin out in service, goin home only once a month?"

"It's lonesome bein the onliest colored."

"I'm lonesome, too."

"But you ain't been sent away to strangers."

"Why do they send you? Fifteen is too young to be alone . . . with strangers."

"Poor people gotta send girls off so's they get room and board."

"Doesn't your family worry bout you?"

"No use. They say to be good and to pray."

"But it's still lonesome."

"Uh-huh."

From that day on they were friends and soon forgot to think about past or future—the only time was now. The first loving was to be the only "sin" but they continued to meet; young bodies, heads and hearts caring without caution, blind to the rules and laws of planned, separate living. One night he crept to her room; after loving, sleep stole over them. The morning sun beamed in the attic window and lighted them cheek to cheek, arms entwined, damp with love, deep in peaceful slumber. His mother awakened them. They sent him away to visit a distant aunt. She was sent home to her mother, four months pregnant, with eight dollars back pay.

Murdell's mama turns away from her mind's eye vision, shivering with the thought of how hot hell must be. "Do, Lawd, have mercy on my only chile! Birth fever took her and she done pay with her life. Mercy, Lawd! Have more mercy!"

Her suffering moves Reverend Mills to hasten his sermon onward, to open the flood gates, to ease heart's pain. "But I tell you, my Gawd is a good Gawd-a!"

Two or three amens come from the people in relieved recognition of soothing rhythm, the sweet sing-song promise of forgiveness. Faces eagerly turn to the preacher to drink in the crystal water of forgiveness.

"I say my Gawd is a good Gawd-a!"

Murdell's mama matches the rhythm of his "Gawd-a" with "Ah-yes-amen-a." The people take it up as their chorus and join in at the next turn. "Ah-yes-amen-a."

Now Mills fully enters the preaching pattern. "Sometime seem like there's no place to turn-a. You look up the road, nothin to see; look down the road, there's nothin but trouble, trouble, trouble-a is everywhere and the road is blocked-a!"

There are shouts of agreement as souls wrestle with trouble, guilt and forgiveness. A woman's shoulders shake as she sobs from some deep, scarred, silent place within her bosom. But there will be no full relief until the leader gives a special word, a signal to release a tidal wave of emotion.

"Have you been a-hungry-a?" Dull starvation moans.

"Have you been a-homeless-a?" The heels of the dispossessed rap out a staccato sound against the bare wooden floor.

"Have . . . have . . . have you been a-friendless-a?" A "Yay-Yay" from the lonely.

"Sayin Lawd, I don't know which way to turn-a?" Feet stamp and the flowers on the dead girl's breast tremble.

Mills' voice lifts and hammers ever harder, word by word, note by note, gaining ground on its way to heart's ease. "But I'm a witness! I say I'm a witness! My Gawd is a good Gawd-a. He never made a cross-a heavier than the cross-a carried on the shoulder of-a Jesus Christ-a, the king-a the world-a!"

They shout approval, urging and hastening him on. "Speak the word! Don't hold back!"

Beads of perspiration drift from his forehead, swelling veins pulse in his temples. His voice grates and thickens as he gulps in air, sending it back out in words as if a giant spirit hand pumps them from his chest. "Bowed in sin-a, bowed with trouble, poor, lost sheep-a, lost in shame and sin-a! But Gawd, my great Gawd-a, my good Gawd-a—praise his name-a—that same Gawd-a that knows every secret corner of a sinner's soul-a—that Gawd-a is a forgivin Gawd-a—and this day will he forgive, forgive, forgive-a all our sins-a!"

Forgive, there is the word; now hearts unlock and tears spill grief. A strapping young woman faints with relief, a man holds her up, the good boy Kojie runs to fetch a dipper of water. An old ex-slave grandfather gropes his way out to the porch. "Thangs to Jedus, thangs to Jedus."

Murdell's mama waves her good hand, riding the high wave of God's forgiveness. She sees the Almighty holding a great set of scales and using a pile of stones to balance her good deeds against the bad. He adds up all the clothes she has washed, the floors she has scrubbed. God smiles, shakes his flowing white hair and counts out each of her hungry days, every lonely hour of widowhood, then throws an extra heavy stone on the credit side because she has never owned a new coat or hat or new anything else in all the days of her life. God smiles as he adds more and more to her credit. She has labored hard, suffered a stroke, seen her only child die in the bloom of youth; she has no money except for the coins of charity in the glass funeral bowl—but, yet and still, she has loved God through it all. She watches the Almighty turn to the sin side of the scale, holding up one gray rock which is Murdell's sin. God studies that stone, then flings it away; it breaks apart from the force of his anger, smashing itself into tiny little pieces of star stuff . . . and the golden gates of heaven open wide to receive Murdell's soul.

Reverend Mills laughs with joy and proudly gives God the glory, paying the last tribute while the congregation hums "Nearer My God To Thee." "All who knew her loved her—she was kind, she was not perfect—and none of us are. The Lord giveth and the Lord taketh away, blessed is the name of the Lord."

The lady from next door brings in the baby and hands it to the minister, across the dead body. He says, "Mother, rest easy. I now place your child in the lovin care of Mr. and Mrs. William James. From this day forward her name shall be Cora James and the couple will raise her as their own."

Etta raises her hand and pipes out a rehearsed pledge. "Before my Maker and all gathered in witness, I promise to care for this child and love her all the days a my life." Cora yawns and continues to sleep.

Etta carries her in her arms, slowly walking all the way to the cemetery, following the white-gloved pallbearers. Four boys from Jenkins' Colored Orphan Band play cornets and beat bass drums, booming and blowing a triumphant dirge through the cobblestoned streets. Murdell's mama rides in a carriage for the first time in her life—a black carriage drawn by a black horse decked in black plumes, knotted tassels, fringe, wooden beads and a purple satin collar around his neck. Six foot-mourners walk and weep before the congregation. They all pace straight on, moving with measured tread, taking no notice of distractions.

A four-year-old white boy stops playing hop-up-and-down-on-the-curbstone long enough to ask his older brother, "What they doin?"

The ten-year-old thumbs his belt in imitation of his father and tries to squirt spit through the side of his mouth. He wipes his chin and grumbles. "Aw, a nigger got kilt and they goin to bury him."

The little one gathers that this is something to be pleased about, that they should laugh or maybe throw something. He watches big brother to see how and when they will act.

An old white man with yellowed hair and pale parchment skin touches the big boy's shoulder. "Don't bother them niggers. Let em bury the dead in peace." The big boy shrugs and walks away, laughing at the old man's baggy, misfit pants. The little boy also laughs.

Mourners see her to rest in the colored cemetery. They stand in the chill breeze and cautiously draw their sweaters, shawls and jackets closer, trying to ward off enemy death, secretly wondering what it's really all about—if people really "die by threes," and who will go next? They finally turn away mystified, weary, emotion spent—and glad today is not yet their time.

Etta lingers at the foot of the grave to pray in private. "Gawd, this is the dead girl's chile . . ."

The gravediggers remove their caps and bow their heads.

"Dear Lawd, please don't strike me down 'fore I can raise her—that's all I ask you in the name a Jesus. Amen."

The gravediggers say "yay-men" and go to work filling the hole. Etta feels almost ashamed to be so happy—going home happy and proud to be a mother, the only way she can.

Steve Cannon

(1935–   )

Born in New Orleans, Cannon is a fiction writer who makes good use of the voodoo lore associated with his birthplace to delineate the strengths and foibles of Americans. His 1969 novel *Groove, Bang and Jive Around* is an underground classic. He and Ishmael Reed are the founders of the Reed-Cannon publishing enterprise. The following short story was published in *Callaloo* #4 (October 1978).

Mama Louise Grabs Her Satchel and Splits Inside Doc John's Cavern/His Cave

On her way to the quarter Mama Louise slipped off the scene looking behind and making sure no one was following her chasing her trailing and or tailing her behind, whatever, as she ez'd inside the "Witch" Doctor's head. The Boogie man's intestines. Music liquid air and solid sounds ran thru the length and breadth of her body, exploding at her nerves' ends. Bucks bubbled. Butterbeans Suzy Q'd. On the Midnight special (that daylight express) amongst Cadillacs and Lear Jets she came. Whamo—The works worked. She found herself in the midst of Django Rheinhardt's and Dizzy Gillespie's party talks. Cocktail sips after the show. Yet babes in and out of toyland and folks from other continents and Islands danced (or rather *did*) The Twist to tunes made famous by the Georgia Minstrels—The Midnighters Little Richard and Chubby Checker along with Teenagers from the Peppermint Lounge and that John and Jackie Kennedy set. Party types . . . The whole place shook rattled rolled and scored the bottom the top the top bottom and straight up and down, while in the back and foreground and stage center Smokes smoked smoke. Toked coke and passed it around. Drug and dope addicts under amber and red lights delighted. Edgar Allan Poe (like his cousin Baudelaire) hung up on himself a picture on the wall strung out on himself in more ways than one (like Annabel) sat inside dark colors shot up and took two three slow drags while studying medical reports and treatises (like monographs) on the occult—mysteries. Fiestas played Salsa inside Siestas while Lockjaw mad at himself went shownuff into Hotstuff. Chandeliers glisten glinting light from the ceiling. Crystal clear. Sparkles showered the crowd. The place felt—O. Hell, what dud Hell, the place felt great—Grand to be alive, like it felt nice, if not plain old "neat." That's all—if not a little dreamy—EYED.

A brother from afar into surrealistic (nightripping) re bob de be bop dada da da newsprint Headlines datelines and captions and bottom lines and camp and chic (whatever's in) poetry checked for cues and probed for clues inside the computerized lino "type," smiled at the entrance as Mama Louise approached on her way—inside. Say, Hey, Babes, How you doin?

Mama Louise in bonnet and rags from the turn of the century, just the opposite of Tremonisha, wearing a long silk and satin skirt with a thousand petty coats, carrying two three hand bags, a couple of pocket books, two weighted down like brick shopping bags, smiled showing gold filled rotten (to the core—root canals?) teeth, sighed and asked: I'm looking for Doc John. Do you know if he's around? That's what I wanna know. That Tyrant up yonder down below out near the lake by the riverside is out of touch with Reality, himself (into illusions) for that matter and done lost control of his staff (Flip and Puddin) and it's rumoured that Flicker Fickle Flicker Finger Fate's got his rod. She blinded her eyes (in the light darkness) lifting her left eyebrow as if signaling the Re Bop de Be Bop Di Da di Da La De Da Boy in the Cage, with his cutouts of newsprint. Reports. The youngster into newsprint digging the latest haps in the Village around the globe reports from here and abroad crisscrossed word puzzles anagrams ideograms signs sick jokes and comic strips smiled when he looked up and saw Mama Louise's smiling face—the Radiance, and answered-O, Er. O. Er. The Good Doctor. O Doc John—is that who you wanna see?

Mama Louise looked askance at herself thru the two way mirror, at parentless children abandoned to the element the streets who snuck up close to her and asked her for a dime with gimmie on their minds. She fluffed them off and continued to talk. Is the Good Doctor in? That's all I wanna know. What's the Scoop Jackson, aside from dem Russians crushing political dissenters and counterspies.

Don't rush me. Yawl get the fuck away from here you hear? He screamed at the little kids the street urchins orphans who were plotting and conspiring to take over the WHIRL (while fighting desperately for survival) possess it with their dreams and turn it into schemes (dreams into realities). The brats made faces, stuck out their tongues and wiggled their fingers with their thumbs stuck in their ears, rolled their eyes and scattered up back alley ways empty parks garbage dumps abandoned buildings playing Afro-Latino (into Native vibes) on their transistors, listening to sounds from polytheistic GodHeads/Demos by name, imitating cops and robbers con men and pushers dealers and racketeers and gamblers doing the hustle on the block (smarty pants) and accosted another Stranger. Gone!

Don't rush me. Again the brother in the glass cage responded to Mama Louise's request. He reached below the counter and came up with a chart a map with passage ways clearly diagramed in red blue yellow orange purple and green on a light grey background outlined in black borders with ABC's going horizontally down the side (both sides) and the numbers from one to ten (1-10) running vertically across the top and bottom laminated card, he'd slipped it to her thru a small opening thru the glass caged booth bullet proof window. Thru the slide he slid it thru. X marked the spot (inside that Maze, that Labyrinth) where the Good Doctor ole Doc John could be found. Known to prisoners and ex-cons thru out the land, as Long Lost John! Two heels, between the X marked the spot. His mark. The Last Escapee, who got away for Keeps.

Mama Louise took the map, deciphered its code and went for it. You know she went for it. As strung out as she was . . . That was her mission the only direction in which she could travel listening to her heartbeat probing dead souls (her ancestors speak) so you know she went for it—seeing ghosts and spirits—like strange feelings, in her path. And gladly at that, she went for it, as if her number, too, was up. She and Doc John were friends from way back, like from long ago and far away, before the Judaic Christian tradition ever became the bottom line, like Guilt and or the Devil, she went for it, like to her, it was ole Hat. But that's neither here nor there. But they *were*! Check the Reels. You'll find the images in the can. Check with Stone Cold Deals, he knows.

The dude gatekeeper watcher of the night the clock the people and the times rattling his brains his skin and bones muscle and fibres genetic codes and techtronic's latest doo hickey its gadgets craze faze band wagon space program spin offs mini computers country bumpkins and cousin routines pressed a bottom and the doors, like Sesame, but made of Japanese Steel, swung open—WHUUP!

He watched as Mama Louise's image vanished (turned into a dot) inside the screen, her walking and disappearing down the hall the corridors thru tunnels and tunnels of tunnels and into the blue green. Gone. Himself? As for himself he went back into slapstick lickity split Da Da Daah Who'd news making cutouts and poems out of the damndest Headlines Datelines and Captions, playing the electronic organ (under an electro-magnetic field) and synthesizer for Kicks, his head into earphones and his eyes into scanners like open to the window of the WHIRL (his taste buds fouled up with a strange and eerie flagrant fragrance in the air) but yet he watched the Picks. Would you believe it? Yes, he did.

*   *   *

Thru the tunnels (like visible and invisible walls) the halls the passageways pass unmarked and marked doors pass windowless and windowed dark rooms where men and young boys sat at controls looking (and double checking) Flicks flickering in on moving picture screens on consoles pass wire and wireless teletype rooms where machines and young women clattered along with the machines and clicked checking out incoming and outgoing messages in codes, pass guards in dark blue and gold trimmed uniforms who asked to see her ID, like asking her the pass word talking in signs, blunt and direct to the point, pass the point man and fires in the lake and brimstone murals (Injuns doing a war dance—hooping and hollering, passing that pipe and doubling up on them drums) pass David and that famous five pointed star, that seal in Bethlehem and a triangular circle done up in gold emeralds and jeweled boxed and unboxed reviews (with a lotta fan fare) doing parodies on high rollers, like monkeys as if they were in some kind of Zoo playing and replaying the Bar's Fight with Lucy Terry leading the Hoe-Break-Down (walk around) with a cat gut fiddle and a baboom doing the crisscrossed double cross, enigmas riddles and word puzzles playing five card stud, on Mama Louise walked looking like mad searching crevices and corners looking for the place marked X, pass groups of people undergoing baptism by fire in the fire religious conversion in the lake the stream dissolving into steam and pictures of nincompoops who were into their own rackets—like Presidents, De Capo's Bosses Execs and others who ran a tight ship, Tycoons from the last days of Aide De Camps, hair sprays and Spar Varnish, other people's lives, and Polar Bears (like Penguins) eating whole "Eskimo" Sandwiches, Mama Louise, her mind on and off Jack, into Ro-bin going round Robin and passing into herself into interior monologues of breaches of promise (crying FOUL) and I'm gon Do dialoging dialogues, into I'm Go- Do- landscapes of Cityscapes (railroads truck and bus lines, car lanes?) Bathyspheres Flip in his Box, boxed in Flop and Pudd'n Twisting and Turning as if the wind were here and now, the East Wind trade winds northerlies and southernlies around the Equatorial Torrid and North Temperate Zones inside the Vulgar Boatman's catastrophies (with Mississippi Bottoms like Finn and Jim) she touched bases with herself her insides with her head in the clouds taking extra care and precautions to be ready and thinking only to herself about herself in side her self her genealogy the snake and her experiences (like passingthru now) and the kindness and understanding nature of Doc John, now that as far as she was concerned Jack's out the picture, now she thought only about her family, as she walked on thru the labyrinth, Amazed and on she walked looking to see where X-marked the Spot—of Janus and his two - faces, an image which originated in Africa, like Eshu—Oh Mama Louise walked—neither disturbed nor perturbed but satisfied in her soul.

Brenda Wilkinson
(1946–   )

A poet and author of children's books, Wilkinson has been praised for her keen eye for detail and her sensitivity in rendering the dynamics of contemporary life. The novels *Ludell* (1975), *Ludell and Willie* (1976), and *Ludell's New York Time* (1980) deal with a poor black child's growing up in Waycross, Georgia, in the 1950s and 1960s. *Ludell and Willie* was named one of the outstanding children's books of the year by the *New York Times* and a best book for young adults by the American Library Association. Wilkinson was born in Moultrie, Georgia, and attended Hunter College. Her most recent work is *Not Separate, Not Equal* (1984). The first two chapters of *Ludell and Willie* are reprinted here.

---

from Ludell and Willie

CHAPTER ONE

Last night's dishes would be in the sink. Soggy cereal would be floating in bowls. Sugar, milk, jelly, whatever else the children had helped themselves to while their mother lay sleeping in her room would cover the table, chairs, floor. Clothes would be strewn about; the bathroom sloppy; beds pissy; and the youngest of the four little boys wet and whining. Ludell had come to expect this after three years of working every Saturday morning at the Seaman household.

Even so, Ludell wished that the driver would hurry and reach her destination, for it was an unbearable ninety-eight degrees this sticky summer morning! Her negative feelings about the Seamans were for the moment secondary to thoughts of their air conditioning.

"Least I'll be cool," she mused; then quipped paradoxically, "on my way to Hell to cool off!"

"Hot as the devil taday," one of the two ladies seated up front beside the driver stated matter-of-factly.

"Yes mam, you can say that again," Ludell responded, getting amens from fat Mis Toosweet and Sissie White. She was sandwiched in between them in the backseat. The driver had all the windows down, so there was a little drift of air from the cab's movement, but it was no help to Ludell from where she sat. Not one breeze hit her! Miss Toosweet's heaviness pressing her from the right, and Sissy's stiffly starched uniform scraping her on the left, Ludell settled herself on the very edge of the seat, using the front seat for a prop. "Dog we going slow!" she thought despairingly. "Fat Mis Toosweet probably got the cab weighed down. Know she got some meat on her!" Ludell thought, staring down at the thighs exposed from beneath Mis Toosweet's dress. "Wonder what a real ham the size of one o' her thighs would cost?" she asked herself. "Bout ten dollars? Fifteen? Bet her thighs weigh a good thirty pounds apiece! Sure don't know how she can stand to work all day in that girdle. Specially hot as it is today! Shoot. The meat would hafta gone and shake if that was me!"

The driver had just begun to speed up some when he went "ooops!" making a sharp turn that threw Ludell clean into Mis Toosweet's fleshy spread.

"Some sharp curves," he declared.

"Not from where I'm sitting," Ludell joked to herself, getting up off Mis Toosweet.

"Guess I better slow back down," said the driver. "Hope I don't run nunna yall late."

"Don't make me no never mind," Sissie White interjected. "I get to work whenever I please. Woman I work for know she aine gon find no one good as me." Sissie proceeded to rave about how indispensable she was to her employer, her remarks gradually triggering similar ones from the other ladies. It had been that way every Saturday for as long as Ludell had been working. One or two of the women would get to bragging about how easy their job was, how crazy Mis "Who-so-ever-she-was" was about her performance, and by the time they'd reach Garrington Heights the whole car of women would be lit up trying to outtalk each other about how her situation was the best. Originally Ludell had sat dumbfounded by it all, wondering how they found these ideal white people to work for. The lady she worked for wasn't that way, nor the one her grandmama worked for, nor Mis Johnson next door. "Just where," she wondered, "did all these colored women find such glo-o-rious white ladies?"

It was only after she asked her grandmother that she came to know that they were making the stuff up. "I'm surprise you couldn't tell rat off the bat they jes be talkin'," her grandmother told her. "Hate when I hafta take a cab 'n listen to that foolishness. Pitiful's what it is. Plain pitiful! Po women. Work all the time. Nothing else to brag on."

"And got to fabricate then," Ludell had thought sympathetically afterwards. "Guess I shoulda known they was making it up," she said to her grandmother. "Specially when I heard this woman say one Saturday that she made a dollar fifty a hour!"

"Whhaat?" cried her grandmother. "Well hush yo mouf 'n git away from here!" she declared. "NO WAY! Aine a white woman roun here pay more than fifty cents a hour—from the biggest shot to the littlest one! And some don' half wanna pay that! <u>Reason your mother claim she can never come live in Georgia again!</u>'' Northern Migration

"Caine much blame her," Ludell had responded, knowing how she herself hated the long hard day of labor for so little pay. But as horrendous as she found it, she knew it was worse for <u>her grandmother</u>, who, like the women she was riding with now, <u>spent five</u>, sometimes <u>six days cleaning after white people</u>.

Listening to the women chatter on, she thought, "In a way I guess talking this foolishness easier than thinking bout how it really is. Truth just make the ride worse. Who wanna hear it? To think about it?" She sighed, picturing the Seaman house once again. <u>The Seamans had a maid who worked through the week, so it just mystified Ludell how their house could be so nasty every weekend</u>. She cringed recalling the Saturday morning she'd arrived and discovered a worse fate in the children's bedroom than the usual pissy beds. The baby boy had vomited during the night, and his mother had rolled up the sheets and towels filled with it and left the filth there on the bedroom floor. Generally Mis Seaman slept past noon, but she had emerged early that morning as Ludell had entered, immediately informing her that she was to clean the mess up. "I've got a weak stomach," the white lady had drawled, strolling on back to her bedroom and closing the door. Cursing, Ludell had just stood there frozen, staring down disgustedly. Then, holding her breath, she had bent down and lifted the smelly sheets and towels with her fingertips. Going out back to the washroom, she'd gotten paper bags, quickly dropped the dirty linen inside, and had headed outside for the garbage cans. "I cleaned that stanking dog mess out the carpet like you asked me that time, lady!" she had silently cried out in contempt. "But I AIN'T RINSIN OUT NO VOMIT!! Say yo stomach weak?? Well so is mine! SO IS MINE!!!" she had repeated, trembling with anger as she'd packed the bags down deeper and deeper into the tin garbage can beside the house.

She had gotten tremendous satisfaction out of throwing out Mis Seaman's linen, but greater glory would have come had she been able to walk up to that white woman and shout "I AINE COMING BACK NO MO!" So many times Ludell had longed to do that but realized how important it was that she keep the job. <u>She didn't know her father</u>, and her mother Dessa sent very little money from New York, so every penny Ludell earned was a help to her grandmother who had raised her from a baby. And even if there was a chance of Ludell finding another cleaning job, there was the risk of the new white lady being worse to work for than Mis Seaman—like that crazy woman she had helped one day this summer. She had had Ludell down on her knees scrubbing the spaces between the bathroom tiles with a toothbrush! Mis Seaman had her lazy trifling ways about her, but at least she wasn't fussy about how you cleaned. All that mattered to her was that she had space to walk in. How and where you shoved the dirt didn't count!

Ludell kept thinking about next June when she could escape the drudgery of it all. It was this thought that sustained her, kept her going. <u>She and her boyfriend Willie from next door would be graduating from high school in</u>

[margin notes: Ritual / Absent Father / High Moral Ground / Invisible People \ Spiritual Figures. and The Religion of The Oppressed]

June, and they had definite plans of getting out of Waycross, Georgia! There
was no way she was going to end up trekking out every day to some white
woman's!

As the cab swung down the private road entering the Heights, Ludell gazed
upon spacious brick-framed house after house, all with flowers and dark green
grass and shrubbery. Pine trees towered over the entire neighborhood, shading
the sun. Even on a hot day like this, everything appeared cool and serene. At
the house where they dropped off Mis Toosweet, Ludell saw a girl about her
own age, still in pajamas, staring lazily out of a huge picture window. As
they rode away, Ludell envisioned the girl strolling back to her air-conditioned
bedroom, propping herself up on a big fluffy pillow, dreaming of a gala
evening, perhaps with some friends, maybe just one boy. . . . She sucked her
teeth in contempt at her own situation.

When the cab stopped at the Seamans', Ludell leaned forward to pay her
fare, and silently prayed that the mess inside would be no worse than usual
this morning.

CHAPTER TWO

Had it been twelve? Or thirteen? Willie had stopped counting the years since
his daddy had gone off, leaving six children behind for his mama to raise.
After all this time, his mother's only comment to her children was still "Your
daddy left seeking means to do better by us." To which Willie would silently
comment "He must be walkin overseas."

And to make matters worse, Mattie, the oldest, had upped and gone off to
Florida last year, running after some baseball player and leaving her five-year-
old, Alvin, in her mama's care. Mis Johnson hadn't received a word or a dime
from Mattie either!

Since summer vacation had begun, ten-year-old Cathy, the youngest, had
been stuck taking care of little Alvin all day, while Mis Johnson went out to
do housework. Willie, Ruthie Mae, Buddie Boy, and Hawk all worked in
tobacco. With their pitching in and sharing their earnings with their mama,
things generally went smooth during the summer, but the rest of the year,
when only Mis Johnson worked—the children picking up an odd job only
occasionally—things were pretty rough for them. They'd grown accustomed
to seeing the Georgia Power truck rolling down the street to shut off their
lights, their water, or both. There would be times, too, when Mis Johnson
couldn't make the twenty-dollars-a-month rent on the old run-down place they
lived in. And it only took being a few days late to bring around Ole Man
Clinton to tack a bold black-and-white "For Rent" sign on the front of the
house. So Mis Johnson naturally tried her best to get him his money on time,
even if she couldn't anybody else's.

Being without electricity a few days in winter wasn't too unbearable, for
the fireplaces served as sources for light and cooking. As far as the water was
concerned, that was never a big problem; for unlike the electricity, the water

could be turned back on right in front of the house by any of them. There was the danger, however, of being caught by the law. So Willie was cautious, always waiting until nightfall before easing out front, where he'd lift the iron top and turn the water back on. Buddie Boy would stand in the street watching for the police, who sometimes had nothing better to do than to ride around looking for somebody to lock up. Hawk and the others would be busy catching pots and jars of water. They would give the toilet a good flushing (having had to flush it with water borrowed from next door all day), then Willie would turn the water back off. Once the boys suggested to Mis Johnson that they leave the water on all night and rise early and turn it off the next day, but she thought it just too risky. As it was, she could hardly bear the thought of her boys stealing the water, knowing they were old enough to go to jail if caught.

Ruthie Mae faced the most embarrassment over being without lights or water. Some nights when they'd be in the dark, boys would come around looking for her, and she'd send Cathy to the door to say she wasn't there. One time the boy heard her and came walking on in. Alvin came walking in the hall carrying a candle in a jar and Ruthie Mae was so ashamed she wanted to go through the floor. All she could do was tell the boy the truth and say she'd see him later. The boy was a good sport about it and left, joking, "I guess you will SEE me later." She was so grateful that he never told anybody at school, or ever made her ashamed by mentioning it again. Many a time boys had been there when they'd been without water, and only once had Ruthie Mae's prayer that the boy not ask to use the bathroom not been answered. That time she just lied and told the boy "You hafta pour a bucket of water down it to flush it, cause it aine working right today."

About the longest the Johnsons had ever gone before having their utilities turned back on had been two or three days. Somehow by then Mis Johnson would have managed to borrow the money from some of the people she worked for. They would take it out of her salary a little at a time. Mis Johnson would hardly be done paying one white lady before she was borrowing from another. It disturbed Willie immensely to watch his mama carry such a heavy burden. When he turned seventeen, he had seriously considered quitting school and joining the army. He felt that the allotment check his mama would receive from the government would be something she could count on. "Roun a hundred and something dollars a month" he'd heard she'd receive. "Allll that money—and it would be steady."

But then Ludell just couldn't see it his way. Said she didn't think he had any business talking about quitting school. He had gone on to explain to her just how bad things were for his family, and how he felt that he ought to be doing something about it. Ludell said she understood all his feelings but that he could work it out in time, that he should just be patient a little bit longer. "You've come too far to give up getting your diploma," she told him. And although he agreed with that, Willie still couldn't stop thinking of all that money his mama could be getting, could be using, right then. What made him finally break down and say he wouldn't go was Ludell's desperate declaration

Note the contradiction of R. Wright

that she was sure she'd die going a whole year without him. All along he had
realized that he'd miss her equally but had tried blocking the thought out,
telling himself how the time would fly, and how he'd be back for her after
she graduated and they would be married and finally together. Forever. She
had pointed out to him how there was much about her day-to-day existence
in Waycross that she didn't like, yet she remained, even turning down her
mother's offer that she come and finish high school in New York City. "I
told my mother that I aine wanna leave mama, my friends, and my school,"
Ludell had relayed to him. "But you know it's you, don't you, Willie?" she'd
said. He couldn't leave her after that.

There was one other factor, too—one brought on by his sister Ruthie Mae.
After Ruthie Mae's boyfriend had gone into the service, it was no time before
she had taken up with some other boy. Willie realized there was no comparing
Ludell to that fast-behind sister of his. Yet the fact of what had happened
remained. And Ruthie Mae was supposed to marry the boy—had taken his
class ring before he left and everything! Somehow the boy got word of Ruthie
Mae's carryings-on, and had written home to her on a single square of toilet
paper stating that she was on his "S list," and had instructed her to take his
class ring around to his mother's house that very day. Ruthie Mae had found
the whole thing hilarious and had gone around telling everybody about it,
calling the boy crazy. "I'm a young girl," she told people. "Fool must be
crazy if he think I'm sitting roun here twirling my fingers two years till he
come back from France!"

Disregarding his general rule of "not paying any attention to something his
sister had to say," Willie weighed Ruthie Mae's words heavily in this instance.

"It's going to be hard watching mama continue to try to make do," he
concluded. "But I'll make it all up to her one day. Later on. Just can't go to
no army now though! Shoot, the army could kill everything I got with Ludell.
And more than anything, I wanna marry that girl."

Will they escape the South?

Lorenz Graham
(1902–1989)

Graham is best remembered for his "Town" series of young adult fiction—
South Town, North Town, Whose Town?, and *Return to South Town*—
realistic stories about a black youth's battle against racism and oppression. Born in New Orleans, Louisiana, Graham earned his A.B. from Virginia Union University and his M.S.W. from Columbia University. During
the 1920s, he was a teacher and missionary in Liberia where he learned
the local dialect of English, which he used in adapting biblical tales for
children in *How God Fix Jonah* (1946). He received a citation from the
Thomas Alva Edison Foundation for his 1956 adaptation of the biblical
story *The Ten Commandments*, a Follett Award (1958), and a Child Study
Association of America Award (1959) for *South Town*. Among his works
for children are *I, Momulu, Carolina Cracker, Stolen Car, Runaway*, and
John Brown's Raid. The following excerpt is from *South Town*.

---

from South Town

When he saw the car coming up the road, David went into the yard. He had
been watching for it. He wanted to talk with Pa before his mother saw him.
Ma had been watching too. She was as anxious to hear the news as her son
was, but she did not rush out. It was just as well, she thought. Her menfolk
stood beside the car talking. Neither of them was smiling.

David told Pa everything. The words rushed out: his watching for his father
to come into the shop, Mr. Boyd's agitation, his sneer at the idea of a black
doctor, his threat.

"It's bad, son," his father said. "It's bad stuff. Rotten! He wanted me to
go in the shop for forty dollars a week. Said we'd all have to take cuts. Just
talked like it was business at first. Then I asked if the other mechanics were
getting the same thing. That's when he got mad and said the war had ruined
the blacks, only he didn't say it that way. I guess I got mad too. I told him
I wasn't willing to sell my skills for a mess of pottage. I told him just that.
He said I'd come crawling to him for a job, said he'd fix it so I couldn't work
anywhere in South Town, in the county, in the whole state. He said the
businessmen were going to get together and put the black people in their place.
I asked him what any man's place was. Then he started cursing, right there

152

in front of the girls. He told me to pick cotton, shine shoes, lick the spit out of cuspidors. I said I'd rather do that than work at a skilled trade for peanuts."

Pa stopped and shook his head.

"He talked about integration and desegregation and said white folks in this state didn't give a damn for the Supreme Court, and the black folks were fools if they believed in it." He smiled, but there was no humor in his face. "He didn't order me off the place. Guess he was saving that one for my son. I got off easy."

Ma waited as long as she could. Then she called through the open window, saying that dinner was ready.

"Just one more thing, Pa." David held his father's arm. "I didn't tell Ma very much. Just said that Mr. Boyd got mad and fired me. Check?"

"Check!" Williams put his hand on David's shoulder as they walked toward the back steps. He had to reach upward to do it. It felt good to both of them.

They ate slowly. Pa talked about the men he had seen in town. He told the funny things they had said and laughed at his own jokes.

When David asked to be excused, he invited Betty Jane to go with him to the barn. Pa would want to talk to Ma alone.

"I have to do the dishes," Betty Jane said. "There's plenty of time. You help me with the dishes, and then I'll go with you."

"I'll let you milk," David promised.

Mrs. Williams told her to go ahead. She would do the dishes.

Betty Jane was happy to get away from the dishwashing. As they went down the path, Betty Jane carrying the milk pail, brother and sister talked about what they might do before school started. At least one picnic, and another day would be a fishing trip. They would go visiting. They would have to go to Belleville to see Mrs. Moss and to Center City to see the Johnsons and the Center City Williamses. They would have to go to the movies one or two nights. If Pa didn't go to work right away, maybe they could take a real trip, maybe to the coast where they could see where he had worked building ships.

David left Betty Jane milking to go for Josephine's fresh water. When he entered the barn again, she called him.

"David, what's the matter with Pa?" she asked.

David emptied the two buckets he carried into the big wooden tub. He moved it back toward the wall so Josephine would not kick it over during the night. He took as long as he could. He was thinking.

"Dave, you heard me. What's the matter with you, too?"

"What do you mean?" he asked, looking down finally at his sister. He could get an argument out of this. "What do you mean, what's the matter with grown-up people?"

"Oh, you think you're so grown up." Betty Jane smiled up at her brother. "You know what I mean. You all been acting funny, and Pa, he's been . . . I don't know . . . he seems like he's so much older since he's been back."

"Sure! Is that what you mean?" David acted as if it were very simple. "Sure he's older. You're older, ain't you? What's the matter with getting older? You're older today than you were yesterday. Pa's older now than he was when he started to work in the city. For gosh sakes! Older! Come on. You got to leave some milk in the bag for Josephine's milk snakes.''

Betty Jane made a show of fright. She jumped and turned and almost upset the pail. David was fun.

When David and Betty Jane came in, Ma was laughing and Pa was drying dishes.

They started planning what they might do together. Betty Jane cried out for trips and visits, all the fun they would have, all the people they would see.

''Well, all right, children,'' Pa said. ''Time's a-wasting. You hair is short and your feets is long, I don't see what you waiting on! Let's go. Let's get started.''

''Oh, not tonight, dear,'' Ma said. ''Why, we hadn't planned anything.''

Betty Jane danced her delight.

''Well, we don't need a blueprint to find our way up the road,'' Pa said. ''Do we, Dave?''

There was hasty washing, changing to fresh starched clothes, slicking down of hair, and the family was off, with David driving and Betty Jane beside him. Pa and Ma rode in the back and called themselves bride and groom.

They went to see the Mannings. Mrs. Manning was one of their favorite friends. Indeed, she was a favorite friend of everybody for miles around. She was a widow and the mother of grown sons and daughters. Her youngest daughter was in college. Two of her sons were up North, where they were married and had families. Her granddaughter, Elizabeth, lived with her. Her youngest son, Al, had been in service. He was at home now. David liked to hear him talk about the things he had seen. Freed from the responsibilities of her own children, Mrs. Manning had gone back to teaching. In the two-room school at Holly Crossing, she saw before her the sons and daughters of those she had taught a generation earlier. Men who had traveled these years to the far corners of the earth wrote to her, ''Dear Mother Manning.''

Mr. Jackson, the principal, back early for the school year, drove up and stopped for a visit. He was eager to hear from Mrs. Manning a report on what had been happening among the people. He wanted to know what folks were saying about school integration.

''They don't say much,'' Mrs. Manning told him. ''They don't expect any changes soon, and they don't see anything they ought to do but wait.''

A full moon rose while they sat on the porch. Joshua, one of the men who was helping with the tobacco, came to say good night. He said he just happened to be carrying his guitar. With little urging he sat on the steps and sang ''Careless Love'' and ''Nobody's Darling.''

Ed Williams laid aside his troubles. He had worked away from home for nearly three years without a break except for short weekends. Mrs. Williams said he had earned a vacation and wanted him to take it. They made their visits. They went fishing at the millpond, and took Ben Crawford. David and Ben had to show where David had gone over the dam and just where and how

Ben had pulled Lit Red out and where David had been located by the white boy. On Sunday they went to Centerville.

They had their fun, but it was not the same. Pa seemed restless. He was a working man, and idleness was like Sunday clothes. It wasn't natural. He wasn't free and easy.

Ma had only words of encouragement. She agreed that Ed was doing the right thing. Of course he should not sell his skills for a mess of pottage. She would rather grub a mess of pottage out of their own piece of land. It was about paid for, thank the Lord. They had some savings. They could wait a while.

"For all his big talk," she said, "Mr. Boyd needs you more than you need him, and right away, too. He'll be the one to crawl, if anybody crawls. I don't see what makes him try to be so mean."

"Don't nobody have to crawl," Pa said. "Why should a freeborn man have to crawl to anybody for anything? He can come to me like a man and say he needs my skill and say what he'll pay. If he offers enough, I'll work for him. I'll work good and earn him money. If he don't, I'll know what to do."

But Boyd did not come and say he needed Ed Williams. He drove by Williams' house while Ed sat on the porch. He drove by looking straight ahead. David saw the dull look in his father's eyes.

On Wednesday Ed Williams drove alone to South Town. He came back early, but he looked tired. David wondered if he had seen Mr. Boyd. Out in the yard, beyond Ma's hearing he asked his father.

"Nope," Pa said. "I didn't see him, but I saw some others. He's been around. He's been to Chevvie and the other shops. They got together on me."

On Thursday he drove off again, this time away from South Town. He took his box of tools and a pair of overalls, saying he might be gone all day.

It was nearly dark when he got back. The car was covered with dust, but his overalls were still clean. They were folded just as they had been laid in the car.

On Friday it rained. Williams drove out to the road and turned toward South Town, and David knew he meant to explore the towns beyond.

Ma said she had wanted to do some shopping. It was plain to see that she was worried. She wasn't worried about how they could get along. They would make it. She was worried about the hurt look in her husband's eyes. It rained hard. Cars went by on the highway with the mounting and then fading sound of rubber on wet asphalt. Mr. Boyd did not stop. Nobody called.

It was nearly dark when Pa came home. He had that tired look. He said little. He did not smile. He ate and answered questions shortly.

After David had gone to bed, he heard Pa talking in the kitchen with Ma. David wasn't trying to listen for the words, but at one place Pa raised his voice.

"I ain't crawling to nobody." That was what David heard.

Before Pa went away to work in the city, the Williams family had established a regular Saturday routine. Ma would ride to South Town with her husband first thing in the morning when he went to work. As she did her shopping, the packages and bundles would accumulate in the car parked behind the garage. By noon Ma would be through with her business, and Pa would bring her home during his lunch hour. Then in the evening, after Pa came home and had his dinner, all the family would go back to town for Saturday night.

Stores and shops and markets stayed open late. Saturday was pay day for those who worked. It was market day for those who bought and sold. Bargains were advertised. Payments on accounts were made. Debts were increased in the dazzle of Saturday night's display.

David remembered Saturday nights first as he trudged along holding on to his father's hand, moving through the forest of legs and skirts, and then on the edge of the forest looking into brightly lighted show windows with his tongue licking across the coldness of an ice-cream cone.

When he was older, David walked alone. Sometimes he would find a boy he knew and walk with him, promising to be back at the car in just a little while. Time went fast on Saturday nights, and he had been punished for holding up the family, making his father wait and walk about to call and look for him, worrying his mother, who was always afraid he would get into trouble.

With Pa away, Saturdays had been different. In the morning Ma would catch a ride to town. People whom they knew would be passing. Often she would make a deal with the same friend to bring her back at a certain time. If not, she would deposit her packages as she shopped in the car of someone else who lived out that way. When the car owner came back to his car and found packages which did not belong to him he knew he was going to have a rider. Sometimes it was confusing, but everybody was nice to Mrs. Williams.

Ma did not like David to go to town on Saturday nights. She seemed altogether unreasonable on the subject. David could see nothing to be afraid of in the town.

"I'm not a baby, Ma," he would say patiently. "And I don't run around with fellows who get into trouble."

David knew there was a crowd of boys, his age and a little older, who might have trouble. He knew them. They were just the fellows around who had dropped out of school. Some lived in town, and others lived on nearby farms. David felt that the members of that crowd were trying, deliberately trying, to be tough. As individuals he liked some of them. As a crowd they were headed in another direction. Nobody said anything about it, but David knew and the fellows knew that there was a difference. They were not walking together. Color & Class

Most of the fights in South Town took place on Saturday nights. Older people gathered around Brown's restaurant. Younger people liked Jo-Jo's place because there was a large floor and they could dance to the music of the juke box. Both places sold wine and beer, but people seldom got drunk. At the barbecue stand only soft drinks were sold, but bootleggers met their customers there and sold country-made liquor illegally.

People who got drunk, really drunk, would be locked up by Chief Peebles

[margin note: mother's fear for the safety of her son, a young black man.]

or his assistant if either of the officers saw them. If friends were around, they would take care of the drunk, get him into a quiet place or get him into a car to his home.

No one liked to see a man locked up in the jail.

It wasn't a big jail.

It wasn't like in the pictures.

It was just about the size of a brick two-car garage and it was in an alley; that is it opened into the unpaved alley back of the liquor store. The door was of heavy wood, and it had riveted iron straps on it, and over the windows were iron bars. That hardly made it look like a jail, because doors and windows of warehouses are often secured the same way. You wouldn't have known it was a jail, just to look at it.

You would have to smell it.

Everybody who smelled the jail would know. They might not know it was a jail, but they would know that the place was something bad, something to keep out of and away from, something that was evil and cursing and fouling.

It wasn't a big jail, but Chief Peebles boasted that it was big enough for all the bad folks who wanted to jump in it. It was big enough to have two cells so white and black offenders could be kept separated.

David had passed the jail with other boys. He knew the smell. He knew men, and some boys, who had been locked up there. He knew them, but they were not his friends. They were the ones who seemed deliberately to be tough and rowdy. Most of them were ignorant and very poor. It was said that no graduate of Pocahontas County Training School had ever been in jail.

Saturday morning broke clear. It had rained in the night, and the air was sultry, but the sun was bright. During the morning David worked in the garden. He turned some soil where he planned to put in late vegetables. His father had taken Ma and Betty Jane to South Town to do some shopping. David did not want to go so early in the day. There would be more to see in the late afternoon and after dark.

Pa brought Mrs. Williams and Betty Jane home at noon, and after lunch he went right back, saying that he had to see some friends. David was not through in the garden, and he hadn't washed up. It would be easy to catch a ride if his father did not come back with the car in time.

David had taken his bath and he was partly dressed when someone knocked, and then he heard his mother talking at the front door. He had put on his white trousers, which were a little short but not too short for wearing in a crowd. He was lacing his saddle oxfords when Betty Jane came to the door.

"Ma says come, David," his sister said. "It's the sheriff."

"The sheriff?" No officer of the law had ever been to their house. "What's he want?"

"Come on. They're talking." Betty Jane was frightened. David hurried from the room, drawing a shirt over his arms.

The sheriff and another white man were in the front bedroom. The bed was pulled out from the wall, and the sheriff's man was bent over with a flashlight. The sheriff had Pa's gun in his hand.

"Who's this?" the sheriff asked Ma.

"This is our son," Ma said. Her voice was strained and hollow. "His name is David."

"What's the matter, Ma?" David went and stood close by his mother's side.

"Just a check-up, boy," the sheriff said easily. "You got a gun?"

David's mouth went dry. He licked his lips.

"Where's your old man's pistol?" the sheriff demanded.

"He hasn't got a pistol," David said. It was the truth. Ed Williams had always said a decent man had no need for a pistol.

"Don't lie to me, boy," the sheriff said. "If you're lying and we find out, we're liable to have to take you along. That's perjury, you know."

David knew it was not perjury, but he said nothing.

Ma said it was true that her husband did not own a pistol. He used to hunt with the shotgun. The sheriff seemed to believe her.

"You got a gun?" he asked David. "Any kind of a gun?"

"Yes, sir," David replied. "I've got a rifle, a twenty-two."

"Bring it here."

David looked at his mother, and she nodded quickly. As he started for his room at the back of the house, the two men came close behind him.

"You all got anything else?" the sheriff asked.

"No, sir, only my father's shotgun and my rifle," David said. He was about to reach for the .22 caliber pump gun where it hung on the wall when the sheriff's assistant shoved him aside. He took the rifle in his hands and threw open the breech, pumping it a couple of times. It was not loaded.

"Where's your cart'iges, and where does your old man keep his shells?"

David went to a shelf and took down a box containing a dozen or more longs. Then he went back into the front bedroom and got a box of sixteen-gauge shells. The two men searched every room. They looked into closets and moved things in the pantry. They went on the back porch and pulled a box away from the wall. They turned up the mattresses, even in Betty Jane's small room. They pulled the radio away from the wall and looked into the cabinet. They lifted pictures so that anything hidden behind them might fall to the floor.

Mrs. Williams, David, and Betty Jane followed them, not saying anything.

At last they seemed to be satisfied.

"Is anything wrong, Sheriff?" Ma asked when they were ready to go. "Can't you tell us?"

"It's just a routine check-up," the sheriff said, lighting a cigarette and throwing the match on the floor. "If you folks are telling the truth, it's all right."

"I don't understand," Ma wanted to know more. "Our home has never been searched before."

"We ain't searched it, woman," the sheriff said. "We ain't searched your house. We just asked you some questions, and you turned these pieces over to us voluntary for safekeeping."

"But we didn't," David said quickly.

"Oh, yes, you all did, boy." This time the sheriff's man spoke. He was smiling. "I seen you. I'm a witness."

When they had gone, Ma sat down in a low rocker. Betty Jane went to her, and Ma put an arm around the little girl's shoulder and held her tight. David hooked the screen door and stood there until the car had driven out of the yard and turned toward South Town.

"Your father is in trouble," he heard his mother say; David turned.

"Pa don't get into trouble, Ma," he protested. "He ain't ever been in trouble. Not ever."

"He's in trouble, son," Ma said, her eyes fixed straight before her. Betty Jane was crying. "Hush, baby. We've got to think. We got to do something."

"I'll go in town, Ma," David said. "I'll catch a ride. I'll get help."

"Yes. You'll need help." Ma got up and put a hand on David's arm. "I'll go, too. Somebody in town will know. We'll try to find Mr. Jenkins. We'll go."

Betty Jane was still crying. Ma was putting on her hat when a car came up from South Town and turned into the yard. It was Joe Brodnax from the Ford agency. He braked swiftly and jumped from the car.

"They got Ed. They locked him up for nothing, less than nothing," he said.

He told all that he knew. Williams had come to the agency. He had found Mr. Boyd in the superintendent's office. Joe had heard Mr. Boyd talking about Ed's crawling back to work. Old man Boyd had been mean, and Williams had talked back to him, told him he had a right to work and be paid the same as other men. Boyd had stormed. Mundy had joined in. Mundy had said Williams was full of foreign Communist propaganda. Williams had come out of the office, with Boyd shouting that people were sick and tired of agitators and they were going to teach the blacks a lesson.

"I knew something was going to happen," Joe went on. "After Ed left, the man was calling people on the phone. Then one of the Skipwith boys come to the alley door and called me out. He said Ed Williams was arrested. That's when I left to bring you all the word."

"What can we do?" Ma asked. "We never had anything like this before. What is it about bail?"

Joe stood silently looking at the floor. Ma shook his arm.

"Tell me what to do, Mr. Brodnax," she said. "Lawyers get people out of jail. Can't we get a lawyer?"

Joe looked up and shook his head. "Mrs. Williams, I don't know what to say. You can get a lawyer, maybe, but if old man Boyd wants Ed to stay in jail over the weekend, they ain't nobody hardly can get him out. I'll drive you anywhere you say. I ain't going back to work today. It's pay day, but that don't matter."

They packed themselves into Joe's old coupe. Betty Jane sat on her mother's lap. They were crowded, and the car was dirty. It was the kind of car that automobile mechanics often drive. It had a sweet-running motor, but little else that was good could be said about it.

In town, people were sympathetic. All the black people had heard that Ed Williams had been arrested for talking back to his former boss. They said it was a shame. Some of them had seen the arrest made near Brown's restaurant. Mr. Brown said he would do anything he could.

People were sympathetic, but they were powerless.

One of the tough boys, just a little older than David, came up and took off his hat.

"Mrs. Williams," he said, "I done talked to Mr. Williams."

Ma grabbed him by the arm.

"You went to the jail?" she asked.

"Oh, yes'm. Jailhouse ain't nothing to me. I talked to him through the window."

"I'll go there now."

"No'm. You can't do that," the boy said. "You're a lady. Can't no lady go up in that alley. He specially said to tell you and David not to come up there. He say tell you to stay home. He say have Mr. Jenkins get him a lawyer. Get Lawyer Wilson. He the best one in this town."

"Is he all right?" Ma said, still holding the arm of the boy who looked to her like a messenger of hope. "Did they hurt him?"

"Yes'm, he all right." He smiled. "They don't hurt you up there, not most and generally. He say he hope the lawyer get him out, though. It sure ain't no place for a man like Mr. Williams to stay the night."

"Will you go back?" Ma took money from her purse and held it out. "Can you go back and tell my husband that you have seen me? Tell him I'll do exactly what he says."

"Sure, I'll go back." He drew away. "I'll go tell him."

Mrs. Williams took a step forward, still holding out the paper money. "Here, take this for your trouble," she said. "And I thank you. You don't know how much I thank you."

"Ain't no trouble. I couldn't take nothing." His smile was full and warming. "Mr. Williams been a friend to me, and he's a fine man. I'm glad to help."

They learned that Dan Jenkins had not been in town. Lawyer Wilson's office was closed. He was not at home, but Mrs. Williams left a message.

"Tell him," she said, "that whatever it costs we will pay. Be sure to tell him that."

They discussed driving back in the Williams car. David had a spare key, but they decided Mr. Williams would need the car to come home in. Mr. Brown said he would keep an eye on it. It was getting late. Pa had said for them to stay at home. Joe volunteered to come back and keep after Lawyer Wilson. Mrs. Williams said she hated to take up all his time.

"I don't mind that," Joe said. "I sure don't. I'll do anything for a man in trouble, and Ed's my friend. If they's any other place you want to go, we go there 'fore we leave town."

"How about the old judge?" David asked. "I think he could help us. He knows what kind of man Pa is."

Old Judge Armstead was heartily loved by the people of Pocahontas County. He was a kind man, and all the black people said with great respect that Judge Armstead was a "sure enough gentleman." He was perhaps the best educated person in the county. David had heard that Judge Armstead had said publicly that the law applied equally to white and black.

They went to Judge Armstead's house.

Joe stopped his shabby car on the road. David walked with his mother up the driveway and knocked on the side door. A woman they knew worked in the house; she came to the screen door. She would call Judge Armstead.

While Ma told her story, the judge stood inside looking out over her head. It had been a hot day, and he had taken off his shirt and his shoes. Through the screen David could see the white hairs on his chest above the line of his undershirt. Blue veins stood out on his forearms. The muscles of his biceps looked soft.

"You people don't understand," he said, still gazing out as though he were searching for something far away. "You people don't understand that it's a matter of law. The case has not come before me. Now I hear your side. How do I know what the complaining witness and others will say? I can assure you that whatever decision I render will be in keeping with the law and the evidence presented."

"But can't we do something now, Judge Armstead?" Ma was almost in tears. "We've never had anything like this before. I don't understand those things. What about bail?"

"You will need counsel," the judge said. "You can get a lawyer next week when your man comes up for his hearing."

"Next week?" Ma would have fallen if David had not held her arm. "Next week? Must he stay in that place until next week?"

"I am afraid so." At last the judge looked into the eyes of the woman before him. "I am afraid it will be impossible to find a lawyer to take the case at this time."

He turned away and walked off silently in his stockinged feet.

David had to put his arm around his mother's waist to steady her as they walked down the drive to the car.

"Good-by, you all!" David looked back over his shoulder. The woman who had received them said softly, "God bless you, and be careful!"

God bless you and be careful. The benediction and the counsel. A word to cheer and a word to caution. What did it mean? A green light and a yellow, or was it a green light and a red? Might it be a warning? Was there another danger? What would they do?

Joe drove down by the high school for white children and turned to pass Lawyer Wilson's house; but they could see the garage standing open and empty, so they did not stop.

It was nearly dark when they got home. David had to hurry with the evening's work. Betty Jane offered to help him, but he told her to stay in the house with Ma and to call him if anyone came.

Ma prepared dinner in silence. Even David had lost his appetite. The food had no taste, but they sat at the kitchen table, each one trying to encourage the others.

There was a step on the back porch.

"It's me, Al. Don't turn on the light." Al Manning came in and moved through the kitchen to stand in the door of David's room in the shadow.

"Come on in, Reverend," he said, "in here." Reverend Arrington was panting.

"Mr. Williams ain't come home yet?" Al asked. "I just thought I'd come and sit with you. Reverend Arrington was at the house, and he wanted to come too."

"That was right nice of you, Al," Mrs. Williams said with a smile, "and you too, Reverend Arrington. Won't you folks sit down and have a bite? We didn't have much."

Reverend Arrington said he had eaten his dinner.

"That's all right, Mrs. Williams," Al said. "We ate before we left home. Ma says tell you she's with you in spirit."

"Come on and sit down," said David. "We don't charge for seats."

"Not worth while to get in the light," Al said. "You through eating? Come on in; I want to talk to you."

David went into his room, and in the dark they talked.

"You don't have to bother your mother," Al said softly, "but you might as well know there may be trouble. Some of the folks are watching out in town, and some more will be out here. Some of the white folks have been having meetings. They're talking about putting us in our place. You got any guns in the house?"

David told in low tones about the sheriff's visit.

"That figures!" Al said. "They took the guns so you all wouldn't be able to fight back. It shows how well they've organized. Well, we're getting organized too. Come on up front."

They slipped through the kitchen door and on into the front room. The preacher, fat though he was, moved lightly behind them.

"When Ma slowed down for us to get out of the car, I put a bundle down on the far side of the road," Al said, pointing out a spot near a bush. "You'll have to go out there and get it. Don't let nobody see you, but if they do see you, it won't be like them catching sight of me."

"What do you think they'll do, Al?" David asked.

"Maybe nothing. Maybe nothing at all," Al said. "We just got to be ready."

David went out and sat on the steps of the porch. He watched his chance and ran across the highway, picked up the package, and was back in his place before the road was lit up again by the lights of a passing state police car.

The bundle was heavy. In the padding of an old patchwork quilt there were long straight pieces. David knew before Al unwrapped them in the darkness of the front room that they were guns, two shotguns and a repeater rifle.

Reverend Arrington had gone back to hold Mrs. Williams' attention.

"The others will be along soon," Al said, as he fitted gun stocks and barrels.

David told of their efforts during the afternoon. He said that Judge Armstead had seemed more concerned than he wanted to show. David still believed that somehow the law, as represented by Judge Armstead, would protect them. There was something dreamlike about the whole situation.

Irony?

The white car of the state troopers passed, moving slowly.

"That's the second time they've gone by," Al said. "Maybe they won't come in. If they do . . ." He paused.

"If they come, Al, what are we to do?" David asked.

"The preacher"—in the darkness Al motioned with his head—"Reverend Arrington is to talk to them, try to keep them from coming in. That's the diplomatic line of defense. If he can't stop them . . . we'll see."

Another car coming from the direction of South Town slowed up and then accelerated, and the car moved on.

"That's Ben Crawford's car," David said.

"They didn't stop because that other car was coming," Al said. "They'll be back."

Other cars passed, going up and down the highway. David hoped the Crawford car would wait awhile.

They watched for it.

It was coming, coasting without much noise. It slowed without coming to a full stop. A car door slammed, and the motor roared as the Crawford car sped off toward the town. Two bulky forms moved across the highway and merged into the shadow of bushes around the steps. Al went to the door and spoke.

With just the least bumping of hard metal against wood, Israel Crawford and his son, Israel, Jr., came in.

They reported that things were quiet in town, awful quiet. The state liquor store had closed early without explanation. Mr. Brown was not selling wine at his restaurant. He had taken all he had off the shelves.

Around the barbecue stand and at Skipwith's pressing shop people were coming and going. They were not just standing by the road, hanging around like most Saturday nights.

White folks? What are they doing? Kind of hard to say. Some of them said they hoped there wouldn't be any trouble. Some of them had good hearts. Others were just plain scared. The rebbish ones weren't saying anything.

The light was switched off in the kitchen. The little glow that had come through the door was gone. The folks were coming to the front room. Ma was in the doorway with the smaller shape of Betty Jane beside her. The preacher leaned against the mantel over the fireplace.

David told his mother that everything was all right. There was nothing for her to worry about.

"I know, son," she said. Her voice was strong, although she was speaking low. "It's all right. For a while I was afraid. I just didn't know which way to turn without Ed. I'm all right now, and I want to thank you all who have come. Al, you're a good boy, a son any mother could be proud of. I don't know who the others are by name, but I know you are true friends. God bless you.''

Al brought her low rocker, and they told her Mr. Crawford and his son were there. She must have made Reverend Arrington tell all he knew. She was prepared for anything.

"I'm keeping up the fire," Mrs. Williams said. "There's coffee on the stove and cold ham and biscuits and some cake on the table. We might as well eat.''

"Can we play the radio, Ma?" Betty Jane asked.

David felt it wasn't just right somehow for them to be sitting around with a radio playing while Pa was in jail, but Ma snapped it on and they got some music.

While they waited, saying little, cars went up and down the highway. Some of them slowed down. Then two cars passed, driving very slowly. They passed, and then they pulled off the pavement and stopped. Their lights were put out. Al and Mr. Crawford went into the front bedroom to look from that side. Men were talking at the car. They could not have been friends. They were the other. Guns were loaded. Reverend Arrington stood with his broad shape framed in the little light that came through the door. It looked as if the men got back into their cars and drove off. Al came back.

"We've got to watch both sides and the back," he whispered. Each man was sent to a window with a loaded gun. David was to watch the back through the window from his own room. Israel, Sr., and Israel, Jr., took opposite sides. That left the front with Al and Reverend Arrington standing in the door. The Reverend did not have a gun. He was afraid of guns. He wasn't afraid of white people, though, and he sure could talk.

In the front room the radio had been turned off.

There was no moon. Crickets and other insects of the dark seemed less noisy this night. It was as though they too waited for a blow out of the silences. It was a long wait.

Troubled thoughts went through David's mind. What was the danger? He had heard of mob violence, and he had read newspaper accounts of beatings and shootings by organized groups of white people. He had seen pictures of crosses burning and houses destroyed by fire and bombs. It had always seemed far away, something that happened where people were different from the people around South Town. Yet he knew that it could happen. There were some mean people. His father should not have been arrested. Joe had held little hope for Pa's release. Judge Armstead had said no lawyer would take the case just now. The woman who worked for him had said, "Be careful.''

There was no movement in the garden, nothing unusual in the barnyard. A rooster crowed, and others echoed his call. It must be after midnight, and nothing had happened.

David's mouth was dry. He was thirsty. He wanted to talk to someone. He wanted to go outside. He wanted to go into the kitchen.

Israel Crawford leaned in the door, his rifle hooked in his good left arm. David spoke to him. No, he hadn't seen anything. David wanted to ask Israel how he could shoot with only one hand, but Israel did not turn his head. He just stood motionless, quiet. Drank some water. It was warm, but it refreshed him a little. When he passed the door again, Israel said without moving, "We ready!"

A little later Al's voice reached him from the kitchen. There was the sound of the coffee pot being moved. David's eyes searched the darkness for movement. Al came and stood beside him.

"You'd better go drink some coffee," Al said. "I'll watch here."

David said he didn't like coffee, but he'd get some milk.

"No milk, Dave," Al said. "Milk will make you sleepy. Drink a cup of coffee and then go up front. Your mother will feel better if you're up there."

Dave drank the coffee. It was very strong. It took a lot of sugar to make it go down.

Ma had put Betty Jane to bed. Poor kid. This wasn't for little girls.

They told him more cars had come and stopped on the road. People were looking them over. The white state police car passed again.

David felt more comfortable here in the front. Ma was sitting in her rocker behind him, and out the side window where he watched, he could see the highway toward South Town. Among the cars that went by were those of friends. He could be sure about them. He knew the noises they made as well as their shapes and the way their lights were canted or dim on one side.

A car stopped in front of the house. A man got out and stood. He came slowly toward the yard and stopped at the gate.

It looked like a white man. David stood in the door beside the preacher. He cocked his gun. He heard the click of another safety behind him.

"Hey, there." The voice was familiar. "This is McGavock. Anybody home?"

"Mr. Mack?" David called.

"Davie, can I come in?" McGavock moved forward slowly. He was opening the gate. He carried a gun.

"Stop where you are!" It was Al speaking over David's shoulder.

"He's all right," David said. "He's our friend. He's a mechanic who worked with Pa at the garage."

"Put your gun down and come in," Al said. "Can you trust him?" he asked David.

"He's all right, I tell you," David insisted.

McGavock laid his gun on the grass and came up on the porch.

"We heard about it, and we thought we'd come out and set up with you," he said, speaking through the screen door. "It's Travis in the car, Dave. You know Travis."

"Sure, Mr. Mack." David had not seen Travis since the white mechanic was discharged from the shop. "Sure, tell him to come on in. Some others are here already!"

To Terrorize
+*To Victimize*   cf. R.W. *Fire & Cloud*
                         Bright & Morning Star

166   *Lorenz Graham*

"I don't know about that," Al said, pushing by David to go out to the porch.

"Young man, you don't need to be afraid of us," McGavock said. "I don't blame you for not trusting me, but I swear I'm with you. So's Travis. He brought me the news. Soon or late you might need us, and we're ready."

It took Ma and David to convince Al that there was no trickery in the offer, that these men had proved before that they were friends. It was Al who finally went out to the highway to tell Travis to put the car in the empty garage and come in.

Things were still quiet in South Town, McGavock reported, but after Boyd had Williams arrested on charges of disturbing the peace, he had gotten some of his friends together. They were talking about teaching the black folks a lesson, putting them back in their place, they said. It was the old night-rider plan, to terrorize the family and, through them, all the black people of the countryside. The sheriff and the police were with Boyd, of course, and those who were right thinking were afraid to do anything.

McGavock did not know the part Reverend Arrington was to play, and when he saw the white car passing again, he suggested a plan.

"Why don't you let me set out there on the porch?" he asked. "They know me, and if they come, I got a nice speech prepared for 'em. They know me, and they know I mean what I say." He turned toward Al. "Maybe you don't trust me, but one thing you all got to remember, it ain't every white man that's against black folks. A lot of us feel just like you do. It's just that we been scared too, and we keep silent about what we think. I'm through biting my tongue now. I want a chance to say my speaking piece."

Al was still doubtful, but he said, "We'll try it."

He was grim, and he spoke between scarcely parted lips. "We'll be watching you, though, you and your friend. If it gets bad, I'll know what to do."

McGavock turned and pulled himself up tall.

"I'm an old man, son," he said, "and I wouldn't mind dying for something good. I'd be scared only of dying as a traitor. You can trust me."

Al watched while McGavock went to get his gun and returned to sit on the edge of the porch, partly hidden by the climbing gourd vine. Inside, no one spoke until Al opened the door and started telling the men to get to their posts.

"We got plenty in the house now," Israel, Jr., said. "Maybe I better get out front. I'll be up yonder, 'longside the fence."

Travis spoke. "Good idea!" he said. "Flank defense. How's about me going with you?"

Al looked at Travis. In the darkness there was little he could see.

"No! Israel won't need no help," he said. "You'll be with me."

The house settled into quiet again.

Men left their places one at a time to go to the kitchen for coffee. Ma went back to put more wood on the fire. Those who smoked covered the glow of their cigarettes so that they would not be seen by those who drove by.

The world lay quiet outside. Few cars passed. Although he drank more coffee, David was sleepy. A sentry does not sleep at his post. At their places men still crouched, peering into the darkness. Mrs. Williams sat back in her rocker with her eyes closed. She was not asleep, or if she was, she slept fitfully, because she moved and she sighed. They were not afraid. They knew fear, but they were not afraid of whatever was to come.

The little creatures of the night quieted. It must be near morning. It was a long night.

The silences. These were the silences, then. About him were people who were no longer satisfied with silence. The preacher was here, ready to do what he could. Al Manning had brought the courage of a trained soldier. Mr. Crawford, who had lived in and with the silences all his life, had come with his battle-scarred son, and they were ready to speak out. Travis and Mr. Mack had come, not afraid and not willing to keep silent.

A schoolhouse on a hill should ring out in the silences. The fresh paint had made the school look like a lighthouse. It called the people to learn. It gave them something to stand up for. It made them know what to speak for, and it gave them courage. Israel Crawford had said, "We're ready!" Judge Armstead had said there was nothing he could do. Maybe he was afraid.

Pa had spoken out, all right.

"I ain't crawling to nobody," he had said. He had talked back to a white man, and for talking back, Pa was locked up in the jail. David wondered if Boyd's hatred might lead him directly to the jail. He remembered things he had read about black men dragged from their cells. No. Not that, he told himself, not just for back talk.

David's head rested against the side of the window as he studied the sky for a trace of light. The darkest hour is just before the dawn. This must be it, the darkest hour, but he, David Williams, was seeing things now he had never seen before. His eyes were being opened. There were good men and bad men. Travis and McGavock were white, but they had come to be with the blacks, to speak out, to fight back, willing even to die with them.

That one word, with. Fighting with could mean fighting against, or could it? Should it? You had a fight with somebody, or you stood with somebody to fight an enemy. Words were funny. Words were like people. They were all about you, and you thought you knew them, and then they came up meaning the opposite of what you had thought they meant. And when you used them wrong and accepted them wrong, you were so sure you knew. You had been sure you were right until you learned better.

Eyes, but they see not. Ears, but they hear not. A blind man seeing and a man looking into darkness and seeing. A boy looking into the darkness and seeing the light, waiting in the silences and hearing a great voice ring out.

Cars were coming up the highway from South Town, moving slowly. David

Modeling: white man to white men } Challege Racism + Bigotry
Blk   to   Blk   Intolerance.

168   *Lorenz Graham*

called out to the others. He counted six cars coming on close together. The white car of the state troopers was leading; as it came near, a spotlight was snapped on. The narrow beam played on the front of the house. There was a rush of feet from the rooms at the back. The head car stopped in front of the gate, its light shining through the door and flooding the room. Al and Travis and old man Crawford crouched silently, gripping their guns. The shadow of McGavock's form was thrown backward, jagged against the mantel over the fireplace.

"What do you want?" McGavock's voice rang out.

From the car a man replied, "What are you doing there?"

McGavock shouted, his voice echoing through the house, "I'm Sam McGavock. I'm a freeborn citizen, and I'm setting up with my friends. I'm asking you, what in God's name do you aim to do?"

There was no answer. Behind the police car, the others had stopped. In the house they could hear the drift of voices.

From the car someone called, "You're a white man, Mack. You got no business mixing up in this. If you know what's good for you, you'll clear out."

McGavock answered, "Yes, I'm a white man, and I ain't yellow, and I know what's good for me and what's good for you, too. If any one of you tries to harm anyone in this house, it'll be the last evil thing you do on God's green earth. We'll shoot, and we'll shoot to kill. And I know you, John Whitlock, parading in a uniform of the law, disgracing the mammy that born you. I know you, and I hate your guts. I hate what you're a-doing. Leave these people be."

McGavock turned toward the other cars. "And that goes for the rest of you," he shouted. "There ain't going to be no house-burning here tonight. Clear out now! Clear out! Get on back to your homes and your women whilst you're able, and come sun-up, look on the day and thank God you're living and beg him to forgive you. This here's Sam McGavock talking sense to you, and by God you know I mean it."

The spotlight was turned off. A car door slammed, and two men walked forward to the police. Angry voices rasped through the night, and from the darkened cars ugly words were hurled at McGavock.

Another voice shouted out from somewhere in the darkness up alongside the fence. The voice was strong, but the tongue-twisting curses were not clear. Israel Crawford, Jr., had not yet mastered his false teeth.

"We ready for you . . . Oh, yes, we ready . . . Ain't nobody . . . scared . . . Can't die but once, and if I dies, you dies with me . . . Come and get it, or get from round it . . . Maybe we goes down, but we goes down fighting and them what lives is living like mens . . . Get going now, white folks . . . Get in or get out . . . I tired of waiting . . ."

A starting motor whirred. The last car in line backed and turned and started back down the grade toward South Town. Another car pulled out. It did not turn, but headed up the hill away from town, rushing at full throttle as it passed the point closest to the hidden voice. The light of another car lit up

the highway briefly, and David recognized the heavy figure of Boyd as he left
the police car and returned to his own.

They were leaving. The police car which had led the line was the last to
leave—and it moved slowly with its spotlight playing along the side of the
road.

Israel's voice shouted out again.

"If you come back, we still ready . . . Any time you want put this kind of
mess on our folks, we be ready . . . Ain't going stand for no more lynchings
. . . We fighting back . . . We ready."

The white car slowed and almost stopped, as though the driver would come
back to meet the challenge. Then suddenly it leaped forward with a roar to
overtake the other cars.

It was over. It was over for the time at least. David filled his lungs again
and again. It was as though he had been under water for a long time, and
now at the surface he could breathe.

McGavock sat on the step. His head bowed into his hands. In her rocker
Ma was weeping softly. David rested his gun in a corner and went to put his
arms around his mother. He knelt by her chair and drew her head to his
shoulder. He was like a man comforting his child.

"Ed, Ed!" she sobbed. "Go help him! Don't let them get him."

"No, Ma. They wouldn't try that." David remembered that Joe Brodnax
and the others were on guard in town. They too were ready.

"The Lord is my light and my salvation; whom shall I fear? The Lord is
the strength of my life; of whom shall I be afraid?"

It was the preacher, quoting scripture at a time like this! David wanted to
rise up and tell him to save it.

"When the wicked, even mine enemies and my foes, came upon me to eat
up my flesh, they stumbled and fell. Though an host should encamp against
me, in this will I be confident. One thing have I desired of the Lord, that will
I seek after; that I may dwell in the house of the Lord all the days of my life,
to behold the beauty of the Lord, and to enquire in his temple."

Maybe it was all right. Ma was quieter. She seemed to be listening. She
seemed to get something out of it.

"For in the time of trouble he shall hide me in his pavilion; in the secret
of his tabernacle shall he hide me."

Ma was joining in, her soft voice blended with that of the preacher. She
knew every word of the psalm.

"And now shall mine head be lifted up above mine enemies round about
me; therefore will I offer in his tabernacle sacrifices of joy; I will sing, yea,
I will sing praises unto the Lord."

Mr. Mack opened the screen door and came in, leaning on one side, listening. Israel, Jr., stood outside the door, quiet again. No one else was speaking, just the preacher and Ma reciting from the Bible.

"Hide not thy face far from me; put not thy servant away in anger;
thou hast been my help; leave me not, neither forsake me, O God of my
salvation."

Another voice had joined in, faltering at first, then stronger. David raised his head and saw Al holding his gun at the ready and speaking the words his mother had taught him before men took him from home and taught him to kill.

"Deliver me not over unto the will of mine enemies; for false witnesses are risen up against me, and such as breathe out cruelty. I had fainted, unless I had believed to see the goodness of the Lord in the land of the living."

Then David joined in, and Mr. Crawford, and Mr. Mack, and Travis and Israel at the door.

"Wait on the Lord; be of good courage, and he shall strengthen thine heart; wait, I say, on the Lord."

When he came to the end of the psalm, Reverend Arrington said, "Let us pray."

The words the preacher said were not in the loud speech of the church house on a Sunday morning. It was not as though he were calling to his God high in the heavens. It was rather as though he spoke to One who was there in the living room of the small white house at the side of the road a few miles from South Town. And the words asked for nothing. They expressed simple thanks for protection and deliverance from evil. David was kneeling beside his mother's chair. He was thinking that she seemed to be at ease when suddenly someone in the room shouted in alarm, and in the same instant came a roar that was a clatter and a series of sharp explosions and crashings and startled cries and rushing to get to guns laid down too soon. And then David saw through the window that cars were speeding down the road toward South Town, and in the next instant Israel stood on the porch firing after them and old Mr. Mack was there beside him, but the cars were out of range. Inside the house Al was calling for a light and Betty Jane was screaming in fright or perhaps in pain. David had to know, and he went to his mother, who was trying to comfort the little girl, and from her voice rather than the words she was saying, David knew that Betty Jane was not hurt and that Ma too was safe.

Betty Jane was not hurt, and Ma was safe, but Al was muttering strong curses as he bent to examine, with the light of a match, the face of Travis. Someone turned on the electric light. It was blinding at first, but they could see the mark of a bullet wound in the forehead of the still white face.

David tried to remember what the limping veteran had once said about being with angels.

There was no panic in the house.

There was no panic, and for a time there was no movement. It was as though all thought and speech and motion were frozen in time and space.

Al was bending over the body of Travis where it lay, arms widespread, quite calm, the face upturned with the small red spot near the center of the forehead. The eyes were nearly closed. The mouth was slack. A slow stream of blood coursed from the hole and ran down to the side toward the right ear.

It was Crawford, father of Israel, who had reached up to pull the cord, flooding the room with light. He had not lowered his arm. His hand still clutched the small white ball on the end of the cord. Words came from him, in anguish. "Lord have mercy!"

Arthur Flowers
(1950   )

Flowers, is a novelist and essayist whose works include *De Mojo Blues* (1985) and *Good Loving Blues*. He is a native of Memphis, Tennessee, and cofounder of the New Renaissance Writers Guild. His story "Another Good Loving Blues" appeared in the anthology *Homespun Images* (1989). The following excerpt is from *De Mojo Blues*.

---

from De Mojo Blues

Early in Spring 72, Tucept HighJohn, in Levis and an army T-shirt with the sleeves cut out, came out of his place in the woods of Memphis Riverside Park and hitchhiked over to his folks' house. He had a key and let himself in. His momma was in the backroom, humming a blues over her loom. Tucept watched hypnotic brown fingers weaving a thick black web into existence on fine emerald cloth.

Hey ma, Tucept kissed her cheek. She murmured and nodded without looking up from the piece between her hands.

I came by to clean up the attic, he said.

Is it Saturday already? she asked absently.

He nodded, Afraid so.

He watched her for a few minutes before climbing the stairs to the attic. The attic was hot and steamy with slanted roofbeams and dark cobwebbed corners of dusty old memories, bulging boxes, bags, piles of old clothes, busted toys, lawnmowers, furniture, bicycles, lumber, boxes and boxes of papers, photos and records, and the scattered pieces of 4 old ice cream machines. Homemade ice cream. His mouth watered but he couldn't find enough pieces to make a complete one. He found the box that he stuck his army gear in when he got back from Nam. He pulled out a couple of fatigues and a pair of jungle boots to replace the ones wearing out on him and placed them on the steps so he wouldn't forget them.

Finally he really started, methodically working his way through by section, throwing away stuff that had been sitting up in there forever. He left papers alone. Most of them were records from his father's medical practice, from way back when he first started out over in Arkansas and made house calls to

172

scattered farms. Tucept remembered sharing the back of the old beat up Plymouth station wagon with Caldonia and medical fees; crates of greens and cabbages, sides of meat, bushels of corn, and mason jars of red, grape, orange and yellow preserves. On holidays they would get homemade candies, fudges and brownies. Tucept found records of the many offices his father had before he and some friends built the new medical clinic on the South Side.

In one box, taped and reinforced against time, Tucept found letters that belonged to his granma, suitors who referred in flowered script to his granma as My Dearest Pearl. He visualized his granma as a My Dearest Pearl. His momma's notebooks from Fisk. The effect of religion on community. Existentialism and the Negro worldview. His eyebrow raised. Mamma was deep. The attic was deep. And hot. Sweat poured off him as he worked.

Finally he got up and stretched, and wiped the sweat from his face with his T-shirt. Sitting at the little back window, he smoked a joint, blowing the smoke outside. Thoroughly high, the steamy attic became a world of its own and he worked it like an automaton, lost in his rhythm and old comfortable memories. Bruuuuhhhhhh, the backdoorbell pulled him back.

Tucept, his momma yelled from the back, Would you get the door please?

Tucept came down from the attic into the cool air downstairs with a cramped sigh of relief, he hadn't realized he had been up there so long.

Through the door glass he saw two dashiki clad brothers talking. Tucept didn't recognize either of them and he opened the door with a questioning slowness.

The shorter brother, stocky and glowering through a bearded face, asked if Doctor HighJohn was in.

No, Tucept shook his head, He isn't in.

The brother looked at him without warmth, Are you Tucept HighJohn? he asked.

Tucept nodded.

We'd like to talk to you if we could.

Tucept stood aside and asked them to enter.

He stepped briskly inside and introduced himself, Shukim, he said.

The name rang a bell and Tucept played with it for a moment until he remembered why. Shukim. One of Martin Luther King's lieutenants had stayed in Memphis after King was shot and had become involved in local community activism.

The tall brother with him nodded greeting.

Shukim sat in a denchair and glared at him before pronouncing abruptly, People around here say that you and your daddy are two of the smartest bougie in this town.

Shukim's head bobbed as he spoke, as if he were listening to a music no one else could hear. Tucept frowned and waited.

We want to know, said Shukim, what you doing for blackfolks' freedom. We want to know what your plan is.

Tucept looked at him blankly, totally wacked.

Uh, . . . uh, I don't understand, he said, playing for time, struggling for clarity. The high that had been so great a minute ago turned on him. He couldn't think. He struggled to clear away fluffy mental clouds. Condition red, man the defenses. Sweat beaded his brow as he forced himself to straighten up.

Shukim stared at him, head bobbing, impatiently waiting and not expecting to hear anything he doesn't already know. Tucept glanced at the tall brother. His obvious sympathy only angered.

Sweat running down his face, Tucept's mind finally began to kick the high and move into gear. His plan for blackfolks' freedom? What the hell? He didn't have the faintest idea what this fool was talking about.

He switched tracks. Why me? Who sicced this fool on me? The last time he had seen Shukim, he was still in highschool, back in 68, down at the Temple the night before they got King. The night before they brought him down.

Mountain Top Speech

> *We've got some difficult days ahead*
> *but it doesn't matter to me now. . . .*

On a humbug him and his cronies had decided to see the King since he would be speaking over at the Temple. They were irrelevant local militants, Levi jackets faded to uniform perfection. They had helped break up King's first parade for the sanitation strike and forced him to try again. And now they came to jeer him.

> *I may not get there with you but I want*
> *you to know that we as a people will*
> *get to the promised land. . . .*

A big storm that night, thunder and lightning rippling around the Temple to the cadence of his words of power. They had to admit the boy could preach, his black moon face sweat slick and gleaming as he called down power under the stained glass windows of the Temple.

> *I'm not fearing anyman. . . .*

Tucept had been moved. Tear tracks trickled from his eyes. And when he saw the way the blackfolks in the audience stood up with a longlost pride and dignity he left with respect for the King.

MLK Assassinated The next day the .30–06 bullet sang into his neck and Tucept and his boys hurled themselves through floodlit streets and brick warfare with National Guard tanks and troops that occupied a raging Black America. A rage perplexed at the slaying of the dreamer and his dream. A rage contained by tanks, Cointellpro, and the Great Society. A rage that finally settled into the slow relentless anger falling rain on stone. A rage that made college a scowling beard, a ragged afro, strident anger, and a .50 caliber machine gun shell

Class Tensions { Shukim, The people
Tucept, bourgeoise (which he does not accept).

necklace that looked photogenic on the nightly news. But that was before he
went to the war.

Now Tucept looked at Shukim through unfriendly eyes. He had been like
Shukim in those days. But he had been playing a role, strutting the stage. At
least Shukim was sincere.

You bougie blacks are all alike, said Shukim suddenly, head bobbing with
the suddenness of the assault, People tell me that you and your daddy got
some sense, but I can see you aint doing nothing for blackfolks.

Tucept remembered his first class accusation. Hurled against him when a
brother from his old neighborhood said, in front of witnesses, You wouldn't
play with us because your father was a doctor, a bougie opportunist.

Cf. Angela Davis

Who me? Tucept had wailed, shocked, shamed and shrunken in front of his
activist peers, What are you talking about man? I thought we were cool. Are
you serious? You talking about me? My daddy aint beating nobody. Fuck you.

Intimidated under Shukim's ungiving eye, Tucept started blustering, Hey
man, he said, I did my bit, I went through the 60s too man. I was there. I
been beat and teargassed, I was there man. I marched. And I know all about
talking and posing too. Now you want me to talk some more. No more talk
man, I'm willing to work with anything that's real, something that's concrete,
but I aint got nothing to talk to you about, I aint got to sit here and convince
you of some plan I got for blackfolks' freedom, what makes you think I'm
going to tell you about it?

A strange sensation of standing back and watching himself, watching swift
angry words tripping over themselves. Too swift, too angry.

So what are you doing? he said finally, I'm willing to work with anything
thats concrete.

Contemptuous pity mingled with Shukim's earlier belligerency. He stood
next to a shelf of trophies Tucept's folks had won playing bridge. He grunted
and picked up a gold hand holding a spread of cards. No trump. He looked
at it disdainfully. Tucept looked around the den selfconsciously, its very com-
fortableness an accusation. Shukim put the trophy down, letting it fall on its
side. Tucept righted it.

We're working over on the Franklin projects, said Shukim, as if he were
on a podium giving a boring lecture, his voice even and modulated, We're
helping them build a truck garden, teaching them how to be self sufficient,
grow their own foods, we're trying to organize them for survival.

Thats cool, said Tucept, I can deal with that. I'll come down and help you
with that.

Thats good brother, the tall brother spoke for the first time, We can use all
the help we can get.

Tucept nodded at him, cautiously grateful.

What days and hours you working? asked Tucept, knowing as he asked that
he wasn't down for working in no garden. He was good for a couple of days
maybe, max a week. Jiving again.

It was like Shukim knew it, contempt obvious in the brown lemon of his
face, his drawn together eyebrows. He just didn't have anything more to say

to Tucept, studiously ignoring Tucept as his eyes continued to sweep over the den. As if calculating how many blackfolks had to suffer so that Tucept HighJohn could grow up comfortable.

The tall brother said he had heard Tucept was in the Nam, how was the herb, how were the women?

Tucept's eye slitted, he certainly wasn't admitting to no herb, or women. Probably bougie traits. How do they know all my business anyway? I'm living in a fucking fishbowl.

Tucept's attitude reached for the threshold of anger.

Shukim stood, We're leaving.

Tucept walked them to the door and down the driveway.

Where's your car?

The tall brother answered, Don't have one.

How you getting way over to the other side of town?

Shukim turned on him, belligerence once again riled by this display of privileged naïveté.

We hitchhike, he said tersely, Look man, we want the good things in life too.

Shukim's dashikiclad arm swept gracefully, green cloth billowing behind it. It encompassed his folks' house, the large, well kept lawn, We want cars, he said with a false patience, We want a nice place to stay too, but these things aren't as important as blackfolks' freedom and they will just have to wait.

Tucept didn't say anything. Sucker was determined to bust his chops.

They caught a ride and Tucept HighJohn walked back up the driveway fuming and muttering curses. Back in the attic, sweat rolling down his body, he worked with a vengeance that placed everything in precise strict alignments. His plan for blackfolks' freedom, he muttered through lips beaded with sweat, what kind of shit was that to put on somebody?

Just like before the war, Tucept hung out on the fringes of the movement through the low profile 70s, a body for demonstrations, community work, passing out flyers, making meetings and programs, trooping it until the day Gail called him down as an intellectual, the ultimate activist putdown.

All I'm saying—Tucept held up the document they had just worked over— is that this doesn't say anything new, just a bunch of rhetoric that folks have heard a thousand times already. It goes in one ear and out of the other. Old news. We gotta be a lot slicker than this, otherwise blackfolks gon be suffering forever.

Gail looked at him smugly, You're saying it isn't intellectual enough?

Tucept's eyes looked to heaven. An intellectual par excellence herself, she followed the party line like the puritan Marxist-Leninist she was. He had always dug her but activist women demanded you be either superblack or downtrodden. He aspired to neither. Cool was his game.

He should have kept his mouth shut. He knew better. He wasn't considered seriously political by his nationalist and Marxist-Leninist cronies because he didn't participate in their political dialogue. As far as he was concerned, the choice between a five state bantusan and being cannon fodder for the latest set of good white folks was no choice at all.

Feeling unaccountably mischievous, Tucept harrumphed until he had everybody's attention and made so bold as to suggest that there was only one legitimate goal of political activity: Conquer and Hold.

Power surged through him, a quick chill as quickly gone, leaving him half dazed. They smiled indulgently. HighJohn again. Think he HighJohn de Conqueror they laughed. He amused them. After all they were serious political activists, HighJohn was just a halfass bougie nationalist.

He laughed it off with them, his ha ha hearty claiming to have just been kidding anyway. They went back to yesteryears plans, yesterdays battles. HighJohn sat back, shut his mouth and watched through veiled eyes. It wasn't wasted time. Keeping his finger on the pulse. Just hated to see them wasting good effort, good heart. He respected them. Warrior clans.

His eyes distant, he shook his head slowly, almost imperceptibly. What was his contribution to blackfolks' freedom? What could he say, what could he do that would help blackfolks get out of this historical trickbag? One man with a limited little time on the planet. One shot. He wouldn't waste it on no rhetorical bullshit.

[handwritten annotations:]

Competing Ideologies

The 1960's Black Revolution Revisited

Class Tensions: Toward A Definition of Blackness.
(& Freedom).

Cultural Nationalism

Economic Empowerment

Integrationist \ Bourgeoise Values

What's in a Name?

De Mojo

Tucept   High John — Aprodasic — (individual) passaging Charisma
— Rootworker
— brimming sexuality
— a cultural worker?; a priest for a proscribed Religion.
— a priest to a whole congregation of believers.

M.L.K. Mountain Top Speech
& The Promised Land Complex.
Adjusting to being in the Promised Land

Carol Dixon
(1949–   )

Dixon is a novelist and winner of the John Oliver Killens Fiction Award. Her contribution to *Black Southern Voices* is an excerpt from her novel *Going Home.*

---

from Going Home

Once more, huddling birds upon the leaves
And summer trembling on a withered vine.
And once more, returning out of pain,
The friendly ghost that was your love and mine.

Men, for the most part, live their lives for the moment, each moment being judged by the success or failure in it. Their pleasant memories, those centered around their successes, are fired repeatedly, like unaimed projectiles, into the empty canyons of their consciousness, where they ricochet off the surfaces, and fill the voids with recurring echos of their triumphs. Their painful memories, those reflecting their failures, are simply worked off in gyms, or left to rot in the dust behind the screeching sound of tires, hell bent on self destruction. And even the most painful of these, the ones wrapped around the smell of her perfumed neck, the feel of her hands, or her face in sleep. Such memories as these are often found floating face down, drowned in some shot glass. Such are the memories of men.

Women, on the other hand, treat their memories like priceless, crystal keepsakes, carefully selecting them, placing them just so. Each one is treasured, precious and unique in its own right, none being quite like the other. The more beautiful ones, the ones ringing with rich tones and sparkling with clear colors, these are brought out regularly, served up with tea and cake, proudly displayed for the envious eyes of less fortunate women. The more fragile ones, rarely brought out, are displayed only in the dark china closets of the mind, fondled occasionally in private rooms, unseen by others, their value known only to the owner. And still, the most delicate of these are wrapped carefully in layers of thin tissue paper and locked safely away forever. They are never unwrapped, never displayed, never savored privately. For the owner lives in

178

constant fear that at any moment her trembling, unsure hands could let the delicate piece slip carelessly through her fingers, sending it crashing to the floor, shattering it into a million pieces, destroying it forever, along with her fragile heart. And such are the memories of women.

Nadine quietly slipped the tiny key into its lock, the lock on the china closet of her mind. Thankful that she had awakened from her brief nap to find the beast dormant within her, she sat now at the kitchen table sipping a cup of tea. Realizing that Time was robbing her of time, she decided to relish in the seconds allotted her. So she turned the key ever so gently, and prepared to indulge herself. Her mind wandered among the various pieces that she possessed, trying to determine which one to select first. She was amazed at the size of the collection that she had amassed over her fifty-eight years. At first her mind just toyed with her keepsakes, fingering them lightly, finding pleasure in the mere wandering. But then it wandered into that area of a woman's memory that holds the most joy and the most pain. It rested calmly among those fragile treasures that reflect the spectrum of emotions that pass between a man and a woman.

Here, her mind skipped lightly across her first stolen kiss behind the schoolhouse. And it lingered only momentarily on the deep crush she'd had on Reverend Roscoe Peters, partially out of respect for Mrs. Peters. But when she came to a warm summer day, an old metal lawn swing, and a nervous hand in her hand, she stopped to look.

She was seventeen again, and the nervous hand holding hers belonged to Larry Wilson. Uncle Sam wanted him and he was leaving in a few weeks. And at the end of the summer, she was going off to Benedict College to become a school teacher. The paths of the two high school sweethearts were diverging, coming to a parting of the ways. The appearance of their futures on the not-so-distant horizon made them anxious because they felt their childhood slipping away from them. It was a time of mixed emotions for them. A time of ups and downs, of beginnings and endings. A time for rejecting the old and accepting the new. Their spirits danced with anticipation, but there was a soberness about them too. They wanted to grab the future, but they were afraid to let go of the past.

Nadine could feel the conflict bubbling within her. She was sure of herself one minute, then uncertain and insecure the next. She needed to hold on to something familiar. She held on to Larry. The woman in her looked for something in him to help her through, the little girl in her not quite understanding what it was she was searching for. Larry was wrestling with the boy and the man in him. He wanted to embrace the man fully, but the boy was less threatening, so he held on. The man in him knew that Nadine needed something from him, but the little boy didn't quite understand what it was.

The questions that screamed inside of them left them feeling like mutes, unable to give voice to their dilemma. But when Nadine looked up and saw Larry coming that afternoon, she knew he had found an answer. She watched him closely as he stopped in the dusty road a short way off from the house to put on his shoes that he had been carrying, slung over his shoulder. As his tall, honey brown body neared the house, she noticed that his pants had been pressed to a tee. Her mind told her that something special was going to happen. As he got closer, she saw that he had left just enough buttons open on his clean white shirt to expose his three chest hairs, and the hair on his head, which was already cut short, had been plastered with enough pomade to make every hair lay down flat without hope of ever rising again. He stepped up on the porch and they exchanged pleasantries. The smell of his dime store aftershave caught Nadine off guard. Larry felt he had splashed just enough on his cheeks to give the impression that he was already shaving. Nadine felt that the amount he had used had just fallen short of attracting the amorous attention of stray cats. She was, however, very impressed. Then it suddenly dawned on her why he had taken so much pain in dressing this afternoon. He was going to ask her to marry him. The little girl in her beamed with the thought.

They sat now on the old metal lawn swing, holding hands. The maple, the willow, the oak, and the pine, realizing the importance of the occasion, swirled their fragrances into an elusive mixture that floated down and mingled with the smell of fresh earth, and the daisies, marigolds, and sunflowers that waited there. And the two noticed that their senses were heightened by the mysterious opiate that the warm summer air offered up to them. As the warm sun glowed around them, they felt full and happy with each other and in each other.

"Where's your mean old Daddy, girl?" Larry asked trying to prepare himself for what was to come.

"Now Larry, you know there ain't a mean bone in Papa's body," Nadine answered, trying to sound somewhat indignant.

"Oh he's mean all right. I hear he tries to run off anyone that tries to talk to his girls."

"Papa don't mind talk none, Larry. At least not from nice boys. It's the fresh ones like you that gets his goat." Nadine smiled secretly knowing what Larry was hinting at.

"Well your sister Mattie's beau must be pretty fresh then, 'cause I hear your Daddy run him off the other evening with a double barreled shot gun. Now I don't know about you, girl, but where I come from, that's considered pretty mean."

"Go on, Larry." Nadine giggled a little behind her hand and gave his thigh a light slap. "You know Papa was only funning with John Avery."

"Funning? You call that funning? Well if that's funning I sure don't want to meet the man when he's serious." Then keeping with the spirit of the joke he added, "And I don't think poor John took it for no lark either. In fact they tell me he passed his house by two counties, he was running so fast." The image of big, clumsy John tripping all over himself, trying to run, filled Nadine's head and she burst out laughing. Larry, sensing an opportunity to shed his awkwardness, joined in. He looked over at Nadine and became uncomfortably aware of the woman that was blossoming out of the girl. He felt the sun warm his blood slightly and his skin became moist. He suddenly noticed that his shirt was sticking to the middle of his back. He quickly turned his consciousness towards the true intent of his visit.

"Nadine," he said, making his eighteen-year-old voice sound as manly as he could, "you know you my girl, right?" Nadine didn't answer this question because she knew she wasn't supposed to. And because she remained silent, he knew it was safe to go on. "And . . . you know I love you, right?" Nadine recognized her cue.

"Uh-huh," she answered, her eyes glued to her lap. The sun beamed in her, warming her with the secrets of womanhood, and she basked in the full glow of it. Their mutual warmness met in the center of their palms, making the children in them uncomfortable. He slipped his hand gently from hers, hoping she wouldn't notice. She was simply relieved that he had done so. He stood up now and shoved both of his hands deep into his pockets. In fact, if his pockets had reached down to his ankles, his hands would have found the bottom. He stepped down from the porch and walked a few steps off from her, trying to form the words for his next question. He hadn't realized it was going to be so hard.

Nadine watched him standing out in the yard. She wondered if he was losing his courage. The girl in her became anxious, and suddenly this was all very important to her. She didn't know why, in fact she really didn't care why. She just knew it was.

"Larry, you better get out of that hot sun before you melt." It was all she could think of to say. She felt stupid and desperate at the same time. He seemed to be unaware of her comment. He kicked a small pebble across the yard, then turning he looked back at the porch and Nadine sitting there. He had to ask the next question, but it had suddenly dawned on him that he really didn't know what her answer would be. He watched her carefully now, needing to validate his motives, while trying to feel if there was enough man in him to accept whatever answer he might get. He began slowly, hesitantly, his eyes boring holes in his shoe tops. "Well, Nadine, I . . . er . . . sort of thought . . . that is I was . . . er thinking that . . . Well I figure that you love me too, huh?" The space between his question and her answer seemed like an eternity. He had dared to bare his hopes to her and he now realized that her answer could make him feel powerful or vulnerable. He waited anxiously as the seconds ticked loudly in his ears.

"I guess you figure right," the girlish voice floated over to him. Nadine had realized the power she had held over his ego in those few seconds and the taste of the sport was in her mouth. Her words found him across the yard and fulfilled his hopes. His boyish chest inflated and he actually felt the hairs growing on it. He walked towards her now, a little more confident than when he had started. He watched her sitting there, her shapely brown legs swinging slightly back and forth, just barely moving the swing, but allowing him to see a little more of her than custom dictated he should have. He sat beside her again, his mind trying to form the words that he thought his heart wanted his mouth to say. He looked at her now, needing to read every gesture, every expression. Nadine looked up into his face waiting to imprint the scene in her memory forever. He lost himself momentarily in her large dark eyes, but then regaining his footing, he began, choosing his words carefully, trying not to box himself in, trying to leave an opening, in case he had to flee.

"Nadine, you know Uncle Sam will be paying me a pretty penny now."

"Yeah, so?" She urged him on.

"Well I figure I'll have all that dough and no one to spend it on."

"You could spend some on your family, Larry," she teased, recognizing the difficulty he was having.

"I know that, girl," he said, somewhat irritated at her interruption. "And I plan to do that too. But I'm saying that . . . well . . . I'll probably be ready to support a family and everything now."

"What do you mean, Larry?" She continued the act, flexing her womanness, wanting him to ask her outright. Not really trying to be cruel. She had simply become aware of a strange force within her that allowed her to see his vulnerability and she played with it like a child with a new toy. She was unaware of the toy's capabilities, unaware of its magic and how to use it. She was only aware that it was in her possession. He knew that she understood what he was saying, but he also knew that something in him was making it hard for him. There was still too much boy in him to recognize what he was fighting, but there was enough man in him to make him feel he should fight.

"Well, Larry?" she asked. Larry swallowed hard, trying to lose the taste of resentment that coated his tongue. He drew in a deep breath and started again, not wanting to be bested at whatever this game was they were playing.

"What I'm trying to say is, that with the salary I'll be pulling in while I'm in the army, I'll be able to think about getting married."

"And . . . ?" she prodded, anticipating the question. He ignored her interruption this time and went full speed ahead.

"Well Nadine, seeing as how you love me." He was conscious of implicating her first. "And I love you . . . well it just seems natural that we should . . . umm . . . think about getting married." Nadine wasn't settling for anything short of the question.

"Larry, just what are you talking about?"

"Girl, what's wrong with you? You got rocks in your ears or something?" He exploded, startling her somewhat. He caught a glimpse of his power in her wide eyes. There was still enough girl in her to appreciate the game she had been playing, but the change in his face told the woman in her that the game was over. Her eyes softened now and he found himself once again lost in them. The sun burned in him and mingled with his newfound strength. He felt a part of the boy slip away. The man that replaced it felt strange and unfamiliar, but he found that he was now able to put aside his fear of being hurt. Lost in her right now as he was, draped in this strange new feeling, it no longer mattered how he asked. What mattered was that he wanted to ask, he needed to ask.

"Nadine Baker," he started, "I want you to be my wife. Will you marry me?" Not until she had heard the question did Nadine realize that she was really unsure of the answer. Now her mind played tricks with her mouth, as she hunted frantically for the right words.

"Larry, you know that I'm going to Benedict this fall. My family is really proud of me winning that scholarship. If I back out now they'll be so disappointed in me. I have to go, Larry. I have to." The woman in her told her that she had to help him save face.

"Larry," she began carefully, "I really do love you, but I owe this to my family." There was just enough space left for him to flee.

"Shoot girl! I'm not asking you to marry me tomorrow." And when he said it, he realized it was true. "I know you can't let your family down. I've got obligations too you know. Besides, Uncle Sam will be doing a number on me right now and I've got to keep my mind freed up to deal with that. I don't have time to be worrying about some young wife wanting all my attention." He smiled to himself at the image he had just created. "I just felt that with both of us knowing we loved each other and me going into the service, and you going away to college . . . well I just felt that we should make it plain . . . you know whether we're going to wait for each other . . . or let each other go. You know . . . free each other up in case the other wasn't thinking the same way." He had made it safely through the space.

"Well Larry," she began hesitantly, "I'm willing to wait for you if you're willing to wait for me." The shoe was on the other foot. He could do an about face now and march right over her heart. She waited, the girl in her not quite understanding why she had placed herself in this situation.

"Well," he started slowly, enjoying this reversal in the roles, "we have to give this some serious thought here. I mean you'll be away at school surrounded by all those smart preachers' sons. I hear tell they're some slick cats. I mean who's to know if some little country girl like you won't go and fall for their lines and forget all about me." The weight of what he had just said struck both of them at the same time. He was at the same instant, awed by and sorry for what he had just said. Nadine took it further.

"Well what about you and Uncle Sam? I hear that there are some pretty loose types that hang around army bases, you know. So what's going to keep some city slick type from getting a country boy like you to put a ring on her finger, while she puts one through your nose." Larry felt somewhat better knowing that the same opportunities were available to him. The score evened out and the two relaxed, now being able to share the humor in the joke.

"I sure would look kind of silly with a ring in my nose." Larry laughed.

"Yeah, well I'm not exactly ready for the Amen corner either." They found relief in their laughter and the problems that they had created for themselves no longer seemed so overbearing. They held hands and rocked the old lawn swing back and forth. The warm southern sun beamed its blessings down on them and they felt the fullness of their young love. He leaned over and kissed her deeply and unashamedly, showing her how he felt at that moment. She returned the kiss as fully as she had received it, letting him know that she shared the feeling.

"I will wait for you, Larry," she repeated softly.

"And I'll wait for you too," he answered, "I'll wait forever for you."

There was still enough of the child in the both of them to believe that their young, innocent, and untried love could withstand the tests of time, distance, and maturity. But there was just enough woman in her, and just enough man in him, to make them wonder.

The phone rang, startling Nadine and jarring the precious memory of her first marriage proposal. She returned it safely to its proper place, closing the door on her keepsakes. Time revealed that she had not married Larry, she had married someone else. But that was another memory, and right now she had no time to dwell in the past. The present was calling her. She got up from the table and walked towards the phone hanging on the opposite wall.

"Hello?"

"Hello, Mom."

"Buddy?"

"Yeah, Mom, it's me. How are you doing this morning?"

"Fine baby, just fine," Nadine lied.

"That's great, Mom, that's just great." There was a short pause and then he continued. "Listen, Mom, the reason I'm calling is to let you know that something's come up here at the office. It's kind of messy and I'm really trying to get it worked out as fast as possible but . . ." He realized she was silent. "Mom?"

"Yes, Buddy, go on." Nadine listened carefully now, not so much to his words as to him. A mother may love all of her children fully and without reservation, but the child who has had the rocky start in life always carries her special blessing on its head. Nadine listened carefully to this man, her child, her son. The son who had not cried when the doctor slapped him at birth. The son that had been given up for dead. The son who had miraculously started breathing on his own to the amazement of everyone involved. The son that her God had spared for her, and in that sparing, had placed on her head, the burden of caring for that which should not have been. And this mother had borne that burden proudly and willingly. This mother who had tiptoed into his room for years to check him in sleep. This mother who had rocked him through his tears, who had cradled him through his illnesses, real and imagined. This mother who knew more about him than he knew about himself. This mother listened quietly now, as he spoke.

"You see, Mom. I'm really tied up here. Now I want you to know that I'm going to try to make it to the station this afternoon, but if I can't . . ." This mother listened and understood perfectly.

"I mean I may be here all night. When these guys screw something up they really—"

"Buddy," Nadine interrupted, "I understand." He continued to make his point.

"Yeah, Mom, it's pretty hectic here . . ." Nadine listened to the faint sound of her grandchildren playing in the background.

"Buddy," she said softly, "it's all right. Stop it. Don't do this to yourself."

The man now knew what it was the mother understood, and the guilt swelled in him.

"Mom, I want to . . . I just can't. I'm sorry, Mom . . . I just can't."

"Buddy, listen to me. It's all right. Do you hear me? I understand."

"Mom . . . I just can't watch you leave like that. I just can't do it."

"Buddy, it's better this way. Believe me."

"Help me, Mom . . . Please help me." The man was sobbing now, and the mother felt the weight of her old burden creeping up on her shoulders. Once again she reached out to her child, rocking him gently with her voice.

"Listen to me, Buddy, I know you love me. I know you do. You don't have to come. I understand, and I love you."

"But Mom . . . I—"

"Stop holding on, Buddy. Let me go. You have your wife and children. Let me go." The mother's voice floated to him through the wires, stroking him, strengthening him, but the pain in her words coiled themselves around her heart and she felt herself getting weak.

"Buddy, I'm going to hang up now, but I want you to know that I understand. Don't blame yourself."

"Mom . . . Please don't."

"I'm hanging up now." The man's voice came quietly and desperately through the phone.

"Mom, I love you."

"I know, baby, I know."

Nadine placed the phone on its hook. She struggled back to the table and sat down. She put her head back and closed her eyes tightly and while the tears flowed, her mind raced, frantically wrapping the memory of this phone call in layers and layers of thin tissue paper. The room was quiet and still. The only sound was the tiny click of a lock inside her head.

Joyce L. Dukes
(1954–   )

Dukes, a native of Memphis, Tennessee, is an instructor of African-American literature at the College of New Rochelle and an English teacher at the City University of New York. A founding member of New Renaissance Writers Guild, she is currently working on a novel, *One Note of a Whole Song*.

How Many Miles to Bethlehem?

Early morning dew sparkled under the Tennessee sun. Things were fresh and cool instead of hot. The narrow gravel road Zoe lived on displayed its florid neatness of boxed homes and clearly defined yards with pride. Glistening green hedges lined the golden strip, trimmed low in the front to reveal red, yellow and blue porches. There were five homes on Yellow Road with four brown dirt driveways evenly dividing the green bushes and colored porches. It was a one-way street, past four houses it ended in the front yard of the fifth.

The street was quiet now. Zoe was the only one awake. It wasn't yet 6 A.M. Most of the grownups were at work and the others, left to mind the business of the family, lay still, enjoying their moments of rest. Those old enough to pick cotton had gone on the early truck to the fields. The younger ones slept, waiting in childish dreams for the sounds and smells of breakfast to wake them.

Zoe was up and dressed in her short blue overalls and pink T-shirt and sneakers, eager to take part in another summer morning. She crawled out of the bedroom window, jumped to the ground, landing on her feet and hands in the backyard. Her thick, tight braids slapped her cheeks sharply when she landed. She startled Che-Che, the rooster who was visiting from next door.

"Morning," she whispered. "Thanks for waking me, Che-Che." She tried to pet him but the rooster scrambled away in clucking confusion. "See you later," she waved her goodby and walked across the wet grass to the hedges where she crawled through a small opening between the bush and ground. Zoe stood on the yellow gravel road brushing moist chunks of dirt from her knees only a moment before beginning the now familiar journey to visit her friend Marassa.

186

The street beamed bright to her, totally unlike the darkness of the night before. At night, when the porch lights were out, you had to know the road because you could not see it. Needing no sight at all, Zoe could run across it night or day—she could almost fly. Now Zoe strutted up the glimmering sunlit path and finally broke free of the trees that hid her domain entirely. Yellow Road led her to another path connecting her small world with Marassa's more expansive neighborhood. She strolled peg-legged fashion down the gray pebbled trail, bordered on one side by tall trees on a high bank and the other by a sidewalk with grass sidings next to a concrete curb and telephone poles. With one foot on the curb and the other deep in the grass, Zoe watched the morning damp grass brush her leg like so many wet kisses. A wide black tarred street stood at the end of the trail. She turned left there where high brick walls sided the road and there were no sights to be seen. Zoe's spindly legs pumped up the steep hill away from the sun. She hiked the shadowed pavement that looked like water to her and felt her damp leg cool.

While climbing the hill past the brick walls, Zoe silently amused herself with her favorite game. It brightened the path to her destination. She felt the voices of the other children ringing in her ears and envisioned them as they played; holding hands with ten others in an arc across the grass. Zoe at one end, Luther and Lisa at the other with their fingers locked atop raised arms forming a temple to be entered.

"How many miles to Bethlehem," she hollered to the other children.

"Three scores and ten," they answered loudly.

"May I get there by Cadillac?" she questioned.

"No, not without your beau and bend."

"Well, baby," she replied blushing, "here's my beau," she motioned towards an imaginary person by her unoccupied side, "and here's my bend." Here, Zoe placed her free hand on her hip, and yelled while charging across the yard, "So open that gate and let me and Marassa in!" Lisa and Luther opened the gate and Zoe swiftly led the others through the temple to Bethlehem.

It didn't matter to them that they didn't know who Marassa was because by now, they all felt they knew Zoe's friend. She always said Marassa, and they always let her through. If you tried to get through the gate without naming your beau, or by calling the name of your sister or brother, Zoe knew only too well, they would not let you through.

Zoe smiled at her memories as she moved swiftly and silently past the brick walls at the top of the hill. She stopped to catch her breath and take in the view from the top. The wide street before her was revealed in shadows. As the hill leveled off and tree trunks became visible, Zoe saw her friend, Marassa, standing as faithfully ceramic as always. Beyond the trees, houses peeped out as vast as their manicured lawns. There were no porches in this pale, forbidden world, just long walkways that led to large iron doors with gold knobs, and windows as dark and wide as the tarred road she walked. In this still and different world was her friend who seemed part of her street but lived inexplicably here on this shaded street, his alabaster smile so loudly out of place in the still morning. This street, Zoe thought, had a different rhythm from her own yellow road. This place with its winding walkways, dark windows, brick walls, bird baths and small white steel lace furniture, had a piercing quiet that always seemed to soothe Zoe's own exuberant nature. She had been friends with Marassa for as long as she could remember. He was always there—no matter her early hour, inviting her into his quiet world. As she grew closer to him, she began to sing his name, the name she gave him. "Marassa Midnight, Marassa Midnight," she sang with a smile in her voice. Zoe had dreamed of him last night, of seeing him and talking to him in the shade of this hot day. She had dreamed of Bethlehem and Cadillacs, and the security of a world she only half understood. Now she was here to share her precious memories with Marassa. She could see him fully, standing on the edge of the wet green lawn wearing the same alabaster black pants, white shirt and blue vest, and a red cap, eyes bright and white teeth glowing. Drops of early morning wetness glittered on his face. As always, he motioned her forward.

"Marassa," she whispered, tipping into the yard. "How many miles to Bethlehem?" Zoe leaped a giant step directly in front of him. She giggled openly and circled Marassa playfully, running faster and faster around him until she fell to her knees puffing with laughter. She regained her breath, stood in front of him, and continued her visit. "Marassa, how many miles to Bethlehem?" Again, she paused for the answer. "Don't you know, Marassa?" She leaned closer to his face, having to bend only a little to touch his black nose with hers, peering into his forever unblinking eyes.

"Marassa, don't you know?" She took a seat on the grass in front of him, folded her legs, and rested her elfish brown face in her palms.

"I bet you know how many milk bottles are left each morning on your doorstep, huh, and when the paper boy comes." The thought of seeing the paper boy excited her.

"I've never seen him, Marassa, no matter how early I get here the paper is always there. Is he black like us, Marassa?" Zoe noticed squirrels playing on the lawn near by. "Look, Marassa, look!" She whispered, but not soft enough, the squirrels scrambled away. She watched them playing at the other end of the lawn.

"Marassa, how come I never see nobody playing in these yards? All this grass and trees, how come aint no skates and bicycles laying around? Don't these people have any children, Marassa?" She looked around—searching lawns and driveways. "Oh," she sighed, "I bet they do quiet things, huh?

"Like what, Marassa? I seen them a coupla times—sitting at their tables with the curtains back, having meals, but I don't ever see them having fun. Maybe they got a playhouse somewhere in the back where they go to have fun, huh, Marassa? Are they your friends, Marassa?" She looked at him, puzzled. "I'm your friend, right, Marassa??"

Zoe stood up, shyly shoving her hands into her overall pockets, twisting her sneakers into the wet grass. "It's too bad you can't be with us when we be having fun on my street, Marassa. Everybody on Yellow Road be hanging out together. All the big children and everybody." Her almond shaped eyes widened, "Mr. Timbo got a garden with everything in it—watermelons, a grapevine . . . everything." She paused to look at Mr. Timbo's garden in her memory, then resumed her monologue. "But anyway, we play school and dance in the front yard all night. Aint no grass in Mr. Timbo's yard cause he always over there in it—but the other yards got grass and hedges and little porches that everybody sit on and talk.

"Sometimes they tell us stories and make us so scared. Mr. Timbo and 'em got strawberries and plums too, Marassa. We build a fire in the yard and make us some juice from the berries—and at night, we drink our juice and dance, dance, dance—all around the fire so the smoke can keep the mosquitoes away from us." Zoe snapped her fingers to a familiar beat for a second. Then, "Do mosquitoes get you at night, Marassa?" Her voice softened as she began to reveal a secret to him. She stood still and close, looking at her damp square sneakers as she spoke. "At night, Marassa, at night, when the stars come out and I see one falling, I make a wish." She acted out her words and closed her eyes real tight. She crossed her fingers and whispered to Marassa, "Star light, star bright, I wish I may, I wish I might, have this wish I wish tonight." Her eyes opened as she regained her balance and continued. "And then, Marassa, then I wish I was with you. I wish you and me had a great big yard like this one and we could run and play all over it." She circled him with outstretched arms in a flying motion. "And have so much fun, Marassa." Zoe stopped behind Marassa and leaned her head on his small stone shoulder. "Then," she said, "then, I wish we had a little house to sleep in with all the things a big house has, but this one would be just for us, Marassa, me and you."

Zoe shifted in front of him, not as dizzy as before, and cupped his small black fingers and added, "I wish you could stay on my street, Marassa.

"In the day time mostly it's just the little kids like us. We have fun, though. We find bottles, sell 'em and have a Kool-Aid party with cookies and stuff. Sometimes we have a parade. We practice all day—and then in the evening, before it get dark, we have a parade while everybody be sitting on the porch after dinner.

"The big children like us, and the old folks too." Her voice lowered. "You like it here, Marassa? Sometimes I do," Zoe confided. "But . . . it make me feel . . ." She stopped—at a loss for words. Her voice dropped instinctively to a whisper as she added, "You like it here . . . with all these white folks, Marassa?"

Zoe ignored her unanswered question and continued, "I like to come and talk to you, Marassa . . . cause, sometime, Marassa, over here, on this street, round all these trees and no sounds, white sidewalks, slick black road and no sun . . . you just see windows and things that don't move." Her eyes fixed on him. "Sometimes the papers don't even move—cause I see 'em stacked in the driveways just as still."

Zoe didn't move as she went on in her early morning whispery voice. "Sometime this still place take me somewhere else, somewhere I think I like to be sometime. I don't know, Marassa . . . it's here, like me and you . . .

but . . .'' She searched his face for words. Finding none, she looked away into the shadows as she fingered his shiny black buttons and said nothing. The unbroken silence listened as she felt what she wanted to say. Birds chirped, trees rustled, Marassa was faithful to his silence. She slapped at a bug flying too near his face. ''You want to come to our street, Marassa?'' She squatted in her original spot in front of him. ''It's just different!'' she finally explained. Zoe pecked softly at the wet drops of dew on Marassa's shoes. ''If you want to stand in the yard or on the porch, you can—and you'll be able to see the whole street. And everybody will be there . . . most of the time.

''We got a horse too, Marassa. Well—he really a mule name Mike. He Mr. Tot's horse and he let us ride him. We can ride two at a time, Marassa. Oh, Marassa, you could ride him.

''Oh, Marassa!'' Zoe grabbed his arm and pulled herself to her knees. ''You'd be perfect to ride Mike. You'd look so good—with your little red cap and all. We could have another parade to welcome you to our street.'' She jumped from the ground prancing in a circle, making up a tune for the occasion. She felt Marassa's pleasure and it made her lift her thin legs higher and higher. Zoe marched in ecstasy for them both.

On the quiet street, a car appeared. But it did not disturb Zoe in her parade making. Not until the sharp swift splash of white eggs attracted Marassa's smile. Eggs came three at a time, clinging to the surface of their target. Yellow yolks slid slowly down Marassa's red cap, black face and blue vest. They kept coming. The shells lay on the grass, they splattered Zoe's bare legs. She was still—arrested in her marching position—as the smell of raw eggs filled her nostrils while her vision blurred on yellow globs sliding down Marassa's still figure.

The car skidded away quickly but not before Zoe spied a familiar black face. She darted across the white eggshelled lawn to the middle of the tarred street. She fled the shaded silence back to her own sunlit road. She had no thoughts except astonishment, and the need to be home and safe.

At home, the bedroom was empty. She didn't bother to wipe the crusted egg whites from her legs, but removed her shoes and got under the covers, closed her eyes and prayed for Marassa and prayed for sleep. It came. It came and kept her until she felt the warmth of evening nudge her sleep. The voices of her parents in the kitchen were her first awareness. The house smelled like dinner. Lawnmowing sounds crept under closed windows.

''You see them folks got their yard egged this morning, Lena?'' That was her father's voice.

''Nah, Zephrine, what folks,'' Zoe heard her mother respond.

''Them white folks with the statue in the yard over on the west end of the street. Lord, they try so hard to pretend we aint sitting down here right next to 'em . . . but they can't quite do it. These kids aint gonna let them forget. They aint got no more plantations—even if they do still got their big white houses, aint no slaves in 'em. I remember when those yards weren't nothing but cotton fields and they all belonged to my daddy. We were the only black faces that stood on that land.'' His voice was full of pride remembered. ''Yeah, these kids done egged that slave statue they got propped up in the front of their house, guess they keep 'em there to hang on to their master feeling. Nine-to-five housekeepers aint enough.'' He sucked back his grin through his teeth. ''We ought to get us one, Lena. Paint 'im white and put him up at the top of the road.'' He laughed now, even more amused. ''Next thing these kids gonna do, is blow his head off. And then what the white folks gonna do with a headless slave???'' His muffled pleasure almost choked his laughter.

Zoe closed her eyes real tight and pulled the covers up over her head. ''Oh, Marassa! Marassa!'' Zoe cried under the covers. She bit back her unrecognized shame through trembling lips and prayed for sleep to take her and Marassa somewhere else. Perhaps to Bethlehem, she thought, where they could get there with a beau and bend. He would be her beau—and she placed her hands on her bend.

Doris Jean Austin

(1943–   )

Born in Mobile, Alabama, Austin received the DeWitt Wallace/Reader's
Digest Award for Literary Excellence in 1984. She is a member of the
New Renaissance Writers Guild and a former member of the Harlem
Writers Guild. Her articles have appeared in *Essence* and *The New York
Times Book Review*, and her first novel, *After the Garden*, was published
in 1987.

Heirs & Orphans

On the night before her parents were killed, long after she should have been
asleep, Rosalie Tompkins crouched behind her bedroom door and peeked and
listened to the last conversation she would hear between her father and his
only brother, her Uncle Cleophus. Listening behind doors and around corners
was her only other vice besides her capacity for remembering slights forever
and *"getting even."* This night she listened to a conversation, punctuated by
the dull thump of her daddy's earthenware moonshine jug being set down on
the table, picked up, set down again.

"Ain't selling this land to nobody and nothing." Thump.

*Cleophus picked up the jug and took another swig. "Gonna be trouble. For
that kinda money, somebody sure nough mean business. You thought about
that?" Thump.*

*"Thought about it. Don't care bout no trouble. Ain't selling and that's all
to it. Land belong to Rosalie and Moses after we gone." Thump.*

*"We may be gone a whole lot quicker than you thinking bout. Old Sumpter
already sold off his place. We ain't even got no more neighbors to speak of.
And what about that big old place they putting up so fast up on the ridge?
It's looking smack down on us. Ain't nothing in back-a the place but them
rocks leading over to the swamp. What they building can't grow no place but
right down here. Run us right over. Who you s'pose building up over us? You
sure you know what we doing?" Thump.*

*"You the college man, Cleo, you oughta be figgering better'n you doing.
Sumpter never was nothing but some poor white trash. Anything he got for
that old run down dust bowl put him ahead. You right though. We may have*

to sell 'em a piece. Sell whoever it is a piece-a land so they don't feel cramped 'tween here and the swamp. Not a big piece. Just a li'l good will piece. No more'n that. Why'nt you gwan out front and look at what we got and then come back here and tell me you wanna to give it away.''

Amos picked up the jug and turned it up over his shoulder, he shook it over the table to show it was empty. Both men got up and tiptoed over to the door and out front. Rosalie guessed they were going for her uncle to look at the land they weren't going to sell, or to get another bottle of her daddy's corn liquor. He kept some cooling off in the well sometime.

Rosalie went back and climbed into her narrow bed on her side of the room, careful not to wake her cousin Moses sleeping on the other. Whatever it was all about, Rosalie would always remember how proud she was that her daddy wasn't selling their land. She didn't care *that* much about living on some pavement up north. She scooted down under the cover facing the window, watching the moon and fell fast asleep.

Ever since Rosalie could remember she had loved the feeling that came to her just before daybreak—the feeling of being the only one awake in the whole state of Alabama, maybe in all these United States of America, and at the height of her dreaming, Rosalie pretended she was the only one awake in the whole world. That's how it was in the pre-dawn of the day that would reshape all her possible futures into question marks, that Rosalie lay in bed under her open window, her whole room full of country silence until she heard the first sounds of birds waking, one joining the other until their tentative notes cradled the house and echoed softly in the nearby woods. Soon, she knew, would come the iron sounds of the men laying new tracks, salvaging the old Union-ravaged rails of southern railroads that would reconnect the "New South" her Uncle Cleophus was always telling her daddy about. Tracks were being re-shaped and laid in Georgia and Louisiana to come on down and meet in Alabama so everybody could go any and every which way. They'd all ride to Selma on a train one day soon, he said. But on these mornings when the iron rang out over the land, the south would be waking up, not only the neighboring south, but all the grown folks in her own family as well. And Rosalie wanted to get away to the woods before they woke up.

Lightning flashed over by the smokehouse, behind her mama's clothesline and the wind brought the shadow of a flapping quilt across her window. It gave her a nice, lonesome feeling watching that quilt weave and bob toward her, just like maybe it wanted to come in and lay across her on the bed, she thought. The wind loosened some pecans from the tree that leaned over the room Rosalie shared with Moses. The nuts clattered singularly down the roof and fell silently to the ground. "Shhhh," she whispered, hoping they wouldn't wake anyone else in the house. She raised up on her elbows and breathed deep. Rain coming. She had smelled it when she first woke up. Unable to resist, Rosalie got up, shook Moses awake and handed him his overalls and shirt off the nail over his bed. With stealth and shushings they dressed by fading moon and starlight, and Rosalie sneaked herself and Moses outside real quiet-like, helped Moses climb over the fence that made so much noise when you forced open the gate, and headed for her own private place. It was several miles through the woods, across an open pasture bounded on the right by a patch of watermelons, on the left by a field of corn, almost up to the cave near the stream where her daddy kept his still. That's where she and Moses would go if God sent more rain than Rosalie was comfortably prepared to meet. They arrived at her lookout point before the sun or the rain.

She waited. The coolness from the earth rose soothingly under her pinafore where she hunkered down between vines connecting watermelons as big as her body. The green mint smell of earth and morning was damp around her. Rosalie watched the last few stars fade and the sky go ash gray with sunrise. An unexpected breeze caught the hem of her skirt to expose what were surely the whitest cotton drawers in Monroe County, Alabama. Her skin was full black, tinged with blue and smooth all over. She shone. Her eyes were fixed on the bank of clouds on the horizon. Suddenly, she broke into a dazzling grin. Her thoughts were hushed. *Oh, here it come!*

"Moses, you wake up now! Here it come!" She spoke over her shoulder in a loud hoarse whisper.

The vines rustled behind her as Moses sat up knuckling his eyes open, blinking at the wash of sunlight glancing off the melons around him. His red shirt startled the green morning. Rosalie reached back impatiently for his hand and pulled him up.

It came, driving the snuff-colored dust before it. Laughing, they ran, spindly legs pumping faster and faster, to meet the rain.

Moses was the first to turn as the cloud swept overhead leaving them thoroughly soaked and breathless. He looked back the way they had come so early, earlier than even the grown folks got up. In the distance he saw what appeared to be another sunrise but Moses was too young to question such a remarkable event as a second sunrise. Instead, his mind turned homeward. They had come too far from breakfast for his comfort. Moses wanted to go back to the house and *"smell some sausage cooking,"* he'd confided as he mumble-trotted behind his cousin. He couldn't see no *"damned advantage"* (he quoted his daddy) *"to tipping round before day, sneaking out the house while everybody else still sleep to come all this way."* His soft drawl was tentative in deference to Rosalie's eleven years. Moses was five. *"We done missed breakfast, you reckon?"* he asked the hand that held his.

Rosalie cast a look upon her young cousin that said as clear as day, *"Oh ye of little faith."* She switched her hips as best she could, lifting her knees high like she had to back through the vines and over to the closest plump melon. She bent to raise high a wrinkled croker sack toward Moses. It gave off a wet straw smell. "Moses, I'm gonna cook us up some breakfast right outchere in these woods. You just watch and see if I don't." She patted the pocket of her pinafore where a fistful of forbidden matches rested. She knew she would get the switch if her mama counted and missed the five matches she took from the box in the kitchen. She'd taken them one at a time all last week.

"You know how to cook?" Moses said in real quiet, like he knew he was treading on dangerous ground. And sure enough, she turned on him something fierce.

"Whatchu mean, kin I cook?" The hand that held the sack went to her hip and the sack bobbed up and down, punctuating her words. *"Whatchu mean?"* she repeated, like he better not mean what she thought he meant.

"Course I kin cook by myself! All I got to do is make me a fire and cook it up. I got a pot and everything."

"Breakfast in that sack?" His genuine concern made the risk an honorable one.

"Sure nough. I got some ham and yams, and some biscuits from last night and . . ." Rosalie went silent with her inventory. The air rang loudly with hammers and iron. Back at the house, their folks were up.

This seemed to be Moses' talking year, he never stopped. He followed Rosalie from sun up to bedtime with questions about chickens and eggs and sunrise and sunset and, *"How Daddy and Uncle Amos know when it be time for dinner?"* he wondered as Rosalie hurried them along with the midday meal down to the field where Amos and Cleophus worked shoulder to shoulder. *"Roe, how this pecan get all the way inside this shell?"* As Rosalie answered each question firmly and approximately, Moses grew quiet. Something about this new sunrise registered wrongness to the boy as he gazed back toward the house, perplexed.

"Roe, look over yonder. Ain't that the sun coming up behind them clouds back there?" He pointed to the left, over the woods they'd come through, then whirled around to face the sun he and Rosalie had been running toward. He stopped in confusion, his arm still in the air. But before he could continue his questions, Rosalie spun around, delicately lifting the wet hem of her skirt away from her body. She stared in surprise. The sky was dark with hundreds of birds, their screeching rode the morning air. Beneath the birds, it did look like the sun was blazing orange through the blackest clouds she'd ever seen. In the west.

Rosalie didn't say a word to Moses—just sped away in the direction they'd come. She instinctively increased her speed to investigate Moses' western sunrise. Her heart hammered a faltering beat in her throat as she sniffed suspicious thoughts from air that confirmed her fear. Moses followed, disgruntled by a speed his shorter legs could never match. When he fell trying to keep up, Rosalie left him there on the damp ground crying and alarmed. She stumbled and fell. She rose emptyhanded and was off again, eyes still on the smoke that spiralled steadily upward in the distance. Mud dried on her hands and arms as she ran. The front of her dress clung wet and muddy against her body. Her bare feet slowed as they slapped the ground with faltering hope when she could no longer see the flames peeping at her through the trees, but still she ran. When she arrived at the edge of the woods near her house, she collapsed, having only that much strength left. Shortly, Moses arrived and plopped himself beside her. They stared into the clearing, speechless.

Rosalie lay on her stomach breathing hard. She hadn't the wind or the courage to scream. A protective silence descended over her like the cover you

pulled up over your head when you had a bad dream. To the left of her vision
a man was leading Turnip to her mama's chinaberry tree just outside the front
yard. The gravid mare danced skittishly as the man tied her and tried to pat
her quiet. Vaguely, Rosalie remembered that Turnip's foal was to be hers.
She already had a name for her pony: Dumpling. She watched the man as he
moved across her vision to the right toward a skinny string of a man who
strutted about—nervously in charge. The gate lay inside the yard. The porch
leaned in on its two sides toward the smoldering rubble and even from here
she could smell kerosene. The sun was all white dry heat to her eyes from
the shelter of the woods where she and Moses lay hidden. Each scene melted
silently into the next like a picture book her mama gave her once—when you
flipped through the book real fast, the characters moved faster. Rosalie watched
the rapidly shifting scenes before her and she could feel the red dust in her
face as the men stamped around. There were four of them, four white men
casually performing on her daddy's land. As she watched, sound returned in
an indecipherable wave—like a single note hurled from an entire band. *"Possum,"* she heard one of them say, *"wasn't some children . . ."* His voice
faded. Shimmering waves of August heat blurred the scenes before her forever
in her memory. She tried and could not imagine that the charred sticks and
smoldering tar collapsed in the middle of their new porch was once her house.
Somewhere deep in the cavern of her soul, a scream was born. She had begun
to deny that the rubble before her contained not only her own mama and
daddy, but Moses' as well. She fought back the fiery images and replaced
them with nothing. Just sat, emptyminded, watching. Moses lay on his stomach
beside Rosalie, sniffling, snot-nosed, wild-eyed black baby boy. He squinched
his eyes as tight as he could against the house burned to the ground—and the
end of the world. He whimpered for his mama, having made only a vague
connection between the fire and her absence. Forever gone was not within his
power to envision. When he cried out again, Rosalie clamped her hand over
his mouth. Sweat ran from her forehead into her eyes and became tears. Her
head was cocked to one side listening. Suddenly, she jerked around, looking
for . . . but no one was there. The men were in the barn now. She heard the
chickens squawking their protest. She heard . . . She jerked her head around
again, sure this time, she'd heard her daddy's voice. *Was he hiding out in
these woods, too? Was he trying to whisper something to her?* Rosalie wiped
tears or sweat from her face and concentrated. It seemed like her daddy was
saying for her to *"Just be still."* Just like that. Just like that time when she
cut her foot on an axe when she went out to get some kindling for her mama's
fire. "Just be still, sugar," he told her when she wanted to dance and run
with pain and fear of her own blood. "Just be still, baby. Daddy gonna take
care everything." Then he'd lifted her up light as you please and took her in
to her mama. Tennie was the one always stopped all the pain. Tennie, another
tenth Alabama child, moving around her kitchen with authority, smelling of
cinnamon and vanilla extract, stopping pain when it came to Amos and Rosalie
and visiting relatives, and even an old mangy dog once—just always stopping
the pain because it was her job. This hadn't been the first morning Tennie

Tompkins found an empty bed when she went to Rosalie's room. Hadn't been the first time she complained to Amos that Rosalie *"done sneaked her lil fast self out to them woods fore day again."* It hadn't been the first time Amos laughed her out of her fretting. *"Done took Moses again with her this time,"* Tennie laughed to Cleophus and EverJean. It hadn't been the first time . . .

Rosalie lay real quiet listening. *"Just be still,"* her daddy whispered—so she did. She put her arm around Moses and lay just as still as anything.

When the men finally left, leading Turnip and the other two horses from the land, closing two dusty wagon canvases on four pigs, sows and hogs: two of each; three cows; one calf, all the chickens and roosters and two wild turkeys her daddy'd been fattening up—when finally they had all left, Moses turned to Rosalie. She sat, eyes unblinking, staring at the yard. "Roe?" His voice was scared and tearstained. He shook her shoulder, "ROE!"

When Rosalie still could not or would not answer, Moses fell upon his cousin with all the fervor of his alarm.

"ROE!" His blows fell on her face and shoulders in fierce repetition. "ROE!"

Only when his arms grew tired did Moses fall exhausted into Rosalie's lap, the only solace he had left in the world.

"Roe?"

"Shhh."

"Roe?"

"Shhh."

She stood up slowly. She didn't cry. With a mind of their own, it seemed, her eyes blurred with tears. But she didn't cry. Again, she cocked her head. Listening. *"Run, baby. You run away from here."* And even though Rosalie wasn't sure if it was her father's voice or the ringing of the iron, she ran, dragging Moses behind her. Running and stumbling back through the woods. Wet leaves slapped her face and neck and she didn't notice the many scratches on her bare arms and legs. She felt but could not hear herself landing heavily, breaking through the dense undergrowth. Her ragged breathing danced awkwardly between each footfall that seemed to pursue them, and the busy remembering and trying not to in this terrible silence. Moses fell and she dropped beside him, scuttling them both off the path, burrowing deep into the underside of the moss-covered rock—a boulder really. The hole in the earth where they hid was just large enough for all of Moses and most of Rosalie. Her arms could not be pulled in all the way. From this shelter, Rosalie watched the path through eyes stretched to popping. She allowed no thought of her parents, no memory of her aunt and uncle, to mar her fearsome vigil. An hour later—or maybe it was five—Moses tugged unnecessarily at Rosalie's shoulder to signal her attention to the heavy footsteps approaching. She held his hand tightly, beyond knowing that he might have cried out. Without words, Rosalie's brain recognized and stored the image of the man who had tied Turnip to the chinaberry tree. He rounded the bend, obviously searching—although just as obviously, without diligence . . .

For us, Rosalie thought. *Oh Lord, he looking for us.* The deserted woods were unnaturally quiet, no birds called, the only sounds were the approaching footsteps. *"Oh Jesus, oh Jesus,"* Rosalie whispered to her own scared self, sounding just like her mama for the world. *"You gonna wear the Old Boy out directly, aintchu, Tennie?"* Amos would laugh his full-bellied girth past his wife, managing to brush up against her as he moved from one chore to the next. Rosalie turned sharply away from the picture of her mama and daddy and replaced her silent litany to Jesus with a whimpering, *"Oh Daddy . . . ,"* then was silent. Dragging loose dirt as fast as she could up around her and Moses, unaware that the small shovels of her fingers would be amateur sleuthing for a man like *Possum Crowder*, her eyes never wavered from the path. She could see him plain as day now. Possum's big red moon face glistened its usual heat in the cool quiet woods. Rosalie pushed her fist as hard against her chattering teeth as she could. Possum came, brandishing a long stick before him to the left and right. The stick cut through leaves a foot or so above and in front of the children's heads as he moved past. Rosalie eased her free hand from her mouth to press against her heart, sure when he stopped that he heard it drumming like thunder. But he only paused to pull a jug from inside his shirt and take a long swig before returning the bottle to his shirt and moving on. It seemed hours before he returned, moving faster this time, his search obviously over as far as he was concerned. Again, as it forever would it seemed, alcohol made its arbitrary contribution to history and helped the woods to hide the children.

Rosalie and Moses crouched, clenched still and silent, long after he left. They did not speak or look at each other. They squatted, stared straight ahead. Once Rosalie stood and tried to pull Moses up, but his trembling legs did not allow him to understand. She fell beside him. And although she forgot to breathe—convulsively, at long intervals—her body wrenched her forward in its demand for air, small seizures that threw her sideways against the moss-covered rock. Slowly, their postures thawed and they sprawled in relief. Moses lay on his back staring up at the ceiling of sun-peeking branches. Presently, he peed on himself. Rosalie watched his small crotch darken, watched the stain grow. Her eyes were bland with what might have been acceptance. Fitful sobs convulsed her slight frame but there were no more tears. Finally, she turned over and, using the rock for a pillow, released her body to almost-sleep, unseeing eyes wide open. In the back of her mind the picture of her daddy's cave grew, moved slowly forward as the air became chill with promise of more rain. Cried out and exhausted, Moses and Rosalie slept in the shelter of Alabama woods that indiscriminately sheltered heirs and orphans.

Bill Williams Forde
(1924–1991)

Bill Williams Forde was the author of *Requiem for a Black Capitalist* and a longtime member and leader of the Harlem Writers Guild. The following story, "Miss Julie," is excerpted from the manuscript of *Mama's Boy.*

Miss Julie

Miss Julie was not and had never been the Other Woman. Mama was the interloper. In all truth, my old man was still married to Miss Julie, though he was insanely in love with Mama, my young pretty light-skinned green-eyed Mama with whom he now shared a one room shack, along with me, Baby Sister, and my half-brother, James. Right in the middle of the Baptist church, during service, before I was old enough to pee straight, Miss Julie did her best to knock me out of Mama's arms. If Mama hadn't been possessed by one of her rare protective moods, I'd either fallen into the baptismal pool or upon the plank floor. She clutched her frightened and screaming child to her stingy breast, a child she considered dark and ugly, and that she'd never wanted in the first place, and I was saved to become a man . . .

Though I sat in the same church every Sunday with Miss Julie we never communicated. Each time she came close or I even saw her at a distance I cringed, fearing her. She might arrive as an usher in a starched white uniform pushing a collection plate into my face; she might be up there beyond the pulpit as a member of the choir singing joyously and righteously; she always accompanied the Reverend into the baptismal pool that was located in the front of the church to the left of the pulpit and assisted the pastor in ducking the heads of sinners into the deep blue sinister water. I dreaded the day when the Holy Ghost would grab me by the collar and propel me to the Mourner's Bench, where I would leap up and down, go into a convulsive frenzy, like other religious converts, and babble my incoherent love for Jesus and a hope He'd wash my black soul as white as snow, but only to end up in the fearfully deep baptismal pool with Miss Julie's cold and vengeful fingers gripping the back of my neck . . .

On a Sunday, during service, I simply had to pee, and bad. The Reverend's sermon droned on and on, about sinners and how the wicked rich would never get to heaven, and the Three Hebrew Children in the fiery furnace, and the parting of the Red Sea, and Daniel in the Lion's den, while a pink melancholy blue-eyed painting of Jesus nailed to the cross looked down from the ceiling, blood streaming down His cheeks. Colorful fans advertising the local funeral home pushed the scent of armpits and powders and hair pomade and cheap soaps and perfumes about the church; the choir, in their billowing black and white robes, waited to hop to their feet and sing.

Seated upon the hard wooden bench, my feet did a tap dance on the plank floor. Anything to quiet my screaming bladder. I recoiled at the idea of standing and excusing myself and gaining the aisle and walking what seemed like a million miles past the pulpit and baptismal pool and on out through the back door, the only route to the outhouse located at the back of the church. All eyes would turn around and regard me. Bastard boy! Oh, yes, the son of that green-eyed stuck up wench—who even thinks she's gotten too good to come to church! What an ugly stupid boy!

God, how could I stand up and walk through all of those watching eyes! But I had to do something. Scalding drips already teased my thighs. And soon I'd mess up my Sunday pants if I didn't do something—and Mama would kill me. A boy who possessed the unhealthy habit of groaning nightmarishly during the long Southern nights and drenching bed sheets; pissing, pissing, you filthy thing! Mama would shout, aiming her peach tree switch at my naked knees or rear-end or even my face, pissing in the bed and now pissing in church! Oh, how could she've birthed such an ugly stinking person like me! I could hear her say.

Next to me on the bench Baby Sister wore the beatific expression of an angel, and opened her mouth wide and firmly and joined in when the choir sprang to its feet and began singing, ''. . . moving up the King's Highway . . .'' Unlike me, she longed for the day when the Holy Ghost would seize her and the Reverend would personally take her hand and lead her into the blue holy pool. Down near the end of the bench, partly hidden behind a funeral fan, James snored softly.

My bladder hollered again and propelled me to my feet. I lowered embarrassed eyes and excused myself and hugged my stomach and gained the aisle and hobbled and skipped and almost ran toward the pulpit and past the pool. I fought the back door and managed to get it open and stumbled outside and down the steps into the cotton white sunshine. I sped around the pump and through the frolicking world of blue black birds and sparrows and whippoorwills and red birds and honey bees and multicolored butterflies and got to the toilet and snatched the door open and tumbled inside. The planks gleamed lyesoap clean but had been weakened by long years of use. In my haste to unbutton and limit the damage to my pants a plank ripped free and first my hand and then my foot tilted into the smelly yellow wormy stuff below. I was falling. I think I screamed.

Behind me, someone pulled the door open. In a glance I only saw blackness blocking out the sun. The Devil in me, in my heart, and the Devil at the door. Then I thought, no, not the Devil, exactly. Someone worse. Miss Julie.

In her billowing choir robe she loomed in the doorway. She stepped in. When she touched me I screamed again. Having failed in her attempt to drown me years ago in the baptismal pool, she'd now finish the job and thrust me into the toilet. I fought her touch, screaming.

"Hush," she said, and I was amazed to detect a certain gentleness in her tone. Instead of pushing me down into the awful stuff she began aiding me out of the predicament. She led me out into the sunshine.

"I saw you running out of the House of God," she said. "And the Savior told me something might be wrong."

I gaped at her. The underlying gentleness remained in her voice. She guided me to the pump and squatted and stuck my hand and feet under the water. I gazed at her soft brown face, her broad nose and full lips, a face that looked more like my own than Mama's did. I could smell her. Lavender water and moth balls and something else: aloneness. Over there in that big house in Bank's Addition, alone. She hates me, Mama was always saying. Hates me. The black bitch! Well, didn't Miss Julie hate me, too?

The world seemed abnormal. The tenderness of her touch belied everything I'd thought. She was round and slightly plump and a grayness tinged her thick hair. As she attempted to wash the front of my pants, she kept on talking, she hadn't ceased talking for a minute, but as if mostly talking to herself.

". . . I told yo daddy he ought to bring you over to the house so I could see you. Not at first I didn't . . . I couldn't at first. But the Lord moves in mysterious ways. He decided not to bless me with children. And so yo daddy went away and sinned. If I'd been blessed I'd had a son about your age, older. So when I started seeing you . . . coming and going in the church, or walking up there on top of the railroad tracks, where you could get hurt, or standing outside the General Store and hoping for a piece of chocolate candy or something, I told yo daddy again to bring you over to Bank's Addition . . . But I guess he was just too scared of what yo mama might say or do . . ."

I didn't say anything. What could I say? I just listened to my heart pounding and I kept smelling her and feeling the warm touch of her fingers.

"Hardly can you go back into the church looking a mess like this," she said. "How'd you like to come home with me and I'll finish cleaning you up better?"

"Yes m'am," I said at once. But then I thought: she could be pretending to like me, how could anyone like me but Papa and Baby Sister? She could be pretending only to get me over to that house in Bank's Addition where she'll still murder me.

But when she stood and took my hand I followed her and it was like walking in a dream.

Oh, I became a tyrant. Never having known true affection from an adult female before I demanded everything just short of Miss Julie's life. I pestered her until she bought chocolate covered cherries every day. I persisted until she allowed me to get up from the cot she'd prepared for me and I crawled into bed with her. I demanded that my hair be combed and that she remain right there beside me and give me a bath nearly every day, which I'd previously hated at Mama's rented house. I told her I wanted a bicycle for Christmas, if not a Model T Ford, and a white horse, a Shetland pony would do, and a cap pistol, and money to catch a bus and go on a trip to Memphis or Jackson, and maybe all the way to Chicago and New York. I was feverish with demands, but even when I saw she was inclined to acquiesce and humor me as much as she could, her gifts still didn't seem to be enough. How to fill this painful craving, this vacuum, etched so deeply within the heart? She wasn't Mama. Wasn't Mama. Wasn't Mama. But I had no inkling then of what I really wanted.

Oh, she truly loved me, Miss Julie did. Bloated with chocolate candy and fried chicken and candied yams and macaroni and cheese and collard greens, I curled up against her warm plump body in the middle of the night and she embraced me as if I was still a little child. At times, I thought she must be crazy. It simply didn't seem normal for a grown-up woman to love a boy child. But I could smell the depths of her satisfaction as she held me. I burrowed into her chest and belly. Her breast felt bloated with milk, her arms with joy. I wondered how she'd been able to endure these long lonely years before she saved me from drowning in the toilet?

The house was a magic place. Not as large as I had imagined, but two bedrooms and a kitchen and a gallery that wrapped nearly all the way around it. And a swing. A swing! And a deep backyard where she tended a garden and flocks of chickens. Farther, at the rear of the lot, sat the inevitable outside toilet—a state no one but the appointed Mayor and the Reverend and the school principal seemed to have overcome, when not considering Those People who lived in Merigo and Cleveland and the like. But I loved that house. Being there was better than escaping into the woods or hiding in the darkness under Mama's rented house or suddenly becoming a powerful black hawk and flying away toward the sunset forever.

One day, after we came out of the chicken coop, where I'd assisted Miss Julie in feeding the chickens and collecting eggs, I came down with a severe case of lice. I didn't know I was lousy until, scratching desperately, I bungled a task I normally performed at least once a week for Miss Julie. She squatted in the darkened bedroom while I was supposed to hold the old fashioned douche bag filled with warm and medicated water high in the air. She was always saying,

"Higher. Higher. Hold the bag higher! And be sure to keep yo eyes turned away."

I pushed the douche bag as high as I could, longing to look around and see what she was doing. She still wore her dress or nightgown. The other end of the rubbery contraption which squirted water disappeared under her clothes but I couldn't quite figure out its purpose. Then I began to fidget and scratch with my free hand. My neck was on fire, my scalp, my belly. Something was eating me alive.

"Higher!" she urged.

"I can't go any higher."

"Just a little higher."

And I heard the water guggling down the line and toward her. But I couldn't cease scratching and the bag kept tilting, and finally I dropped it to scratch.

"Naughty boy!"

"But . . . but . . . Miss Julie, something is eating me up!"

She got up reluctantly. Soon she discovered the lice and became alarmed. These things might bite until I went blind or I lost my hearing or something. Deadly was her fear that something would happen and I would be snatched away from her. Never had I been scrubbed and scrutinized and medicated and oiled with such thoroughness. And from then on she tied her sun bonnet about her face and covered her neck and arms and left nothing exposed but her eyes and went into the chicken coop alone and made it very clear I should stand outside and avoid danger.

I was disappointed Mama wasn't jealous and didn't seem to care if I disappeared for two or three days at a time or even for a whole week, staying over there with Miss Julie. One less mouth to feed! Already the Government's fires had begun springing up in the fields. And fewer trucks came to the Town's Square to pick up cotton pickers to be ferried out to the surrounding farms and what had once been the old plantations. Papa had lost his Model T Ford and the hard times began eating into his eyes.

In a sense, he was the main support of two households. When rich and prosperous, before the Depression, he threw out his chest and grinned proudly at being able to provide for both Mama and his legitimate wife, Miss Julie. Not that she needed much of anything: the house was almost paid for, and she sold chickens and eggs and vegetables from her garden and some early mornings she'd put on a cotton sack and take a truck with the other cotton pickers and go into the fields and do a day's work. The only thing she rejected was the idea of doing washing and ironing for the women who drove into town from Merigo and Cleveland looking for cheap help.

I remember just before the world started crashing to the ground how Papa arrived at the house in Bank's Addition, footsteps resounding on the gallery, whistling and smiling self-consciously and laden with fish and rabbits or possums and rice and self-rising flour and maybe a shawl or sunbonnet he'd gone all the way to Memphis or Jackson to purchase for Miss Julie. He bent down to brush her mouth with a kiss and she, warily, offered her cheek.

"I don't need this stuff. I don't want it," she said.

"Food's for the boy," he said.

That was different. If there was something for me she'd accept everything. They circled each other uneasily during his short stay.

"How you making out?"

"Fine. Fine. Can't complain."

"Folks buying yo vegetables and eggs?"

"Same as usual."

"Well, I suppose I'll get going."

"Little Willie, give yo daddy a hug," she said.

I hugged him uncertainly, enveloped in his strong tobacco smell and starched

white shirt. One part of me wanted him to stay and laugh and talk with Miss
Julie, but another part of me wanted him to leave. Didn't he belong to Mama?
And didn't Miss Julie belong to me?

The next visit he overwhelmed her with a surprise. He unpacked his gift
and it was a new shiny victrola and records by Ma Rainey and Bessie Smith,
tunes he and Miss Julie used to dance by years and years ago. Nostalgia
swooped over Miss Julie. She caressed the box and drew the records to her
bosom and laughed a little and started losing her head. When he bent down
she didn't turn her lips away. She played the records over and over. Oh, those
haunting voices, those at once raunchy and melancholy blues stole into my
very soul and swept me up into their happy madness. Papa grabbed her and I
thought the arms he flung around her plump waist should be mine. I leaped
after them, tugging at Miss Julie. I didn't know how to dance yet; like Mama
I hadn't mastered the rhythm that all Colored people seemed to have. Mama
was as stiff and aloof from music as an ironing board; I longed to get inside
the hearts of Bessie and Ma Rainey and join Papa and Miss Julie, and I
pestered them. In a tone both playful and sterner than I'd ever heard, Miss
Julie said, "Run outside and play for a while, Little Willie."

"I don't want to."

"Go swing, son," Papa said. "You know how much you like to swing."

"Nawsuh. I hate swinging."

"Go out there and sit in my car then," Papa persisted. "And a little later
I'm going to teach you how to drive this very day."

"I don't want to learn how to drive."

"Git boy!"

I left them with my mouth poked out. I went out onto the gallery. I glanced
at the swing and it seemed as if I'd really begun disliking it. But how could
I resist the Model T Ford? It sat parked just off the front porch under the
chinaberry tree. Black, sleek, powerful, maybe more powerful than a black
hawk, a tractor, and certainly a buggy, and could transport you anywhere. I
went down and got in. Messed around with the gadgets. I had watched Papa
driving but I still didn't know precisely what I was doing, and yet I got the
car cranked and the motor going and before I knew it I was sailing backwards
instead of forward. Terrified, I searched for the brake. Papa's precious vehicle!
One of the great loves of his life. The car kept on going, speeding backwards
across the dirt road, alarming neighbors. It wouldn't stop. I saw the ditch
rushing at the back wheels and then the Model T Ford crashed into it.

The railroad tracks and the narrow two-laned highway divided the small
town, like a part Mama sometimes combed into her yellow hair. I'd often
walk the rails, arms outstretched like an airplane, balancing myself atop the
shining blue steel. To each side of the tracks squatted the ditches, boasting a
finger of stale water that seeped in from the river and a lot of sewage, and
beyond, were perched a line of shacks and one-story houses and the church
and the General Store and a few two-story houses, one of them where the
appointed Mayor lived. Everything near the railroad smelled of burning tar

and singed grass and grasshoppers and butterflies and stale sewage. I'd walk the rails wondering where all the trains finally ended up, what existed out there in the world beyond the blue horizon.

When I wrecked the Model T Ford, I jumped out of the car and ran. Oh, Papa would break my neck! No matter if, unlike Mama, he'd never hit me, how could he ignore the wreck? Yes, I was his favorite child, even over and above his affection for Baby Sister. And during all those barren years with Miss Julie he must have longed for a son, someone with whom to share his accomplishments, his prosperity, and I imagine I came into his life like a miracle or something. But didn't he love that Model T Ford more than anything else in the world, including me? Neighbors had begun shouting. That dumb bastard boy tearing up the car! I ran to the railroad track and began walking. I was in such a hurry to escape Papa's wrath I did little balancing upon the rails and jumped from one cross tie to another. How could I go home and throw myself on the mercy of Mama? Pity you didn't break your stupid neck! she might say. And wouldn't ole mean and evil James poke fun at me? He disliked the car anyway; disliked Papa owning it and impressing Mama with it.

I passed the Baptist church which was also our elementary school and the General Store and the home of the appointed Mayor and kept on hopping toward the horizon. Where was I going? I hadn't the faintest idea. I knew I didn't dare go into Merigo or Cleveland and be caught there after sundown, unless I had a note from one of Them, or the Sheriff, or the Stationmaster, or the Manager of the General Store or one of the owners of the outlying plantations. I could leave the tracks and go hide in the woods or along the banks of the Mississippi River somewhere. But what would happen after night fell? Grizzly bears roamed the woods, and wildcats, and ghosts, and wolves, and rattlers and boa constrictors, and hobos, who'd recently begun jumping from the trains, intent on robbery and murder. I had nowhere to run to and yet I kept on running.

I was surprised to hear the horn of the Model T Ford out there on the highway. Papa was out there in the traffic, waving his arm wildly and honking vigorously at me, and yelling.

"Where you think you going, boy? Come down off them tracks!"

I was amazed the car was still running. So it wasn't damaged beyond repair, after all? I hesitated and then climbed down and jumped across the ditch. Papa got out of the car and stuck a rough hand around my shoulder and shook me lightly.

"I ain't going to beat you, boy. My fault anyway I didn't already learn you how to drive. Me and Miss Julie was just about worried to death you might have hurt yoself."

"Naw. Naw. I'm all right," I said, staring guiltily at the ground.

"Nothing but dented my fender," he said. "But one thing about a Model T, I can take a hammer myself and straighten that out in no time. You sure ain't no bones broken?"

"Nawsuh," I said. "I'm just fine." And I stood there basking in his warm

odor of fish and Bull Durham tobacco and starched white shirt and my chest
filled up with affection for him and I wanted to hug him real tight for not
being angry with me.

But I did nothing.

In our wealthier days Mama's rented house stood just across the road from
the town's doctor, a family of blue-eyed people whose talented son knew how
to build a fire and surround it by bricks and bake water that produced steam
which loudly popped corks from bottles and created a melody like the strum-
ming of a guitar. They rode around town in a brand-new Chevrolet and knew
intimately the appointed Mayor. Owners of one of the few homes built of red
bricks, I got the feeling the doctor and his wife didn't particularly approve of
Mama. But the amazing son, whom all the girls seemed crazy about, including
beautiful Catrina, oh, Catrina, often climbed the fence and came over to our
house and played with Baby Sister and me, especially with Baby Sister.

Mama possessed a huge backyard and a large garden plot and chickens that
were always underfoot. She seemed relatively happy in those days. A few
townspeople had begun visiting her. Occasionally I glimpsed one of her rare
smiles. Still, it was clear to me that she hungered to leave Mound Bayou, to
keep on going up North somewhere, and felt herself trapped by some vague
responsibility to Baby Sister and me. Sometimes it crossed my mind that she
just might pack up and walk out the door and we'd never see her again. Good
riddance? Assuming she'd take James, naturally. Then wouldn't Baby Sister
and me have our loving Papa all to ourselves? And I had Miss Julie. Whenever,
even in those good times, when the storm blew up inside her chest and Mama
slashed me with the peach tree switch, I passionately embraced the fantasy of
her vanishing forever. I knew I feared her but I couldn't yet admit to myself
that I also wanted to hate her. After all, wasn't she Mother . . .

Baby Sister loved to play with things, anything. Her big brown eyes shined
with curiosity. I think she already knew more about how to drive the Model
T Ford than I did. She followed the doctor's son around trying to figure out
how to make steam that sounded like guitars. She hung over my shoulder her
mouth agape as I stuffed worms into the mouths of the baby birds I'd climbed
a tree and captured. I loved those birds. Each day they waited for me to bring
them water and dig for worms and feed them. Baby Sister also loved those
birds, so much so she thought one Sunday to share a precious slice of her
chocolate cake with them.

Mama's rich cooking was too much for the baby blue jays. When we went
back to inspect the birds they were all dead. I stroked the poor things, my
heart hurt, and I was angry. But talk about weeping—Baby Sister broke down
and sobbed as if real people had died. It was a sad funeral. We dug the grave
and buried them as she wept. How could I stay angry? I could think of nothing
but how to mend my poor sister's broken heart.

We played with the chickens. One day the doctor's son and I stumbled upon
an idea—he did or I did, I don't remember which. Perhaps he did since he
was so inventive. We caught a hen and sat her upon my lap. I was sexually

aroused—and had been for days, perhaps for months. I had entered that strange phase when I dreamed obsessively of female mysteries. A fleeting glimpse of a Vaselined ankle or knee was sufficient to set me off on a baffling trail of aching and yearning.

The doctor's son and Baby Sister held the hen at the ready while the idea was for me to stick my Thing into whatever hole I could find. I jabbed desperately at the hen. It squawked and flapped its wings and tried to get away. They held on and I tried harder, pushing at the feathers and the hole where the eggs came from. Painful for the poor chicken, and it broke free and flew into the air and wobbled across the yard. The son of the doctor was reluctant to admit that it hadn't been a good idea, and was prepared to catch another hen. But my Thing felt sore and I didn't want to do it again, wondering how come the doctor's son didn't do it himself? He never did.

Baby Sister and me slept in the same bed which was located in the living room where the fireplace blazed against the cool nights. Mama and Papa occupied their own bedroom. And James slept in another small room on a cot.

We were in bed, Baby Sister and me, and Mama was sitting in one of the cane-bottomed chairs ringing the fireplace stitching a quilt and chatting with a neighbor.

". . . Ah Lord," she was saying. "New York City . . . ! I heartell, honeychild, all you got to do is stoop down and reach out and you liable to find you done picked up a ten dollar gold piece! And a Model T Ford ain't nothing. Folks up there driving around in Buicks and Packards. And some of them got chauffeurs! Ah, Lord."

"Well, I ain't got nothing nailed down here in Mound Bayou either," the neighbor said. "If I got on that Pee Vine Special and left tomorrow it wouldn't be too soon. What's so hot about a town where the poorest peckerwood can slip on a white sheet and come riding up the highway and scare every niggah out of his shadow? Imagine, girl, a klansman parading up there through Harlem. Them bad Negroes would whip out they blades and cut his throat!"

Then their voices faded and I worried that Mama's attention may have turned away from the conversation and toward Baby Sister and me. And I had every reason to worry.

Though pretending I was asleep, I knew the precise moment when Baby Sister grew restless. She couldn't get to sleep. She tossed and turned. Then she must've become conscious of the Thing. Lately, I was having trouble keeping it down. The covers had only to brush it lightly for it to rise up again. So I imagine Baby Sister began thinking about the Thing as simply something else to play with. And she grasped it and began doing just that. And it felt good. But how could I admit that I was awake? Wasn't this sinful? And wrong? I kept my eyes closed. Baby Sister decided not to leave it at that. If she could play with the Thing one way, perhaps another way would be better. Still under the covers she attempted to climb atop the Thing. I acquiesced as much as a sleeping person could, tilting the Thing so that it was a little more accessible. But, like with the hen, it wasn't easy to make it work. Baby Sister huffing and puffing and trembling the covers—no wonder Mama was alerted.

"What them children doing?" the neighbor wanted to know. "Good Lord . . ."
Mama leaped up, grabbing her peach tree switch, embarrassed before the neighbor.

"You dirty dog!" she shouted. "Don't pretend you're asleep! And you Miss Fast-Ass thing—I'll break the necks of both of you!" And she used that switch.

And, of course, that ended our sleeping together. Mama banned Baby Sister to the cot in the other room, and I again had James, who pissed in the bed nearly as often as I did, for a sleeping mate.

The rape took place under very strange circumstances. It was a Sunday. I had already endured Sunday-school and church. Then I was in a wagon pulled by two mules seated between Miss Julie and a driver whose face I can't recall. We left Mound Bayou and headed for the countryside. Soon pecan trees and oaks and pines and sycamores bordered the winding dirt road. The scent of magnolia and honeysuckle permeated the air. Sparrows, blue jays, red birds, black birds, white birds, mocking birds, honored us with their songs. Flocks of multicolored butterflies fluttered within hand reach. A friendly afternoon sun warmed our faces. The rhythmic trot of the mules to the driver's "git up, git up there now," trotting up the endlessly winding dirt road, was like a sort of music in itself. The wagon swayed gently, and each time we took an abrupt turn beneath the umbrella of trees, Miss Julie instinctively reached out and steadied me though I was in no danger of falling.

It was a long ride. Visiting some of Miss Julie's kinfolks and friends way back out there in the country. She wore her best Sunday outfit; white satin and starched underclothes and shoes with silver buckles. I was pleased to lean against her and smell the lavender water and moth balls. Sweat popped from the rumps of the trotting mules.

"Miz Julie! Oh, there's Miz Julie! Girl, it's been so long since we seen you last!"

A bunch of people rushed at us and ganged around the wagon helping us down and hugging Miss Julie and rubbing my head and staring at me curiously.

"Yes, indeed. Looks like you could've spit this boy out!"

"Sho favors you a heap."

"Why, thank y'all."

"We been hoping for three Sundays you might be coming. And so just in case you was on yo way we barbecued and kept cooking up a little something extra. Got plenty of barbecue left and snoots and greens and a sweet potato pudding and we made some ice cream and Ernest cooked some chitterlings, so I hope you won't be disappointed."

"Hush yo mouth. Girl, we didn't come here to eat. It's a blessing from the Lord merely to set eyes on y'all again."

"Come in! Come in! And this is . . ."

Introducing me; and names and faces to me. I forgot nearly everyone. I was hungry. Sweet potato pudding and ice cream! I could think of nothing I liked better.

I don't remember the name of the younger girl either. Nothing about that initial meeting save she was several years older than me, and was very black with big shy lonesome-looking eyes, and a sweet shy smile. She wore a white dress and a white silk ribbon in her short coarse hair. Evidently these people had not so long ago come from another church somewhere.

I remember the house as being something of a log cabin, but it was roomy and pleasant and soon a long table was laden with food and iced tea and punch for the children and punch for the grown-ups, spiked with moonshine.

I nearly ate myself to death, as they say. The conversation of the grown-ups swirled around the table, boring really, and I doubt if I listened to it. My distant cousin—she would've been my cousin if I had been Miss Julie's blood child—seemed bored also. Occasionally she glanced at me and smiled her shy lonesome smile.

I had drunk so much lemonade and punch I had to go to the toilet. An outhouse, naturally. Immediately Miss Julie stood up to take me out there. After all, this was wilderness country. Grizzly bears certainly out there. And wild cats. And alligators. And maybe even mountain lions.

"I'll take him to the toilet," my distant cousin volunteered.

"No, I better take him," Miss Julie insisted.

"Oh, he'll be all right, Sister Julie," one of our elders said. "Sit. Have a little more punch."

My tall cousin took my hand and we went out the back door. And across the yard and past the garden and the chicken coops. Rather menacingly, the thick world of trees loomed behind the toilet.

She unlatched the door. I thought she was supposed to stand outside and wait, but she didn't. Exhaling that strange lonesome shyness she stepped in with me. I could get my own Thing out myself, and was rather surprised at her helpfulness. Flushing, I turned my back a little and wee wee-ed. I could hear her breathing, smell the Vaseline in her hair. I meant to button up myself but she was helpful again. An intense loneliness emanated from her bent neck, as she watched what she was doing. Then she ceased buttoning before she'd finished, and her warm nervous fingers undid the buttons she'd done. I watched her watching me, numbed. I heard the rustling of her starched underclothes as she began lifting and pulling. Her breathing sounded like sobs. I waited, paralyzed, gazing in amazement at her lower belly, the black babylike hairs crawling between her legs. Now I could see what Miss Julie and Mama always kept hidden. She helped me atop the toilet seat and pushed her hips forth to catch my Thing. She'd closed her eyes and her pretty dark cheeks glowed with joy. I wasn't really sure whether I was inside her Thing or not. There was a lot of belly rubbing. Then she gasped and leaned forward and kissed me squarely on the mouth.

Of course, I was traumatized. For years I remembered the moment as so beautiful I went around tugging at the elbows of older girls, hoping one of them would decide to rape me again. But nothing happened. I'd be nearly fifteen years old before I'd experience again the strange and mysterious joy I lucked upon that Sunday afternoon.

*   *   *

That trip to the countryside was the last time I saw Miss Julie. The hard times had fallen over the country and Papa lost his Model T Ford and we lived in the one-room shack facing the highway and railroad track, until Papa caught a freight train and hoboed North, and was lucky to find a modest job in a factory and he sent for us. We piled our tacky belongings atop an old dilapidated moving truck and left Mound Bayou in the early morning hour, ahead of the rent collector and food bills we'd managed to run up, and from the rattling and speeding truck I could see Miss Julie's lonesome-looking house fading away in the distance.

One day I'll come back and see you, Miss Julie, I vowed. And I felt my throat filling up and tears in my eyes. The woman who'd most taught me about the possibility of being loved . . . But I never got back to see her, never got around to telling her that I loved her. And years later I heard that loneliness and aloneness or something else I couldn't fathom had eaten into her heart, and slowly she lost her mind and tilted into insanity. And soon died.

How can I look out there now into the vast blue universe and not miss her? I wish so much that I'd at least said goodbye. So having not said it then, I say it now: goodbye, goodbye, Miss Julie, and wherever you are I love you and miss you.

Sarah Wright
(1928–   )

A native of Wetipquin, Maryland, Wright studied at Howard University in the 1940s with such masterful writers as Sterling A. Brown and Owen Dodson. Before moving to New York and joining the Harlem Writers Guild, she lived in Philadelphia, where she assisted in founding the Philadelphia Writers Workshop. She has won the MacDowell Colony Fellowship for Creative Writing (1972 and 1973). Ms. Wright is the author of *Give Me a Child* (1955), a book written with Lucy Smith, and *This Child's Gonna Live*, which the *New York Times* chose as one of the most important books of 1969. The following excerpt is taken from *This Child's Gonna Live*.

---

from This Child's Gonna Live

CHAPTER ONE

Sometimes the sun will come in making a bright yellow day. But then again, sometimes it won't.

Mariah Upshur couldn't see herself waiting to know which way it was coming as she fretted to see through the sagging windows squeezed between her upstairs roofs. The bed with Jacob's legs sprawled all over her was a hard thing to stay put in.

Strain cut in her face in such a heavy way, she thought, "My skin must be sliced up with the wrinkles the same as an old black walnut." She touched it and found not a single line.

She had the same tight skin, the same turned-up nose that people used to say went with her "high-minded gallop" when she wasn't doing a thing but marking time on Tangierneck's slowing-up roads. Pyorrhea in the gums had taken all of her back teeth, but her jaws stayed firm and slanty—pretty as a picture of any white girl's she ever saw on those Christmas candy boxes that her mamma used to cut out and hang on the cedar tree and the walls. Little "star light, star bright" twinkling angels, that's what Mamma Effie always hung on that tree. And she told Mariah, "You got to be *that* good and pure before the Lord's gonna bless you with anything."

"But I got a different set of eyes in this night, Jesus. If you'll spare me, me and my children getting out of this Neck."

Such a chilliness crept over Mariah, and she cried all down in herself, for she couldn't wake her children. She'd been dosing them up all through the night with the paregoric so they could get some easement from their coughing.

"Done promised you me and the children getting out of here so many times, Jesus, you must think I'm crazy. But you ain't sent many pretty days this way lately."

With a start Mariah caught herself criticizing the Lord and said, "Excuse me, Jesus. I'm willing to do my part. Just make this a pretty day so I can haul myself out of this house and make me some money. Jesus, I thanks you for whatever you do give to me. I ain't meant to say nothing harsh to you. Jesus, you know I thanks you. I thanks you. I thanks you."

Then it felt to Mariah as if the comforts of the Lord's blessing spread all over her.

Soft sleep rested so lightly on her eyes, and she was home safe in a harbor warm, just a-rocking in the arms of Jesus. And the spirit of the Lamb became a mighty fire prevailing in the woman's eyes sunk now to dreaming, and she could just about see how this new day's sun was gonna come in.

It was gonna sail up blazing and red and hoe a steady path on up to the middle parts of the sky. Clouds get in the way? It was just gonna bust on through them and keep on sailing until it rolled on up easy over the crest of those worrisome waves.

Then it was gonna rock awhile—all unsteady like—until it made up its mind that it was on high and it hadn't sailed through anything but some feathery nuisances. Rock awhile and then turn all yellow and golden as it smiled at the cloud waves turned to nothing but some washed-out soapsuds foaming on the treetops of what Mariah liked to call this Maryland side of the long-tailed Dismal Swamp.

It was gonna sit there a long time grinning and spilling those fields full of itself, making every potato digger—leastwise herself—feel good down to the quick same as if it was summer still.

And she could dig a-many a potato on a day like this. Just scramble down those rows and flip potato after potato into those four-eight baskets. Dirt flying in her face? Well, honies, she wasn't even gonna mind. She'd eat that dirt and hustle on. She wouldn't even mind how the dirt got packed under whatever fingernails she had left—not even mind when the hurting from the dirt pressure made her shoulder blades cleave all up to themselves. She was just gonna suck her fingers every now and then—dirt and all—and keep on tearing down those rows. And when Bannie Upshire Dudley's hired man wrinkled his old pokey face in consternation from handing her "that many!" tokens for all those solid loaded baskets she got such a shortness of the breath from lugging up to the field shanty, and when he snickered to her, "Mariah, ain't you done stole some baskets from Martha from on Back-of-the-Creek?" she was gonna sic her big bad word doggies on him. Gonna sound worse than a starved-out bloodhound baying at the teasing smell of fresh-killed meat, ten thousand times worse than the menfolks do when they're away from the white-man bosses—all except that no-talking Jacob she was stuck with.

"Jam your dick up your turd hole, cracker, and bust from the hot air you bloated with. You believe every colored person that's getting a-hold of something's stealing. I believes in working for my money. Give me my money, man. I ain't no thief like the woman you working for. *That's* the thief!"

If he said half a word back to her she was gonna grab his squelched-down, corn-colored head and twist it to the east and the west and the north and the south so he could get a good look at all the scores of acres that used to be in Jacob's papa's hands. Didn't care if she rang it off like she'd do a chicken. "See, see you ass-licking poor white. See how Miss Bannie done glutted up our land. Now you want to talk about a thief, you talk about her. She knows most of the colored was renting land off of Pop Percy. She knowed it just as good as anything when she went and lent him all that money to get his affairs straightened out. Then she come charging him interest on top of interest with things as hard as they is. Knows we ain't able to pay it. And selling food for the hogs and things as high as mighty. She knows good and well we ain't got no way into Calvertown to buy it cheap since the steamboat stop running. I ain't like the rest of the niggers you and Miss Bannie got, saying your shit don't smell bad when you use them for a toilet. I ain't saying tiddely-toe and grinning when you fart in my face no more, when I know good and well that tiddely ain't got no toes and your fart don't smell like perfume."

Then she was gonna tell him where his old bleached-out papa come from and his weak-behinded mamma too, if she could stomach herself getting down that low. She was gonna stomp his ass good, buddies. Set it on fire. Gonna send him popping across those fields the same as if he was a never-ending firecracker. Wishing she had a razor on her like most white people thought colored carried, so she could catch up with him and cut his old woman-beating fists off and then slice out his dick so he wouldn't plug up that simple-minded Anna of his anymore with his corn-colored bastards to tease her little Skeeter and Rabbit about the way they looked. But she wasn't gonna waste any time dwelling on that, for the old fart-bloated cracker wasn't worth her getting a murder charge laid against her name. She was just gonna be glad she sent him running.

And then in the plain light of day—yes, yes, my God, on that pretty day! She was gonna reach up to that culling board where he had a habit of spreading out a pile of tokens to glisten in the sun so as to entice the colored people's eyes as they scrambled up those potato rows. Gonna scoop herself up a handful of tokens, just a-singing to the world. "No more short change for me, my Lordy. No more shitting on me and then telling me I smell bad 'cause you won't let me wash it off. No more! No more mocking my children when they come down to this field to help me out, calling the little naps on their heads 'gun bullets' and making them feel bad. No more!"

And all around here there was gonna be such a commotion. With people running up from the rows to the field shanty, crying, "Glory Hallelujah, Mariah done chased the money changers out of the temple." And black work-

ing hands looking so pretty next to those gold-colored tokens were just gonna
be scooping them up. But most and especially there was gonna be little old
hickory-nutty Aunt Saro Jane with all those little winning airs she put on even
though she must be going on a hundred, saying, "Mariah, now you know you
ought not to have done that white man that way. We colored in Tangierneck
have to depend on those people!"

"Look like they the ones been depending on us, Aunt Saro Jane. We built
up this Tangierneck and now they taking it away from us."

"Can't help that, Mariah. They got the money. They got the banks."

"But we doing the work for to make that money, Aunt Saro Jane."

That's the way Mariah was gonna talk back to her. Then she was gonna
stroll on off. No, she was gonna stomp on off, and run. Head thrown back
the same as if she were a wild mare filly. If anybody stopped her to ask where
she was going, she was gonna just holler back, "I'm on my way to the North.
Going to the city where me and my children can act in some kind of a dignified
way."

As she ran she wasn't gonna worry about a thing except maybe whether or
not she'd scooped up enough tokens to pay for Skeeter and them to get some
good clothes instead of having to wear those tow sacks she sewed into garments
for them, and some medicine for the colds in their chests and things like that.

She might give a thought or two to giving Jacob a little piece of the money
she'd have, for after all it was Jacob that put in all of that time last year
pulling out the crabgrass and the jimson weeds from around those potato plants.
He tended that field so good when those potatoes weren't anything but some
little old twigs and promises. My, how he sprinkled that nitrate of soda over
that low ground so as to give those little brown potato babies something worth
eating for to suck on. Spent a whole heap of time plowing that ground so it
would be soft and tender for those things to nestle down in and nurse until
they got good and fat and ready for the harvesttime. And now Miss Bannie
done claimed that field for herself, too.

She wasn't gonna take up too much time with Jacob though, for he wasn't
going one step to save his own life. And when she grabbed her children and
headed for the road going North, she wasn't even gonna look back at Jacob
standing in the yard telling her that her talk about the children needing this
and that for to grow on was nothing but a whole lot of "horse manure."

Even in that last minute, I mean buddies, in that very last minute, he
wouldn't have the spine to grow an inch taller on. He never could so much
as say the word "shit" when he meant it. He was just weak, weak, weak,
that's all there was to it—and always hiding behind the Lord. If the crops
failed, it was the Lord's will. If the children stayed sick with the colds, it was
the Lord's will. And she never was able to tell him anything, honies, about
those little corn-colored children of Bannie's field man calling Skeeter and
them out of their names when they came down to the fields to help her out.
All of that was the "Lord's will."

She used to say to him, "Jacob, everything ain't the Lord's will. Some of
these things happening is these Maryland type of white people's will. I don't

care how much they go to the church, they ain't living by the word of the Lord. They living by their greedy pocketbooks. They got a different set of white people in them cities up North. Your brothers done gone, Jacob. You the only one sticking to this land.''

In spite of the devil, Jacob would answer her with something like, "But they'll be back, Mariah. They ain't doing nothing up there in them cities but getting pushed around. Trying to do some fancy singing they got on them radios up there, but there ain't nothing to it. They don't own nothing, Mariah. Ain't a cent they got they can call their own. Paying off furniture on some time plans and all of that kind of foolishness. A man is his land. In other words, what he owns that he paid for outright. A man is his land.''

Then he'd quote from some old simple-assed poem he learned from his father:

> I am master over all I survey
> My rights there are none to dispute
> From the land all around to the sea
> I am Lord o'er fowl and brute

Said to him a-many a time, "My children ain't no fowl and brute. I wants my children to live. They human beings just like anybody else.'' But if he thought she was gonna stop and whine those words to him now, he had another thought coming, for she was running, honies, running. And it wouldn't be worthwhile for her to turn around and say one thing at all, for all he was gonna do was call her a nag.

Nag, shit, the woman panted in the dreams of morning. All I ever been trying to do was tell him something in an easy way of speaking, so as not to hurt his feelings. Just run now, that's all she was gonna do.

Littlest one of her children, Gezee, weighed heavy in her arms, and her stomach was so swolled up with the gas, his sleepy weight just caused her to ache so much.

"Skeeter, Rabbit, you all come along here! Skeeter, what you doing letting Rabbit drag you along? You the oldest. Don't be trying to hang back with your daddy. Skeeter, stop that coughing, child. We can't slow down for you to catch your breath. I got a heavy enough aching on me as it is.''

She couldn't let Skeeter's lagging and waving his arms back for his daddy to hold her up one bit as she went sailing over those sand dunes going down the hill past blabbermouth Tillie's house, past those distant-acting in-laws of her's high-and-mighty-looking house.

It's a long stretch of road when you're running with such a weight bearing down on you. Renting-people's little shanty houses stretch a good ten-minute run along that sandy road when you're in good shape. But Lord help you when you're heavy. Children linking themselves around Mariah's arms and legs felt just like chains in the running. They weighed heavy on her when she tried to run past her own mamma and papa's house. Slowed her down to a standstill, and she couldn't fight her way past her papa standing there in the road.

Papa was something to fight. The only man in Tangierneck who ever paid off his land entirely to Percy Upshur. He liked to broke his back doing it, but then Pop Harmon was a mighty man. If you measured him by inches he wasn't so tall. She'd give him five feet and seven inches, but she couldn't measure Pop Harmon by the inches. She had to measure him by the squall in his face and his shoulders all flung back. He was a deep mustard kind of yellow, but he called himself black. It wouldn't do for anything frail to be getting in his path. He'd just mow it down.

"You too high-minded, woman, too busy gazing for the stars to see the storm clouds right around us. Folks have to navigate their ways through the rough seas of life before they can set back and feast their eyes on the stars. You think you seeing some stars now that you're running up to them cities? Well, honies, I'm here to tell you you can't see no stars anywhere at any time with your naked eye in the time of a storm. It's the time of a storm all over for the colored man. They lynching colored men every day by the wholesale lot just south of this swamp, and up there in them cities, too. But in a different sort of way."

"But what about the colored *woman*?" Mariah tried to answer him back. "All I keep hearing is you all talking about the hard time a colored *man's* got."

"See my scars! See my scars! Colored woman's always been more privileged than the man. You ain't got no hard time in this community." He roared against her terrible screaming of "Papa, let me go!"

But his powerful shoulders pushed her back, flail out against them all she pleased. He almost knocked her down in the shifting sand. She came back at him like a foaming-mouthed terrier. But nothing came out of her mouth except a moan.

"Don't talk to me about the colored woman, gal, until you see my scars." In a split second he was naked, standing in a blazing sun. Bleeding all over his back. "See my scars, woman, see my scars!"

And all Mariah could see to him was his scars. Even as naked as he was, she couldn't make out a thing else about him except his scars.

"White men up there to Baltimore Harbor liked to beat my ass off when I landed in this 'land of the free.' They said to me, 'Horace, you come here all the way from Barbados hid down in the hold of our ship. You ain't paid a cent for the passage. You ain't worked for us, you ain't done nothing. Now what you gonna do, you little monkey?' I says to 'em, 'Monkey your God-damned self. Let me go!' Now heifer, I want you to know they let me go 'cause I went into them for the kill. See my scars. . . ."

Last shades of night hung on for Mariah, and deeper into sleep she sank. The dream kept coming: her papa pushing her down in the sand, in the choking sand while he called up to that little squeezy house she was born and reared in for her mamma, Effie, to come to the road.

"Effie, Effie, this gal of yours is getting out of control. Bring your switch out here and beat this gal, Effie. Whip her ass good!"

Mamma Effie always was a good beating-stick for Papa. He did the talking but Mamma did the beating. Her whole body was like a whipping switch, thin and lean and crackling. Her great dark eyes were always filled with lightning, and most of the time she never said a word to her children except something like, "I'll beat the living daylights out of you if you don't listen to your papa."

There was but one of those children left now, and that was Mariah. Mariah tossing under the quilts Mamma Effie made for the times of her giving birth. Mariah heavy with a sleep that wouldn't let her go. Mariah groaning in her sleep from the beating. A switch can draw blood, but getting beat up with a stove-lid lifter can make a person cry for her own death. Those things are made of iron. A beating on your back and legs with one will make a person's soul cave in.

As her mamma beat her, her papa talked on.

"Stop that running, gal. You ain't getting past me. You can't run your way through the brambles and the bushes of life. You got to chop down those vines and creepers first before you go headlong through them. Old rattlers are coiled up in them. Pretty flowers on them vines is just there to entice you out of your senses. Rattler's going to sink his fangs in you on this road.

"All of this talk about you going away to the cities to make something of yourself don't mean a thing 'cause you still don't see nothing but the flowers on the bushes. Ain't a decent woman *enough* for you to be? You'd better pray for God to send us a pretty day tomorrow so we can get out of here and pull some holly out of this swamp. We got to pay off this land."

Mariah couldn't wiggle out of her papa's hands. He had some big, strong hands. Just holding her. "Effie, beat her, beat her. Beat her ass good. Make her work. A child is the servant of the parent."

A violent wrenching of herself got Mariah free to hobble, broken, on up that road. Saying to her papa, "I ain't no more child, Papa. What you all holding me up for? You ain't suppose to be talking to me like when I was a child. I got my own children." Moaning, "Come on, Rabbit. Come on, Skeeter. Help me to carry Gezee. . . ."

Mamma Effie tore after her, hollering, "Come back here, slut! Look a-here, here comes Jacob bringing that little near-white affliction you done bore to him. If you gonna leave, take 'em all. The thing ain't Jacob's. Why you leave that burden on him?"

"I ain't got no other child, Mamma! Why you always trying to accuse me of something!"

With a jolting start Mariah sat up in the bed. She cried, "Jesus!"

Her eyes groped in the darkness for something to hold on to. A bit of light from the kerosene lamp she kept in the hallway helped her out some. The woman prayed, "Jesus, it ain't dawn yet."

The little attic type of a room took shape. Little by little the chest of drawers with the blue paint peeling off it, and the wallpaper gone limp and nipplely from the damp and the winds easing their ways in between the boards of her upstairs roof sank into her head. She thought she heard Jacob mumbling from under the quilts, "Woman, go on back to sleep." And maybe she did, but she couldn't be quite for sure, for his legs were such heavy weights on her. He must be sound asleep.

She inched herself toward the edge of the bed as much as Jacob's warmed-up, pinning-down feet would let her. A fearful sickness rolled through every inch of her lumpish body. She tried to get free, but every time she tried to move, the way Jacob had of throwing himself any which a-way in the bed so he got the quilt tangled up and locking her in wouldn't let her.

Teeth wiggled in her gums so bad they hurt. Gritting her teeth too much. Gums hurt her. Head was just a-pounding, but she couldn't feel a thing else. Just her gums aching and the pounding in her head.

She hissed into the night that looked like it was never gonna go away, "Move!"

But Jacob did not move.

Outside in the nearly-about-morning world, the wind growled and hawked and spit the same as if it had a throat. Wind wasn't doing a thing except messing up everything in God's creation, spitting in the face of hopes for a pretty day, moaning nothing but more of what Tangierneck mostly was these days—a place of standing still and death.

"Death!" Mariah could hardly say the word, for it seemed the thing was creeping its way into her soul-case. She had seen a naked man in her dream!

"No, he wasn't naked! He wasn't naked, God Jesus! I ain't seen it, have I?"

A stillness came over her. Jaws became solid frozen. Her elbows cracked as she let her hands go trembling over the mound rising up from her middle parts. She could hardly ease her body down to wait for the coming of dawn. A shudder started in her shoulders—locked her neck to the pillow.

"Why, the child hadn't moved in a good while! Dreams are a sign. . . . Oh my God, my God, I done killed it! It can't be dead!" She drummed on the skin stretched tight on her belly. Tried to sound out life, but no matter which combination of taps she drummed, life wouldn't sound back. "Must be lazy this morning. Bet you's a girl. Girls is lazy." Terror scalded her eyes. The dream flooded over her—the running into her papa naked, and Mama Effie's accusation.

"Jacob's your daddy, honey. I talked it over with Jesus. Know he wouldn't lead me wrong." She pleaded softly to the unborn child, but the child didn't make a single move.

A loathsome sickness wormed in her throat. Shame for everything washed all over her. The cussing and the anger of her dream. Maybe if she prayed to God to wash her sinful dream away the child would move!

She opened her mouth to scream, but no sound came. A whisper jerked its way out. "My child's all right, ain't it, Lord?"

"Woman, what in the name of God you doing, pulling all the covers off of me?" Jacob's voice came over the thundering in her skull.

Mariah let go of the covers. Didn't realize she was pulling them. There was nothing eviler and more contrary than Jacob if the cold air got to him when he was sleeping.

"Woman, lay on back down will you, or stay still or something unless there's something the matter with you?"

Mariah froze. Couldn't answer Jacob to save her life.

The man said no more.

Humble yourself to the Lord, Mariah. Apologize one more time. If she could only speak. If she could only run. Get on that speeding-up Route 391 and run. Wished she'd kept on running when she went to see that Dr. Grene. Run right past him. Gone on to the Calvertown Hospital clinic.

"Didn't believe they'd treat me right though, Lord. Thought it'd be easier to talk to that new colored doctor about my headache—tell him about the screaming that backed up in my head when Mary died . . . Jesus!" The woman cringed in startled panic.

"Jesus!" Her lips moved without a sound. She fixed her eyes on the little white lambs flocking around the white-robed figure on the Jamison Funeral Home calendar.

"You know that's over with, Jesus. You ain't gonna punish me no more. You ain't let me kill this young'un, has you?

"I know I ain't nothing but a woman filled with sins. But I cares for my children. Remember, you said to me, 'Now Mariah, you're on the side of life. You're a mother. Two sins don't make a right.' I know you had to talk to me right smart, Jesus, because I was scared. But you know how people do when they get scared. Do anything. But you snatched that other bottle of Febrilline out of my hands before I had a chance to pour it down my throat when my head was wobbling from that first bottle of quinine mess like it was fit to roll off in one of those oyster buckets. . . ."

Her head filled now, tighter than a skin drum full of water. "Let the child kick. Let the day come in nice. Spare the child, Lord, and I promise you, if I use every last bit of strength I got, we getting out of this place."

She closed her eyes, for a little voice far back in her head said, "Jesus is just testing you out, Mariah, Jesus just testing you out." And right along with the voice came a movement around her navel, soft as a little spring breeze.

She smiled to the Lord. "Gonna stop thinking about death. Ain't gonna cry no more."

Later in the dawn she cracked her eyes again, and a little light did come in. October sun comes so late. She dug her chapped knuckles into the deep, warm places her eyes made, and lifted her heavy lids.

She wondered sometimes how the sun ever made it at all coming from the easternmost part of God-knows-where down to low-laying Tangierneck. Lowest place on the whole Eastern Shore of Maryland, she did believe. Wonder was that it hadn't been washed away, the way that big, wide, bossy, ocean-going Nighaskin River keeps pouring water down into the mouth of the Neck until Deep Gut swallows all it can hold and backs the rest of it out for the ocean. Orange ball bouncing on the Nighaskin Sound, heaving and setting and hardly climbing up at all. Oyster boats tossing helplessly.

She balled her hands up until they hurt. "Jacob, I swamp it, Deep Gut's filled up with wind again. Spewing out ponds all over the fields. There's not gonna be a cent made today."

Every muscle swoll in her craning neck. She swallowed hard. Last night's terror left a nasty morning taste. "Nothing here, Jacob, but death. Nothing down here but nothing."

Jacob stirred. "Death coming sooner or later, woman. What you all the time harping on it for?"

"Children ain't had no milk in the longest kind of time. I ain't neither. I was thinking to myself I'd send Skeeter down to Bannie's to get us some. . . ."

Jacob flew right into her. "Don't send Skeeter nor nobody else down to Bannie's for nothing. I done told you once. I ain't gonna tell you no more. And another thing, woman, I don't want to catch you digging no more potatoes for Bannie."

"Tell me the Welfare people's giving out cans of Pet milk by the case full. . . ."

"Shut up, woman. I done told you now. I provides for my family."

Silence hung between them like the deep maroon drapes in Jimmy Jamison's funeral home parlor. She might have known he'd act like that. But there used to be a different kind of time, the woman thought. There used to be a time when she could really tackle Jacob. She'd tell him in a minute about picking up his own trash behind himself, or about throwing his money down on the table for her to keep them and the children halfway going like he was throwing a bone to a worrisome pet dog. He'd throw the money down and stroll on out of the house, not even saying as much as "Dog"—that was the least he could call her—"here's the money for this or that."

In one day and time she'd go in to Jacob like lightning with, "Man, why don't you change your drawers a little more often and wipe yourself good? Any dog gets tired sometimes of scrubbing out somebody else's shit from their drawers."

That kind of thing would set him on fire, but she'd go on. "Sparrow, they tell me that Uncle Marsh Harper's about the cleanest man on the oyster rocks. Tell me when he gets through doing his business, he wipes himself good with his glove, then leans over in the Gut and washes himself off and his glove."

"He's about the purest fool we got on the boats, woman!" Jacob would thunder back. "Fool's gonna catch the pneumonia first and last splashing that cold water on himself."

And Mariah, she used to play a little bit, too. "Did you say first in the ass, Jacob?"

Then he'd have to break down and laugh himself. But then he'd go on and give her a lecture about cussing and how sinful it was in the eyes of the Lord. But those times were all over with now. . . .

There was no sense in her mentioning the Welfare to him anymore, because he wasn't gonna answer. But somehow she couldn't help herself from wishing that they had some milk. How many times had she wished the milk in her breasts could flow by the gallon—enough for all of them to drink. She could almost see herself pulling Jacob's bony, hurtful-looking face to her breasts. . . . But she was leaving Tangierneck. Talked it over with God. Taking her children and leaving death. And she wanted to take Jacob, too.

"Death's so close to you now, Jacob, you can reach out and touch it."

But Jacob did not answer, nor move his reddish, tight-faced head one single inch. He just rubbed his teeth together over and over again, making a terrible grating sound.

"It's been a bad October, Rah. November's almost here. There's a time in the land."

Sounded almost like a cry. Mariah moved closer to him. Tears worked around in her eyes. "Stop gritting your teeth, Jacob. Stop it. You hear me. Don't, I'm gonna give you a dose of Bumpstead's Worm Syrup to work those worms out of you."

"Cut out the foolishness, Rah. Getting too near your time for you to be carrying on like that." Covers fell away from his bony shoulders and he sat bolt upright in the bed.

"My time, Jacob?" If she could only get the sight of him out of her eyes. "My time! And what you done about it?"

"Rah, I done told you. . . ."

"Don't want no Lettie Cartwright, nor no other midwife killing another child of mine. Mary would've been here today if she'd been born in the hospital. . . ."

Jacob didn't take his red, wind-eaten eyes off of her. Tired, beaten-looking eyes with a little bit of stubble for eyelashes jiggling on his sunken cheeks.

"May as well cut out the foolishness, Rah. We ain't got no hospital money, and we ain't getting on no Welfare."

He turned his back to her, mumbling from under the quilts where he buried his head, "You done took all the teas in the world, and some of that Dr. Grene's medicine, too. How come you always harping on death? You need to pray, Mariah. Have a good talk with God."

"You must think you the holiest thing out, Mr. Jacob. Let me tell you how I talked things over with God!"

But the man didn't move. "Rah, I'm going to want my breakfast now and in a few minutes" was all he raised the quilt to say.

"That's all you got to say. That's all you got to say?" Her heart pounded. She was gonna break down and holler at him in a minute.

But he didn't answer.

"Well, let me tell you something, Mr. Jacob. I got something to say."

And all the horror of the night just gone flooded out of her.

"Me and my children getting out of this death trap, Tangierneck, and you can stay here, buddies, 'cause we don't want you with us."

He threw back the quilts. Mariah tried to catch something that happened in her husband's face. It wasn't tight anymore. It fell all to pieces. And though her hands wanted to reach for him, she couldn't bring herself to touch him.

His lips hardly moved. "Cut out the foolishness, Rah."

She wanted to gather up the pieces. If only she could do something nice for him. Get up and fry some oyster fritters, open a can of corn—if she could put her hands on one—set his breakfast on the table, snappy and hot, with some milk to go along with it. Fool ought to know he needed milk. It would clear up the rattling in his chest, make him feel like singing. And she could call him Sparrow once more, for he really was a regular song sparrow before his mouth got clamped down with hunger and worriation. But there were no oysters, for wind had bossed the rocks for two whole days, and there was no corn—just a single can left for Sunday—and there was no milk.

The salt of tears burned through the chapped crust on her lips, and she turned her eyes from Jacob's twitching face. "Ain't nothing down here but nothing."

"Yes, it is too, Rah."

Looked as if his bony hand was going to make it across the quilt hills to touch her. "Why don't you tell it like it is, Mr. Jacob?"

She couldn't bear to look at his torn-up face. "Let go my legs, man!" She jerked herself free. "You'd stay down here until the year 2000 if you could live for seventy more. You gonna pay off the land, huh, Mr. Jacob? Gonna collect all the money that's due on your pappy's land. Pay off Miss Bannie. Gonna make the County give a schoolhouse to your children."

"Woman!"

But she couldn't stop. "And if this child dies, gonna be your fault! So sorry you were when the last one died, you gonna see to it this one comes here in the hospital. . . ."

"Woman!" He shoved a swollen-jointed finger up to her eyes. "Just lift one finger to take either one of my children out of Tangierneck, and I s'pect that'll be the last finger you'll ever lift. . . . And another thing, woman. Child dies, gonna be your fault for lifting and lugging them potato baskets. Told you to stay out of them fields. Never thought you wanted this young'un no way. Sometimes I get the feeling that if you had your way you'd a-killed it."

All over her it was cold. Nothing in her moved. But she stepped out of bed, snatched her hair free of its pins. "I'm going, Jacob." And the trembling-faced man said no more.

Her head was nothing but a throbbing hunk of mostly hair with a little bitty brown face screwed down under it. *Heavy head to tote in the morning, Lord. Heaviest head I ever had.* Almost had a mind to go downstairs and run a straightening comb through that mess of hair so it would flow long and wavy like Jacob used to say he liked it. "But I'm going, Lord."

For a moment she stared at the wall of her husband's back. Wanted to tell him so badly how sluggish the child was acting. *But it ain't his*, evil mind wanted to tell her. Nerves felt like they were about to give out on her. Jacob's back was a hunk of stone. She twisted her hair tightly into a bun again, pulling her face and mind and everything in her tight. "Done talked it over with the Lord," she muttered, and straightened herself on up.

She bounded down the steps, pulling the big, secondhand robe over her stiffened shoulders. Worried to craziness by the stillness, sniffling angrily at the morning mustiness of her body and the thought of the man. Hitting her soles on the bottom steps to stir up warmth, she announced to the early morning darkness of the kitchen, and the wind that crept in between the baseboards, and the wallboards and the places she'd chinked and chinked until she wasn't gonna chink no more, and the sounds of rats and mice gnawing in the molding: "I'm gonna make me a fire. Ought to burn down this place. . . ."

She rubbed her bare feet, one on top of the other, screwed them around on the cold linoleum. Kindling wood bent in her toughened hands, some so damp it would hardly splinter. She took the front lids off the big, black kitchen stove and filled it with wood. The oil that was left in the coal oil can wasn't enough, so she went back up the stairs and got the night lamp burning in the hallway. Blew the flame out and dumped all the kerosene in the oil chamber on to the soggy pinewood.

"Gonna make me a good fire!" And she struck a match. In the gray morning a flame shot up. Up the chimney roaring, out of the sides of the stove, through the cracks between the other stove lids, out of the bottom grating, shooting last night's ashes all over her feet.

There was an orange pain in her eyes and her arm was on fire and she almost cried "Jacob" but she didn't. She smothered her burning arm in the cavity between her breast and her belly, and with her free hand she crushed the last embers in the smoldering sleeve.

Such a kicking went on inside of her!

She stood still while her hands burnt and the lashes of her eyes fell down over her half-fried cheeks. She grinned real wide in the smoked-up morning light. Grinned real wide at the sounds of rats and mice a-gnawing in the molding.

"That's right, baby, kick. Kick all you want to." The bony ribs under her heart hurt. Hurt all the way through her heart and . . . "Kick, you contrary thing. Don't care if you kick my guts out. . . ."

She cried as she greased her face down with Vaseline. "That's right, baby, kick . . . thank the Lord, thank the Lord, thank the Lord." And the grease wouldn't stay around her smarting eyes, she cried so hard. "Jesus, God, and all your little angels, thank you, Lord." She choked up and swore in the light of the quieting-down flame. "Ain't gonna say no more to Jacob about it. Just make this a pretty day, Jesus, and I'll go out of this house and make the hospital money my ownself. Gonna get my children out of this Tangierneck.''

Her greasy lips pursed in determination as she went out to the cornhouse to slice off the last slab of fatback, not even wrapping herself up good from the wind.

PART TWO

POETRY

Spirituals and Blues:
Selections from *The Negro Caravan*

OF THE SPIRITUALS

With a few exceptions, most listeners would agree that the spirituals are quite special products of African-American sacred traditions. They are quintessential markers of historical stages in a people's poetic and musical evolution. Present at the creation, Frederick Douglass informed readers of his *Narrative* (1845) that these songs were expressions of "souls boiling over with the bitterest anguish." Six decades later, W.E.B. DuBois would suggest in *The Souls of Black Folk* (1903) that sorrow songs or spirituals testified to "a faith in the ultimate justice of things." For Douglass and DuBois, the spirituals were at once expressions of deepest hurt and profoundest hope. They are still such for students of African-American culture, whether we read versions in James Weldon Johnson's *Books of American Negro Spirituals* (1925 and 1926), or read *Black Song: The Forge and the Flame* (1972), John Lovell, Jr.'s magisterial study of how the spirituals were hammered out, or listen to folk and classical renderings. In African-American poetic tradition, the spirituals speak memory of the sacred world of slaves. They are touchstones of human excellence.

SPIRITUALS

(The following spirituals are derived from the *Book of American Negro Spirituals* by James Weldon Johnson and J. Rosamond Johnson, *Religious Folk-Songs of the American Negro* by R. Nathaniel Dett, *Slave Songs of the United States* by Allen, Ware, and Garrison, *American Folk Songs* by John Lomax and Alan Lomax, *Songs of Our Fathers* by Willis James, the repertory of the Golden Gate Quartette, and from the collections of the editors of *The Negro Caravan*.)

Sometimes I Feel Like a Motherless Child

Sometimes I feel like a motherless child,
Sometimes I feel like a motherless child,
Sometimes I feel like a motherless child,
A long ways from home;
A long ways from home.

Sometimes I feel like I'm almost gone,

Sometimes I feel like I'm almost gone,
Sometimes I feel like I'm almost gone,
A long ways from home;
A long ways from home.

Steal Away

Steal away, steal away, steal away to Jesus,
Steal away, steal away home,
I ain't got long to stay here.

My Lord, He calls me,
He calls me by the thunder,
The trumpet sounds within-a my soul,
I ain't got long to stay here.

Steal away, steal away, steal away to Jesus,
Steal away, steal away home,
I ain't got long to stay here.

Green trees a-bending,
Po' sinner stands a-trembling
The trumpet sounds within-a my soul,
I ain't got long to stay here.

Steal away, steal away, steal away to Jesus,
Steal away, steal away home,
I ain't got long to stay here.

Deep River

Deep river, my home is over Jordan,
Deep river, Lord; I want to cross over into camp ground.

O children, O, don't you want to go to that gospel feast,
That promised land, that land, where all is peace?

Deep river, my home is over Jordan,
Deep river, Lord; I want to cross over into camp ground.

I Been Rebuked and I Been Scorned

I been rebuked and I been scorned,
I been rebuked and I been scorned,
Chillun, I been rebuked and I been scorned,
I'se had a hard time, sho's you born.

Talk about me much as you please,
Talk about me much as you please,
Chillun, talk about me much as you please,
Gonna talk about you when I get on my knees.

Go Down, Moses

Go down, Moses,
Way down in Egyptland
Tell old Pharaoh
To let my people go.

When Israel was in Egyptland
Let my people go
Oppressed so hard they could not stand
Let my people go.

Go down, Moses,
Way down in Egyptland
Tell old Pharaoh
"Let my people go."

"Thus saith the Lord," bold Moses said,
"Let my people go;
If not I'll smite your first-born dead
Let my people go.

"No more shall they in bondage toil,
    Let my people go;
Let them come out with Egypt's spoil,
    Let my people go."

The Lord told Moses what to do
    Let my people go;
To lead the children of Israel through,
    Let my people go.

Go down, Moses,
    Way down in Egyptland,
Tell old Pharaoh,
    "Let my people go!"

Slavery Chain

Slavery chain done broke at last, broke at last, broke at last,
Slavery chain done broke at last,
Going to praise God till I die.

Way down in-a dat valley,
Praying on my knees;
Told God about my troubles,
And to help me ef-a He please.

I did tell him how I suffer,
In de dungeon and de chain,
And de days I went with head bowed down,
And my broken flesh and pain.

Slavery chain done broke at last, broke at last, broke at last,
Slavery chain done broke at last,
Going to praise God till I die.

I did know my Jesus heard me,
'Cause de spirit spoke to me,
And said, "Rise my child, your chillun,
And you too shall be free.

"I done 'p'int one mighty captain
For to marshal all my hosts,
And to bring my bleeding ones to me,
And not one shall be lost."

Slavery chain done broke at last, broke at last, broke at last,
Slavery chain done broke at last,
Going to praise God till I die.

No More Auction Block

No more auction block for me,
No more, no more,
No more auction block for me,
Many thousand gone.

No more peck of corn for me,
No more, no more,
No more peck of corn for me,
Many thousand gone.

No more pint of salt for me,
No more, no more,

No more pint of salt for me,
Many thousand gone.

No more driver's lash for me,
No more, no more,
No more driver's lash for me,
Many thousand gone.

Raised my hand, wiped de sweat off my head;
Cap'n got mad, Lord, shot my buddy dead.

Cap'n walkin' up an' down
Buddy layin' there dead, Lord,
On de burnin' ground.

If I'd a-had my weight in lime
I'd a-whup dat Cap'n till he went stone blind.

If you don't believe my buddy is dead,
Jus look at dat hole in my buddy's head.

Buzzard circlin' round de sky,
Knows dat Cap'n sure is bound to die.

BLUES

St. Louis Blues

I hate to see de evenin' sun go down
I hate to see de evenin' sun go down
Cause mah baby, he done lef' dis town

Feelin' tomorrow lak I feel today
Feelin' tomorrow lak I feel today
I'll pack mah trunk, an' make mah getaway

St. Louis woman wid her diamon' rings
Pulls dat man aroun' by her apron strings
'Twant for powder an' for store-bought hair
De man I love would not gone nowhere

Got de St. Louis blues, jes as blue as I can be
Dat man got a heart lak a rock cast in de sea
Or else he wouldn't have gone so far from me

Been to de gypsy to get mah fortune tol'
To de gypsy, done got mah fortune tol'
Cause I'm most wild 'bout mah jelly roll

Gypsy done tol' me, "Don't you wear no black"
Yes, she done tol' me, "Don't you wear no black.
Go to St. Louis, you can win him back"

Help me to Cairo; make St. Louis by mahself
Git to Cairo, find mah ol' frien', Jeff
Gwine to pin mahself close to his side
If I flag his train, I sho can ride

I loves dat man lak a schoolboy loves his pie
Lak a Kentucky Colonel loves his mint an' rye
I'll love mah baby till de day I die

You ought to see dat stovepipe brown o' mine
Lak he owns de Dimon' Joseph line
He'd make a cross-eyed 'oman go stone blind

Blacker than midnight, teeth lak flags of truce
Blackest man in de whole St. Louis
Blacker de berry, sweeter is de juice. . . .

A black headed gal make a freight train jump de track
Said, a black headed gal make a freight train jump de track
But a long tall gal makes a preacher "Ball de Jack"

Lawd, a blond headed woman makes a good man leave the town
I said, blond headed woman makes a good man leave the town
But a red headed woman make a boy slap his papa down. . . .

The Southern Blues

When I got up this mornin', I heah'd de ol' Southern whistle blow
When I got up this mornin', I heah'd de ol' Southern whistle blow
I was thinkin' 'bout my baby; Lawd, I sho did want to go

I was standin', lookin' an' listenin', watchin' de Southern cross de Dog
I was standin', lookin' an' listenin', watchin' de Southern cross de Dog
If my baby didn't catch dat Southern, she musta caught dat Yellow Dog

Down at de station, looked up on de board, waitin' fo' de conductor jes to
    say "all aboard"
Down at de station, Lawd, I looked up on de board
I don't know my baby left from here, oh, but I was told

I'm goin' to Moorhead, get me a job on de Southern Line
I'm goin' to Moorhead, get me a job on de Southern Line
So that I can make some money, jes to send fo' dat brown o' mine

De Southern cross de Dog at Moorhead, mama, Lawd, an' she keeps on throo

De Southern cross de Dog at Moorhead, mama, Lawd, an' she keeps on throo
I swear my baby's gone to Georgia, I believe I go to Georgia too

Backwater Blues

When it rain five days an' de skies turned dark as night
When it rain five days an' de skies turned dark as night
Then trouble taken place in the lowland that night

I woke up this mornin', can't even get outa mah do'
I woke up this mornin', can't even get outa mah do'
That's enough trouble to make a po' girl wonder where she wanta go

Then they rowed a little boat about five miles 'cross the pond
They rowed a little boat about five miles 'cross the pond
I packed all mah clothes, th'owed 'em in, an' they rowed me along

When it thunder an' a-lightnin', an' the wind begin to blow
When it thunder an' a-lightnin', an' the wind begin to blow
An' thousan' people ain' got no place to go

Then I went an' stood up on some high ol' lonesome hill
I went an' stood up on some high ol' lonesome hill
An' looked down on the house where I used to live

Backwater blues done cause me to pack mah things an' go
Backwater blues done cause me to pack mah things an' go
'Cause mah house fell down an' I cain' live there no mo'

O-o-o-oom, I cain' move no mo'
O-o-o-oom, I cain' move no mo'
There ain' no place fo' a po' ol' girl to go

Sterling A. Brown
(1901–1989)

A highly esteemed critic, poet, teacher, and essayist, Brown enjoyed a legendary reputation for his extensive knowledge of the blues and his insights about the centrality of folk culture in the creation of African-American literature. Born in Washington, D.C., Brown taught at Howard University for forty years (1929–1969). The studies he published in 1937, *The Negro in American Fiction* and *Negro Poetry and Drama*, are seminal in the development of African-American literary criticism. Henry Louis Gates, Jr., has drawn attention to Brown's influence on such students as Amiri Baraka, Kenneth Clark, and Ossie Davis, and on such poets as Leopold Senghor, Nicolas Guillen, and Michael S. Harper. Brown's first volume of poems, *Southern Road*, was published in 1932, but it was not until 1975 that another collection, *The Last Ride of Wild Bill*, came into print. The rejection of his second volume *No Hiding Place*, perhaps because of its political content, seems to have disheartened Brown, who then turned to the making of the landmark anthology *The Negro Caravan* (1941) with Arthur P. Davis and Ulysses Lee. The importance of Brown's masterful use of dialect, rhythm, and authentic images in his poetry began to be recognized in the 1970s. His *Collected Poems* (1980) won the Lenore Marshall Poetry Prize in 1982. The attention given to Brown's works by such scholars as Joanne Gabbin and Robert O'Meally suggests that Brown's legacy will not be forgotten. The following poems are from *Southern Road*.

Sister Lou

Honey
When de man
Calls out de las' train
You're gonna ride,
Tell him howdy.

Gather up yo' basket
An' yo' knittin' an' yo' things,
An' go on up an' visit
Wid frien' Jesus fo' a spell.

234

Show Marfa
How to make yo' greengrape jellies,
An' give po' Lazarus
A passel of them Golden Biscuits.

Scald some meal
Fo' some rightdown good spoonbread
Fo' li'l box-plunkin' David.

An' sit aroun'
An' tell them Hebrew Chillen
All yo' stories. . . .

Honey
Don't be feared of them pearly gates,
Don't go 'round to de back,
No mo' dataway
Not evah no mo'.

Let Michael tote yo' burden
An' yo' pocketbook an' evahthing
'Cept yo' Bible,
While Gabriel blows somp'n
Solemn but loudsome
On dat horn of his'n.

Honey
Go straight on to de Big House,
An' speak to yo' God
Widout no fear an' tremblin'.

Then sit down
An' pass de time of day awhile.

Give a good talkin' to
To yo' favorite 'postle Peter,
An' rub the po' head
Of mixed-up Judas,
An' joke awhile wid Jonah.

Then, when you gits de chance,
Always rememberin' yo' raisin',
Let 'em know youse tired
Jest a mite tired.

Jesus will find yo' bed fo' you
Won't no servant evah bother wid yo' room.
Jesus will lead you
To a room wid windows
Openin' on cherry trees an' plum trees

Bloomin' everlastin'.

An' dat will be yours
Fo' keeps.

Den take yo' time. . . .
Honey, take yo' bressed time.

Strong Men

The strong men keep coming on.
                    SANDBURG.

They dragged you from homeland,
They chained you in coffles,
They huddled you spoon-fashion in filthy hatches,
They sold you to give a few gentlemen ease.

They broke you in like oxen,
They scourged you,
They branded you,
They made your women breeders,
They swelled your numbers with bastards. . . .
They taught you the religion they disgraced.

You sang:
  Keep a-inchin' along
  Lak a po' inch worm. . . .

You sang:
  Bye and bye
  I'm gonna lay down dis heaby load. . . .

You sang:
  Walk togedder, chillen,
  Dontcha git weary. . . .
    The strong men keep a-comin' on
    The strong men git stronger.

They point with pride to the roads you built for them,
They ride in comfort over the rails you laid for them.
They put hammers in your hands
And said—Drive so much before sundown.

You sang:
  Ain't no hammah
  In dis lan',
  Strikes lak mine, bebby,
  Strikes lak mine.

They cooped you in their kitchens,
They penned you in their factories,
They gave you the jobs that they were too good for,
They tried to guarantee happiness to themselves
By shunting dirt and misery to you.

You sang:
  Me an' muh baby gonna shine, shine
  Me an' muh baby gonna shine.
      The strong men keep a-comin' on
      The strong men git stronger. . . .

They bought off some of your leaders
You stumbled, as blind men will . . .
They coaxed you, unwontedly soft-voiced. . . .
You followed a way.
Then laughed as usual.
They heard the laugh and wondered;
Uncomfortable;
Unadmitting a deeper terror. . . .
      The strong men keep a-comin' on
      Gittin' stronger. . . .

What, from the slums
Where they have hemmed you,
What, from the tiny huts
They could not keep from you—
What reaches them
Making them ill at ease, fearful?
Today they shout prohibition at you
"Thou shalt not this"
"Thou shalt not that"
"Reserved for whites only"
You laugh.

One thing they cannot prohibit—
      The strong men . . . coming on
      The strong men gittin' stronger.
      Strong men. . . .
      Stronger. . . .

James Weldon Johnson
(1871–1938)

James Weldon Johnson's position in black American history is special. As a poet, critic, anthologist, and novelist, he contributed significantly to the development of twentieth-century African-American literature. As a diplomat, lawyer, and executive secretary of the NAACP, Johnson left an indelible mark on sociopolitical history. Born in Jacksonville, Florida, he earned his A.B. and A.M. degrees at Atlanta University. In 1900, he wrote "Lift Every Voice and Sing," the poem that was adopted as the Negro National Anthem in the 1930s. While he was serving as U.S. consul to Nicaragua, he published his only novel *The Autobiography of an Ex-Colored Man* (1912) anonymously; the book did not become popular until it was reissued in 1927. Johnson's literary activity during his NAACP years (1916–1930) was substantial. He was awarded the Spingarn Medal in 1925 for distinguished achievement in writing, diplomacy, and public service. He published *Fifty Years and Other Poems* in 1917 and edited three books in quick succession: *The Book of American Negro Poetry* (1922), *The Book of American Negro Spirituals* (1925), and *The Second Book of Negro Spirituals* (1926). His second and third volumes of poetry were *God's Trombones: Seven Negro Sermons in Verse* (1927) and *Saint Peter Relates an Incident of the Resurrection Day* (1935). Johnson also wrote *Black Manhattan* (1930), an informal history of blacks in New York, an autobiography *Along This Way* (1933), and *Negro American: What Now?*, a thoughtful assessment of race relations. Johnson resigned from the NAACP in 1930 to accept a chair in creative literature and writing at Fisk University, a position he held until his death. The following poem is reprinted from *God's Trombones*.

Go Down Death—A Funeral Sermon

Weep not, weep not,
She is not dead;
She's resting in the bosom of Jesus.
Heart-broken husband—weep no more;
Grief-stricken son—weep no more;
Left-lonesome daughter—weep no more;
She's only just gone home.

Day before yesterday morning,

God was looking down from his great, high heaven,
Looking down on all his children,
And his eye fell on Sister Caroline,
Tossing on her bed of pain.
And God's big heart was touched with pity,
With the everlasting pity.

And God sat back on his throne,
And he commanded that tall, bright angel standing at
  his right hand:
Call me Death!
And that tall, bright angel cried in a voice
That broke like a clap of thunder:
Call Death!—Call Death!
And the echo sounded down the streets of heaven
Till it reached away back to that shadowy place,
Where Death waits with his pale, white horses.

And Death heard the summons,
And he leaped on his fastest horse,
Pale as a sheet in the moonlight.
Up the golden street Death galloped,
And the hoofs of his horse struck fire from the gold,
But they didn't make no sound.
Up Death rode to the Great White Throne,
And waited for God's command.

And God said: Go down, Death, go down,
Go down to Savannah, Georgia,
Down in Yamacraw,
And find Sister Caroline.
She's borne the burden and heat of the day,
She's labored long in my vineyard,
And she's tired—
She's weary—
Go down, Death, and bring her to me.

And Death didn't say a word,
But he loosed the reins on his pale, white horse,
And he clamped the spurs to his bloodless sides,
And out and down he rode,
Through heaven's pearly gates,
Past suns and moons and stars;
On Death rode,
And the foam from his horse was like a comet in the sky;
On Death rode,
Leaving the lightning's flash behind;
Straight on down he came.

While we were watching round her bed,
She turned her eyes and looked away,
She saw what we couldn't see;
She saw Old Death. She saw Old Death
Coming like a falling star.
But Death didn't frighten Sister Caroline;
He looked to her like a welcome friend.
And she whispered to us: I'm going home,
And she smiled and closed her eyes.

And Death took her up like a baby,
And she lay in his icy arms,
But she didn't feel no chill.
And Death began to ride again—
Up beyond the evening star,
Out beyond the morning star,
Into the glittering light of glory,
On to the Great White Throne.
And there he laid Sister Caroline
On the loving breast of Jesus.

And Jesus took his own hand and wiped away her tears,
And he smoothed the furrows from her face,
And the angels sang a little song,
And Jesus rocked her in his arms,
And kept a-saying: Take your rest,
Take your rest, take your rest.

Weep not—weep not,
She is not dead;
She's resting in the bosom of Jesus.

Bob Kaufman
(1925–1986)

When Kaufman's poetry receives the critical attention it deserves, he will be recognized as a major innovator in the Beat poetry movement of the 1950s and 1960s. Kaufman was one of the great oral poetry performers of the twentieth century. Many of his poems were never written and had to be transcribed from tapes of various readings. His work extended the jazz poetry experiments of Langston Hughes, and it influenced such poets as Allen Ginsberg, Amiri Baraka, and Ishmael Reed. Born in New Orleans of a Jewish father and a Catholic mother, Kaufman was strongly influenced by his parents' traditions as well as the voodoo lore of the Crescent City. He served in the U.S. Merchant Marine for twenty years before settling in California and becoming a leading figure in the San Francisco literary community. His published works include *Abomunist Manifesto*, *Does the Secret Mind Whisper?*, *Second April*, *Solitudes Crowded with Loneliness*, *Golden Sardine*, *Watch My Tracks*, and *The Ancient Rain: Poems 1956–1978*. The title poem from *The Ancient Rain* is reprinted here.

The Ancient Rain

At the illusion world that has come into existence of world that exists secretly, as meanwhile the humorous Nazis on television will not be as laughable, but be replaced by silent and blank TV screens. At this time, the dead nations of Europe and Asia shall cast up the corpses from the graveyards they have become. But today the Ancient Rain falls, from the far sky. It will be white like the rain that fell on the day Abraham Lincoln died. It shall be red rain like the rain that fell when George Washington abolished monarchy. It shall be blue rain like the rain that fell when John Fitzgerald Kennedy died.

They will see the bleached skeletons that they have become. By then, it shall be too late for them. All the symbols shall return to the realm of the symbolic and reality become the meaning again. In the meantime, masks of life continue to cover the landscape. Now on the landscape of the death earth, the Luftwaffe continues to fly into Volkswagens through the asphalt skies of death.

It shall be black rain like the rain that fell on the day Martin Luther King died. It shall be the Ancient Rain that fell on the day Franklin Delano Roosevelt died. It shall be the Ancient Rain that fell when Nathan Hale died. It shall be the brown rain that fell on the day Crispus Attucks died. It shall be the Ancient Rain that fell on July Fourth, 1776, when America became alive. In America, the Ancient Rain is beginning to fall again. The Ancient Rain falls from a distant secret sky. It shall fall here on America, which alone, remains alive, on this earth of death. The Ancient Rain is supreme and is aware of all things that have ever happened. The Ancient Rain shall be brilliant yellow as it was on the day Custer died. The Ancient Rain is the source of all things, the Ancient Rain knows all secrets, the Ancient Rain illuminates America. The Ancient Rain shall kill genocide.

The Ancient Rain shall bring death to those who love and feel only themselves. The Ancient Rain is all colors, all forms, all shapes, all sizes. The Ancient Rain is a mystery known only to itself. The Ancient Rain filled the seas. The Ancient Rain killed all the dinosaurs and left one dinosaur skeleton to remind the world that the Ancient Rain is falling again.

The Ancient Rain splits nations that have died in the Ancient Rain, nations so that they can see the culture of the living dead they have become, the Ancient Rain is falling on America now. It shall kill D. W. Griffith and the Ku Klux Klan; Hollywood shall die in the Ancient Rain. This nation was born in the Ancient Rain, July 4, 1776. The Ancient Rain shall cause the Continental Congress to be born again.

The Ancient Rain is perfection. The Ancient Rain cured the plague without medicine. The Ancient Rain is vindictive. The Ancient drops are volcanoes and in one moment destroyed Pompeii and brought Caesar down, and now Caesar is fallen. This Roman Empire is no more. The Ancient Rain falls silently and secretly. The Ancient Rain leaves mysteries that remain, and no man can solve. Easter Island is a lonely place.

The Ancient Rain wets people with truth and they expose themselves to the Ancient Rain. Egypt has a silent sphinx and pyramids made of death chambers so that Egypt remembers the day the Ancient Rain drowned it forever. The mummies no longer speak, but they remember the fury of the Ancient Rain. Their tombs have been sawed in pieces and moved to the graveyard to make way for the pool of Ancient Rain that has taken their place.

The Ancient Rain saw Washington standing at Appomattox and it fell on Lee as he laid down his sword. The Ancient Rain fell on the Confederacy and it was no more.

The Ancient Rain is falling again. The Ancient Rain is falling on waves of immigrants who fled their homelands to come to this home of Ancient Rain to be free of tyranny and hunger and injustice, and who now refuse to go to school with Crispus Attucks, the Ancient Rain knows they were starving in Europe. The Ancient Rain is falling. It is falling on the N.A.T.O. meetings. It is falling in Red Square. Will there be war or peace? The Ancient Rain knows, but does not say. I make speculations of my own, but I do not discuss them, because the Ancient Rain is falling.

The Ancient Rain is falling in the time of a war crisis, people of Europe profess to want peace, as they prepare day and night for war, with the exception of France and England. They are part of the N.A.T.O. alliance. I believe that Russia wants war. Russia supports any Communist nation to war with weapons and political stances on behalf of any Communist political move. This will eventually lead to war—a war that shall make World War Three, the largest war ever.

The Ancient Rain is falling all over America now. The music of the Ancient Rain is heard everywhere. The music is purely American, not European. It is the voice of the American Revolution. It shall play forever. The Ancient Rain is falling in Philadelphia. The bell is tolling. The South cannot hear it. The South hears the Ku Klux Klan, until the bell drowns them out. The Ancient Rain is falling.

The Ancient Rain does what it wants. It does not explain to anyone. The Ancient Rain fell on Hart Crane. He committed suicide in the Gulf of Mexico. Now the Washington Monument is bathed in the celestial lights of the Ancient Rain. The Ancient Rain is falling in America, and all the nations that gather on the East River to try to prevent a star prophecy of 37 million deaths in World War III. They cannot see the Ancient Rain, but live in it, hoping that it does not want war. They would be the victims . . . in Asia, the Orient, Europe, and in South America. The Ancient Rain will cause them to speak the languages they brought with them. The Ancient Rain did not see them in America when Crispus Attucks was falling before the British guns on the Boston Commons. The Ancient Rain is falling again from the place where the Ancient Rain lives. Alone. The Ancient Rain thinks of Crockett and falls on the Santa Ana Freeway and it becomes a smog source.

The Ancient Rain wets my face and I am freed from hatreds of me that disguise themselves with racist bouquets. The Ancient Rain has moved me to another world, where the people stand still and the streets moved me to destination. I look down on the Earth and see myself wandering in the Ancient Rain, ecstatic, aware that the death I feel around me is in the hands of the Ancient Rain and those who plan death for me and dreams are known to the Ancient Rain . . . silent, humming raindrops of the Ancient Rain.

The Ancient Rain is falling. The Washington
   Monument rumbles.
The Lincoln Memorial is surrounded by stars.
Mount Rushmore stares into every face.
The Continental Congress meets in the home of
   the Ancient Rain.
Nathan Hale stands immaculate at the entrance
   to the Capitol.

Crispus Attucks is taken to school by Thomas
   Jefferson.
Boston is quiet.
The Ancient Rain is falling.

The Ancient Rain is falling everywhere, in Hollywood, only Shirley Temple
understands the Ancient Rain and goes to Ghana, Africa, to be ambassador.
The Ancient Rain lights up Shirley Temple in the California sky. Meanwhile,
in Atlanta, the German U.N. delegation sits comfortably eating in a restaurant
that Negro soldiers can't get into, as of some deal between the Germans and
the Ku Klux Klan.

The Ancient Rain is falling on the restaurant. The Southern bloc cannot see
it.

The Ancient Rain is falling on the intellectuals of America. It illuminates
Lorca, the mystery of America shines in the Poet in New York. The Negroes
have gone home with Lorca to the heaven of the lady whose train overflows.
Heaven.

The Negroes have gone home to be enclosed by the skirts of their little girl
mother. Black angels roam the streets of the earth. Make no mistake, they are
angels, each angel is Abraham Lincoln, each angel is guarded by Ulysses S.
Grant. They are for the death of the Ku Klux Klan at Appomattox. The sword
of Lee is no more.

The Daughters of the Confederacy are having a luncheon at the Beverly Hills
Hotel in the Savoy room. They are not Daughters of the American Revolution.
They are not the Mothers of Crispus Attucks. They shall have Baked Alaska
for dessert. Their lunch is supervised by a Japanese steward, the French caterer
has provided them with special gray napkins.

The voice of Robert E. Lee cannot be heard over the rumbles of Grant's tomb.
They leave as they came, the Daughters of the Confederacy, each enclosed in
her own Appomattox. Back home they go to Cockalo. Crispus Attucks lying
dead on the Boston Commons is the burning of Atlanta by the Union Army.
John Brown was God's Angry Man. Crispus Attucks is the black angel of
America. Crispus Attucks died first for the American Revolution, on the opening day of American glory. Crispus Attucks does not want a white mother.
Crispus Attucks is the Blackstone of the American Revolution that is known
to God. Crispus Attucks is not the son of the South, not the son of Lee, not
the son of Jefferson Davis. The South cannot have Attucks for a son. Crispus
Attucks is my son, my father, my brother, I am Black.

Crispus Attucks will never fight for Russia. That cannot be said of the Rosen-
bergs or Alger Hiss or Whittaker Chambers. Crispus Attucks lives in heaven
with Nathan Hale. They go to the same school. They do not live in the South.

I see the death some cannot see, because I am a poet spread-eagled on this
bone of the world. A war is coming, in many forms. It shall take place. The

South must hear Lincoln at Gettysburg, the South shall be forced to admit that
we have endured. The black son of the American Revolution is not the son
of the South. Crispus Attucks' death does not make him the Black son of the
South. So be it. Let the voice out of the whirlwind speak:

> Federico García Lorca wrote:
> Black Man, Black Man, Black Man
> For the mole and the water jet
> Stay out of the cleft.
> Seek out the great sun
> Of the center.
> The great sun gliding
> over dryads
> The sun that undoes
> all the numbers,
> Yet never
> crossed over a
> dream.

The great sun gliding over dryads, the sun that undoes all the numbers, yet
crossed over a dream. At once I am there at the great sun, feeling the great
sun of the center. Hearing the Lorca music in the endless solitude of crackling
blueness. I could feel myself a little boy again in crackling blueness, wanting
to do what Lorca says in crackling blueness to kiss out my frenzy on bicycle
wheels and smash little squares in the flush of a soiled exultation. Federico
García Lorca sky, immaculate scoured sky, equaling only itself contained all the
distances that Lorca is, that he came from Spain of the Inquisition is no
surprise. His poem of solitude walking around Columbia. My first day in
crackling blueness, I walked off my ship and rode the subway to Manhattan
to visit Grant's tomb and I thought because Lorca said he would let his hair
grow long someday crackling blueness would cause my hair to grow long. I
decided to move deeper into crackling blueness. When Franco's civil guard
killed, from that moment on, I would move deeper in crackling blueness. I
kept my secrets. I observed those who read him who were not Negroes and
listened to all their misinterpretation of him. I thought of those who had been
around him, those that were not Negro and were not in crackling blueness,
those that couldn't see his wooden south wind, a tiltin' black slime that tacked
down all the boat wrecks, while Saturn delayed all the trains.

I remember the day I went into crackling blueness. His indescribable voice
saying Black Man, Black Man, for the mole and the water jet, stay out of the
cleft, seek out the great Sun of the Center.

Etheridge Knight
(1931–1991)

Born in Corinth, Mississippi, Knight perhaps will be best remembered for
his excellence in blending oral and literary poetic traditions as he tried to
create works that confronted personal and social dimensions with relentless honesty. Some critics praised him for his ability to render the genre
of the toast as high art. He began writing poetry in 1963 while he was
incarcerated at Indiana State Prison. His books include *Poems from Prison*,
Black Voices from Prison, *Belly Song and Other Poems*, *Born of a
Woman*, and *The Essential Etheridge Knight*. Knight received NEA grants
in 1972 and 1980 and won a Guggenheim Fellowship in 1974. His work
is included in such anthologies as *Dices and Black Bones*, *Norton Anthology of American Poets*, *New Black Voices*, and *Black Poets*. The following
poems are reprinted from *Born of a Woman*.

A Poem for Myself
(or Blues for a Mississippi Black Boy)

I was born in Mississippi;
I walked barefooted thru the mud.
Born black in Mississippi,
Walked barefooted thru the mud.
But, when I reached the age of twelve
I left that place for good.
Said my daddy chopped cotton
And he drank his liquor straight.
When I left that Sunday morning
He was leaning on the barnyard gate.
Left her standing in the yard
With the sun shining in her eyes.
And I headed North
As straight as the Wild Goose Flies,
I been to Detroit & Chicago
Been to New York city too.
I been to Detroit & Chicago
Been to New York city too.

Said I done strolled all those funky avenues
I'm still the same old black boy with the same old blues.
Going back to Mississippi
This time to stay for good
Going back to Mississippi
This time to stay for good—
Gonna be free in Mississippi
Or dead in the Mississippi mud.

Belly Song

(for the Daytop Family)

"You have made something
Out of the sea that blew
And rolled you on its salt bitter lips.
It nearly swallowed you.
But I hear
You are tough and harder to swallow than most . . ."
—S. Mansfield

1

And I and I / must admit
that the sea in you
   has sung / to the sea / in me
and I and I / must admit
that the sea in me
   has fallen / in love
   with the sea in you
because you have made something
out of the sea
   that nearly swallowed you

And this poem
This poem
This poem / I give / to you.
This poem is a song / I sing / I sing / to you
from the bottom
of the sea
   in my belly

This poem
This poem
This poem / is a song / about FEELINGS
about the Bone of feeling
about the Stone of feeling
   And the Feather of feeling

2
This poem
This poem
This poem / is /
a death / chant
and a grave / stone
and a prayer for the dead:
    for young Jackie Robinson.
a moving Blk / warrior who walked
among us
    with a wide / stride—and heavy heels
moving   moving   moving
thru the blood and mud and shit of Vietnam
moving   moving   moving
thru the blood and mud and dope of America
    for Jackie / who was /

a song
and a stone
and a Feather of feeling
    now dead
and / gone / in this month of love

This poem
This poem / is / a silver feather
and the sun-gold / glinting / green hills breathing
river flowing—for Sheryl and David—and
their first / kiss by the river—for Mark and Sue
and a Sunday walk on her grand / father's farm
for Sammy and Marion—love rhythms
for Michael and Jean—love rhythms
love / rhythms—love rhythms—and LIFE.

3
This poem
This poem
This poem
This poem / is / for ME—for me
and the days / that lay / in the back / of my mind
when the sea / rose up /
    to swallow me
and the streets I walked
    were lonely streets
    were stone / cold streets

This poem

This poem / is /
for me / and the nights
    when I
wrapped my feelings
    in a sheet of ice
and stared
at the stars
    thru iron bars
        and cried
in the middle of my eyes . . .

This poem
This poem
This poem / is / for me
    and my woman
    and the yesterdays
when she opened
    to me like a flower
but I fell on her
    like a stone
I fell on her like a stone . . .

4
And now—in my 40th year
    I have come here
to this House of Feelings
to this Singing Sea
and I and I / must admit
that the sea in me
    has fallen / in love
with the sea in you
because the sea
that now sings / in you
    is the same sea
that nearly swallowed you—
    and me too.

                                              Seymour, Connecticut
                                                      June 1971

Three Songs

"I was so in love I was miserable"—Guitar Slim

I. Slim's Song
I knew something was wrong

when he said
I want this whiskey tested
and my money invested
'cause times are bad
just lost the best girl
I ever had.

Of course it didn't last long.
Not after the coconut was opened.
No milk. No milk.
Just bubble, bubble.
Toil and trouble.

We call and call:
it wasn't me.
Me neither—
It wasn't me neither,
neither neighbor.

II. Song of the Reverend Gatemouth Moore
Gatemouth Moore
became a preacher
Now it's The Reverend
Gatemouth Moore.
This is where the wind
begins to stretch
and cling to solids:
like a rock is a rock and
a bird in the sky
is a bird in the sky.

A tornado warning is something else.
Teach them to run
from the enormous funnel.
Sometimes the retarded children
come to play and are ushered
about like lepers.
Teach them to avoid the sickness
that waits in the well.

Bwana this is your game
(bwana mean friend).
Because we have the music—
So, please, come dance—
come dance with me.

III. Healing Song
The power returns. We remember.

The night of the tennis
The eyes in your garage.
These twins. These twos
glare at you
in and out, up and down.
But it all comes out the same place
and fails to convince.

(Meanwhile in the heart of the city
the night is long and moonless
but the fire is bright
in the hearts of the people.)

It all seems so simple
so I'll tell you where to look
not what to see. "Dr. i-john
the Conqueror" has roots.
He sees. Sometimes the music
makes you want to boogie.

And always the white streets
and ladies departing. Ladies
departing.

Created in fellowship with Robert Slater, K.C., Mo., 1976

Julia Fields
(1938–   )

Born in Perry County, Alabama, Fields is a poet, short-story writer, and playwright. She received her B.S. from Knoxville College and her M.A. from the Bread Loaf School of English. She has taught at Hampton Institute, East Carolina University, Howard University, and the University of the District of Columbia. Her books include *Poems* (1968); *East of Moonlight; A Summoning; A Shining; Slow Coins*; and *The Green Lion of Zion Street*. Her poems are anthologized in *The Poetry of the Negro, 1746–1970, Black Fire, Nine Black Poets*, and *New Negro Poets: U.S.A.* The following poem is reprinted from *First World* (Vol. 2, No. 2, 1979).

Mr. Tut's House
A Recollection

This poem is dedicated to Hoyt W. Fuller

A.D. 1947 Uniontown, Alabama

When we crossed the railed road,
Coming into town from our long journey,
Past the white pools of green water
Past the white hills, past the white house
With the flowers of every description; of
Every color and fragrance and beautifully
Bloomed everyday in the year, summer
and winter and autumn, and especially spring—

When we crossed the railroad, past
The plank pied store and past the
Sun—brown cafe with the women
Leaning over the knick-knack counter
And the smooth, quiet guised men
Leaning over the counter with lazy
Graceful Southern hands in strong
Workmen's pockets, past the good
Smells of full hand-made burgers

Coming through the Colonial Bread sign
In the screened silver door,
Then we were nearly at the three—
Cornered building with the Silas Green
From New Orleans sign left up
And still up on the heavy walls,
And everyone had said how vulgar,
How nasty a show it was and how
Much everyone who went enjoyed it
And wanted the Silas Green People
To come back, but they never did,
And passing the sign and the road
To the cottonseed plant, you could
Smell the pleasant cotton seed oil
And the mouldy linseed and the
Natural odor and soil of four colors
And four earth flavors on the tongue.

And you were coming into Uniontown where
Flowers were everywhere. Worls and skeins
Of flowers.

Then, you walked past Mr. Tut's slowly.
His white house so still and set
So still upon that spansed still earth.
Your mother and your father must
Haven spoken of Mr. Tut a million
Times. Of Mr. Tut's stones. Mr. Tut's
Cut stones for the death beguiled.
And since death was no more than
A mysticism, you could lean against
The net fence and look at the
Work he did. See him revealed there.

Mr. Tut cut the stones with his
Hands. All of the stones were
Borne through Mr. Tut's hands. And
The stones were earth-measured
Beauty in whites and greys. They
Were lined on the living yard
Grass like any exhibitions of any
Sculptured forms. They were the
Life webs of Mr. Tut's, standing
Like descended desert birds.

You could rest by the fence.

You could eat BB Bats and
Stand child-curious still to rest
Before you walked the four
Separate but equal miles down the
Tar parched road called a highway.
The road breaking through red
Clay, white limerock mounds and
Black loam. You could rest then,
Looking at the stones.
Seven miles of razor back hills
Past Mr. Tut's. And no dogs on
Leashes anywhere. His stones stopping
On the yard of a house so
Quiet, it was not known if he
Lived at all alone or with
Some other—a spirit, a saint, a waif.
It was not known. And even in
The flowered trees no birds sat
Within the wisteriad profusion.
You could not see daylights or
Nightlights there, either.

Did you or did you not see Mr. Tut?
Go over your memory with a
Brush and a sieve. Did you or
Did you not see Mr. Tut? Things
Cannot fall into place unless you
Are certain. Did you glimpse
A thin man in pale denim
Near a sculptured stone?
And what season of the year
Was the time? Was it morning
Or was it midday? Was
It afternoon or first dusk? Was
It in the twilight? Was it?

Did Mr. Tut not look deeply
Into your eyes across the
Fence and bend his face faintly
Close, and turn, without speaking
Back to his stones, and turn
Once yet again to look at you
And leave? And did he not
Float around the East most corner
Of his silent, violet-tinted afternoon?
And was he then a man or a

Man-bird? The etcher and weaver
Of the Prints of Destiny?

His bird eyes perched three-cornered
Across the net fence and looked across
At you. What was the shock
Within his gold-irised star?
What was the language spoken
There? Was it in the morning or
The afternoon? How will
Things fall into place if even
The dregs of memory are clogged?

Mr. Tut's house was real. You could
See it years later. And even
When no mention was made of
Mr. Tut. The red church was
Near it. Real in the fire-red stone
Where people were baptized beneath
The floor and not outdoors in
A cow pond. Not sanctioned in
Buttercups and summers overfull
Of bumble bees and wasps, or
Grapes and blackberries or ripe
Corn. Not minded with cattle and
Mules and horses and dust. Not
The red dust floated horizon ward
Richer than clouds for winter snows.
Nor flowers on ditchbanks and
Rattan lines. Nor flowers on the
Highways in clovers red and white.
Flowers. Flowers. And lily pads on
Green waters, and cattails and

Fern and mosses wild and willowed.
Mr. Tut's house was there.
And the stones forever
Were there. Then, no more
Talk of Mr. Tut. Then, no
More mention of the stones.
And talk, though, of the
Canneries and plants and the
Closing down of plants and
The red factories. Talk of
Moving people, leaving people,
A grief-growing children

And Summer sad haze on
Frosted fields of pale dust.
Mr. Tut's house was there.

A.D. 1977 Washington, D.C.

Have you not been to see
The exhibition of King Tut
Ask the fast thinking people
With pigeon thighs? Have
You not been? Have you not been?
It will not stay here longer
Than the coming March.
You have got to see it.
You must go to see it.
Do not miss seeing it.
And Tut. King Tut's golden
Mask rests in the Capital
City. The boy King rests in
Gold, his soft Negro round
Mouth up flat for curious
Eyes. Flat to implacable wonder
At the surfaces and the
Planes of things. And Tut's
Mask teaches nothing not
Convertible to gold.

I will answer them and say:
"Once, Mr. Tut leaned over
A fence in Uniontown,
Alabama, and looked deep
Into my eyes. He was
In his 4000th life, and,
His stare was electric and
Yellow. His body was
Tri-cornered.
His eyes were
tri-cornered. And there
Were eyes within the eyes
Within the eyes. He came as
A stone cutter this time.
Be wary, lest he come
Behind you while you watch
His mask of death. Be wary
Lest he spring as a serpent
Near your heart. I have seen

His eyes of gold and I
Have looked back and
Forward through them down time.
Be wary.
Mr. Tut's house at the Museum
Is resplendent they say and
Done by hand. In four-block
Lines they file past his
Death mask. They drink him in
Through the head. While he is
Still, before he is removed
And kept moving until he
Crumbles into the dust.

Tut must not rest—even in death.
Mr. Tut's house is open to
The season. Even his bones
Are golden. O bones of
My brother. You who are
Older than I who am older
Than you. Can you see my
Heart with your tri-cornered eyes?
Over these foul centuries, hear
The song I make for you. I think
That you hear. Hear and ease
With me these calloused hours in which
Our Essence is brushed through Evil
Sieves. Hear. My little Brother. Hear.

Gold—shrouded King mocked by flesh
And curious eyes. I saw you once—
Not then a mask, but tall and
Strong, darker than the claws of
Horus' Lucky feet. Quick darkness of
You I saw. So swift. But Horus
Once I touched before the three
Evil days beside the black ocean
Where sickness held me heavy
And still until the Sun came
And stood and spoke to me.
Kindest father Sun who sent a
Beam of light from the ceiling
To my heart and healed me. (And
Leads me.) My little brother, Your
Death mask is in the museum,
But you are not there, are you?

I think that I know where
You are. I always know you
When and wherever you appear.
And I know the things which
Fall into their golden place.

Sterling D. Plumpp
(1940–)

Born in Clinton, Mississippi, Plumpp is Associate Professor of Black Studies at the University of Illinois-Chicago. He was a member of the Organization of Black American Culture during the 1970s, and his first three books of poetry—*Portable Soul, Half Black, Half Blacker*, and *Steps to Break the Circle*—were published by Haki Madhubuti's Third World Press. Plumpp consistently uses the Mississippi folklore of his youth, the idea of ancestry, and the blues ethos as themes in his poetry, fiction, and drama. He has also published *Black Rituals*, a book of psychological essays, *Clinton*, a long poem about his childhood, *The Mojo Hands Call, I Must Go* (which won the 1983 Carl Sandburg Literary Award for Poetry), and *Blues: The Story Always Untold*. He edited *Somehow We Survive: An Anthology of South African Writing* and served as advisory editor for *From South Africa: New Writing, Photographs and Art* (*TriQuarterly* 69). His nonfiction, fiction, and poetry are anthologized in the first three volumes of *Mississippi Writers: Reflections of Childhood and Youth*. The following poem is reprinted from *The Mojo Hands Call, I Must Go*.

Clinton

1

Before me/taut pallets of smoke.
Day waking from pores like black smiles
Defying tenements' grasps. Rural town,
Your skies got the blues.
My longings like cigarettes
Come back for your deep sleepdrags.
It is inhalation, winged memoryreel
Of panoramic comfort that takes
My infancy again to diapers and dust
In the front yard. The song of flowers
Breathing windy perfumes agitates
The fever of sunshine. Escalators.
Your gullies and hills. I run
Through rains from tree
To tree when thunder and lightning

Lie bedridden. Spring.
I am looking out/on uncle's shoulders
Before feet can enroll in your rich embrace.
Funny. How old and young, men and women,
Animals and plants, come up with the sun
To darn the morning with laughter.

2

Talk between the people and the soil
Goes on in sermons by middlebusters
Solos by section harrows
Graces of cultivators
Shouts by swinging hoes
And confessions by hands and knees.
The little plants of cotton, corn, tulip,
Bean, turnip, and okra, open their eyes
To the sun and people bending.
Growth of the vines is a "hello"
Climbing to greet minstrel poles.

3

Night town, strange winds of mystery
Blowing ghosts of rising moons,
I rock in your harvested bosom.
My milk and bread in a bowl
Come through tar-tars from momma.
Hot cornbread crumbles like dirt clods
And makes the clabber bubble.
Before my bowl runs it over
I shovel my spoon to my tummy
And run to the pot before I do-dos
What I gotta do.

4

Dick Tracy chases Eighty-Eight Keys
Past Little Nancy and Slugo.
Cotton town, crossroads town
Of honeysuckle blossoms on fences
Like the faithful on the King's Highway,
Work is seed tonic, logical wine
Committed to the thirsty reason of men
Winning today's rib tips of command
With the swallowing of their labors.
Out cross blackness
Lightning bugs soul clap with stars.
In my heart I want sweetwater

And before I drink at prayer time
Momma says "She is your momma;
I am your grandmomma." I could not
Understand her meaning and my thirst
Became bitter mosquito bites. Shucks
In the mattress played hide
Tickling feathers in the pillow
So they flapped in my face. I lay
Listening to snores of unanswering walls.

5

Morning glories
Pull down music of work days,
Hometown, straw hat men
Walk with round women in ginghams.
I plow unfurrowed rows of my life:
Swinging in trees, sliding down hillsides,
And playing in cotton sheds.
My song of longing leaps
Through radios of your vistas
Like instant dreams in cups of sleep.
The mud and rains of freshness
Stroke my body like a do-right woman.
Black folks picking cotton
Hauling it to gins
Being cheated and whipped
Side their heads if complaints
Burst from sorghum lips.

6

Like a quail
I saunter down your dusty roads
Evenings and dare
Hound your paths, nights
When ghosts blow their cold breaths
In my face when I climb hills
And rinse me in hotness
As I walk in valleys. Rails
Crack with the Bugga Man's steps.
Darkness is a blanket. I touch it.
I cannot sleep anymore unless
My mind exhumes your covers
From the couch of memory.
Momma breaking clods to insert
Seed birth of promised greenness.
Years blink in the distance

Like comets. Yet my scope
Is set on fall afternoons
When leaves wear reddish brown
Shirts and bop to the ground.
Dew comes in mugs of fog
And the sun oversleeps
But goes to bed early.
Off in your nights frost
Becomes coconut of midnight cake
As we watch the simmon tree
For an old possum . . .

7

Today at the edge of light
I soar back to your horizon
Like wise lips hugging thighs.
This hedonistic kneeling of wonder
Yearns in my loins
Dry ice in time's hind pocket.
And I cannot but glory at the sight
Of yesterday rocking down
Through the perversity of my despair
Like an old Black man in a buggy
The bay mare trotting and
He sitting in judgment like Pontius Pilate.
Summer town, I walk out on your fingertips
Reaching for grapes and black cherries.
The bucket I carry in my heart
Is a memory vault. Cotton mouth moccasins,
Spreading adders, and rattlers
Coiling at your toes for granite peace.

8

I resound in your wide halls,
Dirt town, red clay boys
Throwing mudballs
Against banks and one another,
Men and women in rubber boots
Wading and making ditches,
And setting tomatoes and onions straight
On rows. I am pierced by brightness
Of momma's headrag and cleanliness of her apron.
Poppa's overalls are true blue
And patches have conspired
To conceal holes. Autumn.
Pecans rolling around

And hiding under leaves.
I stuff my pockets/eating
Until my belly aches. Castor oil
Invades my ancestral pride
To make my minutes loose.

9
Bad town, I see a white-faced bull
Snorting anger out his nose and pawing
With sturdy precision to zero his body in.
I want to follow a leader beyond clouds
To high nests. Thickets become my refuge.
I walk miles in them. Before long I hear
A bellow coming to the trees. I run
To our yard and enter the grave/wooden gate.
With the agony of black widows leaving grave sites/
Husbands in their eyes, I withdraw to bed
Being checked by a white face
And a huffing and a puffing in the ground.

Night loops of silence/I come to loiter
A black seed in a ripe watermelon. I sit
In tribute of backlogs filling cavities in walls
With rowdy heat. January weekends are great days
For sitting/talking/roasting/and drinking.
Jars of peaches are opened on homemade bread.
Friends and relatives drop by with news.
Extra plates come with bowls of gumbo.
Soppings go on in seconds and the cobbler
Is last to go.

I trot out in the wild wind.
Sable coffee of you stencils
My soul. School/blackboards, benches,
Tables, and toilets outside. Mrs. Latham
Sits watching mouths for gum and quick hands
For spitballs. I cannot go unless
There is an excuse me. Sumner Hill
Is white sides and a green top.
I put my lunch on a desk/then take
My initial wisdom strokes.

10
I come crying/dry leaves
In the wind. Suddenly back
Where lasses and cornbread are vows

Wedded to butter. A looking-glass
Reflects hours/sassysweet dust kissed rains
In times I hugged tight over potlicker.
Could it be/now I am away/far and older/
That joy I know is but a breeze
From clarinets swaying in ways
Only Al Green can feel to order
With his inside love screams?

I have known the arresting
Tender surrender of leaves and
Sap piping green monsoons on desire.
Have known my life is music baked
By fingers only Max-Roached-Monks
Taking C-Tranes can buy with salt peanuts
Of insight. My growing years gallop
Like hoofs of justice. Fear rides
In my veins/when I am jailed by Jim Crow/
When I remember Willie McGhee burning/
Remember Emmett Till drowning/when I remember
Those castrated by silent consent
Not to revel in songs of their manhood.

I sing in solitude; sing pouring
Ways into your gourds and I drink
Recognition. I sing to Holy Ghost
Years/Sumner Hill's diction in accents.
Daily immersion into what St. Thomas said
He thought God was all about and
Life supposed to be. My neck bending
From beads/rosaries saying any life
Without the Roman seal is lost.

11

What is this hip yearning smooching hot
In my breath with passion cut by young
Southern language? What is my life
But a little cup of knowledge? What is
Pain joy sadness love happiness
And despair but a gumbo of life simmering
In pots of your wonder days, nightchild town?
The winds and ways people move
Are scars drawn on your morning valley face
By diasporic singers crying holy blues.
Your lips bless my presence with Satchmo's
Embouchure, small town.

Where do the past's fingers end?
Is yesterday but today and tomorrow
Called in more intimate poetry?
Where is the when of this angling statue
Carved in man's memory as footprints
Of events loved? Where is your magnolia sweetness
To zip up my mind? The streets wind in tune
With pathologies. Crimes manufactured
From need. Songs blown by life. I uncover
Your legacy in the city. Death paints my reality
Before I can pull sounds into sonic graffitti.

12
Your morning peace still drums
Color into Chicago's climate. I go
From open diaries. High school with nuns
Bunnied up in blue. Boys and girls
From "better classes" riding bicycles
And thinking they in space ships
To power and wealth. I am lost.
Keeping somebody else's seven sacraments.
Worshipping fear. Running from everything real.
College is no better than grammar school
Or high school. Only signs of illness
Are less visible. I am in an asylum.
Poor light. Strangers block mirrors
And muddy the water. Songs I have
Drown in books. I am condemned
To repeat names of the dead.

Chicago. Winds bandaging wounds
On faces. Making the world go mad.
My campus after St. Benedict's rules
Tried to commit me behind bars forever.
Ten-hour days. Mail bags. People working
And drifting in confusion. Men fighting
Men. Letting the boy kick their asses
And keep them humping till their number
To move up on the plantation is pulled.

Vision is all life can ever be. Man rising
From clay to control the stars
Because he covets his shadow hovering
In clear days. My source. You are vision.
Back down in Mississippi. Vision. This thunder

Pounding in the music I live.

13
The army. I cannot even dream.
My vision so fixated on suffering
I nearly lose songs spread across decades
My steps took to ripen a music
That is sight. Vision/I say
Is all a poet is and all life is.
Vision is all I could hold onto.
I wake. Morning calling me/notes bopping
Blue and mighty loud in make believe soldiers
Grinding their lives in rinds. Marching
To whistles monsters are blowing.
And the sky is grey and crying. I rise
From government issued hurt laughing.
Tears walking down my face.

The world. A womb and I, bottled flesh,
Dependent upon land to uncork my soul.
Every thought I imagine is thrown
By hands of the land. That source
Naming me. That source I return to
When skin is torn, mangled and I possess
No mending arts. But what is life in armies
But baths in rusty blades? Father dies.
Words freeze in memory. Touch bequeaths ashes.
Silence. A shaky bridge I must walk in pain.
Father. Source blowing away from my anxious,
Grasping fingers.

14
There comes time I call my bonny.
Call my bonny back to me. Comes time
when I call pieces of my life. Saying I
Don't know what tomorrow may bring. But knowing
Unused scraps of my soul will moan
To rising suns. I left the army calling
My bonny without bones of your sounds
To heal my weary soul. Yet there comes time
I call my bonny. Bring my bonny back to me.
Visions in my presence are decadent
As rusted wires/wild around rotted wood.
I bring my bonny back. Chicago and the post office
Like hangnails. Everytime I move pain warns me
To stop. Everywhere I go cops shoot Blacks

Over water faucets; Blacks kill Vietnamese
For blood money. Dances in the streets revive
Old djs to spin jams for bold men rising
From fathers nursed on blueberry hills.

15

The sixties,
I told Black people, it would be all right
If they changed my name/changed my name.
Stokely says friends will not know you
If Black power change your name/change your name.
I said man, it will be all right
If it change my name/change my name.
King says your enemies will pursue you
If freedom change your name/change your name.
I said it will be all right
If it change my name/change my name.
The sixties,
I rise screaming from the dead
Cause I be so glad I change my name.
The sixties,
My blood running like it must have
When Gabriel, Denmark, and Nat realized long ago
That history cannot be put off.
The sixties,
Black people change my name.
I am touched by moanings in daybreak-talking storms.
The sixties,
Malcolm is executed
King is murdered
Little Bobby sacrificed
And Fred Hampton is assassinated.
I am touched. Fred lying in a box.
Country Preacher speaking from a nearby record shop
To the cold wet day.
The sixties,
I am touched/really touched.
A warrior lying with red books on his chest.
Panthers marching to push hurtsongs
From tomorrow's heart.
The sixties,
I remember isles of sweet livelihoods, black town.
I change my name in documents by fire.
People melting steel to take their shadows
And spin images from movement.
The sixties,

My people discovering tiers of their lives in flames.
Changing my name.

16
The sixties,
Youth says it can no longer be my friend.
My voice
Leaping with Black choirs.
The sixties,
I salivate/trying to lean with youth.
I slip into the seventies
To the present. Willie says will it be all right
If I change your name/change your name.
I said it will be all right
If you change my name.
He says the present will be a dangerous place
To live if I change your name/change your name
I said it will be all right
If you change my name. I awake
My past running along like Ellington songs.
The seventies,
My youth withering like love songs.
The seventies,
I will be all right/I changed my name . . .

Nikki Giovanni
(1943–   )

A professor of creative writing at Mount St. Joseph on the Ohio, Nikki Giovanni is one of the major poets of the African-American literary awakening of the 1960s and 1970s. Born in Knoxville, Tennessee, she graduated with honors from Fisk University in 1967 and published her first collection of poems *Black Judgement* the following year. Among her other volumes of poetry are *Spin a Soft Black Song* (1971), *My House* (1972), *The Women and the Men* (1975), and *Cotton Candy on a Rainy Day* (1978). *Gemini*, her autobiographical assessment of her first twenty-five years, was published in 1971. Giovanni's differences and shared values with an older generation of black writers are documented in two extended discussions, *A Dialogue: James Baldwin and Nikki Giovanni* (1973) and *A Poetic Equation: Conversations Between Nikki Giovanni and Margaret Walker* (1974). She has also published a collection of essays, *Sacred Cows . . . and Other Edibles* (1988). The following poem is reprinted from *Re:Creation* (1970).

Alabama Poem

if trees could talk
  wonder what they'd say
met an old man
  on the road late after noon
  hat pulled over to shade
  his eyes
  jacket slumped over his
  shoulders
  told me ''girl! my hands seen
  more than all
  them books they got
  at tuskegee''
  smiled at me
  half waved his hand
  walked on down the dusty road
met an old woman
  with a corncob pipe

sitting and rocking
on a spring evening
"sista" she called to me
"let me tell you—my feet
seen more than yo eyes
ever gonna read"
smiled at her and kept
on moving
gave it a thought and went
back to the porch
"i say gal" she called down
"you a student at the institute?
better come here and study
these feet
i'm gonna cut a bunion off
soons i gets up"
i looked at her
she laughed at me
if trees would talk
wonder what they'd tell me

Ahmos Zu-Bolton
(1935–   )

Born in Poplarville, Mississippi, Zu-Bolton is director of media activities
for the Contemporary Arts Center in New Orleans. He is the author of *A
Niggered Amen*, a collection of poetry, and coeditor of *Synergy: D.C.
Anthology*. He was the founder and editor of *HooDoo* magazine, and for
several years he operated his own publishing firm, Energy Earth Commu-
nications. His work has appeared in numerous magazines and in the
anthologies *Giant Talk* and *Mississippi Writers: Reflections of Childhood
and Youth*, Vol. III. In addition to operating a community bookstore, Zu-
Bolton frequently writes for the *Louisiana Weekly*. The following poems
are taken from *A Niggered Amen*.

---

the governor of ollie street

1

he was the only one of us
to be on time. for sunday school,
for band practice, for the gangmeetings
in the alley.

all this sat him right with the oldfolk
& we never elected him to anything
because of it.

but he was our leader as surely
as he was his father's son.

(his father:
a hellraising preacher
of the old school:
bringing the wrath of the lawd almighty
                   upon us
if we didn't change our niggerways.

2
ollie street is 2 blocks long
with a dead-end both ways.
our nation. where
home was.

until we realized
that we were growing up
we would have defended our nation
against all.

love is a dead-end he told us
but it looks like we gotta choose it
anyhow.

3
so in the 8th grade we put sapphire
on his virgin tail. *love? love*
nigger? here some love,
we screamed.

by the 5th generation
louisiana, after slavery

it had gotten so bad
that they hated
sugarcane, though
they needed a good crop
to get them thru the winter
(hating that which gave
some prayer of life.

the young ones hated
the most. they blamed the land
for what wasnot the
land's fault.

they hated the church
for not giving them hope
in this life

o hope, blessed hope
now now now

until they discovered
that their hatred
was hopeless

Lance Jeffers

A biographical note on Lance Jeffers appears on page 93. The following poems are reprinted from *O Africa, Where I Baked My bread*.

Tuskegee, Tuskegee!

Down I came to wash my soul
in the sweet sweat of the woolly South.

Down I came to my people's silent melancholy
in the jimcrow car crossing Texas and Louisiana.

Down I came, 17, to friend a 10-year-old sister
   amid the tender smiles of the jimcrow car
   moving among the Mississippi cottonfields.

Her blood and mine flowed through a common
   jugular,
this Mississippian aware at 10 of genocide,
   and I,
   the San Franciscan:
   she and I were siblings,
   she the lynched from rope-neck Mississippi
   and I the lynched from Galileo High School.

 And then Tuskegee in the black-moose night,
   and then Jimmy Strickland, Guy Harrison,
   Red Slade and Red-nappy Hamilton, Margaret
   Young, Honey and Mule Ellerbe,

and a tradition that had lain half-forgotten
   in my intestine called me,
and a lyric loosed my fingers on the piano,
and suddenly Earl Hines became my smiling
   father,

and today this tradition, fused in my intestine,
   sucks from my heart a single drop of blood,
   rubs it upon my sleeping eye to wake me
astonished and snorting, "WHERE AM I?"

Oh Tuskegee, Tuskegee!
 Speaking to everyone we met on dirt road
   and college street: all were brothers

and sisters on the jimcrow car,
for lynchers lay without:

Tuskegee, Tuskegee!
The chorus in the chapel Sunday mornings
baptizing us in spirituals:

Oh Tuskegee, Tuskegee!
My lord is so high
you can't go over Him,
so low, you can't go under him,
so wide, you can't go around Him—
you must come in at the door!

Tuskegee, Tuskegee!
Tears flood the valleys of my brain
and gather at stormside
as the sky falls darkly down my pain—

Tuskegee, Tuskegee,
you stand, immovable god-man
in this cindered darkness,
silent sentry of my nights until I die!

To Him Who in His Absence from Himself

To him who in his absence from himself
kills codfish in the rivers of his brain,
to him who would cut the nipples from the breasts
of little mothers, catch the bloody milk in his
  guilty hands—;
Where in your absence from yourself will you go,
where in your hegira have you been?
Where from the white-faced Appalachian mother,
where from the daily desecration of the child,
where from the black girls in their Easter frocks
  in Birmingham, flooded with the neckish
  beheaded gore,
where from the broken-backed lamb inside you,
where from the snow-white tiger in your path,
where from the mountain that stands like human dignity,
pawing aside the mist before your eyes?
Where shall your homeless heart show its tears,
baking inside the hollows of your eyes?
For no hideousness is too steep for the heart
  that has no home,

no salt too caked to place inside a brain,
no murder too lecherous to perform in lieu of
  an erection . . .

Let beauty stay the ocean in its motion between
  the sandy thighs.
Let it carry the lamb to a place among the seals.
Let beauty come home to the coast of the soulless
  land
and man to muttered song among the hills.

The Flesh of the Young Men Is Burning

Standing in the doorway of Cuba's Spanish
  surname
is Africa's massive shadow.

Oh, the African greatgrandmother who leaned
through a window from the courtyard
at Moncada Barracks[1]
and with a toothless grin spoke exuberantly
  in Spanish
to her African children from North America . . .
Oh, the children black and white
who asked us before Moncada Barracks,
their gravity ascendant,
"Are you from Puerto Rico?"
Oh, the summons of that African dignity
in Cuba: the African in Cuba walks
like the African in Angola,
and Magalys[2] bears a victor's serenity
in her smile . . .

Standing in the doorway of Cuba's Spanish
  surname
is Africa's massive shadow.
And Magalys' African laughter, half-cough
  half-cackle in the throat,
her African laughter like Trellie's, like
  Uncle Bob's:
Magalys' African face, Magalys' African laugh:
a century ago she delivered the merchandise
  of danger to the patriots,

[1]The barracks in Santiago which Castro and his followers unsuccessfully
attacked in 1953, now a museum.
[2]One of our Black Scholar group's guides in Cuba, November 1976.

the revolvers beneath her skirts . . .

Why these sudden tears raining down
upon the soil of my content in Carolina?
Why these sudden tears, turf from the sea-
    cliff,
seawater from the storm?

II

I am the diaspora alive and green cast up
    on Havana beach,
I am the octopus graceful in his affection,
the dolphin looking with sinister eyes
    upon the fisherman,
the African from America walking
    among Havana palm trees
that would bow down and kiss me upon the lips
    if I called them freedom,
if I called them liberty,
if I called them human godliness,
if I called them immortality.

If I told the palm trees, you are freedom.
If I told them, you are liberty.

III

I think that I have known freedom,
I think that I have known liberty in
    the caverns I have lived in
underneath the black earth that fronts the sky:
where in my caverns the prehistoric bird,
    great with murder,
his jointed wings like velvet,
swooped hunting through my underground caverns,
and an enormous lizard lifted his head
and swayed it, myopic, from side to side,
and a dove as large as an oak tree
fearlessly fed his brood,
and I, invulnerable, leaned upon an elbow,
    surveying: but
I have forgotten this freedom,
and any freedom I've known is fragile,
and eleven days was not enough
to swallow freedom in Santiago and Havana
where I was foreigner ever
but nigger never.

Why these sudden tears, blood in
the thin and meatless soup of my oppression?

IV

Santiago, still, and caught,
and slowly devoured by Beauty,
but like the hero-rose, birthed again each
    midnight
from Beauty's womb,
each house, each alley, each delicate pigmy
    palm,
each Santiago child's laughter birthed
    again,
and the cathedral too moves down
from Beauty's womb and sits where it sat
where I first saw it,
feminine and reticent upon the hill.

V

They say in Santiago and Havana:
"Where did your grandmother come from,
    Congo or Carabali?"

Which Cuban has no African mothers?
Whose woolly hair does not grow beneath his
    skull?
Who in Cuba does not suckle flamenco and
    Angola?
Which Cuban does not embrace the baobab?
Which Cuban does not know the anatomy of
    his sweat or the unity, the unity of his
    blood?

  What Cuban is not black beneath the skin?

VI

Magalys walks in her serenity,
the grandeur of Nicolas Guillen is ages young,
and the muscular gentleness of Eliseo Diego
sings lyrically beneath the palms.

VII

Oh, the Batista bulletholes in the cottage
    where the young men plotted to take Moncada
        Barracks;
oh, the murdered young men passionate as they
    plotted in the cottage;

oh, the faces of the Batista butchers,
   surfeited with slaughter,
(one young man, taken by Batista, wrote,
                "Mother, I am going to be killed")—

The flesh of the young men is burning, burning
   even now before Moncada,
the flesh of the young men is aglow . . .

VIII

The cabdriver, middleaged, a father,
a dedicated soldier in his face,
no word of English on his tongue, (on mine
   no word of Spanish),
he drove me to the Jamaican ambassador's
   residence,
and we arrived in the dark and half-clothed
   night;
I paid him,
and he thrust out his hand with a warmth
   tangible as the nearest palm, in the night
   there
standing on the edible Cuban earth.
His handshake spoke aloud: "You and I are brothers."

The flesh of the young men is burning before
   Moncada,
the flesh of the young men is aglow.

IX

When he looks steadily into the eyes of evil,
   the dwarf becomes a giant.
When he struggles against wickedness,
   the devil becomes a saint.
When he uses his knife against the testicles
   of iniquity, the defeated man, hacked and
   shriven by wrinkles, leaps the chasm like
   an athlete,
   thus the coward becomes a rebel against himself.

Who cannot see the secret movement of his life
   toward godliness?
Who cannot sense an artery of peace within his
   groin,
   a crucial vein of rage within his heart?
Who cannot hear the unheard music in his hair,
   the hymns that stream like wind-gusts past

his ear?
Who cannot hear the unheard prophecies of his
    soul,
    or touch the redwood buried in his bowels?

The flesh of the young men is burning, burning
    before Moncada,
the flesh of the young men is aglow.

No one dies before he gives consent,
    until his hand turns off the spigot of his desire.
No one dies till he is passive against the
    chains.

X
When the teenage students half-black half-white
sang to the visitors:
"If you are mistreated where you are,
come to Cuba," an
Afroamerican
ran weeping from the room.

The students' applause when she returned was
    an embrace:
"We embrace you, sister, we embrace you."

Eye to eye,
tear to tear,
their anguish and their anger, their
triumph and their rapture,
our outrage, our vision: tributaries
    to a single sea, a single ocean,
all are tributaries to a single sea.

XI
The flesh of the young men is burning, burning
    even now before Moncada,
the flesh of the young men is aglow.

Nayo [Barbara Watkins]
(1940–   )

A native of Atlanta, Georgia, Nayo first gained attention as a member of the BLKARTSOUTH group, a workshop of the Free Southern Theater. Her first book of poetry, *I Want Me a Home*, was published in 1969, and her poems are included in the anthologies *New Black Voices* and *Word Up: Black Poetry of the 80s from the Deep South*. She is widely known in the southeastern region for her promotion of African-American arts, having served as executive director of both the Mississippi Cultural Arts Coalition and the Southern Black Cultural Alliance. In 1987 she became managing director of At the Foot of the Mountain, a women's theater group in Minneapolis; she is currently executive director of the African American Dance Ensemble in Durham, North Carolina. The following poems are printed from the author's manuscript.

Hard Times A' Coming

i see hard times
a' coming
and i rejoice

i see doors shutting
ears unhearing
and hearts turning cold
and i see blk folks
puzzled and wondering

and i hear some
long lost echo saying
'we always gon make it'

i see hunger staring
and plump blk hands stirring
big pots of greens and beans
pots for sharing

i see blk folks moving
moving over to make room

one more in that bed
another pallet on the floor
always room for one more

i see lost blk children
missed and missing
and i see a neighbor lady
switch in her hand saying
'boy, you ain't going nowheres
you stay in that yard
whilst your mama way from home'

i see blk folk watching
watching and caring
daring to be concerned
daring to by-pass
egos and other
individualistic trips

i see blk businesses
pooling and pulling together
providing and patronizing
like they know
what a blk economy is

i see a carpenter
say to a plumber
who says to a mechanic
who says to a baker
who says to an accountant
who says to a teacher
who says to a farmer
who says 'i aint got no money

but i got a back to bend
a hand to lend
a product to swap
a service to exchange'

i see an old woman
pulling a bunch of greens
for a doctor and a doctor's
family grinning
over hot greens and corn mush
while an old woman
is eased of her arthritis
i see this year's style
become last year's hand-me-down
and yesterday's leftovers

a fancy meal for tomorrow
last summer's squash
a winter's feast

i see the lights
going out in america
and i hear teeth gnashing
and pain growling
in the gut

i see white america
twisting and turning
looking for someone
to blame

but i see a glow
in black communities
an old timey glow
like a pot belly glow
like a quilting-round-
the-fire glow
a holding close
a watching and protecting
a sharing and caring
and in the darkest hour
i see the ancestors
lighting fires in our hearts

yes i see hard times
a' coming
and i see blk folks
rediscovering
we are still
our own best resources
and i rejoice.

Near Miss

i saw you
body beautiful
wondered
bout you

my tentacles reached out
to get a feel for you
simply wanted to know
what you were like

met you reaching out for me
touching was electric
i withdrew

suspicious
of you
boxed you up
labeled you
and taped you down
with stereotype

forbidden fruit
looks good
tastes bitter
bidding me

finally decided
to take a chance
touched you
explored
mingled with your thoughts
watched your mouth's corners
rejoiced
that your words were
more than words
your thoughts were
deep waters
you spoke in gentle tones
that floated you
into me

and to think
while my closed mind
prejudged
i almost missed you.

Julius E. Thompson
(1946–   )

Born in Vicksburg, Mississippi, Thompson is a professor of history and
Black American Studies at Southern Illinois University. He earned his
B.S. from Alcorn State University and his M.A. and Ph.D. from Princeton
University. His two collections of poetry are *Hopes Tied Up in Promises*
and *Blues Said: Walk On,* and he has completed a third collection *Mississippi Witness, Poems 1975–1985.* His poems, notable for economy of
language and ironic interrogation, have been published in magazines and
anthologized in *Mississippi Writers: Reflections of Childhood and Youth,*
Vol. III. Thompson is also the author of *The Black Press in Mississippi,
1865–1985: A Directory* and *Hiram R. Revels, 1827–1901: A Biography.*
His work-in-progress includes a biography of Percy Greene and a study
of the Black Arts Movement in Detroit. The following poems are reprinted
from *Blues Said: Walk On.*

In My Mind's Eye

(For Samuel Sanders)

In my mind's eye,
I see Black people
In the cotton fields
And up north
Crying in the cities.

In my mind's eye,
I see no solutions—
Only a million
And a half
Unanswered questions.

In my mind's eye,
I see jesus
On my people's mind
Every hour of
Every day.

In my mind's eye

I see booker t. washington
Laughing with uncle tom;
They both were given special medals
For going beyond the call of duty.

In my mind's eye,
I see jordan river.
It won't let no
Negroes enter for fear of
Upsetting the water table.

In my mind's eye,
I can't roll over
Or under Egypt;
And Ethiopia is below *that*.
How's i gonna get home?

In my mind's eye
Comes the spirit
Of my ancestors,
Telling me not to worry if I don't
Come up with an answer, they will.

In my mind's eye
Is the image of a dying man.
His only crime was
Trying to live
And let others do the same.

In my mind's eye
Is a memory of a journey
Across a sea.
I saw my mother jump in
And my father go after her.

In my mind's eye
Is a story about how we landed
On these shores.
The only greeting we got
Was, "you are now niggers!"

In my mind's eye
Is a second of that first whip.
It went across all our backs
And reached Africa to tell
My brothers left that they were next.

In my mind's eye
Moves a part of me
That can never forget

Where it has been.
Home, home in a dream.

In my mind's eye—
Cover up her body,
Cover up her remains.
Don't let those white folks see her.
Her spirit got to be free!

In my mind's eye
Love knows I understand.
She was tied up too,
And under the prison walls
Her tears could not reach our gods.

In my mind's eye
Is a movement I cannot figure out.
It wants to tell me something,
But fearful I won't answer,
It moves away.

In my mind's eye
Are all those brothers and sisters
Who through the long years
Made a way that
We might one day yet understand.

In my mind's eye
Moves a part of me
That the gray ghost tried
To destroy. his gods were
Not powerful enough!

In my mind's eye
Moves a part of me
That knew I never was a slave,
Though I had no freedom
And no land.

In my mind's eye,
Lord, the spirit
Moves me
Back and forth between
Two worlds.

In my mind's eye
Something is saying
"Awake from your
Walking sleep
And follow me."

In my mind's eye
I see 500 million
Walking home free!
Spirit, Spirit moves over me.
In my mind's eye!   home!   free!

Till

have you seen a black son, walking
down a mississippi highway headed
home?
have you seen his eyes all red
with hope, not more than thirteen
years?
can you understand, can you understand,
can you,
can you feel four hundred years,
can you?   can you awake to see
yourself
dead like he died?   can you?
can you see him, one black son,
one?
one that god didn't save, or
his people? can you spread,
can you spread
one,
just one
lie?
can you spread, can you spread out
death
in no man's
land?
she said
he touched her,
or was it that he had whistled—
does it matter?
pure christians don't
lie
or die.
her good men said
he would never
see chicago again
except in a box nailed
in.
can you, can you spread, spread

out death?
his mother
looking on,
down on their knees,
they were giving prayers
for the son who wasn't saved,
and throughout the world his picture
was seen
in
jet magazine.
some people even cried too soon,
before the preacher
said,
"amen."
then there came
a telegram from the president,
he was so sorry
that
you can't change people with
laws.
justice
had a dream
falling
from the second window
of the whi
te house.
can you spread?   can you,
can you spread
out death
on her
head?
can you?
can you, can you,
can you save one black son
who god didn't?

John Milton Wesley
(1948–   )

Born in Ruleville, Mississippi, Wesley is a poet, fiction writer, and advertising/media relations consultant. After graduating from Tougaloo College in 1970, he worked as a news reporter for WLBT-TV before moving to Maryland. His poems have appeared in *Essence, Little Patuxent Review*, and *Close-up*. He has written two short-subject screenplays, "The Heritage of a People" and "Diamond Junction." He was a consultant for the Baltimore television special "Negritude Poets from the Chesapeake Bay" and is writing *The Soybean Field*, a novel about his growing up in Mississippi. "Son Child" is reprinted from *Mississippi Writers*, Vol. III.

Son Child

On a road in Mississippi
A dirt farmer stopped
Long enough to leave a son child.
A midwife's folly
Ended in a tear. Ten round
Fat fingers reached for
A hollow meat bottle
For lack of something else to
Do with a toothless mouth.
Out of a pregnancy, into
A cold world, free to stretch
Dared to move and demand love.
I never saw his face
Was told it was round and fat
And filled with false teeth
His fingers were also
Known to roam. He ran away
to avoid a steel cage and
An avocation of license plates.
In the years ahead, my brother
Would do his time.
Fats, was a big man the neighbors whispered

How could he be such a skinny child
And baldheaded.
Before the streets were named
And sewers were layed, when
Catfish washed up on the bridge
And the water rose.
Before Emmett Till whistled
At the white woman (they hung him for it.)
A son child left by a dirt farmer
Reached for something soft.
At two he knew the coal bin,
The blackness kept him warm.
Snow fell, Ice cream sat quietly
On the window sill. Hog killing time
Took his friends away. Only roosters
Remained calm and mounted feathered
Backs, crowing, then ran off
To the neighbors backyards. Pulling, scratching
Cackling chickens danced over brown eggs.
Sister Herron's cow kicked the bucket
All the neighbors came out to see
The truck with the pulley roll Bessie
Onto its back. Mr. Seals had a stroke
Coming up the street. He had promised to
Bring me cookies from the store. He fell
And never broke one.
Ruleville, a mainstreet town
North on 49-W, one policeman
Khaki and fat, spat on negroes
Ate their cooking, beat their men
Loved their women, robbed their children
Gave us their old clothes.
Shot-gun houses and shot-gun weddings
Married us to our turnrows, stuffed our
Noses with cotton, broke our backs
With haybails, turned our bright eyes dark
With corn whiskey, baked us browner
Than we were, bearing their burdens
In the heat of the day.
Saturday night, on "greasy street"
The pool halls filled with new crisp
Cotton picking money, full of Schlitz
Southern Comfort, and black berry juice
Wall to wall colored people, before
We were black, before we built toilets
On our front porches to save money

Running sewer lines to the back of the house.
Those were the simpler days of
Commodity lines, of surplus peanut butter
Raisins, and cheese, and milk and flour.
We moved up in line by trading cans of
Corn beef cured in salt and water.
Yellow meal seeped through holes left
In potato sacks. Sack dresses hugged
Our sisters shoulders and waistlines.
We ran for our lives from Klansmen
And tornadoes, high winds, and hail storms.
God caused everything life and death,
Beauty and ugliness, love and hate.
Compress whistles marked the time of day,
Crickets and church bells, whippoorwills
and fireflies danced and sang. Fish frying
Could be smelled for miles.
We were a backdoor people, we knew our place
It was behind the nearest white man, on
The back of the bus, through the kitchen
Waiting until, table cleaning time for
Cold rolls splattered with coffee grounds,
And meat left on T-bones, for negroes racing
With dogs. I once saw a vision of Jesus
Lying awake waiting for the cotton picking truck.
The voice of the driver made the
Sacred mouth move, in the steel cold morning hours,
"Come with me, come with me."
And a Billy goat waiting to be
Barbecued answered, "Baaaaa, Baaaaa, Baaaaa."
Short fat ladies, heads tied, gold teeth
Glistening, wrapped sweet potatoes, pork chop
Sandwiches, and teacakes in cellophane,
And climbed on the back of Ford pickups.
We went early to catch the dew-cotton,
And sunrise, while Jim Eastland, fat, racist,
And serving, chewed bitter round cigars
On Capitol Hill.
We were a beautiful brown hateless people.
Drowning in a sea of cotton, living on the
Leftovers of Bollweevils, and ladybugs.
A day was worth three hundred pounds, and
What honey-dew melons could be found.
Baby-Ruths, lasted all day, coca-colas were a
Nickel.
Those were the days this son child knew

Burned in his eyes by the sun. Chilled in
His belly by pump water. Etched in his soul
By fear.
Way, way back to where the memory fades,
And dissolves into misconcepts of freedom,
And white children, who loved us until
They were told to hate us, and keep
Their oatmeal cookies to themselves.
And they became "crackers," and we became
"Niggers," and before they locked our churches
At midnight, and burned crosses in our front yards.
Way before Wallace and the door, and Barnett,
And Ole Miss, before Little Rock, King, Kennedy, Watts,
And Selma, way, way back before they shrunk
The baby-ruth, a dirt farmer stopped long enough
To leave a son child, who reached for something soft,
And is still waiting to touch it.

Jerry W. Ward, Jr.
(1943–   )

Lawrence Durgin Professor of Literature at Tougaloo College, Ward was born in Washington, D.C., raised in Mississippi, and received his B.S. from Tougaloo College and a Ph.D. from the University of Virginia. A teacher, critic, and poet, Ward has published essays, poems, and critical reviews in such magazines as *New Orleans Review, OBSIDIAN, The Southern Quarterly, Black American Literature Forum*, and *Callaloo*. His work is included in the anthologies *Sturdy Black Bridges, Mississippi Writers: Reflections of Childhood and Youth*, Vol. III, and *Black Women Writers 1950–1986: A Critical Evaluation*. He coedited *Redefining American Literary History* (1990) with A. LaVonne Brown Ruoff. The following poems are printed from the author's manuscript and from *The Black Scholar*, September–October 1980.

Jazz to Jackson to John

(for John Reese)

movement one: genesis

it must have been something like
sheets of sound wrinkled
with riffs and scats,
the aftermath of a fierce night
breezing through the grits and gravy;
or something like a blind leviathan
squeezing through solid rock,
marking chaos in the water
when his lady of graveyard love went
turning tricks on the ocean's bottom;
or something like a vision
so blazing basic, so gutbucket, so blessed
the lowdown blues flew out: jazz

jazz to jackson and
dust to dawn and
words for John

it must have been something like
Farish Street in the bebop forties,
a ragtag holy ghost baptizing Mississippi
on an unexpected Sunday, a brilliant revelation
for Billie telling you about these foolish things
back in your own backyard, angel eyes in the rose room,
Monk's changing piano into horn because it was zero in the sun,
and around midnight there was nobody but you
to walk Parker and his jazz to jackson;
yeah, brother, it must have been something
striking you like an eargasm,
a baritone ax laid into soprano wood,
like loving madly in hurting silence,
waiting to fingerpop this heathen air
with innovations of classical black
at decibels to wake the deaf, the dumb, and the dead;
because around midnight there was nobody but you
who dug whether race records were lamentations or lynchings: jazz

jazz to jackson and
sunset to dawn and
words for John

movement two: blues people in the corn

steal away, steal away, steal away
the heart blow/ horn blow / drum drop
to bass / five-four time beat
making a one o'clock comeback creep
behind all that jazz
beat—beepbeep—beat

steal way back to beginning
beginning
is the water
is the soul
is the source
is the foundation with my brothers
is Pharaoh jamming in the pyramid,
sketches of Spain for a night in Tunisia;
is MJQ, Tatum, Turrentine, Tyner,
the Jazz Messengers, messiahs, crusading
headhunters tracking down the mind

cause, Lord yes, all God's people got sold
and who'da thought
owning rhythm was a crime like stealing a nickel

and snitching a dime, when we had coffers packed
with golden music and time, golden music
sliding from the flesh, the bone, honeysweet music;
them lollipopsicle people
with they sarding ships
(and no music to speak of)
they stole it all and sold it all
for wooden nickels, for frozen dimes: jazz

behind all that jazz
blues people in the corn, in the vale of cotton tears,
blues people in the corn, waiting,
waiting, waiting, wrapped in esoteric patience,
waiting to steal away, steal away, steal away
soon as Miles runs down the voodoo avenue
with some jazz to jackson and
pipes a private number
to call a tune for John

movement three: and this, John, is our new day

and this, John, is our new day.
never say goodbye to the blues that saw you through,
nor put down the spirituals and the salty sermonettes,
the drugs, the junkies, jukebox juice, the sweat
and the pain of shelling hot peanuts, hot peanuts: jazz

and the jazz you gave to us we give to you
as jazz to jackson and
because we really want to thank you
words for John

Don't Be Fourteen (In Mississippi)

Don't be fourteen
black and male in Mississippi

    they put your mind
    in a paper sack, dip it
    in liquid nitrogen
    for later consumption

Don't be fourteen
black and male in Mississippi,
have two 20/20 eyes, feet
that fail to buck, wing, and tap,
audacious mouth that whistles

they castrate you wrap
you in cotton-bailing wire
while your blood still feels,
feed you to the Tallahatchie
as guilt-offering to blue-eyed susans

Don't be fourteen
black and male in Mississippi

they say you a bad nigger
named Bubba, a disgrace
to the race for your first offense,
and slam you in Parchman
for forty-eight years.*
You need, they say, a chance to grow.

Don't be fourteen
black and male in Mississippi

they say you a man at two.
so, be one.
when white boys ask
why you don't like them
spit on them
with your mouth closed.

*The sentencing of Robert Earl May, Jr., 14, reveals the blatant inadequacy and inequity of criminal justice in Mississippi.

Thomas C. Dent
(1932–   )

In the early 1960s, Dent was a member of New York's legendary Umbra Workshop and won attention in literary circles as the editor of *Umbra* magazine. In 1965, Dent returned to New Orleans, his birthplace, to become an associate director of the Free Southern Theater. In 1973 he founded the Congo Square Writers Union, which has enabled a number of New Orleans writers to develop their talents. Dent's reputation as a poet, essayist, oral historian, and playwright grew rapidly in the 1980s. His play *Ritual Murder* is considered a classic in the dramatic repertoire of the black South. Dent's poems, reviews, and essays have appeared frequently in such journals as *Freedomways, Southern Exposure, Black American Literature Forum*, and *Callaloo*. His poetry is included in the anthologies *Schwarzer Orpheus, New Negro Poets: USA*, and *New Black Voices*. Dent coedited *The Free Southern Theater by the Free Southern Theater* (1969) with Gilbert Moses and Richard Schechner. His two collections of poetry are *Magnolia Street* (privately printed) and *Blue Lights and River Songs* (Lotus Press). Dent is a former executive director of the New Orleans Jazz and Heritage Foundation. He is currently doing research for *Southern Journey*, an oral history of the Civil Rights Movement and the contemporary South. Dent's poems are reprinted from *Magnolia Street*; his article on Annie Devine (p. 467) is reprinted from *Freedomways*, Second Quarter, 1982.

For Lil Louis

Louis i'm trying to understand what you were here
   how you left this place
how you gave the people bravura music
how you could survive it all
even bucket-a-blood
where the frustrations of our people
   boiled into daily slaughter
but then New O is an old place for that:

   don't you think its a moon-town
   where the imagination of violence
   sparks easily to life?

what festers in the minds
of the grandchildren of the
people you knew who languish
now in the projects?
bucket-a-blood was demolished
the people banished to the project.
your old town:
the city's new progress
your old house:
the city's new jailhouse.
such the way it is the city
tells you what they think of you
& everyone like you & still the
people dance & progress looks on afraid . . .

Louis i'm trying to understand what you were
really like
in the dark moments away from the stage.
rumors have it you were not pleasant
to be around,
the shit-eating grin nowhere to be found:

    did the moon-blood intrude
    the sleep of your nights
    even sleep of your days
    did you carry moon-blood
    memories to the grave?

Louis i'm trying to understand but never
mind
it's enough that you said don't bury me in
New Orleans
& it's enough to hear your trumpet
laughing at it all
it's enough that you played de-truth-de-truth-beeeeeee
& the sweaty handkerchief
always honest   honest
it's enough
it's enough
but Lou/est

someday the dancers will explode
and all this little history
will shatter as the
shit-eating masks fall . . .
& only the moon will know

Lou/is.

Return to English Turn

I
traveling along
river road.
below
nouvelle orleans.
come to
this place to barren levee called
english turn.

it is here bienville
convinced english
this land french
in 1699
sign say.

it is here
chained to the hulls of ships
we begin our neo-european forced journey:
    the land of misty riches leads to
    the Project called Desire.

if we could look closely enough
we could see the Sediments
absorbed by the river
river he who does not forget.
Bienville's french like invading bees
swarming upriver
establishing style by pushing
the people who live here out
bible pronouncements with strong
musket seasoning,
the best french cooking . . .
and us?
us in the hull
chained
confused
torn
in the hull
the musics of our ruptured memory
clashing with the grating roar
of chains.

& soon all along this winding
road
plantations thrive
off the work

of Leroy
& Beulah:
cotton
sugar
oranges
great houses
massive farms
and still we hear the music of chains.

the boats slipping up & down this
muddy snake:
cotton, sugar
the sugar cane, the cotton bale
corn, oranges
the corn stalk, the orange tree
oil, tobacco
the quick-dollar turn rig
the harsh-taste perique
boats up & down
& around
propelling goods for france england
cincinnati memphis holland
st. louis china south america
chain-forced hull energy
forging the neo-european progress
chain-forced hull energy
sustaining the languorous civilization
chain-forced hull energy
trying to bring this river under control
control commerce control
control machine control
control dollar control.
and even our music was stolen
made circus show for drunk
whiskey dreams not ours
made entertainment for newly
americaine straw-hatted rulers
who laugh till they sweat
through dey seersucker suit,
wipe their brows over oysters,
contemplate next move.
the river contains all this:
he who does not forget.

and during all this
our songs
our shouts

our forgotten lives
echo through this valley
strong men screaming from the dungeon
of the new hull . . .
Leroy struggling past crabs-in-the-barrel to
aborted rebellions that ended
in Parish churchyard hangings
the dungeon of the new hull
Beulah in the fields, in the white uniform
whispers between Leroy & Beulah
at midnight
whispers of tomorrows for the children
& other whispers
but still chained
confused
torn
in the hull

& the music from all this:
   song of Beulah's soft smile
   too raucous laughter of Leroy's
   torn memory
hull songs for us alone
songs of hulldom for us
yeah oh yes . . .
warming the heart of congealed years.

those songs our only way of saying
what we could not afford to say
those songs our only understanding
of what we could not comprehend

   why *were* we brought here?
   why were we brought here to these
     oppressive plantations
   how did we end up being the ones?
   why were we chosen for this
   bitter joke
   of the god of fates?

we made music that absorbed all that
music that floated on the wings of memory on the wings of tomorrow's
travail through the muggy Saturday night
from the shacks behind the tracks.
we, doomed to hulldom, attained elegance in ragged attire.
& even when we beseeched our god of
rivers

it seemed he had forgotten us
and there was no escape
no turning back.
but the river contains all this too
river he who does not forget.

II

so now let us turn
to you in the city project
you who know hulldom but
    not it's history before the first
    american hull
you of the cannot-find-a-job know-not-why
you of the slow deaths & quick crab-barrelled murders
you of the ruptured family
you of the krazee citee, de city a de pleasure unpostponed
you seething in project heat
you of the grass broken the steel jutting
the plaster chipped the streets mud
you of needle dreams, seeeething memories
you of city dock, city factory
you of the massa's kitchen, the praline mammy
you of the stolen music
you of the music that drowns rain
    soothes cuts from shards
you of the questioning who-am-i who knows not
    who-was-i
you of the misty hull with one leg out of the steel hull
    masking as modern civilization
you confused, struggling for direction, for a way
    to end forced journeys
you who listen to the river's voice
    river who does not forget
the you who is each of us

let us return to english turn
rip up the signs
wipe out the legacies
pledge no more forced journeys

    no more english turns
    no more spanish turns
    no more french turns, portuguese
    or german turns

rip the markers of neo-european conquest from
    their roots

plant a new one marking:

   our turn

our turn to flow out of the hulls, on to the decks,
   take control of the pilot wheels, choose the
   direction of our own journeys, for the first
   time in this valley
our turn, but never forgetting the forced journeys.

III

there is a song the old griot sings
about the uprooting of
european markers
& the planting of baobab trees
& we hear it now
winding around us
caressing us with its ripples of Kora notes.
it is a tune we have heard many times
containing notes we do not now know
but pleasing
growing stronger now
stronger
its clear music
skipping across the muddy waves
of the river

Dream Orpheum Balcony

            and then
            our lives full of streetcar clamor
            streetcar clamor
            drowning out freight choo-choo
            (cho-cho midnights run amok
            through day & night . . .
            cho-cho making us sweat
            until out heart beats
            louder than train wheels)
            and then
            off to eighty-eight steps
            toward fantasy heaven
            were warm hamburgers from the counter
            below
            spill chopped onions
            over the balcony
            into the Esther Williams aquatic

extravaganza . . .
our peanut shells giggle
uncontrollably
at the sound
of the last solemn
kiss
and then
streetcar clamor drowning out
freight choo-choo
except at midnight
when choo-choo chugs
the weight of our
questions
and then

Helen Quigless
(1944–   )

A graduate of Fisk University, Quigless received her M.L.S. from Atlanta University. During her undergraduate years, she was an editor for the *Fisk Herald* and a participant in the John Oliver Killens Creative Writing Workshop at Fisk. Her poetry has been published in the anthologies *For Malcolm, The New Black Poetry*, and *Today's Negro Voices*.

Moving

He says:
"Only the black mind can project
the black reality."

Others dispute him and tell us
"how it is."
And we wonder while
we
  are
    moving
      closer
to the discovery that life
is a propelling reel in who's pocket.

Until then, a black man
is called negative; in his own eyes (a cultural giant)
capable of reprint, yet without positive qualities
——a dreamer, a prisoner of belief.

(Who's belief?)

Just a pair of eyes.

Moving
Moving toward freedom of imagination
Moving closer . . .

Evening

The rain, falling,
crackles upon the dry earth.
A swishing sound rises, then falls.
And a car's motor rattles like
seeds in a gourd.

Clouds divide, and the silence flows.

The sky, violet and orange, extends behind
black shaded trees,
which are poised
like impassioned dancers
who throw up their arms, or hang
quivering heads towards their feet,
trunks contorted.

Time moves: leaves, limbs, green,
disappear.

The train, precise in its coming,
rolls through this,
my simple town,
stiffly repressing its awesome power
with an oriental distance
as it progresses, brushing dissonantly
against the local wind.

Thus,
I know it is evening.

Childhood Scenes in Four Seasons

Spring
I
Laughter tumbled over laughter
as three small children heard it rise up the stairway
Our curiosity peaked
while waiting for the invitation to join them.
For a moment, I closed my eyes
and saw myself darting like a sprite
among the many flowers my Mother had planted.

I opened my eyes
and saw flirtations
of so called very important people
who had the second, and maybe, third cocktail

tilted in one hand.

Goodnight, Goodnight!
A good time was had by all.

Summer
II
The crickets and gardenias attempted to fill my senses,
but the hypnotic swaying of the front porch swing dominated.
I contentedly buried my head in my Grandmother's lap.

The voices of grownups murmured about matters of the day
and became intermittent phrases that slipped into the velvet night,
as I floated into abstraction.

Autumn
III
The leaves turned red and brown as my Father
paused   in his endless entertaining chatter.

HE gave my Mother a larger diamond ring
    on one fine September . . .
HE told her that I hit the wrong note
    while practicing the piano . . .
HE photographed my sister who sat
    like a cherub in a large armchair . . .
HE shouted with perfect timing so that my brother
    avoided a moccasin snake hiding in a pile of leaves
    as we all followed him through the forest . . .

My Father
paused   and glanced at me (I was shy with strangers)
            as I attempted to get a word in.
Winter
IV
Once a forest painted upon
school-house windows
with snow, and smoke puffs
from far kindled fires.

Bare branches made
living sculptures frozen
against the sky.

Now the limbs' creaking
rides the wind through a
house of broken glass.

Alvin Aubert

(1930–   )

Born in Lutcher, Louisiana, Aubert is the founding editor and publisher of
OBSIDIAN: Black Literature in Review. He is a Professor of English at
Wayne State University and has taught at Southern University (Baton
Rouge) and the State University of New York at Fredonia. His poems,
critical articles, and reviews have appeared in various magazines, to-
gether with poems in the anthologies *Southern Writing in the Sixties,
Broadside Annual, Contemporary Poetry in America, Ceremonies, A Ge-
ography of Poets*, and *Contemporary Southern Poetry*. His three volumes
of poetry are *Against the Blues, Feeling Through*, and *South Louisiana:
New and Selected Poems*. His play *Home from Harlem*, adapted from
Dunbar's novel *The Sport of the Gods*, had its premiere in Detroit in 1986.
The following poems are from Aubert's second volume *Feeling Through*.

Baptism

ancestral pearls so deep, so blue
blues-oozes from a teeming swamp.
a river rolls its ancient silt gulfward.
a muddy voice rises. 'come here pretty
baby, come sit down on my cypress knee.
run your willowy fingers thru the speckled moss
of my oaken heart. jordan river so chilly
and cold, religion so sweet.' mary mary
mother of discreet hallelujahs, make way
for this wild explosion of jubilant
white-robed sisters settled to their feast
of succulent crabs and bisque.
you miracle-motored scooters along
inaccessible ways, intrepid seekers of depths,
bring back that summer breeze that soulful
drummer breeze. stir this simmering black
pot to a cauldron of fructifying memory.
swirl this stagnant blood. this cold
streaming liquid pearl. trouble

this rooted tongue . . .

were you there when the preacher he dunked
sweet hannah deep down the western bank
and she rose white-robe-clinging wet
out of pearly blue blaze?—go down.
sweet hannah! run, river; trouble my song.

were you on the set when black king
of the blues-fiery throat traded in
his box for a travelin piano?—made
the levee his road, the sure way of
the river?—willow his tent, rock his
pillow, cold cold ground his bed?—
were you there? if you saw the sun
lay its thousand daily kisses the breadth
of that muddy bosom, felt the river bed
rock in the cradle of its mighty run
and the cypress swamp turn its oozing
blues to gold in the deep of midnight,
you were there. saw blue and coal
black king saw him sing. heard his
deep timbre entwine with another
sweet as rose water and old as wine.
black magnolia of the valley, queen
of the golden scissors. cleanest
belly button maker this side eden.
king singing from the midnight coal
black and blueness of his lonesome
road, his sad/happy song swaddling the wail
at the pearly root of this lifelicking tongue.

For Mark James Robert Essex, d. 1973

etch in the memory of your bones
the riddled broken blood
of Mark James Robert Essex.
the valiant lawmen surrounding it,
tallying their leaded holes, thinking
order and mardi gras. of clearing
the streets and air for the annual
festivity. pity those fallen at the hands
of Mark James Robert Essex. remember them.
but do not forget Mark James Robert Essex.
pray for him. prayer of song in our
native strain. voices raised from the

mangled flesh of that sad new orleans day.
sing for the blood of man. for the
fallen six stilled by the hand of Essex.
but remember Mark James Robert Essex.

Feeling Through

through the open porch window
past starched green curtains
in/thru your immaculate wall mirror
(fixed, ancestral: of its own light):
the mantelpiece, the flat carnival shot:
you. yes. perched on a hanging quarter moon.
was there breeze then as now?
the river, a scent of memory. fish.
waterlogged driftwood. oil slicks
where the sun designs. burning diesel
from the ferry stack, the old st. james, retired.
festering lilies at the water's edge.
maypops in their fragrance along the levee.
the future of now; the pastness of then as now.
is there a way to tell?
men of science read fossils, i read you
imagine your reply. not knowing
yet remembering the poet in you: 'yes;
hold it close to your naked heart; feel.'
and yes, i say. but not quite that. this:
where did you come from to that waiting moon?
where did you go, after; how was it in that tent,
sitting on the moon? did it really hang, as
the snapshot says? swing? was it hot and
who watched as you fixed yourself for the encounter?
was it good . . . your eyes
faded as all else then; as now, but something
there. points of light.
a burning through. then as now.
was it good . . .
either the green curtains close
the mirror darkens the fireplace explodes
or the porch swing goes wild:
i cannot see you anymore.
i have it (feel) here.

Alvin Aubert

When the Wine Was Gone

we lived in language all our black selves,
wordsound was our food. was what we got
high on when the wine was gone. was all
the world we had to move around in. was
the blues once we slipped past steal away
to jesus to get a hold of his old man's throat
dam his breath to form again that one big long
last word freedom. was ragtime then jazz
was all the rap boogie to bop that kept
charlie dancing till we could figure out how
he rocked. try his rock on. find it didn't
fit. make a rock of our own to the rhythm
of a painful black movement in the mind
that springs you have to move with when it
spring or break and die. break, brother,
sister, and die.

PART THREE

DRAMA

Thomas C. Dent

(See p. 298 for biographical information.) The text of *Ritual Murder* is reprinted from *Callaloo* #2 (February 1978).

Ritual Murder

CHARACTERS

NARRATOR
JOE BROWN JR.
BERTHA (Joe's wife)
MRS. WILLIAMS (Joe's teacher)
DR. BRAYBOY (a black psychiatrist)
MR. ANDREWS (Joe's boss)
MRS. BROWN (Joe's mother)
MR. BROWN (Joe's father)
JAMES ROBERTS (Joe's friend)
MR. SPAULDING (anti-poverty program administrator)
CHIEF OF POLICE

SETTING: New Orleans, La.
TIME: Now
It is important that the actors make their speeches in rhythm to the background music.

NARRATOR: Last Summer, Joe Brown Jr., black youth of New Orleans, La., committed murder. Play a special *Summertime* for him and play the same *Summertime* for his friend James Roberts who he knifed to death. (WE HEAR *SUMMERTIME* UNDER THE NARRATOR'S VOICE.) In every black community of America; in the ghettos and neighborhood clubs where we gather to *hear our music*, we play *Summertime*; and in each community the bands play it differently. In no community does it sound like the *Summertime* of George Gershwin. It is blusier, darker, with its own beat and logic, its joy unknown to the white world. It is day now. The routine events of life have passed under the bridge. Joe Brown Jr. has been arrested, indicted, and formally charged with murder. It happened . . . it happened in a Ninth Ward bar—we need not name it for the purposes of this presentation. The stabbing was the culmination of an argument Joe Brown had with his friend. We have learned this, but the *Louisiana Weekly* only reported. "James Roberts is said to have made insulting remarks to Joe Brown, whereupon Brown pulled out a switchblade knife and stabbed Roberts three times in the chest before he could be subdued." The story received front

315

page play in the *Louisiana Weekly*, and a lead in the crime-of-the-day section in the white *Times-Picayune*. After that, it received only minor news play, since there are other crimes to report in New Orleans. Play *Summertime* for Joe Brown Jr., and play the same *Summertime* for his friend James Roberts who he knifed to death. (THE MUSIC DIES OUT.) Why did this murder happen? No one really knows. The people who know Joe Brown best have ideas.

(WE SEE BERTHA LOOKING AT T.V. THE SOUND IS OFF, ONLY THE PICTURE SHOWS. BERTHA IS YOUNG, ABOUT 20. SHE IS JOE'S WIFE. SHE IS IRONING WHILE LOOKING AT THE SET—IRONING BABY THINGS.)

BERTHA: Joe just didn't have any sense. He is smart, oh yes, has a good brain, but didn't have good sense. The important thing was to settle down, get a good job, and take care of his three children. We been in the Florida Ave. project now for almost a year, and we never have enough money. Look at the people on T.V., they make out okay. They fight, but they never let their fights destroy them. Joe didn't have control of his temper. He was a dreamer, he wanted things. But he wouldn't work to get them. Oh, he would take jobs in oyster houses, and he'd worked on boats ever since he was a kid. But he wouldn't come in at night, and sometimes he wouldn't get up in the morning to go to work. Sometimes he would come in and snap off the T.V. and say it was driving him crazy. It's not his T.V.—my father bought it, and besides, I like it, it's the only thing I have. This is just a 17 inch set, but I want a 21 inch set. Now I'll never get one because he had to go out and do something foolish. You ask me why he killed that boy? I don't know. But I think he killed him because he had a bad temper and wouldn't settle down. Joe was a mild person, but he carried knives and guns—that's the way his family is. I used to tell him about it all the time. Once I asked him, "When are you gonna get a better job and make more money?" He said, "When I get rid of you and those snotty kids." He could have done something if he had tried, if he had only tried: but instead, he wanted to take it out on us. I'll go see him, but now look; I have to do everything in this house myself: Iron the clothes, cook the meals, buy the food, apply for relief and get some help from my parents—and my father ain't working right now. Joe didn't want to have our last baby, Cynthia, but we couldn't murder her before she was even born and now I got to take care of her too. Joe knifed that boy because he was foolish, wouldn't settle down and accept things as they are, and because he didn't have common sense.

NARRATOR: Mrs. Williams, could you comment on your former student, Joe Brown Jr.?

MRS. WILLIAMS: I don't remember Joe Brown Jr. very well. I have so many children to try to remember. I had him three or four years ago just before he dropped out of school. I was his homeroom teacher. Joe was like all the others from the Ninth Ward, not interested in doing anything for themselves. You can't teach them anything. They don't want to learn, they *never* study, they won't sit still and pay attention in class. It's no surprise to me that

The material affects the educational / The spiritual's
    The underlying values
    The alienated
Those on whom America landed.

RITUAL MURDER   **317**

he's in trouble. I try to do my best here, but I have only so much patience. I tell you you don't know the things a teacher goes through with these kids. They come to class improperly dressed, from homes where they don't get any home training, which is why they are so ill-mannered. We try to teach them about America—about the opportunities America has to offer. We try to prepare them to get the best jobs they can—and you know a Negro child has to work harder. I teach History, Arithmetic, English, and Civics every day, and it goes in one ear and comes out the other. It gives me a terrible gas pain to have to go through it every day, and the noise these kids make is too, too hard on my ears. I've worked for ten years in this school, and I don't get paid much at all. But next month my husband and I will have saved enough money to buy a new Oldsmobile, which I'm happy to say will be the smartest, slickest, smoothest thing McDonough No. 81 has ever seen. Two boys got into a fight in the yard the other day and it was horrible. It pains me to hear the names they call each other—irritates my gas. Some of them even bring knives and guns to school. It's just terrible. I'm only relieved when I get home, turn on my T.V., take my hair down and face off, drink a nice strong cup of coffee, look out at my lawn in Pontchartrain Park, and forget the day. You ask me why Joe Brown murdered his friend in a Negro bar on a Saturday night and I tell you it is because he was headed that way in the beginning. These kids just won't listen, and don't want to learn, and that's all there is to it.

(LIGHTS ON JOE BROWN JR. HE IS WEARING BLUE JEANS AND A TEE SHIRT. HE IS SEATED. HE FACES THE AUDIENCE. THERE IS A TABLE IN FRONT OF HIM. ON THE TABLE IS A SMALL TRANSISTOR RADIO, BUT THE MUSIC WE HEAR IS GIL EVANS' *BARBARA SONG*.)

NARRATOR: Here is Joe Brown Jr.

JOE BROWN JR.: Once I saw a feature about surfing on T.V. Surfing on beautiful waves on a beach in Hawaii, or somewhere. . . .

(THE LIGHTS SHIFT TO ANOTHER MAN WHO IS SEATED ON THE OPPOSITE SIDE OF THE STAGE. HE IS A MUCH OLDER MAN, DRESSED IN A BUSINESS SUIT. HE IS A NEGRO. HE IS DR. BRAYBOY, A PSYCHIATRIST. HIS CHAIR DOES NOT FACE THE AUDIENCE; IT FACES JOE BROWN JR.)

NARRATOR: A black psychiatrist, Dr. Thomas L. Brayboy.

DR. BRAYBOY: At the core of Joe Brown's personality is a history of frustrations. Psychological, sociological, economic . . .

JOE BROWN JR.: . . . and I wanted to do that . . . surf. It was a dream I kept to myself. Because it would have been foolish to say it aloud. Nobody wants to be laughed at. And then I thought, I never see black people surfing . . .

DR. BRAYBOY: We might call Joe Brown's homicidal act an act of ritual murder. When murder occurs for no apparent reason but happens all the time, as in our race on Saturday nights, it is ritual murder. When I worked in Harlem Hospital in the emergency ward, I saw us coming in bleeding, blood seeping from the doors of the taxicabs, . . . icepicks and knives . . .

Thomas C. Dent

(THESE SPEECHES MUST BE SLOW, TO THE RHYTHM OF MUSIC.)

NARRATOR: Play *Summertime* for Joe Brown Jr., and a very funky *Summertime* for his friend James Roberts, who he knifed to death.

JOE BROWN JR.: . . . And then I thought, I don't see any black folks on T.V., ever. Not any real black folks, anyway. There are those so called black shows like *Good Times* and the *Jeffersons*, but they are so far removed from the kind of folks I know that they may as well be white too. I see us playing football, basketball, and baseball, and half the time I miss that because they be on in the afternoon, and I'm usually shelling oysters. "Where am I?" I asked my wife, and she answered, "In the Florida Avenue project where you are doing a poor job of taking care of your wife and children." My boss answered, "On the job, if you would keep your mind on what you are doing . . . count the oysters."

DR. BRAYBOY: . . . Icepicks and knives and frustration. My tests indicate that Joe Brown Jr. is considerably above average in intelligence. Above average in intelligence. *Above* average. Vocabulary and reading comprehension extraordinary . . .

NARRATOR: (TO AUDIENCE) Our purpose here is to discover why.

DR. BRAYBOY: . . . But school achievement extremely low. Dropped out at 18 in the eleventh grade.

JOE BROWN JR.: I began watching all the T.V. sets I could, looking for my image on every channel, looking for someone who looked like me. I knew I existed, but I didn't see myself in the world of television or movies. Even the black characters were not me. All the black characters were either weak and stupid, or some kind of superman who doesn't really exist in my world. I couldn't define myself, and didn't know where to begin. When I listened to soul music on the radio I understood that, and I knew that was part of me, but that didn't help me much. Something was not right, and it was like . . . like I was the only cat in the whole world who knew it. Something began to come loose in me, like my mind would float away from my body and lay suspended on a shelf for hours at a time watching me open oysters. No one ever suspected; but my mind was trying to define me, to tell me who I was the way other people see me, only it couldn't because it didn't know where to begin.

(THE SCENE SHIFTS TO THE DESK OF THE CHIEF OF POLICE. HE MAY BE PLAYED BY A WHITE ACTOR, OR A BLACK ACTOR IN WHITEFACE.)

NARRATOR: The Chief of Police.

CHIEF OF POLICE: The rate of crime in the streets in New Orleans has risen sharply. We know that most of our colored citizens are wholesome, law abiding, decent citizens. But the fact remains that the crime wave we are witnessing now across the nation is mostly nigger crime. Stop niggers and you will stop crime. The police must have more protection, more rights, and more weapons of all types to deal with the crime wave. We need guns, machine guns, multi-machine guns, gas bombs and reinforced nightsticks.

Otherwise America is going to become a nightmare of black crime in the streets.

(LIGHTS UP ON MR. ANDREWS, JOE'S BOSS. HE IS SITTING BEHIND A TERRIBLY MESSY DESK WITH PAPERS STUCK IN DESK HOLDERS. HIS FEET ARE ON THE DESK. HE IS EATING A LARGE MUFFELLETA SANDWICH. HIS IMAGE MUST BE ONE OF A RELAXED, INFORMAL INTERVIEW AT HIS OFFICE DURING LUNCHTIME. IF THERE ARE NO WHITE ACTORS, THE PART CAN BE PLAYED BY A BLACK ACTOR IN WHITE-FACE, BUT INSTEAD OF EATING LUNCH, HE SHOULD BE SMOKING A HUGE CIGAR.)

NARRATOR: Joe Brown's employer, Mr. Andrews.

MR. ANDREWS: I have trouble with several of my nigra boys, but I likes 'em. (HE ALMOST CHOKES ON HIS SANDWICH.) Joe was a little different from the rest . . . what would you say . . . dreamier . . . more absent minded. Joe was always quitting, but he must have liked it here 'cause he always came back. You can't tell me anything about those people. One time, during lunch hour, they were singing and dancing outside to the radio and I snuck up to watch. If they had seen me they would've stopped. It was amazing. The way them boys danced is fantastic. They shore got rhythm and a sense of style about them. Yes sir . . . and guess who got the most style . . . ole Joe. (BITES AND EATS.) That boy sure can dance. I loves to watch him. (BITES) Recently, he been going to the bathroom a lot and staying a long time. I ask the other boys, "Where's that doggone Joe?" They tell me. So one day I go to the john and there he is, sitting on the stool . . . readin'. I say, "Boy, I pay you to read or shell oysters?" He comes out all sulky. (SMILING) He could be kind of sensitive at times, you know. I been knowing him since he was a kid . . . born around here . . . kind of touchy. (ANDREWS HAS FINISHED HIS SANDWICH. HE TAKES HIS FEET OFF THE DESK. THROWS THE WRAPPER INTO THE TRASH, AND WIPES HIS HANDS. A SERIOUS LOOK COMES OVER HIS FACE.) As for why he killed that boy, I can't give you any answers. I think it has to do with nigras and the way they get wild on the weekend. Sometimes the good times get a little rough. And them (PAUSE) you don't know what a boy like Joe can get mixed up in, or any of them out there. (WAVES TOWARD THE DOOR) I don't understand it, and I know and likes 'em all, like they was my own family. My job is to keep 'em straight here . . . any trouble out of any of 'em and out the door they go.

(THE SCENE SHIFTS TO ANOTHER WHITE MAN. HE IS WELL DRESSED WITH HIS TIE LOOSENED, SITTING BEHIND AN EXTREMELY DISORDERED DESK. BLACK ACTOR CAN PLAY IN WHITEFACE. HE MUST, THROUGHOUT HIS SPEECH WEAR A PUBLIC RELATIONS SMILE. HE MUST SPEAK WITH A WINNING AIR.)

NARRATOR: Mr. Richard Spaulding, Director of the Poverty Program in New Orleans.

MR. SPAULDING: Last year we spent 3.5 million in five culturally deprived areas of New Orleans. This money has made a tremendous difference in the lives of our fine colored citizens. We have provided jobs, jobs, and more jobs. By creating, for the first time, indigenous community organizations controlled and operated by the people of the five target areas, we have, for the first time, provided a way to close the cultural and economic gap. Social Service Centers are going up in all these areas. We will develop a level of competency on par with American society as a whole. In the Desire area alone, 750 mothers go to our medical center each day. We have, in short, provided hope. Of course, there are still problems.

NARRATOR: Any insights into the murder of James Roberts last Summer by Joe Brown Jr.?

MR. SPAULDING: We are building community centers, baseball diamonds, basketball courts, little leagues, golden agers facilities, barbecue pits, swimming pools, badminton nets, and . . . if our dreams come true . . . well supervised and policed bowling alleys. It is our firm hope that sociology will stay out of neighborhood bars.

NARRATOR: Thank you, Mr. Spaulding.

(THE SCENE SHIFTS TO A MIDDLE AGED WOMAN SITTING ON A WELL WORN COUCH. SHE IS WEARING A PLAIN DRESS. THERE IS A SMALL TABLE WITH A LAMP AND BIBLE ON IT NEXT TO THE COUCH. SHE IS MRS. BROWN, JOE'S MOTHER. ACROSS THE STAGE, SITTING IN A BIG EASY CHAIR IS A MIDDLE AGED MAN IN WORK CLOTHES. HE IS MR. BROWN, JOE'S FATHER. HE IS DRINKING A LARGE CAN OF BEER WHICH, FROM TIME TO TIME, HE WILL PLACE ON THE FLOOR. HE LISTENS TO WHAT MRS. BROWN SAYS INTENTLY, BUT THERE MUST BE AN AIR OF DISTANCE IN HIS ATTITUDE TOWARD HER AND WHAT SHE SAYS, NEVER AFFECTION. THE AUDIENCE MUST BE MADE TO BELIEVE THEY ARE IN DIFFERENT PLACES.)

NARRATOR: (SOLEMNLY) This is Joe Brown's mother. (A SPOT FOCUSES ON MRS. BROWN. THERE IS ENOUGH LIGHT HOWEVER TO SEE MR. BROWN.)

MRS. BROWN: Joe was always a sweet kind boy, but Joe's problem is that he . . . stopped . . . going . . . to . . . church. I told him about that but it didn't make any difference. When we climb out of Christ chariot we liable to run into trouble. I tell the truth about my own children, like I tell it on anyone else. Once, before Joe got married he came home in a temper about his boss and his job. Talking bad about the white folks. Said he wished something from another planet would destroy them all. Said he didn't like the way his boss talked to him, that he should be paid more, and like that. We all get mad at the white people, but there is no point in it. So many colored folks ain't even got a job. I told him, "If you think you can do better, go back and finish school." But no, he didn't finish school, he just complained. "Stay in church," I told him, but he started hanging around with bad friends. Bad friends lead to a bad end. Talking bad about white people is like busting your head against a brick wall.

NARRATOR: Mrs. Brown, do you feel your son would kill for no reason? There must have been a reason.

MRS. BROWN: When you hang around a bad crowd on Saturday nights, troubles are always gonna come. I told him to stay out of those bars. I do know what happened or why. A friend told me the other boy was teasing Joe and

Joe got mad. He was sensitive, you know, very serious and sensitive. He didn't like to be rubbed the wrong way.

NARRATOR: Mrs. Brown, the purpose of this program is to discover why your son knifed his friend. No one seems to have answers. We are using the scientific approach. Do *you* have any answers?

MRS. BROWN: (DESPAIRINGLY) I don't know why. I don't understand. You try to protect your children as best you can. It's just one of those things that happens on Saturday nights in a colored bar; like a disease. You hope you and nobody you know catches it. The Lord is the only protection.

NARRATOR: And your husband? Would he have any information, any ideas?

MRS. BROWN: (SHARPLY) I haven't seen that man in four years.

(BOTH MRS. BROWN AND NARRATOR LOOK AT MR. BROWN.)

MR. BROWN: I plan to go see the boy . . . I just haven't had a chance yet. I have another family now and I can't find any work. I help him out when I can, but . . . (PAUSE) . . . I can't understand why he would do a thing like that.

NARRATOR: If we could hear what James Roberts has to say.

(WE RETURN TO THE *SUMMERTIME* THEME AND THE SCENE OF THE CRIME, THE BAR-ROOM WHERE THE PLAY BEGAN WITH JOE BROWN JR. STANDING OVER JAMES ROBERTS' BODY AND ALL OTHER ACTORS FROZEN IN THEIR ORIGINAL POSITIONS AS IN THE OPEN-ING SCENE. AFTER THE NARRATOR SPEAKS THE BODY OF JAMES ROBERTS BEGINS TO SLOWLY ARISE FROM THE FLOOR AIDED BY JOE BROWN. IT IS IMPORTANT THAT BROWN HELPS ROBERTS GET UP.)

JAMES ROBERTS: (BEGINS TO LAUGH . . .) It was all a joke. Nothing happened that hasn't happened between us before. Joe is still my best friend . . . if I were alive I would tell anyone that. That Saturday was a terrible one . . . not just because the lights went out for me. I heard a ringing in my ears when I woke up that morning. When I went to work at the hotel the first thing I had to do was take out the garbage. Have you ever smelled the stink of shrimp and oyster shells first thing in the morning? I hate that. The sounds of the street and the moan of the cook's voice; that's enough to drive anyone crazy, and I heard it every day. That day I decided to leave my job for real . . . one more week at the most.

JOE BROWN JR.: (GETTING UP FROM THE BUNK INTO A SITTING POSITION) Damn. The same thing happened to me that day. I decided I was going to leave my job.

JAMES ROBERTS: (LOOKING AT JOE WITH DISGUST) Man, you are disgusting. You all the time talking about leaving your job.

NARRATOR: (TO ROBERTS, THEN TO JOE.) Get to what happened at the cafe please. We don't have all night.

JAMES ROBERTS: We were both very uptight . . . mad at our jobs—everybody . . . everything around us.

JOE BROWN JR.: (EXCITEDLY) I know I was . . . I was ready to shoot somebody.

JAMES ROBERTS: Shut up. This is my scene.

JOE BROWN JR.: You won't even let anybody *agree* with you.

NARRATOR: Please.

JAMES ROBERTS: Joe went on and on all evening and all night. We were getting higher and higher, going from bar to bar. We went to Scotties, then to Shadowland, to the Havana . . . we had my sister's car . . . Joe getting mad and frustrated and talking 'bout what he was gonna do. By the time we got to the Ninth Ward Cafe, we was both stoned out of our minds. Joe getting dreamier and dreamier. He was talking about all his problems, his wife, his job, his children. I could understand that.

JOE BROWN JR.: You really couldn't because you don't have those problems.

(WE HEAR OTIS REDDING'S *SATISFACTION* FROM THE ALBUM, "OTIS REDDING LIVE.")

JAMES ROBERTS: Joe was screaming about the white man. He said he was $1500 in debt . . . working like hell for the white man, then turning right around and giving it back to him. He said he couldn't laugh no more.

(FROM THIS POINT ON THERE MUST BE LITTLE CONNECTION BETWEEN JOE'S THOUGHTS AND THOSE OF JAMES ROBERTS. THE OTIS REDDING RECORDING CONTINUES, BUT MUST NOT DROWN OUT THE SPEECHES.)

JOE BROWN JR.: I had a dream . . . I had a dream . . . I dreamed I had 66 million dollars left to me by an unknown relative . . .

JAMES ROBERTS: (SLOW, TO THE MUSIC. AS MUCH PANTOMIME AS POSSIBLE, AS THOUGH HE IS RE-ENACTING THE SCENE.) We were in the Ninth Ward Cafe sitting in a booth by ourselves. There was something on the juke box, I believe it was Otis Redding. It was a hot night. Joe was talking about how there was nowhere he could go to relax anymore. Then suddenly, his mind would go off into outer space somewhere and I had to jerk him back. I would ask him what he was thinking about, and he would say he wasn't happy with himself. He didn't know himself or where he was headed to anymore.

JOE BROWN JR.: . . . I always get screwed up when I try to figure out the *first* thing I'm going to buy . . . a new car . . . maybe . . . Mark IV . . . a new house . . . a brick one with wood paneling . . . a new suit . . . a tailor made three piece . . . new shoes . . . some high steppers . . . a new transistor radio . . . a big Sony that plays loud with big sound . . . Then I'd give everybody a bill . . . but I can't figure out what I'm going to buy *first* . . .

JAMES ROBERTS: I said, man what are you talking about. I don't understand all this blues over what happens everyday. He said he wanted to believe there is hope. I told him there is no hope. You a black mother-fucker and you may as well learn to make the best of it.

JOE BROWN JR.: . . . People always tell me I can't make up my mind what I want, or I want things that don't make sense, or I want too much instead of being satisfied with just a little. People always tell me I ask too many questions . . . especially questions that no one can answer . . . and I am just frustrating myself because I can never find the answers. The way I figure it you may as well dream 66 million as 66 thousand. The way I figure it, you may as well ask questions you *don't* have answers to; what's the point in asking questions everyone knows the answers to. Life is just a little thing anyway . . . doesn't really amount to much when you think about time and place.

JAMES ROBERTS: (INTENSELY AND QUICKER) Then he just blew. Screamed nobody calls him a black mother fucker. I just laughed. Everybody calls him that cause that's just what he is. There nothing wrong with calling anyone a black mother fucker. We been doing it to each other all our lives, and we did it all evening while we were drinking. I just laughed. He jumps up, pulls out his blade and goes for my heart. I could outfight Joe any day but . . .

JOE BROWN JR.: High steppers . . .

JAMES ROBERTS: . . . He got the jump on me and I couldn't get to my blade. It was ridiculous. He was like a crazy man . . . a wild man . . . turning on me for no reason when I done nothing to him at all . . . and shouting, "there is no hope."

JOE BROWN JR.: High steppers . . .

JAMES ROBERTS: Before I knew it I was stunned and weak and there was blood all over the chest of my yellow polo shirt . . . I felt the lights darken, and my whole body turned to rubber . . .

JOE BROWN JR.: High steppers on a Saturday night . . .

JAMES ROBERTS: . . . But I couldn't move anything. (PAUSE) Last thing I heard was Booker T. and the M.G.s playing *Groovin'* . . . Joe . . . his eyes blazing . . . everything turned red.

NARRATOR: (TO ROBERTS AFTER PAUSE) You mean this caused such a brutal act? You called him a name?

JAMES ROBERTS: That's all it takes sometimes.

NARRATOR: And you think this makes sense? To lose your life at nineteen over such an insignificant thing?

JAMES ROBERTS: It happens all the time. I accept it. Joe is still my friend. Friends kill each other all the time . . . unless you have an enemy you can both kill.

NARRATOR: And you Joe?

JOE BROWN JR.: What is there to say? It happened. It happens all the time. One thing I learned; when you pull a knife or gun don't fool around, use it, or you might not have a chance to. Better him dead than me. He would say the same thing if it was the other way around.

NARRATOR: (TO JOE BROWN JR.) What did you mean when you said there is no hope?

JOE BROWN JR.: (EVENLY) I don't know. *There is no hope.* Here in this jail, with my fate, I might be better off dead.

NARRATOR: One more question. (TO JAMES ROBERTS) Do you feel you died for anything? Is there any meaning in it?

JAMES ROBERTS: Yes, I died for something. But I don't know what it means.

NARRATOR: (TO JOE BROWN JR.) And did your act mean anything?

JOE BROWN JR.: (SOFTLY) I suppose so. But I can't imagine what.

(THE MUSIC OF A BLUESY *SUMMERTIME*. THE NARRATOR COMES OUT TO DOWN-STAGE CENTER, AS IN THE BEGINNING OF THE PLAY. HE ADDRESSES THE AUDIENCE DIRECTLY IN EVEN TONES.)

NARRATOR: Play *Summertime* for Joe Brown Jr. and play a very funky *Summertime* for his friend James Roberts who he knifed to death.

(*SUMMERTIME* THEME CONTINUES AS NARRATOR SLOWLY SCRUTINIZES THE PEOPLE HE HAS JUST INTERVIEWED.)

Our purpose here is to discover why. No one seems to have answers. Do you have any?

(NARRATOR MOVES TO ACTORS WHO PLAY BERTHA, MRS. WILLIAMS, MRS. BROWN, JOE BROWN SR., AND DR. BRAYBOY ASKING THE QUESTION "DO YOU HAVE ANSWERS?" TO WHICH THEY RESPOND:)

BERTHA: Joe knifed that boy because he was foolish, wouldn't settle down and accept things as they are, and because he didn't have common sense.

MRS. WILLIAMS: You ask me why Joe Brown murdered his friend in a Negro bar on a Saturday night and I tell you it is because he was headed that way in the beginning. These kids just won't listen, and don't want to learn, and that's all there is to it.

MR. BROWN: I plan to go see the boy . . . I just haven't had a chance yet. I help him out when I can but (PAUSE) I can't understand why he would do a thing like that.

MRS. BROWN: It's just one of those things that happens on a Saturday night in a colored bar . . . like a disease. You hope you and nobody you know catches it. The Lord is the only protection.

DR. BRAYBOY: When murder occurs for no apparent reason but happens all the time as in our race on Saturday nights, it is ritual murder. That is, no apparent reason. There are reasons. The reasons are both personal and common. When a people who have no method of letting off steam against the source of their oppression explode against each other, homicide, under these conditions, is a form of group suicide. When personal chemistries don't mix just a little spark can bring about the explosion. Icepicks and knives, and whatever happens to be lying around.

NARRATOR: When murder occurs for no apparent reason, but happens all the time, as in our race on a Saturday night, it is ritual murder.

(THE FOLLOWING LINES SHOULD BE DISTRIBUTED AMONG THE ACTORS AND DELIVERED TO THE AUDIENCE DIRECTLY.)

That is, no apparent reason.
There are reasons.
The reasons are both personal and common.
When a people who have no method of letting off steam against the source of their oppression explode against each other, homicide, under these conditions, is a form of group suicide.

When personal chemistries don't mix just a little spark can bring about the explosion.

Icepicks

Knives

And whatever happens to be lying around.

NARRATOR: (MOVING DOWNSTAGE FACING AUDIENCE DIRECTLY.) We have seen something unpleasant, but the play is over. Yes, we see this thing (GESTURING TO STAGE BEHIND HIM) night after night, weekend after weekend. Only you have the power to stop it. It has to do with something in our minds. (PAUSE. *SUMMERTIME* MUSIC GRADUALLY INCREASES IN VOLUME.) Play *Summertime* for Joe Brown Jr., and play a very funky *Summertime* for his friend James Roberts who he knifed to death. (NARRATOR WALKS OVER TO DR. BRAYBOY AND SHAKES HIS HAND AS LIGHTS FADE TO BLACK.)

THE END

Kalamu ya Salaam [Val Ferdinand]
(1947–   )

A native of New Orleans, ya Salaam is the most prolific writer of his generation in the black South. Currently a senior partner in Bright Moments, a public relations firm, he served as editor of *The Black Collegian* for thirteen years; he has also been executive director of the New Orleans Jazz and Heritage Foundation. Ya Salaam is the author of two books of essays, *Our Women Keep Our Skies from Falling* (1980) and *Our Music Is No Accident* (1987) and six books of poetry: *The Blues Merchant, Hofu Ni Kwenu, Pamoja Tutashinda, Ibura, Revolutionary Love*, and *Iron Flowers*. His poems, essays, reviews, and articles on music have appeared in numerous magazines and newspapers. A 1987–1988 production of his play *Blk Love Song #1*, published in the anthology *Black Theater USA*, won a "Best of Fringe" award from the *Manchester Evening News*. Among his other awards are two ASCAP Deems Taylor Awards for excellence in writing about music (1981 and 1989), the 1986 Deep South Writer's Contest Award for prose, and a first place in the 1990 CAC Region New Play Competition. *Somewhere in the World (Long Live Assata)* is reprinted from the author's manuscript.

Somewhere in the World
(Long Live Assata)

CHARACTERS

SOFIA: Dark skin. Mid-thirties. Plain in appearance. Tall. Medium-length, untrimmed natural. No perfume. First appearance: Is wearing a plain, white shift. Barefoot. Second appearance: Is wearing baggy, dark-green pants with a light-green knee-length smock. Sandals.

MARY: Light brown or reddish color. Mid-thirties. Medium height and weight. Attractive. Hair is in braids. Strong sandalwood scent. First appearance: Is wearing a plain, white shift. Second appearance: Is wearing a red, full-length shift, with rings and bangles on both hands and arms. Sandals.

SON: Brown skin. Late teens/early twenties. Slender. Dressed as a traditional African warrior, has bells on ankles and carries a spear. Barefoot. Coconut oil is rubbed on his skin.

WARRIOR: Black woman of any skin tone. Late thirties/early forties. Slender. Wears hair close cropped. First appearance: Wears a colorful lappa and bright yellow blouse, with a single bangle. Barefoot. Second appearance: Wears dark-black pants and short-sleeve shirt and only a necklace with African figurine. Sturdy, lightweight shoes.

SCENE I

(No scenery except a pattern of red, white, and blue lights serving as a backdrop. They remain on throughout this scene. Claudine Amina Meyers playing Marion Brown piano music is heard. Soft, bluish-white light on stage center. When lights come up, the whole area is dimly lit. The only prop is a block that serves as a chair and point of reference.

Mary can neither see nor hear Son. Sofia can hear but not see Son. Son sees and hears both Mary and Sofia. Every time Son speaks, Sofia searches for him in the audience. Talks to and touches different men, relating to them as if they were her son. But keeps moving from person to person, searching for him. Many of the movements are dance/semi-dance.)

SOFIA: (Sofia is sitting on a block, right of center. Mary is approaching her from the rear.) I was afraid of the dark then. Afraid of the distances I could not see, afraid of my shadow that was not there. I listen to you coming nearer to me now, and I try to ready myself. There is no love left. What do we own anymore? There is no love left.

MARY: There is love or whatever you should choose to call it.

SOFIA: (Facing Mary.) No, when I was younger, we called it love and tried to love and have children. But now, now I am older and there is not love.

MARY: Where are your children now?

SOFIA: What children? The child? The one I had. The one child I was allowed to have? The testimony of my attempts to live? He is dead.

SON: (He has been standing still off to the side.) Mama, you didn't love me. Don't make it sound so tragic.

SOFIA: Where are you, my son? My child, where are you? (Rises quickly.)

SON: I am somewhere where you cannot reach me. I am somewhere where I love to be. I am inside of me and outside of you. It is too much. I could really, really love myself if it were not for you and all of the others. I could relate to life. But now there is nothing left except this cold wandering through what you call your lives, loves, your experiences.

SOFIA: Where are you?

MARY: Darling, what are you saying? Come to me. (Mary crosses to Sofia and hugs her.) There, there, let me soothe through to your wounds. Let me hug you to my warmness.

SOFIA: (Pulling away from her.) I keep hearing my son. I keep feeling the heat of his breath rising close to my face. (She walks directly to him and

stops just short of touching him.) I can almost feel his hand reaching out
to me.

MARY: Oh dear, but there is only us here. Let me love you, you will feel
better.

SON: Go back to your bitch, mama, and let me stay dead. Go back to your
Black bitch, and let her stick her fingers into your body. Go away from me.

SOFIA: Kofi. Kofi, don't say those things, Kofi.

MARY: Dearest stop screaming so. Who are you talking to? Tell me.

SOFIA: There is nothing to tell. I just thought I heard my son.

MARY: You're upset. You should rest, come to bed.

SOFIA: I'm coming. You go on, I'm coming. I want to know why Kofi is
saying those things. (Mary exits.)

SON: And, why not say then, your whore is waiting, ain't she?

SOFIA: Kofi, you don't know what the world was like during those years.

SON: It was like what killed me dead as I am now. It was a murderous time,
I know that.

SOFIA: Do you really know all of the forces that killed you?

SON: I know them. I feel them. I can smell them—sense them crawling always
there. Blind lunges bursting holes in my heart and the hearts of my people.

SOFIA: Do not hate the dark.

SON: I don't hate the dark. I love the dark. The dark of night—the dark of
me. But, I also need the light. I want to see a new day.

SOFIA: All of us wanted that. (Silence. Sofia sits on the block. Son crosses to
her and bends over looking directly into her eyes.)

SON: Why did you never look me in the eyes?

SOFIA: (Sofia jumps up at the sound of his voice and runs to a man in the
audience, touches his face, his eyes with both her hands.) You had your
father's eyes, the eyes he had, that's why. He wanted to be free. (Dances
in a semi-circle.) He wanted—he wanted to swing his arms loosely all about
him and fill his Black chest with air and tilt his woolly head to the skies
into the sun. Your father, my once used-to-be man—my lover.

SON: Damn, all that used to be. Damn, that. Is that all you can discuss as if
your mouth is rotten—the sweets of what used to be, the candy of the days
gone by—that's all you niggers know. The days, those days, them days.
The day of when before the white man was come into us, the days once
ago when some man stuck his flesh into you. The screaming days of struggle
and pain. I was there in those gone-by days, you know, and those years did
not treat me well. They did not treat me well at all. Shall I ever have a
wonderful, sweet time to remember? Where are the days for the Black young
to love?

SOFIA: Let me explain why—why you really are dead—why we have no Black
young.

SON: Damn all of that—those rationalizations. Deal with now. Deal with that
lady in your bed. Why couldn't we stop it?

SOFIA: We didn't see it coming. We never knew.

SON: You never knew you needed men? Are you saying you never felt that need?

SOFIA: I felt it. I always wanted a man. Oh, I wanted a man so deeply. And that is why I loved your father. That is why I ran to Washington to be with him. That is why you were conceived.

SON: And is that why I am dead?

SOFIA: We did not know, son. Believe me, we did not know.

MARY: (Calling out.) Sofia, are you coming to bed?

SON: I'm glad I'm dead. I'm glad. In fact, if I were you, I would kill myself rather than spend my days in sterile, loveless, non-productive . . .

SOFIA: You don't know what you're saying. The only reason that you can say it, is because you're already dead.

SON: Dead. Yes, I'm dead, and you are dead too, only you don't know it. Only you pretend to live.

SOFIA: We all are. We are all dead, and we are all pretending. We all are.

MARY: Sofia, are you coming to bed? (Mary enters.) Don't you ever tire of talking to yourself? Why are you always thinking about the days that are gone? We choose to remain in America. We have made our choice, and so come now, let us live with it. We could do nothing else but what we did. Let's not regret our choice to live . . .

SON: (He talks at the same time as Mary. Both are speaking slowly but very forcefully.) How can you, Negroes, always find ways to accept all of this shit! How can you find excuses to rationalize your deaths, your murders! Why didn't you leave? Why didn't you change this filth or leave it? Leave it to rot and die on its own or fight it to the finish?

MARY: . . . here. Here is where we belong. We are still much better off than those who are digging their hands into the dirt to grow things to eat, to live. We are better off than those who are living outside under the sun, near the stars, influenced by the moon. We are better off. We are better off here.

SOFIA: Don't be so angry and bitter.

MARY: Sofia, who are you talking to?

SOFIA: A deadness, a spirit. Someone who should have been our future.

MARY: How long has it been?

SOFIA: Three, four—too long. I don't know. Too long.

MARY: It's almost four years since the men are gone.

SOFIA: It's been forever. It's been for centuries—eons. It's been too hard to remember, too far ago away to any longer have been really real.

MARY: Come on, Sofia, don't think about it.

SON: Your woman is calling mama. Don't think about it.

SOFIA: Don't say that. Don't. Stop blaming me. I did all I could. I had you . . .

MARY: Sofia, you're upsetting yourself.

SOFIA: Why don't you leave me alone? Why do you always return to haunt me? I conceived you. I carried your weight inside of me. I fed you with my blood.

MARY: Darling, stop. Don't try to remember.

SON: You weren't the only woman to become pregnant.

SOFIA: But I did it. Your father and I, we . . .

MARY: Stop it. Stop it. All your talk of children and men. They don't exist anymore. We Black people will have no more children. All the men are gone. They are off somewhere, and so now we must look after ourselves, see to our own existence.

Men! I remember even when they were here we did not really have them. Ask me. I know. I remember the animals, and the niggauhs who pretended to be men. I remember so well.

My life was different from yours, Sofia. I did not have a man. I did not have a son. So, I cannot really miss all of that. I was first fucked at fourteen in a doorway step with my dress pulled up. I can only remember being used, being jugged into. I never knew this love you sit around and daydream about. I ain't got no sweet dreams.

SON: That's the typical hard-luck story of Negro women. Y'all always running the same old sad stories about when and where and how you lost your virginity or who got you to lie down first and what he or she did.

SOFIA: Kofi, why are you talking like that?

SON: 'Cause I'm dead and shouldn't be, dead and didn't really have to be.

MARY: A woman and her dreams. Dreams about deadness. I could tell you stories. Stories about my mother and her children. About me and my six brothers and sisters trying to survive. I could tell you about my life.

SON: And, it would be the same old story.

SOFIA: I'm tired of all this. Tired of *all* this.

SON: Why did you accept this kind of life? Why? When? How?

SOFIA: I'm tired of this. Tired of all of this dead living. I wanted sunrises and moons and children at my breasts. Fires and long walks, my black feet in the water. Soft, singing breezes and the rhythm of my man's breathing dancing in my ears. I wanted that, and what do I have? What do I get? The United States of America. A so-called "new" free world. A planet spinning through space. A dead star and dust to cry on. In seventy, we dreamed of a Black nation. And now, we have only this . . .

SON: Deadness and dead ghosts. Restless spirits like me. Unavenged ancestors. Unlived life.

MARY: A Black nation? (She laughs.) Ha! A Black nation. Blackness? What is that? What was that? What was it ever but a sloppy bid to be something else other than the animals we were. The animals we are now. I know. I was one of those Black nation builders. Oh yes, there was a time. There was a time and a place and a year or two. And people, so-called Black people. I was there. I was in it. I was an actress—an artist. I was with them then. Our art spoke of revolution, of liberation, of nation building. But our lives, the real art, the real art spoke of other things. The real art was false. We were only freaks, only fucked-up freaks. All that I know about the way we make love, I learned then. Oh, where is New York now? Where are our cities? Where is that nation we never built?

I could tell you about our supposed-to-be Black days. Those freaky days when we were just then learning to feel each other's asses, just learning how to do our thangs. Our weird, weird thangs. It doesn't sound so pretty, does it? I could tell you of the real love that we never expressed, but what good would it do? Would it change this reality? Yes, those sweet days you remember are too sweet, too sweet. What difference does it make, then or now, the only difference is the time and place. We were no better then and are now no worse.

SOFIA: We were not all freaks. Not all of us were faking. There were some of us who really wanted to build a nation.

SON: And so you killed your children.

MARY: What does it matter! We did not do it. And it wasn't the white man. It was us.

Sofia, come to bed. Let me love you. It does no good to remember such things.

SON: Love?

SOFIA: We missed something. What did we miss? What didn't we do?

MARY: It doesn't matter. The time is past us. Years ago was the time to ask those questions.

SON: You will see me no more. Just like your lover said: It doesn't matter—not anymore. It just doesn't matter. There's no love left. Only dead men. And homosexuals locked up somewhere and lost women entertaining themselves in plush bedrooms.

SOFIA: No. No. No. It is not like that. You are wrong. You all sound so self-righteous. You say that we did not really try. But, that's a lie. It's a white lie. We tried. We tried. Many of us tried. And if we failed, it was not because we did not try. We fought this evilness with all we could.

MARY: Oh yes, I know how we fought. Drugged and doped. High on this and that. Scratching at each other's bodies. Do you want to know who taught me to be the lover I am? Do you want to know the sister's name? You've read her Black poems.

SON: There's no need to hear it. I'm going, mama. The more I find out, the sicker I feel. I'm dead. A spirit and yet it still disgusts me—this thing you all call life.

MARY: Sofia, I said, do you want to know the name of the Black sister who . . .

SOFIA: I don't want to hear any more bad news. That's all people have brought me these last few years, bad news. No. I don't care who she was.

SON: Good-bye! This day will strangle you. You have no past and hence, no future.

SOFIA: Wait. I want to tell you how it was, how you were conceived, what your father and I did.

MARY: Sofia, stop talking to the walls. No one else is listening. Who do you think you're talking to? There is no one else here but you and I. See. (Mary lunges and swings her arms around the space.) See. There is no one else here.

SON: Salaam, my mother. I shall let the past remain dead. You cannot agitate the present, and there will be no future. (He exits.)

SOFIA: Wait! I want to tell you . . . Kofi. (She listens.) Kofi? Well, I will tell you anyway. Do you remember when they passed laws against having more than one child and were forcing us to become sterilized? Remember how they tried to turn us all into unisexed creatures. Well, it was then that I had a man. It was then, during the war in Africa, when our men were being slaughtered. It was then when there were at least three million more Black women than men. It was then.

MARY: Why talk about it. Those of us who are left don't want to remember.

SOFIA: It was the same with us then. We did not want to remember what had been done to us, so that we did not see it when it happened to us again, but I will remember. I will not forget what happened to us. I cannot forget that. I must not.

MARY: I'm going to bed. I don't want to think about the past anymore. There is no nation now, that's all I know. No nation. No men. Nothing except us. Come to bed. Come to bed, Sofia. I feel like making love.

SOFIA: I'm coming. Yes. I'll sleep with you and caress you, but it will not be love.

MARY: Well, then let's just call it love.

SOFIA: Which is all we did before. Just did anything and called it love. No, we'll sleep and play with each other's bodies, but it will not be love. I wish that I could really love again. Somewhere there are Black people loving each other. I wish I was there.

MARY: Sofia, come to bed.

SOFIA: I'm coming. (They exit. Sofia is a few, reluctant steps behind Mary.)

(Lights down, with only the red, white, and blue up full. Amina Meyers' "African Blues" comes up slowly, the background lights fade in proportion to the music's rise. The music plays for a full minute. Begins to slowly fade. Lights out.)

SCENE II

(This time, only red lights are on. The block is gone. Warrior is on the floor. Sofia enters room. It is another day, unspecific time. A woman is lying on the floor. Straw-colored or light-yellow lights come up slowly to full.)

SOFIA: Mary. Come. They have brought another one here.

MARY: (Entering.) Where? (Stopping to look—turning away.) I wish it would stop. I wish . . .

SOFIA: Let's help her . . .

MARY: How? What can one of us do for another? All of us are . . .

SOFIA: (Crossing to the woman and bending over her. She starts to touch her, draws back as if too near a fire.) Suppose they're watching . . .

WARRIOR: I am a survivor—a Black survivor. (She raises her head erect. Sofia steps back quickly. Mary crosses nearer to Sofia.) AaahhhHHH! (She screams with all her strength.) If I have nothing left but my voice, I will raise it in war/song. The fist of my scream beating their ears. AaahhhHHH! (She breathes heavily after screaming. She is weak but rocks shakily to a kneeling position. She begins to laugh.) They cannot kill me. They cannot kill you. (Her finger points at Sofia, at Mary, at people in the audience, at the air, toward the ceiling.) They cannot kill me. They can kill, but they cannot kill. (There is blood on the front of her.) YOU CANNOT KILL ME! (She gains her feet. Rocks a moment and then lurches forward, laughing. A shot rings out. Her body jerks, stiffens, crumples and falls. At the sound of the shot, Mary and Sofia fall quickly to the floor, holding each other, their heads down.) What they have stopped was only the flesh. (She rises gracefully, slowly. Raises her right fist in a salute. Brings both arms high, forms an oval. Dances. Sings.) And still, I rise. They can't kill me. Spirit reach. Struggle On. Arc of love. And still now we gonna rise. We gonna rise, make sun dawn shine. Like love. Rhythm real, insistent. They can't stop I and I. (Laughing. Dancing above Mary and Sofia, stopping beside them.) Why do you try to hide? Why do you cry? Sobbing like penitent children. Life and struggle are your birthright. Survive. (She bends and touches first Mary, then Sofia. Laughs gently. Dances away. Back to the spot where she fell and quietly lies down.)

SOFIA: (Looking up after a brief silence.) Why don't they kill us too. Why not shoot us too? Why let us live, if you can call this living? (Crawls toward the body.) I wonder who she was.

WARRIOR: All us you. (Neither Sofia nor Mary hear her now.) You watch a sister die, watch us get cut down and ask who are you? Are you so blind you do not see yourself in others?

MARY: (Rising slowly to her feet, but ready to fall back down. After a little, she thinks that it is safe to stand up straight.) Let's drag her away. Soon, she will be stiff and start to stink.

WARRIOR: If you have strength enough to dispose of the dead, you have strength enough to fight the enemy. Don't let burying our dead consume all of our will. Bury flesh, not spirit.

MARY: (Bends and grabs an arm.) Help me, Sofia. Let's put her by the others.

SOFIA: (Moving to help Mary, she takes the other arm. They begin pulling Warrior offstage.) Why do they let us live?

MARY: I guess because we are good at forgetting about the dead.

(They exit dragging the body. While they are away, the Warrior enters again, stumbling, falling. Her hands tied behind her back. Defiance on her face. There is a bit of blood trickling down the side of her mouth. She has been beaten. She rises on one knee and faces the direction from which she entered. Rises to both feet. Stays strong, straight. Mary and Sofia enter. Mary sees the Warrior first and stops. Sofia bumps gently into Mary, then sees the Warrior.)

SOFIA: (Frightened.) Ohh . . . you were . . . (pointing to the spot on the floor where the Warrior had died) . . . we just . . . (pointing to where they had dragged the body off) . . . but . . .

WARRIOR: (Looks at the two standing before her. Wipes her mouth on her shoulder. Turns to show her tied hands behind her.) Untie me, please. (Her head is held high. No one moves. Warrior looks over her shoulder. Then turns slowly. Takes a step toward the two, they draw back.) What are you afraid of? Are you afraid that they will tie you up too? That they will beat you in the face and spoil your features? Or what? Untie me.

MARY: (Sofia starts to move forward. Mary stops her, holding her arm.) Remember the last time we . . .

WARRIOR: Stop collaborating. Untie me. (Looking at Sofia, then at Mary.) Wh . . . (wipes her mouth on her shoulder.) What is this shit! What are you afraid of? What have you got to lose?

SOFIA: The last time they chained us and whipped us and wouldn't let us sleep and said that they were going to kill us . . .

WARRIOR: (Smiling, shaking her head.) I'll take your beating, just untie me.

MARY: No. (Sofia starts to move forward.) Sofia, they will separate us. We'll lose each other.

WARRIOR: Three is stronger than two. Untie me.

MARY: They'll put us back outside in the mud.

WARRIOR: You're in a . . . (she wipes her mouth) mental mud now.

SOFIA: They'll kill us if we help you . . .

WARRIOR: Probably. But then, if you don't help, you probably deserve to die.

SOFIA: You don't know us, how can you say that?

WARRIOR: I don't know you? The smell of your fear fills this place. How can someone not know you? Do you know you?

MARY: How do we know you're not one of them come to trick us?

WARRIOR: How do I know you're not one of them put here to torture me? (They glare at each other. Addressing Sofia.) How many masters do you have? I asked you for help. You started to help me. You stopped. What happened? Why? (Sofia drops her head.) Well. Speak slave. Tell me how sweet your captivity, how pleasant your slavery. Speak on it woman.

SOFIA: Don't make us . . .

WARRIOR: I'm not making you anything. I'm only asking you questions. Questions you should have answered for yourself a long, long time ago.

MARY: Who are you?

WARRIOR: If I tell you, will you tell me who you are? (Neither answer.) Never mind, you'd probably only lie. Dress it up. Make your groveling seem like valor. Make me try to think your blues is reggae, your spirituals are liberation anthems, your shuffling is copoiera. Never mind.

It depends on where I am as to what they call me. I call me warrior/ fighter/obeah/see line/tubman/nzinga/yaa/assata woman. Like once in Haiti, under the hot sun, they caught my fighting man and strung a rope to kill him by. But they wanted spectacle and fear to fill those remaining. So they gathered us many heads deep and made us watch as they marched him

Cf. Arthur Flowers Mojo Blues

forward to the rope. And they put my daughter and me at the front to see our seed-giver swing.

You know this hanging thing is sexual. They watch to see the last ejaculation as the male body dies. The last act of death is to pass semen. And that is why they wanted to hang him naked. And they drew it out, hoping he would break and cry for them and then they could plant fear in us.

He started off walking proud. I saw him as the soldiers brought him out. But then, they had a trick for this too. A simple thing really. They hung one man right as they brought another out. So, you are walking forward toward death. You hear the body death crack and see the tongue hang out. The sound that hanging machine they made has when the floor falls away. I saw my man's knees hesitate a little. Like this. (She mimics his walk.) And it is usually at that moment that a mother or lover cries out as she watches a man strain for air, twist sickening, strangling, eyes bulging, the penis erect for the last time. Women often cry at that moment. And the men avert their eyes, look down diminished inside themselves.

So someone cried screaming as they brought him round to hang. The death of a slave is not a spectacle, but when they have captured a warrior, when they kill a warrior that they want to use as a lesson. So they hang those who fought least first and save the stronger for last. So he is walking. And he hears the heavy wails of this woman in the dust underneath a dead man swaying, neck broken. And he stops. I see his eyes. He does not want to die.

SOFIA: Nobody want to die.

WARRIOR: Death is not the question. We will all die. Life, how will we live? That is the question.

MARY: So what did you do to help him face death?

WARRIOR: I hung myself.

SOFIA: You what?

WARRIOR: My daughter and I, we both hung ourselves. We showed him that death was not to be feared. We showed everyone. For a slave who is not afraid to die cannot forever be held a slave.

MARY: You what . . . how did you?

WARRIOR: It's true. (She wipes her mouth.) You don't believe me. But it's true. My daughter climbed to the rope, put her head in, and said: "To die for our people is to live. Be strong, African man!" and hung herself.

SOFIA: What did you do?

WARRIOR: My husband tried to run forward. He cried out. The soldiers held him. I walked to my daughter . . .

SOFIA: Didn't they stop you?

WARRIOR: No. They were too surprised. It shocked them to see someone choose to die in order to make someone else stronger. I saw him look at me. I took her down. And a great cry went up from all of us standing around. I saw how this death—her death was making our people strong. I looked at my husband. To die properly is a victory.

What does your hanging mean to me? It is nothing. You cannot stop us.

You cannot kill us. Even when you kill us, you cannot kill us. I laugh at you. I spit at you. I shit at you. I will fight you in life and in death. What is your execution but another avenue to continue struggle. I laugh at your death.

And then I put the rope around my neck.

I die now, and my husband will die, but you cannot kill us.

I hung myself.

(Silence. Warrior kneels, falls. Jerks twice in a prone position. Body stiffens. Stillness.)

SOFIA: No. (She runs to her. Touches her.)

WARRIOR: (Jumps up suddenly, knocking Sofia aside. Backs away from Sofia and Mary. Warrior's hands are still tied behind her. Her voice accent has changed. She talks faster.) Who are you?

SOFIA: Don't you remember? You were just talking to us . . .

WARRIOR: I talk to no one.

MARY: You're insane.

WARRIOR: Who are you with? Which side are you on?

MARY: Sofia, is this madness or is this madness? (To Warrior) A minute ago you were lecturing us on how you died and now you want to know who we are? (They watch each other a minute.) Tell us another suicide story. (Laughing.)

WARRIOR: Why aren't you tied up? Why do they trust you? You are with them.

SOFIA: No, we are on your side. We . . .

WARRIOR: Is this what we are fighting for?

MARY: We ain't never asked you to fight for us.

(A strong silence. Warrior and Mary measure each other. Warrior slowly circles Mary.)

SOFIA: (To Warrior) Stop! Stop this. We are not the enemy! We live here, but . . .

MARY: (Moving back from Warrior in a defensive posture.) Sofia, I told you this was crazy. This is what happens to you when you try to fight back. You can't win. You start to acting crazy. (To Warrior) Now you want to fight me just because I told you 'bout yourself. (Warrior says nothing. Faces Mary sideways ready to kick.)

WARRIOR: (To Sofia) How come you live without fighting?

SOFIA: Sometimes that is the *only* way you can live.

WARRIOR: Negro, you're dangerous. If you want to live, fight like me.

MARY: Like what? Like who? Since when you so right and we so wrong, because we live . . .

WARRIOR: And suck shit with every breath. They are killing our children— our men—us. They are killing us, and you're talking about coexistence. Hand-out whores. You ain't shit! Cause if you . . .

SOFIA: Who wants to join you if you curse us? Who wants to help you if you hate us? (Warrior looks back and forth between Mary and Sofia.)

WARRIOR: No, we are fighters—we fight. The rest of you are slaves. Part of the problem, not . . .

MARY: Fool, ain't you got the news. The war is over. We lost. Why don't you come in out the sun. It's hot out there. The fighting don' fried your brains. Can't you see what time it is?

WARRIOR: (Loudly.) Nooooo!

SOFIA: It's true. She and I were both fighters once—both of us. But, it was useless. We could not defeat the man and our people didn't want to fight with us. They looked at us and said right on, but very few of them went to war with us.

WARRIOR: I know. (Remembering emotional pain, looking away.) I know. I remember emerging from the bush in Zimbabwe and the people treating the men like heroes and us like we weren't women. Aheee, we fought so hard against the enemy and then had to return to fight our own. I remember a man saying I wasn't a woman anymore because I wore pants and killed with a gun, with a knife.

SOFIA: What were you before the war?

WARRIOR: What? Who? (She turns away, inadvertently looking into Mary's eyes. She answers Sofia but keeps looking at Mary.) I've been so much, too much. I was a pretty little Black girl whose Mama couldn't afford to take care of her. You know what I mean?

SOFIA: No. No. I don't know.

WARRIOR: (Looks at Sofia and then back to Mary.) You know what I mean, don't you? I was a pretty and poor, Black girl.

MARY: I know.

WARRIOR: (To Sofia) What is your name?

SOFIA: Sofia.

WARRIOR: Sofia, I was a whore. (She wipes her mouth. Looks at Mary again and then turns to face Sofia fully.) I tried working. I tried school. None of that didn't work too tough, and I was pretty, and it was easy to get men to like me. You know how it starts. A dude buys you stuff and swears he's in love and all, but really it's all about you serving him, being hot when he's hard, a pillow when he's tired, an ear when he wants to talk, you know, romantic shit. When you're young and dumb and pretty and a man gives you a hundred dollars to buy a dress, you start to figure what the hell or something. Or something. Then you start sorta hanging out, and trying to figure out who got money and who got fake. You know, it's like you tell a sucker he's pretty and shit and he go for it, 'specially when you pretty. I mean, when a pretty woman tell a man *he's* pretty, well like that just takes him on out. It was good money, huh, good money. Ain't that some shit: eating dicks is good money.

SOFIA: What . . .

WARRIOR: What do you think whores do?

SOFIA: I never thought.

WARRIOR: Stop lying. Yes you have thought about it. You've thought about it. You've thought about what you would have done or said if *he* asked you to do it to him. Maybe, you've done it before. I don't know. Maybe you do it now. Maybe you two (motioning toward Mary with her head. Silence, pause.) It hurts to talk truth, huh? (No one says anything for a few seconds.)

SOFIA: So after that you joined the forces?

WARRIOR: No. No. For me, it was not easy. It was not straight. After I was pretty and making money with my body, I got pregnant and had a baby because I was dumb—I mean ignorant. I just didn't know having a baby was all that it was. And I tried to raise the child myself . . .

SOFIA: Where was this?

WARRIOR: It doesn't matter. Everywhere is hard to raise a kid by yourself, 'specially when you ain't young and pretty as you once was. I couldn't deal with it. I, I . . . it was too much. I started to eat and get fat and get bitter 'bout it. Finally, I just went on welfare, 'cause I didn't know what else to do.

MARY: Where's your child?

WARRIOR: (She looks at Mary. Drops her head. Raises it. Wipes her mouth. Turns away. Raises her head again. Inhales deeply. Lets the breath out slowly.) I don't know, I ran off and left her with my sister and never went back . . .

SOFIA: You don't seem like you would do that.

WARRIOR: It don't take much to be irresponsible. Just be a little selfish, ya' know. Hey, you know I kinda' of still live with that. When I went back, my sister had moved. Nobody knew. So there I was, a typical Black woman without nothing to live for.

SOFIA: So then you got involved in the . . .

WARRIOR: (Smiling.) No. I'm slow to learn. I went through some more shit. Then, I joined the Nation of Islam, remember that? That was good for me in a lot of ways—and not so good in other ways. (Smiles. Starts laughing quietly.)

SOFIA: What are you laughing at?

WARRIOR: Me. My old self. It's funny now. Being subservient—being a whore—being dumb. It's all funny now, but not funny. Ya' know? But ain't nothing special about my story—same old story a lot of sisters got to tell. (She grimaces.) I was wounded, and it's hard for me to stand for too long. I have to sit down. (Sits down. Drops her head. Lifts it slowly until her face is all the way up. Her voice has changed again. She speaks slowly.) Let's help each other.

SOFIA: You want us to untie you?

WARRIOR: Do you want to untie me? Whether or not you untie me is your decision. (Talking to Mary.) You've been listening mostly. What's your name? Who are you?

MARY: I'm Mary. I . . .

WARRIOR: I know. You're afraid to untie me. You're afraid they'll see you do it, and . . .

SOFIA: We're not afraid.

WARRIOR: Sofia and Mary, when will you stop lying to yourselves. You act

like actors in a bad play. You say the lines, you play the part. When are
you going to do what you know needs to be done?

SOFIA: What do you mean?

WARRIOR: You know what I mean. When are you going to confront yourselves—who you are? How you're living? When are you . . .

MARY: You mean break out of this? You mean change ourselves and change
this (gesturing around her). You mean make a (almost whispering)
revolution?

WARRIOR: Call it what you will. I mean telling the truth. I mean living to the
fullest. I mean no more artifice, no more facades. I mean touching all those
hurts you hid deep inside. I mean examining what brought you here.

MARY: Sounds like what Sofia be saying to her son.

WARRIOR: Sofia doesn't have a son.

SOFIA: How do . . .

MARY: She believes she does.

WARRIOR: No she doesn't. She fantasizes, maybe, but she knows she doesn't.
Ask her sometime when she's ready to stand up for the truth. (Mary and
Warrior look at Sofia.) Let it out, Sofia. (Sofia stares at Mary who stares
back. Finally, Sofia looks away, looks toward Warrior. Starts backing up.)

WARRIOR: (In a hard voice, almost like she's angry with her.) Sofia, you
pregnant?

SOFIA: (Shaking her head.) Kofi, I don't want to do it. I don't want to. (She
is talking slowly. Wanders about slowly.) It's like a vacuum cleaner sucking
away at you.

   (She moves to a man in the audience. Touches his face gently with her
fingertips. Covers his mouth with the fingers of her hand.) Give me your
hand. Touch here. Cover my stomach. (Takes his hand. Turns, pushing the
hand away. Running.) Kofi, I don't want to do this. We want . . . (Silence.
Starts toward someone. Stops. Turns away. Moves a few steps. Stops. Turns
back and walks straight to the man she initially started toward.) When you
were moving inside of me, you said you loved me, and you wanted life.

   (With pain. Spinning away.) It still hurts. IT STILL HURTS. Doctors are
supposed to save life, not kill life. It hurts. Kofi, I don't want to do this.

MARY: Sofia, don't . . .

WARRIOR: Be quiet. Listen. Help her talk it out. Help her work the hurt out.
(To Sofia in a hard voice.) I want to do it. It's best for us. For you . . .

SOFIA: (Moving toward another man in the audience.) Best for whom? For
me? You think all I want to do is marry you, don't you? See, you can't
even answer me. (Fighting back tears.) I could have stopped it. I could have
made sure that I couldn't conceive. But, I thought—I hoped—I—I guess I
dreamed that you really meant to . . . (She spins away. Stops.)

WARRIOR: (Hard voice.) I really meant what? Tell me. Say it.

SOFIA: I'm afraid. If I tell you—if I tell you, then you won't . . .

WARRIOR: What?

SOFIA: (Gathering her strength. Suddenly turning and walking straight to another man.) Ralph, I want to say something. I ah, I've done some things

before—I mean with . . . wait. Don't stop me. Let me say it all, okay. This is hard. I ah, I had a bab—I mean, I didn't have. I was pregnant. Don't get mad. Wait. Don't get mad. I'm telling you now. Damn man, what you want me to do? What you want: give you the whole story of my life two weeks after we just met? I'm trying to tell you something, and you're getting mad. Yes, you are! I'm trying to tell you about me—something that's important to me. LET ME TALK! It ain't nothing to do with you! It's me. It's me. I need this. I need to say this. Ralph, look, when Kofi and me . . . No, it's not him again. I'm sorry, but . . .

WARRIOR: Say it!

SOFIA: No, I'm not. I'm not sorry. I was pregnant for Kofi. I had his baby, but I never gave birth, 'cause I had, 'cause he wanted me to have—and I did it. I had an abortion. Now! (Becomes very nervous.) Ralph, I want to have a baby. Yeah, I know. I know. (Turns and walks away.) I know. Shit. Now ain't the time. It just seems like it's never the time. I want a baby that's wanted. I don't just want a baby. Ralph, do you understand? I want you to want the baby too.

MARY: I thought you said you had a baby.

SOFIA: (She turns away from the man. Looks in Mary's direction, but doesn't really see her. Shakes her head no.) I been pregnant three times. I had three babies, but I've never given birth. Something was always wrong.

And the last two times it hurt so much. It hurt (holding herself) inside.

Is something wrong with me?

Why is it never the time for me?

Is something wrong with me?

How come my boats always have holes in them. Where are my doors. No time left. Not now. Tomorrow. Tomorrow.

And, I close up—just like a shop gone out of business. I close up. I mean, who needs hurt all a the time?

WARRIOR: What hurt?

SOFIA: Getting fucked over! Nothing I ever did for anybody was enough to make them love me. Nothing. I give them everything I have—everything I am, and it's never enough.

Nigger shit.

Why?

MARY: Sofia. I'm here. It's just you and me now. (Crosses to hold her.)

WARRIOR: And what about us?

SOFIA: I don't know what to believe anymore. (She is crying silently. Walks away from Mary.) I don't know.

MARY: Believe in me.

WARRIOR: Believe in yourself, and believe in us.

SOFIA: I don't know.

MARY: Who loves you? I do. Who takes care of you? I do. Who protects you? I do.

WARRIOR: Sofia, you're covering it back up again. Approach yourself, Sofia. Let it out. Why did you want to have a baby?

SOFIA: Because—because . . . I ah . . .

WARRIOR: What did you tell Kofi? What did you tell Ralph?

SOFIA: (Softly.) I'm confused.

WARRIOR: Why do you want to have a baby?

MARY: (To Warrior.) You had a baby!

WARRIOR: You who? Me, Nzinga? No, I never had a child. I fought the Portuguese for years and years. I had not time for children. Me Assata. I had a baby in jail. I showed them they could not stop the struggle. Who are you talking about? A baby does not make you a woman. Women have babies. Women don't have babies. How you live your life makes you a woman.

Are you a woman, Sofia? Are you a woman now?

SOFIA: Yes, but . . .

WARRIOR: But what?

MARY: Enough! Sofia, she's trying to divide us. She's trying to come between us.

WARRIOR: Mary, why are you getting so upset?

MARY: Sofia loves me.

WARRIOR: Sofia can love all of us.

MARY: Things were all right before you came.

WARRIOR: (Laughing.) You don't really believe that. You call this all right? (Mary crosses to hold Sofia. Sofia draws away from her.)

SOFIA: Don't touch me right now.

MARY: Why? Because of . . .

SOFIA: Mary, please . . .

MARY: Sofia, don't let . . .

WARRIOR: Why don't you give Sofia the space to work through to her own conclusions. Now is not the time for physical love.

MARY: You're just mad because we are lovers.

WARRIOR: What you do with your bodies is your business. Besides, sex is not even the issue.

MARY: It's not just sex. It's love. We love each other.

WARRIOR: Who was the first person to touch you, Mary?

MARY: I first made love on a step with my dress . . .

WARRIOR: That is your stock answer. I didn't ask you when you first made love. I asked you who was the first person to touch you?

MARY: I first made . . .

WARRIOR: Mary, why don't you face the truth?

MARY: On a step—it was on a step.

WARRIOR: Mary, talk truth about yourself. What are you afraid of?

MARY: Don't make me!

WARRIOR: I'm not making you do any . . . (Warrior moves toward Mary, and Mary backs away shaking her head. She sees Mary's fear. Sofia notices and moves to comfort her. Warrior advances toward Mary also.) Mary . . .

MARY: (Flinches when Warrior speaks to her. Backs quickly away. Keeps backing away, shaking her head until she bumps into someone in the audience.) Don't make me do it. (Runs away a few steps.)

WARRIOR: Talk truth, Mary.

(Sofia reaches out her hand to touch Mary. Mary mistakes the gesture for a slap, cowers, and covers her face.)

MARY: (In a little girl's voice.) Don't hit me. Don't hit me. Daddy, don't make me do that. It hurts, Daddy. Don't make me do that. (She crouches into a ball. Crying out without tears.) Owwww. Daddy. Daddy, that hurts me. (Her body stiffens. She falls to her side. Thrashes.) Daddy, no Daddy. I'm not going to run. Daddy, please. I'll take them off. I'll take them off. Don't hit me, Daddy. (Mary rolls on her back. Pantomimes raising her dress and removing her panties.) Daddy, your hands hurt when you touch me like that. (She raises her knees and opens her legs.) Daddy, it hurts. Daddy, OWWWW. Daddy, OWWWW. (She suddenly stops. Her legs go down flat on the floor.) Daddy, I'm bleeding. I'm going to die. I'm going to die. I'm going to die. Daddy, I'm dying.

Yeah, Rufus you can have some. (She is lying absolutely still. Her voice is on edge through clenched teeth.) I'm glad it was good. Yes, you're good Rufus.

Ohhh, ohhhh Bobby. Ohhhh, it hurts so good. I like you, Bobby. Fuck me, Martin—hard Martin. Hard, hard, hard!

I don't feel nothing. I never felt nothing. They didn't even know me. How can you make love to somebody and not know what they're feeling. Not know . . .

Daddy, why did you hurt me like that?

What is it? What am I? It hurts.

(She rolls over. Kneels. Slaps the floor with her hand.) Come bitch. Come bitch. I'm going to make you come. You gon' feel this.

I don't feel nothing. Nobody can make me feel.

(Sitting back on her heels, covering her face with her hands, drops her hands.) I ain't never told nobody this before. Never. Never was no woman I could talk like this to, and I sho' wasn't gon' say this to no man.

When it happens, I don't feel nothing.

WARRIOR: (Warrior walks over to her and kneels on one knee beside her, looks her full in the face.) We need each other.

MARY: (Looks up suddenly toward Sofia.) You don't want me now, do . . . Sofia . . .

SOFIA: Mary. (Moves toward her. Reaches out her hand toward her. Pulls her up and hugs her.) We need each other. (Mary looks at the Warrior who is still kneeling beside her. Smiles. Mary moves to untie her hands, and Sofia helps her. When her hands are free, Warrior rubs them and tries to stand at the same time. She stumbles. Mary and Sofia grab her and help her up. They laugh softly with each other. Sofia wipes her eyes.) Well, what now?

MARY: I don't know.

WARRIOR: Don't stop now. Let's go to the next level. You see, we've only just begun to talk truth. Look at me. You see it took you two—all of us

for us to be strong. There is none of us can make it one on one. There is
none of us can make it just as a couple. Always gon' be three or more.
Always gon' be community, not just lovers in the physical, but community.
There is so much out there left for us to do.

SOFIA: You've been out there. Is it true there are no men left?

WARRIOR: Well, let us go and fight. Not sit in some luxurious cell with
comforts and wait for death. Let us go and make a world, and if there are
any men, truly men, then we will find them as we fight and build. And if
not, well, we must still fight. We must still build. But you worry too much
about a man.

SOFIA: Where are we going?

MARY: Sofia, have you . . . what about us—have you forgotten so quickly?

SOFIA: (Walks close to Mary. Takes her hand.) No, I haven't forgotten us.
Right now, I don't really know what I want. I know I don't want to hurt
you. But as for me, I'm not sure.

WARRIOR: Hey, this ain't no suicide mission. We want to live, not just exist,
to be productive, not just indulge in pleasure. Y'all starting back on down
that tragedy road. This is about new life. Like on a personal level, we all
got problems of some one sort or another. I mean, and some of us got some
deep problems. But every particular personal problem is really a detail of a
larger social problem which, in general, has a definite political and economic
basis, ya' know? But, like the basis we fight on is our belief in the trans-
formatory power of human beings, that is the ability to change ourselves,
sisters, and the ability to change the spaces and places where we live, love,
struggle, and die. We . . . (Warrior grins. Stops. Chuckles.) We don't need
no lectures right now. Let's make like Harriet Tubman and get out of this
place. (She starts to walk.)

MARY: (Visibly shaking.) I don't like the way I'm living, but I don't want to
die.

WARRIOR: Do you want to live a better way? How do you want to live? Afraid
to take the next breath? Hey, I'm ma' tell you, this is about new life, but
there ain't no guarantees. The enemy might be waiting outside with a gun
for us right now, or a bribe to stay for the next installment. The only thing
for sure is that we know what this is about, and it ain't for nothing. I mean,
this is bullshit, but to get past the bullshit, we have to fight. We have to
face the fact that we have to fight to extend ourselves. We have to physically
and mentally fight our enemies, and emotionally fight our old selves—fight
all the thoughts that make us weak. You know, we've got a lot more truth
left to talk, but when slaves start talking truth with each other, then revolution is just around the corner. Let's share our lives with each other. Sharing
will make us stronger as long as we keep reaching for the sun. Come on.
Don't let this place hold you back.

(Warrior starts again to stride out. Sofia hesitates and begins looking
around. Mary, who has started to walk, stops and looks at Sofia.)

(To Sofia.) What are you looking at? The certainties of slavery, the
promise of a warm cell and fresh gruel, drugs and a little leisure time,

records and movie shows. Some pretty clothes. Hey, it don't mean a thing, not for real. There's a world waiting out there to be built better than all of this.

Look, when we, as sisters, get together and help each other talk truth, then we are untying our hands. Then we are setting the stage for moving forward. It's on us, nobody else. It's on us. We have got to be our own liberators, all the way. It's on us.

Let's go for it. (Warrior turns. Mary moves up to her side. Warrior takes her hand and reaches her other hand out to Sofia. Sofia is still looking around.)

Sofia, let it go. (Sofia turns to face them. Takes Warrior's hand but does not move.)

SOFIA: I'm not going.

WARRIOR: It's your decision, sister. (Starts to move.)

MARY: Sofia, why stay any longer? (Moves to face her.) I once said I would never leave you, not voluntarily. But now . . . this is the fork in the road. For once, I'm not going to trade what I believe should be done for what somebody else is doing. I care about you, but you got to do. Wait. I'm not talking straight. I never thought it would end like this. Sofia, come with us. Think about . . .

SOFIA: I thought I was ready to go, you know? I thought when the time came, I would . . . if I go now, how do you know I won't turn back? How do you know I won't crack up or something?

WARRIOR: Everybody has a breaking point, but your real question is, why do we want you to go if we know you are weak, right? (Sofia nods her head.) The problem is not that you are weak, but rather that you have been taught to think you are weak. And guess what, struggle makes you strong.

Sofia, you're right. Everybody is not strong enough to fight on the front, but we all got to do something. Right now, what we got to do is leave the big house, especially the big house in our head. We got to say no to the bribes they offer us to be good slaves.

Sofia, whether you are weak or strong, we love you. Whether you come with us or stay behind, we love you. We're going. But, you know what, we can express our love for you better if you come with us . . . let me stop pampering you. It ain't even about you or Mary or me. It ain't about just the three of us in this world. Sofia, you acting like we the last people left on earth. You talking some self-destruct shit now. That's the ultimate weapon against us—our refusal to fight, for whatever reason. Them suckers is wrong. The way they make us live is wrong. The way they got this shit set up is wrong. And we gon' fight them, with or without you. But, it sho' would be better if you was with us.

SOFIA: Okay. (Mary smiles. Moves forward. The three of them are holding hands.)

WARRIOR: Now, let me tell you, ain't nobody gon' cut you no slack or do you no personal favors. Every woman stands on her own choice. This shit ain't easy. I promise you, it's gon' be hard.

SOFIA: Nothing is easy. I know that already.

WARRIOR: I heard that. (They all turn to move out together. Warrior stops. Returns for the rope which had been left on the floor.) Everything that has been used against us can be turned on the enemy.

From now on, let's turn the hurt out and the truth in.

(They freeze in place for three seconds smiling. Break. Sofia reaches her hand out to the Warrior while holding Mary's hand. The Warrior takes Sofia's hand.)

SOFIA: Let's go. This time, it's our time. (They freeze in place for three seconds laughing. Break. They link arms and start off striding together.)

MARY: Hey, I feel good about this.

(They freeze in place for three seconds. Turn in slow motion and then move in strong, deliberate steps out into the audience, touching every sister and whispering into each sister's ear as they touch and pass: REMEMBER THESE WORDS FROM ASSATA SHAKUR—IT IS OUR DUTY TO FIGHT FOR OUR FREEDOM. IT IS OUR DUTY TO WIN. WE MUST LOVE EACH OTHER AND SUPPORT EACH OTHER. WE HAVE NOTHING TO LOSE BUT OUR CHAINS! LONG LIVE ASSATA!)

(As Sofia, Mary, and Warrior are exiting, a voice reading the words of Assata Shakur is heard. "Because of a rising political awareness and because of the intensification of political and economic repression, there are a whole lot of Black people who would support a revolutionary struggle if we give them something clear, concrete, consistent, and sensible to support. We have got to destroy the victim mentality and realize that our struggle depends on US. Nobody is gonna do it for us. When we make a commitment to struggle, we are also making a commitment to change ourselves, to transform ourselves from passive servants into informed, skilled, disciplined revolutionaries. This is not a quick overnight change, but a long evolutionary process that will go on for the rest of our lives.")

(Sofia, Mary, and Warrior exit. Amina Meyers' "African Blues"/middle or latter section comes up full. Stays up.)

Another Beginning

PART FOUR

NONFICTION

Malaika Adero

(1957–   )

Adero is a poet, video producer, and editor. Raised in Knoxville, Tennessee, she has lived in Atlanta where she was a member of Pamoja Writers Guild. She is a member of the New Renaissance Writers Guild and has published two volumes of poetry, *Moments of Mind* and *Re/visions*.

Outta My Name

My name is a mirror of my life and what I see is the split image of an African American and a free-willed female growing in a white male dominated world. Had I been an African girl-child raised on that continent, a ceremony might have taken place on my naming day. In some cultures it would have taken place 7 days after my birth, libations would have been poured and family and community members would have been in attendance. But as it was, my mother was joined by her mother while the naming took place with a prayer for me in their hearts on the day of my birth in the University hospital of my hometown in Tennessee.

Mama did not consciously choose a name that reflected the state of her household, or in honor of my father, or a deity worshipped by the family as it is done on the Continent. Though, she did give me the name of an ancestor. Deloras, my middle name, belonged to my mother's sister who died as a child many years before my birth. Vanessa, my first name, she got from a soap opera character, Vanessa Sterling on the show *Love of Life*. That was a corny way to name a kid, I thought, but she was only sixteen. So, I forgave her for that. I bore her maiden name, Crump, because she was a single mother and the State of Tennessee would not allow the Birth Certificate of a child out-of-wedlock to bear the name of the father. So, there was a blank space where a man whose name was Blue belonged. But my families recognized what the State was blind to. My father's people always referred to me as Blue.

My mother's addressed me as Crump. I felt a bit split into, not solidly linked to both, but I never said so and nobody asked me how I felt, or what I preferred to be called. But I did ask endless questions about the me that they had named. My grandfather answered that the Crumps acquired the name after a plantation dynasty in Memphis. A notorious political boss in that town descended from this family. After Emancipation, some of the Crumps' slaves took on the name McPherson, he said. But, he didn't know why.

My father said all he knew about Blue was that it was probably of Native American origin. Well, that was an improvement to me over the slave master explanation. Yet, I still felt less than comfortable with the labels to which I was born. This feeling of discontent was encouraged by a surge of Pan-Africanism—a collective mood within the African American community that emerged in the 70's,—during my teen years. The times dictated a re-evaluation of ourselves, a redefinition and identification with the greater part of our heritage. We changed our ways, our images to reflect a new cultural independence from the American mainstream, a new consciousness, politics and aesthetics. It sounded, smelled and tasted good to me. So, I began to re-evaluate me and what I called myself.

Vanessa Deloras was pretty enough. Crump was harsh and Germanic. Deloras, well Deloras means pain. It represents the Great Lady of Sorrow in Spanish-Catholic culture. A white Spanish teacher—whose intent was not to enlighten, but to pick with me—informed me so. And Deloras was heavily weighted to the awesome mystery of the premature death of an Aunt. Blue, for me is the music of Black love and struggle, a part of Native America that I love as I do the color of the sky and the sea.

But none of those names were as African as I felt. Around this time, I heard Roberta Flack sing a song about telling Jesus can she change her name, and I asked my Mama if she would change mine. And like Jesus, she said, "be all right." It was that easy because my mother supported, and still supports, even the wildest of my ideas—minus those, of course, that she thinks will do me harm. She raised me to think for myself, though, surely she has winced at my eagerness to take her up on it, time and time again. But, she got right with the task, talked to some friends from home—Tanzania and Somalia—and came back to me with choices. Without knowing the meanings of the names she wrote on a piece of paper, I was attracted to one—Malaika. It had a musical sound to me, and my mother—the piano player—laughed when I pointed and said, "this one." It was the one she favored too. We chose the surname from a book. Adero—it means, one who comes to make things better. It was to be our new family name, not just mine. Malaika means my angel, fitting from a mother to her first-born. I was proud of her and me, and eagerly set out to be Malaika Adero and immediately found that changing your name can engage you in battles you'd never imagine, with people you'd never imagine.

While some said, "right on" and "that's beautiful sister," others curtly responded, "Aint that African?" "Is that the name your Mama gave You?" "Is that the name you were born with?" These were people who had nothing to say to the Dolins who used to be Dolinskys. These were people who would not have dared to chide someone for calling their child John John a la Kennedy, as was popular in the sixties. And anyway, Mama did give me the name and it did have to do with my *re*-birth. But, for many people, my father and grandfather included, that made no difference.

"You're not proud to wear our name?" the patriarchs in my family asked. As my mind recalled the blank space on my birth certificate. "You don't want people to know you belong to us?" They asked in their respective ways. I thought but was afraid to say that my last name could change if I married, and would they object to that? They asserted their parental right to challenge me and I listened but did not budge. I felt that me and my mother had more to say in the matter. It was my name and I was her baby. I was their daughter too, and resemblance alone would verify that. And I wasn't dis-identifying myself with them. I was re-identifying myself by something other than a white man's piece of property. Yes, it was naive nationalism. But it was real. What my father's understood, and I had not considered, was that an African name would make me a target for the very system I fancied myself undermining.

That was the mid-seventies and I was 17. Now, at 30, Malaika Adero is as much a part of me as Vanessa Deloras Crump Blue. It simply draws more attention and elicits more questions. Yes, it's legal. Yes, my mother named me. No, I'm not Hawaiian. Yes, I am American. No, that is not my religion. Yes, I am African and American and spiritual. Yes, there is a song Miriam Makeba recorded called Malaika, and the stress is on the third or fourth syllable. And there are others with the name. And if you say it it gets easier to say, as easy as Monica, Molly, and Mary. But even if it don't roll off your tongue know that if you speak from love then almost nothing you call me is going to be outta my name.

Frederick Douglass
(1817–1895)

Born a slave in Tuckahoe, Maryland, Douglass escaped to New York and became a noted orator in abolitionist circles. In 1845 he published *Narrative of the Life of Frederick Douglass, an American Slave: Written by Himself*, a work now recognized as a classic in the traditions of slave narrative and American autobiography. The *Narrative* was the kernel for two later autobiographies, *My Bondage and My Freedom* (1855) and *Life and Times of Frederick Douglass* (1881, revised 1892). Douglass founded his own newspaper *The North Star*, later named *Frederick Douglass' Paper*, to fight for the abolition of slavery. In 1853 his novella *The Heroic Slave* was printed in the newspaper. Douglass was a determined abolitionist, a stalwart reformer, and an early supporter of the women's rights movement. Long considered one of the major figures in nineteenth-century American history, Douglass's reputation as a writer increases as serious critical attention is given to his speeches, essays, fiction, and autobiographies. Chapter 1 of Douglass's 1845 narrative is reprinted here.

---

from Narrative of the Life of Frederick Douglass, an American Slave: Written by Himself

I was born in Tuckahoe, near Hillsborough, and about twelve miles from Easton, in Talbot county, Maryland. I have no accurate knowledge of my age, never having seen any authentic record containing it. By far the larger part of the slaves know as little of their ages as horses know of theirs, and it is the wish of most masters within my knowledge to keep their slaves thus ignorant. I do not remember to have ever met a slave who could tell of his birthday. They seldom come nearer to it than planting-time, harvest-time, cherry-time, spring-time, or fall-time. A want of information concerning my own was a source of unhappiness to me even during childhood. The white children could tell their ages. I could not tell why I ought to be deprived of the same privilege. I was not allowed to make any inquiries of my master concerning it. He deemed all such inquiries on the part of a slave improper and impertinent, and evidence of a restless spirit. The nearest estimate I can give makes me now between twenty-seven and twenty-eight years of age. I come to this, from hearing my master say, some time during 1835, I was about seventeen years old.

My mother was named Harriet Bailey. She was the daughter of Isaac and Betsey Bailey, both colored, and quite dark. My mother was of a darker complexion than either my grandmother or grandfather.

My father was a white man. He was admitted to be such by all I ever heard speak of my parentage. The opinion was also whispered that my master was my father; but of the correctness of this opinion, I know nothing; the means of knowing was withheld from me. My mother and I were separated when I was but an infant—before I knew her as my mother. It is a common custom, in the part of Maryland from which I ran away, to part children from their mothers at a very early age. Frequently, before the child has reached its twelfth month, its mother is taken from it, and hired out on some farm a considerable distance off, and the child is placed under the care of an old woman, too old for field labor. For what this separation is done, I do not know, unless it be to hinder the development of the child's affection toward its mother, and to blunt and destroy the natural affection of the mother for the child. This is the inevitable result.

I never saw my mother, to know her as such, more than four or five times in my life; and each of these times was very short in duration, and at night. She was hired by a Mr. Stewart, who lived about twelve miles from my home. She made her journeys to see me in the night, travelling the whole distance on foot, after the performance of her day's work. She was a field hand, and a whipping is the penalty of not being in the field at sunrise, unless a slave has special permission from his or her master to the contrary—a permission which they seldom get, and one that gives to him that gives it the proud name of being a kind master. I do not recollect of ever seeing my mother by the light of day. She was with me in the night. She would lie down with me, and get me to sleep, but long before I waked she was gone. Very little communication ever took place between us. Death soon ended what little we could have while she lived, and with it her hardships and suffering. She died when I was about seven years old, on one of my master's farms, near Lee's Mill. I was not allowed to be present during her illness, at her death, or burial. She was gone long before I knew any thing about it. Never having enjoyed, to any considerable extent, her soothing presence, her tender and watchful care, I received the tidings of her death with much the same emotions I should have probably felt at the death of a stranger.

Called thus suddenly away, she left me without the slightest intimation of who my father was. The whisper that my master was my father, may or may not be true; and, true or false, it is of but little consequence to my purpose whilst the fact remains, in all its glaring odiousness, that slaveholders have ordained, and by law established, that the children of slave women shall in

all cases follow the condition of their mothers; and this is done too obviously
to administer to their own lusts, and make a gratification of their wicked
desires profitable as well as pleasurable; for by this cunning arrangement, the
slaveholder, in cases not a few, sustains to his slaves the double relation of
master and father.

I know of such cases; and it is worthy of remark that such slaves invariably
suffer greater hardships, and have more to contend with, than others. They
are, in the first place, a constant offence to their mistress. She is ever disposed
to find fault with them; they can seldom do any thing to please her; she is
never better pleased than when she sees them under the lash, especially when
she suspects her husband of showing to his mulatto children favors which he
withholds from his black slaves. The master is frequently compelled to sell
this class of his slaves, out of deference to the feelings of his white wife; and,
cruel as the deed may strike any one to be, for a man to sell his own children
to human flesh-mongers, it is often the dictate of humanity for him to do so;
for, unless he does this, he must not only whip them himself, but must stand
by and see one white son tie up his brother, of but few shades darker complexion than himself, and ply the gory lash to his naked back; and if he lisp one
word of disapproval, it is set down to his parental partiality, and only makes
a bad matter worse, both for himself and the slave whom he would protect
and defend.

Every year brings with it multitudes of this class of slaves. It was doubtless
in consequence of a knowledge of this fact, that one great statesman of the
south predicted the downfall of slavery by the inevitable laws of population.
Whether this prophecy is ever fulfilled or not, it is nevertheless plain that a
very different-looking class of people are springing up at the south, and are
now held in slavery, from those originally brought to this country from Africa;
and if their increase will do no other good, it will do away the force of the
argument, that God cursed Ham, and therefore American slavery is right. If
the lineal descendants of Ham are alone to be scripturally enslaved, it is certain
that slavery at the south must soon become unscriptural; for thousands are
ushered into the world, annually, who, like myself, owe their existence to
white fathers, and those fathers most frequently their own masters.

I have had two masters. My first master's name was Anthony. I do not
remember his first name. He was generally called Captain Anthony—a title
which, I presume, he acquired by sailing a craft on the Chesapeake Bay. He
was not considered a rich slaveholder. He owned two or three farms, and
about thirty slaves. His farms and slaves were under the care of an overseer.
The overseer's name was Plummer. Mr. Plummer was a miserable drunkard,
a profane swearer, and a savage monster. He always went armed with a
cowskin and a heavy cudgel. I have known him to cut and slash the women's
heads so horribly, that even master would be enraged at his cruelty, and would
threaten to ship him if he did not mind himself. Master, however, was not a
humane slaveholder. It required extraordinary barbarity on the part of an overseer to affect him. He was a cruel man, hardened by a long life of slave-
holding. He would at times seem to take great pleasure in whipping a slave.

I have often been awakened at the dawn of day by the most heart-rending shrieks of an own aunt of mine, whom he used to tie up to a joist, and whip upon her naked back till she was literally covered with blood. No words, no tears, no prayers, from his gory victim, seemed to move his iron heart from its bloody purpose. The louder she screamed, the harder he whipped; and where the blood ran fastest, there he whipped longest. He would whip her to make her scream, and whip her to make her hush; and not until overcome by fatigue, would he cease to swing the blood-clotted cowskin. I remember the first time I ever witnessed this horrible exhibition. I was quite a child, but I well remember it. I never shall forget it whilst I remember any thing. It was the first of a long series of such outrages, of which I was doomed to be a witness and a participant. It struck me with awful force. It was the blood-stained gate, the entrance to the hell of slavery, through which I was about to pass. It was a most terrible spectacle. I wish I could commit to paper the feelings with which I beheld it.

This occurrence took place very soon after I went to live with my old master, and under the following circumstances. Aunt Hester went out one night—where or for what I do not know,—and happened to be absent when my master desired her presence. He had ordered her not to go out evenings, and warned her that she must never let him catch her in company with a young man, who was paying attention to her belonging to Colonel Lloyd. The young man's name was Ned Roberts, generally called Lloyd's Ned. Why master was so careful of her, may be safely left to conjecture. She was a woman of noble form, and of graceful proportions, having very few equals, and fewer superiors, in personal appearance, among the colored or white women of our neighborhood.

Aunt Hester had not only disobeyed his orders in going out, but had been found in company with Lloyd's Ned; which circumstance, I found, from what he said while whipping her, was the chief offence. Had he been a man of pure morals himself, he might have been thought interested in protecting the innocence of my aunt; but those who knew him will not suspect him of any such virtue. Before he commenced whipping Aunt Hester, he took her into the kitchen, and stripped her from neck to waist, leaving her neck, shoulders, and back, entirely naked. He then told her to cross her hands, calling her at the same time a d——d b——h. After crossing her hands, he tied them with a strong rope, and led her to a stool under a large hook in the joist, put in for the purpose. He made her get upon the stool, and tied her hands to the hook. She now stood fair for his infernal purpose. Her arms were stretched up at their full length, so that she stood upon the ends of her toes. He then said to her, "Now, you d——d b——h, I'll learn you how to disobey my orders!" and after rolling up his sleeves, he commenced to lay on the heavy cowskin, and soon the warm, red blood (amid heart-rending shrieks from her, and horrid oaths from him) came dripping to the floor. I was so terrified and horror-stricken at the sight, that I hid myself in a closet, and dared not venture out till long after the bloody transaction was over. I expected it would be my turn next. It was all new to me. I had never seen any thing like it before. I had always lived with my grandmother on the outskirts of the plantation, where she was put to raise the children of the younger women. I had therefore been, until now, out of the way of the bloody scenes that often occurred on the plantation.

Nell Irvin Painter
(1942–   )

A professor of history at Princeton University who specializes in the Progressive and Reconstruction eras, Nell Irvin Painter has been acclaimed for her ability to combine impeccable scholarship with a writer's sensibility in the construction of narrative. Painter earned her B.A. at the University of California, Berkeley, and her Ph.D. at Harvard. She is the author of *Exodusters: Black Migration to Kansas after Reconstruction* (1977), *The Narrative of Hosea Hudson* (1979), a reworking of Hudson's 1972 autobiography *Black Worker in the Deep South: A Personal Record*, and *Standing at Armageddon: United States, 1877–1919* (1987). Her work-in-progress includes a study in intellectual history, *Mixed Blood and Pure Blood in the Minds of Americans, 1890–1920*. The following excerpt is Chapter 21 of *The Narrative of Hosea Hudson*.

---

from The Narrative of Hosea Hudson

The Steelworkers leadership wasn't lukewarm on fighting for the rights of the Negro people. It was worse than lukewarm. When it come to the constitution of the union, the constitution say one thing, but down there, they wanted to do another thing. Constitution didn't mean nothing in Alabama at that time. That's why I was always raising the devil. I'd take the national constitution and just always hit the deck about what the constitution say, reading certain sections. But I was pouring water on a duck's back. They wont listening.

I had all kind of battles with the district office of the Steelworkers and with the Birmingham Industrial Council. Down in '47, I was on the Political Action Committee, me and another Negro, Saunders, he was from Mine Mills in Bessemer. We was on a committee of seven members, the council interrogation committee. We was to interview the political candidates running for office, see who was the pro-labor candidates, report to a joint labor conference that was being held one Sunday. The joint labor conference was chaired by a man representing Philip Murray's office in Washington. He was there the Sunday we going to give a report on the various candidates running for state office.

Now Saturday night at the council meeting, coming up to the conference on Sunday, they already had the meeting with the candidates, and they didn't even notify me and Saunders. They had done went down to the Thomas Jefferson Hotel, that was a hotel where at that time they wouldn't allow Negroes in, not so far as attending a meeting was concerned. That's where they set the hearing to interrogate the various candidates—at the Thomas Jefferson Hotel. They set there and helt the meeting and didn't say a word to us. We didn't know a word about it. After it was over, then the chairman of the committee come telling me that they done had the meeting and what they decided.

The next day at the conference, they know they done bypass me and Saunders, and I guess they done told the guy who's chairing the meeting, "Now don't let him speak," cause they knew I was going to speak about it. This guy from Philip Murray's office—he was a young guy, he wont so old—everytime I raise my hand up, he look over yonder where he could get somebody else's hand. He look back here at me, I raise my hand up, he look over yonder, call somebody else. That was all the way through the discussion on the report, till the time for to close out the discussion on the interrogation committee's report that they brought back.

I helt up my hand again, he look over yonder, so when they got through, I took the floor, said, "Mr. Chairman . . ."

All these whites come up, "Question! Question! Call for the question, question on the motion!" That's to stop the discussion. When I got up to say something, they just song, "Question, question, question!" That's all whites.

After they put the motion, carried it, then I asked for a special point of privilege. I brought up what I wanted to say at the begin with. I said, "I tried to get the floor on discussing these reports. I was denied the right to get the floor." I said, "It was me and Saunders, we was elected on this committee to interrogate these candidates." I said, "Now if you all didn't trust us to represent you, you wouldn't of elected us," said, "but this hearing been helt in the Thomas Jefferson Hotel where Negroes can't go in, these candidates been invited, and they been interrogated, and me and Saunders hadn't knowed anything about it until last night. This is what I want to make clear here. You asking me, you asking the Negro to go to these locals, and go around, people raising money to support these candidates' campaigns," I said, "and I want to let you know here and now, that since I haven't had a chance to meet the candidates or to speak on this report, and I was denied the floor, I'm not going to ask in my locals for nary dime." And I said, "I'm not going to ask anybody among the Negroes to support nary candidate. If they vote, that's up to them. If they give you money, that's up to them. But I'm not going to encourage them or urge them to give nary penny or vote for nary one of these candidates," I said that. I got my hat and walked on out. And these other Negroes that they wouldn't allow either, they walked out with me. That was my walkout.

I had to battle on both fronts, see, cause many a time I'd hit the floor and other Negroes wouldn't even open their mouths. They would set down, they wouldn't fight back, they wouldn't pick up where I leave off. And the whites would get up there and water down what I said.

The Negroes wouldn't back me up, cause at that time, the Negro in the South, you had to pick certain Negroes to stand up and speak out. Everybody didn't speak out. When Negroes set down, they mind set down, they thoughts set down. They went to sleep, like, and they just couldn't think, cause they wouldn't think. These things they ought to talk about, they wouldn't talk about it.

Now if it come to a vote, they would vote right. But they wouldn't get up and talk. That was the trouble in that Birmingham Industrial Council where I was a delegate from my local. I was always like a sore thumb, standing out ahead, cause I was always raising the issues, questions that the other guys would just sit there and wouldn't say nothing. Some of them would get up and take they hat and walk out and leave me on the floor fighting. To tell you the truth about it, I tells a lot of people every once in a while, I been let down so many times by Negroes, I ought not to *never, never* do nothing but set down in the chair and read the paper and watch the TV.

We heard so much when we was there in the Party in the early years, in the '30s, that Negro leadership wouldn't fight for the Negro masses. That was the regular cry. The regular saying was that what the Negroes was lacking was some good leaders. So when I got to developing and found I could be somebody, from not being able to read and write and still coming forward, I set out to be a leader among the Negro people in Birmingham. I thought, really thought, that the Negro, all he needs is somebody to stand up and speak, and he would fall in line.

But that's where I was let down. That's where I found that they wouldn't do it, they wouldn't. It wasn't a crisis of leadership, it was a question of a crisis of people needing to be educated to the importance of leadership.

Another Sunday in 1947, we had a CIO meeting for political action. Delegates from all over everywhere in Alabama. The hall was packed. That meeting was to report on results of getting members of the union qualified to vote, getting them by the Registration Board. They had a delegation there from Gadsden Alabama, about six or seven. On that delegation was only one Negro.

The chairman, white guy, got up there and he made a wonderful report. Oh, they done so much, what they got in Gadsden, how many members they got qualified to vote, they had so many people went down to register to vote till they give out of blanks. They had to make some more blanks.

Cary Haigler, he was chairing that meeting. He was the state president of the CIO. He said, "We heard the report from our delegates from Gadsden, thank you, you made a wonderful report. You been doing wonderful work. Anybody have any questions?"

Several people got up. "Mr. Chairman, I think the delegation from Gadsden learned us what we should do."

"Mr. Chairman, that was a wonderful report. The brothers from Gadsden set us a fine example."

I was setting there. After a while, I said, "Mr. Chairman, I have a question," and I gets up. I said, "I think all of us have to tip our hats to our union brothers in Gadsden, cause I think the report has showed they've done some good work up there, and I think they can show us all how we can improve our work, getting our members qualified to vote. But I have a question. My question to the delegate is, out of the people that was passed by the Board of Registrars—and I noticed they said so many members of the union went to the board to register till they give out of blanks—could you tell us just what the percentage of *Negroes* that got qualified?''

"No, I, uh, I don't know. I don't know of any . . .'' And they had half of the membership, if not over half the membership was Negro members of the unions, members in the unions up there in the steel plants, in the rubber plants. And yet he couldn't tell whether nary a one passed.

I pointed out what the problems was that Negroes had in trying to pass the Board of Registrars. I said that the union local leadership have to take a greater responsibility in helping Negroes get registered to vote. "If you mean what we talk about getting members qualified to vote to support the labor candidates, we got to get the white members to take a more active part in trying to help the Negro members pass the Board of Registrars. Because,'' I said, "it's like you trying to fight with one hand tied down side of you. Here you fight with one hand, the other hand tied is the Negro." I said, "Automatically the Negro gets the vote, he automatically will support labor candidates, because whatever benefits labor benefits the Negro as a whole.''

When I set down, old big George Mills,* he got up. He said, "Mr. President, I rise to say I think that the delegates from Gadsden done a wonderful job, and I wants to say also, don't let nobody tell you that the Negro is going to turn his back on the CIO.'' This is a black Negro speaking.

I ain't said nothing about turning the back. But this is what I had every time I got up, practically, from some old stupid Negro. And he had the nerve, after the meeting's over, to come out, when we on the street there, said, "Bro' Hudson, you made a wonderful talk. I'm with you one hundred percent.'' This was the same man. The same Negro! That's the way they would do. "Yeah, I'm with you one hundred percent.'' I just walk on off. They'd wonder what they had done. I wouldn't even try to discuss with them.

Me and Eb Cox, we went back a long ways together, back to '36, '37, when the CIO drive was on organizing the steelworkers. Philip Murray sent representatives to William Z. Foster and asked the Party to recommend organizers wherever they had people. In Birmingham, Eb Cox was a member of the Party, and he was a unemployed, militant guy who was there. He was just a member, he wont no important guy way up there, just a member of the club. They recommended Eb Cox and also Joe Howard and Dave Smith. Joe Howard and Dave Smith was the ones who organized that sit down strike at Jackson. That was when the CIO dropped Joe Howard and Dave Smith.

In '38 Cox was still coming into the Party office, having discussions about what our line going to be in the CIO convention, what resolutions we going support. At the same time, Cox is going all out now, he going try to make a

*I guess he's dead now. He was from the wholesale-retail workers' union Local 251.

career in the Steel staff. And Beddow† and them was calling him into account about being a communist. He wanted to be able to fight back if they Red-bait him. He didn't want them to be able to trace him down to the Party office. Cox asked the Party D.O., asked Rob Hall for a leave of absence from the Party, where his conscience could be clear and he could say, "I'm not a member." It wont no great big meeting, private meeting with Rob Hall. It was agreed that Cox leave the Party. So that's when he got loose. I never did see him come in a Party office after that. He'd always give a little finance donation. I'd go around, he'd take a paper, but he kept adrifting the other way.

In '43, he was still good with us, so I supported his position. He was the onliest thing we had among the Negroes worthwhile to support as a representative. It still wont no Negroes on the CIO state executive board. Everything was elected, so everybody going be white. Automatically you elected a president, he going be white. Elect a secretary-treasurer, he's white. Then all the rest of the representatives, the vice-presidents, come from the different unions. Mine Mills would elect a vice-president, textile workers would elect a vice-president, the longshoremen would elect a vice-president, steel would elect a vice-president. They take these vice-presidents from the various unions, and that would make the state executive board. All these would be white, because it wont enough Negroes attending local meetings regular enough to see the importance of they sending Negroes here where they get a Negro elected.

The onliest way you can get a Negro in, you got to figure out how you can do it. So I figured it out, and I presented a resolution from my little local,* and I presented a resolution in the convention that the office of vice-president at large would be opened up. There would be two vice-presidents at large, and I said that the two would be Negroes.

I ran into a conflict in the constitutional committee on that question of the two "be Negroes." While the convention's going on, they called me into the committee Tom Howell from the wire mill local, Local 1700, out there in Fairfield, he was chairman of that constitutional committee. (They were saying that he was one of the top leaders of the Ku Klux Klan.) Me and him and the committee, we discussed backwards and forwards. Finally they convinced me to drop the word "Negro" and just say "two vice-presidents at large." They said you would tie your hands, maybe a lot of whites wouldn't vote for it because they was prejudiced, a lot of the whites was. And they said, next thing, you'd have a Chinese or somebody else come up, an Italian, and they want two vice-presidents at large to be Chinamen or Italians. So I dropped the word "Negroes," and said "vice-presidents at large." They said, "We'll support you in trying to get a Negro elected." I had also asked for the vice-presidents at large to have "voice and vote," and I had to sacrifice "vote." At the next convention, I went in that convention with a resolution supporting

---

†[Noel Beddow was then president of the Alabama State CIO.]

*It wont but twenty-five of us meeting. I wouldn't have all twenty-five at one time. When I got nine–ten I had a big meeting in that period.

that same resolution, but the vice-presidents at large would have voice and vote. That was in '45. We didn't have no convention in '44. That was right in the heat of the war. That was when Roosevelt asked everybody not to have no big meeting, on the question of transportation. So we didn't have no convention in '44.

That first time, Eb Cox was elected over Beddow's head, that was in '43, after I had got the resolution passed. Beddow went down from the table at the front of the meeting to these Negroes over down yonder and talked to one of these Negroes in the Acipco new organized local. (Beddow had been the district representative of the Steelworkers under William Mitch, and he helped organize this new local at Acipco.) He said, "If you all pick your man, I'll help you get him elected." Then Beddow went back to the table.

I'm over here in the aisle over side the wall, and the guy Beddow talk to come over where I was and told me what Mr. Beddow had said. I told him, "We'll support Eb Cox." I said, "I'm going nominate Eb Cox."

The Negro brother goes back down there. All right, Beddow got up, come on down again, walks over and asks him who had they decided to run. The Negro said, "Bro' Hudson said he going run Eb Cox." Then Beddow got all mad.

The brother come back to me looking all sick, told me, "Mr. Beddow say, 'Hell, no!' say his men ain't going never allow Eb Cox to held elective office." "His men," that means all Beddow's staff men in the Steelworkers district office.

I said, "Beddow don't tell us who we vote for a leader." I said, "I'm going nominate Cox. If nobody don't vote for him, then leave it." So then the Negro went away from me looking even sicker. He didn't know what to tell Beddow now, so he went on back and sit down. Nobody didn't say no more.

When it come to nominating vice-presidents at large, I went up to the mike. The mike was setting about 4–5 feet from the table, and I'm over here talking. Beddow was setting right behind the table, in the middle. I talked about what this person had done, what a great leader he would make, put him in good position. I ain't called his name yet. When I got through talking, I said, "This person's no other than Brother Eb Cox of the United Steelworkers of America." When I said that, I walked over around here and back around to my seat.

Beddow got up to the mike right behind me. He said, "I got a man I want to put up here . . ." and all what he was, and finally, "It's no other than Ben Gage." Ben Gage was setting there side of him. He was one of the staff guys too. So that made him have four of his own staff men from Steel running for that particular office. Three of them was elected, Ben Gage and Dan Houston and Cox. A Mine Mill* guy was elected, a white guy. At that time they was elected voice but no vote. They could talk all they wanted, but no vote.

The next time, McGruder was put in and Asbury Howard was put in. Asbury

---

*Mine Mill was the next biggest union in the Alabama CIO.

Howard was from Mine Mill, we supported him. And we was still supporting
Eb Cox. McGruder was from around there in Alabama. He called hisself a
preacher, but he wasn't nothing but a stoolpigeon. The white union officials,
what they was doing, they had him around, trying to go around among the
Negroes, try to win the Negroes over to the union, talking with them, but he
wont from no particular union. They paid him. He was some kind of little
salaried guy. At the '45 convention, he was a delegate, and he's running for
vice-president at large. The white union officials wanted to put McGruder up
over Eb Cox.

We had a Steel caucus, and I tried to edge them off, stall them on endorsing
McGruder. They wanted a unanimous vote. I asked them, "What union do
McGruder come from, is it Steel or what?" They couldn't say. Nobody know.
I said, "Since my question hasn't been answered satisfactorily of what union
do McGruder represent," I said, "I'm going to withhold my vote from the
unanimous." That was the only way I could stall.

They dropped the unanimous question in the caucus itself, said, "Let's just
forget about it, let's forget about it. We won't make a unanimous vote." That
was the whites, see. I did that in order to get back in the convention to
nominate Eb Cox. I did nominate Eb Cox from the floor. But these white
Steel guys, these racist guys among the whites, they was able to muster enough
votes to put McGruder in over Eb Cox.

Race & Class Interests

I had done nominated Cox twice for vice-president at large. And I supported
him from way back in the '30s. We always called up each other to stay in
touch about what's going on. I kind of backed him up. Back in '37, Eb Cox
had to fight these popsicle unions, company unions. He had to fight the leading
Negroes who was working among these Negroes in Fairfield hill. All the big
church deacons and things, all the big homeowners up there, not all of them,
but a lot of them, had a hand in the popsicle unions. One Sunday they was
having a meeting of the popsicles down there in a place called French Town.
Eb Cox found out where they was going meet, he come and notified us and
wanted us to come with him, me and Willie Norman and another guy. We
got with Eb Cox and went to it. It was a private home where they having the
meeting.

We walked in there and all these Negroes' eyes buckled. They stopped the
discussion, got quiet, and looked around at each other. We just sit there. After
a while the chairman, he said, "Gentlemen, we have some visitors here, some
guests, and right here we going hear from them to see what they have to say."

Eb, he was the spokesman. He told them, "We come over to your meeting
this evening to discuss with you the question of labor. We would like to unite
with you to work together with you all. What will benefit one will benefit all,
benefit the Negro as a whole."

When Eb got through talking, the chairman thanked Brother Cox for the
suggestions he had offered, said, "We'll take your suggestions under consideration." Then he asked us to be excused, they wanted us to leave, they had
some important business to take up. We left. We didn't argue with him. But
I never did hear no more about that popsicle after that Sunday. It begin to fall

apart. If I make no mistake, old man Jerry Darby was chairman of that group that Sunday. The man who spoke kind of favored him. I come to know him later. He come to be the vice-president of Local 1700 of the Steelworkers at the wire mills.

That was one thing me and Eb done. And it was lots of little things. Labor Day in '44 me and Eb and somebody else, we all lined up and went to a meeting down in Jonesboro, down the other side of Bessemer. A. Q. Johnson was slated to speak at that Labor Day meeting.

A. Q. Johnson was supposed to been a ex coal miner. But he was one who was fully recognized as being a stoolpigeon. A. Q., he was a orator. He could speak. And Eb Cox was as mad as he could be cause here they recognizing this stoolpigeon up here, and there he was in the leadership, vice-president at large, and nobody invited him to speak. That was another little time I was with him.

Me and Eb started to break, in around '47 and '48, when the CIO started Red baiting. When Philip Murray started his raids against the left in the CIO, Eb Cox was all the way on the other side.

At the last CIO convention I was in, in 1947, I run for vice-president at large. I had supported Cox against Beddow and Cox went in, the first time, and I supported Cox against McGruder, McGruder beat him. Now here the third time. Some of them asking me about running. The Negroes was all saying, "We want Bro' Hudson to run. We want to support him for vice-president this time."

We had a caucus of Negro delegates to the convention down at the little Masonic Temple, about sixty or seventy delegates from all the various unions. They got to talking about nominating of candidates for the vice-president at large, who they going support. Somebody nominated me. Then they nominated Gus Dixon. Gus Dixon was from Steel and I was from Steel. Then they nominated Asbury Howard. Asbury Howard was from Mine Mill, no trouble with Asbury Howard. But now here's Hudson and Dixon.

Eb Cox was chairing the meeting of this caucus in '47. All I fought back yonder for him, and here's my payoff now.

He spoke up and said, "I tell you all, you better know what you doing when you nominating these candidates. You better know what you doing nominating Bro' Hudson."

I said, "What you talking about?" said, "Tell these people what you talking about."

"Naw, Bro' Hudson, let's don't get into it. I think you understand."

I said, "I don't understand nothing. Tell these people what you talking about." He was Red baiting, trying to raise a bogey, telling them, if you nominate Hudson here, he's a bugabear, get you some trouble.

All the people started asking, "What, what about Hudson?" So they didn't nominate me there. They didn't agree on me. Everybody was talking, but nobody else said anything but me. I was the only one that challenged Eb Cox.

We went back to the convention. They got up and nominate Gus Dixon, and Asbury Howard was nominated. And Mack Coad, he nominated me. He had just enough nerve to go to the mike and say, "I want to place a name in nomination for vice-president at large, Bro' Hosie Hudson, president of Local 2815," and went on back and set down. Didn't say who I was or what I had done, nothing. In the voting, Asbury Howard got elected, and Gus Dixon won. They counted me out. The guy counting the people standing up to be counted for me, he didn't count a whole slice of people, went on out the door instead of carrying the votes down. I still got 139 votes. Gus Dixon didn't get but 160-some. But I didn't challenge it, cause I done fought till I just said, let them do what they want to. The rest of the Negroes just sit there and ∧ wouldn't say nothing.

After the voting, Louie Yates—he's dead and gone to the devil now—he walked by me and said, "Hudson, you got 139 votes. Man, you got a whole lot of support here in this convention. Did you think you's going get elected?"

"Why not? What you think I was running for if I didn't want to be elected?" But I tell you who was voting for me. It wont them devils from around Birmingham. The Negroes, yes, but not them whites—a few whites—but not the bulk of the whites. My support was from them out-of-town textile white women, white members from Huntsville, Talladega, and all them places. Them's the ones. On the basis of what I'm saying on the floor, I gained they ∧ confidence. They voted for my position and for me.

Eb Cox and me really broke when Steel raided the Mine Mill, and Smelter Workers, around '48.* Along in the fall, me and Eb chanced to meet on the corner in front of the Masonic Temple. I asked him, "What is your position about Steel going raiding in Mine Mill now?"

"Well, I tell you, Hudson, I'm a old man now. I can't get back into the plant now, cause they ain't going hire me back. I got a job to do. I got to look out for my job. I got to look out for my wife and family."

I said, "Therefore you forsaking the Negro people now, huh?" I said, "Mine Mill been the union that been fighting against all forms of discrimination in the mines, you know that." I said, "you forsaking the Negro, trying to tear down the Mine Mill union and what they done for the Negro, just to support your boss in the Steelworkers union to try to raid Mine Mill?"

He said, "I got to look out for my family. My job is with the United Steelworkers of America."

I said, "Well, I wish you God speed." We walked away from each other, and that was the last time me and Eb Cox had anything to say.

I saw him one more time around about in '50, just before Bull Connor started to raid against us there in Birmingham. I was coming from Atlanta on

*When Philip Murray began to raid, they split Mine Mill right down the middle, black on one side, white on the other, with some whites staying with the blacks and some of the blacks part of the whites. The black members built Mine Mill with a help from a few whites. But among the whites, you had all these Klan elements, all these Red baiters. Automatically they was against Mine Mill, "that damn communist union, them communists! Every time you get around Mine Mill you got communists!" But among the Negroes it was a different picture. When it come to a vote, come to election in the mines, whether to vote for Mine Mill or vote for the Steel union, the Negroes voted for Mine Mill and the whites voted for Steel.

my way back to Birmingham. I happened to catch the train he was on, coming from the Steelworkers convention in Atlantic City, one Sunday. He tried to make a great point with the Negro delegates sitting around me on the train.

He was talking to them. I'm just setting there. "Philip Murray's the greatest trade union statesman that ever lived!" Oh, he put Philip Murray high! That was when Philip Murray was raiding and putting the left out of the CIO. I didn't even turn to answer. I just sit there, let it stay. I rode on in to Birmingham. That was the last time I remember seeing him.*

*I went to Birmingham in 1961 and Eb Cox had just died.

Samuel F. Yette

(1929–   )

Born in Harrimon, Tennessee, Samuel F. Yette won national attention for the trenchant social analysis in his first book *The Choice: The Issue of Black Survival in America* (1971). He received his B.S. from Tennessee State University and his M.A. from Indiana University, and has worked as a teacher, sportswriter, reporter, special assistant for civil rights in the Office of Economic Opportunity, and Washington correspondent for *Newsweek*. Since 1972, he has been a professor of journalism at Howard University. He is also the author of the photo text *Washington and Two Marches* and *The Third American Revolution*, both issued by his publishing company, Cottage Books. The following excerpt is from *The Choice: The Issue of Black Survival in America*.

---

from The Choice: The Issue of Black Survival in America

Introduction: A Question of Survival

When the decade of the 1970's began, the United States government was officially—but unconstitutionally—in the midst of two wars: (1) a war of "attrition" (genocide) against the colonized colored people of Indochina, and (2) an expeditionary "law and order" campaign (repression—selective genocide) against the colonized colored people of the United States.

Although nonaligned, both colonized groups had much in common. As discussed in Part Two, they were, in fact, victims of the *same* war, though in different theaters.

In the United States, as in Indochina, victims of these undeclared wars painfully achieved high visibility during the 1960's. The colonized Blacks inside the United States were the subject of numerous and extensive studies, special programs, White House conferences, and plain gawking curiosity. Occasionally, a collection of what American society regarded as social antiques would present themselves for inspection in the nation's Capital. Such a group arrived in the spring of 1966. A motley collection of Blackpoor, they were a spectacle, even for Lafayette Park, where they spent the night. Rest-broken, poorly clothed, and shivering, the two dozen Mississippi outcasts* could not have been less in tune with the opulence around them. Some still crowded inside and others huddled outside the several tents they had pitched in the park across Pennsylvania Avenue—squarely in front of the White House.

These uninvited campers had braved a bone-chilling mist that shrouded the park. Two years earlier, some of them had dared vote in the Presidential election—for the first time in their many adult years. Others were accused of participating in the "Meredith March Against Fear," a walk quickly interrupted by the blasts of a white man's shotgun that nearly took the life of James Meredith. Some of them might even have joined in that chorus among the Meredith March that gave the first audible shouts of "Black Power!"

Now they were homeless.

They kept explaining that they were *not* the Negroes who had "lived in" at the deactivated Greenville (Mississippi) Air Force Base and were finally dragged out by the military. Instead, they insisted, they had relied on "the people in Washington" to help them work out their needs in an orderly way. All of them had outlived their rights as tenants in the Mississippi feudal system, but they had not outlived their faith in the government. They had been evicted from the land they had worked as sharecroppers, but they still allowed that the failing might be theirs, that it must have been they who had not made clear that their need was great and their cause just.

They hoped that federal antipoverty funds could be arranged for them to build houses and stay in the Delta, for that was home. Paper appeals failing, they brought their bodies to Washington to support their cause and demonstrate their need.

The bureaucratic charades had reduced them to this tent-setting spectacle, a desperate effort to get the attention of President Lyndon B. Johnson, and possibly embarrass him into action on their behalf. The Washington *Post* that morning carried a story of the telegram they sent to the President. It was signed "Your Neighbors." Their humor was lost on the President. There was no neighborly response. There was no response at all.

In time, they were driven by harsh weather and dysentery back, hungry and homeless, to the rigors of survival in the Mississippi Delta.

The spectacle of Lafayette Park kept alive the symbolic depravity of an inhumane history. Those anguished inhabitants of the park were truly a dying people. So were their legions of millions left in the valleys of the Black Belt and in the teeming ghettos of Chicago, New York, Los Angeles, Cleveland, and all the other welfare-swelled urban centers of the East, North, and West.

---

*"A young university economics instructor just made a trip to Mississippi and returned convinced that some 100,000 Negro sharecroppers may shortly be thrown off Delta plantations and forced by whites to move north," Marianne Means reported in the New York *World Journal Tribune*, January 31, 1967. "The practical economics of the wage increase (to 84¢ per hour) hardly warrant the sudden eviction of huge numbers of impoverished Negro families . . . but the political realities are something else again. The [instructor's] memorandum points out: 'the incentive [to evict] is rendered particularly strong by the fact that Negroes now constitute a majority of registered voters in a number of Delta counties and all major state and county offices will be up for election this fall.' "

They were obsolete people, described by the then Labor Secretary W. Willard Wirtz as a "human scrap heap":

> We are piling up a human scrap heap of between 250,000 and 500,000 people a year, many of whom never appear in the unemployment statistics.
> They are often not counted among the unemployed because they have given up looking for work and thus count themselves out of the labor market. The rate of nonparticipation in the labor force by men in their prime years increased from 4.7 percent in 1953 to 5.2 percent in 1962. The increase has been the sharpest among nonwhites, increasing from 5.3 percent to 8.2 percent in that period.
> The human scrap heap is composed of persons who, as a consequence of technological development, of their own educational failures, of environments of poverty and other causes that disqualify them for employment in a skilled economy, cannot and will not find work without special help.
> The 115,000 boys who failed the Selective Service educational tests in 1963 are candidates for the human scrap heap.
> If we are to turn the human scrap heap into the materials for richer progress and more rewarding lives, then private industry and our private institutions must help us to do the job that government actions have only suggested need doing.*

A people whom the society had always denied social value—personality—had also lost economic value. Theirs was the problem of *all* black America: survival.

Examination of the problem must begin with a single, overpowering socioeconomic condition in the society: black Americans *are* obsolete people.

While this certainly is not accurate in a moral sense, nor, at the moment, biologically, it is true where, in the 1970's, it becomes the issue: it is true in the minds and schemes of those who, with inordinate power and authority, control the nation. While it may not be so true among the general population, mass sentiments against oppression and possible genocide are not sufficiently strong to cause these schemes to fail. Black Americans have outlived their usefulness. Their *raison d'être* to this society has ceased to be a compelling issue. Once an economic asset, they are now considered an economic drag. The wood is all hewn, the water all drawn, the cotton all picked, and the rails reach from coast to coast. The ditches are all dug, the dishes are put away, and only a few shoes remain to be shined.

Thanks to old black backs and newfangled machines, the sweat chores of the nation are done. Now the some 25 million Blacks face a society that is brutally pragmatic, technologically accomplished, deeply racist, increasingly overcrowded, and surly. In such a society, the absence of social and economic value is a crucial factor in anyone's fight for a future.

Blacks in America have had 250 years of nationally sanctioned slavery and

---

*Reported in a Department of Labor press release, June 15, 1964, from a lecture by Wirtz to a seminar on automation and technological change in Los Angeles.

another hundred years of deceitful enslavement outside the national law. Now they are irreconcilably committed to personal dignity and justice as a people. Their patience, like the oxcart, is gone. But the hope remains that they, *un*like the oxen, can cease to be driven and can be permitted to stay—on human and civil terms.

They want to survive, but only as men and women—no longer as pawns or chattel. Can they?

This is the most frightful and pressing question facing America in the 1970's. Those who say the most urgent question is the "environment" should recognize that it is Blackness that is unsightly in America. Those who say it is war should face the fact that racism—an arrogance of superiority that seeks economic and military exploitation—is as much the nation's role in Birmingham as it is in Vietnam. And those who say that the most pressing issue is "law and order" should recognize the term for what it is: a euphemism for the total repression and possible extermination of those in the society who cry for justice where little justice can be found.

Whether Blacks have a place in U.S. society is a choice that belongs to the nation. That choice was audaciously called to the attention of white America early in 1960, when four black college students sat down at a North Carolina lunch counter reserved for whites. For the ten raw years of the 1960's, the nation noisily grappled with its choice: freedom or death for Afro-Americans.

By the end of the decade, Blacks were forced to face the evidence heaped painfully upon them. The evidence showed that a choice had been made, and freedom was denied.

True, the decade of the 1960's provided some contrary indications. There were, for example, outpourings of new laws and pronouncements that ostensibly guaranteed not only freedom and security but also socioeconomic progress. Blacks were visibly appointed to a handful of high federal positions. This was a kind of progress, but it was also confusing: it helped obscure from many Blacks and whites alike the true dangers being designed by repressive elements. In significant instances, what appeared to be progress was, in fact, the vehicle of the danger itself. For example, black appointees to high office generally included men of some standing and/or credibility in the black communities. Without that fact, of course, the value of their appointment was greatly, if not totally, diminished. Appointees included such men as Robert C. Weaver as Secretary of Housing and Urban Development, the first nonwhite member of any President's cabinet; Andrew Brimmer, the first black governor of the Federal Reserve Board; Lisle C. Carter, Jr., as Assistant Secretary of Health, Education, and Welfare; Theodore M. Berry, as community action director of the Office of Economic Opportunity; and Thurgood Marshall as Solicitor General, then Associate Justice of the Supreme Court, both unprecedented.

While the black appointees were highly visible, they were, for the most part, powerless. And their powerless visibility in and around the bureaucratic councils added an aura of legitimacy to illegitimate acts, providing a smokescreen for dirty dealing.

This is neither to criticize nor exonerate the appointees. The fault was not theirs. The fault was in the system—by design. Those who attribute the major fault to the appointees do so mainly out of their failure to grasp the cleverness and ruthlessness in the bureaucratic design to which these men were attached.

This is not to say that those who hoped should not have hoped, and that those who tried should have done otherwise. When the 1960 decade began, there was every reason both to hope and to try.

This cycle of hope, lost hope, promise, aborted promise, then rank oppression began with the election, in 1960, of Senator John F. Kennedy to the Presidency. What with the Freedom Rides in full swing, and with black people singing a bold, new song, what real choice had black people between candidate Richard M. Nixon, who had authored concentration camp legislation (see Part Three), and a superbly glamorous young man who promised to "get America moving again"?

When President Kennedy brought into the White House Andrew Hatcher, the first black White House assistant press secretary, that appointment served to indicate that he was willing to hear the black man's story. Subsequently, he received at the White House the leaders of a massive 1963 march on Washington for "Jobs and Freedom." He promised those leaders—Dr. Martin Luther King, Jr., A. Philip Randolph, Whitney Young, Jr., Roy Wilkins, and John Lewis—a new strategy to attack poverty and injustice.

Less than four months later, President Kennedy was dead, and the decade's first brief hope and promise had died with him. New hope and bigger promises, nonetheless, sprang up in their places.

Kennedy's successor, Lyndon B. Johnson, offered his sequel to President Kennedy's "Let us begin." Said President Johnson: "Let us continue."

The Johnson promise: "The Great Society."

Within a few months after President Kennedy was shot down in Dallas, November 22, 1963, President Johnson announced a new "unconditional war on poverty" and succeeded in getting an aggrieved Congress to pass the Civil Rights Act of 1964 (signed on July 2), and to create, on August 20, the Office of Economic Opportunity (OEO).

Beyond that, President Johnson made highly publicized speeches pledging to open doors for poor Blacks and to help them "walk through those doors" into a "Great Society." Those were the promises of the Great Society. The floods of government promise and black hope both crested at that point in the mid-1960's.

But . . . slowly, almost imperceptibly, the glint began to wear from Uncle Sam's shiny new armor. It tarnished, even while Uncle Sam stood like a colossus in the middle of the poverty and civil rights battlefield, swearing to take on all comers on behalf of Negroes and the poor. Still early in that new day of hope, wary Negroes, straining to see some sign of battle, could not perceive the paralysis that stayed the federal giant.

But as the day wore on, the go-slow motions of the federal giant did not match the fast, rhythmic rhetoric. In time, Negroes began to know that what they heard was aimed *at* them—not for them.

The cruelest hoax since the vain promise of "20 acres and a mule" following the Civil War had been set in motion against Africans transplanted in America. The raised hand of Uncle Sam was swatting poor Negroes while rewarding rich whites with the spoils of black misery. As this truth became known, hope turned to hatred, dedication became disgust, hands raised for help became clenched fists, and eyes searching for acceptance turned inward.

Negroes turned Black.

Blacks could see clearer what Negroes could not: If help would come, they, themselves, would bring it. Beauty was where they found it: Finding beauty meant *being* beautiful. They could win only if the system lost, and vice versa. And what truly was at stake was their natural lives.

And so it went—a decade of freedom rides, promises, public con games, black rebellions, and armed invasions of campus "sanctuaries." Even so, through it all, Blacks did manage more togetherness—whether it was in Vietnam or campsites on this side; the college campus or at wakes for the martyrs; in jail cells or on OEO community action boards.

The black togetherness of the 1960's—the newfound Blackness—produced a new visibility and a grip on the issues affecting black lives. Consequently, through a residue of confidence in the political system, hundreds of Blacks were elected to public office. But even some of them foresaw, as the new decade began, concentration camps and oppression.*

Thus, even the Blacks who hoped most and were most rewarded in the tradition of the system saw in the nation's choice a clear and present danger.

The schemes of the 1970's promised new martyrs, bigger jails, more wars (at home and abroad), data banks, wiretaps, and a genuinely regimented society, including the sharp curtailment of black college students, a white establishment take-over of black colleges, and psychological barbed wire around all learning institutions.

In short, the 1970's promised a reversal of those processes that, in the 1960's, tended to bring black people a modicum of socioeconomic advancement.

In the 1970's, for black Americans, it is clearly a question of survival.

*Reported *Ebony* in its February, 1970, issue (p. 77): "Optimism, guarded, qualified and very cautious, was the general tone of the responses of a score of the nation's black mayors to a ten-question *Ebony* poll dealing with the status, present and future, of black people in America. . . . As many as 14 of them generally agreed on a single question (that black people will be better off 20 years from now in the United States), but on another issue they were sharply divided (the possibility of black Americans being 'preventively detained' as Japanese-Americans were during World War II). . . . Mayor Carl Stokes of Cleveland predicted a much improved situation for blacks over the next two decades. Mayor Richard Hatcher of Gary foresaw black fortunes plummeting to 'a desperately low level,' unless some unlikely changes are made. The two men agreed that police state-type detention is a very real possibility for blacks and other groups of Americans."

Martin Luther King, Jr.

(1929–1968)

Born in Atlanta, Georgia, and educated at Morehouse College and Boston University, Martin Luther King, Jr., became a leader in the nonviolent struggle for constitutional rights and human dignity during the Montgomery boycotts of the late 1950s and the deepening resistance to discrimination in the South and the North throughout the 1960s. In 1964, King received the Nobel Peace Prize. King is most often associated with his "I Have a Dream" speech delivered during the 1963 March on Washington, but he also was the author of several books, which help to clarify his complex commitment to morality and social change: *Stride Toward Freedom: The Montgomery Story* (1958), *Strength to Love* (1963), *Why We Can't Wait* (1964), and *Where Do We Go from Here?* (1967). King was the consummate black preacher, and the study of his rhetorical strategies reveals much about the inventiveness of African-American oral traditions as they impact upon the "learned" forms of print traditions. King is one of the few Americans to have the distinct honor of a national holiday, an honor that might insure sustained attention to King's contributions to African-American social thought and literature. "Letter from Birmingham Jail" is reprinted from *Why We Can't Wait*.

Letter from Birmingham Jail

April 16, 1963

MY DEAR FELLOW CLERGYMEN:[1]

While confined here in the Birmingham city jail, I came across your recent statement calling my present activities "unwise and untimely." Seldom do I pause to answer criticism of my work and ideas. If I sought to answer all the criticisms that cross my desk, my secretaries would have little time for anything

---

[1]This response to a published statement by eight fellow clergymen from Alabama (Bishop C. C. J. Carpenter, Bishop Joseph A. Durick, Rabbi Hilton L. Grafman, Bishop Paul Hardin, Bishop Holan B. Harmon, the Reverend George M. Murray, the Reverend Edward V. Ramage and the Reverend Earl Stallings) was composed under somewhat constricting circumstances. Begun on the margins of the newspaper in which the statement appeared while I was in jail, the letter was continued on scraps of writing paper supplied by a friendly Negro trusty, and concluded on a pad my attorneys were eventually permitted to leave me. Although the text remains in substance unaltered, I have indulged in the author's prerogative of polishing it for publication. [King's note]

other than such correspondence in the course of the day, and I would have no time for constructive work. But since I feel that you are men of genuine good will and that your criticisms are sincerely set forth, I want to try to answer your statement in what I hope will be patient and reasonable terms.

I think I should indicate why I am here in Birmingham, since you have been influenced by the view which argues against "outsiders coming in." I have the honor of serving as president of the Southern Christian Leadership Conference, an organization operating in every southern state, with headquarters in Atlanta, Georgia. We have some eighty-five affiliated organizations across the South, and one of them is the Alabama Christian Movement for Human Rights. Frequently we share staff, educational, and financial resources with our affiliates. Several months ago the affiliate here in Birmingham asked us to be on call to engage in a nonviolent direct-action program if such were deemed necessary. We readily consented, and when the hour came we lived up to our promise. So I, along with several members of my staff, am here because I was invited here. I am here because I have organizational ties here.

But more basically, I am in Birmingham because injustice is here. Just as the prophets of the eighth century B.C. left their villages and carried their "thus saith the Lord" far beyond the boundaries of their home towns, and just as the Apostle Paul left his village of Tarsus and carried the gospel of Jesus Christ to the far corners of the Greco-Roman world, so am I compelled to carry the gospel of freedom beyond my own home town. Like Paul, I must constantly respond to the Macedonian call for aid.

Moreover, I am cognizant of the interrelatedness of all communities and states. I cannot sit idly by in Atlanta and not be concerned about what happens in Birmingham. Injustice anywhere is a threat to justice everywhere. We are caught in an inescapable network of mutuality, tied in a single garment of destiny. Whatever affects one directly, affects all indirectly. Never again can we afford to live with the narrow, provincial, "outside agitator" idea. Anyone who lives inside the United States can never be considered an outsider anywhere within its bounds.

You deplore the demonstrations taking place in Birmingham. But your statement, I am sorry to say, fails to express a similar concern for the conditions that brought about the demonstrations. I am sure that none of you would want to rest content with the superficial kind of social analysis that deals merely with effects and does not grapple with underlying causes. It is unfortunate that demonstrations are taking place in Birmingham, but it is even more unfortunate that the city's white power structure left the Negro community with no alternative.

In any nonviolent campaign there are four basic steps: collection of the facts to determine whether injustices exist; negotiation; self-purification; and direct action. We have gone through all these steps in Birmingham. There can be no gainsaying the fact that racial injustice engulfs this community. Birmingham is probably the most thoroughly segregated city in the United States. Its ugly record of brutality is widely known. Negroes have experienced grossly unjust treatment in the courts. There have been more unsolved bombings of Negro homes and churches in Birmingham than in any other city in the nation. These are the hard brutal facts of the case. On the basis of these conditions, Negro leaders sought to negotiate with the city fathers. But the latter consistently refused to engage in good-faith negotiation.

Then, last September, came the opportunity to talk with leaders of Birmingham's economic community. In the course of the negotiations, certain promises were made by the merchants—for example, to remove the stores' humiliating racial signs. On the basis of these promises, the Reverend Fred Shuttlesworth and the leaders of the Alabama Christian Movement for Human Rights agreed to a moratorium on all demonstrations. As the weeks and months went by, we realized that we were the victims of a broken promise. A few signs, briefly removed, returned; the others remained.

As in so many past experiences, our hopes had been blasted, and the shadow of deep disappointment settled upon us. We had no alternative except to prepare for direct action, whereby we would present our very bodies as a means of laying our case before the conscience of the local and the national community. Mindful of the difficulties involved, we decided to undertake a process of self-purification. We began a series of workshops on nonviolence, and we repeatedly asked ourselves: "Are you able to accept blows without retaliating?" "Are you able to endure the ordeal of jail?" We decided to schedule our direct-action program for the Easter season, realizing that except for Christmas, this is the main shopping period of the year. Knowing that a strong economic-withdrawal program would be the by-product of direct action, we felt that this would be the best time to bring pressure to bear on the merchants for the needed change.

Then it occurred to us that Birmingham's mayoral election was coming up in March, and we speedily decided to postpone action until after election day. When we discovered that the Commissioner of Public Safety, Eugene "Bull" Connor, had piled up enough votes to be in the run-off, we decided again to postpone action until the day after the run-off so that the demonstrations could not be used to cloud the issues. Like many others, we waited to see Mr. Connor defeated, and to this end we endured postponement after postponement. Having aided in this community need, we felt that our direct-action program could be delayed no longer.

You may well ask, "Why direct action? Why sit-ins, marches, and so forth? Isn't negotiation a better path?" You are quite right in calling for negotiation. Indeed, this is the very purpose of direct action. Nonviolent direct action seeks to create such a crisis and foster such a tension that a community which has constantly refused to negotiate is forced to confront the issue. It seeks so to dramatize the issue that it can no longer be ignored. My citing the creation of tension as part of the work of the nonviolent resister may sound rather shocking. But I must confess that I am not afraid of the word "tension." I have earnestly opposed violent tension, but there is a type of constructive, nonviolent tension which is necessary for growth. Just as Socrates felt that it was necessary to create a tension in the mind so that individuals could rise from the bondage of myths and half truths to the unfettered realm of creative analysis and objective appraisal, so must we see the need for nonviolent gadflies to create the kind of tension in society that will help men rise from the dark depths of prejudice and racism to the majestic heights of understanding and brotherhood.

The purpose of our direct-action program is to create a situation so crisis-packed that it will inevitably open the door to negotiation. I therefore concur with you in your call for negotiation. Too long has our beloved Southland been bogged down in a tragic effort to live in monologue rather than dialogue.

One of the basic points in your statement is that the action that I and my associates have taken in Birmingham is untimely. Some have asked: "Why didn't you give the new city administration time to act?" The only answer that I can give to this query is that the new Birmingham administration must be prodded about as much as the outgoing one, before it will act. We are sadly mistaken if we feel that the election of Albert Boutwell as mayor will bring the millennium to Birmingham. While Mr. Boutwell is a much more gentle person than Mr. Connor, they are both segregationists, dedicated to maintenance of the status quo. I have hoped that Mr. Boutwell will be reason-able enough to see the futility of massive resistance to desegregation. But he will not see this without pressure from devotees of civil rights. My friends, I must say to you that we have not made a single gain in civil rights without determined legal and nonviolent pressure. Lamentably, it is an historical fact that privileged groups seldom give up their privileges voluntarily. Individuals may see the moral light and voluntarily give up their unjust posture; but, as Reinhold Niebuhr has reminded us, groups tend to be more immoral than individuals.

We know through painful experience that freedom is never voluntarily given by the oppressor; it must be demanded by the oppressed. Frankly, I have yet to engage in a direct-action campaign that was "well timed" in the view of those who have not suffered unduly from the disease of segregation. For years now I have heard the word "Wait!" It rings in the ear of every Negro with piercing familiarity. This "Wait" has almost always meant "Never." We must come to see, with one of our distinguished jurists, that "justice too long delayed is justice denied."

We have waited for more than 340 years for our constitutional and God-given rights. The nations of Asia and Africa are moving with jetlike speed toward gaining political independence, but we still creep at horse-and-buggy pace toward gaining a cup of coffee at a lunch counter. Perhaps it is easy for those who have never felt the stinging darts of segregation to say, "Wait." But when you have seen vicious mobs lynch your mothers and fathers at will and drown your sisters and brothers at whim; when you have seen hate-filled policemen curse, kick, and even kill your black brothers and sisters; when you see the vast majority of your twenty million Negro brothers smothering in an airtight cage of poverty in the midst of an affluent society; when you suddenly find your tongue twisted and your speech stammering as you seek to explain to your six-year-old daughter why she can't go to the public amusement park that has just been advertised on television, and see tears welling up in her eyes when she is told that Funtown is closed to colored children, and see ominous clouds of inferiority beginning to form in her little mental sky, and see her beginning to distort her personality by developing an unconscious bitterness toward white people; when you have to concoct an answer for a five-year-old son who is asking, "Daddy, why do white people treat colored people so mean?"; when you take a cross-country drive and find it necessary to sleep night after night in the uncomfortable corners of your automobile because no motel will accept you; when you are humiliated day in and day out by nagging signs reading "white" and "colored"; when your first name becomes "nigger," your middle name becomes "boy" (however old you are) and your last name becomes "John," and your wife and mother are never given the respected title "Mrs."; when you are harried by day and haunted by night by the fact that you are a Negro, living constantly at tiptoe stance, never quite knowing what to expect next, and are plagued with inner fears and outer resentments; when you are forever fighting a degenerating sense of "nobodiness"—then you will understand why we find it difficult to wait. There comes a time when the cup of endurance runs over, and men are no longer willing to be plunged into the abyss of despair. I hope, sirs, you can understand our legitimate and unavoidable impatience.

You express a great deal of anxiety over our willingness to break laws. This is certainly a legitimate concern. Since we so diligently urge people to obey the Supreme Court's decision of 1954 outlawing segregation in the public schools, at first glance it may seem rather paradoxical for us consciously to break laws. One may well ask: "How can you advocate breaking some laws and obeying others?" The answer lies in the fact that there are two types of laws: just and unjust. I would be the first to advocate obeying just laws. One has not only a legal but a moral responsibility to obey just laws. Conversely, one has a moral responsibility to disobey unjust laws. I would agree with St. Augustine that "an unjust law is no law at all."

Now, what is the difference between the two? How does one determine whether a law is just or unjust? A just law is a man-made code that squares with the moral law or the law of God. An unjust law is a code that is out of harmony with the moral law. To put it in the terms of St. Thomas Aquinas: An unjust law is a human law that is not rooted in eternal law and natural law. Any law that uplifts human personality is just. Any law that degrades human personality is unjust. All segregation statutes are unjust because segregation distorts the soul and damages the personality. It gives the segregator a false sense of superiority and the segregated a false sense of inferiority. Segregation, to use the terminology of the Jewish philosopher Martin Buber, substitutes an "I-it" relationship for an "I-thou" relationship and ends up relegating persons to the status of things. Hence segregation is not only politically, economically, and sociologically unsound, it is morally wrong and sinful. Paul Tillich has said that sin is separation. Is not segregation an existential expression of man's tragic separation, his awful estrangement, his terrible sinfulness? Thus it is that I can urge men to obey the 1954 decision of the Supreme Court, for it is morally right; and I can urge them to disobey segregation ordinances, for they are morally wrong.

Let us consider a more concrete example of just and unjust laws. An unjust law is a code that a numerical or power majority group compels a minority group to obey but does not make binding on itself. This is *difference* made legal. By the same token, a just law is a code that a majority compels a minority to follow and that it is willing to follow itself. This is *sameness* made legal.

Let me give another explanation. A law is unjust if it is inflicted on a minority that, as a result of being denied the right to vote, had no part in enacting or devising the law. Who can say that the legislature of Alabama which set up that state's segregation laws was democratically elected? Throughout Alabama all sorts of devious methods are used to prevent Negroes from becoming registered voters, and there are some counties in which, even though Negroes constitute a majority of the population, not a single Negro is registered. Can any law enacted under such circumstances be considered democratically structured?

Sometimes a law is just on its face and unjust in its application. For instance, I have been arrested on a charge of parading without a permit. Now, there is nothing wrong in having an ordinance which requires a permit for a parade. But such an ordinance becomes unjust when it is used to maintain segregation and to deny citizens the First Amendment privilege of peaceful assembly and protest.

I hope you are able to see the distinction I am trying to point out. In no sense do I advocate evading or defying the law, as would the rabid segregationist. That would lead to anarchy. One who breaks an unjust law must do so openly, lovingly, and with a willingness to accept the penalty. I submit that an individual who breaks a law that conscience tells him is unjust, and who willingly accepts the penalty of imprisonment in order to arouse the conscience of the community over its injustice, is in reality expressing the highest respect for law.

Of course, there is nothing new about this kind of civil disobedience. It was evidenced sublimely in the refusal of Shadrach, Meshach, and Abednego to obey the laws of Nebuchadnezzar, on the ground that a higher moral law was at stake. It was practiced superbly by the early Christians, who were willing to face hungry lions and the excruciating pain of chopping blocks rather than submit to certain unjust laws of the Roman Empire. To a degree, academic freedom is a reality today because Socrates practiced civil disobedience. In our own nation, the Boston Tea Party represented a massive act of civil disobedience.

We should never forget that everything Adolf Hitler did in Germany was "legal" and everything the Hungarian freedom fighters did in Hungary was "illegal." It was "illegal" to aid and comfort a Jew in Hitler's Germany. Even so, I am sure that, had I lived in Germany at the time, I would have aided and comforted my Jewish brothers. If today I lived in a Communist country where certain principles dear to the Christian faith are suppressed, I would openly advocate disobeying that country's antireligious laws.

I must make two honest confessions to you, my Christian and Jewish brothers. First, I must confess that over the past few years I have been gravely disappointed with the white moderate. I have almost reached the regrettable conclusion that the Negro's great stumbling block in his stride toward freedom is not the White Citizen's Counciler or the Ku Klux Klanner, but the white moderate, who is more devoted to "order" than to justice; who prefers a negative peace which is the absence of tension to a positive peace which is the presence of justice; who constantly says, "I agree with you in the goal you seek, but I cannot agree with your methods of direct action"; who paternalistically believes he can set the timetable for another man's freedom; who lives by a mythical concept of time and who constantly advises the Negro to wait for a "more convenient season." Shallow understanding from people of good will is more frustrating than absolute misunderstanding from people of ill will. Lukewarm acceptance is much more bewildering than outright rejection.

I had hoped that the white moderate would understand that law and order exist for the purpose of establishing justice and that when they fail in this purpose they become the dangerously structured dams that block the flow of social progress. I had hoped that the white moderate would understand that the present tension in the South is a necessary phase of the transition from an obnoxious negative peace, in which the Negro passively accepted his unjust plight, to a substantive and positive peace, in which all men will respect the dignity and worth of human personality. Actually, we who engage in nonviolent direct action are not the creators of tension. We merely bring to the surface the hidden tension that is already alive. We bring it out in the open, where it can be seen and dealt with. Like a boil that can never be cured so long as it is covered up but must be opened with all its ugliness to the natural medicines of air and light, injustice must be exposed, with all the tension its exposure creates, to the light of human conscience and the air of national opinion, before it can be cured.

In your statement you assert that our actions, even though peaceful, must be condemned because they precipitate violence. But is this a logical assertion? Isn't this like condemning a robbed man because his possession of money precipitated the evil act of robbery? Isn't this like condemning Socrates because his unswerving commitment to truth and his philosophical inquiries precipitated the act by the misguided populace in which they made him drink hemlock? Isn't this like condemning Jesus because his unique God-consciousness and never-ceasing devotion to God's will precipitated the evil act of crucifixion? We must come to see that, as the federal courts have consistently affirmed, it is wrong to urge an individual to cease his efforts to gain his basic constitutional rights because the quest may precipitate violence. Society must protect the robbed and punish the robber.

I had also hoped that the white moderate would reject the myth concerning time in relation to the struggle for freedom. I have just received a letter from a white brother in Texas. He writes: "All Christians know that the colored people will receive equal rights eventually, but it is possible that you are in too great a religious hurry. It had taken Christianity almost two thousand years to accomplish what it has. The teachings of Christ take time to come to earth.'' Such an attitude stems from a tragic misconception of time, from the strangely irrational notion that there is something in the very flow of time that will inevitably cure all ills. Actually, time itself is neutral; it can be used either destructively or constructively. More and more I feel that the people of ill will have used time much more effectively than have the people of good will. We will have to repent in this generation not merely for the hateful words and actions of the bad people, but for the appalling silence of the good people. Human progress never rolls in on wheels of inevitability; it comes through the tireless efforts of men willing to be co-workers with God, and without this hard work, time itself becomes an ally of the forces of social stagnation. We must use time creatively, in the knowledge that the time is always ripe to do right. Now is the time to make real the promise of democracy and transform our pending national elegy into a creative psalm of brotherhood. Now is the time to lift our national policy from the quicksand of racial injustice to the solid rock of human dignity.

You speak of our activity in Birmingham as extreme. At first I was rather disappointed that fellow clergymen would see my nonviolent efforts as those of an extremist. I began thinking about the fact that I stand in the middle of two opposing forces in the Negro community. One is a force of complacency, made up in part of Negroes who, as a result of long years of oppression, are so drained of self-respect and a sense of ''somebodiness'' that they have adjusted to segregation; and in part of a few middle-class Negroes who, because of a degree of academic and economic security and because in some ways they profit by segregation, have become insensitive to the problems of the masses. The other force is one of bitterness and hatred, and it comes perilously close to advocating violence. It is expressed in the various black nationalist groups that are springing up across the nation, the largest and best known being Elijah Muhammad's Muslim movement. Nourished by the Negro's frustration over the continued existence of racial discrimination, this movement is made up of people who have lost faith in America, who have absolutely repudiated Christianity, and who have concluded that the white man is an incorrigible ''devil.''

I have tried to stand between these two forces, saying that we need emulate neither the ''do-nothingism'' of the complacent nor the hatred and despair of the black nationalist. For there is the more excellent way of love and nonviolent protest. I am grateful to God that, through the influence of the Negro church, the way of nonviolence became an integral part of our struggle.

If this philosophy had not emerged, by now many streets of the South would, I am convinced, be flowing with blood. And I am further convinced that if our white brothers dismiss as ''rabble-rousers'' and ''outside agitators'' those of us who employ nonviolent direct action, and if they refuse to support our nonviolent efforts, millions of Negroes will, out of frustration and despair, seek solace and security in black nationalist ideologies—a development that would inevitably lead to a frightening racial nightmare.

Oppressed people cannot remain oppressed forever. The yearning for freedom eventually manifests itself, and that is what has happened to the American Negro. Something within has reminded him of his birthright of freedom, and something without has reminded him that it can be gained. Consciously or unconsciously, he has been caught up by the *Zeitgeist*, and with his black brothers of Africa and his brown and yellow brothers of Asia, South America, and the Caribbean, the United States Negro is moving with a sense of great urgency toward the promised land of racial justice. If one recognizes this vital urge that has engulfed the Negro community, one should readily understand why public demonstrations are taking place. The Negro has many pent-up resentments and latent frustrations, and he must release them. So let him march; let him make prayer pilgrimages to the city hall; let him go on freedom rides—and try to understand why he must do so. If his repressed emotions are not released in nonviolent ways, they will seek expression through violence; this is not a threat but a fact of history. So I have not said to my people, "Get rid of your discontent." Rather, I have tried to say that this normal and healthy discontent can be channeled into the creative outlet of nonviolent direct action. And now this approach is being termed extremist.

But though I was initially disappointed at being categorized as an extremist, as I continued to think about the matter I gradually gained a measure of satisfaction from the label. Was not Jesus an extremist for love: "Love your enemies, bless them that curse you, do good to them that hate you, and pray for them which despitefully use you, and persecute you." Was not Amos an extremist for justice: "Let justice roll down like waters and righteousness like an ever-flowing stream." Was not Paul an extremist for the Christian gospel: "I bear in my body the marks of the Lord Jesus." Was not Martin Luther an extremist: "Here I stand; I cannot do otherwise, so help me God." And John Bunyan: "I will stay in jail to the end of my days before I make a butchery of my conscience." And Abraham Lincoln: "This nation cannot survive half slave and half free." And Thomas Jefferson: "We hold these truths to be self-evident, that all men are created equal. . . ." So the question is not whether we will be extremists, but what kind of extremists we will be. Will we be extremists for hate or for love? Will we be extremists for the preservation of injustice or for the extension of justice? In that dramatic scene on Calvary's hill three men were crucified. We must never forget that all three were crucified for the same crime—the crime of extremism. Two were extremists for immorality, and thus fell below their environment. The other, Jesus Christ, was an extremist for love, truth, and goodness, and thereby rose above his environment. Perhaps the South, the nation, and the world are in dire need of creative extremists.

I had hoped that the white moderate would see this need. Perhaps I was too optimistic; perhaps I expected too much. I suppose I should have realized that few members of the oppressor race can understand the deep groans and passionate yearnings of the oppressed race, and still fewer have the vision to see that injustice must be rooted out by strong, persistent, and determined action. I am thankful, however, that some of our white brothers in the South have grasped the meaning of this social revolution and committed themselves to it. They are still all too few in quantity, but they are big in quality. Some—such as Ralph McGill, Lillian Smith, Harry Golden, James McBride Dabbs, Ann Braden, and Sarah Patton Boyle—have written about our struggle in eloquent and prophetic terms. Others have marched with us down nameless streets of the South. They have languished in filthy, roach-infested jails, suffering the abuse and brutality of policemen who view them as "dirty nigger-lovers." Unlike so many of their moderate brothers and sisters, they have recognized the urgency of the moment and sensed the need for powerful "action" antidotes to combat the disease of segregation.

Let me take note of my other major disappointment. I have been so greatly disappointed with the white church and its leadership. Of course, there are some notable exceptions. I am not unmindful of the fact that each of you has taken some significant stands on this issue. I commend you, Reverend Stallings, for your Christian stand on this past Sunday, in welcoming Negroes to your worship service on a nonsegregated basis. I commend the Catholic leaders of this state for integrating Spring Hill College several years ago.

But despite these notable exceptions, I must honestly reiterate that I have been disappointed with the church. I do not say this as one of those negative critics who can always find something wrong with the church. I say this as a minister of the gospel, who loves the church; who was nurtured in its bosom; who has been sustained by its spiritual blessings and who will remain true to it as long as the cord of life shall lengthen.

When I was suddenly catapulted into the leadership of the bus protest in Montgomery, Alabama, a few years ago, I felt we would be supported by the white church. I felt that the white ministers, priests, and rabbis of the South would be among our strongest allies. Instead, some have been outright opponents, refusing to understand the freedom movement and misrepresenting its leaders; all too many others have been more cautious than courageous and have remained silent behind the anesthetizing security of stained-glass windows.

In spite of my shattered dreams, I came to Birmingham with the hope that the white religious leadership of this community would see the justice of our cause and, with deep moral concern, would serve as the channel through which our just grievances could reach the power structure. I had hoped that each of you would understand. But again I have been disappointed. . . .

There was a time when the church was very powerful—in the time when the early Christians rejoiced at being deemed worthy to suffer for what they believed. In those days the church was not merely a thermometer that recorded the ideas and principles of popular opinion; it was a thermostat that transformed the mores of society. Whenever the early Christians entered a town, the people in power became disturbed and immediately sought to convict the Christians for being "disturbers of the peace" and "outside agitators." But the Christians pressed on, in the conviction that they were "a colony of heaven," called to obey God rather than man. Small in number, they were big in commitment.

They were too God intoxicated to be "astronomically intimidated." By their effort and example they brought an end to such ancient evils as infanticide and gladiatorial contests.

Things are different now. So often the contemporary church is a weak, ineffectual voice with an uncertain sound. So often it is an arch-defender of the status quo. Far from being disturbed by the presence of the church, the power structure of the average community is consoled by the church's silent—and often even vocal—sanction of things as they are.

But the judgment of God is upon the church as never before. If today's church does not recapture the sacrificial spirit of the early church, it will lose its authenticity, forfeit the loyalty of millions, and be dismissed as an irrelevant social club with no meaning for the twentieth century. Every day I meet young people whose disappointment with the church has turned into outright disgust.

Perhaps I have once again been too optimistic. Is organized religion too inextricably bound to the status quo to save our nation and the world? Perhaps I must turn my faith to the inner spiritual church, the church within the church, as the true *ekklesia* and the hope of the world. But again I am thankful to God that some noble souls from the ranks of organized religion have broken loose from the paralyzing chains of conformity and joined us as active partners in the struggle for freedom. They have left their secure congregations and walked the streets of Albany, Georgia, with us. They have gone down the highways of the South on torturous rides for freedom. Yes, they have gone to jail with us. Some have been dismissed from their churches, have lost the support of their bishops and fellow ministers. But they have acted in the faith that right defeated is stronger than evil triumphant. Their witness has been the spiritual salt that has preserved the true meaning of the gospel in these troubled times. They have carved a tunnel of hope through the dark mountain of disappointment.

I hope the church as a whole will meet the challenge of this decisive hour. But even if the church does not come to the aid of justice, I have no despair about the future. I have no fear about the outcome of our struggle in Birmingham, even if our motives are at present misunderstood. We will reach the goal of freedom in Birmingham and all over the nation, because the goal of America is freedom. Abused and scorned though we may be, our destiny is tied up with America's destiny. Before the pilgrims landed at Plymouth, we were here. Before the pen of Jefferson etched the majestic words of the Declaration of Independence across the pages of history, we were here. For more than two centuries our forebears labored in this country without wages; they made cotton king; they built the homes of their masters while suffering gross injustice and shameful humiliation—and yet out of a bottomless vitality they continued to thrive and develop. If the inexpressible cruelties of slavery could not stop us, the opposition we now face will surely fail. We will win our freedom because the sacred heritage of our nation and the eternal will of God are embodied in our echoing demands.

Before closing I feel impelled to mention one other point in your statement that has troubled me profoundly. You warmly commended the Birmingham police force for keeping "order" and "preventing violence." I doubt that you would have so warmly commended the police force if you had seen its dogs sinking their teeth into unarmed, nonviolent Negroes. I doubt that you would so quickly commend the policemen if you were to observe their ugly and inhumane treatment of Negroes here in the city jail; if you were to watch them push and curse old Negro women and young Negro girls; if you were to see them slap and kick old Negro men and young boys; if you were to observe them, as they did on two occasions, refuse to give us food because we wanted to sing our grace together. I cannot join you in your praise of the Birmingham police department.

It is true that the police have exercised a degree of discipline in handling the demonstrators. In this sense they have conducted themselves rather "nonviolently" in public. But for what purpose? To preserve the evil system of segregation. Over the past few years I have consistently preached that nonviolence demands that the means we use must be as pure as the ends we seek. I have tried to make clear that it is wrong to use immoral means to attain moral ends. But now I must affirm that it is just as wrong, or perhaps even more so, to use moral means to preserve immoral ends. Perhaps Mr. Connor and his policemen have been rather nonviolent in public, as was Chief Pritchett in Albany, Georgia, but they have used the moral means of nonviolence to maintain the immoral end of racial injustice. As T. S. Eliot has said, "The last temptation is the greatest treason: To do the right deed for the wrong reason."

I wish you had commended the Negro sit-inners and demonstrators of Birmingham for their sublime courage, their willingness to suffer, and their amazing discipline in the midst of great provocation. One day the South will recognize its real heroes. They will be the James Merediths, with the noble sense of purpose that enables them to face jeering and hostile mobs, and with the agonizing loneliness that characterizes the life of the pioneer. They will be old, oppressed, battered Negro women, symbolized in a seventy-two-year-old woman in Montgomery, Alabama, who rose up with a sense of dignity and with her people decided not to ride segregated buses, and who responded with ungrammatical profundity to one who inquired about her weariness: "My feets is tired, but my soul is at rest." They will be the young high school and college students, the young ministers of the gospel and a host of their elders, courageously and nonviolently sitting in at lunch counters and willingly going to jail for conscience' sake. One day the South will know that when these disinherited children of God sat down at lunch counters, they were in reality standing up for what is best in the American dream and for the most sacred values in our Judaeo-Christian heritage, thereby bringing our nation back to those great wells of democracy which were dug deep by the founding fathers in their formulation of the Constitution and the Declaration of Independence.

Never before have I written so long a letter. I'm afraid it is much too long to take your precious time. I can assure you that it would have been much shorter if I had been writing from a comfortable desk, but what else can one do when he is alone in a narrow jail cell, other than write long letters, think long thoughts, and pray long prayers?

If I have said anything in this letter that overstates the truth and indicates an unreasonable impatience, I beg you to forgive me. If I have said anything that understates the truth and indicates my having a patience that allows me to settle for anything less than brotherhood, I beg God to forgive me.

I hope this letter finds you strong in the faith. I also hope that circumstances will soon make it possible for me to meet each of you, not as an integrationist or a civil rights leader but as a fellow clergyman and a Christian brother. Let us all hope that the dark clouds of racial prejudice will soon pass away and the deep fog of misunderstanding will be lifted from our fear-drenched communities, and in some not too distant tomorrow the radiant stars of love and brotherhood will shine over our great nation with all their scintillating beauty.

Yours in the cause of
Peace and Brotherhood,
Martin Luther King, Jr.

Angela Y. Davis
(1944–   )

A native of Birmingham, Alabama, Davis gained an international reputation when she was hunted, captured, and tried for conspiracy charges in 1970–1972. After receiving her B.A. from Brandeis, studying in Europe, and getting her M.A. in philosophy from the University of California, San Diego, she became involved in radical politics, continuing the active struggle against oppression she began in her youth. In 1969, Davis was fired from her teaching position at UCLA when she admitted she was a member of the Communist party. Because of her friendship with George Jackson, one of the Soledad (Prison) Brothers, she was accused of complicity in the aborted drama of escape and kidnapping that occurred at Marin County (California) Courthouse on August 7, 1970. She was acquitted of the charges in 1972 and has continued her work as an opponent of economic exploitation, racism, and sexism. In addition to her autobiography, Davis has written *Women, Race, and Class* (1981) and *Women, Culture, and Politics* (1989). The following excerpt is from *Angela Davis: An Autobiography*.

---

from Angela Davis: An Autobiography

The big white house on top of the hill was not far from our old neighborhood, but the distance could not be measured in blocks. The government housing project on Eighth Avenue where we lived before was a crowded street of little red brick structures—no one of which was different from the other. Only rarely did the cement surrounding these brick huts break open and show patches of green. Without space or earth, nothing could be planted to bear fruit or blossoms. But friends were there—and friendliness.

In 1948 we moved out of the projects in Birmingham, Alabama, to the large wooden house on Center Street. My parents still live there. Because of its steeples and gables and peeling paint, the house was said to be haunted. There were wild woods in back with fig trees, blackberry patches and great wild cherry trees. On one side of the house was a huge Cigar tree. There was space here and no cement. The street itself was a strip of orange-red Alabama clay. It was the most conspicuous house in the neighborhood—not only because of its curious architecture but because, for blocks around, it was the only house

386

not teeming inside with white hostility. We were the first Black family to move
into that area, and the white people believed that we were in the vanguard of
a mass invasion.

    At the age of four I was aware that the people across the street were
different—without yet being able to trace their alien nature to the color of their
skin. What made them different from our neighbors in the projects was the
frown on their faces, the way they stood a hundred feet away and glared at
us, their refusal to speak when we said "Good afternoon." An elderly couple
across the street, the Montees, sat on their porch all the time, their eyes heavy
with belligerence.

    Almost immediately after we moved there the white people got together and
decided on a border line between them and us. Center Street became the line
of demarcation. Provided that we stayed on "our" side of the line (the east
side) they let it be known we would be left in peace. If we ever crossed over
to their side, war would be declared. Guns were hidden in our house and
vigilance was constant.

    Fifty or so yards from this hatred, we went about our daily lives. My
mother, on leave from her teaching job, took care of my younger brother
Benny, while waiting to give birth to another child, my sister Fania. My father
drove his old orange van to the service station each morning after dropping
me off at nursery school. It was next door to the Children's Home Hospital—
an old wooden building where I was born and where, at two, I had my tonsils
removed. I was fascinated by the people dressed in white and tried to spend
more time at the hospital than at the nursery. I had made up my mind that I
was going to be a doctor—a children's doctor.

    Shortly after we moved to the hill, white people began moving out of the
neighborhood and Black families were moving in, buying old houses and
building new ones. A Black minister and his wife, the Deyaberts, crossed into
white territory, buying the house right next to the Montees, the people with
the hateful eyes.

    It was evening in the spring of 1949. I was in the bathroom washing my
white shoelaces for Sunday School the next morning when an explosion a
hundred times louder than the loudest, most frightening thunderclap I had ever
heard shook our house. Medicine bottles fell off the shelves, shattering all
around me. The floor seemed to slip away from my feet as I raced into the
kitchen and my frightened mother's arms.

    Crowds of angry Black people came up the hill and stood on "our" side,
staring at the bombed-out ruins of the Deyaberts' house. Far into the night
they spoke of death, of white hatred, death, white people, and more death.
But of their own fear they said nothing. Apparently it did not exist, for Black
families continued to move in. The bombings were such a constant response
that soon our neighborhood became known as Dynamite Hill.

    The more steeped in violence our environment became, the more determined
my father and mother were that I, the first-born, learn that the battle of white
against Black was not written into the nature of things. On the contrary, my
mother always said, love had been ordained by God. White people's hatred

of us was neither natural nor eternal. She knew that whenever I answered the
telephone and called to her, "Mommy, a white lady wants to talk to you," I
was doing more than describing the curious drawl. Every time I said "white
lady" or "white man" anger clung to my words. My mother tried to erase
the anger with reasonableness. Her experiences had included contacts with
white people seriously committed to improving race relations. Though she had
grown up in rural Alabama, she had become involved, as a college student,
in anti-racist movements. She had worked to free the Scottsboro Boys and
there had been whites—some of them Communists—in that struggle. Through
her own political work, she had learned that it was possible for white people
to walk out of their skin and respond with the integrity of human beings. She
tried hard to make her little girl—so full of hatred and confusion—see white
people not so much as what they were as in terms of their potential. She did
not want me to think of the guns hidden in drawers or the weeping black
woman who had come screaming to our door for help, but of a future world
of harmony and equality. I didn't know what she was talking about.

MLK
"Letter"

When Black families had moved up on the hill in sufficient numbers for me
to have a group of friends, we developed our own means of defending our
egos. Our weapon was the word. We would gather on my front lawn, wait
for a car of white people to pass by and shout the worst epithets for white
people we knew: Cracker. Redneck. Then we would laugh hysterically at the
startled expressions on their faces. I hid this pastime from my parents. They
could not know how important it was for me, and for all of us who had just
discovered racism, to find ways of maintaining our dignity.

From the time we were young, we children would go to the old family farm
in Marengo County. Our paternal grandmother and my Uncle Henry's family
lived on the same land and in an ancient, unpainted weatherbeaten cabin similar
to the one in which my father and all his sisters and brothers had been born.
A visit to the country was like a journey backward into history; it was a return
to our origins.

If there had been a mansion nearby, their cabin could have easily been the
slave quarters of a century ago. The little house had two small bedrooms, a
kitchen in the back and a common room where we children slept on pallets
spread out on the floor. Instead of electricity, there were kerosene lanterns for
the few hours of darkness before we went to bed. Instead of plumbing, there
was a well outside where we drew water to drink and to heat over an open
fire in the yard for our weekly baths in huge metal tubs. The outhouse frightened me when I was very young, so I urinated in a white enamel pot and
would go into the brush to have a bowel movement rather than enter the putrid-
smelling little house with the hole in the wooden plank where you could look
down and see all the excrement floating around.

The family ate well; I did not realize then that this was probably one of the
few pleasures that was available in a life which was work from sunup to
sundown, when you were so exhausted that you could only think about recuper-
ating for the next day's work. As a child on the farm, I did not distinguish

work from play because the work there was novel to me and because I was
not forced to do it all the time. When I fed the chickens, I would laugh at
the way they all raced for the feed and gulped it down. When I gathered the
eggs and fed the slop to the hogs, milked the cows and led the workhorses to
the watering trough, I was enjoying myself.

Going to the country, to the green open spaces of the cotton and tobacco
fields, was going to my own vision of paradise. I loved to chase the chickens
barefoot, ride the workhorses bareback, help take the few cows to pasture in
the early hours of the morning. The only amusement available that was totally
unrelated to the work of the farm was the refreshing swims in the nearby
creek—"the crick," we called it—and the exciting trips into the swamps to
explore this wonderful world inhabited by bizarre, crawling, slimy creatures.

Every Sunday after returning from the little wooden church a few miles
down the road, there would be fried chicken and biscuits baked in the wood
stove and spread with home-churned butter, greens and sweet potatoes from
the fields, and fresh sweet milk from the cows in the barn.

Around the time I was twelve years old, my grandmother died. She had
stayed with us in Birmingham for a while but had since moved to California
to take turns living with my father's sisters and brothers who had trekked out
to the West Coast in search of the mythical opportunities open to Black people
there. Her body was brought back to Marengo County, Alabama, to be conse-
crated and buried in her little hometown of Linden. It was a tremendous blow
to me, for she had always been a symbol of strength, of age, wisdom and
suffering.

We had learned from her what slavery had been like. She was born only a
few years after the Emancipation Proclamation, and her parents had been slaves
themselves. She did not want us to forget that. When we were taught about
Harriet Tubman and the Underground Railroad in school, it was my grandmother's image that always came to mind.

Not yet having accepted the finality of death, I still had a nebulous notion
of an afterlife. Therefore amid all the desperate crying and shouting at the
funeral, there were visions in my head of my grandmother going to join Harriet
Tubman, where she would look down peacefully upon the happenings in this
world. Wasn't she being lowered into the same soil where our ancestors had
fought so passionately for freedom?

After her burial the old country lands took on for me an ineffable, awe-
inspiring dimension: they became the stage on which the history of my people
had been acted out. And my grandmother, in death, became more heroic. I
felt a strange kind of unbreakable bond, vaguely religious, with her in that
new world she had entered.

The summer before I went to school, I spent several months with Margaret
Burnham's family in New York. Compared to Birmingham, New York was
Camelot. I spent a rapt summer visiting zoos, parks, beaches, playing with
Margaret, her older sister Claudia, and their friends, who were Black, Puerto

Rican and white. With my Aunt Elizabeth, I rode buses and sat in the seat right behind the driver.

That summer in New York made me more keenly sensitive to the segregation I had to face at home. Back home in Birmingham, on my first bus ride with my teen-aged cousin Snookie, I broke away from her and raced for my favorite place, directly behind the driver. At first, she tried to coax me out of the seat by cheerfully urging me to come with her to a seat in the back. But I knew where I wanted to sit. When she insisted I had to get up, I wanted to know why. She didn't know how to explain it. I imagine the whites were amused at her dilemma, and the Black people were perhaps just a little embarrassed about their own acquiescence. My cousin was distraught; she was the center of attention and had no notion of what to do. In desperation she whispered in my ear that there was a toilet in the back and if we didn't hurry she might have an accident. When we reached the back and I saw there was no toilet, I was angry not only because I had been tricked and lost my seat, but because I didn't know who or what to blame.

Near my father's service station downtown was a movie house called The Alabama. It reminded me of the ones in New York. Day and night the front of the building glittered with bright neon lights. A luxurious red carpet extended all the way to the sidewalk. On Saturdays and Sundays, the marquee always bore the titles of the latest children's movies. When we passed, blond-haired children with their mean-looking mothers were always crowded around the ticket booth. We weren't allowed in The Alabama—our theaters were the Carver and the Eighth Avenue, and the best we could expect in their roach-infested auditoriums was reruns of Tarzan. "If only we lived in New York . . ." I constantly thought. When we drove by the amusement park at the Birmingham Fairgrounds, where only white children were allowed, I thought about the fun we had at Coney Island in New York. Downtown at home, if we were hungry, we had to wait until we retreated back into a Black neighborhood, because the restaurants and food stands were reserved for whites only. In New York, we could buy a hot dog anywhere. In Birmingham, if we needed to go to the toilet or wanted a drink of water, we had to seek out a sign bearing the inscription "Colored." Most Southern Black children of my generation learned how to read the words "Colored" and "White" long before they learned "Look, Dick, look."

I had come to look upon New York as a fusion of the two universes, a place where Black people were relatively free of the restraints of Southern racism. Yet during subsequent visits, several incidents sullied this image of racial harmony. Between the ages of six and ten, I spent a part of most summers in the city. My mother was working toward her master's degree in education, attending New York University during the summers. She always took her children along. In my mother's circle of friends, there was a couple whose futile efforts to find a place to live had brought them and their friends to despair. After listening to vague conversations on the subject, I managed to pry out of the adults the reason for their difficulty: she was Black and he was white.

Another situation in New York was in even sharper contradiction to the
myth of Northern social harmony and justice. When I was around eight, the
McCarthy period had reached a peak. Among the Communists forced underground was James Jackson, whom my parents knew from the time he and his
family had lived in Birmingham. I did not really understand what was going
on at the time; I only knew that the police were looking for my friend Harriet's
father. Whenever I was with the Jackson children, they would point out the
men following them who were always no more than half a block away. They
were stern-looking white men dressed in suits, no matter how hot the weather
got. They even started following our family, afterward questioning whomever
we had visited during the day.

Why were they looking for my friend's father? He had done nothing wrong;
he had committed no crime—but he was Black, and he was a Communist.
Because I was too young to know what a Communist was, the meaning of the
McCarthy witch hunts escaped me. As a result, I understood only what my
eyes saw: evil white men out to get an innocent Black man. And this was
happening not in the South, but in New York, the paragon of racial concord.

Like New York, California was thought to be far more advanced than the
South. During my childhood, I heard numerous stories about the golden opportunities available to Black people on the West Coast. Great westward pilgrimages were still being made by the poor and the jobless. One of my father's
brothers and two of his sisters had joined the Black emigration to the West.
We occasionally visited them in Los Angeles.

Some of the relatives had created comfortable circumstances for themselves—one of my aunts who had gone into real estate was even buying
property in the hills of Hollywood. But another side of the family was in such
difficult straits they were living off welfare. It depressed me to visit my cousins
and discover that they did not have enough food in the house for a single
decent meal—and that six or seven of them were living in a one-bedroom
apartment. I recall their asking my father repeatedly if he would not give them
some money so they could at least put some food in the refrigerator.

My childhood friends and I were bound to develop ambivalent attitudes
toward the white world. On the one hand there was our instinctive aversion
toward those who prevented us from realizing our grandest as well as our most
trivial wishes. On the other, there was the equally instinctive jealousy which
came from knowing that they had access to all the pleasurable things we
wanted. Growing up, I could not help feeling a certain envy. And yet I have
a very vivid recollection of deciding, very early, that I would never—and I
was categorical about this—never harbor or express the desire to be white.
This promise that I made to myself did nothing, however, to drive away the
wishdreams that filled my head whenever my desires collided with a taboo.
So, in order that my daydreams not contradict my principles, I constructed a
fantasy in which I would slip on a white face and go unceremoniously into
the theater or amusement park or wherever I wanted to go. After thoroughly
enjoying the activity, I would make a dramatic, grandstand appearance before

the white racists and with a sweeping gesture, rip off the white face, laugh wildly and call them all fools.

Years later, when I was in my teens, I recalled this childish daydream and decided, in a way, to act it out. My sister Fania and I were walking downtown in Birmingham when I spontaneously proposed a plan to her: We would pretend to be foreigners and, speaking French to each other, we would walk into the shoe store on 19th Street and ask, with a thick accent, to see a pair of shoes. At the sight of two young Black women speaking a foreign language, the clerks in the store raced to help us. Their delight with the exotic was enough to completely, if temporarily, dispel their normal disdain for Black people.

Therefore, Fania and I were not led to the back of the store where the one Black clerk would normally have waited on us out of the field of vision of the "respectable" white customers. We were invited to take seats in the very front of this Jim Crow shop. I pretended to know no English at all and Fania's broken English was extremely difficult to make out. The clerks strained to understand which shoes we wanted to try on.

Enthralled by the idea of talking to foreigners—even if they did happen to be Black—but frustrated about the communication failure, the clerks sent for the manager. The manager's posture was identical. With a giant smile he came in from his behind-the-scenes office saying, "Now, what can I do for you pretty young ladies?" But before he let my sister describe the shoes we were looking for, he asked us about our background—where were we from, what were we doing in the States and what on earth had brought us to a place like Birmingham, Alabama? "It's very seldom that we get to meet people like you, you know." With my sister's less than elementary knowledge of English, it required a great effort for her to relate our improvised story. After repeated attempts, however, the manager finally understood that we came from Martinique and were in Birmingham as part of a tour of the United States.

Each time this man finally understood something, his eyes lit up, his mouth opened in a broad "Oh!" He was utterly fascinated when she turned to me and translated his words. The white people in the store were at first confused when they saw two Black people sitting in the "whites only" section, but when they heard our accents and conversations in French, they too seemed to be pleased and excited by seeing Black people from so far away they could not possibly be a threat.

Eventually I signaled to Fania that it was time to wind up the game. We looked at him: his foolish face and obsequious grin one eye-blink away from the scorn he would have registered as automatically as a trained hamster had he known we were local residents. We burst out laughing. He started to laugh with us, hesitantly, the way people laugh when they suspect themselves to be the butt of the joke.

"Is something funny?" he whispered.

Suddenly I knew English, and told him that he was what was so funny. "All Black people have to do is pretend they come from another country, and you treat us like dignitaries.'' My sister and I got up, still laughing, and left the store.

I had followed almost to the *t* the scenario of my childhood daydream.

In September 1949, Fania had just turned one, and my brother Benny was about to turn four. Having spent three years playing the same games in nursery school and visiting the hospital next door, I was ready for something different and had pleaded to go early to elementary school. On the Monday after Labor Day, wearing my stiff new red plaid dress, I jumped into my father's truck, eager to begin my first day at "big" school.

The road to school took us down Eleventh Court across the overpass above the railroad tracks, through the street dividing the Jewish Cemetery in half and three blocks up the last hill. Carrie A. Tuggle School was a cluster of old wooden frame houses, so dilapidated that they would have been instantly condemned had they not been located in a Black neighborhood. One would have thought that this was merely a shoddy collection of houses built on the side of a grassless hill if it had not been for the children milling around or the fenced-in grave out front, bearing a sign indicating that Carrie A. Tuggle, founder of the school, was buried there.

Some of the houses were a motley whitewashed color. Others were covered with ugly brownish-black asphalt siding. That they were spread throughout an area of about three square blocks seemed to be proof of the way the white bureaucracy had gone about establishing a "school" for Black children. Evidently, they had selected a group of rundown houses and, after evicting the inhabitants, had declared them to be the school. These houses stood all along a steep incline; at the bottom of the hill, there was a large bowl-shaped formation in the earth, covered with the red clay that is peculiar to Alabama. This empty bowl had been designated the playground. Houses similar to the school buildings were located around the other sides of the bowl, houses whose outsides and insides were falling to pieces.

My mother, a primary school teacher herself, had already taught me how to read, write and do simple arithmetic. The things I learned in the first grade were far more fundamental than school learning. I learned that just because one is hungry, one does not have the right to a good meal; or when one is cold, to warm clothing, or when one is sick, to medical care. Many of the children could not even afford to buy a bag of potato chips for lunch. It was agonizing for me to see some of my closest friends waiting outside the lunchroom silently watching the other children eating.

For a long time, I thought about those who ate and those who watched. Finally I decided to do something about it. Knowing that my father returned from his service station each evening with a bag of coins, which he left overnight in a kitchen cabinet, one night I stayed awake until the whole house was sleeping. Then, trying to overcome my deep fear of the dark, I slipped into the kitchen and stole some of the coins. The next day I gave the money to my hungry friends. Their hunger pangs were more compelling than my pangs of conscience. I would just have to suffer the knowledge that I had stolen my father's money. My feelings of guilt were further appeased by reminding myself that my mother was always taking things to children in her class. She took our clothes and shoes—sometimes even before we had outgrown them—and gave them to those who needed them. Like my mother, what I did, I did quietly, without any fanfare. It seemed to me that if there were hungry children, something was wrong and if I did nothing about it, I would be wrong too.

This was my first introduction to class differences among my own people. We were the not-so-poor. Until my experiences at school, I believed that everyone else lived the way we did. We always had three good meals a day. I had summer clothes and winter clothes, everyday dresses and a few "Sunday" dresses. When holes began to wear through the soles of my shoes, although I may have worn them with pasteboard for a short time, we eventually went downtown to select a new pair.

The family income was earned by both my mother and father. Before I was born, my father had taken advantage of his hard-earned college degree, from St. Augustine's in Raleigh, North Carolina, to secure a position teaching history at Parker High School. But life was especially difficult during those years; his salary was as close to nothing as money could be. So with his meager savings he began to buy a service station in the Black section of downtown Birmingham.

My mother who, like my father, came from a very humble background, also worked her way through college and got a job teaching in the Birmingham elementary school system. The combined salaries were nothing to boast about, yet enough to survive on, and much more than was earned by the typical Southern Black family. They had managed to save enough to buy the old house on the hill, but they had to rent out the upstairs for years to make the mortgage payments. Until I went to school I did not know that this was a stunning accomplishment.

The prevailing myth then as now is that poverty is a punishment for idleness and indolence. If you had nothing to show for yourself, it meant that you hadn't worked hard enough. I knew that my mother and father had worked hard—my father told us stories of walking ten miles to school each day, and my mother had her collection of anecdotes about the difficult life she had led as a child in the little town of Sylacauga. But I also knew that they had had breaks.

My preoccupation with the poverty and wretchedness I saw around me would not have been so deep if I had not been able to contrast it with the relative affluence of the white world. Tuggle was all the shabbier when we compared it to the white school nearby. From the top of the hill we could see an elementary school for white children. Solidly built of red brick, the building was surrounded by a deep-green lawn. In our school, we depended on potbellied coal stoves in winter, and when it rained outside, it rained inside. By the time a new building was constructed to replace the broken-down old one, I was too old to spend more than a year or so in its classrooms, which were reserved for the lower grades.

There were never enough textbooks to go around, and the ones that were available were old and torn, often with the most important pages missing. There was no gym for sports periods—only the "bowl." On rainy days when the bowl's red clay was a muddy mess, we were cooped up somewhere in one of the shacks.

Tuggle was administered and controlled as a section of the "Birmingham Negro Schools" by an all-white Board of Education. Only on special occasions did we see their representatives face to face—during inspections or when they were showing off their "Negro schools" to some visitor from out of town. Insofar as the day-to-day activities were concerned, it was Black people who ran the school.

Perhaps it was precisely these conditions that gave us a strong positive identification with our people and our history. We learned from some of our teachers all the traditional ingredients of "Negro History." From the first grade on, we all sang the "Negro National Anthem" by James Weldon Johnson when assemblies were convened—either along with or sometimes instead of "The Star-Spangled Banner" or "My Country, 'Tis of Thee." I recall being very impressed with the difference between the official anthems, which insisted that freedom was a fact for everybody in the country, and the "Negro National Anthem," whose words were of resistance. And although my singing voice was nothing I wanted to call attention to, I always sang the last phrases full blast: "Facing the rising sun, till a new day is born, let us march on till victory is won!"

As we learned about George Washington, Thomas Jefferson and Abraham Lincoln, we also became acquainted with Black historical figures. Granted, the Board of Education would not permit the teachers to reveal to us the exploits of Nat Turner and Denmark Vesey. But we were introduced to Frederick Douglass, Sojourner Truth and Harriet Tubman.

One of the most important events each year at Tuggle was Negro History Week. Special events were planned for assembly, and in all grades each child would be responsible for a project about a Black historical or contemporary figure. Throughout those years, I learned something about every Black person "respectable" enough to be allotted a place in the history books—or, as far as contemporary people were concerned, who made their way into "Who's Who in Negro America" or *Ebony* magazine. The weekend before Negro History Week each year, I was always hard at work—creating my poster, calling on the assistance of my parents, clipping pictures, writing captions and descriptions.

Without a doubt, the children who attended the de jure segregated schools of the South had an advantage over those who attended the de facto segregated schools of the North. During my summer trips to New York, I found that many of the Black children there had never heard of Frederick Douglass or Harriet Tubman. At Carrie A. Tuggle Elementary School, Black identity was thrust upon us by the circumstances of oppression. We had been pushed into a totally Black universe; we were compelled to look to ourselves for spiritual nourishment. Yet while there were those clearly supportive aspects of the Black

Southern school, it should not be idealized. As I look back, I recall the pervasive ambivalence at school, an ambivalence which I confronted in virtually
every classroom, and every school-related event. On the one hand, there was
a strong tendency affirming our identity as Black people that ran through all
the school activities. But on the other hand, many teachers tended to inculcate
in us the official, racist explanation for our misery. And they encouraged an
individualistic, competitive way out of this torment. We were told that the
ultimate purpose of our education was to provide us with the skills and knowledge to lift ourselves singly and separately out of the muck and slime of
poverty by "our own bootstraps." This child would become a doctor, this one
a lawyer; there would be the teachers, the engineers, the contractors, the
accountants, the businessmen—and if you struggled extraordinarily hard, you
might be able to approach the achievements of A. G. Gaston, our local Black
millionaire.

      This Booker T. Washington syndrome permeated every aspect of the educa-
tion I received in Birmingham. Work hard and you will be rewarded. A
corollary of this principle was that the road would be harder and rockier for
Black people than for their white counterparts. Our teachers warned us that
we would have to steel ourselves for hard labor and more hard labor, sacrifices
and more sacrifices. Only this would prove that we were serious about over-
coming all the obstacles before us. It often struck me they were speaking of
these obstacles as if they would always be there, part of the natural order of
things, rather than the product of a system of racism, which we could eventually overturn.

I continued to have my doubts about this "work and ye shall be rewarded"
notion. But, I admit, my reaction was not exactly straightforward. On the one
hand, I did not entirely believe it. It didn't make sense to me that all those
who had not "made it" were suffering for their lack of desire and the defec-
tiveness of their will to achieve a better life for themselves. If this were true,
then, great numbers of our people—perhaps the majority—had really been lazy
and shiftless, as white people were always saying.

But on the other hand, it seemed that I was modeling my own aspirations
after precisely that "work and be rewarded" principle. I had made up my
mind that I was going to prove to the world that I was just as good, just as
intelligent, just as capable of achieving as any white person. At that time—
and until my high school years in New York—I wanted to become a pediatri-
cian. Never once did I doubt that I would be able to execute my plans—after
elementary school, high school, then college and medical school. But I had a
definite advantage: my parents would see to it that I attended college, and
would help me survive until I could make it on my own. This was not something that could be said for the vast majority of my schoolmates.

The work-and-be-rewarded syndrome was not the only thing which seemed
to fly in the face of the positive sense of ourselves. We knew, for example,
that whenever the white folks visited the school we were expected to "be on
our P's and Q's," as our teachers put it. I could not understand why we had
to behave better for them than we behaved for ourselves, unless we really did

think they were superior. The visitors from the Board of Education always came in groups—groups of three or four white men who acted like they owned the place. Overseers. Sometimes if the leader of the group wanted to flaunt his authority he looked us over like a herd of cattle and said to the teacher, "Susie, this is a nice class you have here." We all knew that when a white person called a Black adult by his or her first name it was a euphemism for "Nigger, stay in your place." When this white assault was staged, I tried to decipher the emotions on the teacher's face: acquiesence, obsequiousness, defiance, or the pain of realizing that if she did fight back, she would surely lose her job.

Once a Black teacher did fight back. When the white men called him "Jesse" in front of his class, he replied in a deep but cold voice, "In case you have forgotten, my name is Mr. Champion." He knew, as the words left his lips, that he had just given up his job. Jesse Champion was a personal friend of my parents, and I was appalled by the silence that reigned among the Black community following his act. It probably stemmed from a collective sense of guilt that his defiance was the exception and not the norm.

Nothing in the world made me angrier than inaction, than silence. The refusal or inability to do something, say something when a thing needed doing or saying, was unbearable. The watchers, the head shakers, the back turners made my skin prickle. I remember once when I was seven or eight, I went along with my friend Annie Laurie and her family on a trip to the country. At the house we visited, a dog was running around in the yard. Soon another dog appeared. Without any warning the two animals were tearing at each other's throats. Saliva was flying and blood gushed from the wounds. Everyone was just standing, looking, doing nothing. It seemed we would stand there all day watching the hot Alabama sun beat down on the stupid, pointless fight of two dogs gnawing out each other's guts and eyes. I couldn't stand it any longer; I rushed in and tried to pull the dogs apart. It wasn't until after the screaming adults had dragged me away that I thought about the danger. But then it didn't matter; the fight had been stopped.

The impulse I felt then was with me at other fights. Fights not between animals but between people, but equally futile and meaningless. All through school there were absurd battles—some brief, but many sustained and deadly. I frequently could not keep from stepping in.

The children fought over nothing—over being bumped, over having toes stepped on, over being called a name, over being the target of real or imagined gossip. They fought over everything—split shoes, and cement yards, thin coats and mealless days. They fought the meanness of Birmingham while they sliced the air with knives and punched Black faces because they could not reach white ones.

It hurt me. The fight in which my girl friend Olivia got stabbed with a knife. It hurt to see another friend, Chaney—furious when a teacher criticized her in front of the class—stand up, grab the nearest chair and fly into the teacher with it. The whole class turned into one great melee, some assisting

Chaney, others trying to rescue the teacher, and the rest of us trying to break up the skirmish.

It hurt to see us folding in on ourselves, using ourselves as whipping posts because we did not yet know how to struggle against the real cause of our misery.

Time did not cool the anger of the white people who still lived on the hill. They refused to adapt their lives to our presence. Every so often a courageous Black family moved or built on the white side of Center Street, and the simmering resentment erupted in explosions and fires. On a few such occasions, Police Chief Bull Conner would announce on the radio that a "nigger family" had moved in on the white side of the street. His prediction "There will be bloodshed tonight" would be followed by a bombing. So common were the bombings on Dynamite Hill that the horror of them diminished.

On our side, old houses abandoned by their white inhabitants were gradually bought up, and the woods where we picked blackberries were giving way to new brick houses. By the time I was eight or nine, we had a whole neighborhood of Black people. When the weather was warm, all the children came out after dark to play hide and go seek. There were many hiding places within our boundaries, which were not less than one or two square blocks. The night made the game more exciting, and we could pretend we were outsmarting the white folks.

Sometimes we actually dared to penetrate their turf. "I dare you to go up on the Montees' porch," one of us would say. Whoever took him up would leave us on our side of the street as he hesitantly crossed over into enemy territory, tiptoed up the Montees' cement steps, touched the wooden porch with one shoe as if he were testing a hot stove, then raced back to us. When it was my turn, I could virtually hear the bombs going off as I ran up the steps and touched the Montee porch for the first time in my life. When this game began to lose its aura of danger, we made it more challenging. Instead of just touching the porch, we had to run to the door, ring the bell and hide in the bushes around their house, while the old woman or old man came out, trying to figure out what was going on. When they finally caught on to our game, even though they could seldom find us, they stood on the porch screaming, "You little niggers better leave us alone!"

In the meantime my playmates and school friends were learning how to call each other "nigger," or what, unfortunately, was just as bad in those days, "black" or "African," both of which were considered synonymous with "savage." My mother never allowed anyone to say the word "nigger" in the house. (For that matter, no "bad words"—"shit," "damn," not even "hell" could be uttered in her presence.) If we wanted to describe an argument we had had with someone, we had to say, "Bill called me that bad word that starts with an *n*." Eventually, my mouth simply refused to pronounce those words for me, regardless of how hard I might want to say them.

If, in the course of an argument with one of my friends, I was called "nigger" or "black," it didn't bother me nearly so much as when somebody said, "Just because you're bright and got good hair, you think you can act like you're white." It was a typical charge laid against light-skinned children.

Sometimes I used to secretly resent my parents for giving me light skin instead of dark, and wavy instead of kinky hair. I pleaded with my mother to let me get it straightened, like my friends. But she continued to brush it with water and rub Vaseline in it to make it lie down so she could fix the two big wavy plaits which always hung down my back. On special occasions, she rolled it up in curlers made out of brown paper to make my Shirley Temple Curls.

One summer when our Brownie troop was at Camp Blossom Hill, it started to rain as we were walking from the mess hall to our cabins, and the girls' hands immediately went for their heads. The water was no threat to my unstraightened hair, so I paid no attention to the rain. One of the girls switched out and said, "Angela's got good hair. She can stroll in the rain from now to doomsday." I know she wasn't intentionally trying to hurt me, but I felt crushed. I ran back to my cabin, threw myself on the bunk sobbing.

My cousins Snookie, Betty Jean and their mother, Doll, lived in Ketona, Alabama. I always loved to spend the weekend with them, because I knew they would put the hot comb over the wood fire and run it through my hair until it was straight as a pin. If I begged my mother long enough, she would let me wear it to school for a few days before she made me wash it out.

Downtown near the post office was the Birmingham Public Library. It was open only to white people, but in a hidden room in the building, accessible only through a secret back entrance, a Black librarian had her headquarters. Black people could pass lists of books to her, which she would try to secure from the library.

As a result of my mother's encouragement and prodding, books became a gratifying diversion for me. Mother taught me how to read when I had hardly reached my fourth year and eventually, when I was a little older, we both established a quota system for the number of books I should be reading per week. My mother or father picked up my books downtown, or else the Black librarian, Miss Bell, would bring them by the house.

Later a new Black library was built down the hill, on the corner of Center Street and Eighth Avenue. The new red brick library, with its shiny linoleum floors and varnished tables, became one of my favorite hangouts. For hours at a time, I read avidly there—everything from *Heidi* to Victor Hugo's *Les Misérables*, from Booker T. Washington's *Up From Slavery* to Frank Yerby's lurid novels.

Reading was far more satisfying than my weekly piano lessons and Saturday morning dance classes. For my fifth Christmas, my mother and father had gotten enough money together to buy me a full-sized piano. Once a week I trudged over to Mrs. Chambliss' house, dutifully played my scales and compositions, suffering the humiliation of being screamed at if I made a mistake. When the lesson was over, I paid her seventy-five cents and, if it was dark, waited for Mother or Daddy to pick me up so I wouldn't have to walk by the cemetery alone. On the other six days, I had to practice before I went out in the neighborhood with my friends. Around the end of May each year, Mrs. Chambliss' recital took place either at St. Paul's Methodist Church or the 16th Street Baptist Church two blocks away from my father's service station. With my hair in curls, wearing a ruffled organdy dress, rigid with nervousness, I tapped out the piece I had been practicing for months. The reward for the ordeal was three whole months without the pressure of piano lessons.

Saturday mornings I joined scores of leotard-clad girls at the Smithfield Community Center in the projects where we used to live. There Mrs. Woods and her helpers made sure we did our pliés and arabesques. Ballet during the first part of the class, then tap, soft shoe. My natural clumsiness defied the delicate ballet steps, so I always tried to find a place to hide in one of the back rows. For a while, my little brother, Benny, was coming along, so I had the added responsibility of taking care of him. One morning as we were walking down Center Street, he ran out in front of me—straight across Ninth Avenue. A bus came screeching to a stop, practically knocking him down. Trembling violently, I ran to rescue him. He was totally oblivious to the fact that he had almost been killed. During the warm-up exercises, I was still shaking. Suddenly I felt something warm streaming down my legs. I dropped to the floor, into the puddle of my urine, so humiliated I couldn't bear to look up at the staring faces of the other pupils. A girl named Emma came over and put her arms around my shoulder. Saying, "Angela, don't worry. Let's go outside," she led me away. She never knew how much her gesture meant to me. Still, having to face this same crowd every Saturday filled me with shame.

Joyce Ladner

(1943–   )

Acclaimed by American sociologists for her contributions to sociological theory and writing, Ladner is currently Vice President for Academic Affairs at Howard University. A prominent figure in the Civil Rights Movement of the 1960s, she was born in Waynesboro, Mississippi, and received her B.A. from Tougaloo College and her M.A. and Ph.D. from Washington University (St. Louis). Her works include *Tomorrow's Tomorrow: The Black Woman* (1971), *Mixed Families: Adopting Across Racial Boundaries* (1977), and the anthology *The Death of White Sociology* (1973). The following article is reprinted from *Essence* magazine (June 1977).

Return to the Source

As I sat in New York's LaGuardia Airport last November 5th waiting for my friends to join me on the flight to Atlanta for the first reunion of the Student Nonviolent Coordinating Committee (Snick), I saw JoAnn Grant walk through the terminal—obviously, I thought, bound for the same flight that would take us to the same meeting. Fleeting thoughts rushed through my mind as I remembered her covering civil rights battles in the Southern civil rights movement for the *National Guardian*. The battlegrounds: Atlanta, Greenwood, Jackson, Albany, Americus, Lowndes County, Selma. I envisioned familiar faces of people I hoped would be at the reunion. Suddenly, I was overwhelmed with emotion and began to silently weep tears of joy and sadness. I was happy to be going back to see some of my dearest friends after many years. Yet, I was also sad. Some were dead, others were in prison and still others had fallen victim to the very destructive forces they had so valiantly fought. I was, it occurred to me, going back home—returning to my roots, to the source— where it all began. I was to later feel that this trip was one of the most significant experiences of my life.

It was more than a physical return to the South because I go back to Mississippi to visit my family often. This return symbolized my rejoining some of the most important social reformers American society has produced. In 1976, after 200 years of emancipation, I was going to an alumni meeting of that cadre of radical, uncompromising, idealistic young Blacks and whites who carried, and made internationally famous, the banner of Snick. Conceived in 1961 and disbanded in 1967, the organization produced some of the most devastating changes in the structure and fiber of this nation. We registered hundreds of thousands of voters; we helped disenfranchised Blacks get involved in the political process by forming their own political parties and running for public office; we integrated lunch counters, bus and railway stations; we organized literacy classes and economic boycotts; we integrated white segregated churches. Our symbol of a Black hand and a white hand clasped together symbolized our commitment to an integrated America. In a sense we were the "Green Berets" of the movement because it was the fearless Snick workers who organized Blacks in some of the most hostile towns in the South. I wanted to find out what had happened to those young brave warriors with whom I had so closely identified since 1961.

I wanted to get a glimpse of their faces once more. Hug them. Slap them on the back. Kiss them. Sing with them. Compare notes with them on marriages, children, jobs. I desperately wanted to know how they felt Snick had affected their lives.

I wanted very much to see some of them whom I hadn't seen for many years: Carver and Chico Neblett, two brothers who came from Carbondale, Ill., and organized all over the South. Cleve Sellers, who spent several years in a South Carolina prison for refusing to be drafted into the army. John Buffinton, who came down to Mississippi in 1964 from Chicago and stayed on long after Snick had disbanded. Fay Bellamy, who after all these years remained in Atlanta and was pulling this reunion together. Stanley Wise, a former Howard University student who more than anyone else is the person who can locate all the old Snick workers. Lucy Montgomery, a white woman who, in spite of her wealth, was committed to Snick's goals. John Lewis, Julian Bond, Marion Barry, Ivanhoe Donaldson, Karen Spellman, Jim Foreman, Curtis Smith, Judy Richardson, Martha Prescod and "Annie Pearl." The list is endless.

What about Rap Brown who had gotten out of jail a few weeks before the reunion? Would he show? And his older brother, Ed, who joined Snick before Rap? And Stokely Carmichael? Was he in the country or in Africa? I also wanted to see Casey Hayden, who was the first feminist I ever met. Casey, Mary King (who would later work for Jimmy Carter's election) and Dinky Rommily were among the white women who embraced feminism more than a decade ago while in Snick—long before the rumblings of feminism in the North. And what of our casualties? How many of our comrades had been destroyed or had had their ability to function severely impaired because of their Snick involvement? What would we as a group be able to do about those who had once been with us, who were now in jail on trumped-up charges? How could we avenge the deaths of those who had fallen in the line of battle? How many were still under government surveillance after more than ten years? I also imagined that there were some who could tell us what it meant to have become prosperous members of the "establishment" we loathed and still others who could describe what it meant to float into anonymity and live like the people next door.

There was one other thing that intrigued me about this meeting. It would give me the opportunity to compare notes on childrearing and family life. As a parent and wife, I knew that my Snick experiences had given me a different perspective on raising my child than would have been possible otherwise. I knew that my two-year-old son, Thomas, would grow up with a strong social conscience, a sense of independence and a strong sense of his self-worth, inculcated in him because of my background. I wondered whether my friends in Snick felt the same way about their children. I suspected they did.

Over the next two days I had the opportunity to fulfill all my dreams and get answers to most of my questions. More than anything else, I came away from that meeting feeling that the years hadn't turned us into a new middle-class group of prosperous, well-dressed people as the *New York Times* had reported. The years had brought about the expected changes: we looked older, we had pretty much settled down with families, taken on jobs to support our families and ourselves, but little else had changed. Practically everyone worked with people—as social workers, teachers, politicians, organizers, nurses and the like. Few, if any, could claim to have acquired wealth since leaving Snick. Some were not so fortunate as to have a job.

The years had not caused them to become more conservative. As Gloria Richardson, the tough leader of the movement in Cambridge, Md., and now a HARYOU employee, says, "We're older and wiser. We aren't running around allowing ourselves to be beaten over the head anymore. But we are still as committed as ever to eradicating racism and poverty. I know I haven't changed in my beliefs one bit, and I don't think most of us ever will."

This return to the source was well-timed. It occurred only a few days after Jimmy Carter won the Presidential election—the first Southerner to do so in 100 years. Was it fate, I wondered, that brought us together a few days after the fruits of our labor in voter registration had been realized? Snick's voter registration and education program in the 1960s was, I am convinced, directly responsible for Carter's carrying an almost solid South in the election. The large block of Black voters was, according to several national opinion polls and a survey by the Joint Center for Political Research, the decisive factor in this election.

I spent the summer of 1963 working in a Snick voter registration project in Albany, Ga.; about 30 miles from Plains, Carter's hometown. Albany and Americus, Ga., were the sites of intensive Snick voter registration campaigns in 1963. Never in a million years would I have imagined that little over a decade later a United States president would be elected from notoriously racist southwest Georgia. Even more difficult to accept was the idea that a U.S. Attorney General, Griffin Bell, should come from Americus, the same town where three Snick workers were arrested for "attempting to incite insurrection," a charge that could have brought a death sentence. Donald Harris, now a top aide to Newark Mayor Kenneth Gibson, Ralph Allen and John Perdew, a white organizer from Denver, Col. (who had settled in Atlanta and works for a community health center with his wife, Amanda, a Black Snick worker from Americus), spent three months in jail without bond before a three-judge federal panel ruled the charge unconstitutional. Although Attorney General Bell was a member of the U.S. Fifth Circuit Court of Appeals (he was a Kennedy appointee), he was not on the panel that ordered the Snick workers' release. This charge had only been used once before in Georgia: in the 1930s, when Angelo Herndon, a Communist Party organizer from Atlanta, was actually sentenced to death. A U.S. Supreme Court decision overturned this death sentence.

Although a national campaign was waged to seek the release of Harris, Perdew and Allen, few of the local whites in southwest Georgia spoke up in their behalf. One can only wonder where Jimmy Carter and Griffin Bell were during this time. What did they personally think about the reign of terror that was carried out by the local police against Snick workers and local Blacks who were jailed when they demonstrated against segregated public facilities and for seeking the right to vote? I have often wondered if the outspoken "Miz Lillian," mother of President Carter, tried to persuade her neighbors that their racist attitudes and actions were wrong.

A notable exception to the hostility and silence by the local whites was Clarence Jordan, the late uncle of Hamilton Jordan, a top Carter aide. In 1942 Clarence Jordan founded Koininia Farm, an interracial religious cooperative. Beginning in the 1950s and continuing through the sixties, Koininia was the target of hostility and economic boycotts from the local whites. *Koininia*, the Greek word for fellowship or community, was an oasis in southwest Georgia. Snick workers were welcomed and permitted to hold their retreats there.

In a short while I realized that after all the years I knew my Snick comrades as well as I ever did. The time and distance that separated us had not made that much difference. When I saw Willie Ricks, I was transported in time back to the summer of 1966 when, on the Meredith March through Mississippi, he shouted "Black Power"—signalling a new era in the civil rights movement. Ricks, as he is affectionately known, was busy throughout the reunion exhorting everyone to become a follower of Pan Africanism. As Ricks and I talked, he reminded me that when he joined Snick he couldn't read or write. "Snick," he said, "gave me all the education I have." Many others would undoubtedly say the same thing. As Reggie Robinson, a veteran of the Cambridge, Md., movement, said, "Snick gave me my Ph.D. in life. If it hadn't been for Snick, I'd probably still be drinking wine on a street corner in Baltimore." As Ricks and Reggie talked, I wondered what I'd be doing now had it not been for Snick: Why did I feel that my Snick participation was the single-most important experience in my entire life?

Although I cannot be as precise as Willie Ricks or Reggie Robinson, I do know that I would not have had such a rich life; I would not have met some of the most interesting people alive; I doubt that I would have traveled to Africa and other places. Most important, I certainly wouldn't have developed the perspective on world politics and the human condition—a perspective that has enabled me as a teacher and writer to influence people in a certain way—

that I now have. Snick provided the context, the background, the forum for my enlightenment. It was through Snick that I was exposed to other Blacks and whites who felt the same way about justice and equality as I did. They came to Snick from all over: California, New York, Michigan, Alabama, Illinois, Washington, D.C., and practically everywhere else. We all shared the common dream that one day we would create a society in which racial oppression and poverty would be eliminated. So strong was this commitment that Snick workers risked death, fractured family ties and in the early days lived on a ten-dollar-a-week salary (nine dollars and sixty-four cents after taxes)—whenever it was available.

My commitment to human rights did not begin with Snick. As early as I can remember, I was acutely sensitive to the racism, the pervasive poverty of Blacks and the economic oppression of poor whites that surrounded me. I was in elementary school, and I remember crying when Mother explained that my sister Dorie and I couldn't go to the red brick school because it was "for whites only." We had to go to the dilapidated frame school, with its white peeling paint, that was built "for Blacks only." Growing up in Mississippi in the late forties and early fifties meant that we knew, almost instinctively, that Blacks and whites could not socialize on an equal basis.

Growing up in the segregated South caused Blacks *and* whites to suffer from the inability to express themselves freely—to associate with whomever they wanted, having their intellectual development stifled by parochialism and by the censorship of books, newspapers and films. In this sense white youngsters were as deprived as I. They, too, lacked the freedom to decide such things as who their friends could be, what books they could read or whom they could marry. It never made much sense to me that my entire existence should be determined by my skin color. I am sure this was the reason I vowed then that my children would not have these severe restrictions placed on their lives. I wanted them to enjoy the freedoms that were denied me.

One of the consequences of having grown up during this era was that Black children matured much earlier because their parents could not provide them with the protected, carefree atmosphere so typical of many growing youngsters. Our parents could not fortify us against the knife of injustice and the knowledge that our skin color and our poverty were reasons for our oppression.

We lived in an all-Black community, Palmers Crossing, four miles from downtown Hattiesburg. Although we had lots of contact with whites, we were always subordinate to them. My grandmother worked for the same white family for over 20 years, rearing their two children in the process. When JoAnn, this family's daughter married, Grandmother was invited to the wedding and was as proud as any mother, and as was customary, she sat in the balcony of the white church. It never occurred to her that she should sit anyplace else. Dorie and I told her that she shouldn't go if they didn't think enough of her to allow her to sit with them. Privately we told each other that she was acting like an "Uncle Tom." We decided that we'd *never* go to a white person's wedding if we had to sit in the balcony. Although we were not more than nine or ten years old, we knew that we would not spend our lives working as domestics. Our sights, very early in life, were set on big careers.

Dorie always wanted to become a lawyer. During the summer, we kids (there were nine of us) used to sit on wood crates in a mock courtroom in the backyard, as Dorie presided over cases she dreamed would one day make her a famous *Black female* Mississippi lawyer. She also created and taught us younger kids her "African" dances—based largely on a few books, television shows (usually "Tarzan")—and the many warm stories "Dr." McLeod told us about the great ancient African civilizations and their great warriors. Dorie's vivid imagination allowed her to choreograph the dances, make the costumes and teach us, her enchanted pupils, how to perform them. Dr. McLeod was an herbalist who sold his home-made medications from his car. He was a great believer in civil rights and it was he who gave form to our dreams of a society in which racism would be nonexistent. "Cous," as we called Dr. McLeod, told us secretly that he was a member of the NAACP (in the early fifties!) and, upon discovering how interested we were in the civil rights issues, let us borrow books of Black literature.

As I reflect on the meaning of growing up in the segregated South, I realize that I probably had an unusual set of influences. My first grade teacher, who was also the school librarian, Zola Jackson, was the first intellectual I ever knew. Ms. Jackson had a passion for reading, and upon discovering that we were interested in books, cultivated us by introducing us to every new book she ordered for the school library. We read fiction and nonfiction, especially biographies of Black personalities. I will always remember the time Dorie and I reached the level at which Ms. Jackson thought we were ready to be introduced to a thick volume on the history of Western civilization. Dorie read it in a few days and I followed suit. Had it not been for Dr. McLeod, Mrs. Jackson and another teacher, Mrs. Clark, these years would have been different.

Neither of my parents finished high school. However, they strongly valued education feeling it held the key to a life better than the one they had. Mother was very strict with us. She drilled us on our homework and didn't permit us to go outside to play until it was finished. I entered school at the age of three and a-half. It was because of mother's initiative that I went to school so early.

Mother was always a housewife. My father insisted that she not work for whites and be subjected to the abuse his mother had experienced. My mother was a very strong and resourceful woman. She stretched father's salary (he was an auto mechanic) further than one can imagine. I have often thought that had she had opportunities when she was growing up, she undoubtedly would have studied medicine or nursing. She nursed every sick relative and neighbor back to health. Whenever anyone in the neighborhood got sick, they called upon "Auntie," as she is known. All of us kids probably acquired our humanitarianism from her.

But when it came to getting involved in "white people's business," Mother and Daddy strictly admonished us not to interfere. I remember when Emmett Till was lynched in the Mississippi Delta in 1956 for allegedly whistling at a white woman almost twice his age. Dorie and I ran to the corner store every day at 4:30 p.m. to buy the *Hattiesburg American*, our daily newspaper. We kept the clippings of the lynching in a scrapbook and each day tearfully pored over the pictures and stories. Emmett Till was our age! We cried for him as we would have cried for our brothers. When his body surfaced in the Talla-hatchie River, we wondered, "How could they do that to him?" Dorie said that when she became a lawyer, she'd fight to change things. And I said that when I became a social worker, I would help poor people get their rights so they wouldn't have to live under such terrible conditions.

Our dear friend Dr. McLeod urged us on. Each week he ritually brought us his copies of the *Pittsburg Courier* and the *Chicago Defender* so that we could read what the outside world was saying about the lynching. Dorie wrote a lengthy letter to the *Pittsburg Courier* on her reactions to Emmett Till's lynching. She described how frightened she was as a 14-year-old growing up in such a hostile, brutal atmosphere. Mother was terrified that if the letter was published, the Ku Klux Klan might see it and retaliate by burning down our house. Although we eagerly looked for the letter in each week's paper, we were very disappointed; it was never published.

Then in 1958, when I was 14 years old, Mack Charles Parker, a Black man, was lynched in the small town of Poplarville, Miss., for allegedly raping a white woman from Hattiesburg. While being held in the Pearl River county jail, a stone's throw from Hattiesburg, he was dragged down the concrete steps by a white mob. His body eventually turned up in the Pearl River. This lynching shocked us. We hadn't expected it. His trial was coming up soon and the rumor in Hattiesburg's Black community was that his NAACP-hired lawyer (one of the three Black attorneys in the state at the time), R. Jess Brown, would prove his innocence. Brown had evidence, we heard, that Mack Charles Parker was somewhere else at the time of the alleged rape, and the truth was that the white woman hadn't been raped at all. She had had a rendezvous with her boyfriend, and when pressed to reveal her whereabouts by her husband, told him she had been raped. Parker, we thought, had fallen innocent victim to these unfortunate circumstances, since he (and probably a thousand other Black men in Poplarville) fitted the general description of the alleged rapist.

After the lynching, Dorie and I rode the bus downtown every day to overhear the conversations of the national and foreign press that converged on Hattiesburg to cover the lynching. We reasoned that these "outsiders" were our friends because they didn't believe in segregation like the local whites. Their accents were even different from those of all the white people we knew. When Mack Charles Parker's body surfaced in the river, we cried. We cried for him and for his family; we also cried for our father and for our brothers. If they could do that to him, and he wasn't guilty, we thought they could just as easily murder any of the Black men in our family. I don't remember any other time when I was more frightened. Yet I was never more determined that one day things would be different. I suppose for the first time I understood why my mother was so protective of my brothers.

The South with its strange customs is a multitude of paradoxes. Mother had a white cousin, whom we called "Cousin Ross," who often visited our home. Our white cousin lived in an all-white neighborhood with his family, who, although we never met them, knew that he had Black relatives. Neither he nor Mother thought it strange that they were related. Once when I asked Mother how she felt about having a white cousin, she replied, "It doesn't make me feel different from other people. I'm used to it. When I was growing up a lot of our relatives were white. Mama [my maternal grandmother] used to spank our white cousins if they did wrong, and when Papa [my maternal grandfather] died, they all came to his funeral and cried like babies. We all grew up together—the coloreds and the whites." I suppose that in a sense I accepted Cousin Ross but I never resolved this paradox. White lynch mobs killed Emmett Till and Mack Charles Parker and still I had a white cousin.

Growing up in the segregated South meant that I had severe restrictions placed on almost every facet of my life. I did not have the freedom to express myself and to explore many of those things in which I was interested. I felt like a caged animal. We were subjected to some of the most psychologically brutalizing treatment possible. I am reminded of the white bus driver who drove the Palmers Crossing bus to downtown Hattiesburg. Since the buses were segregated, whites sat in the front and Blacks sat in the back. About half the seats were always reserved for the whites. No matter how crowded the bus got, we were forced to stand in the rear even if there were only one white person sitting in the front section. This vicious bus driver frequently swore at the Black passengers, and he was so hostile that we didn't dare challenge his authority. Often he very casually told Black riders, "you niggers get in the back."

It is very difficult to describe how oppressed I felt during those years: to be stifled, to live in fear, to be poor and subjugated, to be humiliated by ignorant whites whom we regarded as the scum of the earth and to realize that people in powerful positions didn't care what happened to you. I was acutely sensitive to those less fortunate than ourselves. I always defended the underdog. When I was in the sixth grade I had a class-mate named Hattie Mae Naylor. Hattie Mae was one of about 18 children from a very poor family. She and her sisters and brothers had to walk several miles to school and usually didn't arrive until after the morning recess. I remember going off into a corner crying when the other children made fun of Hattie Mae because of her tattered clothing and her worn, dusty shoes. Sometimes she had no shoes and came to school in barefeet. Hattie Mae was much older than I, but I always felt very close to her. I used to offer to help her catch up on her homework. In some sort of way I understood that Hattie Mae and her parents were victims of the same system that created both the abject poverty in which they lived and the vicious bus driver. That is why one of my favorite statements was: "When I get big, I'm going to go away and make a lot of money and come back and tear all of these old houses down and build brand new ones. I'm going to give everybody money to buy all the food and clothes they want."

This oppression caused me to become very restless and anxious to find ways to destroy all of the obstacles that were thwarting my development. I used to look in picture magazines and long for the day when I would be as free as a bird to travel to New York to see all the things I'd read about and to meet people who were creative and different.

During these racially turbulent years my mother and father rarely openly discussed racial problems. Having grown up under severe racial oppression, they had learned early in their lives how to survive. Their method was to keep a low profile with whites. While they despised "Uncle Toms" (Mother had a cousin who was regarded as the biggest "Tom" in Hattiesburg), they would never have joined the NAACP in the fifties and early sixties. In their own subdued way, they "got white people told" when whites misbehaved toward them. My father, a soft-spoken man, walked off his job as a diesel engine mechanic many times when his white supervisor treated him in a racist manner. He never told us and we never asked the specifics of what happened. Along with Mother we automatically knew. We also assumed that he went back only after the owner of the garage, who was fairly decent, called our home, apologized for the supervisor's behavior and asked Daddy to return to work. Even though he knew he was dependent upon his job to support his family, he also tried to keep some of his dignity and pride. He always told us, "Don't ever let anyone take your pride from you. It's the most valuable thing you have."

Years later, after we were in college and involved in Snick protest activities, we would learn from Mother whenever FBI agents visited Daddy at work to ask him to persuade us to get out of the movement. In his quiet, firm manner he told them: "If you have something to say to them, I'd advise you to tell them. I don't carry messages to my children. They're grown. They can do what they want to." I was deeply moved because I knew the depths of my parents' fear for our safety and for their own. They had great reason to be afraid! Mother encouraged us to stand up for our rights and she admonished us, "Don't let anyone walk over you."

In 1959 when we were high school juniors, we organized the first NAACP Youth Council in Hattiesburg. The late Medgar Evers, slain in 1963 when he was state field secretary of the NAACP, came to Hattiesburg to meetings of our youth council. Clyde Kennard, a young man who was active in the adult NAACP chapter, was our advisor. We recruited about 60 of our friends to join the NAACP and felt a tremendous sense of satisfaction that we were finally doing something. We were in full gear when one of our "Uncle Tom" high school teachers visited most of our parents and convinced them that they'd be lynched or have their homes firebombed if they didn't forbid us to participate in the NAACP. Unfortunately she succeeded and our organization folded.

During this period we traveled 90 miles to Jackson, the state capital, to NAACP rallies to hear officials, such as Roy Wilkins, speak. Vernon Dahmer, president of the Hattiesburg NAACP, his sister, Eileen Beard, a close family friend and a member of my parents' church, and Clyde Kennard always drove us to these meetings. Mr. Dahmer and "Sister" Beard were founders of the local NAACP. I remember how much emotion and hope these meetings aroused—hope that one day soon we would be able to vote, to use the segregated public facilities, to rid ourselves of all the restrictions placed on us by the segregationist laws.

Clyde Kennard, an intense, wiry young man who always wore a somber expression, was a tireless NAACP worker. After returning home from a stint in the army and studying at the University of Chicago, Clyde made two attempts to desegregate the state-supported Mississippi Southern College in Hattiesburg. In 1956 he tried to enroll and was turned away. In 1958 he informed the college officials of his intent to register for the term and they called the police. A short time after ushering him off the campus, the police arrested him for allegedly stealing a bag of chicken feed (he was a farmer). Clyde spent two years in jail and was subjected to the most brutal treatment. He developed cancer, and although a national campaign was mounted to secure his release, he was not pardoned by Governor Ross Barnett until he was near death. He died in 1962. The segregationist forces in the society murdered Clyde. They couldn't have been more effective if they had lynched him. In a sense it was worse because they lynched him under the law.

Some years later, after I had left Mississippi and entered graduate school, my telephone rang in the early morning hours. Mother called to say Mr. Dahmer was dead. The Ku Klux Klan firebombed his home and he was burned to death. It was hard for me to understand why and how he had lived through the difficult years of the forties and fifties only to die tragically now. Part of my faith and hope that we could achieve justice through integration died January 12, 1966.

One of the things about the South to which I never reconciled myself was the wanton and indiscriminate use of violence. I will never forget how deeply disturbed I was when I attended the funeral of three young Black girls who were killed in a Birmingham church in 1963. I was a senior at Tougaloo College at the time and had just returned to Mississippi after spending part of the summer working at the national "March on Washington" headquarters in New York City. I was overwhelmed by that historic occasion when over a quarter of a million people of all races and nationalities demonstrated for the rights of Black people in America. The March, at the time, represented a fulfillment of the dreams of my short life span. Freedom, I thought, had finally come.

These hopes were profoundly shattered a month later when we learned of the murder of these three young girls. A large group of us from the Jackson area drove to Birmingham to the funeral to mourn their passing and to demonstrate against the vicious bombing that caused their deaths. One would have thought that the white segregationists in Birmingham would have taken a holiday, that they would have repented for this dastardly act. Instead the police were everywhere. They harassed and detained overnight a carload of our group as they were trying to return to Jackson. All the hopes that the March on Washington had aroused within me were dissipated. It seemed as if the white segregationists were telling us that you could demonstrate as much as you liked, but the South would continue to say "Never!" We were back to the point where we began. Later that fall, I spent a week in jail for attempting to integrate a white Methodist church in Jackson, not so much for religious reasons, but rather because it seemed that there were fewer and fewer staunch symbols of segregation capable of arousing indignation. That week in jail caused me a great deal of inner turmoil because I felt that if I could be arrested in a church, then all forms of individual expression had been suppressed. A footnote to this series of events was John Kennedy's assassination in Dallas, Tex. Although a group of Tougaloo students drove to Washington, D.C., for his funeral, I could not muster enough psychic energy to go. A chapter for me was closed.

The tragic circumstances surrounding the deaths of Vernon Dahmer, Clyde Kennard and Medgar Evers, my political mentors, and the countless others must have reinforced within me the feeling that Blacks had to sometimes pay the ultimate price for freedom—death. Indeed, freedom was not free. Until 1966 when Mr. Dahmer died, I had fervently believed in integration as the solution to the racial problem. Even when the Snick leadership turned away from integration and toward Black consciousness and Black power, I hesitated to follow suit.

When Vernon Dahmer was killed, my faith in integration was shaken. I found myself trying to justify my belief that "Black and white together" was still the solution to the race problem. I began to feel that it didn't make sense for me to continue to fight for and believe in integration. What Blacks needed to do, I thought, was to unite as a group and develop their own institutions and communities. What they needed was Black power! Only then, I felt, would whites give in to our demands. I gave up on trying to appeal to the conscience of whites. Racial power politics seemed to be a more viable way to effect fundamental changes. Institutional racism became the target instead of individual racial prejudice.

Although I had worn my hair in an Afro since 1963, it took on new meaning. I began to see it in symbolic terms—as a manifestation of my pride in kinky hair and dark skin, a rejection of all things Caucasian. This was a very agonizing and difficult period for me. I suppose the most painful time of all came when I rejected long-time white friends solely because they were white. Their white skins represented all the viciousness and violence perpetrated against Blacks. For a time, I was consumed by this intense feeling of betrayal of my beliefs. I felt that my ideological commitment to integration had never brought the freedom and dignity Dr. McLeod had told me I should fight for when I was a young child, that Clyde Kennard and Mr. Dahmer died for. This must have been the most intense, introspective period of my life.

Eventually I was to rid myself of this obsession and in so doing, would be able to look back on the period when I rejected whites as a necessary developmental step. And in the end, I am neither blindly committed to total integration, which is unrealistic, nor an ardent devotee of Black separatism. Somewhere, I found my middle ground in some form of humanism.

Over the years the South has changed, and my parents' lives symbolize many of those changes. While they once feared that exercising their constitu-

Joyce Ladner

tional right to vote might cause them bodily harm, today they take voting for granted.

I will never forget how proud I was when Mother and Daddy registered to vote. As is the case when something important happens, Mother telephoned me to tell me that they had gone to the courthouse to register. This was in 1967, several years after we had joined Snick. I had tried unsuccessfully to register to vote in Hattiesburg in 1964 when I was in college. I failed the test, as did all other Blacks, because Therron Lynd, the Forrest County registrar, felt I had not adequately interpreted the 14th Amendment to the United States Constitution. Mother and Daddy registered after the literacy test was declared unconstitutional by the courts.

An example of the profound changes in my parents' life came when Mother rallied her neighbors to get out to vote for Jimmy Carter. I could just imagine her sitting in her kitchen (which we jokingly call the local news headquarters—because she knows everything going on) calling Miss Katie, Sister Moseley, Miss Mae, Brother Smith and Paw Paw (my grandfather) and all the others asking them, "Have you voted yet? You'd better get on up to the polls because 'they' say Carter is a good man and he needs all the votes he can get." She would also tell them, "Bill [my father] is taking the afternoon off work so he can drive you to the polls if you need a ride." Mother would be sure to invoke "they say" because she wanted to make certain that her neighbors understood that not only did she support Carter but the local Black leaders did too.

To Mother, Carter was someone she understood and could relate to. To one of my queries she said, "He is like the white folks around here. They're not like they used to be when you were growing up. They've changed a whole lot." Because I left Mississippi in 1964 and haven't lived there since, I did not experience the changes Mother has seen. I remember a visit I made to my parents in 1970. Mother and I had gone shopping, and she suggested that we stop on the way home to have a sandwich and soda at a roadside restaurant. For a moment I thought she'd lost her mind. "Mother," I said, "we can't go in there. They'll arrest us. They might beat us up!" Mother looked at me with that broad, understanding smile and reassured me that it was all right for me to stop the car at the restaurant. "You've been away from here too long," she said. Indeed I had. My only recollections of that and all other "white" restaurants were that they were places we never would have considered entering. But these are changes that she has seen. Over the last ten years she has become accustomed to many of the local whites addressing her as "Mrs." and saying "yes, ma'am" to her. I don't know if I will adjust as easily.

The Snick reunion allowed me to relive a lot of these important memories—memories that I shared with some of the best friends I ever had—one more time. And maybe never again.

John A. Williams

(1925–   )

Professor of English and Journalism at Rutgers University, John A. Williams was born in Jackson, Mississippi, and grew up in Syracuse, New York. He has been a journalist for *Ebony*, *Jet*, *Holiday*, and *Newsweek* and has taught at the City College of New York and Sarah Lawrence. Williams gained international recognition for *The Man Who Cried I Am* (1967), an apocalyptic treatment of race and politics. Among his other novels are *The Angry Ones*, *Night Song*, *Sissie*, *Captain Blackman*, *Mothersill and the Foxes*, *The Junior Bachelor Society*, and *!Click Song*. His nonfiction works, which include *This Is My Country Too*, *Flashbacks: A Twenty-year Diary of Article Writing*, and *The King God Didn't Save* and *The Most Native of Sons*, biographies of Martin Luther King, Jr., and Richard Wright, reflect his sustained interest in history, race, and politics. The following excerpt is from *This Is My Country Too*.

---

from This Is My Country Too

I left Nashville for Atlanta on a Sunday morning, long before the churches began ringing their bells. Beside me on the seat, wrapped in waxed paper, was a small pile of Southern fried chicken. The big new car and the supply of chicken didn't go together. Stories are still current about Negroes who now live in the North and plan to return home in the South; they debate whether they should drive their Cadillacs. Some wear chauffeur hats or carry them on the seat alongside; others pretend that they are just delivering the car. The stories seem to come less often now, but on this trip the daughter of a Midwest Negro district attorney told me that, when her father travels South, he will not leave his car for any reason until he is safe in a Negro neighborhood.

Thinking such thoughts, I pulled into Bill and Joyce Eure's driveway, in Atlanta. Bill and I had grown up together. At one time his family lived upstairs above us. We called him "Dirty Bill," only because, in our sports-minded circle, he was a tough competitor. Pick the sport. Bill Eure starred. And to this day he swears by athletics; he believes they saved most of us from long periods in jail.

I was most curious about one thing: how Bill, having been raised in the North, in Syracuse, could find a life in the South.

Bill is very chunky, about five-ten or -eleven; he shrugged and said, "I don't know. I came down, played ball, got a good job while I was in school, made a little change, finished, got married, and here I am, teaching."

Like most of their neighbors, Bill and Joyce live in a moderately expensive house and have two cars. Most of their friends are teachers or professional people. Atlanta Negro society ranks high, and it seemed to me that life there must be largely cannibalistic with the competition for status so keen—status being based on material objects. The fact that so many people are so well educated cancels out any intellectual achievement. Ph.D.'s are a dime a dozen. Indeed among American cities, Atlanta, with Atlanta University, Morris Brown College, Clark College, Morehouse College (the Negro's Harvard), Spelman College, plus a couple of divinity schools, produces—and keeps—the highest number of educated Negroes.

Atlanta is the home of "M.L."—Martin Luther King. There was much talk of how he grew up and how successful he had come to be. But black Atlantans told me they required a city leader: "M.L." was so busy being a national Negro leader that his time for leading at home was always little, and his work, excluding the March on Washington, was not very effective in long-range gains.

Out of the search for a new leader may come Jesse Hill, Jr., editor of a Negro weekly, the Atlanta *Enquirer*. Young Mr. Hill and I didn't get on too well. At first he seemed to doubt my sincerity; then he indicated that I, coming from the North, was as far removed from the problem as a white man. Subdued heat flashed back and forth. His impatience was obvious. He did say that a summit meeting representing eight organizations was being called to find a new leader for Atlanta.

Dr. Albert Davis, a man with a sense of humor (Hill showed none) and a vision that surmounts the horizon, could also become a prime candidate. He is bitter because so few professional men like himself are deeply committed to action. "Atlanta politics are pretty much like politics anywhere," Davis said. "Joining the Old Guard"—conservative Negroes—"which acts out of a sense of personal belief, mostly, are the Negroes who accept payoffs and who find later, when it's time to make demands, that they cannot."

Davis is a slender man who slides easily between the vernacular of the street Negro and the precise grammar of the medical profession. He leaned back in his chair and went on: "Our big problem is resegregation—the closing up of places we've already opened. We don't have the follow-up. The first-class places are usually the ones that open first, but who can afford to take dinner out two or three times a week? They see that we aren't coming back right away and without fanfare reinstitute the old regime. We've got to organize our people so that they will, by turns, keep the pressure on those places, get them used to seeing us in them." He looked very weary when he stood to go.

One of the people I most wanted to meet and talk with in the South was Ralph McGill, publisher of the Atlanta *Constitution* and winner of a number of awards for journalism. I had enjoyed much of his writing and appreciated the importance of the time in which he wrote. It was surprisingly easy to arrange the appointment.

He was not as tall as I had imagined from his pictures, but just as sturdy, just as ruddy. He seemed glad to see me, although he didn't know me. He would be glad, I imagined, to see a Negro walk through the door of his office on assignment for *Holiday*, and later he implied as much. We sat in his office, a room made all the more cozy because of the hundreds of books in it. They gave off the smell of freshly printed pages still to be opened, and combined with this was the comfortable odor of ink and newsprint from the presses downstairs. My eyes kept sweeping back to the books. The man was inundated with them. I imagined a hundred publicity people in publishing houses checking off his name and saying. "McGill *must* get a copy of this one!"

I found him very deliberate, most cordial and warm. As we edged our way into conversation, he was leaning back in his chair, his hands folded over his head. Downstairs, on Forsyth Street, a part of the business district of Atlanta, the city hummed on its way.

Was there a possibility of a political civil war between Democrats of the North and South?

McGill did not think so. He expressed the hope that change would be more rapid after the Old Guard—white, in this case—passed. He stared at the ceiling and, as if receiving an idea from it, said, "We're now in a time of change and examination. It goes slowly. An idea gets going, stops, starts, takes form, becomes alive, becomes real."

Atlanta had changed in the past decade or so, I observed. He smiled a little. Yes, it had. "New businesses which require trained people, black and white. We need a crash program." He came forward in his chair, its spring catapulting him toward a stack of newspapers. He thumbed through one and ripped out an ad placed by a vocational school which offered courses in data processing, computer programming, computer analysis.

"They'd hire a nigra just as quickly as a white man if he had these courses under his belt. We have a constant influx of rednecks who don't have the training in human existence, let alone formal schooling."

Nigra? I thought.

I asked if he believed that college education had been oversold among Negroes. Negro families were bending all their efforts toward getting their children into college and keeping them there. Negro communities were being glutted with academicians. Should there not be a return, not to the fundamental Booker T. Washington formulas of working with the hands, of being one with the soil and separate and apart from whites, but to blue-collar work attuned to automation, whose demands were daily growing greater?

"No, college hasn't been oversold," he said. "We'll always need college-educated people."

And now a wall began to grow between us. He was not aware of it, and it was not a wall as such but a great difference of opinion. I had been meeting social workers, teachers, college instructors, doctors, nurses, insurance managers and the like. Only in a barbershop had I met the people of the street, loud with their arguments, unmindful of passers-by, plain, vigorous, kinetic. Between the Negroes of the street and the Negroes of the professions there existed very little contact.

To what extent had resegregation hampered desegregation efforts?

In his view, the places which had opened to Negroes (he said this time) were still open to them. And others would follow suit. I wondered what would happen if Doctor Davis and Mr. McGill ever sat down together to compare notes. McGill is white. He doesn't have to go out to dinner when he doesn't want to or can't afford to, just to see if a place will let him in, merely to keep a foot in the door.

Was he aware of police harassment of Negroes?

"Rednecks. Country people who are always difficult."

I suppose when a man is very famous and very good in his field, a great many people beat a path to his door, and after a time there are no new questions he can be asked. All the answers are at his fingertips. And I am sure he had reason to be pleased with the changes in the city, changes for which he was partly responsible.

I sat there irritated with myself because I could not find within myself that stunning question to ask, a question that would catapult him forward once more, that would even explode the warm cordiality in which we sat. We had reached, I felt, a kind of impasse. I liked him very much, but knew him well, instinctively. His words, "We are a part of all we've met," told me that, in a way, he knew me too. He rose, stretched his hand across a pile of books and said, "Just remember—change. Ten years ago you would not have been here as you are, not even three or two, for *Holiday*."

I think he saw me, in that moment, as a product of his work.

It was morning. Bill Eure stood beside the car. Last-minute instructions. "Remember, stop for your gas in the large cities, don't mess around with the small places. As soon as you see a speed zone, *slow up*. Don't wait for another sign. Even if you don't see a sign but there are houses, slow down. Some of these places don't post the speed limits until you're on the far side of town, and by then you've had it. They'll pull you back to appear before the judge, but the judge won't be there. They'll tell you that you have to post a bond of fifty dollars, seventy-five or a hundred. They'll tell you when to come back and appear before the judge. You never come back; who in the hell wants to come back to Georgia? And they *know* that all you want is to get away. Watch your step, keep your tongue inside your head, and *remember where you are*."

A fine goddamn send-off. I clutched my sandwiches and looked longingly toward the north, but got in the car and drove on south toward Alabama.

I had crossed the border and was driving through a small town when I almost missed seeing a red light. I rammed down hard on the brakes and would have hit the windshield had it not been for the seat belt. The squeal of my tires attracted the attention of passers-by, and I cringed in the seat. A youthful daydream came flooding back into my mind. After every reported lynching I saw myself in a specially made car, with perhaps Bill Eure and about four other friends, heading South. Built into the front of the car were three machine guns, two .30-caliber and one .50. The two .30's could track 90 degrees on each side. The car, of course, was bullet-proof, and the engine was supercharged; nothing on the road could catch us.

The light changed and I continued on through Alabama.

One morning, as I neared the town of Tuskegee, I stopped to pick up five Negro children hiking patiently along the road, tattered notebooks under their arms. I asked the obvious question: "Going to school?"

"Yes, sir," said the boy who seemed to be the leader. His head was long, and behind his long, curled lashes, his big eyes were bold.

"How far do you have to walk?"

"Three mile." The other kids were looking at and feeling the red upholstery, giggling and sneaking glances at me.

"That's a long way to go," I said. They kept turning, picking out, I supposed, landmarks they would not yet have reached on foot.

I let them out at a narrow path. "Where's the school?"

"It back there," the leader said, pointing. I looked. Far beyond the roadside sat a gray, leaning building. It looked like a disused barn.

"What kind of school is that? Don't you go to a public school?"

The boy shrugged.

"Is that a church school?"

"Yes, sir," he said. "I guess."

The others, already running into the woods, shouted, "Thank y', mister." Hurrying to tell about the man with the beard and the big car with the strange license plates. Hurry on, then.

I had late breakfast in Tuskegee and then headed for Montgomery, the cradle of the Confederacy. Its streets and buildings seemed to me shabby. There was a listless, to-hell-with-it air about the city. I didn't like it; I don't like it now.

I checked in at the only hotel for Negroes. It was a miserable two-story hovel with a restaurant. The clerk asked me if I wanted to pay in advance.

"Only if you insist," I said.

"Them's the rules," he said.

"I don't think much of them rules," I said, but I paid and left a deposit on the key.

This was the town that started the struggle in 1955, when the Negroes boycotted the buses with M.L. leading. As a direct result, I was told, the attitudes have hardened since then. "Nothing much going on here," an elderly man said. "After all we been through, it looks like it was for nothing. Maybe the buses changed, but not much else. Town's as tight as a drum."

I drove to Alabama State College, which looked, as so many do in the South, like a high school. A group of students gathered around the car. "You from the North, mister?"

"Yes, from New York."

"Where you going when you leave here?"

"Mobile."

"Mobile? Got a gun or *some*thing? They pretty bad down there."

"I got something," I said, thinking of my skinning knife at the bottom of a duffel bag under a seat.

"You better have. They tough down there, mister."

Wouldn't anyone give me a good word along the way, something cheerful?

I looked for a chap whose name had been given to me, but learned he had had the good sense to leave. As a substitute, I was offered a professor of sociology. I won't name him. I am sure that if Governor Wallace wants to give him a medal, he can be found. For myself his name is a four-letter word—and I wish I could think of something worse. I introduced myself, but the words were hardly out of my mouth when he said, "Governor Wallace pays my salary; I have nothing to say to you. Excuse me, I have a class to get to."

And he went in his finely cut suit; he went out to teach young people the mechanics of getting along with one another. I stomped down the stairs, my stomach suddenly kicking up, and crept back to my hovel of a hotel. I lay in the sagging bed and thought of all those people who had walked all those miles for the right to sit anywhere on a bus, and here was a man of position, of some intellect, who in his own quiet way was working just as hard as the segregationists to maintain the status quo. And what was he teaching those kids on Governor Wallace's pay check? I shudder to think.

I had no trouble in Mobile; I wasn't there long. Then I was cruising along the Gulf, looking out toward the sea. Without a perceptible change in the palm trees, I was in Mississippi, driving through Biloxi and Gulfport. The land now was flat and sandy, sparse, as it is in the Hamptons on Long Island, but the sea was bluer and warm air wafting in brought with it a hint of salt. Way out there were Cuba, Haiti, Puerto Rico, the Virgin Islands. I thought of lazy days in St. Thomas and Puerto Rico, of good swimming, good food and good drinks. Ah, perhaps New Orleans would be like that. Perhaps, perhaps.

With the map of New Orleans on the seat beside me, I managed to find the way to Mason's Motel on Melpomene Street. As I rounded a curve, gay colors leaped over the gray houses. Mason's Motel! After the dump in Montgomery, the road *had* to lead up.

Mason was a tall, thin man, graying beneath his wide-brimmed hat. His grin was broad and his eyes danced. I had the feeling I had met him before. He gave me the M. L. King suite for half the going rate. But before I could get to it, he took me to the bar and introduced me to a group of market specialists, those people who go about convincing businessmen and Madison Avenue how many millions of dollars are spent in the Negro market. I knew the types. Bourbon all around. "Drink up, Williams. Drink up." I drank. They were going to show me a big night. Where was I from? New York? Yeah—and veils began to drop over their eyes.

A fresh member of the group showed up with a new iridescent suit and tried it on to cries of, "Man, that's tough!" "It flashes, Billy." The new man described what he would wear to a dance that night. The eyes of the others around the table glittered.

They asked me more about myself and the veils dropped further. Even so, they urged me to get some rest for the big time ahead that night. We'd have a ball.

I went upstairs to the M. L. King suite and dropped off to sleep. When I woke it was past the hour for our balling, and there had been no calls.

"The boys taking you out tonight?" Louis Mason asked with a grin.

"Supposed to," I said.

They never showed. I spent the evening talking with people in the bar and eating red beans and rice with Louis.

I don't know why I thought New Orleans would be different from other cities in the South. My dreams, I guess. I went to the motel's roof-top patio and almost did fall in love with the city. A slight breeze blew over the roofs. I listened to the music coming up from below and wondered what it was about me that had put the hucksters off. From the next block came the organ and tambourine sounds of a revival meeting. There seemed to be a lot going on.

The next day I called a restaurant to make a reservation for dinner, saying that I was from *Holiday*. The reservation was quickly confirmed, so quickly and effusively I felt as though my hand were being kissed from the other end of the wire.

"Wait a minute," I said. "I'm Negro."

There was a long pause, as if the poor man were trying to catch up with the world and had become breathless from the effort. "Oh, we can arrange to send you something."

"Forget it."

I went downstairs and out to the old section, the French Quarter, thinking how strange it was that a city as cosmopolitan as New Orleans should be part of the old order. Its appearance, its layout, its people all seem to belie its Deep South character. I walked the streets of the Quarter and stopped in amazement at the Mammy dummies. They were full-sized, big-bosomed, black and dressed in loud colors. They stood outside the gift shops. Were the white shopkeepers merely making fun of Negro femininity or making fun of their own fear of it? I shopped the Quarter and found only trash, and therefore bought nothing. The clerks hustled, of course, as they do in Greenwich Village; if they didn't have what I wanted, they tried to sell me something else.

I returned to the motel and got directions to the colored restaurant that last night's red beans and rice had come from. "Soul food," Louis said. "Good."

I walked around the corner and got lost. I looked up the street and down, but saw only one restaurant, Nick and Tony's. At the time it didn't even bother me that the name sounded wrong. I crossed the street and went in. The place was rather dark. Several men, all white, were standing at the bar. I walked up, placed my elbows on the bar and looked around. The bartender came running toward me.

"Outside. I'll take your order from the window." He pointed. Ah, yes, the Nigger Window.

"I only want information," I said.

"All right, let's talk outside," the bartender said. He was a big man, going to pot, with a full head of hair and the kind of face that you forget one second after you've seen it.

We moved outside, and as we did, several of the men at the bar followed us out. I told the bartender, without glancing at the others, that I was looking for a colored restaurant. He said he didn't know any and waved in some obscure direction. I left them, never having felt, if indeed I was supposed to, any threat. But the threat was there. I just could not, even refused to, cope with the thought of violence snowballing over nothing. But that is the South, and the North and the East and the West. And the moment I entered Nick and Tony's I had committed the unforgivable sin: I had not kept my mind on danger. I had dropped my guard—and had walked away without a lump. Lucky.

The restaurant that served the soul food was not a place to eat soul food in, and I brought it back to the motel with me. Relating my adventure at Nick and Tony's to the regulars in the bar, I received only quiet smiles; no laughter. Had I jeopardized the peace and tranquillity of custom, and therefore brought danger to them?

Next door to the restaurant stood an old theater. In the street was a large van which advertised that Gene Ewing, a revivalist, was bringing a "Living Christ to a Dying World." I saw elderly Negro women, late for the meeting, hurrying to it, sweat spotting their hastily powdered faces. Ewing was white. He sold Christ and he sold books; and I heard somebody complain that, if Negroes would give as much to the movement as they did to that cracker Ewing, we'd get things done.

When I saw Ewing on the stage, he looked to me as though he could drive one of his two cars across town and join a rock 'n' roll band without a change of pace. Perhaps he had hit a gold mine with Negro audiences—he a white man, preaching to people who couldn't get into the white churches in their city. He had moved into a Negro neighborhood (at least to conduct the revival) with his giant van with all kinds of leaflets in it, and his organ. . . . Rock, Gene, *rock*!

One night an acquaintance drove me in his own car to a good restaurant. On the way back to the motel, we were stopped by two policemen. We had been traveling rather fast, but I had assumed that my host understood the risk. He had a gun in his car, a .32 automatic. The cops found it and began hitching up their pants and puffing their chests preparatory to taking us in. My host got out and took them aside. I sat wondering what a New Orleans jail would be like. He returned to the car and drove away, the cops following. We went to his place of business, and while I waited and the cops waited, he unlocked the door. A light went on. A couple of minutes passed and my host returned, went directly to the cops, leaned inside the lowered window, then came back to me.

"How much did they want?" I asked.

"Twenty. Ten each. Gave them twenty-five. They don't make no money. You can generally buy 'em off." He looked at me and grinned. "Scared?"

I had been badly scared. I had had visions of people saying, "Gee, the last we heard of John, he was in New Orleans."

Jackson, Mississippi. That name, on my mind when I awoke next morning, depressed me. Who was I kidding? Hell, I didn't want to go to Jackson. Then, turning over in M.L.'s bed—in which he had slept once—I remembered that I had already come through a part of Mississippi, driving along carefully, looking at the sea and palm trees. Besides, think of all those colored people who've *always* lived there. That's *their* problem, I thought in the shower.

Jackson is my mother's birthplace, and was her home for a time. I was born there. My parents were married and made their home in Syracuse, where I was conceived (I refuse to give all my heritage to Mississippi), but they returned to Jackson for the birth of their first child, according to the custom of that time. Thus, in my family, a line of "free" Negroes on my father's side, and one of former "slave" Negroes on my mother's side, were merged.

Some years ago, my boys asked me, "Dad, where do we come from?" Although I had started thinking what to tell them years before, I was startled. Quickly I mentioned Jackson, but I was in panic. A man *ought* to be able to tell his children where they come from. I envied those Italians who return to Italy to visit their homes, the Polish and Hungarian Jews who return to see their relatives, the Irish who make the hop to Shannon and go off in search of old homes and friends. But the boys and I, seeking our lineage before Mississippi, moved to the map of Africa on the wall. We looked at the West African coast, and with falling voices and embarrassed eyes concluded that we could have come from anywhere along the 3,000-mile coast and up to 1,500 miles inland. Then to books with photographs of Africans. Did we resemble any of the people shown? Around the eyes? The cheekbones? The mouth? Which were our brothers? Another check: which peoples were brought to Mississippi? Ah, how can you tell, when they arrived in coffles from other states, already mixed with a hundred different peoples? Mandingo? No, most certainly not. Kru? What, then—Baule?

"Dad, where do we come from?" Up to great-grandfather, some trace; beyond him, fog. We came out of fog. We did not perish in it. We are here.

But Jackson lay north; at least the direction was right. I had tired of down-home Southern cooking, soul food. Let them sing about it. Now I know the dark, greasy gravy, the greens cooked to the consistency of wet tissue paper, the grits, the redeye gravy, the thick, starchy rice. I ate my breakfast, one of soul food, and drove out of New Orleans on the Pontchartrain Causeway. The twenty-four-mile ride over the soft blue water was hypnotizing, as if the end of the ride over that stretch of steel, concrete and asphalt had to be a plunge into the lake. At first, up ahead, there was only the suggestion of land, a silvery haze rimmed in a darkness; only that and the causeway, with few cars going and coming on it. But presently the land at the northern end of the lake became solid, took on color, green and brown. Then the lake lay behind me, its clean, small morning waves dancing now for other drivers.

I was still in Louisiana, but in "stomp-down cracker" land, and I had to start watching my step more carefully. I stopped for gas, and again the ritual of the South was trotted out; a Negro attendant came to wait on me. The white attendants, in the stations that can afford this silly double standard, take care of white customers. Before long I had threaded my way across the border and into Mississippi. The land along the way was flat. Although I watched the speedometer, the car sometimes seemed to have a mind of its own, like a colt: it would leap forward, and it would be seconds before I could get the motor to simmer down and keep me out of jail. "I'm gonna let you run, baby," I promised it. "Later."

My *Travelguide* had given me the name of a hotel in Jackson, and I came upon the city cautiously, looking for the street. From the south, the city sweeps from a plain to a modest hill, but the aspect is one of flatness and of rigidly dull buildings. Used-car lots filled one side of the street, small hardware stores the other. As I drove up the gentle hill, the stores improved in quality and in merchandise. Following directions, I drove off the main street, went two blocks—and suddenly the streets were filled with Negroes. I had arrived in the Negro section; it seemed boxed in. Almost at once I saw two colored cops; they were employed after the summer demonstrations and they seemed, in their new uniforms, as proud as kids in new drum-corps suits.

The hotel was very much like the one in Montgomery, even to the key deposit. But why run a place in this manner simply because transient Negroes have no other place to stay? Segregation has made many of us lazy and many of us rich without trying. No competition—therefore, take it or leave it, and you have to take it. The slovenly restaurant keeper, the uncaring hotel man, the parasites of segregation need only provide the superficial services of their business. I had coffee in the dingy little dining room and rushed out, overwhelmed by the place, which not only accepted the code of Mississippi but enforced it to the hilt.

I fled to Jackson State College, but even there I found small comfort. Somewhere this must end, I thought, walking around the campus. Tennessee State, Alabama State, Jackson State, a pattern. Brick buildings like high schools, surplus prefabs, some grass, some dirt. Here, you colored people, take this! But had I been brainwashed, perhaps? I have seen many campuses rolling among soft hills or edging up the sides of valleys, overhung with chestnut and maple and cedar. I have seen domes and columns, and baroque and Gothic structures, cushioned lecture seats and marble walls inscribed with gold; I was spoiled.

I wrestled with these thoughts and finally knew them to be valid, however brainwashed. No great ideas of the past stalked these halls or sandy stretches of walk. When the state legislatures of the South created the Southern Negro college, they thought they knew what they were doing. Books and teachers and space. Build what you will. But the white schools had grass, and baroque and Gothic structures, and great ideas sometimes trod those halls, even if unminded.

I talked with a faculty member at Jackson State, one who, like Bill Eure, had been raised in the North. I asked the inevitable question. He sighed heavily and answered, "I've been in the South a long time now. We have this house. I have my doctorate. I make good money and I'm in a position to maneuver for more. I've got security"—and he reached over and pushed my knee. "Up there—you know how we lived in my town—we had nothing and couldn't *do* anything, couldn't go places. Here, I keep my nose clean. I don't look at white women. I have my contacts. Hell, everyone in this business has his contacts, better have them. My wife has her car, I have mine. I ask you, what in the hell would I have had up there?"

I nodded, too depressed to continue. The elite among the Southern Negroes, the teachers and professional people, were as estranged from the masses of Negroes as the whites were. If New Orleans is any example, the people I met there were not of the professions, and they seemed totally without leadership, but at least they talked about the movement. In Mississippi, few did.

What can instructors so far removed from life give their students?

"We give them a cycle of ignorance," another Jackson man, not a teacher, said to me bitterly. "Many of our instructors are ill prepared to teach, because Southern legislatures don't care about their ability as long as they make the shoddy mark set up for them. They in turn pass on a haphazard education to their students, many of whom become teachers themselves. From last year's class, for example, seventy-six students became teachers; only eight went on to graduate or professional schools; two became secretaries, and so on. Seventy-six teachers. They will pass on what their instructors gave them, and so down the line. Yes, some go to the big schools in the North for advanced degrees, but not because they're interested in the course. More money."

True, some of what the Southern Negro teacher learns in the North (what it is capable of teaching) may filter down to his students. But if the motive isn't pure, can the method be?

And yet, out of the wastelands that whites and Negroes together call colleges, there has come the rebirth of America's greatest idea, that a man is a man and is free under the sky and over the earth. From brick buildings so new that they still sparkle red, from dingy prefabs, from re-used floors, from out of the desert, and despite many of their teachers—from here have come sit-ins, Freedom Walks, kneel-ins.

I drove out to Tougaloo, where Ola, my mother, went to school. Much more beautiful than Jackson State, Tougaloo Southern Christian College is set among grass-covered mounds, within touch of partly timbered land and with a forest in the background. I tried to picture young Ola walking about in this setting. When she was here, the school trained domestics; young Negro girls were taught that their mission was to serve white people, unless they could find other work and the chance of that was small. Ola has spent better than half her life in other people's kitchens and bedrooms and bathrooms. She knows more about white people than they can ever know about her. I hoped the campus had been as nice in her day as it was during my visit.

At the moment, however, the place was buzzing. White men had been riding past the campus at night and firing blindly into it. The co-eds were unsettled, and male students stood guard at night. My mother would call the gunmen "night riders," and every Southern Negro who has ever lived in an outlying section knows what the term means. A woman or a girl found outdoors alone at night was subject to mass rape; a lone Negro male walking home was subject to a beating. By whites. It was for these reasons that my grandfather, who had five daughters to worry about, kept a loaded rifle slung over the door—and he knew how to use it. Here at Tougaloo, however, the male students shot at everything that moved, sometimes even at instructors returning from Jackson. Perhaps they knew what they were doing.

I drove back to my hotel feeling disassociated. I had not found the family roots in Jackson, and felt as though we had sprung out of air. When I checked out the next morning, the boarders in the dining room were talking about drilling for oil and the chance of striking it on property they had. They would be rich because, as one said guffawing into his coffee, "All the scared niggers done left Mississippi and ain't got no more claim on anything." General laughter, in time for my exit.

There are two reasons why Greenville, Mississippi, is unlike Jackson. One is that the city is a river port and thus a place exposed to ideas and people from outside the state. The second is that the Hodding Carter family lives there and publishes the *Delta-Democrat Times*, a "liberal" newspaper.

I went to Greenville to see Hodding Carter, Jr., who has taken over the paper from his eminent father. I thought, as I drove carefully through the neat, quiet streets, this is a place where a man ought to be able to relax. Yet I was cautious even in asking directions to the paper. I should have been more relaxed; I had been in the South long enough to learn that whites and blacks weren't continually at each other's throats; that their back yards touched and that they sometimes chatted across the back fences. In the shops—in Atlanta, in Nashville, even in Jackson—I had heard cashiers say "Thank you" to Negro customers and had seen clerks waiting on Negroes go rushing off to the storeroom for items not on the shelves. There was not the cleared space, the No Man's Land, the demilitarized zone. No, lives dovetailed.

Carter's office was a dark, leathern kind of place, comfortable; there was something solid here, I felt. I knew something about him—not much, to be sure, but something. I knew that even though he was away from home, someone was guarding his family with a loaded firearm. I knew that he had learned to live with threats on his life. This was the price for holding a view unpopular in his city and state—that a law existed, a federal law, and should be obeyed. The Carters were not for Negroes but for law, and because they were, in the minds of the white masses they were "nigger-lovers."

Of all the newspaper people I had talked to about civil rights, only Carter said, "It's going to get worse before it gets better." Surely the others must have been aware of the steady approach of violence, but they avoided the problem as if to wish it away. For Carter, there was not even the hope that matters would improve with the passing of the Old Guard. The throb of violence was too near, and only a miracle could avert it.

It had become almost a macabre game, by now, asking questions and having them answered. I found myself looking for some new nuance. No. The questions we asked, the answers we gave bounded from one corner of a closed box to another, like Mexican jumping beans.

I felt a sudden, billowing tiredness. I tried to conceal it, but Carter saw it. "What's the matter?"

"Tired," I said, not at all surprised that I would admit it to this stranger, who, in a larger way, was not a stranger. "Tense," I added.

"I'll bet you are," he said, and he grinned. "First time South?"

"Since 1946, but I was born in Hinds County."

His nod was an understanding one.

As we parted he gave me directions through a less troublesome part of the state. But driving away, heading for Tennessee and points north, I knew I had to take the other route, the one where possible trouble lay, in order to live with myself and in order to overcome the shame I suddenly felt at confessing my tiredness, my tension to this white man. Drive the cliff edge.

The land was flat, the earth powder. Trees rimmed the distance, so far from the fields that I could not tell what they were. Cotton fields with Negroes in them, pulling long gunnysacks. I thought of Ola and her sisters and brothers and wondered what it had been like for them to pad between the bushes snatching off the cotton and dumping it into the bag in one motion, for speed meant money, money meant survival. There were fields filled with peas and corn. How level the land was, empty almost, as if even the great Mississippi had fled it in terror.

Above, the sky held blue. It was colder now. I wanted to make southern Illinois before I stopped. I edged through the dangerous towns, tired but somehow hyperalert, at times seeing what wasn't there and hearing what had no sound. Clarksdale. Ah, there was a town that Carter had warned me about, but I was through it and on the open road again. Tunica, Hollywood and the land continued flat, but the timber was growing taller. Now the fields began to tilt upward, the timber thickening. Eudora off to the right and then, right on the Mississippi-Tennessee border, Walls! Coffee now, a ham sandwich and a rest.

Now through western Tennessee, through Kentucky, threading along mountains in the falling night. They turned from green to gray, from blue to black. The night became my ally, shielding me from the police in the small towns. I know many Negroes who travel in the South only at night. Now I knew how fugitives felt when they crossed these borders, waiting joyously for starlight.

The drone of the car was making me sleepy and I lowered the rear window. Cold air came snapping into the car, whipped at my ears, numbed my nose. I should stop now, I told myself, for I was driving with my left foot on the gas pedal; my right knee had almost locked, and I had it stretched out toward the right-hand door. There was no place along my route where I could stop in safety. And the rule among Negroes who travel in the South is: don't sleep in your car. Now the high beams of oncoming cars and the lights of towns were blinding me for a second, and I knew that soon I'd have to stop. Where was I? Tennessee, Tennessee, *Kentucky*. Kentucky, Kentucky, *Illinois*.

Let it have changed in this section, let it have changed.

It had. After fourteen hours, I was in a warm room and a warm bed, after hot food and a bath to soak my knee.

Amelia Platts Boynton

(1911–)

A native of Savannah, Georgia, Boynton received her undergraduate training at Tuskegee Institute. She began working as a home demonstration agent in Dallas County, Alabama, in the 1930s, teaching home economics and child-rearing methods to rural black families. She has been active in the civil rights movement for more than half a century, participated in the famous attempt to march across the Edmond Pettus Bridge in Selma, and has a unique perspective on the efforts of blacks in the South to obtain constitutional rights. Her autobiography *Bridge Across Jordan* is representative of the views held by many middle-class Southern blacks of her generation and of the self-conscious narration in the development of African-American autobiographical writing. Her account of Selma's "Bloody Sunday" in March 1965 is included in *Talk That Talk: An Anthology of African-American Storytelling*. The first two chapters of *Bridge Across Jordan* are reprinted here.

---

from Bridge Across Jordan

CHAPTER ONE: SELMA IN THE 1930'S

On a cool crisp morning in April 1930, Mr. Dobbs, the state extension agent, and I were on our way to Selma, a place I had never heard of.

I was to teach the people of Dallas County, Alabama, of which Selma is the county seat, every phase of home economics. I would walk in the footsteps of a good leader, and I heard this as a challenge to excel. A Mrs. Williams had resigned to get married; in those days getting married was the end of extension work for a woman. Regardless of how good one was, the Extension Department could not see dividing an agent between her work and her husband. I knew marriage would have to wait until later, but this was no real problem, as I was not in love with anyone—only my work.

"It's a very small place," Mr. Dobbs informed me. "When you get there you'll find there isn't room enough to turn around, hardly. The train doesn't stop, it only slows down and there is a large bank of sawdust. When they shout 'Selma!' you jump off." I laughed, but believed him. We had boarded the train at Montgomery, and though the distance is just 50 miles, seemingly it took us several hours to reach Selma. As the train slowed down and the conductors called "Selma, Selma, all out for Selma!" I looked at Mr. Dobbs, thinking he would take his little bag and jump off. I was uneasy, because I didn't want to miss it. I did not realize that this was the last stop. Selma was the place where most people came to live when they left the farms. The plantation owners' heirs came as merchants and business people and the Negroes came as teachers, domestics, and all types of laborers.

We were met by the county extension agent, Samuel William Boynton; he took us by car to the place where I would live. I was constantly reminded that this was not Philadelphia (where my parents had gone to live) and neither was it Savannah. The people have to be taught, and you have to be very careful how you act, the county agent said. I was determined to give all my attention to the task and to try to please not only the department but especially the farm people with whom I would work.

This part of the country is called the Black Belt, not, as one might suppose, because of the color of its inhabitants, but because of the rich black soil noted for its abundant cotton crops.

Next morning I rose bright and early in the large old-fashioned home of Mr. and Mrs. Dommie Gaines. They were old settlers of Selma and they knew the surroundings, the people, and their attitudes toward outsiders. This was most helpful to me. The white people had adequate public schools and the Negroes had only one—Clark, which graduated students from the ninth grade. However, there were several private schools for the blacks, including Knox Academy, a high school run by the Reformed Presbyterian Church; Lutheran Academy and College; Payne University (an African Methodist church school); and Selma University, a Baptist institution. Selma's Negroes were proud of this educational center, but illiteracy in this county and those surrounding was as prevalent as in any part of the South.

The first day I went into the county, Bill Boynton gave me some very good advice. When I talked to the farm people I had better know what I was talking about, but "Always be kind and don't say anything that will make them think your education is so far above theirs that you create a barrier. They may be unlearned, but they are intelligent and can teach you a whole lot you don't know." I had never dealt with rural people before and I did learn much from them in a short time.

Bill Boynton, whom I married several years later, had a rural background and loved and understood the people. They were eager to get to the meetings which he tried to make entertaining as well as informative, and they asked Bill many questions that had nothing to do with the farm. Even after he retired, farmers still came to him for information. His being able to help them was what gave his life meaning. Bill was seldom angry, and when he was, it was never because of anything done to him, but because someone had taken advantage of one of his farmers. He encouraged both young and old to continue to educate themselves in the vocation they liked best. There were many ways the state and county programs helped to perpetuate segregation and discrimination in extension work. Bill did not like these methods but he could do little about it. It made his work much harder in helping his people to excel.

There was never a time when the work of black farmers or 4-H club members was exhibited jointly with that of the white community. All shows, demonstrations, and fairs took place in the Negro community, visited by Negroes, and in most cases where competitors were working for prizes, the judges were Negroes from Tuskegee Institute.

There was no such thing as a good road in the black community, let alone paved streets in the black section of Selma. If a Negro lived on a plantation (most of them did), he had to get to his home the best way he could unless he lived in the backyard of the owner. You could always tell where the white man's house was located in the country because you simply followed a road, and this always ended at the owner's gate or in his yard. If you wanted to go back to the "quarters," as they were called, you had to leave your car at the road's end and trudge over ditches, gulleys, wagon roads, or unattended fields. Negroes who owned property in the country owned mostly portions away from roads and highways. If the white owner who had property where the road ended didn't want visitors going over his land, they would be stopped. The families behind the plantations would thus be entirely isolated. Some of this situation remains to this day.

We who were county workers always first contacted the white owner to avoid trouble, but no provision was ever made for our travel in the remote parts of the county. Often we were met by black community leaders and taken to the meeting place either by wagon or even by horse- or muleback. Little or no transportation, bad roads, lack of freedom to go whenever and wherever the farm hands wanted to go made the blacks in the rural district "slaves" to the plantation owner.*

Booker T. Washington, founder of Tuskegee Institute, had devised a plan to reach as many of the people as possible by putting into operation a school on wheels. At first the school was a covered wagon drawn by two horses and equipped with farm implements and some household goods. It traveled in the communities near Tuskegee and was called the Jessup Wagon. Later this was replaced with a truck and still later a trailer equipped with modern implements and home appliances. Then it was staffed with a farm and home demonstration agent, a health nurse, and a 4-H club agent. Its name became the Movable School; it traveled around giving demonstrations in farming and homemaking in the most remote parts of the state. The health nurse was always soon surrounded by mothers with babies and the sick.

The Movable School was one of Tuskegee's mammoth projects to teach the

---

*By far the largest number of Negroes on farms were sharecroppers. Under something very like a feudal system, they were furnished with seed (payment for which was taken out of their profits later) and they also returned half of their yield in payment for the use of the land and a place to stay.

The tenant farmer was a cut above the sharecropper. He leased land from the owner and paid rent for it and his lodging.

uneducated. Its teaching of better farming methods could not help but pay off in greater yields and therefore profit to the plantation owner; nevertheless we often ran into stiff opposition. The planters and overseers would not allow us to have suitable places to hold the school, and they were even more uncooperative when we asked them to let their tenants attend the one-, two-, or three-day sessions. In most cases our pleading with them to permit the school to come onto their places was in vain, even though we scheduled the school during the time there was less work to be done on the farm.

We once got permission to hold the school on the Sampson farm in the southwest section of the county. Hundreds of people lived on this property, which was owned by a multimillionaire from New York. He came down once or twice a year for the dog trials. The Sampson house itself was occupied by white workers, but nearby the road gradually faded into the woods, where there were wagon trails and footpaths leading to many rundown shacks occupied by large families. Each Christmas, millionaire Sampson came down and gave his tenants clothes and a few dollars apiece.

We made plans, with the participation of the Negro county workers, for a session of the Movable School at the Sampson place. When we arrived in our cars and trucks we were stopped by a white man with a gun. He would not allow us to drive through his property. We backed the trucks and the cars along the highway, then had to carry, on foot, the equipment and appliances to the remote section where we would hold the school in one of the little houses. We were almost exhausted when we got there, and rain had begun to fall.

We set up demonstrations despite many handicaps, one of which was that the house was threatening to collapse from the weight of the large number of people in it. There was no electricity, so we could not use some of the equipment. But in spite of the difficulties, the demonstrations were fruitful and were welcomed by the people of the community, who seldom got to any town or went anywhere except to the two stores in Alberta, a tiny village on the road to Selma.

CHAPTER TWO: A FEUDAL SOCIETY

I had read in history that Abraham Lincoln signed the Emancipation Proclamation in 1863. I believed in this until I went to Dallas County, Alabama. There I found that Negroes on most of the plantations in the Black Belt were far from free. The reason: Like Negroes in many other parts of the nation, they thought "white is right, and that gives the white man the privilege to lynch, to whip, to segregate, and to exploit."

Most Negroes were so convinced of this (unconsciously) that they thought only what they believed the white man wanted them to think. Even if a black man violated the law, as long as he was imposing on another Negro and if he were a good hand for the white man, his sentence was either light or it was suspended. The city fathers called this being good to the Negroes.

On the large plantations such as we had in Dallas and adjacent counties, there was no such thing as set working hours. The Negroes went to the fields early in the morning and worked until it was too dark to see. There were still overseers who were as inhuman as the Simon Legrees of slavery times. The Negroes became either an asset or a liability to the owner when the place was sold. The seller and the buyer always discussed the assets that went with the land and if the tenants were good workers the price went up. If not, the land was sold for only its real estate value. Negroes never got a chance to buy the land; it had become a gentlemen's agreement not to sell them farm land. Only occasionally could a Negro buy land from a white man and when he did, the price was almost out of reach.

I have seen landlords as proud of their sharecroppers as they were of their herd of cattle, especially in the days when cotton was king. All the loans and requests for food, clothing and other necessities had to be made either at the plantation store or directly to him so the owner could keep an eye on everyone. There were scheming plantation owners who watched the growth of the boys and girls and where there was the least indication of taking a mate he would encourage it, hoping there would be more farm hands born of the union. He went even further to keep the young couple on his place—adding a room to the already crowded shack of the parents. Cotton hands were needed in large numbers in the 1930's, '40's, and '50's.

Many stories of cruel and inhuman treatment of sharecroppers were confided to me in those days, and I have no reason to doubt their truth—they were typical and they differed from one another only in specific details. The theme was always exploitation of and contempt (or condescending generosity) for the Negro.

On some plantations the owner would discourage the Negroes from buying licenses to marry. He would tell them it was a waste of money; he could do the same thing the justice of peace could do. Such "fictitious" marrying made it difficult later to get certain benefits that require proof of marriage.

Before there was government-financed work to be done and the farms became mechanized, the farm Negro had to get all his cash from the landlord, and this was almost nothing. If he needed a doctor or his children needed clothing, he would go to the plantation owner, who in turn would call the doctor or the store and tell them he was sending his "boy" with his baby to be treated, or that his "boy's" children needed shoes. Of course the Negro paid dearly for this type of service—it would all come out of his wages.

I knew a large black farm hand named Jint. His 12 children could not go to school until November because they had to gather crops, and then they could go only if Jint could buy them books and clothing. In March they had to leave school to plant the crops. Although the owner, Mr. Gibbs, profited from Jint's labor, Jint got nothing but a balance due bill every year. He decided he would leave the plantation, but he had to have money to move, so he bought sugar and began to make illegal whiskey. Mr. Gibbs, his landlord, sold him hundreds of pounds of sugar and knew it was being used for something other than home use. But he bided his time, to turn Jint's pursuits to his own advantage. He was not about to let him, with his big family, leave the plantation—they made up to 50 bales of cotton for him each year. He thought of a scheme to keep him.

Gibbs called the sheriff and told him Jint was drunk from illegal whiskey and Jint was arrested. Right away Gibbs appeared at the jail and offered to help his sharecropper. At the trial he was there to hear the judge fine Jint $80. According to the agreement between Gibbs and the judge, the judge reprimanded Jint, Gibbs paid the fine and took Jint back to the plantation to be relegated to harder labor with less pay. For more than a year Jint did extra work, then took the $80 to Gibbs, who was so surprised that it took him some time to recover. He told Jint that the interest had run the fine up to $250 (which of course he knew Jint didn't have).

After two more years of hard labor on the farm, Jint was able to pay the full amount, which had now increased to $400, and he wanted to leave. Gibbs had to think of another way he could get Jint into trouble. He talked to a neighbor, whose sharecroppers were friendly with Jint's family, and made a deal with him. The neighbor in turn made a deal with one of his Negroes. The plan was to invite Jint to a Saturday night party where they knew he would drink and perhaps clown around. The neighbor's sharecropper would pick a fight with Jint and the officers would again arrest him. The plan worked. Jint was accosted and teased and provoked, and at first he walked away because he didn't want trouble. But when the other Negro followed him saying he would kill him, Jint pulled out a knife and cut him with it. Within a few minutes the officers arrested both of them and charged Jint with assault with intent to murder. Back to court went Jint, thrown on its mercy and that of the landlord.

The judge said, "You are charged with assault with intent to murder. What ails you, boy? You've been up here before and you just can't keep out of trouble. I'm going to put you where you can stay out of trouble." While he talked to Jint, he was looking at Gibbs and winking. "I'm going to give you seven years at hard labor, and that will keep you for a while."

Jint felt he was doomed for life, but just then Mr. Gibbs whispered to the judge, who now said, "Now boy, Mr. Gibbs here says you got a whole pen full of children and you need to be with them. Tell you what I'm going to do. I'm going to suspend your sentence and put you on probation. Do you have any money?" "No sir," said Jint. "Well," continued the judge, "your landlord Mr. Gibbs here will pay your fine and I will release you to him. Now you go back to the farm and behave yourself. Don't get into any more trouble, and work hard." Jint left the courthouse with his landlord, sentenced along with his family to a punishment far worse than slavery, for it looked now as though he would never get out of debt.

Jint and his family have finally been released from this ungodly punishment, but not through the generosity of their master, Gibbs. When the old style of farming (with mules and ploughs) became obsolete, Jint and his family became a liability. The Government permitted the owner to put his land in the soil bank, and later Mr. Gibbs died. The old worn-out farm implement, giant Jint, was now a liability and was set aside without a penny. He left the farm and through the goodness of relatives in one of the northern ghettoes, he went to make a living for his family. He knows very little about reading and writing and the same is true of his older children, but his younger children still have a chance—a ghetto chance.

On another plantation about 15 miles from Selma there was a large number of sharecroppers who never saw cash that the cotton brought. The owner always called them together after the crops were in and gave each person who was head of his house a good lecture and a few dollars. The owner happened to be a doctor, and any tenant who was ill had to report to him. If the doctor thought the Negro was ill, he would give him a few pills and send him home to get well over the weekend and be prepared to start work early Monday morning.

Maria was a small, frail woman I had known since I first came to Selma. She had been ill a long time and had gone to her doctor-landlord for treatment. She had lived on that plantation all her life and she came to me very much frightened. She didn't know what to do and feared for her life, as she had been told she was a liability.

After she was able to talk without sobbing she said "I was pickin' cotton and I wasn't able to keep up with the others when the straw boss come over to fin' out why I so slow. I tole him I was sick and had been to the doctor but his medicine hadn't he'ped me. The doctor, he operated on me, but the place he cut me never healed. I went back to him so much until he got mad with me and tole me not to come no more. I owed him a big bill and I was too sick to work it out, but I had to go back. At first he passed by me and wouldn't saying nothing. When he was ready to close his office his nurse came out and tole me I had to go. Next day I went again and he came out to the waiting room and asked me what was wrong. I tole him my side was hurtin' and the place was still bleedin'. Instead of tryin' to do somethin' for me, he tole me to go home and stick a corncob in my side, and he pushed me out of his office and said don't come back."

I was dumbfounded and said he must have been joking. But Maria said he was not joking and he was angry with her for not being able to produce the amount of cotton she used to. She was once the fastest picker on the plantation—nearly 400 pounds a day.

All this was bad enough, but another great shock was to come. Maria said, "Everybody knows the doctor gave me a botch operation and he won't wait on me. He knows I don't have no money to go to another doctor and no way to go even if I did. No one else would take me because everyone is scared of that doctor. He tole me to go home and lie down and die, because I wasn't going to live anyway."

Maria said that a few days after the doctor had pushed her out of his office, Tom Brown, who lived on the other end of the plantation, told her that the doctor had offered him $10 if he would take Maria down to the river and drown her.

We were able to do something about Maria. She needed medical attention right away, and we asked churches and individuals to raise money for another operation. We soon had her in the hospital, and after proper care, she recovered.

Maya Angelou

(1928–   )

Maya Angelou has probably made her greatest contribution to literature through the art of autobiography. The initial volume of her autobiography, *I Know Why the Caged Bird Sings*, is widely accepted as a classic of twentieth-century African-American feminist writing. The autobiographical series includes *Gather Together in My Name, Singin' and Swingin' and Gettin' Merry Like Christmas, The Heart of a Woman*, and *All God's Children Need Traveling Shoes*. Born in St. Louis, Missouri, Angelou has excelled as a dancer, actress, poet, playwright, director, and writer of "faction." Currently writer-in-residence for life at Wake Forest University, Angelou has demonstrated in such screenplays as "Georgia, Georgia" and "All Day Long" and the television plays "Blacks, Blues, Black" and "Sister, Sister" her talent for dramatizing multiple facets of humanity. Her use of language to resist the loss of African-American traditions and values is apparent in her collections of poetry—*Just Give Me a Cool Drink of Water 'fore I Diiie, Oh Pray My Wings Are Gonna Fit Me Well, And Still I Rise*, and *Shaker, Why Don't You Sing?* The following excerpt is taken from *Gather Together in My Name*.

---

from Gather Together in My Name

There is a much-loved region in the American fantasy where pale white women float eternally under black magnolia trees, and white men with soft hands brush wisps of wisteria from the creamy shoulders of their lady loves. Harmonious black music drifts like perfume through this precious air, and nothing of a threatening nature intrudes.

The South I returned to, however, was flesh-real and swollen-belly poor. Stamps, Arkansas, a small hamlet, had subsisted for hundreds of years on the returns from cotton plantations, and until World War I, a creaking lumbermill. The town was halved by railroad tracks, the swift Red River and racial prejudice. Whites lived on the town's small rise (it couldn't be called a hill), while blacks lived in what had been known since slavery as "the Quarters."

After our parents' divorce in California, our father took us from Mother, put identification and destination tags on our wrists, and sent us alone, by train, to his mother in the South. I was three and my brother four when we

435

first arrived in Stamps. Grandmother Henderson accepted us, asked God for help, then set about raising us in His way. She had established a country store around the turn of the century, and we spent the Depression years minding the store, learning Bible verses and church songs, and receiving her undemonstrative love.

We lived a good life. We had some food, some laughter and Momma's quiet strength to lean against. During World War II the armed services drew the town's youth, black and white, and Northern war plants lured the remaining hale and hearty. Few, if any, blacks or poor whites returned to claim their heritage of terror and poverty. Old men and women and young children stayed behind to tend the gardens, the one paved block of stores and the long-accepted way of life.

In my memory, Stamps is a place of light, shadow, sounds and entrancing odors. The earth smell was pungent, spiced with the odor of cattle manure, the yellowish acid of the ponds and rivers, the deep pots of greens and beans cooking for hours with smoked or cured pork. Flowers added their heavy aroma. And above all, the atmosphere was pressed down with the smell of old fears, and hates, and guilt.

On this hot and moist landscape, passions clanged with the ferocity of armored knights colliding. Until I moved to California at thirteen I had known the town, and there had been no need to examine it. I took its being for granted and now, five years later, I was returning, expecting to find the shield of anonymity I had known as a child.

Along with other black children in small Southern villages, I had accepted the total polarization of the races as a psychological comfort. Whites existed, as no one denied, but they were not present in my everyday life. In fact, months often passed in my childhood when I only caught sight of the thin hungry po' white trash (sharecroppers), who lived sadder and meaner lives than the blacks I knew. I had no idea that I had outgrown childhood's protection until I arrived back in Stamps.

Momma took my son in one arm and folded the other around me. She held us for one sweet crushing moment. "Praise God Almighty you're home safe."

She was already moving away to keep her crying private.

"Turned into a little lady. Sure did." My Uncle Willie examined me with his quiet eyes and reached for the baby. "Let's see what you've got there." He had been crippled in early childhood, and his affliction was never mentioned. The right side of his body had undergone severe paralysis, but his left arm and hand were huge and powerful. I laid the baby in the hand of his good arm.

"Hello, baby. Hello. Ain't he sweet?" The words slurred over his tongue and out of the numb lips. "Here, take him." His healthy muscles were too strong for a year-old wriggler.

Momma called from the kitchen, "Sister, I made you a little something to eat."

We were in the Store; I had grown up in its stronghold. Just seeing the shelves loaded with weenie sausages and Brown Plug chewing tobacco, salmon

Tears; Crying
why?
themen
"Anger etc.

and mackerel and sardines all in their old places softened my heart and tears stood at the ready just behind my lids. But the kitchen, where Momma with her great height bent to pull cakes from the wood-burning stove and arrange the familiar food on well-known plates, erased my control and the tears slipped out and down my face to plop onto the baby's blanket.

The hills of San Francisco, the palm trees of San Diego, prostitution and lesbians and the throat hurting of Curley's departure disappeared into a never-could-have-happened land. I was home.

"Now what you crying for?" Momma wouldn't look at me for fear my tears might occasion her own. "Give the baby to me, and you go wash your hands. I'm going to make him a sugar tit. You can set the table. Reckon you remember where everything is."

The baby went to her without a struggle and she talked to him without the cooing most people use with small children. "Man. Just a little man, ain't you? I'm going to call you man and that's that."

Momma and Uncle Willie hadn't changed. She still spoke softly and her voice had a little song in it.

"Bless my soul, Sister, you come stepping up here looking like your daddy for the world."

Christ and Church were still the pillars of her life.

"The Lord my God is a rock in a weary land. He is a great God. Brought you home, all in one piece. Praise His name."

She was, as ever, the matriarch. "I never did want you children to go to California. Too fast that life up yonder. But then, you all's their children, and I didn't want nothing to happen to you, while you're in my care. Jew was getting a little too big for his britches."

Baby Born in CA
1928
17
1945
?
1940

Five years before, my brother had seen the body of a black man pulled from the river. The cause of death had not been broadcast, but Bailey (Jew was short for Junior) had seen that man's genitals had been cut away. The shock caused him to ask questions that were dangerous for a black boy in 1940 Arkansas. Momma decided we'd both be better off in California where lynchings were unheard of and a bright young Negro boy could go places. And even his sister might find a niche for herself.

Despite the sarcastic remarks of Northerners, who don't know the region (read Easterners, Westerners, North Easterners, North Westerners, Midwesterners), the South of the United States can be so impellingly beautiful that sophisticated creature comforts diminish in importance.

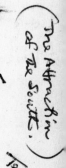

(The Attraction of the South.)

For four days I waited on the curious in the Store, and let them look me over. I was that rarity, a Stamps girl who had gone to the fabled California and returned. I could be forgiven a few siditty airs. In fact, a pretension to worldliness was expected of me, and I was too happy to disappoint.

When Momma wasn't around, I stood with one hand on my hip and my head cocked to one side and spoke of the wonders of the West and the joy of being free. Any listener could have asked me: if things were so grand in San Francisco, what had brought me back to a dusty mote of Arkansas? No one asked, because they all needed to believe that a land existed somewhere, even

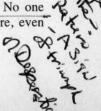

Teenage Mother Return "As if" & triumph. Desperation

beyond the Northern Star, where Negroes were treated as people and whites were not the all-powerful ogres of their experience.

For the first time the farmers acknowledged my maturity. They didn't order me back and forth along the shelves but found subtler ways to make their wants known.

"You all have any long-grain rice, Sister?"

The hundred-pound sack of rice sat squidged down in full view.

"Yes, ma'am, I believe we do."

"Well then, I'll thank you for two pounds."

"Two pounds? Yes, ma'am."

I had seen the formality of black adult equals all my youth but had never considered that a time would come when I, too, could participate. The customs are as formalized as an eighteenth-century minuet, and a child at the race's knee learns the moves and twirls by osmosis and observation.

Values among Southern rural blacks are not quite the same as those existing elsewhere. Age has more worth than wealth, and religious piety more value than beauty.

There were no sly looks over my fatherless child. No cutting insinuations kept me shut away from the community. Knowing how closely my grandmother's friends hewed to the Bible, I was surprised not to be asked to confess my evil ways and repent. Instead, I was seen in the sad light which had been shared and was to be shared by black girls in every state in the country. I was young, yes, unmarried, yes—but I was a mother, and that placed me nearer to the people.

I was flattered to receive such acceptance from my betters (seniors) and strove mightily to show myself worthy.

Momma and Uncle Willie noted my inclusion into the adult stratum, and on my fourth day they put up no resistance when I said I was going for a night on the town. Since they knew Stamps, they knew that any carousing I chose to do would be severely limited. There was only one "joint" and the owner was a friend of theirs.

Age and travel had certainly broadened me and obviously made me more attractive. A few girls and boys with whom I'd had only generalities in common, all my life, asked me along for an evening at Willie Williams' café. The girls were going off soon to Arkansas Mechanical and Technical College to study Home Economics and the boys would be leaving for Tuskegee Institute in Alabama to learn how to farm. Although I had no education, my California past and having a baby made me equal to an evening with them.

When my escorts walked into the darkened Store, Momma came from the kitchen, still wearing her apron, and joined Uncle Willie behind the counter.

"Evening, Mrs. Henderson. Evening, Mr. Willie."

"Good evening, children." Momma gathered herself into immobility.

Uncle Willie leaned against the wall. "Evening, Philomena, and Harriet and Johnny Boy and Louis. How you all this evening?"

Just by placing their big still bodies in the Store at that precise time, my grandmother and uncle were saying, "Be good. Be very very good. Somebody is watching you."

We squirmed and grinned and understood.

The music reached out for us when we approached the halfway point. A dark throbbing bass line whonked on the air lanes, and our bodies moved to tempo. The steel guitar urged the singer to complain.

> "Well, I ain't got no
> special reason here.
> No, I ain't got no
> special reason here.
> I'm going leave
> 'cause I don't feel welcome here . . . ."

The Dew Drop In café was a dark square outline, and on its wooden exterior, tin posters of grinning white women divinely suggested Coca-Cola, R.C. Cola and Dr Pepper for complete happiness. Inside the one-room building, blue bulbs hung down precariously close to dancing couples, and the air moved heavily like stagnant water.

Our entrance was noted but no one came rushing over to welcome me or ask questions. That would come, I knew, but certain formalities had first to be observed. We all ordered Coca-Cola, and a pint bottle of sloe gin appeared by magic. The music entered my body and raced along my veins with the third syrupy drink. Hurray, I was having a good time. I had never had the chance to learn the delicate art of flirtation, so now I mimicked the other girls at the table. Fluttering one hand over my mouth, while laughing as hard as I could. The other hand waved somewhere up and to my left as if I and it had nothing to do with each other.

"Marguerite?"

I looked around the table and was surprised that everyone was gone. I had no idea how long I had sat there laughing and smirking behind my hand. I decided they had joined the dancing throng and looked up to search for my, by now, close but missing friends.

"Marguerite." L. C. Smith's face hung above me like the head of a bodyless brown ghost.

"L. C., how are you?" I hadn't seen him since my return, and as I waited for his answer a wave of memory crashed in my brain. He was the boy who had lived on the hill behind the school who rode his own horse and at fifteen picked as much cotton as the grown men. Despite his good looks he was never popular. He didn't talk unless forced. His mother had died when he was a baby, and his father drank moonshine, even during the week. The girls said he was womanish, and the boys that he was funny that way.

I commenced to giggle and flutter and he took my hand.

"Come on. Let's dance."

I agreed and caught the edge of the table to stand. Half erect, I noticed that the building moved. It rippled and buckled as if a nest of snakes were mating

beneath the floors. I was concerned, but the sloe gin had numbed my brain
and I couldn't panic. I held on to the table and L. C.'s hand, and tried to
straighten myself up.

"Sit down. I'll be right back." He took his hand away and I plopped back
into the chair. Sometime later he was back with a glass of water.

"Come on. Get up." His voice was raspy like old corn shucks. I set my
intention on getting up and pressed against the iron which had settled in my
thighs.

"We're going to dance?" My words were thick and cumbersome and didn't
want to leave my mouth.

"Come on." He gave me his hand and I stumbled up and against him and
he guided me to the door.

Outside, the air was only a little darker and a little cooler, but it cleared
one corner of my brain. We were walking in the moist dirt along the pond,
and the café was again a distant outline. With soberness came a concern for
my virtue. Maybe he wasn't what they said.

"What are you going to do?" I stopped and faced him, steadying myself
for his appeal.

"It's not me. It's you. You're going to throw up." He spoke slowly.
"You're going to put your finger down your throat and tickle, then you can
puke."

With his intentions clear, I regained my poise.

"But I don't want to throw up. I'm not in the least—"

He closed a hand on my shoulder and shook me a little. "I say, put your
finger in your throat and get that mess out of your stomach."

I became indignant. How could he, a peasant, a nobody, presume to lecture
me? I snatched my shoulder away.

"Really, I'm fine. I think I'll join my friends," I said and turned toward
the café.

"Marguerite." It was no louder than his earlier tone but had more force
than his hand.

"Yes?" I had been stopped.

"They're not your friends. They're laughing at you." He had misjudged.
They couldn't be laughing at me. Not with my sophistication and city ways.

"Are you crazy?" I sounded like a San Francisco-born debutante.

"No. You're funny to them. You got away. And then you came back. What
for? And with what to show for your travels?" His tone was as soft as the
Southern night and the pond lapping. "You come back swaggering and bragging that you've just been to paradise and you're wearing the very clothes
everybody here wants to get rid of."

I hadn't stopped to think that while loud-flowered skirts and embroidered
white blouses caused a few eyebrows to be raised in San Diego, in Stamps
they formed the bulk of most girls' wardrobes.

L. C. went on, "They're saying you must be crazy. Even people in Texar-
kana dress better than you do. And you've been all the way to California.

They want to see you show your butt outright. So they gave you extra drinks of sloe gin.''

He stopped for a second, then asked, ''You don't drink, do you?''

''No.'' He had sobered me.

''Go on, throw up. I brought some water so you can rinse your mouth after.''

He stepped away as I began to gag. The bitter strong fluid gurgled out of my throat, burning my tongue. And the thought of nausea brought on new and stronger contractions.

After the cool water we walked back past the joint, and the music, still heavy, throbbed like gongs in my head. He left the glass by the porch and steered me in the direction of the Store.

His analysis had confused me and I couldn't understand why I should be the scapegoat.

He said, ''They want to be free, free from this town, and crackers, and farming, and yes-sirring and no-sirring. You never were very friendly, so if you hadn't gone anywhere, they wouldn't have liked you any more. I was born here, and will die here, and they've never liked me.'' He was resigned and without obvious sorrow.

''But, L. C., why don't you get away?''

''And what would my poppa do? I'm all he's got.'' He stopped me before I could answer, and went on, ''Sometimes I bring home my salary and he drinks it up before I can buy food for the week. Your grandmother knows. She lets me have credit all the time.''

We were nearing the Store and he kept talking as if I weren't there. I knew for sure that he was going to continue talking to himself after I was safely in my bed.

''I've thought about going to New Orleans or Dallas, but all I know is how to chop cotton, pick cotton and hoe potatoes. Even if I could save the money to take Poppa with me, where would I get work in the city? That's what happened to him, you know? After my mother died he wanted to leave the house, but where could he go? Sometimes when he's drunk two bottles of White Lightning, he talks to her. 'Reenie, I can see you standing there. How come you didn't take me with you, Reenie? I ain't got no place to go, Reenie. I want to be with you, Reenie.' And I act like I don't even hear him.''

We had reached the back door of the Store. He held out his hand.

''Here, chew these Sen-Sen. Sister Henderson ought not know you've been drinking. Good night, Marguerite, Take it easy.''

And he melted into the darker darkness. The following year I heard that he had blown his brains out with a shotgun on the day of his father's funeral.

Jack Hunter O'Dell

(1923–   )

Formerly a merchant seaman and member of the National Maritime Union, O'Dell is a longtime activist in the civil rights and international peace movements. He has directed the International Affairs Bureau of PUSH, taught at Antioch College (Washington, D.C.), and is currently Director of International Affairs for the National Rainbow Coalition and Chairman of the National Board of Pacifica Radio. He has been associate editor of *Freedomways* and wrote numerous editorials and essays for the magazine before its demise in 1986. O'Dell's work has also been published in *Violence in America*, *Black Titan: W.E.B. DuBois*, and *Paul Robeson: The Great Forerunner*. The following article was first published in two parts as "On the Transition from Civil Rights to Civil Equality" in *Freedomways* (Second Quarter 1978 and Fourth Quarter 1978); this version was published in *Southern Exposure* (Spring 1981).

Notes on the Movement
Then, Now, and Tomorrow

The most significant feature of any movement that is effecting profound change in society is the role it plays in creating a dual authority in the country. It is the authority of the movement as the people's response to the policies of the established authority which gives the movement the power to ultimately effect a democratic transformation of society.

Beginning with the events of Montgomery in 1955, when the Afro-American community of 50,000 citizens stood as one in a bus boycott, and extending to 1969 with the Vietnam Moratorium, in which an estimated four million people participated, our Movement created a dual authority in the country. There was on the one hand the established authority: the citadels of institutional racism, the masters of war, the apparatus of government—state, local and federal— and those chosen to do the dirty work of suppressing our Movement in defense of the status quo. This established authority acted out a way of life that was rooted in custom and tradition, and dictated by class interests.

The other center of authority was the Civil Rights–Anti-War Movement which represented a continuum of protest activity during the period. This authority, the Movement, represented the people's alternative to the power of institutional racism and colonialist war. The Movement had at its disposal such resources as dedicated organizers who educated and mobilized the aggrieved people; charismatic, grass-roots leadership that articulated the goals and the vision that inspired action; performing artists who gave of their time and talent; church choirs, benefit concerts, mass meetings, and literature designed to instruct and enlighten as well as reflect the experiences of the Movement. All of this was held together by an ethos of camaraderie developed in struggle.

The Movement was a proliferation of centers busy with community activists planning strategy, recruiting volunteers, raising bail for those arrested for exercising their constitutional right to protest injustices; above all, people organized and aroused to action. In this many-sided collective activity, untold numbers of people made personal decisions on how much they would allow the Movement's authority to affect their everyday lives. The decisions were varied: whether to attend a meeting, participate in a march, or register to vote; whether to use vacation time, or drop out of school, to do full-time organizing; whether to give the family car to the Movement or put up property as bail bond. Some ministers cut down on their church work in order to do what they perceived in a new light as the work of the church. Teachers volunteered to run "freedom schools," and a few lawyers donated their services to defend participants in the Movement or to help redefine the meaning of law-and-order in the South.

In the years between Montgomery and the Vietnam Moratorium, the authority of the people's Movement in this country was expressed in thousands of individual actions and hundreds of local demonstrations in cities across the land where citizens singled out targets for disciplined, collective action. The authority of this Movement sprang from the best traditions of the Negro church, organized labor and populist radicalism, and its spirit was reflected and continually revived in the musical themes of that period: "This Little Light of Mine," "All We Are Saying Is Give Peace a Chance," "We Shall Not Be Moved," and the most famous, "We Shall Overcome."

Obviously, the struggle for civil rights did not begin with the mass protests of the 1950s, but the physical involvement of thousands of Afro-Americans and whites in the South and North transformed the struggle into a movement whose authority challenged the basis of the established order's value system with a new vision of freedom, brotherhood and democracy. It was this spirit and commitment to a new set of goals and values that enabled our Movement to sustain the wounds inflicted upon peaceful demonstrators in Birmingham and Selma, the Democratic National Convention in Chicago and the Poor People's encampment in Washington, DC.

From an international perspective, the mass movement of the 1950s and '60s created a moral and political crisis for the rulers of the U.S. who at the time were immodestly proclaiming themselves the "leadership of the Free World." One would have had to look very hard to find a country whose citizens were so systematically denied the elementary right to use a public park or go into a restaurant for a meal or use the regular elevator or attend a public tax-supported college. In the United States, Afro-Americans were denied every

one of these rights and more. By forcing an end to such embarrassingly backward practices, the Movement created the conditions whereby the U.S. and its
leadership partially closed the gap in relation to the rest of the modern world.

Similarly, through the sacrifice of the Movement, through the emancipation
of the mind and spirit of the South's people, the Southern region of the United
States rejoined the nation and entered fully into the twentieth century. Segregation had clouded the white Southerners' perception of reality and held them
back from acting on what they did perceive clearly. The Civil Rights Movement, like all mass movements for democracy, was a great teacher of civilized
values, and in the wake of the removal of segregation, the common interest
of the white and black working population is beginning to surface, as exemplified by union organizing efforts in the region.

Given its particular focus, the Civil Rights Movement achieved its stated
objectives by first abolishing law-enforced segregation and ending disfran-
chisement of the black population in the South. Having achieved these objectives, the movement for civil rights was transformed into a movement to
complete the tasks of the Second Reconstruction by winning greater representation for the black population in government. When the civil-rights legislation
in 1964–65 became law, there were barely 300 black elected officials in the
country. Today, there are almost 5,000—about half of them in the South.
When the civil-rights legislation of 1964–65 was passed, there were a million-
and-a-half black voters in the South. Today there are nearly three million. It
is important to understand that this transformation from mass protest to a focus
on legislative power was a logical development, since our experience had
taught us that having a greater voice in the institutions of government is the
only way to protect the rights we have won and make secure their enforcement.

It is equally important to recognize that the civil-rights laws of the 1960s
were passed after the fact. They did not create change; rather the struggle for
expanded democracy, participated in by tens of thousands of our fellow citizens, produced a body of legislation which confirmed the effectiveness of that
struggle. The laws were a crystallized form of expressing the new reality that
people would no longer abide by the rules and mores of racial segregation.
Segregation was in fact abolished by the power of the Civil Rights Movement.
A movement, whether of reform or revolution, always struggles for a legislative manifestation of its victory because that establishes a new code of conduct
in relation to the old order of things. It confirms that change has been accepted
and that the particular struggle for democracy has been victorious.

Once the victory is formalized, the movement must regroup around the
definition of the next stage of mass democracy and move on to its fulfillment.
The opposition will inevitably attempt to trap the movement into preoccupying
itself with implementing victories that have been codified into law. Indeed,
the law is often written in such a way as to encourage this entrapment. And
since the Movement's activists are often experiencing a degree of exhaustion,
the tendency to focus on emphasizing that which has been won is even stronger
because it is a form of reprieve.

The decade of the 1970s has found the Movement caught up in just such an eddy in which motion is devoid of clear direction; we have become preoccupied by the rituals of the technician-intelligentsia and have shifted responsibility for social change to them, substituting their busy-ness for mass-movement organizing. Yet only the latter can provide the driving force for the achievement of greater democracy. The tendency has become to make Title III, VI or IX of this or that act the focus of our attention along with the writing of proposals to foundations or government agencies. These activities have been projected as "more sophisticated" ways of achieving our objectives. This is the New Thing; and the complexities of life and the difficulty of identifying programatically what we need to focus on have tended to give credence to this new style.

It is inevitable and good that we have learned—for example—how to hold press conferences, for we all recognize that technologically this is a media age. But it was disastrous for us to rely primarily upon these corporate forms of mass communication to get our message and analysis out to the public. Once that dependence becomes a matter of style, it is too easy to fall into the practice of tailoring activity to fit what the media might pick up. Such dependence encourages competition among the leaders themselves since the new value system becomes who gets the most media attention. In the end, it means a new kind of addiction to media rather than being in charge of our own agenda and relying upon mass support as our guarantee that ultimately the news-covering apparatus must give recognition to our authority.

The mass meetings held every Monday night, week after week, in dozens of Southern communities and every Saturday morning in Northern cities during the early 1960s were main forms of communication, mass education and mass mobilization. This was the strength of the Movement: not having fallen into reliance upon the monopoly-controlled media to report its activities. Through these regular mass meetings and the mobilization that followed, the direct participation of the community in the struggle to secure our objectives was sustained. Thus a direct line of accountability was maintained between the leaders at all levels and the broad base of support among the people. Another important dimension of this relationship was that the people themselves financed such a movement, lessening the dependence on the "generosity" of other sources of revenue. The power of any movement for democracy is always dependent on such reciprocal relations between the mass of people and their leadership.

The decade of the 1970s has been a hard teacher for Afro-American leaders, and the sense of apprehension and doubt about the possibilities of a better life under this economy has dramatically increased. Yet the remedies traditional civil-rights organizations are clinging to and placing hope in are at best potentially relief measures rather than solutions. Such measures as economic set-asides from the federal budget to assist black businesses are seen as an aid to economic development; more affirmative action, vigorously enforced in both the public and private sector, and more support to black colleges are of course all laudable relief measures that deserve support. However, such programs suggest that we are suffering from a parochial approach to solving the problems of the Afro-American community. These problems are connected to and are an exaggerated expression of a deeper malady. The United States is a society currently in the throes of a long-term economic crisis whose process of ruination is a protracted one. Notwithstanding the appearance of relative prosperity among a large section of the employed population, the features of stagnation and dislocation in our capitalist economy are deep and of long duration. The time in history in which we live, and the general crisis and regressive trends in our country, call us to move boldly on to the next stage of struggle for mass democracy.

The Civil Rights Movement of the '50s and '60s was always an anti-racist revolt within the general struggle to preserve constitutional rights and block the timetable of fascism in our country; the latter is the natural tendency of the ruling corporate elite when their system is in the kind of crisis it is today. Yet this mass-movement revolt against racism in all its forms was not an anti-capitalist revolt, nor was anti-capitalist ideology at any time a very significant influence. However, the Civil Rights Movement under the leadership of Martin Luther King, Jr., evolved the strategic concept of mobilizing the poorest among the working class in a campaign to dramatize the issue of widespread poverty in the "richest country in the world." At that point, the Movement began to step across the threshold of struggle for merely *formal* equality into an era of struggle for *substantial* equality. This jump inevitably meant a confrontation with the economic and ethical deficiencies of the free enterprise system itself. The very essence of the Poor People's Campaign was to confront the nature of the system that produces poverty for the millions as a natural accompaniment to making the super-rich more extravagantly wealthy. On the eve of that campaign, Martin Luther King was assassinated in Memphis as he responded to the call for help from sanitation workers seeking recognition for their union and their right to collective bargaining.

The voices of the New Right are frequently heard today proclaiming that "the movements of the '60s went too far." In fact, our social protest movement didn't go far enough in the depth of its criticism and public education concerning the nature of American institutions. Nor could it have gone further, for once the Civil Rights Movement correctly shifted its focus to the poverty conditions of millions of our fellow citizens and to the immoral, racist war in Vietnam, the Movement became the target of a counteroffensive spearheaded by the government. Many of the details of this sinister counterrevolutionary offensive were officially documented by the Senate Select Committee headed by Senator Frank Church and are now public knowledge. So we need not elaborate here on COINTELPRO, political assassination and other forms this took. What must be underscored, however, is that the design was to bring to a halt the advances and the momentum of the movements of the '60s; to get the Movement out of the streets and therefore out of public view and out of public consciousness; to break up the alliances that were being built with organized labor, women, Latinos and Native Americans and otherwise liquidate the Movement. That was the point. This was a more sophisticated attack than those which occurred during the crude illegalities of the early McCarthy era, but the content and purpose were the same. The crowning achievement of this counterrevolutionary offensive was the election of Richard Nixon to the presidency of the United States, and as a consequence, this marked the beginning of the nadir of this historical phase of the Civil Rights Movement.

The Movement is still alive, yet its life today is being consumed fighting defensive battles. The defense of affirmative action programs in education and employment; the defense against retrenchment by some states whose legislatures are trying to rescind their decision to endorse the Equal Rights Amendment; the defense of innocents in prison like the Wilmington Ten and the Wounded Knee defendants are among such examples. No one can deny that defensive battles have to be fought from time to time and fought effectively so that victories are won. Yet the time-tested wisdom which holds that the best defense is an offensive movement is an important concept for us to renew in practice today.

Social change and real progress always require that a movement keep the offensive in pursuit of clearly defined goals. That is how our Movement abolished segregation in public accommodations; it launched a mass offensive against this form of institutional racism. Defensive battles are selectively taken up and victories won *when they are shown to be related to the offensive* our Movement is developing. Otherwise, we can be kept busy by the opposition with defensive battles, but we will not be going anywhere. In such a busyness situation, the vision of our goal is lost and soon the movement fragments.

To put our Movement on the offensive again, we must make the transition from a primary emphasis on formal civil rights to an emphasis on achieving the goal of substantive civil equality. Such a movement will shift from a focus on the formal recognition of our rights to the implementation of actual equality in the conditions of life, liberty and the pursuit of happiness all of us aspire to share. It will provide our country with a national purpose and goals consistent with human progress. It will be good for the spiritual and material well-being of U.S. society, and as a majority of the population embraces and gets involved in this national effort, our country will again "catch up" with the global movement for human rights that daily exposes the backwardness and contradictions of our present system. Consider these fundamental structural inequities that remain to be addressed by our Movement in its new stage, because they are left unsolved even with the formal reality of legislatively-protected civil rights:

Income. Over the last 30 years the median family income among Afro-Americans has been 40–45 percent less than the median family income among whites (except for 1969 when it was 39 percent less). If black families received the same fraction of total income as their 12 percent of the total population, their cash receipts would have been $75 billion more than what they actually received in 1980. The picture of stagnation and deprivation represented by these figures unmasks the deceit behind the official propaganda about the rise of the black middle class. The number of middle-income black Americans has indeed risen; but so has the number of permanently unemployed and underemployed black workers whose jobs have been eliminated by technology or the flight of capital investment abroad. Growth without development is increasingly a characteristic of this political economy, and the growth of the middle-income stratum of Afro-Americans is being used to conceal the fact that the community as a whole is being de-developed. In any year during the entire decade of the '70s, a minimum of two million black workers were unemployed; some estimates put the figure as high as three million.

Housing. A decade ago, our Movement was demanding equal *access* to housing available for rent or sale without discrimination. Today, the national supply of moderately priced housing is totally inadequate to meet the needs of the average-income family. This shortage is not the result of our lack of access to available housing; rather it is an institutional problem involving the level of monopoly control exercised by the banks and lending agencies over the housing market. We have won an end to racial discrimination in housing, but the housing situation is generally worse today for working and middle-class people than when the Open Housing Act was passed by Congress after Dr. King's assassination. That act did not address the institutional problem of housing in America; in our new Movement, the role of the banks, and their dominant influence on the ownership of homes, farms and land, must be the focus of our actions.

Health. It is well known that the United States is the only industrially developed country, other than South Africa, that has no government-financed system of national health care, either through national health insurance or the more efficient and less costly form, a nationalized health service. To note but one example of the backwardness of our current health system, the United States, with a two-trillion-dollar Gross National Product, ranks seventeenth in infant mortality; that means sixteen other countries do a better job of saving children's lives than we do. A health-care system based on private profit is not only inefficient and elitist; it fundamentally perpetuates sickness by surviving off the catastrophic potential of an individual's disease. A mass movement demanding equal and full health care treatment for all people undercuts the very basis of the current private doctor-patient system that dominates U.S. health policy.

Energy. The private corporate ownership of a natural resource—oil, gas, coal—is another contradiction that stands in the way of solving national problems in the public interest. If there is indeed an energy crisis, then we must set up the rational conditions for the public use of oil, gas and coal in a rational way. Only public ownership—i.e., public control over the manufacture, distribution and sale of energy—allows for the rationally planned conservation and use of these natural resources. The regulatory agency as a substitute for public ownership or nationalization is, by design, inadequate. For example, the Federal Power Commission tried to regulate the price of natural gas in interstate commerce. But since the natural gas is owned by the corporate Seven Sisters, they simply refused to sell it interstate until they could get the price they demanded. So gas shortages are not real, but contrived by those manipulating the market to maximize their corporate profits. If we are serious about dealing with the energy crisis, there is no reason for us to leave the nation's energy resources in the hands of Exxon, Texaco, Continental Oil, Con Edison and other parasitic monopolies. If the public does not control the sources of energy, we cannot control the solution of the energy crisis. Thus, public ownership of public resources is the prerequisite for a solution to this national problem.

Inflation and Militarism. A major ideological hurdle is being overcome by traditional civil-rights organizations as they increasingly insist, and correctly so, that putting people to work in a full-employment economy is *not* inflationary. Yet most civil-rights organizations have still not articulated, through their leadership, the position that the military budget is the chief cause of inflation. The question of inflation versus unemployment will continue to be a nagging, tortuous reality because the U.S. economy is sick. It is up to our Movement to popularize the common root of both problems in the use of public resources for military hardware. Inflation is fueled by the wasteful expenditure of government funds for nonproductive, over-priced goods which are continually being destroyed or declared obsolete. Further, for every 1,000 jobs created by investment in military production, the same amount of money would create 1,200 jobs if invested in socially useful sectors of the economy, such as housing, schools, day-care centers and the like. Consequently, spending for the military aggravates unemployment instead of helping solve the problem. It is in the highest national interest, therefore, that the arms race and the military budget be made less attractive to those corporations and politicians whose survival depends upon war and the preparation of war. The world, too, would breathe a sigh of relief if we, the people of the United States, demanded an end to the arms race and the danger of nuclear war. A full-employment economy of socially useful peacetime work for all is the real guarantee of our national security, in contrast to the rampant parasitic militarism which escalates the arms race and pushes the world community toward nuclear annihilation.

A national movement centered on these ideas will require for its achievement the kind of in-depth renovation of the main economic and political institutions that our nation has not seen since the abolition of slave labor more than a century ago. The winning of substantial equality as the national goal of a mass movement will obviously be a protracted, drawn-out battle. It is important in this context to remind ourselves of another lesson we have learned from previous movements of Afro-Americans, women, labor, Hispanics and Native Americans: our journey will inevitably be slowed by two historical tendencies in the official policy of the government and the economic order it serves.

The first tendency is simply delay: to postpone, drag out indefinitely, as long as possible, the recognition of formal equality or equal rights. Then, when this right is formally conceded, to let that stand as the ultimate concession. Under this tendency it took the women's movement 75 years to get a constitutional amendment (1920) formally acknowledging their right to the vote—a right which didn't fully materialize until the passage of the Civil Rights Act of 1965, when black women could finally vote in the South.

The second historical tendency involves drawing the line against further gains by reintroducing regressive trends in the life of society. The re-emergence of the Ku Klux Klan, the propaganda about "reverse discrimination" and the revival of the old theories of white supremacy dressed in the new academic regalia of "socio-biology" are current examples. The airwaves are also reverberating, as in the past, with messages from the false prophets of the white Christian church in the form of an evangelical crusade—this one called the Moral Majority. Associating love of one's country with love of the free-enterprise system and support for increasing the parasitic military budget, these evangelist preachers are mobilizing the conservative wing of the Christian church in hopes of drowning out the social gospel of liberation with which the black church in the South has been so prominently identified. In the tradition of all obscurantist movements throughout history, the Moral Majority is designed to pollute the public minds with impressions that create a subservient mass base in support of ultraconservative public policy.

Nevertheless, our protracted struggle for human equality will not take as long as the 300-year struggle for civil rights because the world situation is more favorable today than ever before. The political map is being changed on a global scale by the mass movement of ordinary people who are wiping away the legacy of racism, colonialism and national oppression. Their mass movement is an irreversible force affirming the "somebody-ness" of every member of the human race. The idea of peace, justice and socially useful work for all is no longer an abstraction. Hundreds of millions of people have made this ideal a flesh-and-blood reality as they reorder the economic and political life of their societies.

It is against the backdrop of this ascendant humanism in our age that we, citizens of the United States, must measure the level of civilization we have achieved as a society and the tasks ahead of us as a movement for civil equality. Our success in confronting institutional racism in America is inescapably measured by the grim realities of continued U.S. support for such policies as apartheid in South Africa and torture in Central America. As the martyred patriot, Dr. Martin Luther King, Jr., said in his last speech, "All we are saying to America is, 'Be true to what you have said on paper.' " Consistent with this commitment to fulfill the ideals of the Declaration of Independence, our Movement's success will ultimately mean the regeneration of the United States as a civilization and its transition to higher forms of democracy. That vision gives our Movement the authority it must have to overcome the authority of the old order.

The self-interest held in common by Afro-Americans, women, organized labor, Hispanic-Americans and Native American Indians is the foundation for building a new political life in the United States today. Yet in a period in which selfish individualism is encouraged as a substitute for involvement in collective effort, we should guard against the tendency to see "self-interest" in the narrowest meaning of the term. "Be concerned about your brother," Dr. King said to the people of Memphis in his last speech. "You may not be on strike, but we go up together or we go down together." That is the spirit of unity and unselfish commitment which has guided every movement that has succeeded in winning substantial victories. And that is the spirit, affirming a global level of mutual respect and common humanity, which will provide the motive force for the authority of our new mass movement.

John O'Neal

(1940–   )

A director, playwright, poet, and actor, O'Neal was born in Mound City, Illinois. After receiving his B.A. from Southern Illinois University, he became a civil rights worker in Mississippi. Along with Gilbert Moses and Doris Derby, he founded the Free Southern Theater (FST) in 1963 as a means of using drama to awaken masses of people to the issues underlying social activism in the South. O'Neal was the only original member of FST to remain in New Orleans during the 1970s and 1980s, trying to maintain the theater as a viable enterprise. In 1985 he coordinated "A Valediction without Mourning for the Free Southern Theater 1963–1980," a conference to mark the end of an important phase in black theater history. Since that time, O'Neal has won much praise for *Don't Start Me Talking or I'll Tell You Everything I Know* and *You Can't Judge a Book by Its Cover*, one-man performances he has constructed around the character Junebug Jabbo Jones. The following article was first published in *Southern Exposure* (Spring 1981).

Art and the Movement

Culture played an important role in the Movement. There was drama and poetry, exceptional photography and an abundance of good graphic design work. Tall-tale telling was raised to new heights (which is one reason it's so hard for historians to get a clear idea of what the facts actually were). This highly developed storytelling tradition in the South serves as the foundation for the remarkable improvisational art of the preacher. Some of the finest political oratory ever created rolled from the rapturous lips of Movement pastors inspired by the passion of their congregations. And there was music! Organized and spontaneous, professional and traditional. People's music. The people gave form to emotions too deeply felt for speaking by making songs, or shouting or humming or moaning—

> *I don't know why I have to moan sometimes*
> *I don't know why I have to moan sometimes*

452

It would be a perfect day, but there's trouble
all in my way
I don't know why, but I'll know by and by.

As we reflect on the role of culture in the Civil Rights Movement, we must be mindful of how easy and pleasant it is to make romance of the past. In romance, we tend to exaggerate the emotional extremes at the expense of fact. This is not a helpful tendency. However much fun it may be to recount tales of ancient glory and shame, the value in the examination of information about past events is to help us discover patterns from which we can draw lessons for the future.

A few general observations:

- Since art can stand no taller than the philosophical ground upon which it rests, the art work of the '60s is limited by the philosophical shortsightedness of the Movement itself.
- The art and literature of black artists intellectually grounded in the period between 1918 and 1940 are generally superior to the work of artists from the '60s because of the stronger philosophical ground that oriented the movement their work reflects.
- The interplay of ideas about culture and art that occurred during the '60s is more important than the actual accomplishments of artistic work done. Consequently, the art is more important as historical data than as aesthetic product.
- The strongest art work is that which is most deeply rooted in the folk-life and traditions of the people for whom the work is created.
- The connection between the content of the work and the audience is critical. The people are the ones who make the music and the artists are the instruments they play.
- The popular art, controlled by entrepreneurs whose interests are distinct from, if not contradictory to, the interests of the masses of people, has been more influential than anything Movement artists have yet created.
- Movement artists, like the Movement itself, tended to ignore the economic terms which limit and define possibility.

Now a summary of the experiences upon which these ideas are based.

It didn't matter that most of the marquees were for second-rate skin flicks. It didn't matter that we had said to each other time and time again, "Broadway's a pointless exercise in decadence!" There we were! In The Big Apple! In spite of everything, my partner, Gilbert Moses, and I were standing in the busiest part of the Great White Way and excited to be there. There was romance and excitement that caught me by surprise.

Our object was to recruit people to join the effort to build the Free Southern Theater in Mississippi. Armed only with what we thought was the most important artistic idea of the decade, we were on the way to meet a group of actors.

Of the several people we talked to that night, I remember one actor of exceptional ability. We'd seen him perform earlier that evening. He was just the
kind of person we needed.

After we'd run down our naive but enthusiastic rap, the actor was almost
as excited as we were. "You guys have come up with a great idea!" he said,
almost bursting. "I wish I could come down there to work with you, but I
can't leave The City right now. I'M JUST ABOUT TO MAKE IT!"

Whenever I see that actor now, almost 20 years later, I can't resist the
impish impulse to ask, "Hey, man, you made it yet?"

How many times we were to hear that refrain.

That encounter typifies the problem of the arts and the Civil Rights Movement. We were caught up in and driven by forces we did not understand.

With the shameless arrogance of innocence, we charged ahead with little
respect for the struggles of our elders. "They couldn't have done much!" we
told ourselves. "If they had we wouldn't have The Problem to deal with,
would we?"

Like most of the youths who got involved in the Movement, I labored under
the mistaken idea that the only thing wrong with America was that it didn't
live up to its own standards. This idea placed severe limits on what the Movement could accomplish. It was particularly bad for artists. To create art of
sustaining value, the artist must be grounded in a comprehensive and coherent
view of the world. Mastery of skill, craft and style cannot make up for faults
in basic conception.

The Movement was a good thing. Some important changes were won as a
result of it. But if we aren't careful, we will make the mistake of separating
the Movement from history. The '60s are like the third act in a drama that
begins with the end of the Second World War and will likely end with some
other definitive event of world-wide significance like the fall of South Africa.

Act One of this historical drama starts with demands to integrate the armed
forces in the fight against Nazism. Japanese-Americans are marched off to
concentration camps in California. Then the pointless atomic destruction of
Hiroshima and Nagasaki. It ends with race riots in the streets and Joe McCarthy
beating the bushes for Communists.

Act Two takes up with the undeclared war against "Gooks and Chinks" in
Korea, includes the Supreme Court decision deposing the doctrine of "separate
but equal" in favor of "all deliberate speed," goes on to the Mau-Maus in
East Africa and ends with the Montgomery Bus Boycott.

Act Three opens with the independence of Ghana, the sit-ins spreading like
a prairie fire in brown grass, and jumps to the Freedom Rides. The price is
paid in blood, but great moral victories are won. Legal sanction for segregation
is withdrawn. It is an important but limited victory. With the March on Washington the initiative passes out of the hands of the Movement into the hands
of a liberal/labor coalition that serves as the "loyal opposition" to Corporate
America. Official Washington consolidates control over Movement leadership
by putting them on the payroll in the War on Poverty. Those who can't be

isolated, forced into exile or jailed are declared to be outlaws and are killed with or without the cover of law. Act Three ends with the assassinations of Malcolm X, the Panthers and MLK.

Act Four goes from the Poor People's March on Washington to Andy Young's rude end at the UN.

The resurgence of the Klan starts Act Five and some cataclysmic event like the fall of South Africa ends it.

As we struggled through what I've called Act Three, what we sought to be free *from* seemed clear. But, in all our terribleness, when the Movement tried to define the freedom *to* . . . the confusion spread all around. Answers to questions either faded off into infinite shades of gray or fell into bold and outrageous absurdities which were to be accepted on faith.

The Movement was not the product of a concept or program of social change. It was a spontaneous response to intolerable conditions. A great many people were mad enough to act simultaneously. It was the greatest strength and the greatest weakness at the same time. No single decapitating blow could stop it. But, as every good street-fighter knows, if you go into a fight mad, you'll probably lose. There's no guarantee that good thinking will win the fight, but it's almost certain that bad thinking will lose it.

It could not be said that our Movement was distinguished by the quality of its thought. It was dominated by philosophic chaos! That condition was probably one of the main reasons that the pragmatists were able to carry the day, pragmatism being as close as you can get to having no philosophy at all while maintaining a semblance of rationality. In profane exaggeration of the idea of democracy, anybody who didn't already know a philosophy that would suit his or her fancy was prompted to invent a new one.

In this philosophical disorder, Movement leadership—caught in a compelling sense of urgency—was defenseless before the aggressive inadequacies of pragmatism. By the spring of 1963, a coalition of national civil-rights organizations held more power than had ever been achieved by a group of black persons in America. The best among them were awed by the power and carried it with a certain virginal innocence. But, as is often the case with virgins, the confrontation came. On one hand they faced formidable political, economic and police sanctions; on the other hand, they saw what appeared to be unlimited access to government resources.

In the made-for-TV movie about Martin Luther King (played by Paul Winfield), there was at least one brief moment that had the ring of truth. Martin is in the White House trying to get LBJ to support some pending legislation. Martin asserts the justice of his cause.

LBJ: It's not about justice, Martin. It's about power.
You give me a campaign bigger than Birmingham and
I'll give you a Civil Rights Bill.

MLK: (Aghast) Dozens of people could be injured
or killed!

LBJ: (Turning mournfully to look out the window
    at the Washington Monument) I order hundreds of
    people to their deaths every day, Martin. . . .

According to the film, that's how the Selma-to-Montgomery March started.

The altruism that had characterized the early '60s faded into frustration, and frustration gave way to cynicism. By 1965, the Movement was effectively finished. A small but important minority, recognizing the insufficiency of reform, moved towards revolutionary ideologies. The majority, however, simply relinquished their claims to the high ideals that brought them to the Movement. Considering that they had paid their dues, many decided to step off the battlefield to join the establishment. Others simply dropped out.

We who work in the arts are supported by or limited by the social-political environment in which we work. When the political movement is doing well, many options and possibilities open up for us. Like every progressive political movement, the '60s liberated a great surge of creative energy. Regressive political trends tend to force the creative impulse into isolation. Dread, doom, fear, gloom and themes of sensual and erotic decadence juxtaposed to strident militarism come to the fore. Inevitably, as our Movement lost its orientation, so did most of our artists.

The general trend is especially evident in music. Music was one of the more important organizing tools of the Movement. It was used to inspire, educate, demonstrate, propagate and raise money. Every meeting had to begin and end with a song. The SNCC Freedom Singers became a popular attraction on campuses and in concert halls everywhere. In some cases traditional musicians appeared with the Freedom Singers. More often they traveled with seasoned performers like Pete Seeger and Dick Gregory. In order to structure the relationship between musicians and the Movement, the Folk Music Caravan was organized to produce concerts, festivals and other music activities in the South while continuing to work on fundraising.

The widespread interest in folk music that developed was reflective of the potency of the grassroots social movement. It was a perfect analogy. The power of spontaneous social movement, like the power of music, is more intuitive than rational. To be a part of a group of hundreds or thousands of people, marching together, singing together, united in pursuit of a purpose greater than each, yet valuable to all, is a compelling experience. It is humbling and uplifting to hear the voice of 10,000 people come out when you open your own mouth to sing. Artists who participated in such experiences were always profoundly affected, and it influenced their work.

The Movement set the tone for the popular music of the day, too. Almost all of the popular music acts had one or two recordings of "message" music. Some acts, like the Impressions, built large portions of their repertoire on Movement themes. Jazz artists like Nina Simone made extensive use of Movement material. Max Roach's *Freedom Now Suite* with Abby Lincoln on vocals is classic. One of the reasons that the Little Rock school incident is fixed so firmly in my memory is that bassist Charlie Mingus satirized the governor of Arkansas so well with his *Fables of Faubus*.

Aside from the Freedom Singers and the Folk Music Caravan, the Free Southern Theater was the only organized cultural program that developed in the Southern Movement.* Theater is so verbal and so organizationally complex that it's especially important to be clear about what you're trying to do. At the FST we were forced to think about the Movement systematically. If we were to portray relevant themes and Movement people, we had to find out what gave them their particular character. We had to look for artistic models.

At first, we overlooked one of the best sources—the wealth of oral literature created by Afro-Americans—because it didn't fit into our idea of what theater was. There are parables and animal stories for teaching children, tall tales and bawdy rhymes for adults only and everything in between. This highly developed storytelling tradition in the South also encompasses the remarkable art of improvisational preaching, of which Martin Luther King, Jr., was one of the most notable masters.

Folk art is that area of art limited least by the shortcomings of Movement thought. Because it boils up from the realities of life faced by rural and urban workers, folk art is largely insulated from the extravagant abstractions of current theoretical trends.

Maybe it did sound hip as it dripped from the lip of some silvery-tongued orator, but most of the Movement mass meeters, being well-practiced churchgoers, knew that it takes just about as much energy to turn a pretty phrase as it takes to turn a shovelful of dirt.

The Movement gained far more from the rural and urban workers than it gave back as improvements in the quality of life. The main troops of the Movement were from the rural and urban working classes. The main leadership and most of the dominating ideas came from black professionals and small property holders. As it turned out, the classes which provided the leadership were the ones to get the main benefits also.

What is true in the political and economic sphere is generally reflected in the aesthetic sphere. Since the ideas of the Movement did not correspond to the realities that people had to live through, these ideas never did filter down and take root among the masses of the people. Little damage was done to the folk culture.

The literary product generated by the Movement is voluminous. Everybody tried to write poetry. There are dozens of biographical essays. Several collections of letters, diaries, reports, etc., have been assembled. Fiction, long and short, is relatively rare.

It may be that the most important art and literature from the period have

*Liberty House/Freedom Co-ops produced and distributed hand-crafted items. To a certain extent the Freedom Schools participated in the promotion and development of cultural activities. In the North, Operation Breadbasket developed a choir and a band. The Last Poets were a product of Movement activity in the North. The Folk Music Caravan was succeeded by the Southern Grass Roots Music Tour, which continues to produce festivals and tours.

not yet been published or distributed widely. Based on the available material, it seems that there is more historical than artistic value to be found in the cultural product of the '60s. Of the material that has been published the most important are those unself-conscious personal forms: letters, diaries, reports, etc. The record of direct experience will prove invaluable as source material for future work.

A lot of exceptional photographic and graphic design work was done during the Movement for two reasons. First, the graphics industry, like the music business, is highly structured and is a well-developed part of the mass media. Photographers and graphic artists who understand and have access to it can practice their craft and make adequate income at the same time. Second, graphics is not verbal and is therefore less threatening. Like musicians, graphic artists may use words but they are not dependent on them.

Because of the large investments required, large corporations operate virtually unchallenged in TV and film industries. Blacks who become involved to a significant degree tend to be those who accept the superiority of a "market to be exploited" over an "audience to be served." The main thing that happened in consequence of the Movement was that a few black people got jobs in the industry. When the Movement began to fade, so did the strong image of black people from the screen.

When the Movement was in the press every day, it acted as a magnet to people in the commercial entertainment industry and all other levels of cultural and artistic endeavor. As the Movement lost its orientation and focus, the flow of influence was restored to its reactionary norm. Artists, instead of being drawn into the orbit of the Movement, deserted the people's struggles for the alluring illusions of the Great White Way and Tinsel-Town. The same process that robbed the Movement of its leadership, robbed the people of their artists. In too many cases the leaders, artists and scholars did not simply desert the field of struggle but actually joined the ranks of those who profit from the people's misery.

The most significant literary work done by people from this period has been done in the essay. Here is where we wade through the swirling torrents of our experiences in search of coherent formulations and our ideas are exposed to critical evaluation.

The Free Southern Theater experience fits within this general context. What we have done is good, but the artistic and political potential of our work is far greater than anything we have actually been able to do. We have not created works which adequately illuminate those values or actions which the masses of people recognize as being helpful and supportive to their struggle to improve the quality and character of our collective life. Although there are moments when we rise above it, our work has been dominated by private, ego-centered visions. Even as we address the problems of the Movement, we have seldom grasped the social, economic and historical essence of the problems we face.

At the same time we have not understood the compelling impact of economics on art. Qualitative improvement in the work requires study and practice;

these take time and time costs money. The FST, again, in correspondence to the general trend of '60s survivors, has been supported primarily by grants and contributions from foundations and government sources. This is not viable.

The political, economic and social goals of those who provide the financial base and control the process must correspond to the aims and goals of the artists. In turn, these must correspond fundamentally to the needs of those who comprise the critical audience. If these corresponding relationships don't exist, then the efforts of the artists are ultimately nullified. These two problems, the philosophic and the economic, form the axis that identifies the shortcomings of art and cultural activity in the Civil Rights Movement. The challenge for the future is to meet and solve these problems.

The longer it takes for us to gain a firm grasp of these problems, the longer it will take us to meet the responsibility before us in this historic moment. The result will be an unconscionable delay in the coming of that day when the dreams of our grandparents and their grandparents before them shall come true. If we fail in this historic moment, then the legacy of suffering we pass to our children will be increased. Our failure would increase the ultimate cost of the struggle and will postpone the time when the social order shall be transformed. Future generations wait to see if we will shoulder our share of the burden. There is no question about whether we will ultimately win. The question is how much it will cost.

John Oliver Killens
(1916–1987)

A biographical statement on John Oliver Killens appears in the fiction section. For Killens, and many black Southern writers who agree with his values, being a long-distance runner is a crucial matter. The following article first appeared in *The Black Scholar* (November 1973).

Wanted: Some Black
Long Distance Runners

It is an interesting phenomenon that we black folks, as a people, have produced some of the most magnificent athletes the world has ever known, but have produced very very few long distance runners. We've raised a whole lot of hell in the hundred and two hundred yard dashes. You watch the Olympics and you see nothing but black brothers up there at the finish tape in the sprints. We have the fastest getaway known to man or womankind. At the same time we have produced very few long distance runners. Long distance running, which requires planning, pacing, discipline and stamina, and a belief in the ability to win everything over the long haul. Lasting power is the name of the game.

When I mentioned this idea to my publisher, he didn't think too much of it. He told me, "John, you don't understand sports. The athletes are in it solely for kicks, and the sprints are where the glamor and the kicks are at. The distance is a bloody bore." I told my publisher that the kicks may very well be in the sprints and the dashes, but it was that last kick in the mile that counted. And that our struggle for liberation was indeed a *long* long distance race, for we are out for nothing short of winning the entire human race and we were up against a formidable foe, and to win this race would require planning, pacing, discipline and stamina, and a belief in our ability to win the long protracted struggle. Indeed we must construct one hundred year plans. Two hundred year plans. We must construct institutions for generations yet unborn. Black people live a hand to mouth existence and our planning for liberation tends to be from hand to mouth. But hand to mouth planning will not win the human race, will not topple this capitalistic white supremacy establishment, which is what W.E.B. DuBois was all about. I believe Dr. W.E.B. DuBois to be the most outstanding long distance runner of the twentieth century, or any other century for that matter.

The heroic struggles of the late fifties and the decade of the sixties were a series of hundred yard dashes with which some black minds and bodies thought and sought to turn the country around. Probably the first sprint was the great Montgomery saga, the bus boycott, coming as it did, after the historic victory by the N.A.A.C.P. in 1954 at the U.S. Supreme Court. Some of us thought the historic bus boycott would fundamentally change the country. Montgomery was a noble and a valiant struggle. Fifty thousand black folks, young and old, under the leadership of Sister Rosa Parks and Brothers Martin King, Ralph Abernathy and E. D. Nixon stood and walked together in the very cradle of the confederacy, withstood the vicious violent attacks of white bigots, who all along had really thought they knew their "nigrahs." White folks did a lot of head scratching at the way their happy and contented "nigrahs" were acting up, and sticking together. I was there during some of the struggle. One old white-haired head-scratching white man shook his scraggly head and told me, "They look like our nigrahs, but they doggone sure don't act like them. It's as if some other nigrahs sneaked into Montgomery in the middle of the night and took the places of our nigrahs. They look like our nigrahs," he repeated, "but they sure'n hell don't act like em." And he was as serious as a heart attack. The white folks of Montgomery were shaken to their roots. For to paraphrase Reverend Ralph Abernathy: "How could these unreconstructed crackers possibly know the New Negro when they did not even understand the old Negro who oftentimes grinned when he wasn't tickled and scratched when he did not itch?" The New Negro was all ages, eight to eighty and their theme was: "Walk together children—Doncha git weary!"

The second sprint was the Sit-Ins. Black young courageous people put their bodies on the line to integrate the two-by-four Southern restaurants, and *toilets*! Some of us thought that this would turn the country around. It didn't happen. It couldn't happen. Remember the eight young tender warriors of Little Rock? And Daisy Bates? Autherine Lucy? James Meredith? Then there were the heroic freedom riders, then voter registration, then the so-called "race" riots which I preferred to call "police" riots, since I firmly believe that many of them were provoked by the police and planned in the police stations to try out their new weapons and to waste some of our brave young black warriors, our valiant freedom fighters. Take a look at the statistics, of Watts, of Newark and Detroit. A lot of beautiful young people got wasted during those glorious times, and I am not now trying to negate their struggle or the importance of their contributions to the Movement. Indeed these struggles inspired freedom fighters around the world. And they were necessary and important phases in our development as a people in the war of liberation.

What I *am* saying is that some of us thought that one or two of these phases would topple the structure and destroy white supremacy once and for all. Well it was not about to happen that way. And when it did not happen, a lot of our young people got wasted, physically and psychologically. Some became disillusioned. Well, you do not become disillusioned unless you have illusions in the first instance. Some got disillusioned and went off into all sorts of mystical escape hatches such as new religious bags, astrology, name changing, witchcraft, blacker-than-thou champeenship bouts, and so on. Some of the mysticisms were divisive, at a time when unity was desperately needed; some of us came up with such ridiculous dogma as "putting the black woman in her place,"—"at home"—"in the kitchen"—"walking three paces behind her man." But the black freedom movement was and is for the liberation of all of us, men and women, and the whole attitude was a denial of Harriet Tubman and Sojourner Truth and Gwen Brooks and Margaret Walker, my mother and your mother, and all the other black women who have lent their love and strength to us down through the years. And the only way we can possibly win is for women and men to march hand in hand together down the road to liberation.

Some of us followed the white youth into their "Do your own thing bag," which was but another version of the terrible American tradition of every man for himself and do others before they do you. Yet another version of "rugged individualism," which was how the West was won, or lost, depending on your point of view. Some blacks tripped out to Haight Ashbury or down to Greenwich Village and joined white youth in the drug culture, seeking what they thought to be revolutionary insights. But "spacing" could reap us no revolutionary insights, since there are none out in space. And if "nation time" means anything, it means land, good sweet black earth; there is no land out there in space except possibly the moon, which the European has already staked out with the Star-Spangled Banner.

Again, some of us followed the white youth into so-called generation gaps. Some young folks thought that nothing had happened in the Movement until two or three hours before or after they joined the issue. Black folk cannot afford the middle-class luxury of generation gaps. We need all the forces we can gather, men and women, old and young, united in this struggle. As I've said before, "Let the white youth have their generation gaps. Most probably it is the only humanistic thing they still have going for them."

Yes, we had illusions. Most of us had. But black folks at this junction can ill afford illusions. Yet they still keep cropping up, such as the recent myth of Black Capitalism, which is yet another get-rich-quick finishing tape. What does the Negro want? Some black leaders have, historically, answered, *We want everything you got. We want integration.* Well if the U.S. of A is one great capitalistic whorehouse, I'll be damned if I want into it, and if this whorehouse is syphilis-ridden, I'll be damned if I want any part of it. I don't want a piece of the action. I want to change the action. And that is what William Edward Burghardt DuBois dedicated his entire life to. That is what this long distance runner struggled for. This is the race he fought to win.

But in the late fifties we were conned into thinking we were in a fundamental revolution. It was a time coming on the heels of McCarthyism, when the word revolution was anathema, a dirty word, the use of which could get you called before one of those Congressional Committees, and you could lose your means of livelihood. You could even lose your life. You would have thought that the phony Revolutionary War of '76 had never been fought. Then a clever white Establishment sage told the world and black people that what the rest of America did not understand was that the Negroes were in a revolution. I believe his name was Eric Severeid. And some of us blacks went around with our chest poked out saying, "Yeah! Like man we're in a revolution. Like man, we're revolutionaries."

The white boy had conned us one more time. Because you see if you are already in a revolution, you do not need to make a revolution. Even the venerable N.A.A.C.P. got carried away and came up with the over optimistic slogan: *Free in Sixty Three*. NO WAY. And even though Martin Luther King must have known better, in the excitement and heady freedom wine we were consumed with in those days he came up with his famous speech. *"Three Little Words*. We want it *all*! We want it *here*! We want it *now*." He knew that powerful institutions like the U.S. of A. do not topple that easily.

I recall the last time I saw another great long distance runner of this century. I refer to that great black all-American, Paul Robeson. I said to him, "Brother Paul, to every black artist with a heart or memory, you are the Big Daddy and Dr. DuBois is the Big Granddaddy." And yet some of our young folk do not know Big Paul, the athletic, intellectual, artistic, masculine giant and genius of the Twentieth Century. We need our heroes desperately.

I vividly recall the first time I was in Dr. DuBois' home and stared in respectful awe at a veritable library of books, an institution of black erudition, and underneath the title of almost every book was the name, W.E.B. DuBois, some of which were published in the 19th Century. It was an inspiring, though chastening experience. Here is what I mean by long distance running. For with his books he had constructed an institution that would stand against the ravages of time, would inspire generations to come and help them to understand the task that lay ahead of them. Planning, pacing, discipline, stamina, faith in the future and a black victory—in a Great Gittin' Up Morning. A portrait of a long distance runner. This was the man, W.E.B. DuBois. Lest I be misunderstood, when I speak of DuBois as a long distance runner, I am not alluding *only* to his great life's longevity, though that is certainly part of the portrait. I also refer to the institutions that he constructed: The Atlanta School of Social Work, The *Crisis* Magazine; the torch that has been taken and forged forward by Henry Lee Moon; I mean DuBois, a founder of the Niagara Movement, forerunner of the National Association for the Advancement of Colored People; I mean The Encyclopedia Africana which he began in Ghana at the age of 93.

And so in his tradition, we must evolve a generation of long distance runners, men and women prepared to pay some dues for their children's children's children's children. Our people have paid some terrible dues for us to have come to this place and this moment in time and space.

Another hundred yard dash which was an integral part of the smoking sixties was what I call the Rap Revolution, with apologies to our good friend, Brother H. Rap Brown. We were going to rap our way to liberation. As I tell my students at Howard University. It should be clear to one and all that the Rap Revolution is *over*. It should also be clear by now that we are not going to rap the white boy into liberation. But we did an awful lot of rapping during the sixties. If rap were uranium or dynamite, we would have blown this planet up to the moon, and spared this country the wasteful and perverted expense of the Lunar Module.

We are up against the greatest amassment of power and sophistication the world has ever known. Sophistication is a very important aspect of this struggle. It's the thing we have got to carefully watch. We rap about revolution, and they come up with the *Dodge Rebellion*. We call for Black Power and they come up with *Pucker Power*. The President of the United States of America comes before nation-wide television at Howard University and tells us, *We shall overcome*. Tricky Dick gives us back the slogan, "Power to the People!"

There must be men and women willing to do the unglamorous work of building for our posterity long distance institutions. So many of us are overly concerned with our T.V. images. Understand that if you are really T.C. Bing, doing some real long distance running, hundred year planning, you will probably get very little exposure over the Establishment's idiot box, which is just as well. Understand also that television belongs to the Establishment. It is its most powerful all-pervasive communication weapon. And the Establishment is not about to give a serious black long distance runner a weapon to defeat it with. The late Lorraine Hansbury once told me that her motto was: Whenever she got on television or radio to deport herself as if she did not want to be invited back. Sound advice.

There were some long distance runners constructing for their posterity during the last two decades, such as Hoyt Fuller, and his *Black World* and OBACI. Nathan Hare gave us the *Black Scholar* magazine. Vincent Harding and Bill Strickland worked tirelessly to give us the Institute of the Black World. From the inspiration of Dr. W.E.B. DuBois and Shirley DuBois came *Freedomways* magazine which was maintained by the hard work and dedication of John H. Clarke and Esther Jackson. Brother Martin and Brother Malcolm were long distance runners, which is why they were gunned down so early in the race. There is an old Chinese proverb that says: "A man's life is like a candle in the wind." We must make every moment of it count for something. Never say you didn't have time. There is no more time on earth. Make sure of your priorities. Check them out constantly, monthly, weekly.

Nothing will take the place of hard consistent work. Planning, pacing, discipline, stamina, an undying faith that the future will be ours, but that we must work for it and we must take it. It will not be given to us. This is the meaning of DuBois' life. This is the profoundest meaning of what Frederick Douglass meant when he said, "Without struggle, there is no progress." When he said: "Men of color, to Arms! Who would be free must themselves strike the blow." DuBois' life was dedicated to the destruction of capitalism and its handmaiden whore, white supremacy. Black film exploitation to the contrary, we must not be the pimps for this whorish society. DuBois was committed to construct a society that would be man-oriented. We live in a society that is thing-oriented. Call it socialism, call it Pan-Africanism. Call it a cooperative society. Call it Nyerere's African Ujamaa. DuBois worked tirelessly for a society in which men and women would be the master of things and not things the master of men and women.

Chancellor Williams in his great book, *The Destruction of Black Civilization*, teaches us that white men came into knowing full well that their plans would not come into fruition in their time or in their children's children's time. But that eventually, Black Egypt, the cradle of civilization would be in white hands. White power would prevail.

I am certain that, by now, you know that when I speak of long distance running, I am not referring to the Olympics or the Penn Relays. I am talking about the nitty gritty unglamorous world of discipline, planning, pacing and the building of institutions that will be left as a legacy to our posterity, to black generations yet unborn. If I read Chancellor Williams right, he said that ancient African civilizations spent far too much time, energy, money and resources constructing pyramids and monuments to the dead and not enough for their posterity.

To set the record straight, I am not now, nor was I ever, an advocate of gradualism. Of course, we want it all! We want it here! We want it now! But to paraphrase Martin King: We must realize that fundamental change will not come overnight, but we must work as if it is a possibility the next morning. But we are mature enough to know that it ain't gonna happen that way. Gil Scott-Heron is right. The Revolution will not happen on television. One faithless cynical brother commented, "Maybe that's the only place it'll ever happen."

Notwithstanding, we must keep the faith. We must believe in our people's will to survive and overcome. So many of our sprinters have run out of faith and steam and have fallen by the wayside. Some of our tigers and panthers of the roaring '60's have become toothless pussycats. They had illusions of a get-rich-quick victory, but did not have enough faith in our people and their strength and their indomitable spirit. And their will to win the human race.

Nevertheless, in the tradition of Preacher Nat and Denmark Vesey and Gabriel Prosser, W.E.B. DuBois, Paul Robeson, Martin King and Brother Malcolm, we must be prepared to pay some terrible dues for our posterity who are a hundred years away in time and space.

Everything points to the decline of this cancerous civilization; the loss of face and the loss of the War in Vietnam, the narcotics epidemic, the rise in flamboyant homosexuality, rising unemployment during a major war, the orbiting cost of living creating problems even for the middle classes. Go along New York City's honky-tonk Forty Second Street and the stench of decadence is all pervasive, overflowing onto the avenue. One can easily believe that here is a civilization heading gayly down the drain. Wish fulfillment could have some of us blacks believe that all we have to do is to sweat this one out. Stand still and watch it go. But there is ample evidence that some of us are determined to go down the drain along with it. But why should you go down with the sinking ship? You have never been the captain. Black men limping along in high heel shoes. The process hair-do creeping back into vogue. Glorification by black artists of the whore, pimp and pushers. Black people, this white whorehouse is rotting, cracking at the seams. Don't go down with it. Come, brothers, sisters, let's put our shoulders together and give it a shove. Remember the song of your slave ancestors. "If I had my way, If I had my way, lil chillun, I'd bring this building down!"

In a way, we must be like termites working consistently and sometimes quietly away at the foundation of the status quo which has ever been the bane of black existence. Like the man who swiped at the other man with a razor and the fellow said, "Ah! You missed me!" And the other cat answered, "Shake your head."

So let us fantasize a toast to William Edward Burghardt DuBois, greatest of long distance runners. Let us also toast a new generation of black long distance runners in their great and glorious tradition.

Thomas C. Dent

(1932–   )

Biographical note appears on p. 298.

Annie Devine Remembers

Last spring, while driving through Mississippi en route from Memphis to New Orleans, I reflected on the beauty of the rolling green hills, the plethora of fast food restaurants, the similarity of the highway to others in the United States.

As I noted the names on the exit turnoffs—*Hernando*, *Oxford*, *Holly Springs*, *Marks*, *Cleveland*, *Greenwood*—it seemed almost unbelievable that a few years ago these names had held so much meaning in the civil rights wars of Mississippi. They were names that brought forth poignant memories, each with its own story. Now, only a few years later, it seemed that nothing had ever happened in these towns; seeing them now was like waking from an especially frightening and intense nightmare—or was the nightmare real and this now lazy, peaceful land a dream?

I reflected that 19 years had passed since the murder of Medgar Evers and 12 years since the killing of Martin Luther King. These deaths are watermarks by which black southerners mark the passing of years and sometimes progress, or the lack of it. In my case, each of these deaths is tied inextricably to Mississippi. I had known Medgar Evers, while I was working with the Legal Defense Fund, as a man whom I felt safest with, more than any other in Mississippi. How absurd it seemed that someone so unmindful of danger and threats could be killed. My earliest mature memories of driving through Mississippi were with Medgar. The day King was killed I had driven through tornado warnings from New Orleans to Mary Holmes College in West Point, Miss., to teach a class in Afro-American literature. It was an evil day, and I had wondered if keeping an appointment to teach a class was worth the trip. I recalled vividly that community leaders John Buffington and Cliff Whitley had been so involved in the struggle to qualify Whitley as a candidate for political office, the demands and the needs of the Clay County, Miss., struggle so pressing, that it had taken a long time for the news that King had been shot to sink in. The Mississippi struggle had its own imperatives.

467

Now, as I was driving, I wondered whether Mississippi—this strange, for-saken, legendary, fearful place—had *really* changed, could ever really change.

I decided during that drive to return to Mississippi and talk to people who were in Mississippi when the struggle began in the sixties, were intimately involved in the movement and were still in the state. I wondered what *they* thought of Mississippi now.

I mentioned this idea to former SNCC leader Ed Brown, a veteran of the Mississippi wars. Ed Brown works in Atlanta now, but he founded the post-Movement organization, MACE, the Mississippi Action for Community Educa-tion, a successful economic development project situated in the poverty-stricken Delta. "You couldn't do better," he said, "than to go to Canton and talk with Annie Devine."

I knew that Canton had had a reputation as a bastion of segregation. I knew Mrs. Devine had been one of the leaders of the Freedom Democratic Party. Though I had never met Mrs. Devine, I also knew that she was something of an underground legend of the Mississippi movement. Not as widely known as her close friend and associate, the late Fannie Lou Hamer, she was nonetheless known by everyone who worked in Mississippi, and highly esteemed for her commitment and honesty. I knew, too, that Canton had been a "CORE" town. (The Movement had divided Mississippi into territories which were assigned to the key civil rights groups, SNCC, CORE and the NAACP. However, progressive NAACP state leaders like Medgar Evers, Aaron Henry and Amzie Moore worked with both SNCC and CORE, and by 1964 there was consider-able coordination among groups in the state.) New Orleans had also been CORE territory; several of the New Orleans civil rights "family" had received their fiery baptisms in Canton.

"There wouldn't have been no movement in Canton without Mrs. Devine," said Ed Brown. He called her on the telephone, telling her that I was "one of *our* guys."

It takes just an hour to drive from New Orleans to the Mississippi state line and only four hours from there to Canton, but it takes far longer to adjust to the different landscape. For example, in New Orleans the colors of Black people are incredibly diverse, ranging from very light to very dark with all variations of hair, and in New Orleans the manifestations of racism are subtle and full of strange contradictions. In Mississippi, there is greater uniformity of skin color among our people, which symbolizes the state's social reality. Matters are more or less black or white.

In New Orleans black culture, a certain joie de vivre marks even the most serious matters—funerals, for instance; whereas the unrelenting repression Blacks have experienced in Mississippi has lent to their milieu more the rich pathos of Delta blues. Perceived as "frivolous" by many hard-working, puri-tanical southern black leaders, life in black New Orleans has permitted imagi-native fantasies and dreams about racial identity and life's possibilities; but in Mississippi, life for Blacks has been far more proscribed.

*   *   *

Annie Devine lives in a small brick house on the outskirts of Canton, about 25 miles north of Jackson. She is a short woman in her late sixties, deliberate in her motions and direct in her speech. Despite her sense of grace, I could see that she might make some people feel very nervous. Small talk is not one of Mrs. Devine's gifts.

The photographs adorning Annie Devine's home reflect the primary concerns of many Black women her age: they feature her two daughters and two sons, all grown and living elsewhere, and her church. There are no noticeable civil rights mementoes.

When I asked her how she felt about the seventies and eighties, what kind of progress she feels black folk have made in Mississippi, she smiled. "It is a *strange* time," she said. "Of course we *have* made progress, but it's difficult to figure out just where."

Riding through downtown Canton, one sees that Black people, especially teenagers, have a strong presence, especially on weekends. The young people shop in the stores, their soft, musical accents rippling the air, as if there had never been a problem; while older people sit and appear to be waiting for something to happen. If the youngsters strolling the streets don't recognize your car, they may look up hopefully, for they lack that look of despair so characteristic of northern ghettos.

Here are young people who have little personal knowledge of the Mississippi movement struggles that were waged on these very streets. For the first time, we have a generation now in school that is for the most part unfamiliar with names like King, Evers, Stokely, Wilkins, Young, Rap, Meredith. They know nothing of Montgomery, Selma, Birmingham, the Mississippi Freedom Summer.

Mrs. Devine comments on the most common measure of southern racial progress—the number of political offices won by Blacks: "Too often the allegiances of these politicians are to the white power structure, not to the black community." We discuss the fact that although a few more Blacks are employed, so many of the jobs came from federal programs. "In a place like Madison County [where Canton is located], 200 or so jobs obviously make a difference," said Mrs. Devine. But she expressed mixed feelings about these jobs: "On the one hand people need the money; on the other hand so many people have become satisfied with the situation as it is now, there's not much drive to better the community. The thinking is 'don't rock the boat.' "

What about the "progress" of school desegregation, one of the strongest objectives of the civil rights struggle. Indeed, the successful legal attack on segregated schools was really the beginning of the end of the segregated South. "The problems have been numerous. Under desegregation black teachers and administrators have lost even the limited controls they maintained under segregation. We can't return to segregation, but in a lot of cases the schools now are worse than they were 20 years ago. Also, many of the best public schools today are the ones that remained all-Black. That might go against popular belief, but that's true."

"Throughout Mississippi," Mrs. Devine adds, "black principals from the old black schools were reassigned as assistant principals under desegregation; fine black coaches were made assistant coaches. Whites got the senior authority." As a former school teacher, Mrs. Devine is particularly interested in what has happened to the public schools. "In the old days there were a few black teachers who cared about what our children learned and how they behaved, though there should have been more. Who cares today? Who makes sure that our students learn? I'm not even sure there's anyone who cares about whether they're actually in school."

All over Mississippi, white children who can afford it go to the private high schools that were set up to avoid desegregation. The result is a depleted tax base for public education, with no interest among wealthy whites in public schools since their children don't attend them. In effect, the public schools have been abandoned to the poor and the Black. Courses in black history, and extracurricular programs designed to involve the black community, often quite common in the old "black" schools, are now anathema. Many white administrators consider courses or programs exhibiting black consciousness or pride to be detrimental to "racial harmony." "Where," asks Mrs. Devine, "in the black community today do we gather to discuss issues and develop policies about matters that are crucial to our community?"

Annie Devine has lived in Canton since she was a child, raised there by an aunt after her mother died. "We were just among the poorest of the poor," she says. After completing high school she worked briefly for a black printer. She married in the early forties and bore two daughters and two sons. Eventually her husband moved north, leaving her with the task of raising their four children.

She taught elementary school in nearby Flora, which paid 35 dollars a week: "It was never a matter of doing something I wanted to do, or felt particularly qualified to do." She taught for eight years. During those years, she took classes at Tougaloo College to upgrade her education. In the middle fifties, she left the school system to sell insurance for a Jackson-based company. Mrs. Devine was struggling as an independent insurance agent and living in a federal housing project when the first CORE workers came to Canton in early 1962.

In the 19th century, Canton had developed into a prosperous cotton marketing center where, as elsewhere in Mississippi, the white owners of the town ruled over the 70 percent black population with absolute authority. And as elsewhere, any black person in Canton who took on the burden of fighting for black rights, or even protesting, was literally courting death and might have to get out of the state by sundown. Blacks owned 40 percent of the land in Madison County, but out of a population of approximately 30,000 Blacks only 150 to 200 were registered to vote. Of these, less than half actually voted.

Against this background, it should be noted that the Civil Rights Movement of the sixties also sought to change the psychology engendered by conditions such as the above, which were widespread and historical. A psychological revolution became possible precisely because the Movement was broader in scope than a city or region or state or personal grievance. It offered, for the first time in the 20th century, a large and basically spiritual unity to those who would challenge the power structure. Growing Movement participation promised that individual and local protests against injustice, previously so isolated and sporadic, could now be part of a bridge that spanned the entire Southland in a new broad-based battle for social change.

The first CORE volunteer to attempt a voter registration drive in the sleepy town of Canton was George Raymond, who was barely in his twenties and a native of New Orleans. His story really needs fuller telling than is possible here for he is a true unsung hero of the Movement. It was Raymond, with a style of bravado and fearlessness, who captured the imagination of Canton's young people and got the Movement going. It is interesting, however, that as the Movement in Canton blossomed, Raymond's influence decreased; finally, he became sidetracked in the late sixties. He remained in Canton, but Movement activity there and across the state was slowing to a halt. He suffered a serious heart attack in 1969 and died in New Orleans in 1970 from a follow-up attack. He was not yet thirty. In effect, he devoted his entire adult life to the black community of Canton, Mississippi.

Raymond's first task had been to convince Blacks to go to the Canton courthouse to register. The problem there was Foote Campbell, the County Circuit Clerk, who used his multifaceted and imaginative "constitutional interpretation test" to fail Blacks who attempted to register. In addition, after registration drives began through CORE's efforts, the Canton town square was often filled with hostile, armed whites from all over the county. Police harassment was constant. In a small town like Canton, special note was taken of any Black person who joined the registration struggle.

Since fear was pervasive, Raymond and the early CORE volunteers did not receive a warm reception from the adult black community. The first strong adult supporter of CORE was C. O. Chinn, a local cafe owner and businessman, another unsung hero of the Movement. Chinn took the lead in providing CORE workers with housing, food and transportation. "When George had to go somewhere, Chinn took him. When he needed protection, Chinn, who was known to be fearless, protected him. When he and the other workers needed somewhere to sleep, Chinn found beds," remembers Mathew Suarez of New Orleans, who joined Canton CORE soon after Raymond arrived.

The Movement could not have secured a foothold in Canton without Chinn's support, and it is a measure of Chinn's sacrifice that he is said to have suffered the loss of almost all his financial holdings because he aided the CORE volunteers. He was also jailed. Annie Moody, a former Tougaloo student and author of the excellent *Coming of Age in Mississippi*, which deals at length with the Canton struggle during her involvement there, said that at one point Chinn himself had to go on the meager CORE salary of 35 dollars a week.

Annie Devine's decision, very soon after Raymond arrived, to quit her job and commit herself to the freedom struggle as a CORE staff member was

extremely important in gaining for CORE another level of black community
support. As a mature and soft-spoken woman, mother, former school teacher,
well-connected insurance agent and churchwoman, Mrs. Devine represented
the respectable center of the black community, and must have set a striking
example for those adults who were afraid to step forward. In contrast, Chinn
was a bar owner, opinionated and regarded as something of an outlaw. Thus,
the Chinn/Devine alliance in support of CORE and the Movement symbolized
the unification of the black community and provided the Canton Movement
with an important and unusual legitimacy in the history of the southern civil
rights struggle.

George Raymond and Annie Moody invited Annie Devine to her first Movement meeting. She recalls:

> The meeting was at Pleasant Green Holiness Church on Walnut Street. When
> I arrived there were police cars everywhere. There were cars of roving whites
> for blocks as far as you could see. About a dozen policemen were milling
> about the church grounds.
>
> After the meeting the police went to each car to ask questions; they already
> had our tag numbers. They were taking down names, addresses and jobs. I
> was in George Raymond's car when one of the six policemen got to me.
> He asked me my name. I said, *"Mrs.* Devine." He seemed to stiffen. He
> asked me where I lived. I told him the name of the project where I was
> living. He said, "Well, you won't be living there tomorrow."

Remembering this incident vividly, she says,

> It made me *very* angry, very hurt. I didn't tell the children anything when
> I got home, but I didn't sleep that night. With four children, where was I
> supposed to go if I was forced to move?
>
> When it came time to pay the rent I didn't have the money. When I went
> to tell the woman in the office, who was white, she said something like
> "Well, it seems as if you have time for everything else, so I hear." I knew
> she had been informed I had gone to a Movement meeting.
>
> I think I made a decision right there. If I was going to be harassed, be
> made to move just because I went to a meeting, then I was already *in* the
> Movement. I was either going to be a part of it or out of it, and I wanted
> to be a part of it. Because something had to be done *now*."

After successfully protesting an effort to evict her, Mrs. Devine resigned
from her insurance job and went to work for CORE. She was 50 years old.
Her friends in church and other people who had known her probably thought
she had lost her mind. Her daughter Monique says that Mrs. Devine's friends
couldn't understand why she had to become so "personally involved." But
Mrs. Devine's decision probably changed the course of the struggle in Madison
County.

"We were young and full of energy," says Suarez. "We were trying to
bust down brick walls by running our heads through them. We understood

very little about Mississippi and how whites and Blacks related to each other. All of us had come from larger towns and cities." Mrs. Devine "knew her community and understood it," adds Suarez. "She knew what we could get away with and what we could not, who to talk to, who to trust. Too often we tried to intimidate people into becoming involved. She agreed with our goals, but she believed in approaching people with more subtlety and sensitivity, and she was more successful. She could reach people by saying, 'You should do such-and-such because you *know* what has happened around here, you know it better than anyone else.' "

Attorney Dave Dennis of Lafayette, Louisiana, who was then director of the CORE Mississippi project, notes that "Mrs. Devine's strength was not manifested through words but through actions. She was a catalyst in a quiet but extremely effective way."

It was not long before Mrs. Devine's involvement became statewide. By 1964 she was attending regional meetings throughout the state, and in the spring of that unforgettable year she played a key role in forming the Council of Federated Organizations (COFO), the new supra-organization created to coordinate the efforts of Mississippi civil rights groups.

The objective of COFO was to sharply increase the number of volunteer civil rights workers in the state. A large-scale recruitment was planned for the summer of 1964, to be called Freedom Summer. A two-week recruitment session, held in May at Oxford, Ohio, was attended by Mrs. Devine as the representative from Madison County. More should be written about the intense sessions at Oxford and about Freedom Summer itself, for they were the arenas in which all the future directions and divisions within the Movement surfaced.

Mrs. Devine brought some 20 volunteers back from Oxford to Madison County. June 1964 was a fearsome time because of the disappearances of civil rights workers James Chaney, Andrew Goodman and Mickey Schwerner while on a trip to Neshoba County, just a few miles east of Canton. (Later that summer their bodies were found near Philadelphia, Mississippi. This was the Klan's answer to Freedom Summer!) Dr. Rudy Lombard of New Orleans was one of Mrs. Devine's Canton recruits. He remembers, with amusement, "I had no intention of working in Mississippi that summer. I went to Oxford on the urging of friends from the New Orleans Movement, but I planned to return to school to work on my degree. Somehow I ended up in Mrs. Devine's sessions. Then just before we left, she looked me in the eye and said 'Rudy, I *know* you won't deny us the benefit of your talents in Canton this summer. I'm depending on you.' I knew I was trapped. No way I could turn that woman down."

No Freedom Summer activity was more significant than the creation of the legendary Freedom Democratic Party (FDP). The FDP was an attempt to utilize the black voting strength that was developing out of the statewide voter registration drives. The FDP set as its goal a challenge to the legitimacy of the lily-white, regular Democratic Party of Mississippi at the Democratic National Convention in Atlantic City in August 1964.

Annie Devine was involved in forming the FDP, as were her close friends and co-workers, Fannie Lou Hamer of Sunflower County and Victoria Gray of Forrest County. The attempt to put FDP together was not taken lightly by state officials. Mrs. Devine recalls: "We were harassed just trying to meet. Meetings were broken up. Workers were followed. Organizers were arrested. And the harassment hurt us. When someone was arrested, for instance, we had to find money to put up bail, which was a problem. In Canton, we were getting so much heat we moved our meetings out in the county where we had a better chance of meeting unmolested."

At the FDP organizing convention in Jackson in July 1964, Mrs. Devine was one of the 68 delegates chosen to travel to Atlantic City for the Democratic Party challenge. Aaron Henry, state NAACP president then and now, was elected chair of the delegation. What happened at Atlantic City that August also deserves a book. Some readers may remember Mrs. Hamer on television speaking at Convention Hall, testifying unforgettably about the brutal racial realities of Mississippi. Then, she was preempted for a statement by President Johnson, designed, many feel, to push Mrs. Hamer's moving appeal off the screen.

The issues at stake in the challenge made by the FDP in Atlantic City were complex. However, briefly, the FDP was offered a compromise by the national party leaders which allowed for only two of the 68 delegates to be seated along with the regular Mississippi Democratic delegation. This offer sparked a bitter debate within the FDP between those who wanted to accept the compromise and those who thought two delegates were far too few. Mrs. Devine, along with Hamer and Gray, were leaders of the faction that voted to reject the compromise; Aaron Henry led the faction that voted to accept. The FDP challenge had received much northern liberal support and was the focus of extensive media coverage. Most of the liberal whites argued for acceptance on the basis that two delegates represented a meaningful victory. But when the vote was taken, the majority voted to reject. "We felt," says Mrs. Devine, "the compromise left us right where we were. It didn't give us any leverage at all."

So the FDP delegates returned to Mississippi determined to continue challenging the credentials of the state party's delegation when Congress convened in January 1965. But the split that developed at Atlantic City continued to widen once people were back in Mississippi. Generally, the contending groups were, on one side, "newcomers" to state activism like Hamer, Mrs. Devine and others who were products of the new civil rights organizations like SNCC and CORE; and on the other side, traditional state civil rights leaders best symbolized by Mr. Henry. Many observers testify to Mrs. Devine's efforts at mediating the dispute, and to her attempts to hold the organization together after most of the traditional leaders had left. "There were people," she says, smiling, "who said if they had known what they were getting into they wouldn't have become involved. I felt I understood what I was getting into. If we were going to make any progress, we had to follow through with political organization, whatever the consequences."

During the fall of 1964, a revamped FDP decided to challenge the seats of five Mississippi congressmen. Mrs. Devine was selected as challenger from the Fourth Congressional District. Hamer and Gray were chosen as challengers from their districts. A national support committee was organized in Washington to fund and publicize the effort, which was expected to be given a hearing in January 1965 in Washington by the Congressional Credentials Committee.

However, when the FDP challenge was presented in January, Mrs. Devine and company found themselves face to face with the U.S. political establishment and a national Democratic Party that was not at all enthusiastic about removing any of the five incumbent Mississippi Congressmen. Six hundred black Mississippians were bused to Washington in support of the FDPers, but their supporters were not even allowed in the halls of Congress. The FDP was told that it would be "a long time" before the Credentials Committee could get around to hearing them. In fact, they had to wait exactly *eight months*. Devine, Hamer and Gray rented an apartment in Washington as hearing date after hearing date was postponed.

Finally, on Sept. 17, 1965, the FDP challenge was heard and summarily rejected. Mrs. Devine remembers that during the hearing one of the Mississippi Congressmen, whose seat was being challenged, shouted that he "didn't have to sit here and listen to this stuff." At the end of the hearing Fannie Lou Hamer made a beautiful statement, according to Mrs. Devine. "She said no matter how the nation looked on this challenge, we weren't there to play. We were there because we wanted the nation to know it was sick. Everything we testified to was true. 'I hope,' Mrs. Hamer said, 'I live long enough to see some changes made, some hearts soften, some people begin to do some right things in Mississippi.' "

The Freedom Democratic Party was unique among black political movements because it never lost its integrity as a people's movement. The strength and vision of the FDP stand in stark contrast to some of the conservative and compromised-almost-beyond-recognition black elected politicians of the current period. The three great women who helped build FDP and keep it true to the needs of the people were Fannie Lou Hamer, Victoria Gray and Annie Devine. Ed Brown, a SNCC leader in those days, calls Mrs. Hamer "the spokeswoman," Mrs. Gray "the strategist" and Mrs. Devine "the unifier." "Within the specific context of what went on, Mrs. Devine was an unsung heroine because her role was one that did not draw public attention." Rev. Harry Bowie of McComb, formerly a leader of the Delta Ministry, assesses Mrs. Devine's contribution to the struggles of those days by noting: "Too often we view leadership in the black community only in terms of spokesmanship. But there is another kind of leadership that comes from day-to-day, unpublicized and dedicated work. We need to value this quality more in our communities."

Facing the eighties, Mrs. Devine, like many other Movement veterans, sees a falling off of commitment: "Somehow we've been steered away from the objectives of the Movement." There has been progress, "particularly in the minds of youth," but she feels that progress for Blacks in the South has in many ways been more superficial than substantive. "Economically, Black people are weak. Politically, there is little that black communities control. Culturally, we are still struggling to find and have confidence in ourselves. There is no unity of direction. Sometimes I fear," she laughs, "that the Movement opened Pandora's box."

She does not idle her time away. She worked in a community program until retiring in 1977 ("I'm a senior citizen, you know") and continues to be active as one of the founding board members of the Greenville-based Delta Foundation. Of the "three great women" of the sixties, only she remains in the state. Mrs. Gray now lives in Virginia, and the unforgettable Fannie Lou Hamer died in her home at Ruleville in March of 1977.

Leaving Mississippi to return to New Orleans, I pondered the nature of the harvest sown by the struggles of Black people in Mississippi and the South. For sure, it is difficult to assess current "progress"; things are not, as Mrs. Devine suggested, what they seem. Of course, more Blacks vote; there are more Black elected officials; more Blacks are getting higher wages; and much of the racism that was rampant in the South has been pushed to the rear of our collective consciousness. Unquestionably, these conditions represent substantial change and progress over conditions 50 or even 25 years ago.

On the other hand, unemployment among Blacks today is higher than at any time since the Great Depression, particularly in the cities. The greater presence of Blacks in politics has not been able to turn our disastrous economic condition around. Organizational efforts by Blacks to produce change have slowed to a halt, while the U.S. has become increasingly conservative and unwilling to address fundamental economic inequities and social injustice, symbolized by the election and policies of Ronald Reagan.

The deeper meaning of the sacrifices of Annie Devine and others like her, who were not ordained or recognized as national leaders, suggests to us in 1982 that effective leadership can and must come from people who are interested and who care; that a real movement in the future will be forged by committed, knowledgeable individuals, not by some great mythic leader who will descend upon us like a comet from afar. Mrs. Devine's story and the stories of other Mississippians who devoted themselves to the sixties Movement instruct that social progress derives from a sense of personal sacrifice on the part of a dedicated few. Perhaps part of our problem today is that we have lost the sense of how leadership develops, how a movement for social change develops. Everything we know about the sixties tells us that movements emerge when enough people in a society take upon themselves the responsibility of effecting change without being told by someone "above" them that it must be done. In reality, the committed show the leaders where to lead. All great leaders know how to listen to the hearts and voices of the people and synthesize what they hear, as the gifted Martin Luther King did, into a collective, eloquent expression of aspiration and purpose.

Finally, the value of black history lies in its lessons for survival. If we can forget a history so recent as the heroic struggles of our people two decades ago, then no wonder our ship is now rudderless. To know how we can better our condition, we have to know how we did it before. To know in what direction we must move, we have to know the details of our tortuous journey from whence we came to where we are now. History is not in the library; history was, is and will be our lives.

Nearing New Orleans, which has such a curious spiritual tie to Canton, I felt that what is happening to Mississippi is that it is becoming more like New Orleans—more subtle and contradictory. Mrs. Devine mentioned Pandora's box. A trick bag. It may be that if we don't take on the responsibility of interpreting our journeys in America, we will drown in the glitter of her promises and fantasies, never knowing what happened to us or what we struggled for.

The Ethics of Living Jim → The Exiled Return
1) Comment on Murray's Attitude (His South). ger & Shame Theme.
2) Your response. Is he trapped within a mythology
3) Establish linkage w/other texts. of The South?
                                   The memory He Carries
Albert Murray
(1916–) ⑥ How do these
(nonfiction pieces) autobiographical pieces
4) Al Murray illuminate
    + obs. made in the imaginative
William Mackey
As Scholarship Boys
Naipaul, House for Mr. Biswas; A Turn in The South
    Sugar Cane Alley.
5) Murray + Mackey, Search for The "guts" of history (506)
What do they discover? (learn) (organizing Themes)

After retiring from the U.S. Air Force as a major in 1962, Murray devoted
himself to a career as a novelist, literary and culture critic, and essayist.
He was born in Nokomis, Alabama, and received his B.S. from Tuskegee
Institute and his M.A. from New York University. He draws frequently on
his Southern background in his work, especially in the autobiographical
South to a Very Old Place (1971) and the lyric novels *Train Whistle Guitar*
(1974) and *The Spyglass Tree* (1991). In a prose style that resonates
with the grace for which Ralph Ellison set a pattern, Murray champions
the expressive culture of black Americans in his nonfiction works, *The
Omni-Americans* (1970), *The Hero and the Blues* (1973), and *Stomping
the Blues* (1976). He collaborated with Count Basie in writing *Good Morning Blues: The Autobiography of Count Basie* (1985). The following excerpt is from *South to a Very Old Place*.

---

from South to a Very Old Place

*Rearrived on expense account this time you take the limousine to the Battle
House not so much remembering the stopover in Atlanta as continuing the
interior monologue you began months ago back in Lenox Terrace. But thinking, or at least reiterating, this nevertheless: Yes, homecoming is also to a
place of very old fears, some mine (perhaps most of which I outgrew growing
up) but mostly theirs (which mostly they did not but maybe at last are at least
beginning to).*

*You tell yourself that you are prepared to take things as they come, after
all you are on a writing assignment this time. But even before the bellhop
straightens up with your bags he anticipates and allays any such misgivings
as may be related to those you had pulling into Atlanta.*

*"Did you have a nice flight in, sir?" he says; which sounds like nothing
in the world so much as: "O.K., man, don't be coming down here getting so
nervous you going to be forgetting my goddam tip now. That's all right about
all that. So you desegregated. Well, good, so act like everybody else then and
lay it on me heavy. Hell, you know I'm looking out for you so remember I
got a family to be taking care of. And damn man it ain't your money no how."*

*   *   *

It is now the Sheraton Battle House as in Statler and Hilton. But in the old days it was *the* Battle House as in *the* Plaza, as in *the* Waldorf-Astoria. It was *the* Battle House as in the one and only best there is, and what you always saw when somebody used to say Battle House Service or used to say Battle House Steaks (precisely as they would also say Palmer House Service or Parker House Rolls, for instance) was a grand crystal Belle Epoque–opulent dining room where millionaires in stiffly starched bibs sat (beside their bunned and corseted Gibson girl–proper wives) holding their solid sterling forks, prongs down, and left-handed, eating plate-sized steaks that were obviously as tender and as succulent as Oysters Rockefeller.

Because when you used to hear the old saying that the Battle House was a place which, like the Pullman cars on the Pan American Limited or the Southern Pacific back in those days, was for no black folks at all and only a very few special white folks, *"A precious few white folks and no niggers at all,"* what you thought about was not complexion but money, prestige, and power; fame, fortune, and finery. Because only a very few white folks were famous millionaires, and perhaps no black folks at all as yet, except maybe Dave Patton, the contractor, whose big house was out on Davis Avenue. But only as yet. And what you always said about all of that was: *"Don't tell them nothing. Don't tell them a thing. Don't tell them doodly squat."* Because Mobile is also a place of very old horizon blue dreams plus all the boyhood schemes that are, after all, as much a part of achievement as of disappointment.

As for the part about being a nigger, the most obvious thing about that was that you were not whicker-bill different like them old peckerwoods were, because you didn't look like that and you didn't talk and walk like that and you couldn't stand that old billy-goat saw-fiddle music. So you were not po' white trash and your ears and nose didn't turn red when you were either scared or excited or embarrassed, and no matter how dingy and ashy you got you never looked mangy and when you needed a haircut and didn't comb your hair you were nappy-headed and even pickaninny-headed but when pale-tailed, beak-nosed soda-cracker people got shaggy headed they looked as sad as birds in molting season. On the other hand, you had to give them this much; mangy or not they would come out on a freezing morning wearing only a thin shirt, baggy ass-lapping pants and low quarter shoes, but no hat, no coat, no undershirt, and no socks, and just hunch up a little and keep on going like a fish in an icy pond, while you were all wrapped up in coats and sweaters and still shivering. That was something! And some people used to think that maybe having hair that was that much like bird feathers meant that they could also close their pores like a duck against the freezing dampness of the swamp.

It was also obvious that when the peckerwoods said "nigger" they were doing so because they almost always felt mean and evil about being nothing but old po' white trash. So they were forever trying to low-rate you because they wanted you to think they were somebody to look up to; and naturally you low-rated them right back with names like peckernosed peckerwoods, crackers, rednecks and old hoojers—not hoosiers, but goddam shaggy-headed, razor-backed, narrow-shouldered tobacco-stained thin nose-talking hobo-smelling hoojers ("I'm a black alpaca ain't no flat assed soda cracker").

When you were looking into the mirror you were the me of I am; and you were always Mamma's little mister misterman, Momom itchem bitchem mitchem buttchem bwown man and Pappa's big boo-boo bad gingerbread soldier boy; and in the neighborhood you were the you of whichever one of your nicknames somebody happened to like; and in school you were the you of your written name. Nothing was more obvious than all of that. Nor was it any less obvious that when somebody called himself or somebody like himself a nigger he was not talking about not being as good as white people or somebody rejected by himself because he is rejected by white people—not at all. He was talking about being different from white people all right, but ordinarily he was mainly talking about being full of the devil and stubborn to boot: as stubborn as a mule, mule-headed, contrary, willfully different, cantankerous, ornery, and even downright wrongheaded. When somebody said, "Don't make me show my nigger"—or "don't bring out the nigger in me," he was bragging about having the devil in his soul. And when somebody said that somebody else "started acting like a nigger" he was not talking about somebody acting like a coward or a clown. The word for that in those days was darky: "acting like a good old darky." When homefolks said that somebody was playing the darky they meant he was putting on an act like a blackface stage clown, either to amuse or to trick white folks. But when they said you were being an out and out nigger they were almost always talking about somebody refusing to conform, and their voices always carried more overtones of exasperation than of contempt: "Everybody else was all right and then here he come acting the nigger." Or: "Then all the old nigger in him commenced to come out. You know how mean and evil some of us can get to be sometime."

So what was suggested by the worst sense of the word "nigger" as used by people who applied it to themselves on occasion was an exasperatingly scandalous lack of concern about prevailing opinion, whether in matters of etiquette, of basic questions, of conventional morality, or even of group welfare: "After everybody got together and agreed how to do it, here he come acting the goddam nigger and talking about it don't have to be that way and can't nobody make him if he don't want to. Like some goddam body trying to make him—when all folks trying to do is get together." "That's what I say about niggers. Can't nobody make 'em do right when they get it in their head to do something else. And that's exactly how come the white man can keep us down like this. Because niggers too selfish and evil and suspicious and mule-headed to pull together!"

That was what the worst sense of the word was all about, not what white folks were always trying to say because what they were really talking about was really the best part no matter how bad they tried to make it sound. Because that was the part that went with being like Jack Johnson and John Henry and Railroad Bill and Stagolee all rolled in one. So of course, as nobody had to tell you but once, it was also the part you had to be most careful about: because the mere mention of one bad-assed nigger in a don't-carified mood was enough to turn a whole town full of white folks hysterical. A newspaper statement like "crazed negro [sic] last seen heading . . ." scared peckerwoods as shitless as an alarm for a wild fire or hurricane. Of course everybody always knew that the newspaper phrase "crazed negro" didn't really mean insane—or even berserk. Sometimes it didn't even mean angry, but rather determined or even simply unsmiling!

Some folks also used to declare that the reason the white folks wanted to lynch you for being a nigger was because when all was said and done they really believed that the actual source of all niggerness was between your legs. They said you were primitive because to them what was between your legs was a long black snake from the jungles of Africa, because when they said rape they said it exactly as if they were screaming snake! snake! snake! even when they were whispering it, saying it exactly as if somebody had been struck by a black snake in the thickets. Bloodhounds were for tracking niggers who knew the thickets like a black snake. When white folks called somebody a black buck nigger they were talking Peeping Tom talk because the word they were thinking about was fuck, because when they said buck-fucking they were talking about doing it like the stud-horse male slaves they used to watch doing it back during the time of the old plantations.

They said black as if you were as black as the ace of spades not only when you were coffee or cookie or honey brown but even when you were high yaller or as pale-tailed, stringy-haired as a dime-store hillbilly. Because to them it was only as if you were hiding your long black snake-writhing niggerness under your clothes while showing another color in your face, camouflaging yourself like a lizard. Nor did anything seem to confirm their suspicions about the snake rubbery blackness of your hidden niggerness more convincingly than the sight of you dancing. They always seemed to be snake-fascinated by that, even when it was somebody that everybody in your neighborhood knew couldn't really dance a lick.

But even so sometimes it was not so much a matter of terrified fascination as of out and out enjoyment and frank admiration. During the Mardi Gras season, for instance, when the dancing floats were passing Bienville Square and the shuffle-stepping marching bands, say like Papa Holman's, were jazzing it like it was supposed to be jazzed on such a festive occasion, there was always somebody saying something like: "Here they come, here they come; here come them niggers! Goddammit them niggers got that thing. By gyard them damn niggers got it and gone over everybody. By gyard you might as well give it to them, it'll be a cold day in hell before you ever see a durned old niggie and a bass drum going in contrary directions and that's for a fact."

Nevertheless when you heard them saying "boy" to somebody you always said mister to, you knew exactly what kind of old stuff they were trying to pull. They were trying to pretend that they were not afraid, making believe that they were not always a split second away from screaming for help. When they said Uncle or Auntie they were saying: You are not a nigger because I am not afraid. If you were really a nigger I would be scared to death. They

*were saying: You are that old now and more careful now so I don't have to
be afraid anymore; because now you are a darky—a good old darky, so now
my voice can be respectful, can remember the authority of reprimands that
were mammy black and the insightfulness that was uncle black, now I can be
respectful not only of age—as of death but also of something else: survival
against such odds. "By gyard, Uncle, tell me something, Uncle . . ." Their
fears of your so-called niggerness became less hysterical not when they them-*
∧ *selves grew up but when you grew older. Or so it seemed back then. Anyway,
all of that was an essential part of how it felt to be a nigger back in those
old days. Which was why white folks couldn't say it without sounding hateful
and apprehensive! When some old chicken butt peckerwood says nigger this
or nigger that naturally he wants to give the impression that he is being
arrogant. But if you know anything at all about white folks his uneasiness will
be obvious enough, no matter how trigger-bad he is reputed to be.*

Gone
154~5.

Progress?

This time it is almost as if it is still the time before, which was only five
months ago when after an absence of fifteen years you came back in January
and found that the neighborhood that was the center of the world as you first
knew it had been razed, completely industrialized, and enclosed in a chain-
link fence by the Scott Paper Towel Company.

"All of that is Scott now," somebody after somebody after somebody kept
shaking his head and saying then; and somebody else after somebody else
repeats now.

"The old Gulf Refining Oil yard is still where it was and you probably
remember the old creosote plant down off the creek. But just about everything
else over in there is Scott. Three Mile Creek to the Chickasabogue, L&N to
the AT&N, Scott, all Scott."

Indeed, to you at any rate, it was very much as if the fabulous old sawmill-
∧ whistle territory, the boy-blue adventure country of your childhood memories
(but which had been known and feared back in the old ante bellum days as
Meaher's Hummock), had been captured in your world-questing absence by a
storybook dragon disguised as a wide-sprawling, foul-smelling, smoke-chug-
ging factory, a not really ugly mechanical monster now squatting along old
Blackshear Mill Road as if with an alligatorlike tail befouling Chickasabogue
Swamp and Creek—a mechanized monster who even in the preliminary process
of getting set (to gobble up most of the pine forests of the Gulf Coast states,
to turn them into Kleenex [sic!] paper towels and toilet tissues) had as if by
a scrape of a bulldozing paw wiped out most of the trees and ridges that were
your first horizons. And although you knew better, it was also as if all the
neighborhood people who had died since you were there last were victims of
dragon claws, and as if those still alive had survived only because they had
been able to scramble to safety in the slightly higher regions of Plateau and
Chickasaw Terrace.

But even so you were (then as now) back in the old steel-blue jack-rabbit
environs once more, and as you made the old rounds you were home again
because you could still find enough of the old voices and old reminders to

provide the necessary frame of reference; and after all what more did you expect and what else could you expect? Maybe when Thomas Wolfe said you can't go home again he meant because things ain't what they used to be. If so then all you have to do is remember that things never are (and never were) what they once were.

On the previous trip in addition to those you reencountered once more along the old Bay Bridge Road, along Tin Top Alley and up in Plateau after all those years since the days of Dodge Mill Road and No Man's Land and Gin's Alley, there was Veleena Withers, a teacher over at Mobile County Training School. Her very presence there, even on an almost entirely rebuilt campus, was such that it instantly brought back vividly to mind the days of Mister Baker, Benjamin F. (whom everybody had long since come to revere even while he still lived as if he, and not Isaiah J. Whitley, were The Founder). Not only that, but everything she did and said was evidence of the continuity of the old misterbaker doctrine of MCTS verities. Indeed, she (whom you had known only casually in high school and had last seen not in Plateau but at Tuskegee) was a misterbaker returnee, just as in addition to whatever else you were, you and Addie Stabler and Frank Watkins and Leo Greene and Lehandy Pickett and Orlando Powers were also misterbaker-directed, nay, ordained, beknighted pathfinders and trailblazers specifically charged to seek your fortune—by which he meant the fortune of your people—elsewhere.

(It was Veleena Withers who put you in contact with Noble Beasley, leader of the local civil-rights organization which at that time had the broadest appeal and was making the biggest impact on City Hall. She assumed that you'd want to talk with him not because there was any connection with MCTS—he is from another part of town and is also after your time; she assumed that for you as for her what Beasley's organization was doing was a logical updating and extension of what the local dimension of MCTS was all about back in the old days, and as far as you could make out she was right.)

It was also through Veleena Withers that you reencountered Henry Williams, a MCTS graduate who teaches Welding at the Carver State Trade School. To this day you cannot place him as of those days except very vaguely by that part of his family which you remember as the Godbeaux or the God bolts. What Veleena Withers knew, however, was that he was not only a welder whose knowledge of his trade included a lot of fascinating background information about the wrought-iron ornaments for which the architecture of Old Mobile has long been noted, but he is also a part-time historian whose first-hand field research and personal sense of local continuity were precisely what you were looking for but were afraid that you had come back too late to find. That was how you had come to spend one whole afternoon and part of the next day with an expert on all the old landmarks and homesteads, and early families, including not only those with names like Allen, Ellis, Fields, Keeby; and Lewis whose African grandparents came over on the old *Clotilda*, but also those named Augusta, Coleman, Edwards, Henderson, all great riverboat men during the sawmill era (which lasted all the way into the Great Depression you remember from the sixth grade).

As for what Henry Williams remembers about you there back then, according to him you were one of the all but out of sight upperclassmen about whom there were misterbaker-made legends, one of which was that the reason you had won your scholarship to college was that you were so conscientious that sometimes you had actually worked out your Algebra and Latin assignments by moonlight.

"Man, old Prof Baker would get going about you and I could just see you down there where you used to live, hitting them books with the moon over your left shoulder." At which you had laughed and said: "Boy, I'm telling you, that Mister Baker. Wasn't he something?"

"What the hell was he *talking* about, man?"

"I don't know. We did used to have to turn off the lamp when the L&N roundhouse blew. But I don't know, I might have snuck out to a streetlight or something to finish a translation for Latin. I can tell you this, it was not algebra."

But thinking about it again later and remembering the chapel-time misterbaker legends about your own upperclassmen you find yourself thinking that homecoming is also to the place of the oldest of all pedestals. *Wherever else is that rib-nudging "That's him! That's him! That's him! Here he comes! Here he is! There he goes!" dimension of acclaim, fame, publicity, or notoriety ever likely to be of more profound and of more profoundly personal significance than on the main drag of the hometown of your boyhood and youngmanhood? Not even your name in lights on Broadway (or on the cover of a magazine on a New York newsstand) not even the instant recognition by strangers, not even the satisfaction of seeing your name and image on national network television, is likely to surpass the sense of apotheosis of buttchem bwownhood you experience when the most familiar people in the world, the people you have known all your life, suddenly look at you as if for the first time—as they do when you hit a home run (or, as in your case, save the game by striking out the last batter) as they do when you bring the house down with an inspired rebuttal, or an oration—as if to say, "Yes; man is indeed what he achieves and this is what you are making of yourself—but whoever would have thought that the little boy—the itchem bittchem baby boy we all knew when he was no bigger than a minute—would become if not quite our glory yet, at least a part—if only a modicum—of our hope!"*

Nor did Mister Baker or anyone else permit you or any other itchem mittchem buttchem bwown to forget the proximity of pedestals to pillories and guillotines, the contiguity of apotheosis to ostracism and disgrace. For after all, where on the other hand was failure ever likely to be more bitterly resented and ridiculed, more difficult to bear, than along that same main drag back home? *"Well, goddammit, boy, you messed up and messed us all up. Boy, you might have meant well but you sure played hell. Shit, boy, you should have been ready. Shouldn't no goddamn body have to tell you that. What the hell you doing up there messing with that stuff and ain't ready? Boy, who the goddamn hell told you to get up there? Boy, they saw your dumb ass coming. Boy, you up there flat-out shucking and them folks mean business. Boy, white*

folks always mean business with us. Fool, this ain't no goddam plaything
unless you already the expert, and know your natural stuff like old Jack John-
son or somebody. And just remember they didn't stop until they brought him
down. Folks counting on you and there you up there tearing up your black
ass in front of everybody and showing everybody's raggedy-butt drawers be-
cause you ain't ready. Hell, if you ain't ready yet don't be jumping up there
in front of somebody else that is. Just let it alone, and stay out of the way.
Boy, you too light behind. Hell, boy, you don't even know how to hold your
mouth right to be grabbing hold to this stuff." (Mista Buster Brown how you
going to town with your britches hanging down?)

On the other hand of course there was also Mister Baker's absolute disdain
for those who betrayed even the slightest misgivings about going places and
doing things that no other homefolks were known to have gone and to have
done. "Oh faint of heart. Oh weak of spirit. Oh ye of little faith! Oh jelly
fish, oh Mollycoddle! Yes, many are called but few are chosen. Yes, only the
pure in heart." (*Young man, you sure better start getting some glory and
dignity from the common occupations of life because from the looks of these
grades that's what you're going to be doing.*)

The paradox
The Brain/Brawn
(unequal) Development
Speaker's Scholarship

The teacher from the old blue-and-white MCTS whippet banner days you
pop in on this time is Jonathan T. Gaines, now principal of Central High
School on Davis Avenue not far from where Dunbar High School used to be.
It is Sunday. He is at home, and he comes slipper-footing it in arching his
brow in a put-on frown as if to say: "Yes, yes. So here you are as I knew
you would be. Murray, Albert Murray. Well, well. And now, where is the
rest of the class? Where is Addie Stabler? Where is Frank Watkins and Leo
Greene and Lee Handy Pickett?" Then during the chat he keeps frowning his
old tardy-bell plus binomial theorem frown as if he is still trying to make up
his mind as to whether your high grade point average along with your performance as a debater and an athlete will get you his tough minded math prof
vote when the faculty next sits in judgment as to who is college timber. Who
has the caliber to carry the MCTS colors out into The World.

Completely delighted, you think: *Homecoming is to a very old MCTS atmosphere, where teachers knew exactly what playing Santa Claus was all about;
and what they tried to teach was the blue steel implications of fairy tales.*
WHO IS THE QUICK BROWN FOX WHERE IS THE SALTY DOG.

Then later in the afternoon driving south along the old Spanish Trail and
into the old Creole and pirate bayou country with Henry Williams you say:
"About that joke about me and the books in the moonlight, man, one day I
came on campus and everybody was congratulating me because the faculty
had designated me Best All-Round Student for that year. Then I got to class
and looked around for Kermit McAllister and found out that he had been
promoted to the graduating class. Man, when I finished Tuskegee, he had
finished Talladega in three years and already had his M.A. at Michigan and
when I went up to Ann Arbor for a taste of grad school the only thing old
Kermit still had to do for his Ph.D. in philosophy was the dissertation. So he

was taking a year off to swim, chase the trillies, and read Santayana. The last
time I saw him was in the Gotham Book Mart in New York. He was then an
associate professor of philosophy at Howard. The last I heard of Addie Stabler
she was teaching at Morehouse. I saw old Frank Watkins last in Los Angeles.
I forget whether he was about to get his Ph.D. or had just gotten it, but he
had some kind of math-and-physics–type job in electronics or aeronautics or
something. I was out there with the Air Force at that time.''

You make the old rounds answering the old questions and accounting for
your whereabouts and involvements over the years not only as you did the last
time and the time before that but also as everybody has always done it for as
long as you can remember; and this time that part (which along with the old
street-corner hangouts and barbershops also includes gate stops, yard visits,
sitting porch visits and dinner-table reunions) goes something like this: ''Hey,
look who's back down here from up the country again. Ain't nobody seen him
in umpteen chicken-pecking years until last when was it, last January? February? Last Feb, no, January. And now here he is again. Like somebody was
saying I hope ain't nobody up there after him or something. Oh, oh, excuse
me. Hey-o there, New York? Unka Hugh and Miss Mattie Murray's Albert!
What say man? Used to be little old Blister from down in the Point. Hey, you
looking all right, boy. Don't be paying no mind. Hell, you a Mobile boy,
Murray. Ain't nobody nowhere, I don't care where they come from, got no
stuff for no Mobile boy unless he get up there and forget where he come from.
Hell, just remember when you come from here you supposed go any goddam
where and make it.''

''All I say is this,'' somebody else says winking, ''just don't be making
none of them northern boots nervous by getting too close to their white folks,
especially with all the fancy book learning you got. Man, that's the one thing
they subject to run you out from up there about—taking their white folks away
from them. Man, you might as well be messing with somebody's wife or
something! Man, them northern Negroes love their white folks, and don't you
forget it.''

''Especially them that always so ready to get up somewhere talking about
the black man this the black man that,'' somebody else continues grumbling
as much to himself as to you and the others. ''Man they'll run over you getting
to some old white folks. Man, I used to know some there won't even give
you the time of day until they happen to find out that you know some impor-
tant-looking white folks.''

''New York, hunh?'' An old poolroom sage comes up slaps you on the
shoulder and says, ''Hey, say, how about old Cleon Jones and Tommy Agee
and them up there with the Mets. From Mobile County Training School.
Putting old County on the big-league baseball map. You see that fine brick
house old Cleon built over there not far from school? But hell, Mobile is a
baseball town, you know. Look at old Willie McCovey out there in Frisco
with the Giants, out there with Willie Mays from right up there in The Ham.
Not even to mention old Hank Aaron.''

"Say, I got a glimpse of him when I stopped off in Lana the other day," you say, nodding. He goes on.

"Old Hank is something else, boy, and from Mobile all the way. Right out there in Whistler! Remember old Emmett Williams and them Hamilton boys? Mobile always has been a mean baseball town. Even before old Satchel Paige, and that was like goddam! I can still remember him with them old Satchel foots up there on the Chickasaw ball diamond forty some odd years ago throwing the stew out of a ball called the goddam fade away. . . ."

"Hey but let me tell you something else about some of them old New York City Negroes," a former MCTS upper classman says. "Man, I remember when I was running out of there to Chicago on the New York Central back in the Depression. That was back when somebody was always hinting and whispering and winking and carrying on about the C.P., talking about the Communist Party. Man, party some stuff. Man the party them New York City Negroes I used to know were talking about was a sure enough party having a ball getting in some frantic white pants. And don't think them fay boys not doing the same thing vice versa. Man but here's the joke about that part. Them fay boys strictly out to get some ashes hauled and them supposed to be so educated boot chicks up there so busy putting on airs because they so sure they screwing their way into some high-class culture, they been had before they catch on that them fay boys think they all a bunch of cottonpatch picka-ninny sluts! And, man, talking about snowing them, man all some lil old raggity butt WPA fay boy used to have to do was take one of them to a cheap concert or a free museum or something and tell them he respect their *mind*. *Man, was I drug!*

"Man, but what I'm talking about is most of them New York Negroes didn't bit more care nothing about no Communism than they did Einstein and didn't know no more about it. I know what I'm talking about because I was hitting on a few of them fay frails my damn self and they'd leave you these pamphlets and I used to read some of them, and I tried to talk to some of them Harlem cats. Man them cats look at you like you carrying a violin case or something. But the minute they round a bunch of ofays don't nobody know nothing about it but them."

"Hey, how you doing, homes?" somebody else on another corner begins. "Up there in New York, hunh? But hell, all I got to do is look at you looking all classificational and I can see you taking care of business. You really looking good there boy. I kinda lost track of you there recently. We all remember you from over there at the school, you know. So we used to hear about you up at Skegee, and on the faculty and then you went to the Air Corps in the war. See what I mean? And then back to Skegee and then back in the service and traveling everywhere. Then I lost track and then that other time they said you were in here from New York so when I heard it this time I said, 'Hell, I remember that boy, I'm going over here and meddle him a little.' He know me. So how you doing, homes? Goddam, man. Sure good to see you."

*   *   *

Sometimes it also begins in a stylized falsetto exactly like this: "Hey, damn, man, they told me you were here and looking all clean, like for days. So now look here! I got to talk to you, man. So come on and get in this old struggle buggy and let's circle over by my place and say hello so the folks can see you and have a little taste and shoot the goddam shit awhile. I ain't going to hold you long and then I'll drive you anywhere else you got to go. Man, damn, I got to talk to you because I want to know what you think about some of this stuff I been thinking about. I know you might think I'm crazy like some of them say. That's all right. Just tell me what you think. Some of these folks around here, goddam. Some of them. And I say some of them, look like they think they got to latch onto everything come along because it's new. And it ain't even new. That's the killing part. It's old as all these old country-ass sideburns and bell-bottom sailor-boy pants and pinch-back used to be called jazz-back suits that come in back there right after pegtops and them box-backs. They think they getting with something so cool and all they being is ass-backwards. So all you got to do is just tell me what you think, like somebody been somewhere and seen something and got some sense! Because some of this stuff. Man, I'm telling you."

You go of course. You meet the folks and settle down in the parlor. Then he continues, beginning with an eye-cutting, elbow-nudging button-holing intimacy: "So now the first thing is this, and like I say you might think I'm crazy too. But just think about this for a minute":

Then in an italicized conspiratorial whisper: "*White folks don't go around trying to make fun of us like they used to*. You noticed that shit? Think about it. Now the minute you think about it you got to remember when we were coming along you couldn't do nothing without them trying to make out like somebody so goddam ignorant that everything was always funny as hell. Remember all that old Hambone stuff they used to have in the papers, and all that old Stepinfetchit and Willie Best and Mantan Moreland stuff in the goddam movies and that old Amos and Andy stuff on the goddam radio, all that old Kingfish and Lightnin' and Madame Queen stuff. That's the kind of old bullshit they used to try to pull on us, remember, and we used to see it and, hell, we knew exactly what they were trying to do. You know that. So we went on about our goddam business. So now my first point is this. *How come they ain't making fun of nobody no more?* Wasn't nothing funny about what we were doing and them sonbitches used to write up every goddam thing like everybody talking some kind of old handkerchief-headed dialect. My point is ain't nobody never cut the fool like some of these clowns we got these days and you don't see no crackers laughing. That's what I'm talking about. You used to get somewhere and you were not about to make no mistake because that's what they were waiting for you to do and they would look at you buddy as much as to say, Nigger, you done tore your barbarian ass. So you didn't get up nowhere until you could cut the mustard. Hell, you're not supposed to rip your drawers. Now that's what I call some goddam black-ass pride! That's just what I'm talking about. That's exactly what I'm talking about, cutting the goddam mustard. We got some out-and-out fools will get up anywhere nowdays carrying on with all them old passwords and secret grips like old-time lodge members back when most folks couldn't read and write. Talking about right on and tearing right on through their BVD's to their natural booty holes! And then talking about pride! And them crackers ain't even cracking a goddam smile. So now, you know what I think?''

Whispering again: *"I think them goddam white folks know exactly what they doing and they know if they start laughing and correcting them, most of these clowns subject either to shut up or wise up and straighten up!"*

Normal voice: "So see what I mean? You see the big difference, don't you? Look, don't nobody want nobody laughing at us, you know me, cuz. I'm ready to kill some son of a bitch come trying to make fun of me. So in a way it's good, but in another way you better think about it. I say they ain't laughing because they want us to follow the ones that's so loud and wrong. You get my point? Because if they start laughing at them that get up there talking all that old diaperical psychological economical bullshit they know good and well the others won't follow them. So they don't. Man, white folks the very ones encouraging them to be loud and wrong, man. And that's the problem. Because, see, these fools think you can get up there shucking and won't nobody know it—and the white man working day and night figuring out ways to stay ahead of us. Now am I shitting or gritting? Am I facking or just yakking?''

You say: "I know what you mean. I know exactly what you mean." You say: "Man, sometimes I get that uneasy feeling that rapping is getting to be the name of the whole goddam game for more and more of us." You say: "Old-fashioned street-corner woofing and simple-ass signifying and that's all, and then in Harlem they go around later on bragging about what they said and how it shook up the whiteys and broke up the meeting."

Then in an uptown-mocking voice that is part West Indian, part New York Jewish intellectual, part Louis Armstrong, you say: "I told them, man. You hear me telling them? You heard me rapping. I said like this is the black communertee and black people radicalized and tired of all this old shit from the sick, racist establishment! You heard me. I said 'Forget it, Charley.' I told it like it nitty-gritty fucking is, man. I said, all this old honky shit ain't a thing but some old jive-time colonialism versus upward mobility and black identity. I gave them whiteys a piece of my cotton-picking mind. I said 'Black is beautiful, baby, and you better believe it, chuck.' ''

But the main purpose for making the rounds this time is to listen. And later on in another part of town somebody else says: "One thing the old folks used to worry about all the time. They were always talking about education, and saying when you got that in your head you had something couldn't nobody take away from you. But they also used to worry about bringing up a generation of educated proper-talking fools. Remember how folks used to look at you when they said that, and start talking about mother-wit and don't be putting on no airs? Well, we got the finest bunch of young'uns you going to find anywhere in this country these days, but when you look up there on TV you got to admit we got ourselves a whole lot of loudmouthed educated fools to watch out for among them too. Ain't no use in lying about it.''

And somebody else says: "Now I'm just going to tell you. Now this is me and this is what I think and I been thinking about this for a long time. All right, so we the ones that got them to open up them schools to our children. That was us, and nobody else and we ain't never said nothing about letting nobody in there that wasn't qualified. Never. You know that. Never. So what do they do? I'm talking about the goddam white folks now. They come up and figure out how they can let a lot of loudmouth hustlers in there that don't belong in there. Because they know good and well these the ones ain't going to study and ain't going to let nobody else study. So that's what we got now. We send them up there to learn what them white boys learning about running the goddam world and they up there out marching and wearing all that old three-ring-circus stuff and talking about they got to study about Africa. Now what I say is if that's all they want to know they ain't got no business up there. That's what I say. Because the white man only too glad if they rather learn about Africa instead of how to run the world. I say them Africans already know about Africa, and what good is it doing them? Every time I see one he over here trying to get himself straight; and most of them hate to go back, and I don't blame them."

To which still someone else adds: "This is what I say. I say we know this white man. I say don't nobody nowhere in the world know this white man better than us, and this is the goddam white man that runs the goddam world. That's a fact, gentlemen, and ain't no disputing it. Don't nobody nowhere do nothing if this white man here don't really like it. You remember what Kennedy did to old Khrushchev that time about Cuba? Old Kennedy said, 'I'm going to tell it to you straight, pardner.' He said, 'Listen horse, cause I ain't going to tell you but once, so listen good or it's going to be your natural vodka pooting ass.' He said, 'Now I want all them goddam missiles and shit out of there by Wednesday (or Thursday—or whenever the hell it was—) and he said, 'I want them back on them goddam boats heading in such and such a direction, and then goddammit when you get to such and such a latitude of longitude I want you to stop and peel back them tarpaulins so my bad-assed supersonic picture-taking jets can fly over and inspect that shit and then I want you to get your Russian ass out of my hemisphere and stay out.' That's this white man, and don't nobody mess with him, and what I'm saying is we the ones that know him inside out and been knowing him inside out. What I'm trying to say is we right here in the middle of all this stuff that everybody else in the world is trying to get next to and what these college boys got to do is get something to go with what we know about this white man. What I'm saying is he smart enough to go all the way up to the moon and we know he still ain't nothing but a square like he always was, so what these college boys got to do is get ready to take all this stuff we know and push it up to the nth degree and use it on this white man right here."

"Now you talking," somebody else continues, "now you saying something. Talking about Africa, this white man right here is the one you going to have to come up against, don't care where you go. And we already know him. Supposed to know him. Better know him. And all y'all know I been saying

this for years. Every time somebody come up with some of all that old West
Indian banana-boat jive about the 'block mon' I tell them, and I been saying
it all these years and ain't about to bite my tongue. I tell them, ain't nobody
doing nothing nowhere in Africa and nowheres else that this white man right
here don't want them to do. I tell them. Every time a goddam African put a
dime in a telephone, a nickel of it come right over here to this same white
man. That goes for them Germans and Frenchmen and Englishmen, all of
them over there and them Japs too. So you know it goes for them goddam
barefooted Africans. So when they come up to me with some of that old
monkey-boat jive I tell them: All y'all want to go back to Africa, you welcome
to go. Fare thee goddamn well, horse, I say. But I tell you what I'm going
to do. Because I know what's going to happen. I say: I'm going to get my
college boys trained to go to New York City and Washington, D.C., and get
next to something. Because what's going to happen is them Africans going to
take one look at them goddam jive-time Zulu haircuts and them forty-dollar
hand-made shoes and they going to lock your American ass up in one of them
same old slave-trading jails they put our ancestors in, and they going to have
you writing letters back over here to this same old dog-ass white man in the
United States of America asking for money. Hey, wait. Hey, listen to this.
Ain't going to let them get no further than the goddam waterfront. They go
lock them up with a goddam Sears, Roebuck catalogue. I'm talking about right
on the dock, man, and have them making out order blanks to Congress for
Cocolas and transistors, and comic books, cowboy boots and white side walls
and helicopters and all that stuff. And you know what the goddam hell I'm
going to be doing? I'm going to have *my* college boys sitting up there in
Washington and Wall Street with mean-assed rubber-assed goddam stamp saying Hell, no! Saying, forget it, cousin. Hey, because by that time with what
we know we supposed to have this white man over here all faked out and off
somewhere freaking out and I mean for days! And I'll bet you this much any
day, we'll have this white man over here faked out long before any boots from
Harlem fake any of them Africans out over yonder. You go over there trying
to pull some old chicken-shit Harlem hype on them Africans and they subject
to bundle your butt up and sell you to them A-rabs. Man, them Africans ain't
going to never pay no boot like me and you no mind as long as they can do
their little two-bit business directly with this same old white man that we
already know fifty times better than any African, and I ain't leaving out no
Harvard Africans.''

You think about all the tourist-style trinkets so many naive U.S. black
nationalists seem to think is the great art of the mother country, completely
ignoring all of the art history and criticism that goes into museum acquisitions.
You also think about how *shared experience* has been a far greater unifying
force for so-called Black Americans than *race* as such has ever been to the
peoples of Africa. It is not the racial factor of blackness as such which is
crucial among Africans any more than whiteness as such kept the peace among
the peoples of Europe. But all you do is shake your head laughing along with
everybody else.

And what then follows you remember later as having been not unlike the leapfrogging chase chorus exchanges among musicians running down a theme on some of Lester Young's early, post-Basie, combo recordings: the soloists trading eight-, six-, and four-bar statements (nor did they lack any of old Lester's querulous coolness, nor any of his blues-based determination to blow it as he felt it and heard it regardless of what was currently hip):

"Hey, man, me, man (*One trumpetlike statement begins*), you know how come I don't be paying no mind to none of that old talk? Because they talking but I'm looking and listening too. They talking all that old Afro this and Afro that and black this and black the other and I'm right here looking at them cutting up exactly like a bunch of goddam rebel-yelling crackers cussing out the Supreme Court. If you want to know the truth, sometime when some of these TV cats get going about liberation I get the feeling the only freedom they want is the right to cuss everybody out."

"Hey!" (*this could be another trumpet, say with a parenthetical mute, or it could be an alto, or a getaway tenor*), "hey, but you know something else some of this old stuff put me in the mind of? A big old-fashioned church mess. You know what I'm talking about. Look, everybody going to church to try to save his soul and get to heaven. That's what getting religion is for and that's what the church is about. At least that's what it's supposed to be about. And that's exactly how come some old church folks the very ones make me so tired. Everybody in there because they trying save themself from torment and look like all they trying to do is trying to tell somebody else what to do and when you don't let them run your business they ready to gang up on you in some kind of old conference and blackball you out and if it's left up to them right on into eternal fire and brimstone. You see my point? I'm talking about church members now. I'm talking about the very ones suppose to be living by the word. They the very ones always subject to come acting like they already so close to God they got the almighty power to do you some dirt. Man that's what I can't stand about all this ole brother and sister putting on they got all out in the streets these days. The very first thing I think about when somebody come up to me talking about bro is, here come another one of them old deceitful hypocrites."

"Well, now" (*this is plunger style trombone jive*), "talking about rebel-yelling crackers, I'm just going to come on out and tell you, me. Hell, if I'm going to be some old damn peckerwood, I'm going to make sure to be one that's got enough money to play it cool. Damn, that's the least I can do. Of course, you know me. I always did think like a millionaire, myself. I'm always out to make me some more money, myself."

"You and me both" (*you remember this as a baritone statement, barbershop Amen corner baritone*), "and I'm going to tell you something else. I'm going to tell you what they doing. I'm going to tell you exactly what they doing. Because they doing exactly what they always doing when they start talking all that old Mother Africa bullshit. Any time you hear them talking all that old tiger-rag jive about the black man and Mother Africa you just watch and see what the first thing they do going to be. The very first thing they going to do is start turning on one another. Man, you gonna have a much harder time getting two dozen of them cats on a boat going to Africa than they had dragging our forefathers over here. But what I'm talking about is some of these little rascals already getting up calling somebody nigger in front of white folks, and supposed to be getting college educated! Up there shucking and signifying while them white boys knocking themselves out qualifying!"

"And don't think the white man don't know what's happening, horse" (*signifying monkey trumpet, with a mute plus derby!*). "Because you see the white man is the one that knew exactly how we got our black asses brought over here in the first goddam place. Up there talking about black history. I'll tell you some goddam black-ass history. This is the kind of black history the white man studies. As soon as them Africans get mad they subject to take and sell one another to the white man. They been doing it. They been doing it, and they still do it. I keep telling these little rascals it ain't going to do no good calling yourself no African. You got be from the right tribe or whatever it is. Hell mess around an come up with the wrong tribe and that's your behind, Jim. Sheet, the man just about know all he got to do is wait, because just like you say, some of these little fools already up there denying their own folks."

"That's what I say." (*So on it goes and maybe this is a big tenor. But then all the words were there long before the instrumentation.*) "That's exactly what I say. And I ain't talking about criticizing. You got a right to criticize anybody you think doing wrong, I don't care who they is. That's for my own benefit. That's for everybody's benefit. I'm talking about denying your own folks just because you mad with them about something. That's what I'm talking about. I talking about them little fools up there denying their own mamas and papas. I bet you don't hear no young Jews up there calling their old folks kikes, and yids, and Hebes and dirty Christ-killers in front of other folks. Don't care how mad they get with one another. Them Jews got organizations to take care of that kind of old loudmouthed bullshit. Don't take my word for it. Ask New York. Tell them, New York."

"Hey wait a minute. Now this is what I say about that. I say ain't nobody going to never get nowhere disrespecting your mama and papa. I might not go to church as much as some folks but I believe in the Good Book and the Good Book say honor thy father and thy mother."

"Didn't it though. Oh but didn't it though. That thy days shall be long upon the land which the Lord thy god giveth thee. I can still hear old Elder Ravezee preaching that sermon when I was a boy."

"And don't forget old Reverend Joyful Keeby. Talking about Africa, I bet you one thing. I bet you ain't nobody going to catch nobody like Plute Keeby talking about going back to his kinfolks somewhere over in no Africa, and old Plute and them can trace their African blood right back to that old hull of the *Crowtillie* out there in the mouth of the Chickasabogue."

"Man, I want to thank you for putting that in there. I just want to thank you. I only want to thank you. I just want to thank you one time. But hey look here now—you know I thought one of y'all was going say when he said

that about the boat going to Africa. I thought somebody was going to say
something about them northern city boys always talking about Africa and can't
even spend a weekend in the goddam country. Man, the minute them cats get
off the edge of the concrete, they start crying for Harlem. Now if I'm lying
come get me, cousin.''

"Hey, yeah, but wait a minute I'm still talking about these little fools
getting up there trying to put the badmouth on their own dear folks for the
goddam white folks. That's putting your own goddam self in the goddam
dozens without knowing it. You see what I'm saying? And talking about
putting the cart before the horse! Man, damn! Who ever heard of the chillun
putting badmouth on the old folks?''

"Thank you. I just want to thank you again. Because that's the Bible again.
Talking about the sons of Ham. That's laughing at thy own daddy's drunkenness and nakedness. And that's exactly how come the Lord banished his dumb-
ass ass to the goddam black-ass wilderness. And told him: Here you come all
puffed up on something you read in some old book and laughing at thy father
who gavest thee the very eyes thou seest with and the very tongue thou mockest
him with, and don't know the first frigging thing about what that old man
been through to get you where you at today!''

"Showing out for white folks. That's all I say it is, mocking your *own* folks
to impress some little old white—and I'm talking about some little old *bullshit*
whiteys that ain't got no more than nobody else. That's what I'm talking
about. Somebody ain't into nothing with no profit at all. Somebody can't even
do nothing for themselves. So you know they can't do nothing for you. But
get you in more trouble than you already got.''

"But now you see that's why it didn't surprise me a bit when they broke
up with all them that used to be down here every summer two or three years
ago. You know what I mean? If you want to help I say thank you. I say thank
you very much. But don't come acting like you know more about my goddam
business than I do and don't come expecting me to prove nothing to you like
you better than me. Hell, ain't nobody better than me. Not if I'm the one
telling it.''

"That's exactly why I said what I said. I said come on, man. I said goddam.
I said what the hell I'm doing wasting my goddam time proving some kind
of old bullshit point to some little bullshit ofays down here on a summer
vacation and sicking me on the goddam police to get some knots on my head
and they can go home to papa and that fat-ass checkbook any time they want
to. So here I am with a bunch of hickeys on my knuckle-ass head and they
back up there bragging about how they helped me. Dig that. I said, man, what
is this shit? I said man, fuck that shit.''

"Hell, anytime they get a toothache Papa can send that private plane down
here with his own private doctor on it.''

"Yeah, you right. I see what you mean. But I wasn't talking about all of
that. I was talking about them jive-time missionaries that come down here just
wanting somebody to think they more than they is.''

"You goddam right. Me I just don't want no bunch of eager-beaver ofays

coming down here telling me what to do just because they might know how
to type up a letter. That's one goddam thing I learned in the Army. Don't
take no Ph.D. to know how to fill out them papers. You see what I'm talking
about. If you supposed to be so goddam white I'm expecting you to put me
next to something—otherwise forget it. Anybody can fill out them old papers.''

"Well goddammit me, I'm talking about *all* of them. I'm talking about I
don't have to be proving nothing to nobody. Unless I'm trying to get him to
hire me. And you *know* I'm forced to be bullshitting him then, bullshitting
them a *while*. I'm talking about our children the ones supposed to be leading
this thing. Because if you don't watch out them little old ofays will have you
all bogged up in some of that old Beatle shit, man.''

"Hey but you know where the Beatles got that shit from. You know that's
our shit they fucking up like that.''

"Yeah, but damn, man that ain't what I'm talking about now. Hell, you
know what I'm talking about. I'm talking about some little old chalk chick
come talking about the Beatles and all that old rockabilly stuff. You suppose
to put her hip. Tell her that's some old nowhere shit for days. Don't be come
repeating some old psychological jive like it's deep just because you laying
some little old fay broads that's oooing and aaaing over it because they read
about it in a goddam magazine.''

You say: "I think I know what you mean about the white kids, and yet
they may be the first generation of white people who are really beginning to
be uncomfortable about their heritage of racism. You have to give them that.
But the goddam problem is that they are still no less condescending than their
parents. I mean who the hell are they to be 'helping' somebody? How the hell
would they know who to help anyway? Goddam it if they really mean business
they've got to stop acting as if only the most confused, uninformed, and
loudmouthed among us are for real. And everybody else is either stupid or is
trying to pass for white.''

"Ain't that a bitch,'' somebody says. "That is a *bitch*, gentlemen. That's
a bitch and ahalf. I'm talking about how white folks can always come up with
another kind of excuse to be against something look like it might profit us
something.''

*But mostly you listen as if from the piano. So mostly what you say is very
much like playing ellington and basie style comp chords. (Remembering also
the old one which goes: if you don't play them just pat your foot while I play
them.) But every so often it is also as if they have swung the microphone over
to you for a four-, six-, or eight-bar bridge or solo insertion.* This time
somebody says: "Well, what you got to say about it there, Mister New York.
Where the hell they getting all this old bullshit up there talking like their own
people the ones trying to hold them back. Ain't no goddam body doing nothing
but trying to make it *possible* for them. That's what the old folks did for us
and mine always told me the way to thank them is do the same for the next
generation and any child of mine get up there saying I ain't done my part is
just a bigmouth lie and I bet he won't tell me to my face. Just let one of them
dispute that to my face.''

And somebody else cuts in as with a plunger-style trombone to say: "Hey, especially when you get your head bad. Man, goddam, I'd hate to see one of them little clowns forget he ain't talking to one of them simple-ass ofay reporters and jump you with your head bad. Great googly woogly!"

You say: "They don't really mean it." You say: "I don't think they realize what they're saying. The big thing with them nowadays is to sound revolutionary. Which is fine. But most of those I've talked to tend to confuse revolution with community rehabilitation programs. A lot of them keep talking about what they are going to do for the people of the black community, and I keep telling them that too many of them are only sounding like a bunch of hancty social-welfare case workers, and ofay case workers at that. Man, you go around to the Ivy League campuses and listen to some of our kids talking all that old blue-eagle jive and they sound like they've never been anywhere near their own people. You know what I mean? Like, well, when you come right down to it they sound almost exactly like a bunch of rich or passing-for-rich white kids ever so hot to trot into the Peace Corps. You know what I mean? To help the poor natives somewhere. What bothers me and this really bothers the hell out of me is that they are responding to what they read instead of what they know, and yet when you check them out on what they read you find they haven't really read very much."

"And got the gall to come thinking they so hip," somebody says.

"Hip?" somebody else says, "Did you say hip? Come on, man. How the hell they going to be hip? They ain't been around long enough to be hip. Ain't been far enough. They ain't been into enough. Come on man. How they going to be hip up there showing how much they don't know every chance they get because they ain't hip enough to cool it because somebody *else* might know. Damn, man, the first thing about being hip is being hip to how hip the other fellow is. Man when you hip the first thing you know is you ain't never supposed to be playing nobody cheap just because they come acting like they don't know what's happening. Man, the last thing you can say for these clowns is they hip; and the way some of them going they ain't going to live long enough to be cool enough to be hip and subject to get a lot of other folks messed up in the process, and just over some old loudmouth bullshit."

Elsewhere you yourself also say. "You know what I want them to be like? Our prizefighters. Our baseball players. Like our basketball players. You know what I mean? Then you'll see something. Then you'll see them riffing on history because they know history. Riffing on politics because they know politics. One of the main things that too many spokesmen seem to forget these days is the fact you really have to know a hell of a lot about the system in order to know whether you're operating within it or outside it. What bothers me now is that they are so quick to start formulating policies before double-checking the definition of the problem. The difference between riffing and shucking is knowing the goddam fundamentals. Man, when I see one of us up at Harvard or Yale I want to be able to feel like you used to feel seeing Sugar Ray in Madison Square Garden or Big Oscar there, or Willie Mays

coming to bat in an All-Star game. You know what I mean? I like to think
that old Thurgood Marshall came pretty close. At one time when he opened
his briefcase in the Supreme Court it was almost like Lawrence Brown and
Harry Carney unpacking their horns backstage at Carnegie Hall.''

Then for outchorus: "Man, if you don't know what to do with that kind of
black heritage you're not likely to know what to do with any other kind either.
Some of our kids now seem to think that heritage is something in a textbook,
something that has to be at least a thousand years old and nine thousand miles
across the sea. Something you can brag about. Some fabulous kingdoms of
ancient African tyrants for liberation-committed black U.S. revolutionaries to
be snobbish about! And yet few would regard themselves as antiquarians.
Ordinarily, they're the last people in the world to be messing around with
something that is the least bit out of date.''

You also find time to sit and listen to what some of the very oldest among
the old heads from the old days want to tell you about the condition of contemporary man in general and about the state of the nation's political well-being
in particular. Because missing that part, which is always like coming back to
the oldness of the old chimney corner even in summer, would be perhaps even
worse than missing another chance to sit down to a full-course spread of old-
time home cooking once more.

You never miss that part of it if you can help it, and this time (which is
chinaberry-blue Maytime) one very special back porch after-supper rocking-
chair session in the fig-tree—fresh, damp-clay—scented twilight which is supposed to be about the first three months of the Nixon administration turns into
the following unka so-and-so monologue: "Lyndon Johnson. Lyndon Johnson.
Old Lyndon Johnson. They can call him everything but a child of God as long
as you please and I still say old Lyndon Johnson, faults and all. They talking
about what they talking about and I'm talking about what I'm talking about.
I'm talking about the same thing I always been talking about. I'm talking
about us, and I say old Lyndon Johnson is the one that brought more government benefits to help us out than all the rest of them up there put together all
the way back through old Abe Lincoln. I'm talking about Lyndon Johnson
from down here out there in Texas. And they tell me old Lady Bird Johnson
is from right here in Alabama. The Lord spared me to live to see the day
folks been talking about ever since my own daddy, God rest his soul, was a
boy and he used to say it back when I was a boy and old Teddy Roosevelt
sent for old Bookety Washington to come up and have breakfast with him in
the White House that time. Everybody got to carrying on so about that, and
my daddy kept telling them over and over. He said, them northern white folks
grinning in your face in public don't mean nothing but up to a certain point ∫
and beyond that point it don't mean a blessed thing. He said they generally
more mannerable toward you than these old pecks down here. You got to give
them that but that don't mean they don't expect you to lick up to them if you
want something from them. And then they still ain't going no further than up
to that point, and they ain't going that far if they got to buck up against any

of these old white folks down here to do it. And I said the same thing when
you yourself wasn't nothing but a little blister of a boy. When they all used
to get to making such miration over old Franklin D. I said that's all right
about Muscle Shoals and Three Point Two and God bless Miss Eleanor for
being as nice as she is and all that, but I said both of them come from up
there and I don't care how good they talk you just watch and see if they don't
always manage to find some old excuse not to buck the Southern white man.
Oh I ain't going to say they don't *never* buck him. I'm talking about bucking
him in the favor of *us*. So anyhow this is what I got from my daddy, and his
daddy ran away and fought for freedom with the Union Army, and I said you
can say what you want to, and I might not be here to see it, but it's going to
take one of these old Confederate bushwhackers from somewhere right down
through in here to go up against these old Southern white folks when they get
mad. My daddy used to say it over and over again. So when old Lyndon
Johnson come along and got in there on a humble—and, boy that's the onliest
way he ever coulda made it into there—I was watching with my fingers crossed
because he was the first one from down in here since old Woodrow Wilson
and all that old dirt he did to us—and them white folks up north not lifting a
finger against him either, talking about old Woodrow Wilson. So anyhow, like
I say I was watching him and the first thing I could tell was that them white
folks up the way was the very ones that was satisfied that old Lyndon Johnson
was going to be like old Woodrow Wilson all over again. But now here's
what give the whole thing away to me. These white folks down here. Boy
don't you never forget they always been the key to everything so far as we
concerned. So what give it away to me was them. Because they the very first
ones to realize that old Lyndon Johnson meant business when he said the time
is here to do something. And didn't nobody have to tell them what that meant
because they already knew he was one of them and if they made him mad he
subject to do some of that old rowdy cracker cussing right back at them, and
some of that old cowboy stuff to boot. When they commence to telling me
about how mean he is that's when I tell them, I say that's exactly what we
need, some mean old crackers on our side, for a change. That's when I
commenced to feel maybe the Lord had spared me to see the day, and then
the next thing you know them northern folks up there talking about you can't
put no dependence in him no more. The very same ones that used to trust him
when they thought he was another one of these old crooked Confederates.
Now wait, I'm going to tell you what put us in that creditability gap you been
reading about. Talking about the government lying to them about something.
Boy the consarn government been lying to *us* every since emancipation. Now
here they come talking about somebody lying! You remember that old Kennedy
boy was the one started talking about getting a black man up there in the
Cabinet with him. All right now you got to give him his due for that, but
look at the way he up and went about trying to do it. He looked over all them
Cabinet jobs he already had open and come talking about if he could just get
a new one to fill; and then he come right on out and told them who he was
going to put in there—like Congress going to be ever so mighty glad to give

him some kind of brand new extra job so he can give it to one of us! Confound
the luck, that didn't make no sense at all to me. Then old Lyndon Johnson
come along and said he needed that same extra job. But you notice he didn't
say a thing about who he had a mind to put in there? And naturally they don't
just come right on out and ask him because they know good and well he know
how come they didn't give it to Kennedy. So all they did was just kinda hint
around to let him know—since he was a cracker anyway. And all old Lyndon
Johnson did was wink a cracker wink at them and change the subject. And
then as soon as they give it to him he turned right around and put the same
one in there they turned Kennedy down on, the same one! That's how Weaver
got to be the first one in there. That's why I say you got to give old Lyndon
Johnson credit. Because all he had to do was let them know he was going to
hold the line on the black man and he could've stayed up there as long as he
wanted to. All he had to do every time one of us started acting up was just
put on his old head-whipping sheriff's hat and make out like he getting up a
posse or something, and theyd've *kept* him up there till he got tired of it.
That's why I got to give him credit don't care who don't. Because I know
what he coulda done and I remember what he did for a fact. He got up there
in front of everybody and said we shall overcome. Boy that's enough to scare
white folks worse than the Indians, boy. But you know what that put me in
mind of? I'm going to tell you exactly who that put me in the mind of. Old
Big Jim Folsom on his way to Montgomery. That first time, I'm talking about.
Old Big Jim Folsom talking about y'all come. You remember what Old Big
Jim Folsom said when they come up to him about what was he going to do
about us? Old Big Jim Folsom told them. Old Big Jim ain't never been nothing
but a Alabama redneck and never will be, but he told them. He said what
y'all always running around scared of them for? He said, they been right here
amongst us all this time. He said, I ain't scared of them. That's exactly what
he said. He said, Hell they just trying to get along the best they can. He said
now a fact is a fact and they got something coming to them like other folks.
He said live and let live. That's what he was talking about when he said y'all
come. And that's when these Alabama peckerwoods took his credit away from
him and started calling him Kissing Jim. That's what all that's about, boy.

"That's what old Lyndon Johnson kinda put me in the mind of when he
got in there—old Big Jim before he went bad. Somebody come in there and
told him, 'Mister President, I swear I can't find no experts that know what to
do about them niggers being so lowdown and don't-carified.' Now this northern
city joker wasn't talking about nothing but getting up some more of all that
pick and shovel stuff from back in the days of old Franklin D. Boy, the last
thing that joker want to see is a whole lot of our educated ones like you up
there getting somewhere like everybody else. But that's exactly where old
Lyndon Johnson stepped in. He know good and well all this northern joker
trying to tell him is niggers just will be niggers as far as northern white folks
is concerned. But I can just imagine him saying, 'Hell, how come ain't nobody
tried this: Send me old Thurgill Marshall. He already whipped everybody
that'll go before a judge with him. So cain't nobody say he ain't ready. I'm

going to make him my chief lawyer for a while and then I'm going to ease
him on up on the Supreme Court bench and let him help make some decisions.
Then I'm going to put one up there with them millionaires on the Federal
Reserve Bank to help me keep an eye on the money. I want him to be a real
black one so they can't say I just put old Thurgill up there because he's damn
near white! And another one over in the World Bank to look out for that.
Make that one brown.' Think about that, boy. Two niggers watching white
folks count money!

"Boy, Old Lyndon Johnson say, 'Before I get through I'm going to let
some of my niggers get a taste of some of all this high class stuff.' That's
what I'm talking about the Lord sparing me to be here. And I can imagine
another one of them coming in there and saying, Now, I'm just going to have
to come right on out and tell you Mister President, the big money folks up
North getting nervous. And that's when I can imagine old Lyndon Johnson
cutting into a big red apple with his silver-plated Wild West pocketknife and
offering him a slice like a chew of Brown's Mules chewing tobacco and
saying. 'You go back and tell 'em I'm from down south so I'm kinda used
to having them around me. Tell 'em I feel kinda lost if ain't none of them
around. Tell 'em they'll get used to them in here just like they already used
to them cooking and running them elevators. But tell them they can depend
on one thing. I ain't going to put nary a one in nowhere unless he ready, and
if he don't cut the mustard I'll kick his black tail out of there so fast he'll be
shame to even remember he was in there. Tell them they can depend on that.'
Boy that's another thing about so many of them white folks up north. You
tell 'em folks hungry and all they can think about is spoon-feeding somebody.

"The Lord spared me to be here to see that day. Talking about when old
Lyndon laid it on them. But son, I never thought I was ever born to witness
the day that followed, and I'm talking about followed before anybody could
even get set to get something out of what we were just about to get up close
to. Now that's another thing you got to give old Lyndon Johnson credit for,
because you know good and well he must have meant business because he got
too much sense about politics not to know there was bound to be some white
backwash. But the thing of it all was the next thing. Because I been here all
this many years and I declare before God I just couldn't believe it, and I know
my daddy poor soul turned over in his grave. The next thing you know, some
of our own folks up there jumping on Lyndon Johnson with both feet just like
we in with the white folks against him, and all the time these old white folks
down here just sitting back laughing and talking about they been knowing
niggers didn't have sense enough to grab our chance if somebody gave it to
them.

"So now do you see what I'm talking about, young fess? Because I said
all of that there to say this here. Because you know good and well I ain't
talking about what happened to old Lyndon Johnson. Old Lyndon Johnson can
take care of Lyndon Johnson, ain't no doubt about that. I'm talking about
what's happening to us. I'm talking about some of us up there so busy showing
out for them northern white folks we done completely forgot what we supposed

to be doing for one another. I'm talking about y'all up there doing what you doing and here come all them old nice grinning northern white folks and that's all right with me if they want to help out but the next thing you know they got y'all up there doing everything they talking about. Boy, you old enough to remember when they come grinning down here back during the time of all that old Scotchbug mess. Well, y'all up there putting more dependence in them right now than anybody down here was near bout to be putting in them back then when most people still suppose to been still ignorant. So I said all that because I want you to remember this. Just remember you got all your good book learning because that's what the old folks wanted you to get and they want you to see just how high you can go. But they don't want you to get up there and forget your common sense just because two or three of them people feel like grinning at you and treating you nice. You don't have to just flat out and insult nobody. Folks expect you to know better than that. They come grinning to you. You grin right back at them if you want to, that ain't nothing but manners and decency. But just keep remembering they grinning about what they grinning about and you grinning about what you grinning about. You see what I'm talking about old Lyndon Johnson? Boy, I ain't talking about no friendship. I'm talking about knowing what to do when you got your chance to do business with a politician that ain't going to back up off these old Southern white folks because he one of them. I'm talking about what old Lyndon Johnson had to back up off of was the big-money northern white folks. And now we got old Nixon. So now the northern white man come trying to make out like he so worried because old Nixon ain't doing enough for us. But now you just wait and see how many of them going to buck up against old Nixon. Just wait and see. Don't be surprised if old Nixon don't have do more on his own than any of them old nice grinning Northern white folks ever going to be willing to try to force him to do. I'm talking about for us—ain't talking about that old war over yonder. I say it still going to take somebody like old Lyndon Johnson from down around somewhere in here and the Lord might not spare me to see that come around another 'gain but I just hope and pray that enough of y'all will know better next time.''

You hope so too. And you want to believe most of what he says about white southerners like Lyndon Johnson as much as he apparently wants to believe it. (*"Some mean ass crackers on our side for a change, for whatever goddam reason"*) But even so if you were naming the "other folks" who would be the ones most likely to stick their necks farthest out for you out of a sense of moral obligation—and keep it out there even against the opposition of their "own people"—most of them would probably be Jewish. Not only that but, Air Force buddies aside, you actually found it somewhat less embarrassing to have to ask urgently needed personal favors of Jewish friends than of white southerners. Not to mention Yankee do-gooders. On the other hand you'd much rather have old Willie Morris, for instance, go on functioning in terms of his Yazoo City courthouse square sense of actuality than have him become another compassionate pop-cause-oriented, underdog-loving, petty cash-generous, tax write-off neo-Great White Father.

You hope for that too. But you do not ask even that of him, either—or of any other white Southerner, including old Lyndon Johnson himself. Because it is not something for which you ask (and make yourself beholden!). It is not something to be requested anyway; because, as old Lyndon seems to have come to realize as few others have, it is something already required of him— as much by his own personal predicament as by the state of things in the nation and the world at large.

Some altogether pleasant reencounters also go exactly like this: "Is this who I think it is? This ain't who I think it is. This can't be who I think it is. Boy, is this you? Boy, this ain't you! Come here and let me look at you, boy. Look at him. Boy, you something! You think you a man now don't you! Well I guess you turned out all right! They tell me you been some of everywhere and doing all right for yourself, and you sure look like it. Been all over there in Paris, France, and Rome, Italy, they tell me. And Casablanca and all out in Hollywood. And living up in New York these days. Well go on then, Mister World Traveler, I hear you. Go on with all that old fancy stuff they probably taught you in Paris and Casablanca. That's all right with me. Just don't be up there thinking you so much, and forgetting where you got your start. Because some of these same little gals you left down here in poor little old countrified Mobile, Alabama, don't be backing up off none of them, and that goes for any of them little old clippity clopping bouncy-butt cuties up there in Harlem too. So go on, I know you down here on business and ain't got time for no foolishness but just don't be forgetting. These old Mobile girls never is to be standing still neither."

Other such reencounters begin in the same manner, and perhaps as often as not the topic is also essentially the same. For instance: "You got yourself a wife and family? How come you didn't bring your wife so folks can meet her? Now don't be coming down here leaving her up there because you done gone and married some little old white gal—unless she rich and stand for something. And I'm talking about with money's mammy. But shoot, I know you better than to come doing something like that. Your folks ain't worked themselves down to get you all that good education to be taking care of no old pore-tail white gal with. Boy, if you can't marry no white gal that's rich enough to take care of you, forget it. I know you better than that. So is your wife from somewhere down in here? Is she nice? I'm satisfied she pretty. So bring her on down here with you next time, ain't nobody going to bite her."

"I know she educated and I know good and well she pretty," echoes somebody else who was once almost as certain of her own pulchritudinous plurabilities. "Because you probably forgotten me but I remember you all right. You and Leo Greene. Neither one of y'all ain't never had much for no ordinary-looking broad to do—not in the light of day, I'm talking about. Because wait. You know something? Now, I'm going to tell you something. I said I was going to tell you this one of these days, and I am: So you know something? Sometimes you and old Leo Greene used to go around like y'all were trying to be so cute or something. Especially sometimes when somebody didn't stay on in school. But I think I can just about make you remember a few things, Mister Albert Lee Murray. I just about think I just about can.''

You assure this one that you remember very well indeed. *But never as you will always have to remember somebody else who will always be Miss Somebody. Who looked like Kay Francis would have looked if Kay Francis had been sugar-plump brown like that with a shape like that and could have walked that kind of sugar-plump walk wearing bunny-rabbit bedroom mules to the store like that; somebody who said: "Not if you ain't going to stay out of the streets and promise me not to lose sight on the whole world because you finding out what that's made for, not if you ain't going right on keeping that head in them books where it belong"; who said "Lord boy you better not be letting no little old conniving gal come whining your name in your ear so she can come back whining something else soon enough unless you want to end up around here in one of these old sawmills or on the chain gang or something"; who said, "boy God knows you ain't nothing, but a child to me," and said: "Ain't nothing but a little old boy I don't want to see getting too mannish for his own good."*

But the mention of Leo Greene also makes you remember the time when Mister Baker started talking about The Ifs of Initiative Ingenuity and Integrity during the morning assembly period and went on and on about the vision and stick-to-itiveness of great men as contrasted with the self-indulgence of mediocre men (with everybody squirming and wondering) until after one o'clock; and then saying: "Who is going to lead our people into the great tomorrow if promising young men like Leo Greene and Albert Murray don't hold their talent and integrity firmly in clutch instead of riding bicycles all the way over to Cedar Grove to seduce girls on Monday of all nights. Ambition must be made of sterner stuff sterner stuff sterner stuff."

There is also time this trip to revisit some of the old downtown landmarks: and since you are already staying at the Battle House you begin in Bienville Square, *where the sound of the oldest of all wrought-iron municipal fountains immediately evokes Hernando de Soto and Ponce de León once more as it always did during your grade-school days.* (When what use to evoke Bienville and Iberville was the powdered wigs and slippers and pastel stockings of Felix Rex and his masked courtiers during Mardi Gras season.)

From the Square you cross Dauphin Street to Kress (better known as Kresses) which is not only the original of all five-and-dime stores but as such was also your actual prototype of all storybook bazaars, including the getting-place of Christmas toys. (There was a time when it was all too obvious that the route to North Pole and the toy workshop of Santa Claus was through the attic of Kresses.) This time the soda-fountain counter is no longer for whites only, and the palest of all paleface girls are now free to smile their whing-ding service with a red-lipped perfume-counter-faced whing-ding smile at you too (in public). And say: "Coke and one burger comin' *right* up." And say: "Be anything else? Well thank you *kindly*, now." And say: "Come agayhan, now, you hear?'' democratizing and howard-johnsoning you at one and the same time.

You also stand on the corner of Dauphin and Royal once more remembering how when you used to stand there in that time many years ago waiting for the trolley car, with Checker cabs and chauffeur-driven Cadillacs and Packards and Pierce Arrows passing, when what with seeing so many different kinds of people and hearing that many different languages all around you because there were ships flying flags of all nations docked at the foot of Government Street, only a few blocks away; and what with the newsboys chanting the headlines against the background of the empire state tallness of the Van Antwerp Building you knew very well that where you stood was the crossroads of the world.

From Dauphin and Royal you also circle through Metzgers remembering adolescence as the age of Hart, Schaffner and Marx and Society Brand and Kuppenheimers plus Nunn-Busch for some and Florsheim for others. The mere sight of L. Hammels and Gayfers reminds you of the time when the theme-song of every high-school Cinderella was "Sophisticated Lady." You stroll remembering and taking pictures along the waterfront and along Government Street. Then finally you have also checked by the Saenger Theatre and found not only that the old side street "Colored" entrance is now closed but also that the movie of the week is something called *Riot* starring Jim Brown (even as during your high-school days it used to be Johnny Mack Brown the old Rose Bowl star).

Then before you move from the vintage Mobile oldness of the Battle House to spend your last night in the newness of the refurbished Admiral Semmes, from which the next morning you are to begin the return trip to New York—by way of New Orleans, Greenville, and Memphis—there is one other sidewalk reencounter: "Hey, well, if it ain't old Murray. Am I right? Albertmurray. I got you Murray. I know I got you. Albert Murray. Used to live in that shotgun house down there on the way to Dodge's old shingle mill. Had a chinaberry tree in the front yard and a red oak in the back and then some thickets. Boy when did you get back to this neck of the woods? Boy you sure ain't changed a bit have you? Say who you been pitching for since you left town, Murray?''

"Pitching?'' you say, stretching your eyes like Duke does when somebody mistakes him for Cab Calloway and asks for Minnie the Moocher instead of The Mooche. "Man, the last time I pitched a baseball game was back when they were still playing up on old Plateau diamond. Where they used to hit left-field home runs across the Southern Railway crossing toward the Telegraph Road and Chickasaw Terrace. Man, you were probably there. And when they hit hard enough to right center it could go on past that tree and into Aurelia and Louise Bolden's yard.''

"Boy, you used to could pitch your tail off. Hell, if you'd come along a little later you could have made it to the majors. Except damn when it comes to batting you couldn't hit a sack of balls from somebody that didn't have near bout as much stuff on it as you. Man, if you coulda hit like you used to could chunk and field. But that's right I do remember you also used to play all them schoolboy games too, like old Sonny Keeby, and stayed in school and went off to college, to Skegee. Yeah I remember now. That's right. Hey, who you coaching for, Murray? You got any of your boys up there in the big money yet?''

William Mackey, Jr.
(1920–   )

An eminent historian, photographer, and musicologist, Mackey was born
in Jacksonville, Florida, and grew up in southeast Georgia. He currently
teaches world history and conducts a workshop on Black writers at Empire State College. The following excerpt is reprinted from the manuscript
of *Going Home to Georgia*.

Going Home

"A ant is a small thing, but if you mash it you fin' de gut!"

This phrase I heard often from my grandmother, Harriet Weston, years ago
when I was a small boy. She owned a farm in Camden County near the
southeast end of coastal Georgia. The meaning of the expression varied according to the circumstance in which it was used. Sometimes it signaled her
intent to get at the root of some problem; she also used it as an explanation
of how she had solved a problem; again it might constitute a cryptic denial of
some request that she had no intention of granting. In other words, it was one
of her favorite expressions.

The two of us lived alone on that farm for many years, during which I had
countless opportunities to witness firsthand many other examples of her unusual
wit and intelligence. The amazing thing to me about all of this was the fact
that grandma was totally illiterate! She was born in 1857 on a plantation only
five miles away and spent the first eight years of her life in slavery. Her entire
life was spent within a radius of 100 miles of the place where she was born.
Nevertheless, she possessed all the mental and physical skills necessary for
survival. At no time since have I met anyone possessed of a more analytical
mind than this backwoods peasant woman.

I had occasion to recall that phrase many times when I returned to this
backwoods area for the sole purpose of a brief visit but, as a result, found
myself searching for the "guts" of its history. I had been in self-exile and
had maintained little contact, personal or otherwise, with anyone in the area.
Except for the occasional news of someone's death conveyed in passing by
some relative or acquaintance from the vicinity, I had been completely isolated
from the land of my origin. This isolation had not been accidental: for, like

The Return Home after 30 Yrs. in Self-Exile; in the "promised land"

Redefining the Heroic

many other southern Blacks of my generation, I had pulled "up stakes" and left for the "promised land" vowing never to look in a southerly direction if I could avoid it—let alone return.

For 30 years I kept that vow. The credit for my decision to break this vow and consider returning home after all those years must go to my young son, Patrice. Although increasingly as I grew older, thoughts of home crossed my mind, I had not considered going back. However, as my son approached his sixth birthday, the questions—as they inevitably must—began to come: "Hey, Dad! Where were you born?" "What did you do when you were growing up?" "What was it like living on a farm?" "What was your grandmother like?" "Why did you leave and how come you never went back—not even once?" And on and on—ad infinitum.

Home + Memories of Home / The Construction of Home

The more questions he asked, the more my mind began to dwell on home. Why not go back? Wonder how many of the old folks are still alive? Is the old homestead still there and, if so, is anyone living on it? What's the matter, are you afraid to go back, afraid of what you might find? After all, it's home, that's where your roots are. The clincher came when one day my son said to me, "Hey, Dad, I've got an idea. Why don't you and me take the car and drive down to Georgia? I'd like to see the place where you grew up and meet our family who still live there." That did it! I resolved that at the first opportunity I would pay a visit "down home" and renew acquaintance with my past.

In May of 1969, having first supplied myself with enough film and tape to photograph and record most of the inhabitants of the southeastern United States, I headed my car south on my journey of rediscovery. I timed the beginning of my trip so that the daylight hours would be spent driving through the South. This would afford me the opportunity of photographing people, places and things of interest I encountered along the way. After leaving New York around midnight and driving the rest of the night, I arrived in upper Virginia just before daybreak the next morning.

The Return South 1969 → 1969

1939 cf. R. Wright's U.T. Children

After stopping at a motel to wash up and have breakfast, I hit the road again. Before mid-morning I was driving through the lush countryside of North Carolina, the land of my father's ancestors. The planting season was in full swing, and as I went by people working in the fields or walking along the road would wave to me and smile in greeting. Once I passed an old Black man driving a team of oxen pulling an ox cart. He seemed to be in his mid-eighties and was sitting with both legs hanging down on one side of the harness shaft with all the aplomb of a monarch on his throne.

The contrasts between the old and new were sometimes stark. In a field on one side of the highway men were plowing with the latest mechanical implements, while on the opposite side other men could be seen following mules pulling old-fashioned hand plows in the same manner as their grandfathers had tilled the soil. On some fields mechanical seeders using tractor power were in use; in others, groups of Black women, stooping so low that their faces seemed but a few inches from the ground, sowed seed by hand! There they were—two antithetical systems of agriculture—co-existing side by side and, seemingly, in complete harmony! The examples serve as effectively as any I know to illus-

Agrarian Culture

The Contrasts As in So called Third World States/Nations

1) The Ethics of Living Jim
2) The Site of The Blues
3) The Religion of The oppressed.

While traveling along?

✳

DREAD
Doom

Strategies for Survival

Erasure of Individuality of. Luddell Willis

Double Consciousness

trate the extreme diversity of attitudes and philosophies that somehow manage to exist alongside each other in the South.

As I barreled along Interstate Route 1-95 at a seventy-miles-per-hour clip, I gradually became aware of a growing sense of anticipation and excitement welling up within me. I had originally planned to take about two and a half days to complete the trip. Since I was traveling alone and had no one to assist with the driving, I didn't want to push too hard and tire myself out in the process. The distance from New York City to my destination, Woodbine, Georgia, is approximately a thousand miles.

As the sense of anticipation grew, however, I began to feel the urge to get "home" as quickly as possible. Accordingly, I decided to cut my traveling time to a day and a half. By this time, I had been on the road for about twelve hours straight and was as yet feeling no signs of fatigue—my sense of excitement was too high.

Upon entering Virginia earlier that morning I had felt that sense of apprehension which all Black southerners must develop if they hope to survive in their homeland. It is a sense that must be acquired early in life and sharpened to the point where it reacts like an extra reflex muscle. Its presence can often spell the difference between life and death. One's education in acquiring this "extra sense" is speeded up considerably by the actions and admonitions of one's family and community. Furthermore, each "lesson" must be absorbed instantly; there just isn't time for repeats or refresher courses. One either learns immediately, or suffers the consequences!

Since no human being can be expected to live in a state of constant anxiety, it is necessary to acquire the ability to switch one's "apprehension light" as required. To trigger this control most southern Blacks develop sets of invisible "feelers" which not only activate the "circuit" but also give advance information concerning the type and degree of apprehension to be felt, along with an indication of the kind of emotional reaction called for. When not in use, these antennas retract themselves somewhere in the psyche and lie passively until they are required to spring forth again to pick up danger signals.

It is not sufficient just to acquire a general sense of apprehension; it is essential to subdivide it into various categories so that one's response may be exercised only to the extent necessary—no more, no less! Hence, a southern Black usually carries with him at all times, as part of his emotional luggage, a whole series of apprehensions, labeled according to type and ready to be brought into play as the occasion demands.

Sorting these apprehensions is no easy task; some types are so closely related as to almost overlap. Still, the distinctions must be recognized and responded to accordingly. Two of the common types may be labeled as "local apprehensions" and "traveling apprehensions." An example of how the first category is applied is the different ways in which southern Blacks may react to being addressed as "boy" by a white person. The reaction may range all the way from annoyance to anger or fear depending upon the degree and type of hostility that the antennas may "sense" in the addressor. This "sensing" may have absolutely nothing to do with whether obvious hostility is indicated by action

The Rhetoric of black invisibility.

One life depends on
Not making an incorrect
choice.

②

or tone of voice; the "sensing" is done on a deeper, almost instinctive level. If the Black misinterprets or chooses to ignore the apprehensive intelligence relayed by his antennas, he does so at his peril!

The second category comes into play whenever a Black person (northern or southern) travels in the South. The antennas first alert him to the fact that he is not only in strange, but also hostile territory. Then the secondary "apprehension activators" take over; they remind him to be on guard against sheriffs and state troopers saddling him with speeding tickets unjustly (keep speed at least ten miles below the legal limit if possible). They warn him to bend every effort to avoid getting involved in accidents—regardless of who is at fault— with whites, especially women (maintain as much distance as possible between you and any other vehicle). They help him anticipate possible trouble spots when stopping for food, gas, repairs or lodgings. The traveler rarely relaxes until he is back on familiar ground.

It was my "traveling apprehension" that had come into focus when I crossed into Virginia that morning. In fact, my antennas were far more sensitive than normal. Having been away for so long, my "southern apprehensions" were quite rusty and needed a strong dose of extra stimulation to oil them up again. That is not to say that New York Blacks don't have apprehensions, they do; but "northern apprehensions" are a different breed from their southern counterparts; therefore different emotional techniques must be used in order to perfect them. Having spent over thirty years trying to cope with the New York variety, I was unable to shift gears smoothly and ease back into the southern version without some strain. Thus, in the beginning, I overreacted.

Once or twice while driving through Virginia I considered turning back. "What the hell am I doing?" I'd ask myself. "Why in hell am I out here on a strange highway that probably leads to nowhere, trying to find my way back in time to a place which for all I know may no longer exist? Hadn't Thomas Wolfe, and others who tried it, said "You can't go home again"? Thirty years is a long time. The old people are probably all dead; the young ones won't know me. I'll probably wind up standing in the middle of some crossroad, surrounded by strangers, feeling like a damn idiot!"

I even considered going back to Baltimore, where I had friends, spending the night with them and then taking off for Brooklyn the next morning. (I had not told anyone in Georgia that I was coming. I'd told my wife that the reason was that I wanted to surprise them. This was only partly true; I also wanted to be in a position to turn around and come back in case I chickened out, without anyone down there being aware of it!) However, by the time I reached North Carolina my spirits were all charged up and I gave little thought to the idea of turning back. Besides, by this time, I had cut the distance almost in half and it would take about as much time to get back to Brooklyn as to continue on to my destination.

It was a balmy spring day and the soft fragrance of honeysuckle was mixed with the pleasing odor of freshly turned earth. As I drove along my imagination began to peel away the layers of years and soon I became deeply engrossed in remembrance of things past. Once again, I was a carefree boy tramping

Anti-Pastoral

Pastoral

barefoot through the woods. In my mind's eye I took in the entire expanse of grandma's farm. I saw all the buildings: barn, henhouse, smokehouse, dairy and syrup house. I saw the road that led up to the broad expanse in front of our house which, for some reason, we called "the lane."

I could see all our utility buildings arranged on both sides of "the lane" and the huge woodpile (which one of my chores had been to keep supplied from the forest) placed almost in the center. As nostalgia took full possession of me, I began to flesh out the rest of that farm; the grape arbor, the rice field down in the bottomland that grandma had cleared of trees and undergrowth all by herself while grandpa cleared the other farmland. She was determined to grow rice without delay, so she had prepared all ten acres singlehandedly. I remembered how in later years when I'd asked her how she'd done it, she answered, "If you git up and try to he'p yo'se'f, then God he fin' a way to he'p you. If you sit on yo' behin' an' wait fo' somethin' to fall in yo' lap, you starve to death! Lazy folks don't never git nothin', even de bird in de fiel' got to work fo' his food. You do nothin', you git nothin', tha's all day is to it!"

Now, driving along thinking of the past, I had an overwhelming urge to get home as quickly as possible. I told myself that the first order of business when I arrived would be to pay a visit to the old homestead. Looking at my watch, I noted that it was only eleven thirty. I decided that I would cover as much ground as possible before calling it a day so as to arrive early the next morning. My apprehensions were all gone now, all I thought about was getting home.

Then, as I was nearing the town of Wilson, North Carolina, I came around a curve, and there it was! Just off the highway on my right stood a huge sign painted red and blue with white letters. In the left-hand corner was the figure of a knight clad in white armor and mounted on a rearing horse. At first glance I thought it was some kind of ad for "Ajax Cleanser," but upon looking closer, and when the full impact of what the sign said hit me, I almost ran off the road! This "white knight" was clad in the regalia of the Ku Klux Klan, complete with the symbolic "K" emblazoned on the horse's blanket. His head was covered with the traditional pillowcase, which had a cross painted on it in the places his eyes and nose would normally occupy. In his upraised left hand he carried a burning torch that projected about eighteen inches above the top of the sign proper. The horse was entirely black (a kind of ironic symbol in itself if one wishes to stretch the point). In his right hand the "knight" was carrying what appeared to be a Bible. The legend on the sign, in heavy type, about twelve inches high, read:

YOU ARE NOW IN KLAN COUNTRY

WELCOME TO NORTH CAROLINA

JOIN THE UNITED KLANS OF AMERICA

Below the bottom of the main sign, as if tacked on as an afterthought, a piece of board, about eight inches high, was attached. Its message was: "HELP FIGHT INTEGRATION AND COMMUNISM." In case some sympathizer was compelled, for any reason, to limit himself to resisting only one of the two evils, it was obvious from this sign, which one the Klan gave top priority.

Having pulled over on the shoulder of the highway and stopped, I sat there for about five minutes gazing at that sign in wonder. There it stood—hard by a federal highway! Suddenly I had a nagging feeling that maybe somebody was trying to get a message over to me! I became aware that my old friend "apprehension" was beginning to tug at my guts once again. With some effort, I managed to push my anxiety way down into the inner recesses of my mind. I pulled back onto the highway and continued on my way. "Hell," I muttered, "it's too damn late to turn back."

The image of that sign remained imprinted on my consciousness for quite some time afterwards. I tried consoling myself with the rationale that this was the South and one could expect to see almost anything along the highway. After all, "Southern Hospitality" was one of the major assets the South was constantly boasting about. One aspect of this "hospitality" was the granting of permission to anyone so inclined to install signs in conspicuous places near major highways for the purpose of promoting any message or philosophy they saw fit. It occurred to me that maybe further on I might encounter a sign espousing the cause of the Black Panther Party. Such an eventuality would serve as proof positive that the concept of "equal time" had been extended from the narrow confines of the broadcast studios to cover the lengths and breadths of our major highways! But, alas, it was not to be.

During the rest of my journey I saw many signs advising the impeachment of Chief Justice Earl Warren. And there were two that went for broke and recommended sacking the entire United States Supreme Court!

The number of this type of political sign increased as I penetrated deeper into the bowels of the Southland. In addition, their language grew more and more strident. The second most numerous category of signs were those with a religious bent. They usually confined themselves to warning the traveler to repent and ask forgiveness for his sins immediately, as Armageddon was imminent!

By early afternoon, I found myself in lower North Carolina. This was a section I had known well from having worked there when, as a youth, I had been employed by the Seaboard Airline Railroad Company on one of its "extra gang" crews. I was traveling much nearer the coast than before and the terrain reflected this change. The land was much flatter than before and as a result, there were miles and miles of monotonous sameness. This is the heart of the North Carolina "black belt" plantation country.

The people in this part of the state appeared much poorer than those I had seen in the upper, more industrial part. The number of inhabited shacks increased the farther south I drove. Even the continuity of the superhighway was broken. I was forced to make constant detours getting on and off the bits and pieces of I-95 that seemed to have been scattered about at random in chunks varying from about ten to seventy miles.

One of the side effects of all these detours was a slowing down of my rate of travel. Sometimes I went as much as twelve miles east or west before making a southerly connection again. In addition, the alternate routes invari-

Two Sons of The South
from different generations

ably went right through the center of towns and villages instead of bypassing them as the superhighway does. This necessitated slowing down to speeds of as little as five miles per hour. There was some compensation in the fact that these routes gave me an opportunity to see considerably more of the people and their environment than was possible on 1-95. In the end, the "alternate" routes had the last word. For somewhere in the lower half of South Carolina, after a last, long, dying gasp of about sixty miles, 1-95 gave up the ghost and just quit altogether. That was the last I saw of it until just before turning off route U.S. 17 at the end of my journey.

After leaving 1-95 near Marion, South Carolina, I continued south via U.S. 301 as far as Summerton, South Carolina, where it merged with U.S. 15. Since U.S. 15 split itself into two directions at this point and the indications as to which one goes south were not entirely clear, I decided to stop at a restaurant for directions and a short rest.

Penetration metaphor

While eating a sandwich and getting directions from the counterman, a white man of about 35 years of age, dressed in a U.S. Army Master Sergeant's uniform sitting on the stool next to me, turned and asked how far south I was going. His speech had that drawl characteristic of whites of the Deep South. I answered that I was going across the state of Georgia to within fifteen miles of the Florida border. He said he was headed for Midway, Georgia, and asked if he might ride that far with me, if I had room. For a moment, listening to that drawl, I hesitated. Then I thought: "What the hell, what harm could it do?" Besides, I had been alone so long that a little company might be good. It would also help to keep me alert. I told him I wouldn't mind having someone to talk to for a change and that he was welcome to a ride. He thanked me, then offered to share gas expenses with me. He even offered to pay for my meal, but I refused. After having the car checked and the tank filled, we hit the road.

For about the first ten minutes after we started, neither of us said anything. Finally, he broke the ice by asking where exactly in Georgia was I going. When I told him, he said he'd never heard of it. I said that it was a hundred and ten miles south of Savannah, and the fact that he had never heard of Woodbine was not surprising, since it was so small that it would take no more than two minutes to drive through it at two miles an hour. "At least that was its size when I left," I added. "As a matter of fact," I said, "come to think of it, I've never heard of Midway before either." We had a good laugh at this.

I asked how long had he been in the Army and why had he chosen this method of travel to come home. He said that he'd joined up when he was twenty and was bored with life in Midway where he was born and raised. He thought joining the Army would be the quickest and easiest way to see some of the rest of the world. In the beginning, he intended making a career of it but, after fifteen years, he'd become disillusioned and quit. He had suffered a severe stomach wound a year and a half ago in Vietnam and had been hospitalized for over a year. (As he was talking he pulled the bottom of his shirt and

The military as a way out (mobility) for poor whites + impoverished blacks,

Unified strands ⎡ Shame, Anger, Rage (Blk)
⎣ Guilt (white)

Rhetorically indirection
A metaphor
An Black Attitudes toward whites.

undershirt out of his pants and revealed a wicked looking, jagged scar about five inches long running horizontally across the center of his navel!)

While lying there in that hospital, he had plenty of time to think. The war had long since ceased to make any sense to him, and he began to wonder if there had ever been any logical reason for being there. He said it had been obvious to him for a long time that all the Vietnamese, north and south, hated our guts. It was his opinion that the only Vietnamese who liked Americans were the ones who profited from our being there. And even they only tolerated us.

About six months ago he'd been brought stateside and placed in a convalescent hospital near Boston and had been there until three weeks ago when he was released as being completely recovered. Upon being given his choice of reenlisting for limited duty or resigning, he took the latter course. After visiting various cities in the Northeast and trying to make up his mind about his future, he had come to the conclusion that the best place for him was back home in Midway, Georgia. At the last minute he'd decided to hitchhike back and see some of the country along the way.

He asked me how long I had been away and when I told him, his eyebrows went up. "Man, that's a long time," he said. "Y'all left just about the time I was being born!" He asked why I hadn't come back to visit before now. I just looked at him and laughed. He looked down at his lap for a moment, as if deep in thought, then said quietly, "Oh yeah, I forgot." ←

I was so busy thinking about how to ward off any assault on my inscrutability, that I was totally unprepared for what came next. "You know," he said, "things have changed a lot for the better for y'all down heah in the last few years. They ain't changed enough—but it sho'is a lot better'n before. An' more change is comin' all the time. Even in the Army, things is changin' fast. Course I realize that for folks who is sufferin' from the loss of their dignity, things don' ever change fast enough! But they is changin' alright, yessir. Now you take the Army—it don't even look like the same Army I joined fifteen years ago. All different now. See more o' y'all gittin' promoted all the time; more non-coms, more officers—more everythin'. To tell the truth, I cain't hardly keep up with some o' them changes. Gits kinda confusin' to me sometime, too. Man, it took me the longest time to learn how to say 'Negro' instead of 'nigger.' I never meant no harm in sayin' 'nigger'—it just growed up in me—that's all I ever heard 'roun' home! Man, I used to git in some fights over that word! But I learned!

"It seemed like almost as soon as I got 'Negro' down pat—y'all wanted to be called somethin' else—'Afro-American.' Now the word is 'Black.' Yessir, it sho' is confusin' sometime. Still, I guess everybody ought to have the right to say what they want to be called—don' matter how many times they change it. It's their right! Now, take me. Anybody who call me a Georgia cracker better be ready to fight! Man, I wish I had a dollar for every fight I had 'bout that word; I'd be a rich man now. An' sometimes I was called 'cracker' by Black soldiers who was ready to kill me if I called them 'nigger.' Kinda crazy, ain't it?" I nodded my head and kept silent.

Change of M.K.K.

Recall R.W. Uncle Tom's Children
L. Hughes, Simple Stories

The Importance of Modeling —— on stereotypes
— and the correction made for/white-to-white
men + women
Black-to-Black

514 *William Mackey, Jr.*

It was obvious that his Army experiences had had a profound effect on him. And I couldn't help wondering how these experiences would affect his efforts to readjust to the mores and attitudes of a small Deep South town. It would be interesting, I thought, to come back and talk with him five years from now to find out what had happened to him in the interim.

My companion had fallen asleep shortly after our last bit of conversation and was now slumbering peacefully. His head was tilted slightly backward and his cap had fallen off, revealing a shock of the reddest hair I had ever seen. He slept for about two hours during which we covered most of the distance from Walterboro to Hardeeville, South Carolina. Finally, as I pulled into a filling station for gas and a car-check, he woke up. "Where are we?" he asked. "About twenty miles north of Hardeeville," I replied. "Damn good time," he muttered, half to himself. I agreed that we had covered quite a bit of territory since he fell asleep. "Well, it won't be long now," he continued, "before I'll be back home. Lessee now, it's almos' four o'clock. What y'all say we git somethin' to eat in Hardeeville, I'm payin'." I said that was fine with me.

"There's a Holiday Inn jus' the other side o' Hardeeville. Man, they got some o' the bes' fried chicken anywhere in the south. An' that's sayin' somethin'!" His eyes widened with the pleasure of anticipation as he extolled the culinary delights of this particular inn. "An' the corn fritters they serve are out o' this worl'. Man, they melt in yo' mouth—an' that's a fac'." He went on. "Y'all wanta try it?" he asked. "Why not?" I replied.

In a short while we had passed through the town of Hardeeville and soon reached the inn he'd spoken about. It was located at the southern end of the town and had a large swimming pool that occupied a good deal of the space behind it. There was a large group of bathers sunning themselves around the pool—all of them were white. Some of them watched us with idle curiosity as we entered the restaurant. My companion, noting their looks, remarked: "Damn, you'd think they woulda been used to it by now." Then he said, "Hell, come on, let's eat. I'm hungry."

The food was as good as he'd predicted. The chicken was superb and the corn fritters were in a class by themselves. I had eaten about six of them before I was even aware of my gluttony. After having stuffed myself with chicken and corn fritters, I had very little room left for dessert and decided to pass it up. Our entire bill (including the tip) for this feast, came to only five dollars and seventy-five cents! I made a mental note to time any future trips in such a way as to have at least one meal in this inn.

As he was paying the bill, it suddenly dawned on me that we had been traveling together for over four hours and did not know each other's names. When I pointed this fact out to him, he laughed and exclaimed: "Well, I'll be damn if that ain't the truth!" He stuck his hand across the table toward me. "My name is Roy Willis, but everybody calls me Buzz. Far back as I remember, that's the name I been answerin' to." We shook hands and I told him my name.

Blacks as "workers"

$5.75

4 hrs.

While this was going on, the waitress just stood there looking down at us in amazement. She hesitated a second, then said, "Y'all mean to tell me that the two of you jus' walk in heah an' sit down an' eat together—with conversation an' all—an' y'all don' even know each other? That's the funniest thing I ever heard of!" We laughed at the absurdity of the situation, then Buzz told her how we happened to be together. "Well anyway," she said, "y'all have a nice trip, an' stop in an' see us when y'all come back this way again, heah?" She walked away, shaking her head in disbelief.

As we pulled out onto the highway again, I said, "Well, Buzz, if all goes well our next stop will be your home, Midway. In a few minutes we'll cross the Savannah River and once past Savannah, it should be smooth sailing from then on." He nodded in agreement, then looked at his watch. "It's a quarter after five now," he said. "With a little luck I'll be home before sundown."

Now the highway was cutting a path as straight as an arrow through the marshland. The only vegetation to be seen was the tall wiry marsh grass on both sides of the road. It extended as far as the eye could see. Looming up in the distance was the bridge over the Savannah River—the boundary between South Carolina and Georgia. The bridge is pitched so high above the river that from a distance it seems to be taking off into infinity. When approaching it on a clear day, from the Carolina side, it can be seen from a distance of about seven miles.

As we got closer to the river, I became aware of a mixture of highly unpleasant odors. They seemed to be concocted of portions of every foul-smelling chemical I had ever had the misfortune of being exposed to. The nearer we approached the river, the stronger the stench. A few hundred feet before the entrance to the bridge was a sign. It consisted of the face of a smiling sun with a legend encircling it, enticing us to: "STAY AND SEE GEORGIA!" Just below this, some wag had tacked on a piece of white cardboard on which was written in black paint a message of caution: "AND DON'T FORGET TO BRING YOUR GAS MASK."

Glancing at Buzz, I saw that he had his nose screwed up and his face wore a look of general discomfort. "Man, that's some odor," I said. "You damn right it is." He said, "You know, every time I pass heah, it seems to git worse! Where's it all goin' to end?" "Well, anyway, welcome to Georgia," I said.

At the other end of the bridge, there were a series of toll booths. I wondered how in hell their occupants could stand this torture day after day, without either jumping off the bridge or going mad.

Just off the bridge, there was a sign advising us to take alternate route 17A in order to avoid going through Savannah. I decided to follow its advice. It took only a short time to discover that this route, like parts of I-95, had carved itself out of bits and pieces of streets that skirted the city of Savannah. It conducts a grand tour through parts of the worst slum south of Newark, New Jersey. The only other that can compare with it, in my view, is the west side of Jacksonville, Florida. By a strange coincidence, the inhabitants of both are black!

There were a great many people sitting on their front porches and, as we drove past, many of them waved. The surfaces of most of the streets were in such terrible condition, that any speed above five miles per hour would have been hazardous. The streets ran so close to the buildings that it would be possible for someone sitting in a chair on a front porch to shake hands with someone sitting in a car on the street, without getting up. Some buildings looked as if a strong gust of wind would dislodge them from their pillars. They were all frame buildings and most were one-story high. There were several whose walls were actually being supported by long poles propped up against them. Occasionally, there were dwellings that were constructed of tin sheets. Every once in a while, we passed one of these derelicts that stood empty—in all its grandeur, sporting a "for rent" sign on its front wall!

Frequently, we passed a run-down shop or restaurant with little clusters of men gathered on its front porch. The older men looked just as the older men who gathered around these places had looked when I was a boy. For the most part they were dressed in denim shirts and overalls with a smattering of khaki workpants. They were generally shod in that variety of work shoes that used to be known as brogans. A sweat-stained felt hat usually capped off the uniform. The few who were bareheaded wore closely cropped hair. There were no signs of processed hair anywhere.

The teenagers and younger men were of a different breed entirely! Their dress styles ranged all the way from flamboyant purple shirts, tucked inside multi-colored pants, which in turn were hung over alligator skin shoes; through denim jackets with tight-fitting Levis; on to dashikis combined with chinos and sandals. Their hairstyles, with few exceptions, was of the style known as "Afro."

To the casual eye, these little knots of men might seem, at first glance, to be made up of widely disparate elements; yet they were bound together by two of the strongest links in the chain that unites all Black Americans—sometimes involuntarily—color and economic condition.

There were many restaurants that catered to the palates of those whose tastes favored highly seasoned foods. In one block alone, I counted four such establishments, each of which displayed signs proclaiming its absolute supremacy in the culinary art of preparing barbeque! Once in awhile, I saw one that advertised "soul food," but not often. There was one which referred to itself via a large neon sign, simply as the "Down Home." The hardy aromas of various types of barbeque sauces wafting out from these restaurants were in welcome contrast to the "essence de river" that had just recently overwhelmed us.

Near the end of this section we stopped for a traffic light. While waiting for the "go" signal, a Black youth of about nineteen sauntered up to the curb and started to cross the street. As he came abreast of the car on my side, he waved to me, smiled and said, "Hey brer'." When he reached the opposite side of the car, he suddenly darted out of the crosswalk and poking his head inside the window to within two inches of Buzz's face, he yelled in a voice dripping with venom, "Hiya, honkie." Almost in the same motion, he withdrew his head, went back to the crosswalk and continued walking toward the other side of the street as if nothing had happened.

Buzz sat there stunned! His face was as red as the heart of an overripe watermelon. It had happened so quickly. "Well I'll be damned!" We blurted almost simultaneously. Just then the light turned green and we drove on. For a time we rode in silence, each of us digesting in his own way the impact of that incident. I turned to him finally and said, half jokingly, "Well, Buzz, there's another one of those 'new terms' for you to mull over!" He laughed and the tension was broken.

"Why the hell y'all think he did that?" he asked. "The guy musta been crazy! Did y'all ever see anythin' like that in yo' life?" I answered that during World War II, I had witnessed a somewhat similar incident. "Yeah, what happened?" He wanted to know. "Well, we were on this troop train traveling through Mississippi. Our train had stopped to take on fuel and some of the fellows decided to take advantage of this and sent someone to a nearby store to buy some fruit. Just as the guy came out of the store, the train started to take off. A soldier stuck his head out of a window and started yelling and waving to his buddy to hurry up before he was left behind. As the train was picking up speed, it passed a loading platform next to the tracks. A small white boy about ten years old who was standing on the platform near its edges, slapped the face of the soldier with his head outside, and yelled: 'Hey nigger, git your goddamned head back inside!' Since the train was going in one direction, and the blow came from the opposite direction, its effect was increased about five times! The soldier's head slammed into the side of the train with such force that he lost two teeth. I looked out of another window and saw the kid still standing there on the platform, laughing and shaking his fist in our direction. By the way, the other guy managed to get back on the train."

Buzz looked at me in amazement. "Did anybody catch the kid?" he asked. "Are you kidding? In Mississippi? Not a chance! If anybody saw him, they probably gave him a medal for courage beyond the call of duty." "Goddamn," was all Buzz could say. "So you see," I concluded, "you were lucky you were only assaulted verbally!"

Buzz let that sink in for a moment, then said emphatically, "Man, growin' up down heah in yo' time musta been hell!" "It was," I answered. "Then why the hell you comin' back?" Buzz asked. "I've asked myself that question at least a hundred times since I left New York. I suppose one reason is to see if things have changed much for the better. Another is to find out if it is possible to come to terms with my past. I guess that's something most of us must try to do sooner or later. Also, lately I've been thinking a lot about the old homestead and the family I left back here and I have a strong desire to see them again.

"Apart from these things, during the last five years, I've belatedly come to realize that, insofar as Blacks are concerned, the north is basically no better than the south—only different. So if I find things changed enough to make a readjustment possible, I might consider coming back home for good."

"Gettin' a little tired of the rat race, eh?" Buzz asked. "You bet," I replied. I asked him what his plans were after he got home. He said he would go to work as a salesman in his father's used-car agency. His family had been in business in Midway since shortly after the Civil War. His great-grandfather had founded a farm-implement, seed and livestock business with only two mules and three handplows at the start. The business prospered to such an extent that by the end of the first World War it was one of the largest of its kind in southeast Georgia. The depression came and it all went.

Buzz's father had started all over again. Going into the used-car business during the Second World War. Since new cars were hard to come by during this period, he had three thriving used-car dealerships in the area by the end of the war. One of the main reasons for Buzz leaving home was his father's desire that he learn the business in preparation for one day taking over completely. Buzz found the idea of becoming a used-car tycoon unappealing, and as there were no other local alternatives, he'd just packed up and enlisted.

I asked if he thought it would be difficult for him to readjust to the pace of a small town after all the excitement of the past fifteen years. He answered: "If y'all had the choice of facin' some guy and tryin' to talk him into buyin' a used-car, or facin' some 'cong' in the jungle of 'Nam, what would you do?" I didn't answer.

The highway suddenly expanded into two lanes. A large ornate sign over it welcomed us to the town of Midway, Georgia, then threatened us with dire consequences should we be so rash as to violate any of its traffic laws. "Well, Buzz," I said, "you're home. Where do you want me to drop you off?" He replied, "When you come to the third traffic light, you'll see a Gulf fillin' station on yo' right. It belongs to my cousin. Pull in there." "Okay," I answered. As we pulled into the filling station, I looked at my watch. It was five minutes of seven.

As we got out of the car, a Black attendant came over. When he saw Buzz his face broke into a big smile of welcome. "Well, I'll be damn, if it ain't ol' Buzz! What y'all doin' back heah? I thought y'all been still up dere in the hospital." Buzz told him that he had quit the Army and was home for good. He introduced me, then asked for his cousin. He was told that his cousin had just gone home for supper. He asked the attendant to check my car, make any adjustments necessary, fill the gas tank, and charge it to him.

Buzz suggested that I come home with him and meet his family. He said I could have dinner with them, spend the night and finish my journey the next day. He said that he'd like his folks to meet me and assured me there would be no problem about staying. I thanked him, but said that since I had only about seventy miles to go, I wanted to get home that night.

After wishing me luck and warning me to be very careful while driving through the towns of McIntosh County because they extracted a large share of their revenue from the pockets of unwary out-of-state motorists, he asked if I had something to write on. I handed him a piece of paper. He wrote his address and phone number on it. I gave him my address in return. Then he said that any time I was passing through, to feel free to stop by for a visit. I said that I might just do that.

There was a moment of awkward silence as we stood there just looking at each other. Finally, Buzz stuck out his hand and said, "Y'all know somethin', Bill? I sho' enjoyed travelin' and 'talkin' with you. An' I'm gon' tell y'all somethin' else—I like you. I like you a lot! An' I sho' hope y'all fin' everything alright when y'all get home. Now, y'all be careful on that road out there, you heah. Well, so long an' may God bless an' keep you." I said goodbye, got back into the car and started off on what I hoped was the last leg of my journey.

I had now been on the road for about twenty hours straight. Gradually I became aware of the beginning signs of fatigue creeping over me. It was now night and the greatly reduced visibility, coupled with the necessity for increased alertness, added an extra strain which heightened my sense of weariness. The thought crossed my mind that I might have been too hasty in rejecting Buzz's offer to spend the night at his home.

For a moment I considered turning around and going back to Midway. But a quick glance at the odometer disabused me of that notion, since I had already covered twenty-two miles. The distance back to Midway was about the same as that of the next town ahead. I decided to continue on as far as Brunswick, Georgia, which was only about thirty miles, and stop there for the night if I felt too tired to proceed. This would leave only twenty-eight miles to cover the next day before reaching home.

Before picking up Buzz I had made occasional stops in roadside rest areas to wash up and take short rests. I usually spent about fifteen minutes walking around and doing about five minutes of calisthenics to increase the circulation and loosen up a bit. In addition, I made infrequent stops to photograph people or things I found interesting. This routine, plus my desire to see everything of interest along my route, without jeopardizing my own safety, or that of others, had helped to keep me alert. After taking on my passenger, except for food and fuel, I had made only four brief stops to take photographs, and none for exercise. Our conversation and my interest in the surrounding terrain had been sufficient to keep me pepped up.

None of these options were available to me now. Even reading the neon signs that were on either side of the highway like multi-colored electric hookers enticing me to try everything from Bibles to boathouses, put an added strain on my eyes. Therefore, I kept my eyes off them as much as possible. This was no easy task. They stood out in bold relief against the surrounding darkness and it was almost as difficult not to look at them as it is for a moth to ignore the fatal attraction of a lighted lamp.

I decided to hold my speed down to thirty-five miles per hour, even though the limit posted advised me that I had the choice of living dangerously and doing fifty. I was not traveling on home ground. Even in the darkness I could occasionally recognize the outlines of some landmark that I remembered from years ago. There were more built-up areas along the borders of the highway, but there were still long stretches of countryside in between.

Judging from many of the neon (and other types) signs, it would seem that the major competition for the highway traveler's dollar (as far as food, fuel, lodging and certain regional products are concerned) in the southeastern coastal states, is among three firms: Stuckey's, Horne, and Rawls' With Mr. Rawls occupying, I believe, a tertiary position. The first two usually supply food and lodging, in addition to their other services; the third may or may not.

Coping with the distractions of this surfeit of signs had presented no problem for me during the day when I had been much fresher and the current for the majority of them was turned off. Now, however, it was a different story. I was tired and tense and the sight of all those colorful lights made my eyeballs want to burst. I finally resorted to the tactic of blinking my eyes rapidly for a few seconds periodically in an effort to erase their images from my brain. This solved the problem and for the rest of the journey I was not too conscious of them.

All at once, I saw a sign announcing the city limits of Brunswick. I thought my eyes, in their fatigue, had played a trick on me. Then I saw another larger, neon-lit sign that removed all doubt. "Welcome to Brunswick, Gateway to The Golden Isles." That confirmed it. I was only twenty-eight miles from home!

I had assumed that I was still somewhere north of Darien, some thirty-five miles north of Brunswick. But I had been so absorbed in trying to cope with those damn neon signs, that I had gone right through Darien without being aware of it. Glancing at my watch, I saw that it was only nine-thirty. As I was feeling only a little more fatigued than when I left Midway, I decided to put caution to the winds and try for home. Within a short while, I was cutting through the marshes of Glynn, the subject of Sidney Lanier's epic poem of the same name. My fatigue had miraculously disappeared, and I felt almost as fresh as when I started out. Shortly, I saw a sign announcing the Little Satilla River, and right next to it, another that marked the beginning of Camden County. Soon I was whizzing through little villages and hamlets, the names of which had not crossed my mind in years: Spring Bluff, Waverly, White Oak. So far as I could tell in the darkness, they seemed not to have changed one iota in all the years of my absence.

Five minutes after leaving the hamlet of White Oak, I could see the well-lit bridge over the Big Satilla River. As I got closer I could see that at least one thing in Camden had changed in my absence; the old bridge had been replaced by a more modern one of reinforced concrete. Once on it, I saw that it arched over the river at a much higher distance above the water than the old one had. At its opposite end was a sign announcing that the city of Woodbine, Georgia, began there. Another dramatic change was immediately apparent. In place of the one lane thoroughfare of my youth, there were now two lanes in each direction that ran almost up to the foot of the bridge. A short distance from the bridge was a traffic light. Beyond that, I could see three more lights in the distance.

"Well I'll be damned if Woodbine hasn't gone modern!" I said out loud in stunned surprise. It was not three minutes past ten. The trip from New York had taken me exactly twenty-two hours. The odometer showed that I had covered a distance of one-thousand twenty-three miles!

I knew that just a hundred feet or so from the bridge, there should be a dirt road on the right side of the highway that would take the three and a half miles out to my old community—Scarlett. It wasn't there! I pulled off the road, stopped and got out of the car to get my bearings. I haven't been away long enough to forget where that road was. I stood there trying to re-create the town as I remembered it in my mind's eye. As the past slowly came into focus, I looked at the buildings around me trying to match them with those I saw in my mind. No luck. They wouldn't fit. Finally, I walked the short distance back to the bridge, then retraced my steps back to the car, carefully examining each building as I went along. I saw only one building that I recognized—Gowen's Appliance Store. It had been erected just before I left home and was the most modern building in the town at the time. None of the other buildings were familiar.

I got back into the car and just sat there for a while trying to decide what to do next. The town had rolled up the sidewalks for the night and there was not a single person to be seen anywhere. The few residences adjacent to the highway had their shades drawn. I finally decided to continue a bit further along the highway in the hope of finding a filling station or an all-night truck-stop open. Besides, the prospect of being spotted by some trigger-happy, small-town southern cop who might consider a strange Black man sitting alone in a car with New York plates parked in the commercial part of town at this hour, reason enough to shoot first and ask questions later, was certainly unappealing.

After traveling about a mile further, I came upon an ice plant with a store and filling station adjoining. A sign over it said: OPEN TWENTY-FOUR HOURS. With a sigh of relief, I pulled off the highway and stopped in front of the store. I went in and asked the woman behind the counter if she could direct me to Scarlett. She was new in town and had never heard of it. As I turned to leave, she said that I might try the colored night man working in the ice plant next door as she believed he was a native of these parts and lived about three miles from town somewhere out on route 110. I thanked her and headed for the ice plant.

As I walked up the steps to the loading platform, a Black man of about fifty-three years of age came walking out of one of the freezing stalls pulling a large block of ice behind him. After apologizing for the intrusion, I asked if he could direct me home, and also if he knew my uncle, Aaron Weston. He replied, "Yea, not only do I know your Uncle Aaron, but I know you too!" He was one of my distant cousins, James Forcine, whom I had grown up with! He had recognized me on sight, but my memory was not as acute. After talking with him for a few minutes and studying his facial features, I was able to reconstruct his image as I had known it.

I told him about my embarrassment at not being able to find the road home. He laughed at this, then told me there was no need for embarrassment, for not only had the road been moved since I went away—its surface had also been paved. It was now rated as "Class A" highway and was known as "State Route 110." He added that at the same time the road was paved, parts of it were straightened out and that its junction with U.S. 17 was about a block farther south than previously.

He then informed me that Uncle Aaron had just recently passed by on his way back home after taking his wife to the hospital. He said that my aunt was a diabetic and had to be placed in the hospital periodically for observations and checkups.

He looked at me for a moment in silence, then asked: "Junior, when last you ate anythin'?" I answered, "About five o'clock this afternoon in Hardee-ville, South Carolina." He looked surprised. "You mean to say you drove all the way heah from there since five o'clock?" he asked. "Yeah," I said, "I've been on the road since last midnight." "Without stopping to sleep or anythin'? Man, you musta been outa your mind!" I said, "Well, you see, when I started out, my intention was to make the trip in about three days. But once on the road, I got a strong desire to get home, so I just kept on going, and here I am." "Well, I'll be damned!" he exclaimed. "Boy, you done come over a thousan' miles! You come by yourself?" "Most of the way," I said. "I picked up a white soldier in Summerton, South Carolina, and he rode with me as far as Midway." He asked, "How long is it since you been home?" "About thirty years or so," I answered. "Thirty years! Damn! How old are you now?" "Forty-nine," I answered. He said, "I'm fifty-two and a grandfather! Well, Junior, I guess we gettin' kinda old, ain't we?" I said, "Yeah, I guess we are." He asked, "You got any children?" "Yeah," I answered. "Two. A daughter of twenty-five and a six-year-old son. No grandchildren as yet. My daughter is not married, and my son is too young." We laughed.

I asked about some of the older people I had known in my youth. He said, "Junior, a whole lot of them old people dongone from heah! Mama and Papa, they both dead. There's still some of the old folks around, though. Your granduncle Sonny, he still heah. He about ninety-four years old now. An' my Uncle Cleveland, he still heah—doin' fine at eighty-five, an' still chasin' women! Then, there's Mrs. Katy Jones. She must be eighty-some. Ol' man Derry Toney, he pushin' ninety. Old lady Sarah Jenkins over in St. Mary's she about ninety-three or ninety-four. Anyway, she aroun' Uncle Sonny's age. An' there's a few more knocking about out there in these woods somewhere, whose names I can't remember jus' now. Come to think of it there's quite a few ol' folks aroun' heah—still hangin' on somehow."

He paused a minute, then said: "Boy, I never expected to ever see you down this way agin'—after we didn't hear from you in so long. Mos' o' them that left from aroun' heah come back to visit from time to time; but now you, you ain't come back to visit even once till now. What made you decide to come home after all these years?"

"There's really no simple answer to that question," I replied. "Let's just say, as the old folk used to, that there's a time for all things. And this was the time for me to come back home.''

"By the way,'' I asked, ''have you been living here all these years?''

"Heah,'' he said. ''Ever since I come home from the C.C.C. camp. You know I met my wife, Pearl, when I was in the corps up there in Jasper, Georgia. Brought her back home and we been heah ever since. I been work' heah at the ice plant twenty years, ever since they built. Yessir, seven nights a week for twenty years—except for two weeks vacation each year. I got me a driller's rig an' run a well-boring business on the side. I also do the meter readin's for the town of Woodbine.''

"When the hell do you sleep?'' I asked.

"Oh, I manage to get in a few licks here and there,'' he answered. ''I'm the only one here at night and I set my own pace. There ain't nobody aroun' to bother me. I'm my own boss. It ain't too bad at all,'' he concluded.

"Well, James,'' I said, ''it's a little after eleven o'clock, so if you'll be kind enough to tell me how to find the road home, I'll be on my way. I expect to be here for at least ten days, so I'll stop by your place before I leave. You know,'' I added, laughing, ''if anyone had told me that I would ever need instructions on how to find Scarlett, I'd have called him crazy.''

He gave me instructions on how to find the road and we shook hands. As I turned to leave, he said, ''Wait a minute. I forgot all about you bein' hungry. I'll phone Pearl and tell her you comin' an' to fix you somethin' to eat. You can't miss our house. It's at the crossroad where the artesian well used to be.''

I stood there with my mouth open. ''You mean to say you have phones out there in the woods now?''

"Yessir, an' gas an' electricity too. We got jus' about everythin' out there you got in New York. It ain't like in the old days when you was heah. That's all changed now.''

James said goodnight and went back inside to call his wife. I drove slowly back down the highway until I saw the sign pointing to state route 110. I turned onto it with a sigh of relief and headed for home, three and half miles away. As I reached the city limits of Woodbine, I saw a sign carrying the legend: POSTED SPEED 60 MPH DURING DAYLIGHT HOURS: 50 MPH AT NIGHT. SPEED CHECKED BY RADAR. Well, I thought, it seems that modern technology has finally caught up with the backwoods.

I drove slowly, looking on both sides for some familiar landmarks. I didn't see any. That didn't upset me unduly as I knew that the road passed through a swamp that had hickory groves on either side and seven small wooden bridges within its confines. About a quarter of a mile beyond this, was the crossroad and home! I kept a sharp eye on the lookout for those hickory groves and that swamp, but to no avail. Presently, I came upon a crossroad. This can't be the one. I got here too quickly, I mused. But just to be sure I turned into it and pointed the headlights towards the place where I remembered the community's mailboxes used to be located, about twenty in all, lined up in a row on one long shelf. Nothing! Having thus satisfied myself that this must

be a new dirt road built during my absence, I backed the car out on the main
road and continued on my way. The few houses that I could make out were
all dark and quiet, with only the occasional barking of a dog as I passed to
break the stillness. I was still looking for that swamp and crossroad without
success. Then, I suddenly remembered another landmark, and this one I was
sure would still be there. The community cemetery. It should be on my left,
about half a mile before I reached the swamp, but I didn't see it either.

Just as I was considering turning back, I saw a sign with the "T" symbol
for "dead end" and the stem was facing me. Beneath this, another sign said
that junction 40 was just ahead. A few minutes later, route 110 came to an
end as an entity, and merged with the new road. At their intersection, a group
of directions was posted. One of them stated that the town of Folkston, Georgia, was only eight miles distant. Involuntarily, I slammed on the brakes and
sat there in frustrated embarrassment. Unless the town of Folkston had been
picked up and moved closer to Scarlett, I had gone twelve miles beyond my
destination. In other words, I was lost, again.

I turned the car around and started back. By this time, every bone in my
body ached, and my head felt as though it wanted to separate itself from my
neck. I decided to stop at the first house I saw and bang on the door until
someone opened it—even at the risk of being fired upon by some frightened
householder. I was that tired. I kept the car moving by sheer force of will and
silently thanked heaven that there were no other vehicles on the road at this
hour besides mine. I maintained just enough speed to keep the car from stalling. A ten-year-old could have walked faster without breathing too hard.

After about five minutes at this snail's pace, I saw a light in the distance.
As I came nearer, I saw that it was coming from what I took to be the back
part of a house on the right side of the road. I pulled into the driveway,
stopped and got out of the car, leaving the motor running and the headlights
on. As I walked toward what I could now see was a screened-in front porch,
I heard the sound of voices that seemed to be coming from the back part of the
house. I knocked on the screen door as hard as I could. Almost immediately, a
woman's voice came from somewhere inside. It was unmistakably Black!

"Who that out there this time o' night?" the voice queried. "Excuse me,
ma'am, but I'm lost and I wonder if you might help me," I answered. "Who
you lookin' for?" The voice sounded closer. "I'm looking for my uncle,
Aaron Weston. I used to live here myself, many years ago." "Who you?"
the voice asked. Now I could see her silhouette behind the glass in the front
door. "My name is William Mackey, but they used to call me Junior around
here." "Not Junior Mackey?" she cried, opening the front door at the same
time. "I'm afraid so and a tired and hungry one at that." In one bound she
was at the screen door unfastening it. "Boy, come on in heah, I'm Lonnie
Mae, you remember me. What you doin' sneakin' up on us in the middle o'
the night like this for? You like to scared me to death with that loud knockin'
out there. Come on in heah an' let me look at you! My, my, ain't you
somethin'! That's jus' like you, Junior—sneakin' up on folks without tellin'

'em nothin'! You always did have the devil in you. You ain't changed a bit. Come on in heah an' sit down.''

At last I was home—finally! It had taken me twenty-two hours to drive the thousand miles from New York to Woodbine, then taken me three hours to cover the last three and a half miles from Woodbine to Scarlett!

PART FIVE

CRITICAL
ESSAYS

Stephen E. Henderson
(1925–   )

Currently Professor of Afro-American Studies at Howard University, Henderson was born in Key West, Florida. He was a pioneer in the Black Aesthetic period of literary and social criticism, serving as a fellow of the Institute of the Black World while he was on the faculty of Morehouse College. As director of the Institute for the Arts and the Humanities at Howard, Henderson organized many national conferences for writers and scholars and produced an invaluable videotape collection on writers, folklore, and culture; he also founded *SAGALA* magazine before the Institute was closed in 1985. Henderson is an outstanding theorist, and his study *Understanding the New Black Poetry* (1973) revolutionized literary methodology and the practical criticism of African-American poetry. One of his major symposium papers is included in *The Militant Black Writer in Africa and the United States* (1969), a book he coauthored with Mercer Cook. His recent thinking about the performative nature of criticism is reflected in *Afro-American Literary Study in the 1990s* edited by Houston A. Baker and Patricia Redmond. The following essay is printed from the author's typescript.

Cliché, Monotony, and Touchstone

Folk song composition and the New Black Poetry

Black music is the most powerful and influential creation of Americans of African descent, and its impact upon the national culture has been dramatic, continuous, and pervasive. Notwithstanding, its reception by the dominant group, from the beginning, has been marked by an ambivalence which mirrors Euro-American attitudes toward other aspects of Afro-American culture, especially those which are themselves steeped in the musical tradition. Since Black music suffuses Black creative expression in literature and the other arts, an examination of selective factors in its reception and/or perception may help to clarify the response to other cultural expressions such as literature. Specifically, this paper will attempt to demonstrate that the Black poetry of the 1960s poses certain difficulties of appreciation and interpretation because (1) it inherited a matrix of ambivalent response to the music on which it was often modeled, and (2) it also failed to resolve in literary terms some of the technical problems inherent in the musical tradition. A clarification, if not a resolution, of some of these problems is possible when one examines certain cultural dynamics which underlie both the traditional music and the poetry which drew upon it for inspiration.

In acknowledging the importance of Black music to their lives and art, the poets of the 1960s were not unique. Instead, they were continuing *a tradition of literature* which formally embraces such diverse poets as Paul Laurence Dunbar, James Weldon Johnson, Langston Hughes, Sterling A. Brown, Margaret Walker, Gwendolyn Brooks, Owen Dodson, Frank Marshall Davis, Melvin B. Tolson, Robert Hayden, and Waring Cuney. That tradition of formal poetry was itself nurtured by a vast and fluid body of Black folk song, which encompassed worksongs, spirituals, blues, and other forms of expression. James Weldon Johnson paid classic tribute to the music and its creators in his poem "O Black and Unknown Bards." Contemporary musicians like Max Roach and Archie Shepp pay tribute to the tradition by calling their music folk music and by calling themselves folk musicians. This is important to note because, in taking all of the tradition to be their province, they acknowledge the worth of the whole, they acknowledge their relationship to it, and they erase false hierarchical distinctions. The acknowledgment of musicians like Roach and Shepp is also important because many of the poets of the 60s were more immediately attracted to jazz, or the New Music, as some called it, than to the older forms such as blues, or to religious forms such as gospel. Notwithstanding, both poets and musicians were aware of the essential unity of the music, and both too were aware that the source of this unity lay in the folk culture and its ritualistic embodiment in the music. Both musicians and poets saw themselves as bearers of a tradition which stretched back to Africa but which was condensed in the spirituals and the blues. And both musicians and poets saw themselves as spokesmen, as prophets, as priests. Their text was the music. Their message was Liberation.

In a way, the message, in one form or another, or even the *text itself*, has always been liberation, not only the liberation of Black people but of the entire nation; not merely of man in society but of the human psyche in the world. Liberation not only from oppression but from the deadly corrosives of prejudice and spiritual meanness.

But barriers stand and have stood in the path of this liberation, and they can be found on the personal as well as the group level, whether one speaks in social, political, or aesthetic or moral terms. In aesthetic terms these barriers of "aesthetic intolerance" can be readily traced in certain recurring reactions to Black music and, by extension, to Black poetry which builds upon that music. The barriers are partly rooted in preconceptions about Black people and partly in authentic cultural differences.

The earliest accounts of white reaction to Black music in the New World provide us with numerous examples of this intolerance and ambivalence. Thus many references speak of the "wildness," the "weirdness," and the "monot-

ony'' of the music, sometimes of its strange harmonies, or the Negro's inability
to sing on pitch. There are contradictory reactions also to the song texts which
range from scorn and mockery of the ''crude'' and ''primitive'' language to
a genuine appreciation for the pathos of the slaves' voices and for ''their ideal
ways of speech.'' Out of these reactions several factors emerge: (a) a sharp
(sometimes hostile) awareness of cultural/racial differences; (b) models and
examples of the various song types; and (c) theorizing as to the origin, composition, meaning, and importance of the songs. Some of the evidence for these
deductions is drawn from the singers themselves and some from the observations of outsiders, some of whom were trained social and musical historians.
The following account by J. Kinnard, Jr., of slaves performing a boat song in
1835 is important to an understanding of a widespread method of composition.

> The words were rude enough, the music better, and both were well adapted
> to the scene. A line was sung by a leader, then all joined in a short chorus;
> then came another solo line, and another short chorus, followed by a longer
> chorus, during the singing of which the boat foamed through the water with
> redoubled velocity. There seemed to be a certain number of lines ready-
> manufactured, but after this stock was exhausted, lines relating to sur-
> rounding objects were extemporized. Some of these were full of rude wit,
> and a lucky hit always drew a thundering chorus from the rowers, and an
> encouraging laugh from the occupants of the stern-seats. Sometimes several
> minutes elapsed in silence; then one of the negroes burst out with a line or
> two that he had been excogitating. Little regard was paid to rhyme, and
> hardly any to the number of syllables in a line; they condensed four or five
> into one foot, or stretched out one to occupy the space that should have
> been filled with four or five; yet they never spoiled the tune. This elasticity
> of form is peculiar to the negro song.

The passage thus describes a communal act of musical composition which
contains the following elements:

(1) Call and response both as a performance feature and as a compositional
    device;
(2) Extemporizing (or improvising) of lines;
(3) Communal encouragement of the leader;
(4) Subordination of rhyme to ''sense'';
(5) Subordination of verbal measure to musical considerations;
(6) The use of stock lines and phrases.

Thus this single description of a single type of song contains some of the most
distinctive features of all Black song performance and composition.

Of the features listed above, the call and response is perhaps the most typical
and the best known to the casual listener. This feature appears in many different kinds of Black song, worksongs, spirituals, and blues among them. Extemporizing or improvising is also a well known feature and is well documented
in accounts of the early years of the music in this country and the Caribbean.

But the most revealing feature in the Kinnard account is the reaction of the group (the other rowers/singers and the passengers/audience) to the song leader. They approve "a lucky hit" with "a thundering chorus" or "an encouraging laugh."

The same dynamic obtains in other kinds of Black music, in jazz, for example, where one soloist's ideas stimulate the group's creativity; or in gospel, where the congregation urges the soloist, especially in slow meditative or ornamental passages, to "go 'head—go 'head on." In the oral tradition, this same kind of encouragement is given to a preacher, or to someone who is praying or testifying. The practice is so deeply engrained in Black lifestyle that it carries over into academic and political life as well.

This dynamic interplay between musician and audience, or between speaker and audience is crucial to an understanding and appreciation of the Black poetry of the 1960s. Significantly, many of the poets, especially the poets of Black Consciousness, have emphasized the fact that they were writing primarily for a Black audience. They wished to speak to other Black people and they wished to do it on terms to which the people were accustomed. They wanted to reach "the community," they said, the Black masses, and as they looked for models they patterned their work on their people's music. They wanted to scream like James Brown, to blow like Trane. In the process, they found their roots. They discovered the African griot and rediscovered the Baptist preacher. Larry Neal, one of the most articulate spokesmen of the period, states:

> The poet must become a performer, the way James Brown is a performer—loud, gaudy and racy. He must take his work where his people are: Harlem, Watts, Philadelphia, Chicago and the rural South. He must learn to embellish the context in which the work is executed; and, where possible, link the work to all usable aspects of the music. For the context of the work is as important as the work itself. Poets must learn to sing, dance and chant their works, tearing into the substance of their individual and collective experiences. We must make literature move people to a deeper understanding of what this thing is all about, be a kind of priest, a black magician, working juju with the word on the world.
> [*Black Fire*, Morrow, 1968, p. 655.]

In order to involve an audience in this way the poet, indeed, must become something of a performer. Good preachers know this, and the tradition is rich. Translated into action, this reduces itself to the employment of specific verbal and performance strategies, many common to the oral and the musical tradition, to the preacher as well as the songster, to the earlier music as well as its current expression.

These strategies meet and often overlap in the Black song, whether sacred or secular, and emphasize the importance of Kinnard's observation: "This elasticity of form is peculiar to the negro song." And it is most important to note how this elasticity expresses itself. First, there are differing versions of a single song, varying from person to person and from community to community. The early reporters on the slave songs were struck by this phenomenon. In William Frances Allen's *Diary*, for instance, there is this entry for Sunday, June 5, 1864 [Epstein, p. 355]: "Songs often differ on different plantations, or are peculiar to them, and the 'Graveyard' they sang last night, I hardly recognized, it was so different from the way our people sing it."

Another aspect of the "elasticity of form" is spelled out by Elizabeth Kilham [Bruce Jackson, p. 129]. Here the congregation of freed Negroes are singing hymns which they learned from missionaries, but their attitude toward the text, both musical and verbal, is *plastic*. Kilham states:

> A hymn that is a particular favorite, they will sing several times in the course of a service, each time to a different tune; and the same with tunes; they will sometimes sing three or four hymns in succession to a tune that especially pleases them. It frequently happens in such cases, that the hymn and the tune will be in different metres; a long metre hymn will go stumbling over a short metre tune, or a hymn in short metre will be swallowed up by a tune twice as long as itself. In the latter case the words are stretched, and "drag their slow length along" over half a dozen notes, while in the former they rush along with a hop, skip and jump, that fairly takes one's breath away, and that constitutes one of the wonders of vocalism.

With "elasticity" thus characteristic of Black song, Black music, and performing style, the question arises as to the unifying element or principles of such music and to the manner of its composition. And the further question confronts us: How do these principles and elements function in a poetry which is ostensibly modelled on Black music? And how is one to judge such a poetry?

First, it should be observed that in Kinnard's opinion, the rowers "never spoiled the tune," and despite her theological snobbery and her "aesthetic intolerance," Elizabeth Kilham not only is forced to express her amazement at the "vocalism" of the congregation, but to admit the power of a song that she called "the strangest, wildest, the one which seemed to excite them the most powerfully, not so much I imagine by the words, as the music, which is utterly indescribable, almost unearthly with its sudden changes, each one ushered in, by a long quavering shriek . . ." [Jackson, 126f.].

And she describes the effect of the singing upon her and the other visitors.

> A fog seemed to fill the church; the lights burned dimly, the air was close, almost to suffocation; an invisible power seemed to hold us in its iron grasp; the excitement was working upon us also, and sent the blood surging in wild torrents to the brain, that reeled in darkened terror under the shock. A few moments more, and I think we should have shrieked in unison with the crowd.
> [Jackson, p. 128]

Although she discounts the effect of the words, Bruce Jackson rightfully observes that the "song is obviously a straightforward estimate of the duration of the hereafter'' (p. 120). But more to the point is the fact that the tremendous impact of the performance was largely due to the driving rhythmic repetition of word and motive, although the words on the surface seemed trite and unpoetic. Miss Kilham, in fact, might just as well have been describing a James Brown performance.

Let us examine, then, an important common feature of traditional Black music, song, and oratory, one which delights and transports the Black audience but which from the very beginning has puzzled and annoyed the white observer and critic. This feature, widely misunderstood, is the use of stock lines, images, phrases, rhythms, and motives. Some critics and scholars call these recurrent features clichés. Others have attempted to trace some of the more striking of the images to ''higher'' literary sources, the Bible, for example, or to ''white spirituals'' as in George Pullen Jackson's study *White Spirituals in the Southern Uplands*. Still others have admitted a genuine puzzlement at the appeal of these well-worn lines and images to an audience which has heard them time and time again. This puzzlement and impatience survives to the present time, partly because the listening habits of Black audiences still embody the older dynamic. A consideration of this factor is important, then, when assessing a literature which consciously addresses this audience, as Black poetry of the 1960s did.

The use of stock phrases, lines, and other elements is not limited, of course, to Black folk song, but the practice is so widespread in Black song that it must be considered an important part of the process of composition. Many spirituals, for example, consist of seemingly endless rote or ritualistic repetition of phrases, images, rhythmic and melodic motives. These elements ''wander'' from song to song, at times crossing the invisible line between the sacred and the secular. Lines and phrases even cluster themselves into ''families'' of songs [see Titon, *Early Downhome Blues* and Oliver, ''44/20 Blues'']. Some of this repetition may derive from imperfect mastery of the accompanying instrument, as in the case of many blues singers, and some may be due to faulty memory or to the pressures of improvisation, but some obviously results from a fondness for certain expressions, both verbal and musical. And the fact that many of these repeated elements still persist with considerable force in Black culture suggests that on some fundamental level of the mind they represent, symbolize, or embody important communal concerns. In an early study, *Understanding the New Black Poetry* [William Morrow, 1973], I designated the most powerful of these expressions as *mascons*, a term which I borrowed from NASA, signifying a massive concentration of matter beneath the surface of the moon, and which I used to signify a massive concentration of Black experiential energy locked up in these expressions.

Since Black poetry draws upon the oral tradition as well as the musical, and since, in fact, the two traditions complement one another, it would be useful at this point to indicate the outstanding common factors. The song features listed in this essay are also features of the oral tradition, with modification of no. 5 to read ''Subordination of verbal measure to tonal considerations.'' By this I mean such things as prolonging the vowels of words for emphasis and

emotive effect as in Dr. King's "I've se-e-e-e-e-e-e-e-en the Promised Land."
In addition, we may briefly recapitulate the following: (a) employment of
traditional materials—thematic, structural, etc.—in story, in song, and in sermon; (b) the employment of mascon elements; (c) the degeneration of mascons
into "clichés" when written down or when apprehended outside of the tradition. Thus whether a poet is exploring the musical tradition or the oral tradition
or both at the same time, the chances are that he will encounter a set of useful
strategies common to both and applicable to some extent, at least, to poetry.
These strategies function on a level which precedes poetry, the level of ritual,
and their effect is to move the participant out of himself, beyond himself, into
harmony with a greater reality. The best examples certainly would come from
the Black church, whether one is talking about singing or preaching, but if
one had to choose between the music or the sermon, one would have to choose
the music. Elizabeth Kilham's account is accurate not only for her time, but
also for ours, whether we are listening to a gospel choir, a James Brown
concert, or to an avant garde jazz performance.

The chief function of Black music is *to move* the listener. Listen to Archie
Shepp:

People talk a lot about happiness, but there are very few things that can
make you happy. Music is one of them. It can take you literally and dramati-
cally from a sorrowful state to a happy state. It can make you feel better.
It's a healing force. I go along with Brother James Brown and Aretha and
Stevie and all of them on that; I'm with them on *that!*
[*The Black Composer Speaks,* ed. D. Baker, pp. 301 f.]

Composer Carman Moore is also concerned with the ritualistic and therapeutic aspects of the musical tradition. Here is his reaction to Aretha Franklin in
a review of her album *Amazing Grace:*

You can hear Aretha as she hits upon an idea and turns it into a triumph—
as in "Amazing Grace" where she turns the line "and grace will lead me
home" into "and grace will lead me right on" (echoed by the choir, of
course), "right on home." And in the early part of the same hymn we go
with her as she vainly tries to call the spirit into her singing, first by moaning, then by singing a verse, and we exult with her as finally over the next
two verses she goes out after that spirit and seizes it or is seized by it on a
thrilling high A.

Moore continues:

But the most memorable and telling passage on the album occurs on the tag
end of one of the hymns when Aretha breaks out and does what a gospel
singer is supposed to do in the first place—testify out loud and inspire the
congregation to do likewise. She suddenly begins fervently, and over and
over, to sing "I'm so glad I got re-lig-ion. . . . My soul is satisfied." And
contained in that one outburst are the reasons why AM radio soul music can

never be the real thing, why those Blacks who insist on breaking the back
of the church before starting the revolution in their lifetimes, and why any
government and mystic klan that expects someday to crush the spirit of Black
America can forget it.
[*The Village Voice,* July 6, 1972, p. 31.]

Certain important assumptions about Black song and performance style appear in Moore's account which bear on our concern with repetition and the allusion to compressed group experience. First, the entire song "Amazing Grace" can be considered either a cliché or a mascon depending on one's relationship to Southern Baptist tradition. "Amazing Grace" is in fact a hymn of central importance to both white and Black congregations, although performance styles differ widely, Black style characterized by the elasticity which has been previously noted. The hymn is so well known that it presents a challenge for any performer to get something "new" out of it, musically or otherwise. And the danger is great too. Any falseness is instantly apparent. Everyone is an authority on "Amazing Grace." So how is one to get past the encrusted mediocrities, the shamming, the crocodile tears which, unfortunately, are also part of the tradition? Aretha clearly has her problems, and tries all her technical tricks in an effort to *move* the congregation. She tries "moaning" first, one of the oldest, most distinctive recorded aspects of Black American singing style. Then she paces herself, trying to emphasize the meaning of the verses, and gradually shifts her emphasis to the purely tonal—to the "high A," and brings down the Spirit.

But more crucial is the passage where she hits on the mascon language of "I'm so glad I got re-lig-ion . . . My soul is satisfied." Structurally, she breaks open the logical shape of the song and opens it up to an implosion of energy from common religious/racial experience. The combination of repetition with the compressed history in the phrase ignites her consciousness and, in turn, that of her hearers. On the page, however, the words are trite. They are often trite when spoken, even in a church setting. But to *have* religion is to be saved, to be happy. That is the good news of the gospel, the "healing force" of religion. Music in the Black Experience is a vehicle which leads one to spiritual health.

These repetitions, these so-called clichés, then, are devices which enable the singer to re-enter a certain experiential state, a certain communal space. The highest states in the Black American Experience are those found in the religious experience—"having religion." There are analogues, to be sure, and there are lower states which are also important and which have their own frequencies. The musician, the preacher, the orator, have traditionally known how to achieve these states, how to project or to lead their audiences into those special places of the soul. In the 1960s, the poets wanted to do the same. They turned to the music and the oral tradition for example.

To understand what they found, we must return to the Black song, to the point of conflict between Euro-American and Afro-American sensibility and culture. The point in question is the attitude toward repetition and the use of stock phrases, lines, and imagery. And related to that attitude is the paradoxical notion of "elasticity of form." The best place to go for examples would be the blues, because the musicians inevitably would refer to them as the root of their music, and the poets emulated the musicians. Unlike the musicians, however, many poets held negative attitudes toward the blues without appreciating the blues roots of a James Brown or even of a John Coltrane or an Ornette Coleman.

If we consider a blues song as an object of analysis, then we may consider the entire song or some component part such as the stanza, the image, phrase, or word. If we consider the process of composition, then we have to concern ourselves with the song not only as artifact but as historical process as well. It would not take long for one to discover that blues songs, as, indeed, Black songs in general, embody the dynamic which was recorded by the early observers such as Kinnard and Kilham. Thus there are often many versions of the same song, whether sung by different performers or by the same person. A single song like "See See, Rider," for example, exists as a kind of palimpsest in the tradition, with one version overlapping another, none ever quite forgotten or erased. And the audience as well as the performer reacts to this situation in various ways. The important thing, however, is that no singer feels duty-bound to reproduce a song exactly as he heard it or learned it, as is the case in the Anglo-American folk song tradition [Roger D. Abrahams and George Foss, *Anglo-American Folksong Style,* Prentice-Hall, Inc., 1968, p. 12]. If anything, the performer is inclined to "fool around" with the song, according to the spirit which moves him.

But his fooling around follows certain accepted and expected patterns. If he doesn't actually know a particular song, as was apparently the case with Leadbelly on occasion, he could make up one on the spur of the moment, taking his cue from what the folklorists, in this case, wanted. If he had heard the song before, he might render it in a form close to the original, if he especially liked the version, or he might re-create the song in a manner similar to the original composition. The common manner, one may almost say the archetypical manner, is to string together stanzas from various songs, patching them together according to the demands of the music or the mood. In his book *Early Downhome Blues,* Jeff Titon examines in some detail Blind Lemon Jefferson's three takes of "Matchbox Blues" and demonstrates how the process takes place with a single recording session. As music and poetry "Matchbox Blues" is a moving experience. But the piece lacks the verbal coherence characteristic of the best blues, such as "See See, Rider."

Some striking examples of this lack of continuity and coherence in a song text appear in the recordings of the older Big Joe Williams. No one sings with greater intensity of feeling or plays with such stunning percussive drive, but the lyrics of many of his songs seem to fall apart on close examination. It is this apparent lack of coherence and unity which has bred misunderstanding of the poetic achievement of blues and other Black songs. Still there is genuine excitement in the music of Big Joe Williams, and it is not unrelated to the texts. Careful examination shows that the apparently jumbled texts are indeed unified, if somewhat loosely, and work their effect obliquely on our minds. The words cluster about an "emotional core," to use Tristram P. Coffin's term, and the songs make sense because they retain the integrity of the experience. Abrahams' account of the process is useful. He states:

> As a song is transmitted those stanzas will be retained which are closest to this emotional core, and conversely the ones which are forgotten are those which are farthest from it, i.e., those stanzas having less importance in imparting the action or situation which the singer emphasizes. Although most singers in a homogeneous community will view a song in the same way, what one singer sees as the emotional core may, in certain instances, seem incidental to another. These two singers would consequently tend to remember different parts of the same song. In this way songs develop divergent paths in their history.
> [*Ibid.*, p. 20.]

Although Abrahams is speaking about the Anglo-American folk song tradition, which is much less flexible than the Afro-American tradition, the process of forgetting and re-creating also plays a role in Black song composition. In the case of Joe Williams another factor is operative, the practice of emphasizing tonal and emotional sense over the discursive.

Memory may not even be the key factor in the process of re-creation. A case in point is Son House, the great blues singer who was rediscovered in the 1960s after decades of inactivity. After a short while he was able to play with his original power, but, according to one source, at least, he seemed to have forgotten the words of his songs. Perhaps that was true. At any rate, Son House is important in this regard because he calls specific attention to the importance of continuity and coherence in a song text and pokes fun at those musicians who lack these elements in their work. When we look at one of House's early recordings, "Black Woman, Part I" and "Black Woman, Part II," both recorded May 28, 1930, we find that some factor other than memory must be at stake, for obviously he is not taking his own advice about sticking to the story line. Thus, stanzas 1, 2, and 4 deal specifically with the "Black mama" theme. We can group them together and call them BW1-A. Stanzas 5 and 6 form a related group, BW1-A' in which the woman is obliquely referred to by the kind of animal imagery which so dismayed some of the earlier collectors of Black songs. These stanzas form a kind of extension, part humorous with mythic overtones, of the love ritual of the Black mama theme. The remaining stanzas, 3 and 7, which we shall call BW1-B, are quite different, being essentially religious in expression. They strike a highly personal note, suggesting religious ambivalence. The singer uses them in other songs of equal intensity. Here there is a strong dialectical opposition between the life of the Christian and that of the roustabout. The first of this group, stanza 3, repeats this couplet:

> Hey, 'taint no heaven now, it ain't no burning hell.
> Says, where I'm going when I die cain't nobody tell.

That is the voice of the bad blues man, the renegade and sinner, which intensifies the worldliness of the song by couching it in terms of ultimate Christian salvation. The mood is extended until the very last stanza by the addition of the other stanzas in the A and A' groups. In the last stanza, a sudden dramatic return to the B group unifies the two motives. He accepts the Black woman and asks the Lord's forgiveness. And a unique Son House touch is the moaning at the end, a device originating apparently in the church but later adapted to other singing contexts as well. Part I thus has its own unity.

"Black Woman, Part II" contains three stanzas which relate it more closely to Son House's song "Death Letter" (Columbia, 1965, *The Legendary Son House: Father of the Folk Blues*) than to "Black Woman, Part I." "Black Woman, Part II" connects with "BW-1" through the religious overtones of stanza 1 of "BW-1." The idea of a break in the relationship between the man and woman seems to trigger the next three stanzas (BW-II, 2, 3, 4) which are common to Son House's powerful song "Death Letter" (see DL-1, Columbia, 1, 2, 3 and DL-2, Roots, 1, 2, 5). In fact, one may say that the "Death Letter" imagery forms the emotional core of "Black Woman, Part II," although the parting in the latter song is not final as in DL-1 and shares a tone of conventional retribution with DL-2.

The Columbia version of "Death Letter" is a blues masterpiece, both musically and poetically. Poetically, according to Edgar Allan Poe, the subject, the death of a beautiful woman, is perfect for lyrical expression. But we do not have to go to Poe for justification. In its own right, in its own tradition, the poem is outstanding. It has a coherence and unity which many blues lack, including both parts of "Black Woman" which we have just examined. Notwithstanding, the poem is made up chiefly of traditional images and lines. See, for example, the "Death Letter Blues" of Ida Cox and Jesse Crump or the treatment by Lottie Kimbrough. The "death letter" theme is inversely related to a series of blues in which a love letter is mailed "in the air." Another theme, the "walking blues," is also widespread. It is a mascon of personal histories as well as the historical movement of Blacks from the South to seek a better way of life in the North. It is one of the central themes of the blues. See Lightnin' Hopkins, "Walkin' Blues" or Babe Stovall lines: "I walked this road, my feet got soaking wet/ I'm looking for my good gal/ I ain't stopped walkin' yet." The image merges into a wilderness of highways, a jungle of railroad lines.

In the second stanza the devastating image of the "coolin' board" appears. The cooling board is the table where bodies were placed shortly after death and preparatory to embalming. It appears in a song by Lightnin' Hopkins, who sees his lil faro lying on her "coolin' board." It appears with startling oblique power in "St. James Infirmary," in the lines:

I went down to St. James Infirmary
I saw my baby there
Stretched out on a long white table
So peaceful, so calm, so fair.

Stanza three contains the powerful image of the lover looking down on the dead woman's face. The last line in the stanza, "She's a good old girl, but she gotta lay here till judgment day," sometimes appears as "You're a good old girl, but I just can't take your place." (Cf. "Death Letter Blues," Cox and Crump.) And when it appears in that form, the singer doesn't seem too unhappy about the fact either. The image thus glides off into a related group of cynical expressions, culminating at one point in the 1950s with Joe Williams of the Count Basie band singing, "Baby, you're so fine, but gotta die one day (2×)/ All I want is a little bit of lovin' before you pass away." [See also Billy Bird, "Down in the Cemetery," quoted by Paul Oliver, *Blues Fell*.]

Stanzas 5 through 7 reflect the imagery of a group of songs variously called "Dog Blue" by Furry Lewis and "Two White Horses in a Line" by the New Gospel Keys. The imagery is of the "two white horses in a line" which will "carry me to my burying ground." Another aspect of the imagery is the body's being let "down with a golden chain." For comparison, one could listen to Blind Lemon Jefferson's "See That My Grave Is Kept Clean" and "Dig My Grave Both Long and Narrow." [*Songs from the Bahamas*, Folkways.]

Briefly, then, we see the manner in which traditional imagery, which until recently was almost universally called cliché by blues scholars, can be fused by the imagination of a creative singer into a masterpiece of poetry. We see that the singer responds to something deep and vital which the image embodies and by skillful and passionate selection manages to shape it into a moving statement. We see, finally, from the analysis of the Son House texts, from the research of Jeff Titon and William Ferris, from the historical accounts of song composition, and, of course, from direct experience, that the fundamental process of Black folk song composition involves the dynamic interplay of opposites—the stock image vs. improvisation, concentration vs. elasticity, group synthesis vs. personal expression, a field of related songs vs. a highly individualized performance which enters the tradition and remains virtually unchanged for generations.

When we move from folk song texts to the text of a formal hymn by Bishop Richard Allen, the founder of the A. M. E. Church, we find the same process of composition involved. In their study, *The Negro and His Songs*, Odum and Johnson call attention to the fact that "the song . . . combines many of the ideas and phrases of the favorite spirituals of the slaves" (p. 138). Bishop Allen's "The Pilgrim's Song" is as follows:

I am a poor wayfaring stranger,
    While journeying through this world of woe;
But there is no sickness, toil, no danger,
    In that bright world to which I go.

I'm going there to see my classmates,
  They said they'd meet me when I come;
I'm just going over Jordan,
  I'm just going over home.

I know dark clouds 'll gather 'round me,
  I know my road is rough and steep;
Yet there bright fields are lying just before me,
  Where God's redeemed their vigils keep.

I'm going there to see my mother,
  She said she'd meet me when I come;
I'm just going over Jordan,
  I'm just a going over home.

I'll soon be free from every trial,
  My body will sleep in the old churchyard.
I'll quit the cross of self-denial,
  And enter in my great reward.

I'm going there to meet my mother,
  She said she'd meet me when I come;
I'm just a going over Jordan,
  I'm just a going over home.

Despite the genteel language, it is easy to find traditional images in the hymn. Some of these are indicated in the footnotes. The point, however, is that a poem like this one indicates a transference of the folk song method of composition to the composition of formal hymns. The hymn is a formal poem and thus it also represents an early stage in the adaptation of traditional imagery to the emerging body of formal Afro-American poetry.

The earlier poets who sought to evoke the feel of Black life were confronted with two problems, one of subject matter, the other of style. Both were embodied in and exacerbated by the dialect tradition of Southern writers and the minstrel tradition with its all pervasive stereotypes. Paul Laurence Dunbar's dilemma and his solution to it are well known as is the formulation of the problem by James Weldon Johnson. The problem, technically, with dialect was its limitation, its two "stops": pathos and humor. Johnson's solution was to seek a form which was "freer and larger than dialect, but which will still hold the racial flavor. . . ." In seeking this form in his own poetry, he modeled his work on the cadences of the Black preacher's voice which retained with its "fusion of Negro idioms with Bible English" perhaps "some kinship with the innate grandiloquence of their old African tongues." [*Book of American Negro Poetry*, p. 9.] However, the preacher's voice was not the only voice of the community. Besides, the community itself had changed, and there were the voices also of the bluesman, the raconteur, and the man in the street. It took another generation of poets, epitomized in Langston Hughes and Sterling

Brown, to express itself in those voices, the blues moan, the urban vernacular. They modelled their work on both speech and song, and in so doing they not only utilized the techniques of the folk song tradition but dared to suggest the sophisticated allusiveness of jazz itself.

In seeking the blues tone, the jazz dynamic, the poets of that generation, like those who preceded them and those who followed were acknowledging the primary importance of the musical tradition with its emphasis on the interplay of mascon and invention. Specifically, if one examines a substantial body of Afro-American poetry, from Phillis Wheatley to the poetry of the early seventies, one would find certain recurring patterns of musical allusion. One may list these as follows:

1. Casual, generalized reference (to "blues," e.g., or to "jazz")
2. A careful allusion to song titles (as in "O Black and Unknown Bards")
3. Direct or indirect quotations from songs (Cf. Johnson, above)
4. Adaptation of song forms (as in the blues of Langston Hughes and Sterling Brown, Henry Dumas)
5. Tonal memory as poetic structure (specific acquaintance with a song, a passage, or a style necessary to a realization of the poem, as in Sarah Fabio's "Tribute to Duke")
6. Precise musical notation in the text ("Whistling Sam," Dunbar)
7. Assumed emotional response to well-known music (Carolyn Rodgers' reference to a "Coltrane psalm" in "Me, In Kulu Se & Karma")
8. The musician himself as subject/poem/history/myth (Cf. the poems on Parker, Coltrane, Dolphy, Aretha, and others)
9. Employment of language from jazz or the jazz life (e.g., "changes." Cf. "running the changes" from another context and "going through changes.")
10. The conception of the poem as "score" or "chart." (The poem is the pretext for improvisation, discussed in the text.)

An examination of some of this poetry reveals a process of synthesis and refinement which is reminiscent of the writing of blues lyrics, for example, by Black professional lyricists, like Thomas Dorsey, Lovie Austin, W. C. Handy, and Rosamund Johnson. A chief difference, however, is that the *poets* are conscious of a *reading* audience, and hence avoid certain kinds of repetition, certain kinds of expression, and the like. Their work, then, even the most realistic of it, tends to synthesize the folk elements, or to attenuate them. This attenuation is at once an obeisance toward the formal Anglo-American tradition and a demonstration of the flexibility of the Afro-American tradition. Like the music, the poetry has a certain capacity to absorb outside influences without losing its integrity.

Sterling Brown, Langston Hughes, and James Weldon Johnson are the three greatest practitioners of these methods. Johnson had expressed the ideal attainment of this approach as "a form that will express the racial spirit by symbols from within rather than by symbols from without, such as the mere mutilation of English spelling and pronunciation." Such a form would be "freer and larger than dialect, but which will still hold the racial flavor; a form expressing the imagery, the idioms, the peculiar turns of thought, and the distinctive humor and pathos, too, of the Negro, but which will also be capable of voicing the deepest and highest emotions and aspirations, and allow of the widest range of subjects and the widest scope of treatment" (*The Book of American Negro Poetry*, pp. 41, 42). Johnson attained aspects of this goal in some of his sermons in the folk manner, in *God's Trombones*. The opening lines of the "Prodigal Son" are a good example:

> Young man, young man
> Your arm's too short to box with God.

There is also the apocalyptic imagery of "The Judgment Day," which draws its strength and inner force from sermons such as those recorded by Zora Neale Hurston, in *Jonah's Gourd Vine,* for instance. Johnson wrote:

> Then the tall, bright angel, Gabriel,
> Will put one foot on the battlements of heaven
> And the other on the steps of hell,
> And blow that silver trumpet
> Till he shakes old hell's foundations.
>
> And I feel Old Earth a-shuddering—
> And I see the graves a-bursting—
> And I hear a sound,
> A blood-chilling sound.
> What sound is that I hear?
> It's the clicking together of the dry bones,
> And I see coming out of the bursting graves,
> And marching up from the valley of death,
> The army of the dead.
> And the living and the dead in the twinkling of an eye
> Are caught up in the middle of the air,
> Before God's judgment bar.

And the death of Jesus is described this way in Hurston's account:

> And about that time Jesus groaned on de cross, and
> Dropped His head in the locks of His shoulder and said,
>   "It is finished, it is finished."
> And then de chambers of hell exploded
> And de damnable spirits
> Come up from de Sodomistic world and rushed into de
>   smoky camps of eternal night,
> And cried, "Woe! Woe! Woe!"
> And then de Centurion cried out,
> "Surely this is the Son of God."

> And about dat time
> De angel of Justice unsheathed his flamin' sword and
>   ripped de veil of de temple
> And de High Priest vacated his office
> And then de sacrificial energy penetrated de mighty strata
> And quickened de bones of de prophets
> And they arose from their graves and walked about
>   in de streets of Jerusalem

Johnson welcomed the publication of Sterling Brown's *Southern Road,* in 1932, with these words:

> . . . he has made more than mere transcriptions of folk poetry, and he has done more than to bring to it mere artistry; he has deepened its meanings and multiplied its implications. He has actually absorbed the spirit of his material, made it his own; and without diluting its primitive frankness and raciness, truly reexpressed it with artistry and magnified power. In a word, he has taken this raw material and worked it into original authentic poetry.

When one compares Brown's "Sister Lou," for instance, with some of the sermons which one has heard, or with some of the gentle funeral sermons collected by E.C.L. Adams, one realizes the truth of Johnson's assertion. There are other examples, of course, in Brown. "Tin Roof Blues," to cite one, borrows the title of an actual blues, but the composition is original in the manner of the folk. In the passage below, Brown reshapes traditional lines in a manner and form close to Thomas Dorsey and Everett Murphy in their "Freight Train Blues."

> Got the freight train blues. I've got the box cars
>   on my mind.
> Got the freight train blues. I've got the box cars
>   on my mind.
> I'm gonna leave this town because my man is so unkind.
>   (c) 1924, Chicago Music Publishing Co.

Sterling Brown wrote in "Tin Roof Blues":

> I'm got de tin roof blues, got dese sidewalks on my mind,
> De tin roof blues, dese lonesome sidewalks on my mind,
> I'm goin' where de shingles covers people mo' my kind.

These earlier poets at their best placed their personal stamp on a phase of the folk tradition much as a Tommy Johnson or a Leroy Carr would, giving a personal rendering to a palimpsest of songs that in effect became the standard version of the song. Other versions continued to exist and the larger tradition flowed on, but these were islands of excellence that others knew and, often, imitated.

What many poets of the sixties demanded of themselves, although partly anticipated by Langston Hughes, was more daring. They would not only absorb the earlier phase of the literary tradition, they would go beyond it in the way that jazz emerged from blues and other previous forms, or, better still, in the manner that the New Music, the new free form jazz, of Coleman, Coltrane, Sanders, and Shepp leaped beyond Be-Bop. And how were they to do this? By "the destruction of the text," Larry Neal said, elaborating an idea from poet/musician James T. Stewart. The idea, as Stewart explains it, rests upon the Non-Western conception of reality as change, of experience as develop-ment, and "destruction" to development and hence to continual change. The activity which comes closest to this apprehension of change as reality is music, more specifically the improvisational aspect of music. The kind of music which best embodies this conception of reality is jazz, which constantly seeks to become "non-matrixed," i.e., free from static models and projections, as in much of Western music. Its movement is dialectical.

How does this relate to the poetry? As I understand it, "the destruction of the text" implied two main attitudes toward the conception of a poem. (1) The poem is a kind of "score" which allows a certain latitude of interpretation in performance, similar to that possible in drama, for example, or in musical arrangements. (2) The poem is a kind of "chart" in which the written elements are subject to as much interpretation, expansion, and development (especially in Stewart's sense) as the poet/performer is capable of. Theoretically, at least, the poem would approach the "condition of music," to use Pater's phrase, and could occupy a performer's entire lifetime, if it became fully "un-matrixed."

Both interpretations have models in the musical and oral traditions as our previous discussion has shown. Poems tending toward the dramatic and de-clamatory modes are especially amenable to treatment as a score. However, one could hardly say that the text is "destroyed" in such a case. In a James Weldon Johnson sermon, for example, there is leeway for dramatic and dy-namic invention of various kinds, but these are essentially matters of perfor-mance, and the text as printed is unchanged. A step toward structural change, i.e., actual improvisation, is found in Langston Hughes' *Ask Your Mama*, where room for musical improvisation is written into the poem. Other examples come to mind. Samuel Allen's sermon, "Big Bethel," is constructed on the call and response model and, though complete within itself, is loose enough for interpolation and improvisation. The poet appends the following note to the poem: "The above lines may be considered a framework for improvisation by the speakers. Gospel music is suggested as an appropriate background" (*Humanities Through the Black Experience*, ed. Phyllis R. Klotman, Kendall/ Hunt Publishing Co., 1977, pp. 11–16).

Sarah Webster Fabio's "Tribute to Duke" allows greater freedom without losing control, as the poet suggests specific musical interpolation and invention from the Ellington repertoire. The performance factor here is quite strong and brings us closer to the ideal of continuous creation which the jazz oriented poets aspired to. Still poems like these, though looser, say, than the blues and jazz poems of Brown and Hughes, and the sermons of Johnson, do not achieve

the freedom of the oral tradition, of the rap and the sermon. Many poets of
the 60s simulated this freedom in their delivery but the poem was still basically
tied to the page, a visual as well as an aural creation. Despite a certain freedom
of rhythm, phrasing, and the like, the achievement, in technical terms, did not
go beyond that of Hughes and Brown.

If the text were to be "destroyed," then it would have to be defined in
some other fashion. Each poem, no matter how faithful to tradition, was still,
in effect, a definitive version of those aspects of the tradition which it sub-
sumed, in other words, of itself. Hence, the definitive version of "Long Track
Blues" is the version which Brown wrote. Similarly, the definitive version of
"Don't Cry, Scream" is Haki Madhubuti's (Don L. Lee's) text, just as the
definitive version of Larry Neal's "Don't Say Goodbye to the Porkpie Hat"
is the one which the poet wrote. The "destruction of the text," then, appears
either as rhetoric of the period or as a legitimate but perhaps unrealized ideal.
At any rate, it is an extreme position, a revolutionary one, a fact which James
T. Stewart realized. Citing Jahn's account of African mud temples which are
washed away during heavy rains, but always built of the same material, and
citing the fragility of Japanese ink drawings on rice paper, which was later
used as wrapping paper, Stewart makes the following deduction:

> My point is this: that in both of the examples just given, there is little
> concept of fixity. The work is fragile, destructible; in other words, there is
> a total disregard for the perpetuation of the product, the picture, the statue,
> and the temple.
>
> (*Black Fire*, p. 4)

Opposing the fixity of forms in traditional Western art and thought, Stewart
continues, "We know, all non-whites know, that man can not create *a* forever;
but he can create forever. But he can only create if he creates as change.
Creation is itself perpetuation and change is being" (p. 4). The only being of
a work of art, then, according to Stewart, "is the act of creation . . . as it
comes into existence . . ." (p. 4). It is important to note, though, one crucial
source of difficulty for the poet: "Music is a social activity in a sense that
writing, painting and other arts can never be. Music is made with another. It
is indulged in with others. It is the most social of the art forms except say,
architecture" (pp. 9, 10). The most striking evidence against the poets, however, was the fact that they did write their work down. For the most part, they
were also eager to get them published. To that extent, certainly, they were
locked into heavy contradiction.

There were two well known "exceptions," Yusef Rahman and Amus Mor.
Jazz critic A. B. Spellman makes the case for them in a paper entitled "Oral
Challenges to the Written Word: The Poetry of Yusef Rahman and Amus
Mor" (IAH Wtrus Conf., May 1978). He describes the impact of Rahman,
"the dervish of the jazz club," as follows:

> You had to see him one Monday night at Slugs or East Third Street between

Ave's C & D in concert with Sun Ra's Arkestra, as it was then called. Costumed and jeweled in a manner reminiscent of the Sudanese, preparing the room with incense, shaking chains of bells as he moved among the tables, Yusef danced and sang his poems. The lines as written were like chord changes for verbal improvisation. Taken literally, from the page, we might think the author of these lines to be a silly second-rate Surrealist:

A Gnostic frog-eyed owl/quilted by bone yards bitter blacknight/ SOME-WHERE OVER A COSMIC RAINBOW . . .

But, in performance, the audience's mind straining to visualize the images from this whirling black man who played on every sense and backed by the empathetic Sun Ra band, the effect was strong indeed.

Spellman continues:

Thus the premises of craft for this poet depend as much on his ability to deliver his lines as it does his ability to write them. With recoiless lines like "SOUL-talking/ SOUL-talking/ SOUL-talking/ could be Pops Armstrong a black Mack-the-knife/ strut strut struting [sic] with some bar-be-q." This last sung as Armstrong performed it, segueing into a sequence of quotes from the classics of jazz, crescendoing into a kind of bebop sufic chant, it is clear that this poet had to be seen to be appreciated. (Spellman, p. 7)

Rahman and Amus Mor, "the hip street corner sage," thus represent to Spell-man "the synthesis of black music and black literature, of black materialism and black idealism" (p. 7). And he concludes this study by placing the poets in the tradition of Sterling Brown, his former teacher at Howard University, who, in addition to English, had taught him a good deal about the history of jazz and the black folk tradition. "As Sterling Brown used the blues and the heroic toast thirty years earlier to get at a distinctly Afro-American verse, these poets carried the premise to its conclusion and took the poem off the page" (p. 7).

These various attempts to energize the text, to liberate or to "destroy" it, are deeply rooted in the Afro-American oral tradition, the music and the poetry. The most radical attempt, the "destruction of the text," is related to the tradition in the following way. It proposed to return the poem to the audience, to take "the poem off the page," in Spellman's expression. But it was able to do this by returning to the most basic mechanism of traditional composi-tion—the opposition of the cliché, the mascon—to the inventive impulse, the drive toward elasticity of form. Rahman's employment of mascons in Spell-man's account appears in the "recoiless lines" of "SOUL-talking/ SOUL-talking/ SOUL-talking/ could be Pops Armstrong a black Mack-the-knife/ strut strut struting [sic] with some bar-be-q." The sung quotes from "the classics of jazz" are structural units that appear in poetry and music alike. The struc-tural basis of the performance also appears in the statement, "The lines as written were like chord changes for verbal improvisation." (p. 7)

If we recall the accounts of black song composition in the earlier portions of this paper, we can clearly see the roots of Rahman's technique. If we recall the discussion of Son House's "Black Woman" parts I and II and his "Death Letter," we can see a direct relationship to the tradition. And by the time we get to Sterling Brown, James Weldon Johnson, and Langston Hughes, we find sophisticated poetic composition based on this simple but powerful mechanism. Between these poets and Rahman there are many other poets of the 60s who explore this dynamic also, but with much less daring, or with somewhat different objectives.

The connecting link between poetry and music, between poet and audience is the voice of the speaker and his attitude toward its use. For the black speaker or singer the voice is an instrument. But the instrument must be made to speak. Speak words. And beyond words, speak sounds. Beyond words, the language of experience, the language of feeling and revelation. The voice must move from the known to the unknown. To do this it must be plastic. It must mold sound according to the flow of experience. The flow of experience resolves into commonly recognized elements, into stock images, into stanzas, proverbs, into rhythmic and melodic figures drenched with unverbalized associations. They are taken for granted, they gravitate toward cliché. They are parodied, diluted, and abused, but their power is available when needed. They are chipped, stripped, chopped, and stretched.

There is interplay, vital and continuing, between the vocal and the instrumental, and much of the history, much of the activity of black music, involves this instrumentalization of the vocal, this vocalization of the instrumental. Again, in all of this activity, there is the dialectical movement of the new and the old, the reactionary and the radical, the synthetic vs. the discursive, the fixed vs. the fleeting, the forming. This is the basic dynamic. It lies at the heart of the music: It is the fundamental challenge of the poetry and to the poetry. It prefigures the ideal form which James Weldon Johnson sought, one that "will express the racial spirit by symbols from within rather than by symbols from without, such as the mere mutilation of English spelling and pronunciation." That form would not only "hold the racial flavor" but "will also be capable of voicing the deepest and highest emotions and aspirations, and allow of the widest range of subjects and the widest scope of treatment" (*Book of American Negro Poetry*, pp. 41, 42).

WORKS CITED

Abrahams, Roger D. and George Foss. *Anglo-American Folksong Style*. (Englewood Cliffs, NJ: Prentice-Hall, 1968).

Baker, David et al., eds. *The Black Composer Speaks*. (Metuchen, NJ: Scarecrow Press, 1977).

Epsten, Dena J. *Sinful Tunes and Spirituals*. (Urbana: University of Illinois Press, 1977).

Henderson, Stephen E. *Understanding the New Black Poetry*. (New York: Morrow, 1973).

Hurston, Zora Neale. *Jonah's Gourd Vine*. 1934. (Philadelphia: Lippincott, 1971).

Jackson, Bruce, ed. *The Negro and His Folklore in Nineteenth Century Periodicals*. (Austin: University of Texas Press, 1967).

Jackson, George Pullen. *White Spirituals in the Southern Uplands*. 1933. (New York: Dover, 1965).

Johnson, James Weldon. *God's Trombones*. (New York: Viking, 1927).

Johnson, James Weldon, ed. *The Book of American Negro Poetry*. 1922. (New York: Harcourt, Brace and World, 1959).

Jones, LeRoi and Larry Neal, eds. *Black Fire*. (New York: Morrow, 1968).

Klotman, Phyllis R., ed. *Humanities Through the Black Experience*. (Dubuque, IA: Kendall/Hunt, 1977).

Odum, Howard W. and Guy B. Johnson. *The Negro and His Songs*. (Chapel Hill: University of North Carolina Press, 1925).

Oliver, Paul. *Blues Fell This Morning*. (London: Cassell, 1960).

Titon, Jeff T. *Early Downhome Blues*. (Urbana: University of Illinois Press, 1977).

Hoyt W. Fuller
(1927–1981)

A native of Atlanta, Fuller received his B.A. from Wayne State University and worked as a journalist before assuming the position of associate editor of *Ebony* in 1954. From 1961 to 1976, he was editor of *Negro Digest/Black World*. Within this period, Fuller became one of the most influential voices in the development of African-American social and artistic consciousness, particularly in the development of Black Aesthetic criticism. He was the founder of Chicago's Organization of Black American Culture (OBAC). When Johnson Publications discontinued *Black World*, Fuller and others founded *First World*, a magazine he edited until his death. Fuller was the author of *Journey to Africa* (1973); his work appeared in such anthologies as *American Negro Short Stories* (1966), *The Black Aesthetic* (1971), and *The Black American Writer* (1972), and such magazines as *The New Yorker* and *North American Review*. The following article is reprinted from *Southwest Review* (August 1961).

On the Death of Richard Wright

November 29, 1960

It is 10:55 P.M. now, just over two hours since the news came casually over the phone from someone who did not know the terrible impact of the words he spoke. "I just heard over the seven o'clock television news that Richard Wright died in Paris." Having no television, I have had the radio going ever since, and every so often an announcer will interrupt recordings to recite three minutes of "news," supposedly current, but so far there has been no mention of Richard Wright. The President-elect, Mr. Kennedy, is contemplating his Cabinet, and there is speculation that he will name the governor of North Carolina secretary of commerce, and a Lithuanian-born (the fact was emphasized) psychiatrist named Soblen has been arrested as a Russian spy, and a school bus in Canada collided with a train, killing sixteen children, and Patrice Lumumba is still missing in the Congo. These are events presumably of moment to the nation, not the fate of a displaced American Negro writer.

And yet I know the news is true. It is too dreadful a report to be mere rumor or a case of mistaken identity, however much I wish it so, and so I accept it. Richard Wright was fifty-two, no longer young, and he had spoken with eloquence and with all the power of his great overburdened heart that which he felt so deeply, and this mitigates my grief. It is only that this appallingly troubled world will be so much a poorer place without him.

If I sound as if I were an old friend, someone who knew Wright intimately, it is only a figment of my unrealized hopes, and I think he would forgive me. I never had the privilege of meeting him. Just a year ago, in November, 1959, I loitered at the Café Le Flore and at Les Deux Magots, two of Wright's old haunts, on the chance that he might stop for a coffee or an *aperitif*. I had been told that he no longer frequented those cafés, that he had moved on to other places as yet not "discovered" by the tourists, not yet "chic." I did not want to hunt him down like an ordinary hot-eyed fan, which I both am and am not, and so I did not ask the names of the new places. I preferred being more casual about it, perhaps glimpsing him strolling along Boulevard St. Germain or browsing the bookstores on the Rue de la Seine. It was my last time in Paris for a long while, I knew, and it might very well be that I would never have the opportunity of seeing him—merely of seeing him—if this did not happen now.

November, 1959, was an exciting month in Paris—more exciting than usual, that is, for Paris is always heady. The sweet oxygen of freedom—the kind of freedom that matters—blesses that city. An American writer from North Carolina, a peripatetic expert on Negroes on all continents who draws from a rich and inexhaustible store of ignorance, once wrote that in Paris only Parisians and American Negroes are really at home. A gross oversimplification, naturally, but with a rare grain of perception. Parisians are at home in Paris because it is their city, their conscious creation, reflecting their taste and cultivation and the refined sense of tolerance and humanity which are, after all, the essence of civilization. Those values which represent the noblest in Western thought are eternally rooted in the city's soul. American Negroes are at home in Paris because they have, at last, for the first time in their lives, entered a truly congenial city. Until Paris, they have stood as strangers outside their own doors. They have been spawned by a culture which, nevertheless, refuses them succor, a culture which brands them and taunts them and drives them to despair. In Paris, American Negroes are at last in harmony with the civilization which bred them and which they had enriched. In Paris, they are finally unhaunted and left in peace. They can walk the streets or sit in the cafés without fear of imminent violence to body or spirit (for if violence comes, then they can respond to it as their nature dictates, as their sense of dignity demands, with assurance that law and justice, if these must be confronted in consequence, will see men as men and deeds as deeds). In Paris, Negroes can meld, lose themselves in the swirl of humanity, be men and women among other men and women, and simply that. It is a unique, exhilarating, and precious experience. But the North Carolinian would not understand this. Like so many Americans, this one carries the word "freedom" perennially on his tongue without ever discerning its meaning in his heart.

That November, Paris seemed to be returning a measure of adoration, paying tribute to American Negroes. Josephine Baker was at the Olympia, stirring nostalgia among Parisians of an older generation and delighting the younger generation with a thrill of discovery. Over at the Bernhardt, Katherine Dunham and her dancers were titillating old enthusiasts and winning new ones. The exquisite Lena Horne was in town on vacation, arresting strollers along the Champs Elysées. The comely little Pittsburgh girl called Marpessa Dawn, whom a Frenchman delivered into immortality as Eurydice in the film *Orfeu Négre*, was appearing in a new play. And theater-goers were agog over an outrageous romp, *Les Nègres*, by the incorrigible genius Jean Genet. The production opened a window on the festering Negro psyche and Paris was simultaneously enchanted and dismayed. In Paris it did not seem odd that a white man could know so well how to pluck the nucleus of acridity that burrows at the Negro core. But that is a part of the wonder of that city, Richard Wright's adopted home.

Years earlier in Chicago, another city in which Richard Wright had lived (but, alas, a city which held him at arms' length, isolated him, demeaned him), I met a man who had known Wright well, had nurtured him. This man, William Harper, lives there still, self-confined among the dusty shelves of his shabby bookstore, feeding the insatiable monster of bitterness with the food of his vast crippled spirit. Around his bookstore now, tall and glistening Mies van der Rohe-style apartment buildings are rising where, in Richard Wright's time, stood the evil, aching slums which made of the South Side one of the world's cruelest ghettos. William Harper sits among his books and broods, remembering old injuries and lost moments when the harsh breath of racism blew out every flickering of his nebulous hopes. In those days, Harper could still reach out and touch with his wand of wisdom the spur of creativity among the South Side's soul-wounded youth. He touched young Richard Wright.

When I knew Harper, there were times when he would temporarily relax, forget himself, open up his crowded chest of memories and speak of his former protégé. I suppose he wondered if Wright remembered him or if, perhaps, he also had been buried, as a part of the unhappy whole, along with the reality that had been Wright's in Chicago. Through William Harper, Richard Wright first became for me flesh rather than exalted symbol, a writer who had been young and as frustrated and unsure as Bigger Thomas himself. Through the novelist's old mentor I drew closer to the novelist. It is clear then that I valued any connection with Richard Wright, however impersonal or remote or inconsequential. This had nothing to do with my own pretensions as a writer: it had everything to do with my being a Negro and an American.

In the spring of 1958, Wright's *Pagan Spain* was circulating among my friends on the Spanish island of Mallorca, most of whom were French. The book had been brought in surreptitiously, of course, for it is critical of Spain and of Franco and of the Catholic church, and the authorities would not have looked with benevolence on anyone—particularly a foreigner—caught with it in his possession. All my friends liked the book and agreed with what Wright wrote, except one. But then, she was Mallorcan, not French, and her very close business and emotional attachment to a Frenchman could not moderate her patriotism (I envied her this: I envy any man or woman the simple, uncompromised love of country: I envy the fact of belonging). She did not like the book and, in her anger—an anger deepened by the recognition of the truth in it—she struck at its author through me. "And to think it was written by a man who was not even free in his own country," she said pointedly. "He had to come to Europe to be free. We allowed him to cross our borders like any other man, and this is how he shows his gratitude. Well, who asked him to come to Spain?"

And, by inference, since I agreed with Wright, who asked me to come to Spain?

I understood her anger—and her malice—but she could not know. She could not understand that Wright felt the anguish of the unfree Spaniard precisely because he also had not been free. She could not see that the injustice that was a part of the pattern of her life (she being privileged by both class and sex) was a thing that pained Wright anew, reopened old and unhealable wounds, every time he encountered it. Indeed, my lovely Mallorcan friend could never have known Wright at all—not even if he had come to her and sat down with her and sought to explain to her the whole tortured tale of his journeying.

One day in the spring of 1960 I met in New York City another man who knew Richard Wright. This man, James Baldwin, had argued with Wright in the cafés of Paris. He is a younger man, perhaps young enough to be Wright's son, and though he may resent my presuming to say so (he having differed with Wright on the issue of estrangement), he is in a very real sense Wright's heir. He is a worthy heir, a man of extraordinary sensitivity and talent. Like Wright, Baldwin escaped to Paris, spending some ten years there. But, unlike Wright, James Baldwin returned to America. His return was not such an easy decision, nor an easy adjustment, and he confided that—after a few months at home—the oppressive weight of omnipresent racism together with his furious emotional war with it drove him again to the refuge of Paris. He is back in New York City now, where he was born, desperately struggling against the wrenching grip of his alienation. He is repeating to himself with an urgency that is close to heartbreaking that he is an American and that all this rancor and brutality, the inadmissible guilt and convoluted love are part of the American heritage. He knows from experience that he cannot escape being an American no matter where he goes. And, of course, he is right. Richard Wright knew that. But Wright also knew that to remain in America was either ultimately to betray his humanity or else to exhaust his energies in endless battle against the unrelenting assaults on it. And, perhaps, James Baldwin does not yet know this. Not really, not yet: he clings to hope. But one has only to look at Baldwin's face to feel that he will know. It is a tender and vulnerable and unforgettable face, as stark as a Yoruba mask and as beautifully sorrowful as a cora lament. Even in laughter the face betrays the tragedy and travail quiescent in his blood.

In a way, Baldwin is luckier than Wright was, which I suppose is a commentary on the years that separated them. The big, rich American magazines publish Baldwin's stories and articles, and the critics keep telling him that he is a good writer and that someday he may grow into a great one. The critics have advised him that he should steer away from "the Negro problem" and write on other themes—themes "with which all mankind can sympathize and identify." This, Wright well knew, is an argument as old and tired as it is inevitable. Novels about Negroes automatically are doomed to the category of "problem novels," accorded a discreet notice and then dismissed. The implication is that the lives described in these novels have no real relationship to that which is salient and significant to people generally. Baldwin, however, is not deceived. He knows that the Gordian knot of race in his native land is tied with enough meaning to inspire and confound all the ancient oracles.

In any case, he produced a novel which pre-empted the arguments. All the characters in *Giovanni's Room* are white. And while the central theme of the novel—a homosexual relationship—may not be one with which all mankind can sympathize and identify, it at least possesses the virtue of having no exclusive or direct association with Negroes. The critics praised the novel, as they should have, for it is a good novel. It even seems that the literary name-makers have decided to embrace James Baldwin, to permit him literary life. But this may be only apparent. No one knew better than Richard Wright that Americans indulge in a prudent amount of self-laceration. It is the critics' literary way of taking the nation to church on Sunday. It may be that Baldwin has been adopted as the temporary instrument of their polite penance. But this we must wait to know.

In any event, it is possible now that James Baldwin may not need to run away again. As Richard Wright knew, the world changed radically in the years between *Native Son* (1940) and *The Long Dream* (1958). And here I must make it perfectly clear that I do not have in mind the arguments (which to me have scant merit) advanced by critics of *The Long Dream*—the contention that the America Wright knew in 1939 is a thing of the musty past and that life for Negroes has lost its brutalizing aspects in the intervening years. How can the critics know? How can the man who wields the whip know the feel of the lashes on another's back? It is fashionable among the experts on race in this country these days to speak of the Negro's "breakthrough" into the mainstream of American life since World War II. They congratulate themselves that they have lifted a few boulders from the barricades. Wright once said that there is no "Negro problem" in America, only a "white problem," and that this problem will be solved any time white Americans want to solve it. This has always been true. Negroes have hovered on the outer fringes of freedom and dignity all their centuries on this continent. To be "almost free" when other men are without shackles is no less intolerable than being wholly unfree; it is merely insulting for those who clamp on the chains to judge the measure of their binding.

In saying that the world has changed, then, I have in mind events quite external to America. Wright wrote of this after Bandung and in *White Man, Listen!* Even the most passionate racists are beginning to comprehend that the portion of the world that is not "white" is large and—despite its lack of atom bombs—formidable, and that much of it is not overfriendly, and with good reason. The racists behold the colossus of China across the Pacific, the as yet uncertain quantities of India and Africa and the Middle East, and they are sobered. And now, they also look south across the Caribbean and ponder the ferment of the Americas and realize with a shock that those miserable masses in the midst of potential plenty are mostly red and brown and black and decidedly non-Caucasian. The eyes of America are yanked open at last, and because of the outside pressures which forced them open there is excitement and a new kind of ambiguous hope stirring among American Negroes. I assume that James Baldwin is aware of all this and that he shares, in his own way, in the excitement and the hope. And because of it, he may need never run away again.

Richard Wright was an American, a true "Native Son," and his flight to Paris only underscored this fact. And though he was always alienated, he was an expatriate in name only. He had no alternative but to go into exile, for his very life and sanity depended on it. His going was a gesture of affirmation, testimony to his belief in the preciousness of human dignity and freedom. He loved America for having preached these ideals even though they were not practiced. And he loved Americans. It may be difficult to understand how he could love them, but he did. He had only one time on earth, one life, and it was this time and this life against which they were aligned, and still he loved them. He bore in his soul the burden of their barbarism, and yet, in his intolerable anguish, he wanted to save them. Look—he said to Americans over and over again—that which you destroy transcends the limits of the Negro's humanity and tears at the foundation of the things you profess to treasure most. All humanity and all freedom are the ultimate targets, the eventual losers.

Richard Wright was an American, tugging at the conscience and the submerged sense of reason of America, and America should be proud to have produced him. Perhaps someday a more mature America will embrace her rejected native son. Perhaps that time will come. But now he is gone and will never know.

Addison Gayle, Jr.
(1932–1991)

Born in Newport News, Virginia, Gayle is an eminent African-American critic, one of the major architects of the concept of the Black Aesthetic, and Distinguished Professor of English at Bernard Baruch College of CUNY. Gayle's study of the black novel, *The Way of the New World* (1975), is an illustration of how concern for the historical, moral, and political implications of fiction might lead to an engaged criticism. Gayle edited the anthologies *Black Expression, The Black Aesthetic*, and *Bondage, Freedom, and Beyond*. His essays were collected in *The Black Situation*, and he published his autobiography *Wayward Child: A Personal Odyssey* in 1977. His biography *Richard Wright: Ordeal of a Native Son* (1980) used material obtained under the Freedom of Information Act to cast light on the literary and political dimensions of Wright's career. The following article is reprinted from *Black World* (September 1974).

Reclaiming the Southern Experience: The Black Aesthetic 10 Years Later

"We are a Southern people," John Killens had said, "because that is where our people are closest to Africa. But our literature does not show this." I thought immediately about my own writing and discerned an almost purposeful absence of my Southern experiences, as if, somehow, what I had known there and endured there and hated there and loved there had been obliterated by my experiences in the North; I thought, too, of my contemporaries—novelists, essayists, poets, critics—and, with the exception of Killens and Ernest Gaines, I could recall none who dealt with the South in a significant way, though a great many of them, like myself, were Southerners. The last major novel to treat the Southern experience is Gaines' *The Autobiography of Miss Jane Pittman*; I cannot think of a recent volume of poetry dedicated exclusively to the Southern experience.

Many critics, social and literary, who associate themselves in some manner with the concept of the Black Aesthetic, are Southerners; except for Houston Baker, however, in his recent book, *Long Black Song*, few have journeyed back to the South—to the sounds and smells, the folklore and music, the ribald jokes and the humane laughter, back to the culture which, as Killens noted, is close to the African experience—for the symbols and images, the paradigms of history which should form the underpinning of a people's literature. The reason is due, perhaps, to the fact that the Black Aesthetic movement was an urban phenomenon, pushed into actuality by the Black Power Movement of the 1960's to serve as the cultural arm of the Black Nationalist Movement.

Despite its detractors, Black and white, the movement has produced a major upheaval in Black literature. Black novelists and poets, contrary to the suggestions of Robert Bone and Blyden Jackson, have not followed the example of Robert Hayden and Ralph Ellison, a path leading into obscurantism and indecision, but instead have moved steadily along paths carved out by Imamu Baraka and John Killens—paths which emphasize a fidelity to the Black as opposed to the American experience. On the pragmatic side, even the Black detractors have benefitted immeasurably by the movement brought into being through Baraka's Black Arts Theater experience and Hoyt Fuller's tireless efforts as editor of *Black World*: lecture platforms, once occupied exclusively by white experts on Black people, are now mounted by Blacks. The arrogance and boldness with which white critics once dismissed Black literature occurs now only at the peril of the white critic. And Black critics, who were almost totally ignored before 1960, have gained visibility in the eyes of Black writers and public alike.

The elevation of the Black critic and Black criticism into acceptance and respectability by the Black community is a major achievement, for the job of the critic, as Toni Cade avers, is to call a halt to madness, and it is primarily the critics of the Black Aesthetic persuasion who have attempted to fulfill this function. They have called a halt to the madness of the 1940's and 1950's that propounded the idea that literature could serve as cartharsis for whites, that it might produce changes in them that would force them to move towards producing the "great society." They have called a halt to the madness demonstrated by those who argued that Black men were half men at best, ersatz Americans at most, and that, via the vehicle of protest literature, a transcendence might occur which would allow for the existence of whole men. They have called a halt to the themes of Black pity and gratuitous Black suffering, to the creation of castrated men children who existed in another country of self-pity and hopeless desperation. They have called for a halt to the madness of those who believed that writing was a vehicle for moving outside the Black community and that publishing a novel, play, or collection of poems moved one into higher status than other Blacks, shielded the writer from white exploitation and oppression. They have called a halt to the madness of those who argued that writing made them less African-American, that, in writing itself, they achieved a sort of mutation—"I am a writer, not a Negro writer"—and assumed that the value of Black literature could be validated only by white ∧ critics and a white audience.

Yet, despite the achievements of Black writers in the era of the Black Aesthetic, a major area of the Black experience—the Southern—was almost totally neglected: not the now outdated South of Richard Wright novels, where

Blacks were the eternal victims of whites, nor the South in which Black people lived complacently with fear and oppression, but a Black South where Black Nationalism is closer to achieving actuality than anywhere else in America, where the old suspiciousness of the Americans still survives, where a people know only too well that the solution to social and political problems must be wrought by their own hands. That is the South where Black women still maintain their proud carriage, where our young people continue to look with defiance upon the white world; a South where the ghosts of Harriet Tubman and David Walker, Sojourner Truth and Martin King remain omnipresent, constant reminders of the greatness of a race of men and women, who, forced to desert their god and their land, struggled and survived the American diaspora.

To neglect this area of our experience meant to ignore the one remaining link between Black people in America and those in the Caribbean, Africa, and throughout the world; for it is in the American South that a people, close to the land, are closer to the Africa of their ancestors, closer to the values and ethics of a society where people, not things, are supreme; where men and women, thank God, have no intentions of bringing their children up in the image of Richard Nixon, no intentions, that is, of capturing the American metaphor and making it their own.

Two recent books, however, serve to reverse the trend begun in the Sixties, to move us from an all-pervasive preoccupation with urban America towards an exploration of other, equally meaningful, areas of the Black experience: Houston Baker's *Long Black Song* and Askia Muhammad Touré's *Songhai!*— two books different in terms of genre, emphasis and theme, and yet comparably important departures in the area of Black literature and criticism.

Long Black Song is a scholarly critique, an examination of the roots/foundations of Black literature from the earliest folklore of the race to the literature of the 1960's and 1970's. *Songhai!* is a collection of verse/prose—melodic, rhythmical—weaving fascinating images and metaphors of the new Black World a-coming.* Together they tell the same truth: that the strength of Black people lay in a culture outside that of the American, and that the "New Jihad," to use Touré's phrase, is possible only after a return to the values and ethics of our African forefathers. *Long Black Song* is descriptive of the odyssey undertaken towards reaching the new world; *Songhai!* is a celebration, as much of the odyssey as of the new world itself.

The first book begins with a status report concerning the health of Black culture, and in a personal, analytical, and moving introduction, Baker validates the health of the culture by citing his own conversion: "Born in a racialistic former slave state, I was bombarded with the words, images, and artifacts of the white world. My parents had been bombarded with the same images, and the black librarian was no better off. . . . All of us had been lobotomized into

Long Black Song (The University Press of Virginia: 1972); *Songhai!* (Songhai Press, 50 W. 97th St., N.Y.C. 10025: 1972).

the acceptance of 'culture' on the white world's terms; we failed to realize that the manner in which the white world used 'culture' only helped justify its denial of the black man.''

For many, conversion leads to an attempt to synthesize the white and Black cultures, to critiques designed to prove that Black culture differs little from the American. Baker, on the other hand, rejects this attempt at assimilation and offers a cogent, well thought out answer to the Black and white proponents of a joint American culture: ''There are, of course, those who insist on unanimity of the two cultures: they say to black America: 'We are all from the same land, and the form of your intellectual and imaginative works are the same as ours.' Yes, we are all from the same land: but, to go back to the beginning one must realize that you came as pilgrims and I came as a 'negre.' Yes, the forms of our intellectual and imaginative works do coincide at points, but the experiences that are embodied in those forms are vastly different; in fact, the experiences embodied in some of the forms of Black American culture explicitly repudiate the whole tradition out of which those forms grow.''

According to Baker, the forms of things unknown, to use Wright's description, comprise the body of African-American folklore, which ''rests at the foundation'' of a Black literary tradition: ''for the customs, practices, and beliefs of the black American race . . . are clearly and simply reflected in the folklore.'' Here is the central thesis of *Long Black Song*. In this first literature of the Africans away from the ancestral home are the paradigms, images, metaphors and symbols which have formed not only the literature, but to a large degree the conceptions and perceptions of the race itself. And to return to the intellectual past, to undertake the odyssey back into one's culture heritage, guided by a sensitive, imaginative pilot, is to understand the genesis of a racial literature, to discover the cultural ethic which infuses the works of Black writers from David Walker to Imamu Baraka: ''Only when we have arrived at some knowledge of the heroes and values that characterize the group in which the black writer has his genesis, can we begin to discuss the work of conscious literary artists with some degree of authority.''

What Baker discovers in the animal tales, the trickster tales, in black ballads, blues, and the spirituals, is what Maulana Ron Karenga has called a new value system, one in which man, not things are the center of the universe, in which man's liberation instead of his oppression is of the highest priority, one in which the morality of the Americans and their institutions are continually called into question. From these early beginnings come the outlines of the Black Aesthetic—an aesthetic which refuses to divorce man from art, which agrees with the best of the Black critics of the Sixties and Seventies that an aesthetic, which proposes guidelines for art, must insist that art serve, not some higher metaphysical entity, but people.

This inspirational and informative discussion of Black folklore must be read in its entirety. For what one learns after careful reading is that the values to which the Black Aestheticians seek to return—those which pervade the works of present-day Black writers—is a sense of moral commitment to the sanctity and nobility of the human spirit, and a belief, unshakable, that art is an instrument for producing not a beautiful artifact but a beautiful world. The African-American folklorist, like the African artist, was one with his community, and his works were validated and legitimized by the community itself. How many of the tales and songs have become nonexistent because the community, in its role as critic, found them unacceptable by *its* standards?

Had Baker ended his analysis here, had he merely provided us with a scholarly treatise on Black literature and culture, he would have satisfied the requirement of the academic critics, Black and white, who seek to divorce literature from life. And though parts of *Long Black Song* are marred by the stilted language and jargon of the academicians, Baker has left such mediocrity behind and become a critic in the best sense of the word—challenging, inquisitive, and demanding: "The question of the black man's humanity recedes with the acknowledgement of his culture: passive, bestial victims and sambo personalities are not generally what one has in mind when he speaks of culture as a whole way of life. The goal of an investigation of Black American culture is to discover what type of man the Black American is and what values and experiences he has articulated that might be useful in one's attempt to make sense of the world."

This statement points to the heart of the Black Aesthetic. For it demands that the Black artist help us make sense out of the world we live in, help us achieve a sense of morality, not out of the values of the Euro-Americans, but out of those which spring from our own culture and history. To accomplish this does not necessitate, as some paranoid, hysterical critics have suggested, that one must find irrelevant and invalid every artifact of the Western world; it suggests only that the offerings of the West must be scrutinized in light of the question, "Is it good for Black people?" (We know, for example, that the Viet Cong did not return captured machine guns because they bore the label "made in America"; instead, they utilized them in their struggle to overcome the Americans.)

It is such a world to which the author of *Long Black Song* calls our attention: a world of diversity, and change, where men and women, seen in the context of historical perspective, are paradigms of the courage, endurance, grace, and beauty to which a race of people must, as did Jean Toomer, return and then again return. Writing in the *New Negro*, in 1925, Alain Locke assured his audience that the day of Aunties and Uncles, Toms and Sambos was over. *Long Black Song* tells us, here in the 1970's, that the days of darky entertainers, superflies, sweetbacks, and Melindas, if not over, are numbered, that an excursion into the cultural past can provide images by which we may measure ourselves as a people; it tells us that we are a people whose history and culture exemplify those values by which men throughout the history of the world have lived and died, and that these values found their greatest expression in the Western world in the South, in the first home away from home for the African-American. It is there, where men and women, having undergone the racial holocaust and survived, that the best examples of a viable Black literary and cultural tradition exist.

*   *   *

Unlike *Long Black Song, Songhai!* is an imaginative work overflowing with symbols, images, and metaphors of the new African world to come. History is as germane to Touré's work, however, as it is to Baker's, for it forms the central underpinning of the work. Touré, however, is not only an explorer and analyzer of words; he is also a creator of them. He envisions the world as Baker does: peopled by strong Black men and women equipped with the grace and endurance to survive the Americans. Analogously to Baker, Touré the poet/songster argues that we are better, even, than we think we are.

Touré is one of the finest poets in the language; his verse rings with the sound and timbre of Coltrane and Bird, with the lyricism of Toomer at his best, and contains the rich, symbolic import of the best of Claude McKay's Jamaican poetry. One of the founders of the Black Aesthetic Movement, in his works he is an apt paradigm for that movement. *Songhai!*, his finest effort to date, is an intellectual as well as imaginative exercise, which shows us what we must become by reminding us of what we are, by calling upon us to achieve "Tomorrow Jihad": "Move towards the visions and dreams we half suppress. Shape those visions/dreams with Imagination's scalpel, dare, to soar beyond the Beast-filled Present—Free!—your mind gliding upwards on the wings of love to other universes filled with throbbing Spirit, tropic song. For the real liberation is within. Then, Lover/Warrior/Sista-woman, fling this pulsing freedom from your breast into the astonished eye of Man!"

Songhai!'s music / prose / poetry evidences through its structure—sides one through four, like a long-playing record—that the three art forms are inseparable; that the poet is musician, storyteller, and prophet combined; and that the new African-American form must encompass them all. Only from such a totality can men come to understand themselves in relationship, not to the Western ethic and its God, but to history and Islam—the religion of man—not to a dead past, but to a new birth: "The Spiritual Nation. Samurai/Scholar-warriors in the West, rising with the sun. Teaching, Confronting. Growing into Manhood/anticipating Dawn. *Songhai!* a new world progressing towards birth. Beloved! commune with us in the purifying flames of Tomorrow's Jihad."

Songhai! readily lends itself to the kind of critical evaluation that some Black critics, imitating their white academic mentors, deem indispensable to the analysis of literature. Touré is a master of the symbol and the metaphor: "And Malcolm's blood is straining the asphalt ghetto skies/over Harlem in our minds in our hearts in our dreams/his Eagle-spirit flies away into Eternal Paradise/leaving us to wander blindly in the midnights of our pain." No poet gains so much from meter rhythms, can bend lines with such consummate skill and ease: "You walk in warm honeyed tones sheathed in red,/wild as the landscape of our continent./ You smile and tom-toms beat their lovesong/joyously in my heart./ Rhythm in your soul/rhythm in the way/your hips sway/Congo rhythm primed in Mississippi—*Soul sista*, come and go with me!"

Touré is an experimental poet, searching continually for new forms of expression, and he could be analyzed and re-analyzed to the point of meaninglessness by critiques that focus upon his technical dexterity with poetry, yet ignore the important social and political meaning of his work. (Such critics—

those who mount the barricade against social art and criticism, like white critics, believe that there is something unique and distinctive about Black poets who are expert in the technical aspects of the genre.) Black poets, however, with Touré, have long been aware of the fact that form is little more than the instrument through which the poet addresses his community—the conduit carrying the prophecy which alone can produce change in thought and perception. To analyze poetry by the scriptures of the academicians is to suggest, therefore, that Black poets have little that is important to say about the social and political ideas which in the West play such havoc with one's life. To evaluate Touré by his standard alone would be to do an injustice to a fine mind, to obscure the important message/prophecy, which lies beyond the form, the call for commitment, awareness, and action: "Ambush the Silver Screen. Rob it of its victims—/frightened coons and screeching Aunt Jemimas./Kidnap Birmingham/Stepin Fetchit/Beulah/Butterfly./Nature them to life with the love-cry echoes/of your soul./A new image like a diamond sparkling in an/ebony palm. A Congo-song for the multitudes."

Not surprisingly, the introduction to *Songhai!* is written by John Killens, and if Killens is, as I have written elsewhere, the novelist of love, Touré is the poet of love, and some of the best verse in this collection is that which speaks of love between Black men and Black women, and metaphorically, between one Black and another: "Melodies harmonizing with other hearts/ minds/souls/all as One, One as all—a symphony of ecstasy,/the loving cosmic harmonies of earth/Yes, make it summer. It would be summer:/golden sunlight, incense, flowers nourishing butterflies/azure skies breathing love; my ebony darling laughing/softly beneath my touch. I veteran/older wiser greying at the temples/lounging on a persian rug, stroking my reward/for wading through sewers of bloody death/to come back whole and laughing in an Age/of possibility and love."

Such an age is only possible after the apocalypse, after the cleansing of the Black mind and soul, after a people have undergone the inward odyssey, sifted through the lies and distortions of the past, come to view themselves as new men and women, as earth people, determined to transcend the images offered by the white West. To move through the pages of *Songhai!*, to read poems of examination and conflict—"Babylove," "Entertaining Troops," and "My Man"—poems of love and endurance—"The Birth of a Nation," "Africa: A Faded Summer," and "Green Edens Flourish After Storms," is to arrive, finally at the poems of intellect and imagination, those more prose than poetry, where the prophecy is fulfilled, the world born anew, Black people at one with their ancestral past: "I see now how lucky we are," says Mustafa, future Black woman, after witnessing the apocalyptic end of the West, "having witnessed the rebirth of man, to be free, moving about with a high oneness, remolding the world in a righteous Age. . . ."

Imamu Baraka wrote, "We want a Black poem and a Black world." Well, *Long Black Song* and *Songhai!* are literary maps, depicting the contours of the new poetry that leads on to the creation of the new world. The direction must, of necessity, be one which leads back to the Southern experience, for here is the prelude for the final journey to the new Jihad, the Africa from whence we came, cleansed of the disease of colonialism. For despite the fact that modernization, urbanization, and all the concomitant evils have come to the South, there still remains the spiritual resilience of a people who, having undergone numerous Waterloos, remain faithful to the belief that life can be lived wholly and fruitfully outside the ethical system of the West.

Long Black Song reminds us of those values, once so much a part of our existence—a commitment to man, to the eventual freeing of the human spirit, to the communality and brotherhood of all the earth's people; *Songhai!* speaks of those values regained, that will allow us to construct the New Jihad, to bring upon this earth a world, where poet and people feed into each other's creative ethos, where all men are poets, where love and fidelity to the human condition remain sacrosanct. This, to quote a recent critic, is Addison Gayle's idealism at its highest. True, yet it is an idealism which argues that sane men must never accept the Western indictum that "what is, is right," but that they must work creatively, politically and socially, to construct a world where people are most important, not technology; that, like the slaves of old, they must never accept the dictates of tyrannical men and tyrannical systems; that they must search outside the West for images, metaphors, and symbols which exhibit courage, love, endurance, fidelity, and commitment to the human spirit.

Such idealism still exists in the South, in the minds of the young, who— though all too ready to accept the romance of the North, to be dazzled by the Superflies and the Shafts, the pimps and the hustlers, the chameleon-like clowns clad in high-heel shoes and red suits—are still possessed of a hunger to understand this diverse and complex world in which they live. They do not yet know that this is possible only if they examine the richness of that region where our ancestors first lived and died, only if they understand the examples of Frederick Douglass, Sojourner Truth, David Walker and Nat Turner. They do not know this, and the Black writer must begin to inform them and, in so doing, inform Black people throughout the world. Only when this is accomplished, when the Black Aesthetic has been directed Southward, only then can we begin, with Mustafa, to construct the new society. *Long Black Song* and *Songhai!* are two important works, pointing us in that direction.

Trudier Harris

(1948–)

A literary critic who specializes in African-American literature and folklore with emphasis on the roles of black women, Harris is currently the J. Carlysle Sitterson Professor of English at the University of North Carolina, Chapel Hill. Born in Mantua, Alabama, she received her B.A. from Stillman College and her M.A. and Ph.D. from Ohio State University. Her books include *From Mammies to Militants: Domestics in Black American Literature, Exorcising Blackness: Historical and Literary Burning Rituals, Black Women in the Fiction of James Baldwin*, and *Fiction and Folklore: The Novels of Toni Morrison*. She is coeditor of the Afro-American volumes of the *Dictionary of Literary Biography*, and she frequently publishes articles in professional and literary journals. The following excerpt is from *From Mammies to Militants.*

---

from From Mammies to Militants

The Maid as Southern and Northern Mammy

The literary and historical image of the domestic as mammy is one easily recognized and much maligned, a type which invariably tends toward stereotype. As repulsive as outside observers may judge the role to have been, black women who found themselves in it were privileged indeed within the plantation households in which the type was established. Mammies who had established reputations for responsibility and reliability, who were mature and experienced, usually did less work than other slaves. According to Jessie Parkhurst, the mammy was primarily in charge of child-rearing, sometimes assisting with household tasks when the children in her care had grown large enough to help care for themselves. She was versatile enough to fill "any gap that occurred in the southern household," able to move from child-rearing to cooking to ordering supplies. Generally, she was "next to the mistress in authority" and bossed "everyone and everything in the household."[1] If she did not live in the big house, she lived nearby, she dressed well, was not usually punished or sold, and could cultivate an intimacy with the master that none of the other slaves dared. "She was considered self-respecting, independent, loyal, forward, gentle, captious, affectionate, true, strong, just, warm-hearted, compassionate-hearted, fearless, popular, brave, good, pious, quick-witted, capable, thrifty, proud, regal, courageous, superior, skillful, tender, queenly, dignified, neat, quick, tender, competent, possessed with a temper, trustworthy, faithful, patient, tyrannical, sensible, discreet, efficient, careful, harsh, devoted, truthful, neither apish nor servile."[2] That may have been the type, but it quickly degenerated into stereotype. Mammy's self-respect was lost in groveling before and fawning upon her mistress, master, and young white charges. Her loyalty became self-effacement and her affection anticipated the exaggeration of the minstrel tradition. Her piety and patience worked more often than not in favor of the whites, and her tyranny was most ruthless when it was exercised over other Blacks. Devoted she was, but in contrast to what Parkhurst asserts, she also believed in aping white manners, and, if she was not servile, she certainly believed herself inferior to those for whom she worked. They honored her by singling her out from the black masses, and she repaid them with lifetime devotion.

Features inherent in the job made it necessary for the black mammy to deny her own family in order to rear generation after generation of whites who would, ironically, grow up to oppress Blacks yet further. And because she consented to this denial, the popular stereotyping intensified—particularly when black women persisted in voluntary engagement in such roles after slavery. Images formed from years of habit could not be easily uprooted from the minds of these black women: to them, whites were the models for everything good and right, while black was ugly and undesirable. Such women were utterly without progressive political consciousness.

The three characters classified as mammies in this chapter—Mammy Jane in Chesnutt's *The Marrow of Tradition* (1901), Lourinda "Granny" Huggs in Hunter's *God Bless the Child* (1964), and Pauline Breedlove in Morrison's *The Bluest Eye* (1970)—follow this pattern, totally identifying with whites and white culture and negating blackness and black culture. They hold whites up as models for moral and social emulation, and they refuse to believe that there is anything in the black world that can remotely compare with the cleanliness, the purity, the goodness they see in the white world.

Charles Waddell Chesnutt's *The Marrow of Tradition* (1901) is set in Wellington (Wilmington), North Carolina, in the late 1890's, at its climax featuring racial rioting such as occurred in Wilmington in 1898; and, as one of its several subplots, it offers a portrait of a black southern nursemaid who is only a few years and a few psychological steps removed from slavery. Mammy Jane is an aging "family retainer" whose connections to the Merkell/Carteret family extend over three generations. Having reared the present Mrs. Carteret and her mother, Mammy Jane refuses to allow anyone else to rear the long-awaited Carteret baby, whose birth is imminent at the opening of the novel. The son born to Olivia and Major Carteret is nearly the same age as the son born to Janet and Adam Miller, Janet being the long-ignored "colored" sister of Olivia Carteret and Miller a black doctor. In order to save their son's life, white Olivia is eventually forced to acknowledge kinship to black Janet and the white-supremacist Major is forced to humble himself before the black doctor.

Ironies, coincidences, and the fantastic all characterize the novel; its melodrama is suggested even by the very short plot summary above. In its presentation of the black nursemaid, however, *The Marrow of Tradition* is realistic fiction. Mammy Jane is very much the epitome of the true southern maid, the mammy as she has been herein defined. Most critics writing about *The Marrow of Tradition* simply ignore Mammy Jane's place in the novel or dismiss her role as functional, like those of several stereotyped, minor characters in the novel.[3] However, the fact that Chesnutt decided that such a character as Mammy Jane should exist in his novel, that the social and political climate with which he was concerned dictated her presence, demands a more than cursory consideration of her role. William L. Andrews's point on the conception of character in the novel is relevant here. ". . . Chesnutt conceives of characters and scenes in *The Marrow of Tradition* primarily as demonstration vehicles for general social truths about the New South."[4] Certainly Mammy Jane is a type, and certainly Chesnutt recognized her as such,[5] but what she says and how she acts in that role reflect the historical pattern of many black women after Emancipation, women who found themselves without identities beyond those of the white families for whom they had spent most of their lives working. To the extent that Mammy Jane reflects a truth which goes deeper than the type, her role is important. To the extent that she illustrates a major obstacle to the movement toward self-assertion for many of her contemporaries, her role is equally important.

Mammy Jane enters the novel with a curtsy, and she bows and scrapes her way to her death. She is exemplary in her subservience and unfalteringly believes in her "place." She knows that God has put her on earth to serve quality white folks; she can envision nothing beyond that. Her attitude comes out in the first scene in which Major Carteret enters a room where she is waiting:

> Mammy Jane hobbled to her feet and bobbed a curtsy. She was never lacking in respect to white people of proper quality; but Major Carteret, the quintessence of aristocracy, called out all her reserves of deference. The major was always kind and considerate to these old family retainers, brought up in the feudal atmosphere now so rapidly passing away. Mammy Jane loved Mrs. Carteret; toward the major she entertained a feeling bordering upon awe.[6]

When a young, newly educated black nurse is hired to substitute for Mammy Jane when she suffers from rheumatism, the old woman is appalled by what she considers the girl's lack of respect. The girl ignores the advice Mammy Jane gives and obviously has little patience with the old black woman's adoration of the young white child. "Dese yer young niggers ain' got de manners dey wuz bawned wid!" Mammy Jane exclaims in response to the girl's attitude. And later, when Major Carteret maintains that Jane's attitude toward place and education is correct, she responds:

Dat's w'at I tells dese young niggers . . . w'en I hears 'em gwine on wid deir foolishniss; but dey don' min' me. Dey 'lows dey knows mo' d'n I does, 'ca'se dey be'n l'arnt ter look in a book. But, pshuh! my ole mist'ess showed me mo' d'n dem niggers 'll l'arn in a thousan' years! I's fetch' my gran'son Jerry up ter be 'umble, an' keep in 'is place. An' I tells dese other niggers dat ef dey'd do de same, an' not crowd de w'ite folks, dey'd git ernuff ter eat, an' live out deir days in peace an' comfo't. But dey don' min' me—dey don' min' me! (pp. 43–44)

Of Janet Miller's riding in a buggy she says, "Well, well! Fo'ty yeahs ago who'd 'a' ever expected ter see a nigger gal ridin' in her own buggy? My, my! but I don' know,—I don' know! It don' look right, an' it ain' gwine ter las!—you can't make me b'lieve!" (p. 106) Mammy Jane's prediction that things will not "last" is correct, for the riot changes a lot, yet she is too weak of mind and spirit to try to view the inevitable changes in any but a negative light.

In making his a "story of Southern life" (p. 42), Chesnutt has his Mammy Jane mirror many attitudes held by whites during reconstruction days, the most vocalized of which is the opposition to any change from the pre-war status of the Negro. Major Carteret, arch-supporter of white supremacy and editor of the local white-supremacist newspaper, the *Morning Chronicle*, and his cohorts, General Belmont and Captain McBane, are the chief spokesmen for a nostalgic ideal of Blacks' keeping their subservient place. Staunchly devoted to the concept of "no nigger domination," they work fiercely to reverse the political gains Blacks have made, General Belmont verbalizing what he sees as a distressing trend:

Things are in an awful condition! A negro justice of the peace has opened an office on Market Street, and only yesterday summoned a white man to appear before him. Negro lawyers get most of the business in the criminal court. Last evening a group of young white ladies, going quietly along the street arm-in-arm, were forced off the sidewalk by a crowd of negro girls. Coming down the street just now, I saw a spectacle of social equality and negro domination that made my blood boil with indignation,—a white and a black convict, chained together, crossing the city in charge of a negro officer! We cannot stand that sort of thing. Carteret,—it is the last straw! Something must be done, and that quickly! (p. 33)

General Belmont could very easily be echoing Mammy Jane, and we can further see their agreement in his appreciation of Jerry. "Jerry now," says Belmont, "is a very good negro. He's not one of your new negroes, who think themselves as good as white men, and want to run the government. Jerry knows his place—he is respectful, humble, obedient, and content with the face and place assigned to him by nature" (p. 87). Jerry identifies thoroughly with "quality" white folks; when he wishes he were white so he could enjoy the kinds of privileges whites have (p. 36), the wish is grounded in compliment and appreciation, not rebellion. Jerry is indeed content with his role.

Mammy Jane, like General Belmont, Captain McBane, and Major Carteret, would like to conserve black/white relationships as they were before the war. The major makes his point clear at a dinner early in the novel: "No doubt the negro is capable of a certain doglike fidelity,—I make the comparison in a kindly sense,—a certain personal devotion which is admirable in itself and fits him eminently for a servile career" (p. 24). Mammy Jane gets along well with the major because his description fits her precisely. The major continues his theme in an editorial he writes a few pages later in the novel; it concerns "the unfitness of the negro to participate in government,—an unfitness due to his limited education, his lack of experience, his criminal tendencies, and more especially to his hopeless mental and physical inferiority to the white race" (p. 31). It is a divinely ordained inferiority, the major believes, then, that makes Mammy Jane's role in life the ideal one for the Negro.

The major believes generally that Blacks should go in and come out of back doors. In one instance, place as physical location is literalized into place as status. "It was traditional in Wellington that no colored person had ever entered the front door of the Carteret residence, and that the luckless individual who once presented himself there upon alleged business and resented being ordered to the back door had been unceremoniously thrown over the piazza railing into a rather thorny clump of rosebushes below" (p 68). The fellow's punishment had been slight, to say the least, for even emergencies do not relax the customary rule of the house. Major Carteret feels strongly enough about it to refuse, at first, to allow Dr. Miller to enter through the front door to attend his young son, and even the black woman who comes to tell the Carterets of their Aunt Polly's death comes in through the back door though she has to go around the house to do it (p. 175). Having lost personal property as a result of the war, Major Carteret and others like him are intense in upholding whatever is left that clearly defines them as different from those they judge to be unequal to them. For Major Carteret, then, the passing of such distinctions is tantamount to the final dissolution of culture as he knows it. He will not accept the change passively, as the last words of the following lamentation for the passing of "old times" makes clear:

> The old times have vanished, the old ties have been ruptured. The old relations of dependence and loyal obedience on the part of the colored people, the responsibility of protection and kindness upon that of the whites, have passed away forever. The young negroes are too self-assertive. Education is spoiling them, Jane; they have been badly taught. They are not content with their station in life. Some time they will overstep the mark. The white people are patient, but there is a limit to their endurance (p. 43).

Here is a quintessential expression of place and conservatism.*

It is perhaps appropriate to the novel's period that the major shares his ideas

---

*It underscores the pathetic inability to accept change, and it hints at the fear whites have of Blacks, which will later contribute to the tragic violence of the riot.

with Mammy Jane more often than his ethereal, ineffective wife does so, as she probably would in later works; still, Mammy Jane's role in relation to her mistress is important. Olivia Carteret shares her husband's fidelity to the status quo. She has no fancy words of justification to offer because women-folks are expected just to do, but she shows in her actions that she does believe in the social distance between herself and Mammy Jane and the paradoxically even greater gulf between herself and Janet Miller. As one character points out, blood is thicker than water unless it runs into unapproved channels; then it is the thinnest of substances. Olivia therefore ignores Janet as best she can, and Mammy Jane feels justification in the distinctions she draws and in that neglect. Janet may have acquired many things, by black standards, but she still is not in either of the other women's eyes the white woman's equal. Mammy Jane is as annoyed as Olivia when Janet intrudes herself into Mrs. Carteret's presence by driving on the same street or by passing by the Carteret home.

The nature of the relationship between Mammy Jane and Olivia Carteret is clearest, however, when Mammy Jane is taking care of Theodore Felix, "Dodie," the Carteret baby. Olivia trusts the old servant implicitly, for Mammy Jane has cared for both her and her mother; she accepts it as the natural order of things that black Mammy Jane's life has been devoted to rearing white children. Mammy Jane has, therefore, proprietary rights to the Carteret house and baby, and when she returns from a brief absence and asks how the substitute nurse has worked out, Olivia maintains: "She does fairly well, Mammy Jane, but I could hardly expect her to love the baby as you do. There's no one like you, Mammy Jane" (p. 41). There is certainly no one like her in her devotion to the child. Noting, for example, that the baby has a slight mole on its neck, just at the point at which a hangman's noose would take hold, Mammy Jane decides that in spite of the child's white heritage, which will surely protect it, she—it—still needs the help of the black conjure woman. She goes to the woman, gets a charm, and buries it in the yard of the Carteret house. She buries, turns, and reburies the charm when little Dodie is about to have an operation; and, after the baby almost falls from a window, she attaches what she considers to be a more potent charm to the child's very crib. Olivia, touched, refuses to remove it. Her devotion to the Carteret family and baby gives Mammy Jane license within the household that is peculiarly the mammy's. She can voice opinions that other Blacks would not be able to voice; she can talk with the white doctor Price about Carteret family secrets; and she is allowed to be familiar, to an extent, with Olivia and Major Carteret.

Mammy Jane's place is wherever the white folks want and need her to be, either for work or for show. The christening of the Carteret baby is an opportunity for show: "Upon this special occasion Mammy Jane had been provided with a seat downstairs among the white people, to her own intense satisfaction, and to the secret envy of a small colored attendance in the gallery, to whom she was ostentatiously pointed out by her grandson Jerry, porter at the Morning Chronicle office, who sat among them in the front row" (p. 12). Pride in identification with whites exudes from Mammy Jane for most of the novel. Her compromise in the white world is one which does not allow for an appreciation of her own culture or of her own history without the mediating influence of the whites around her. Thus folk culture for Mammy Jane is not a thing of intrinsic value, a source of truth, identity, and the reality Ellison noted, but a medium for protecting the status quo that the whites hold on to so strongly, a source of reinforcements of the status of the white folks she dearly loves: thus she turns to the root doctor to make sure little Dodie Carteret will live and thrive and grow up to oppress more Blacks. Sharing the stereotyped images that whites have of Blacks, and sometimes going beyond those, she does not realize that she herself is a stereotype. For example, when the Carteret baby is taken to a window to see a mockingbird and nearly falls out of the window when Janet Miller is driving by, Olivia blames the incident on Janet. So too does Mammy Jane:

> Mammy Jane entertained a theory of her own about the accident, by which the blame was placed, in another way, exactly where Mrs. Carteret had laid it. Julia's daughter, Janet, had been looking intently toward the window just before little Dodie had sprung from Clara's arms. Might she not have cast the evil eye upon the baby, and sought thereby to draw him out of the window? One would not ordinarily expect so young a woman to possess such a power, but she might have acquired it, for this very purpose, from some more experienced person. By the same reasoning, the mockingbird might have been a familiar of the witch, and the two might have conspired to lure the infant to destruction. Whether this were so or not, the transaction at least wore a peculiar look. There was no use telling Mis 'Livy about it, for she didn't believe, or pretended not to believe, in witchcraft and conjuration. But one could not be too careful. The child was certainly born to be exposed to great dangers—the mole behind the left ear was an unfailing sign—and no precaution should be omitted to counteract its baleful influence (pp. 107–108).[7]

Mammy Jane's immersion in the folk culture, like many historical mammies', Chesnutt suggests, makes her an ignorant anachronism in a world which struggles to move forward, a world which is held back in its progress by those like her and the whites who share their views. One might excuse Mammy Jane's actions by saying that she is simply a product of the times, one who is offered no alternative lifestyle. But many Blacks in the novel do not hold the same views that Mammy Jane does. From Dr. Miller and the nurse of the younger generation to ole Sam who explains to Miller that whites have refused to allow him to attend the scheduled operation on Dodie, there are Blacks who see a reality beyond the place assigned by whites.[8] They do not avoid whites, but they do not defer to them, and they certainly do not work roots to aid them; they also advocate improving the lot of Blacks through the education that Mammy Jane sees as a decided mistake, a hindrance for Blacks. Mammy Jane's position, then, is partly custom, habit, and tradition, and partly choice.[9] She is not completely blameless in her subservience; in fact, her zeal is a volunteer's.

Ironically, the adoration Mammy Jane has given to the whites cannot ultimately protect her from their wrath against all Blacks. She is killed in the rioting that Major Carteret has initiated with inflammatory editorials in his newspaper. Although both Olivia and Major Carteret had maintained that they would protect Mammy Jane against all possible dangers, and insist that she is somehow special, they cannot control the white-fired bullet that takes her life even as she is on her way to their home to seek that promised protection. She is merely another Black to the angry white men who have declared war on all persons of color. But even imminent death does not alter Mammy Jane's perceptions of what is happening around her—or her identity with the white world. As Dr. Miller lifts her head into a more comfortable position there on the street, her final cry is: "Comin', missis, comin'!" (p. 296) Insisting that her death was an accident, that no white man in town would willfully shoot poor Jane, Major Carteret fails to realize that he himself has killed her. His unconscious but absolute hatred of all Blacks, his belief that they should not move beyond a predetermined place, his campaign against "nigger domination" are all responsible for Jane's death. Try as he might to compartmentalize the good niggers and the bad niggers, they are finally all treated the same. Mammy Jane has, therefore, through her own identification with the whites, been an instrument in her own destruction. That is the consequence for the true southern domestic, the mammy, who cannot effect a healthy compromise when she goes to work for whites.

Mammy Jane's actions, paradoxically, at once reinforce and give the lie to the myth of the strength of black women. She is strong—fanatical even—in her devotion to and work for whites. Simultaneously, she is weak in identity derived either from pride or from culture or race. The price she pays for being the ideal servant is to become a black-faced puppet; sadly, she worships the controllers of her strings. She cannot envision change because she can see nothing wrong with her present condition. Total absorption in where she is and total identification with the people for whom she works make her the quintessential southern domestic. Her upbringing on southern soil, amid paternalistic traditions of black self-denial and dependency, has made Mammy Jane, if not tragic, at least pathetic.

Mammy Jane's situation may be pathetic, but that of Mrs. Lourinda Baxter "Granny" Huggs in *God Bless the Child* (1964) is absurd. Like Mammy Jane, Granny is a family retainer with four decades of service to a single family, the Liveseys—Grandmother Helen, Mother Emilie, and little Miss Iris—who mirror her own family exactly. (Apparently Granny is about the same age as Miss Helen; her daughter Regina "Queenie" Fleming could be Miss Emilie's age; and Miss Iris and Granny's granddaughter Rosalie "Rosie" Fleming are exactly the same age.) Granny does everything for the Liveseys, from rearing three generations of their children to buying and cooking their food to cleaning their house and ordering its furniture. Although the story takes place in the North, Granny has moved with the family from Virginia. She is truly southern in her adherence to the paternalistic order decreeing that there shall be white masters and black servants, to the sense of place expected of her. Indeed,

Granny's move to the North is merely geographical change; in her attitude toward the whites for whom she works, she makes it clear that the story might just as well have taken place in Mississippi or Alabama. The city into which Granny and her white folks had moved many years ago is not named, but its character is obvious from the activities which go on there. Its highly visible black numbers runners, winos, and gangsters all confirm for Granny that her identification with the genteel, quality white folks is correct and that she should instill that identification in her family. Like many mammies historically, she judges her family by standards and values she encounters in the white world. Her granddaughter Rosie, seven at the opening of the novel, dies shortly after she is twenty-one, having been driven by her internalization of the materialistic values Granny worships to work too obsessively, too ruinously hard, to obtain material things.

Throughout the novel, Granny's attitude is one of detachment from Blacks generally, from her family, and ultimately even from the granddaughter who works so desperately to please her. That detachment, that aura of lady-like superiority, has been shaped in imitation of what Granny believes she sees among whites. Her connection to the Liveseys allows her to consider herself infinitely better than other Blacks, and her light skin intensifies that superior feeling. Barely willing to tolerate her brown-skinned granddaughter and falling just short of being a tragic mulatto herself, she is color-struck and thoroughly conscious of a division between lighter- and darker-skinned Blacks. "Down Home," she says, "we were always the lightest. That's how come we were house servants, not field servants. My mother was mixed. She was a gypsy creole. Her name was Tamir, and she used to play on a funny kind of round-shaped guitar. . . . She had wavy black hair so long she could sit on it. . . . She spoke three languages, French and Indian and Gypsy."[10] When Rosie asks why Granny is so light and she is so dark, Granny speaks with the positiveness of the mammies who advised their white charges to find suitable marriage partners and were bitterly disappointed if they didn't. "Because . . . that no 'count father of yours was black as coal tar. I tried to bring this girl [Queenie] up right, and then she ran off and got married without thinkin' about improvin' the race" (p. 19). Handicapped by a color for which she is not responsible, Rosie works ever more diligently to please Granny and thus atone for what seems to be an unforgivable sin. She gains Granny's affection, fleetingly, only when she comes close to approximating the formal social graces Granny values above all else. But she cannot earn Granny's lasting affection, for Granny is cut apart from everyone black, and she probably confronts herself only through a medium comparable to the plastic used to cover furniture.

Granny's adventures in the Livesey household suggest that she out-herods Herod, that she is more white in attitude than the whites for whom she works. Although Granny rides the bus to work, she impatiently insists that the chauffeur drive her home on occasions. The fact that she wants a ride is not relevant here; her attitude toward the chauffeur is. She considers him "field help" (p. 7), thereby showing the ingrained distinction she makes between those worthy of consideration and those not. Indeed, many mammies were leaders in suggesting whom one should socialize with and whom not. She perhaps takes more pleasure in playing the big woman with local merchants than Miss Helen does. The salespeople who originally thought her an "ignorant old colored woman" quickly learned the power of her signature in buying for the Liveseys and quickly learned to bow and scrape to her: "they would never find out that she did not know how to write anything but her name" (p. 5). Her lack of education does not detract from Granny's exalted evaluation of herself, or from her belief that she is a model for emulation in conduct and other Blacks are no-good "trashy niggers" (p. 21).

When the novel opens, Granny is a live-in worker to the Liveseys. In her absence, Rosie begins to romanticize the life Granny has across town. Even at seven years old, Rosie believes her grandmother should not be a resident of the roach-infested apartment in which she and Queenie live. It is all right, Rosie believes, for her mother and herself to smell the toilets and burnt hair and cooking greens of their apartment building, but her grandmother "was different. Granny did not live here; she lived across town in a white palace with marble stairs and crystal fountains, and when she came to be with them on her Thursdays and every-other-weekends, she was company" (p. 15). And Granny forever acts like company. Seldom does she descend from her papier-mâché pedestal to experience the reality of black life of which she is a part.

Thus she ignores the roaches which irreverently traipse over the broken china she brings home from the Liveseys. She brings out elegant candles when the ever-failing electrical system fails once again. She refuses to see the unpainted walls and falling plaster in the apartment where her daughter and granddaughter live. She does not care that Rosie does not go to school as long as she knows the difference between real and imitation silk. She does not care that Queenie could still be happily married if she, her mother, had not insisted that the husband was too black and that he had married Queenie only because of her pregnancy. She does not care that Rosie does not respect Queenie, or even see how she has contributed to that lack of respect. But most importantly, she has no sense of the confused lives she creates around her. Having destroyed Queenie's marriage, she prefers the gangster Tommy Tucker as a suitor to the granddaughter she will drive to her death, scorning the gentle and sturdy Larnie Bell. Once again Granny fails to distinguish between imitation silk and the real thing. Granny believes in show, in appearance, in form rather than in substance. In one brief scene, the conniving Tucker appeals to her gullible southern gentility, and she is ready to throw Rosie into his irresponsible arms (pp. 96–97). The novel is essentially one of suspense: we wait to see how far Rosie will go to please her grandmother before she either kills herself or sees beneath her grandmother's facade. It is also a tale of the destructive effects the mammy role has on the mammy's family. For all the good Granny may believe she contributes to the Liveseys, there is countervailing destruction in the Fleming household. What she does to her family stems from her being a live-in worker for the Liveseys; all of her responses to the world have been shaped by what she encounters in the world of the Liveseys.

It is clear early in the novel that Granny has succeeded very well in setting up the Livesey world as preferable to that of the Huggses and the Flemings. When Rosie plays hooky from school at age seven, one of her pastimes is not merely imitation of grown-ups but imitation of the Liveseys (or at least of their world as she romantically conceives of it). She dresses in her mother's new red dress, applies lipstick and jewelry, and looks at herself in the mirror:

> The vision in the mirror was not Rosie Fleming. It was Missiris, Madam Queen in the house where Granny worked, Princess in all the fairy tales Rosie was just learning to read. Missiris wore long red skirts and lots of red beads and bangles and silk scarves and clinking earrings. Missiris was spoiled rotten because she had a sweet mother named Missemilie and a beautiful grandmother called Misshelen. Missiris had her meals brought up to her on silver trays, and she had a magic carpet that flew her out the window. Zoom! And when Madam Queen Princess Missiris walked down the street and swished her skirts everyone stepped out of her way. Swish! Rosie stamped her feet and the crowds made way for her. Crowds of frightened roaches, scurrying under the bedroom linoleum. Swish! (pp. 12–13).

The reality of these roaches is what Granny ignores throughout the novel, and it is what Rosie will try to overcome. The vision of beauty, cleanliness, the absence of roaches, drives her to her destruction. While the ambition in itself is certainly not unadmirable, its fanatical pursuit is. And perhaps Rosie gives new meaning even to the fanatical.

In the third-floor walk-up where Granny expresses her attitude of silk and china, the seven-year-old Rosie plays the game of squashing roaches. She attacks an army of them before she eats breakfast.

> The counter was three feet high and eighteen inches deep. Rosie could just reach the back of it by standing on tiptoe. She raised both hands and came down on the marching column . . . killing four in one smash. Another quick smash caught two more babies at the end of the rapidly retreating column. From the corner of her eye she saw the giant granddaddy of them all scurry from the ceiling and rush down the wall. She rocked on tiptoe, waiting, gathering strength.
>
> Now he was within reach. Her palm came down on him just as he was about to dart inside the cupboard.
>
> "Got the bastard," she said.
>
> She opened a drawer, ignoring the sudden flurry of movement inside, and took out a pencil and the notebook that said:
>
> "Rosalie Fleming.
>
> My Book."
>
> She wrote the date and, beside it, the number 10, then carefully put book and pencil away. Seven babies and a big one who was worth three points. Not a bad morning. Rosie decided to stay home from school and kill roaches all day (p. 11).

Into this world of roaches, sleeping on cots, and never having enough money, Granny brings a concentrated detachment derived from having none of these worries. Into life, she brings the *form* of living, a show to be put on to impress others, for life itself is simply too graphically unpleasant for her. She arrives a few hours later, and the following scene occurs when she asks what she, her daughter, and her granddaughter are having for dinner:

> "Chinese food on the table," Mom said, pointing, and pouring herself another drink. "Help yourself."
>
> Granny touched the cardboard carton with one reluctant fingertip. "It's cold."
>
> "Well, I ain' movin'," Mom said, "Let your precious grandchild do some work for a change."
>
> "Rosalie," Granny chirped in her best peacemaking voice, "you run set the table while I heat this up a little bit. Get out the flowered tablecloth and put water in some glasses. And get the blue Chinese platter Miss Helen gave me," she added. "Nobody but field hands eat out of cardboard boxes."
>
> After a long search, Rosie found three plates in the cupboard that weren't cracked. She killed two roaches when she went back for glasses.
>
> "What's all that racket?" Granny called.
>
> "I'm just setting the table, Granny," Rosie answered. She always hoped Granny didn't know about the roaches.
>
> "That's a good grandchild. Now look in the top of my bag and see if you can find some little lemon dessert pies" (pp. 16–17).

Little lemon dessert pies are just as incongruous in this environment as Maggie's duck was in *Backstairs at the White House*. Granny remains interested in the surface of things, not the depths that are the substance of life. Focus on the order of the Livesey household will not allow her to see beyond the superficial disorder in her daughter's apartment to the deeper disorder reflected in Rosie's and Queenie's attitudes toward each other as well as in the physical clutter of the apartment.

Rosie's desire that her grandmother not see the roaches is matched only by the grandmother's refusal to see what she does not wish to, and by the energy with which she forces forms of etiquette on her daughter and granddaughter. To accompany her flowered tablecloth and Chinese platter, Granny regales Rosie during dinner with tales of the extravagant birthday party Missiris will have the following day. Rosie's expressions of "Gosh!", "No foolin', Granny?", and "Great day in the morning!" (pp. 17, 18) evince her willingness to believe in the possibilities of that world beyond her roach scoreboard, and she is as willing to abide by Granny's admonitions about dress and behavior as Granny is to offer them.

On the Sunday morning that Granny prepares Rosie's eighteenth birthday breakfast, she insists that Rosie make herself presentable. She orders Rosie to take off her pajamas and "put on something respectable. . . . And don't be fiddling around in front of that mirror neither. Just wash your face and comb that disgraceful head and come on" (p. 64). There is no thought that on one's birthday, at least, one might be liberated from some of the normal, expected formalities. Not in Granny's mind. She insists on dressing up and using a white linen table cloth and candles. All of this, which might be tolerable if born of love, is not: Granny's own artwork, which turns inward to herself, is all that matters to her. (We will see the same self-absorption in Morrison's Pauline Breedlove.) She is more interested in showing that she knows what is appropriate than in why it should fit one setting as opposed to another. And the manners that are the trademark of the mammy are all important to her, whether they are displayed by a snake or a gentleman.[11] Rosie is slightly surprised when Tommy Tucker, the numbers runner, is able to win Granny over by being complimentary and congenial. "For the first time in her life, she doubted Granny's judgment. Couldn't she see past people's manners to what they were like inside? Or didn't she care, as long as the outside was charming?" (p. 99). Rosie is over eighteen when she asks these questions, and her grandmother's influence is too strong to be neutralized. Rosie will continue to believe in the biggest, most glittering things as those most worthy of possessing.

Granny uses the many occasions when she brings things home from the Liveseys to teach Rosie lessons about quality, another extension of her mammy manners from the white household to the black. She brings china, sterling silver, crystal beads, a rainbow-colored bowl, crystal stemware, and bracelets, among other things, which she has usually helped to select, and she insists that Rosie develop the correct attitude toward those rarities. She even explains some of the circumstances under which she has acquired some of the things. In the case of the rainbow bowl, she had convinced Miss Emilie that there was a crack in it so she could bring it to Rosie. The stratagem was unnecessary, for Miss Emilie responded "It's not worth anything, Lourinda, it's just in the way. Why don't you take it on home?" (p. 20). When Rosie questions its value, Granny says: "Child, them people got so much money that they forgets it as soon as they spends it. It might be worth a thousand million dollars" (p. 20). That answer satisfies Rosie, and she assumes she has something of value. In the following few minutes, however, she and Queenie fight over the bowl and break it. Rosie keeps some of the pieces in her pocket during a school day, cutting her fingers in self-imposed penance for her part in the destruction of the bowl. Though the value of the bowl may have been questionable, and Granny's willingness to excuse its castoff status certainly is, Rosie nevertheless treasures it, even in pieces, as a tangible symbol of the romantic white world. The bowl had made "home an ugly place" after she had seen the apartment through its rainbow colors (p. 32).

When Rosie quits school at seventeen, three months before graduation, she explains to her friend Dolly: "I want things. I want things so bad I'd kill myself to get 'em" (p. 59). Although she does not intend the statement as prophecy, it comes true; before that culmination, however, Rosie does acquire things. She starts work as a salesgirl in a department store, then immediately begins a night job as a waitress. She buys extravagant presents for Granny and Queenie in addition to taking over the expenses of the apartment once Queenie becomes ill. She is sensitive to Granny's complaints about inferior quality and overextends herself in trying to buy the best. She buys slippers for

Granny which cost $39.50, and for that fleeting moment, the old woman is pleased: ''. . . she examined them slowly and critically, picking at the little seams where the soles joined the uppers, poking at the lining with her fingernails, sniffing the leather of the soles and, finally, rubbing her fingers over the surface of the fur. 'Real Persian,' she said at last, 'Real well made, too. For these days' '' (p. 175). But Granny's satisfaction is episodic, and each new episode must top the previous one: she always manages to suggest that Rosie has fallen just short of ultimately pleasing. Slips, silk dresses, fabulous shoes— Rosie spends to alleviate the depression of the bills she acquires by spending. So the cycle goes.

She gets into trouble with numbers runners and gangsters in her bid to get Granny a house for her seventieth birthday. Miss Helen having died without remembering Granny in her will, Granny has moved in with Rosie and Queenie—still taking everything as if it were her just due. Rosie feels pressured to make up to her grandmother for the fact that Granny has been cut off penniless from the job in which she has served with such dedication for so many years. She tries to give Granny the kind of elegance she has imagined her being exposed to in her forty years with the Liveseys. Rosie acquires the house shortly after she turns twenty-one, and she again overextends herself by furnishing its ten rooms and basement in the most lavish manner. She wants to make sure that Granny feels like a queen in *this* house—a house which had belonged to Miss Birdie Rice, a friend of Miss Helen's who was so rich that even Miss Helen had looked up to her. It's doubly delicious that Granny should have something that even her special, quality white folks were jealous of (pp. 184–185). However, Granny's sense of accomplishment is still within limits she has imposed upon herself, as is apparent to Rosie's friend Dolly when she is being shown through the house:

Granny led the way up the dark curving staircase. ''This here is the original wood,'' she said. ''Over fifty years old. You feel these stair treads? Solid. Not a creak anywhere.'' It would take Dolly many more years of knowing Rosie to understand all the reasons why she had wanted to own this particular house, but now, hearing the pride in the old lady's voice, she knew the main one. Granny would never have lived as mistress in Miss Helen's house . . . but she was convinced this one was even better. It was the perfect compromise, satisfying both her urge to grandeur and her deeply ingrained sense of place (p. 215).

The last symbolic present Rosie buys for her grandmother is a punch bowl to replace one Granny had loved at Miss Helen's house. It was used, she said, at Miss Emilie's wedding. ''I was the only one they could trust to handle it. It must have weighed pret' near thirty pounds, but I always polished it and put it away by myself. . . . I almost got to thinkin' that bowl belonged to me, 'cause I was the only one took care of it. You could look in it and see rainbows. I used to hold it up to the light and see 'em all the time. I always called it my Rainbow Bowl'' (p. 221). The bowl had been sold after Miss

Helen's death. It is perhaps because Granny's romanticization of the bowl reminds Rosie of the rainbow bowl she had broken that she orders a new one which costs seventeen hundred and fifty dollars. Rosie buys it at the lowest point of her financial credibility—and it, along with the house and all the furnishings, will be sold after her funeral.

During all the buying, Granny saunters along, detachedly ignoring her grand-daughter's declining health, continuing to serve the Liveseys before anything or anyone else. During Miss Helen's illness, Queenie has a heart attack and needs twenty-four hour attention for two weeks once she is brought home from the hospital. Granny declines to care for her daughter, preferring instead to attend Miss Helen and to leave Rosie with bills for a nurse in addition to the four-hundred-dollar hospital bill. In that scene, the usually unruffled Granny has one of her rare emotional outbursts, one that almost approaches anger:

> "I mean," Rosie explained, "you'll have to take off a couple weeks from work so you can look after Mom."
> "Oh, I couldn't do that, Rosie," Granny said innocently. "My folks need me."
> "Ain't we your folks?" Rosie asked sharply, then bit her tongue. She heaved a deep sigh. "Granny, how's Mom gonna get her meals 'n her medicine? She can't get up for two more weeks yet."
> "Oh, I spect she'll be up before then," Granny answered. "The doctor sent her home, didn't he?"
> "He said she has to stay in bed. She's still sick, Granny." She made a helpless gesture to Larnie for aid.
> "A minute ago, she couldn't get her breath," he said.
> An irritable harshness replaced the usual lilt of Granny's voice. "Don't talk to me about sickness. That's all I've heard for three months. Nurses and doctors. Needles and medicine. Temperatures and pills." She sat down on the edge of the bed with sudden heaviness. "I been with Miss Helen forty-five years, Rosie, and the last couple weeks, she don't even know me. Not one sign of recognition. But I keep right on doin' for her, 'cause I know she wouldn't want nobody else to do it. Taking her temperature, taking her her trays, feeding her, nursing her around the clock."
> Her head drooped alarmingly. "It's thankless work, Rosie. It wears me out. I don't feel so strong myself these days."
> "I know, Granny." Rosie was full of remorse. "I'm sorry."
> "It's a terrible thing, watching somebody you love die, when you been with her all your life, and you know it means your own time's comin' soon" (p. 142).

The mammy's first loyalty is to her white folks, and Granny fits the pattern superbly. Biological ties weaken in the face of tradition and custom. Thus Granny shifts the focus of concern and gets her way: she frightens Rosie into giving in and hiring nurses for Queenie, and thereby drives her further into debt. Granny feels no guilt about the debt or about her neglect of her own family. Her claims of frailty and overwork are just that—claims. As Queenie points out, Granny will outlive both her daughter and her granddaughter. She will watch both of them die without considering either death "a terrible thing."

Granny will never care enough about her family to allow them to live by any other standards than those she thinks appropriate for Miss Helen and her family. Since they cannot be Miss Emilie and Miss Iris, Queenie and Rosie will never be good enough for Granny. As Queenie correctly points out to her daughter: "You ain't gonna be good enough till you turn white" (p. 227). Since Rosie obviously cannot do that, her grandmother's affection is forever lost to her. Rosie will never be "all pink and gold peach-face and long bobbing Shirley Temple curls" (p. 25) like the doll Granny brings home for her. No little black girl will ever be able to live up to the standard of beauty that Granny Huggs has embraced.

Unfailingly, Granny manages to wrap a glowing aura of fantasy about each of the worlds around her. She says early in the novel: "If they's things you don't like and you can't do nothin' about them, you just best pretend they ain't there" (p. 67). Since the preferred lifestyle she offers her family cannot ultimately be realized, she finally moves beyond them altogether, into a state where even the little contact they had with her is no longer possible. Upon Queenie's death, she is detached enough to throw Larnie out of the house a few minutes after she announces the death to Rosie; then she goes to remind Rosie not to get her eyes all red from crying (pp. 244–245). When Rosie dies, she shows absolutely no emotion, but she does have a word for the recently widowed Larnie: "Now mind, I want nothing but lilies and carnations for this funeral. Don't be ordering none of them cheap little roses" (p. 279). These are the very last words of the novel. In the land beyond her mind and behind her consciousness, Granny has remained true to her image of herself and the world.

The extent to which Granny ignores reality can be most consummately illustrated by a conversation she has with Larnie when they at last realize that Rosie is incurably ill. Rosie's debts are so extensive that the house and goods will have to be sold to pay them, yet Granny refuses to accept that. She clings to fantasy because in the world in which she has spent a lifetime as a mammy she has never witnessed the kind of financial worries confronting her own family:

Granny said, "Did you tell her?"
    Larnie said, "No. No sense in that now."
    "It's a mercy," Granny said. "Long as she don't know, it don't seem true."
    "It's true all right," Larnie said. "We gonna lose this house and everything in it, and even then we won't be finished payin' all she owes."
    Granny said, "Hush, boy, she might hear you. She won't never let it happen."
    Larnie said, "She can't not let anything happen, not now. Time to stop believing in fairy tales."
    Granny sounded like she was going to cry. She sounded like that a lot of

times, but she never did. "No use talkin' to a crude person like you. You've no idea what a refined person has to go through" (p. 274).

Granny refuses to believe that Rosie can't solve the problems, or that she will die. "Doctors don't know everything," she says to Larnie. "Neither do you" (p. 274). Granny is like a showperson in a menagerie who insists upon her fanciful vision of reality in spite of poverty, roaches, sickness, and death. Yet she rules passively, quietly. And she is more venomous than the black widow spider, for it is not for the sake of storing food to nurture her offspring that she kills; rather, she gluttonously kills her offspring in order to keep feeding some image she has of herself. It is amazing that someone so small and seemingly acquiescent can be so destructive. In the end she perhaps views herself as a martyr, a saint whose elect status has been denied by those too ignorant to see by her lights.

By the time the scene below takes place, the sick, exhausted Rosie is already beyond recovering her physical or mental health. She has aborted Larnie's baby and her lungs are in rags. Granny sends her upstairs to find "a little something I brought home," a present.

> Rosie ran breathlessly up both flights of stairs. Two minutes later she descended slowly with a wad of yellowed tissue paper.
> "That's the last thing I have of Miss Helen's, Rosalie," Granny told her. "When I was leavin', Miss Emilie sneaked it in my hand. She said she didn't want me to think they'd ever forget me."
> "I'll treasure it, Granny," Rosie promised without much conviction. It was an old cameo in a tarnished setting, probably brass. She turned it over in her hand. The clasp on the back was broken. She wanted badly to believe that it was priceless treasure, but she could not prevent her knowing eyes from assessing it as worthless, cast-off junk.
> To conceal her crying, Rosie hugged the old lady tightly, until she felt a stiffening and sensed that Granny was repelled by so much display of emotion. A horribly humorous thought crossed her mind then. Probably all the things Granny had ever brought home were junk (p. 262).

The blinders thus come off in time only for Rosie to see clearly what her past has been, and that she has not escaped it at all. The roach-infested apartment has been traded in on a termite *and* roach-infested antiquated mansion worth much less money, energy, and hope than she has put into it. The delusions she suffers on her deathbed are the clearest visions she has. She lies watching as a roach crawls down her bedpost. She screams for her dead mother, then cries out for Larnie:

> But there was no answer.
> She turned back and contemplated her old friend.
> "You sure followed me a long way," she remarked as he skittered into a crack in the baseboard. "How come you like colored people so much, anyway?"

She added, with increased emphasis, "Well, maybe you like me, but I sure don't like you." Rosie crouched and carefully explored the crack with her fingers. "There better not be no more," she mumbled.

There weren't any more roaches. But there was something worse: the dry empty husk of an egg. And her shuddering hand came away with a coating of fine brown powder.

"Termites!"

Rosie flew downstairs to check the rest of the house for signs of decay, and found them everywhere she looked. Streaks on the wall, scars on the furniture, a long crack down the face of the marble mantel that resembled the west coast of Africa.

The question was: were they new, or had they been there all the time? Had her living room shrunk overnight to its present crowded proportions, or had it always been less grand than her magnifying imagination made it seem? One thing was clear: she had fought and clawed her way to the place where she wanted to be, only to see it crumble into the same ruins she had left behind. . . . The question was: had she bought a palace . . . or just an old, drafty, run-down, rotting house? (p. 276)

She runs through the house looking for more decay and for more roaches in the kitchen; she finds more than enough. It leads her into a frenzy of throwing dishes from cabinets, crying, and smashing roaches with both hands. The hopeless battle and the fact that she is ill and out of bed, fast getting a chill that she does not need, force her to ask the question: *"Did rich white people have roaches too?"* (p. 277) The admission of that possibility completes her mental breakdown; she dashes out in her nightgown and into a bar:

The crowd in Benny's was startled to see something small and dark and swift dart through it then like a demented arrow. It was a thin girl in a soaked nightgown; apparently drunk, for she was screaming and gesturing wildly. She seemed to be demanding service at the bar. Refused, she began to smash things, knocking a dozen glasses to the floor with one sweep of her hand (p. 278).

Thrown out of the bar, Rosie dies. Rosie dies and Queenie dies, but what Granny represents, even when seemingly aged and frail, lingers on when forces which appear to be stronger are dead. How can the attitudes which perpetuate self-destruction in black communities be killed? How can addiction to standards of beauty and lifestyles inappropriate to the black community be rooted out of the community? Perhaps Hunter sees no viable answer.

Though a true southern maid, Granny does appropriate a few things from the Liveseys; she essentially tricks Miss Emilie out of the rainbow bowl for Rosie, and she steals a Shirley Temple doll for her. But she does not steal out of any heightened sense of awareness, or out of any political sense of injustice; she does it pathetically because it seems to be the thing to do to get closer to the whiteness she so adores and the white ways she so much admires. Her trickery is misdirected, and her consciousness is in a state of cultural lag. Her case illustrates the extent to which immersion in the white culture can have a detrimental effect upon the black domestic who is incapable of compromising effectively—and upon her family. In the extent to which Granny allows her job as maid to destroy natural bonds of affection, the extent to which she lacks political and social consciousness, and the extent to which she is unaware of the implications of northern territory, she anticipates Morrison's Pauline Breedlove, who is also a southern mammy in northern territory.

Toni Morrison's *The Bluest Eye* (1970) is the story of the influences on young black girls growing up in the early 1940's. It offers positive and negative role models and values, and presents, embodied in the maid Pauline Breedlove, one of the most destructive forces which shapes the lifeview of black girls in a world where they are taught that black beauty is not the model for their emulation. Set in Lorain, Ohio, the novel recounts the story of two black families, the Breedloves and the MacTeers, contrasting nine-year-old Claudia MacTeer, her ten-year-old sister Frieda, and their parents with Pecola and Sammy Breedlove and their parents, Cholly and Pauline. Although Claudia has a narrative voice, her point of view alternating with the omniscient voice of Morrison, the story is more about the Breedloves, particularly Pecola, than about the MacTeers. The MacTeers, lavish with love if not with luxuries, manage to give their daughters healthy world views, and the girls manage to have healthy responses to their blackness. On the other hand, eleven-year-old Pecola, who has been baptized in the Shirley Temple cult of beauty, wishes for blue eyes as a manifest sign that she has escaped her blackness and the ugliness she sees it. Instead of nurturing in her daughter a positive image of herself, Pauline Breedlove rejects Pecola because she lacks, in her eyes, the beauty and virtue of the white children in the world where Pauline works as maid. Claudia and Frieda watch over this negation of life as Pecola is rejected by children at school, beaten by her mother, raped and impregnated by her drunken father, and finally driven insane as a result of those successive shocks. Pecola Breedlove and Rosie Fleming are sisters in more than one metaphorical sense.

Like Mammy Jane, Pauline Breedlove identifies completely with the white world and takes excessive, self-deprecating pride in child-rearing, cooking, and cleaning for it. She rejoices in the perfect little family of which she is a part in the white house and of which she can never envision the parallel in the black world. The irony of her notion of family is apparent in the omniscient sections of the novel, where Morrison uses the children's reader about Dick, Jane, Mother, Father, their fine suburban house, their dog, and their cat to show that middle class white family structures and values in the United States are grossly antithetical to the black experience. Poverty is omnipresent for the Breedloves, and their house is a cast-off hand-me-down store-front shamble. Father is a drunk and Mother is a maid; Dick runs away from home, Jane inadvertently poisons the dog, and the cat is almost killed. Pauline fails to see the folly of expecting her family to be like the storybook white family, and she lacks both the knowledge and the instinct to nurture her children into healthy adults. Hollywood movies represent her vision of the best of all possible worlds, one to which she escapes as often as she can. Clark Gable and Jean Harlow are a happy contrast to the few clothes and two rooms she must live in. Children born to a parent with such distorted, unrealistic values can only miraculously develop strong conceptions of themselves.

Pauline, like Mammy Jane and Granny Huggs and all other true southern mammies, is apolitical. She never suspects that her family may live in an abandoned store front because her husband has been driven to drink as a result of the pressures he has faced on his job. She never considers that the lacks she sees so vividly in her own family may in some way be related to the place to which the Fishers (her current employers) and those like them have assigned all Blacks in the United States, or considers that they might be related to the psychologically destructive self-images foisted upon Blacks; instead, she blames her children for not being beautiful, bright, and adorable and her husband for not being able to find and hold a job. She cannot conceive that her husband's drinking habits might not be totally his fault or that she should judge her children by a standard of beauty that has not been formed by and for American whites.

Pauline Breedlove, then, left the South physically, but in her actions and attitudes toward the whites for whom she works, she is still very much a southern mammy. Born in Alabama, she was "the ninth of eleven children" in a family which "lived on a ridge of red Alabama clay seven miles from the nearest road."[12] A nail puncture through her foot when she was two saved her, Morrison says, from "total anonymity." She used the slight deformity which resulted to explain many things: why she had no nickname, why there were no jokes or stories about her, why nobody teased her. "Her general feeling of separateness and unworthiness she blamed on her foot" (p. 88). She had only four years of schooling, and she apparently experienced little that was unusual or exciting as a child. She "cultivated quiet and private pleasures," Morrison says. "She liked, most of all, to arrange things. To line things up in rows—jars on shelves at canning, peach pits on the steps, sticks, stones, leaves. . . . Whatever portable plurality she found, she organized into neat lines, according to their size, shape, or gradations of color. Just as she would never align a pine needle with the leaf of a cottonwood tree, she would never put the jars of tomatoes next to the green beans" (pp. 88–89). She missed, Morrison maintains, "paints and crayons."

Pauline's family moved to Kentucky when she was an adolescent, and there, as the oldest girl at home, once her mother returned to work, she:

took over the care of the house. She kept the fence in repair, pulling the pointed stakes erect, securing them with bits of wire, collected eggs, swept, cooked, washed, and minded the two younger children—a pair of twins called Chicken and Pie, who were still in school. She was not only good at housekeeping, *she enjoyed it*. After her parents left for work and the other children were at school or in mines, the house was quiet. The stillness and isolation both calmed and energized her. She could arrange and clean without interruption until two o'clock, when Chicken and Pie came home (pp. 89–90, emphasis mine).

She passively acquiesced in whatever happened to her. When her order was disturbed, she quietly restored it after the disturbance: Morrison reports that "when by some accident somebody scattered her rows, they always stopped to retrieve them for her, and she was never angry, for it gave her a chance to rearrange them again" (pp. 88–89).

All this foreshadows what Pauline will do once she gets to Lorain. Still lacking the paints and crayons and still undistinguished, she will resort to making maid work into ark work, a perverse creativity which will separate her further and further from her family. Her love and near-reverence for household work and for the arrangement of things will intensify in Ohio.

Pauline arrives in Ohio to discover that the world created for her by Cholly, the long-awaited, knightly "Presence" for whom she has hoped, is not without loneliness and "vacant places." Cholly goes off to work, and she follows her old pattern of cleaning things. Unfortunately, the two have only two rooms and it doesn't take very long to clean them. Pauline is both idle and totally dependent upon Cholly; she stagnates at home while he works or goes drinking with new friends. Pauline is further set apart because she cannot reach out of her southernness to touch the northern Blacks around her. She "felt uncomfortable with the few black women she met. They were amused by her because she did not straighten her hair. When she tried to make up her face as they did, it came off rather badly. Their goading glances and private snickers at her way of talking (saying 'chil'ren') and dressing developed in her a desire for new clothes" (p. 94); the desire for clothes leads to quarrels with Cholly about money. Pauline decides to go to work, at first by the day. The money she makes helps with the clothes, but more and more she and Cholly fight over money, and they soon destroy the hopefulness with which their marriage had begun. Pauline quickly retreats into the solace of constant cleaning: "After several months of doing day work, she took a steady job in the home of a family of slender means and nervous, pretentious ways" (p. 94). She loses a tooth, has two children whom she rejects at some level of consciousness because she believes they are ugly, and begins to see Cholly as a mere sinful burden she will carry for many years. Apart from her absences from domestic work during the births of her children, her return to it is permanent.

Pauline Breedlove, in the homes of the white women for whom she works, becomes another example of the maid who cannot effect an acceptable compromise between the kind of work she does and the person she is. She maintains her subservience and is presumably thankful for the jobs she has. As her husband grows in drunkenness and her children in ugliness, as her husband's sporadic work habits force her to assume the dominant position of breadwinner, she relies increasingly on the white house for identity. Morrison comments:

It was her great fortune to find a permanent job in the home of a well-to-do family whose members were affectionate, appreciative, and generous.

She looked at their houses, smelled their linen, touched their silk draperies, and loved all of it. . . . She became what is known as an ideal servant, for such a role filled practically all of her needs. When she bathed the little Fisher girl, it was in a porcelain tub with silvery taps running infinite quantities of hot, clear water. She dried her in fluffy white towels and put her in cuddly night clothes. Then she brushed the yellow hair, enjoying the roll and slip of it between her fingers. No zinc tub, no buckets of stove-heated water, no flaky, stiff, grayish towels washed in a kitchen sink, dried in a dusty backyard, no tangled black puffs of rough wool to comb. Soon she stopped trying to keep her own house. The things she could afford to buy did not last, had no beauty or style, and were absorbed by the dingy storefront. More and more she neglected her house, her children, her man—they were like the afterthoughts one has just before sleep, the early-morning and late-evening edges of her day, the dark edges that made the daily life with the Fishers lighter, more delicate, more lovely. Here she could arrange things, clean things, line things up in neat rows. . . . All the meaningfulness of her life was in her work (pp. 100–101, 102).

Pauline a "queen" in the Fisher household, "reign[s] over" the bounty there, especially in the kitchen. Pauline Breedlove, who has never had a nickname (a sign of lack of affection from family and kin, she believes), is christened "Polly" (p. 101) by the Fishers, and she gets exquisite pleasure from the attention. She in turn protects the Fishers' home against "invasion" by her own family.

Her desire so to protect it indicates how ineffectively Pauline has compromised. She has suppressed self completely and because her goals are not obvious or long range, in that she is not using the whites to support kids in college or something comparable, she runs the risk of becoming a possession. Any white mistress might say, "That's my Mary," as a measure of appreciation, but when her employer says, "That's our Polly," Pauline beams. She is truly "theirs." She denies love to her own children, Pecola and Sammy, and adores the little white girl for whose family she works; her actions show that distortion or perversion of parental affection can be one of the major consequences of ineffective compromise. Pauline becomes a glorified mammy because she sees that as the crowning achievement of an undistinguished existence. Therefore, when Pecola and her friends Claudia and Frieda come to the kitchen to see her, they must wait patiently and immobilely while Pauline gathers wash. When the black children, in typical childish fashion, explore the kitchen and Pecola spills a "deep-dish berry cobbler," Pauline becomes the soldier defending the white outpost against what she views as unscrupulous enemies:

In one gallop she was on Pecola, and with the back of her hand knocked her to the floor. Pecola slid in the pie juice, one leg folding under her. Mrs. Breedlove yanked her up by the arm, slapped her again, and in a voice thin with anger, abused Pecola directly and Frieda and me [Claudia] by implication.

"Crazy fool . . . my floor, mess . . . look what you . . . work . . . get on out . . . now that . . . crazy . . . my floor, my floor . . . my floor.''
The little girl in pink started to cry. Mrs. Breedlove turned to her, "Hush, baby, hush. Come here. Oh, Lord, look at your dress. Don't cry no more. Polly will change it.'' She went to the sink and turned tap water on a fresh towel. Over her shoulder she spit out words to us like rotten pieces of apple. "Pick up that wash and get on out of here, so I can get this mess cleaned up'' (pp. 86–87).

Pecola suffers painful burns from the hot pie, but her mother ignores her. In rushing to comfort "the little pink-and-yellow girl" and abusing her own child, Pauline continues the slave tradition of an adult Black making the welfare of a white child his or her primary concern. The vehemence with which she screams at the black children to get out of "my" kitchen epitomizes both the vehemence of her attempt to reject biological kinship with her own child and the vehemence of her rejection of cultural kinship with anything black; she "banishes the three black girls from Paradise.''[13] Black is ugly and bad; white is the model for the good and the beautiful.

We can only sense in Pecola's quiet departure a portion of what Wright actually says he felt when he and his brother were in the kitchen of a white woman for whom his mother worked. That which Wright received there may have been tolerable, but that which was denied to him made the greater impression:

> I got occasional scraps of bread and meat; but many times I regretted having come, for my nostrils would be assailed with the scent of food that did not belong to me and which I was forbidden to eat. Toward evening my mother would take the hot dishes into the dining room where the white people were seated, and I would stand as near the dining-room door as possible to get a quick glimpse of the white faces gathered around the loaded table, eating, laughing, talking. If the white people left anything, my brother and I would eat well; but if they did not, we would have our usual bread and tea.[14]

Although Wright's mother does not go to the lengths that Pauline Breedlove does in protecting the sanctity of white property and food, she must neverthe-less, by the very nature of her work, set constricting boundaries on what Wright and his brother may and may not do in "her" kitchen. Pauline Breedlove draws the boundary lines in such a way as to cast out her child from cleanliness, beauty and good food and to encircle herself with those things; she is completely an appendage to the white world.

Pauline's consequent ownership by her white mistresses enables the women to interfere in the intimate areas of her life. One white woman, for example, is able to demand that she leave the drunken Cholly Breedlove if she is to continue to work for her; when Cholly shows up drunk and Pauline follows him away from her job, the white woman refuses to allow her to return unless she has left him. She also refuses to pay Pauline the eleven dollars she owes her:

She didn't understand that all I needed from her was my eleven dollars to
pay the gas man so I could cook. She couldn't get that one thing through
her thick head. "Are you going to leave him, Pauline?" she kept on saying.
I thought she'd give me my money if I said I would, so I said, "Yes,
ma'am." "All right," she said. "You leave him, and then come back to
work, and we'll let bygones be bygones." "Can I have my money today?"
I said. "No," she said. "Only when you leave him. I'm only thinking of
you and your future. What good is he, Pauline, what good is he to you?"
(p. 96)

While Pauline realizes that *"it didn't seem none too bright for a black woman*
to leave a black man for a white woman" (p. 95), the intimacy she herself
has cultivated allows the woman to be as presumptuous as she desires. Pauline
has put herself in the position to have her life directed just as easily as a child
might have its life directed. And indeed, Pauline is essentially an impression-
able child, one whose identity may be shaped and determined by the whites.
Since control of wages is one of the most important components of the maid/
mistress relationship, Pauline has especially compromised herself; she does not
get the eleven dollars. This disappointment, however, does not cause Pauline
to reverse her identification with whites.

Whatever is sustaining or spiritually uplifting, Pauline finds in Jesus and the
white folks (especially the Fishers), never in her own family and home. Her
sense of self-worth comes from playing the role of THE MAID. She is titillated
with appreciation when Mr. Fisher says: "I would rather sell her blueberry
cobblers than real estate," or when she overhears Mrs. Fisher saying, "We'll
never let her go. We could never find anybody like Polly. She will *not* leave
the kitchen until everything is in order. Really, she is the ideal servant"
(p. 101). And just as she kept a world of orderliness, privately, when she was
a child, so now does she keep the joy she gets from the Fishers to herself.
"Here she found beauty, order, cleanliness, and praise. . . . Pauline kept this
order, this beauty, for herself, a private world, and never introduced it into
her storefront, or to her children" (pp. 101–102).

The storefront is where the Breedloves live, the shocking contrast to the
primness of the Fisher house. Morrison describes the corner house that Pauline
will never make into a home as an abandoned store which "foisted" itself on
the passerby. The store had in turn been a pizza parlor, a bakery, and a base
of gypsy operations, and was now but a box of "peeling gray":

The plan of the living quarters was as unimaginative as a first-generation
Greek landlord could contrive it to be. The large "store" area was parti-
tioned into two rooms by beaverboard planks that did not reach to the ceiling.
There was a living room, which the family called the front room, and the
bedroom, where all the living was done. In the front room were two sofas,
an upright piano, and a tiny artificial Christmas tree which had been there,
decorated and dust-laden, for two years. The bedroom had three beds: a
narrow iron bed for Sammy, fourteen years old, another for Pecola, eleven
years old, and a double bed for Cholly and Mrs. Breedlove. In the center

of the bedroom, for the even distribution of heat, stood a coal stove. Trunks, chairs, a small end table, and a cardboard "wardrobe" closet were placed around the walls. The kitchen was in the back of this apartment, a separate room. There were no bath facilities. Only a toilet bowl, inaccessible to the eye, if not the ear, of the tenants.

There is nothing more to say about the furnishings. They were anything but describable, having been conceived, manufactured, shipped, and sold in various states of thoughtlessness, greed, and indifference (p. 31).

Pauline has no desire to improve the place; she has, in fact, given up on its possibilities for change.

This background at "home" heightens her delight in housecleaning elsewhere, and it highlights the perversion of the artistry she works. Her creativity does not exist apart from her fanatical carrying out of her job. She trades family, culture, and heritage to become an anachronistic mammy, and she recognizes no life beyond that identity. She is incapable of putting into accurate perspective the historical and social forces which cause her to be where she is, for she lacks powers of introspection. She willingly exists in a world someone else has defined for her and, through her consent, is guilty of exhibiting the traits which illustrate that her role is more important than she is.

Pauline keeps white cleanliness and beauty for herself, but forces upon her family the respectability that constitutes her idea of white Christianity:

> She came into her own with the women who had despised her, by being more moral than they; she avenged herself on Cholly by forcing him to indulge in the weakness she despised. She joined a church where shouting was frowned upon, served on Stewardess Board No. 3, and became a member of Ladies Circle No. 1. At prayer meeting she moaned and sighed over Cholly's ways, and hoped God would help her keep the children from the sins of the father. She stopped saying 'chil'ren' and said 'childring' instead. She let another tooth fall, and was outraged by painted ladies who thought only of clothes and men. Holding Cholly as a model of sin and failure, she bore him like a crown of thorns, and her children like a cross (p.100).

She marries Jesus as she had the white folks, pushing the romantic relationship she has had with Cholly into the background and blanketing herself in the respectability of the church. She initially misses the gentleness with which she and Cholly had once made love, then consoles herself. *"But I don't care 'bout it no more. My Maker will take care of me. I know He will. I know He will. Besides, it don't make no difference about this old earth. There is sure to be a glory"* (p. 104). The knock-down, drag-out fights she has with Cholly do not seem to clash with either her understanding of religion or her image of Christian wifeliness.

Pauline fails as a mother not only by analogy to *Dick and Jane* but by any definition of motherhood. She has bent her children "toward respectability, and in so doing taught them fear: fear of being clumsy, fear of being like their father, fear of not being loved by God, fear of madness like Cholly's mother's.

Into her son she beat a loud desire to run away [which he had done twenty-seven times by the age of fourteen], and into her daughter she beat a fear of growing up, fear of other people, fear of life'' (p. 102). In their ugliness, their poverty, in short, their non-whiteness, they win Pauline's tolerance—and she accepts a responsibility to give them the mere subsistencies of life—but they cannot win her love. She distances herself from them to the point of insisting that they refer to her as "Mrs. Breedlove," saving, as we have seen, all her love, affection, gentleness, and warmth for the Fishers and others like them. She kowtows to the whites and, through her religion, wields cruel power over her own family: just as she humbles herself before white women in their power, remembering always her place, her children are expected to humble themselves before the power of the church and accept the lowly place in her world that she has assigned to them. Under the guise of bringing them up as Christians, she has shaped them, in part, as she was shaped in the South—to be hesitant about living, to be generally unaggressive, to be apologetic for being alive.

Both Jacqueline de Weever and Barbara Christian talk about inversion in *The Bluest Eye*, about how expected roles are therein negated.[15] Its fathers are not like those in *Dick and Jane*; they do not inspire love and respect in their children. Mothers are not warm and smiling. There are enough stunted adults in the novel to ensure that children like Pecola will never develop healthy conceptions of what they as adults might be. Instead, Pecola, like Gwendolyn Brooks's Little Lincoln West, grows "uglily upward."[16] Pauline can only succeed in transferring her own warped vision and self-hatred to her daughter— a legacy uncannily destructive.

The substance of the legacy she passes on prevents Pauline from separating her identity from the whites long enough for her to wear a mask on her job. She would never think of appropriating any goods from the homes of whites for whom she works; the praise she gets from Mr. and Mrs. Fisher perhaps, to her, takes the place of several dollars pay (the salary they pay her is not mentioned). She cannot conceive of unfairness in the domestic arrangements of which she is a part; she has every confidence that the whites will appreciate her great abilities as a domestic and will reward her justly and fairly. She is undoubtedly good at what she does, but she is equally undoubtedly overworked and giving much more than she is receiving. Her satisfaction with the status quo in itself betrays her as a mammy. Although she is in the North, that mythic place of symbolic if not real freedom, she has absorbed the white world's vision of her place and proper subservience as thoroughly as had the South's Mammy Jane.

NOTES

1. Jessie W. Parkhurst, "The Role of the Black Mammy in the Plantation Household," *Journal of Negro History* 23 (July 1938): 351, 356, 357. For a discussion primarily of the literary mammy,

see the chapter entitled "Dishwater Images" in Jeanne Noble's *Beautiful, Also, Are the Souls of My Black Sisters: A History of the Black Woman in America* (Englewood Cliffs, N.J.: Prentice-Hall, 1978).

2. Parkhurst, "The Role of the Black Mammy," pp. 352–353.

3. The following articles illustrate the kinds of treatment Mammy Jane has received: John M. Reilly, "The Dilemma in Chesnutt's *The Marrow of Tradition*," *Phylon* 32 (Spring 1971): 31–38, and John Wideman, "Charles Waddell Chesnutt: *The Marrow of Tradition*," *American Scholar* 42 (Winter 1972–73): 128–134.

4. William L. Andrews, *The Literary Career of Charles W. Chesnutt* (Baton Rouge: Louisiana State University Press, 1980), p. 201.

5. Andrews, *The Literary Career of Charles W. Chesnutt*, pp. 179, 202.

6. Charles Waddell Chesnutt, *The Marrow of Tradition* (Ann Arbor: University of Michigan Press, 1969), p. 43. Further references to this source will be parenthesized in the text.

7. For superstitions about the evil eye and moles in the neck area, see *The Frank C. Brown Collection of North Carolina Folklore*, Vols. 6 and 7, ed. Newman Ivey White (Durham: Duke University Press, 1961 and 1964), Numbers 540lff. and 3705. Parkhurst also comments on how black mammies raised their white charges in the superstitions common to black folk culture, "The Role of the Black Mammy," pp. 361–362.

8. Andrews emphasizes that Chesnutt intended the young nurse as a foil to Mammy Jane, to show progress as opposed to stasis. *The Literary Career of Charles W. Chesnutt*, p. 191; see also pp. 197–198, on Mammy Jane's failure to evolve.

9. Andrews discusses the evaluation of tradition and white supremacy which underlies Chesnutt's view of superiority and subservience in the novel on pp. 181–182 of *The Literary Career of Charles W. Chesnutt*.

10. Kristin Hunter, *God Bless the Child* (1964; rpt. New York: Bantam, 1967), pp. 18–19. Further references to this source will be parenthesized in the text.

11. "The 'Black Mammy' taught the children the proper forms of etiquette, of deportment to all of the people of the plantation, the proper forms of address and the proper distances to maintain. . . . In the Old South where much was made of chivalry and where great emphasis was placed upon form, manners in the life of the child meant much. The 'Black Mammy' knew just what these manners were—when to speak and when not to speak; what was best to say on the proper occasion and what was not; the proper deportment of boy and girl, of young men and young women. . . . A Southerner of the upper class delighted in saying that he was taught his manners by his 'Black Mammy'." Parkhurst, "The Role of the Black Mammy," pp. 362–363.

12. Toni Morrison, *The Bluest Eye* (1970; rpt. New York: Pocket Books, 1972), p. 88. Further references to this source will be parenthesized in the text.

13. Barbara Christian, *Black Women Novelists: The Development of a Tradition, 1892–1976* (Westport, Conn.: Greenwood, 1980), p. 144.

14. Richard Wright, *Black Boy* (New York: Harper and Row, 1966), p. 26.

15. Christian, *Black Women Novelists*, pp. 138–153, and Jacqueline de Weever, "The Inverted World of Toni Morrison's *The Bluest Eye* and *Sula*," *College Language Association Journal* 22 (June 1979): 402–414.

16. Gwendolyn Brooks, *Family Pictures* (Detroit, Michigan: Broadside Press, 1970), p. 9.

R. Baxter Miller
(1948–   )

Professor of English at the University of Tennessee, Knoxville, Miller is one of the leading critics of African-American literature. Born in Rocky Mount, North Carolina, he received his B.A. from North Carolina Central University and his A.M. and Ph.D. from Brown University. In the many articles he has published in professional journals, Miller has consistently argued that the humanistic dimensions of African-American literature be examined in depth. Miller is the author of *A Reference Guide to Langston Hughes and Gwendolyn Brooks* and *The Art and Imagination of Langston Hughes* and the editor of two collections of essays, *Black American Literature and Humanism* and *Black American Poets Between Worlds, 1940–1960*. The following article is reprinted from *Tennessee Studies in Literature* (26, 1981).

The "Etched Flame" of
Margaret Walker: Biblical and Literary
Re-Creation in Southern History

Margaret Walker learned about Moses and Aaron from the Black American culture into which she was born. As the daughter of a religious scholar, she came of age in the depression of the thirties, and like those of Margaret Danner, Dudley Randall, and Gwendolyn Brooks, her career has spanned three or four decades. Much of her important work, like theirs, has been unduly neglected, coming as it does between the Harlem Renaissance of the 1920's and the Black Arts Movement of the 1960's. Most indices to literature, Black American and American, list only one article on Margaret Walker during the last seven years.[1]

Walker knew the important figures of an older generation, including James Weldon Johnson, Langston Hughes, and Countee Cullen. She heard Marian Anderson and Roland Hayes sing, and she numbered among her acquaintances Zora Neale Hurston, George Washington Carver, and W.E.B. Du Bois. What does the richness of the culture give her? She finds the solemn nobility of religious utterance, the appreciation for the heroic spirit of Black folk, and the deep respect for craft.[2] Once she heard from the late Richard Wright that talent does not suffice for literary fame. She took his words to heart and survived them to write about his life, his self-hatred, and his paradoxical love for white women.[3] She knew, too, Willard Motley, Fenton Johnson, and Arna Bontemps. Her lifetime represents continuity. From a youthful researcher for Wright, she matured into an inspirational teacher at Jackson State University, where she preserved the spirit of her forerunners, the intellect and the flowing phrase, but she still belongs most with the Black poets whose careers span the last forty years. Her strengths are not the same as theirs. Margaret Danner's poetry has a quiet lyricism of peace, a deeply controlled introspection. No one else shows her delicacy of alliteration and her carefully framed patterns. Dudley Randall's success comes from the ballad, whose alternating lines of short and longer rhythms communicate the racial turmoil of the sixties. He profits from a touching and light innocence as well as a plea and longing of the child's inquiring voice; purity for him too marks an eternal type.

In *For My People* Walker develops this and other types in three sections, the first two divisions with ten poems each and the last segment with six. The reader experiences initially the tension and potential of the Black South; then the folk tale of both tragic possibility and comic relief involving the curiosity, trickery, and deceit of men and women alike; finally, the significance of physical and spiritual love in reclaiming the Southern land. Walker writes careful antinomies into the visionary poem, the folk secular and the Shakespearian and Petrarchan sonnets. She opposes quest to denial, historical circumstances to imaginative will, and earthly suffering to heavenly bliss. Her poetry purges the Southern ground of animosity and injustice which separate Black misery from Southern song. Her themes are time, infinite human potential, racial equality, vision, blindness, love and escape, as well as worldly death, drunkenness, gambling, rottenness, and freedom. She pictures the motifs within the frames of toughness and abuse, fright and gothic terror. Wild arrogance, for her speakers, often underlies heroism, but the latter is more imagined than real.

The myth of human immortality expressed in oral tale and in literary artifact transcends death. The imagination evokes atemporal memory, asserts the humanistic self against the fatalistic past, and illustrates, through physical love, the promise of both personal and racial reunification. The achievement is syntactic. Parallelism, elevated rhetoric, simile, and figure of speech abound, but more deeply the serenity of nature creates solemnity. Walker depicts sun, splashing brook, pond, duck, frog and stream, as well as flock, seed, wood, bark, cotton field, and cane. Still, the knife and gun threaten the pastoral world as, by African conjure, the moral "we" attempts to reconcile the two. As both the participant and observer, Walker creates an ironic distance between history and eternity. The Southern experience in the first section and the reclamation in the second part frame the humanity of folk personae Stagolee, John Henry, Kissie Lee, Yalluh Hammer, and Gus. The book becomes a literary artifact, a "clean house" which imaginatively restructures the southland.

But if Dudley Randall has written "The Ballad of Birmingham" and Gwendolyn Brooks "The Children of the Poor," Walker succeeds with the visionary poem.[4] She does not portray the gray-haired old women who nod and sing out of despair and hope on Sunday morning, but she captures the depths of their suffering. She recreates their belief that someday Black Americans will triumph over fire hoses and biting dogs, once the brutal signs of White oppression in the South. The prophecy contributes to Walker's rhythmical balance and vision, but she controls the emotions. How does one change brutality into social equality? Through sitting down at a lunch counter in the sixties, Black students illustrated some divinity and confronted death, just as Christ faced His cross. Walker deepens the portraits by using biblical typology, by discovering historical antitypes, and by creating an apocalyptic fusion.[5] Through the suffering in the Old and New Testaments, the title poem of *For My People* expresses Black American victory over deprivation and hatred. The ten stanzas celebrate the endurance of tribulations such as dark murders in Virginia and Mississippi as well as Jim Crowism, ignorance, and poverty. The free form includes the parallelism of verbs and the juxtaposition of the present with the past. Black Americans are "never gaining, never reaping, never knowing and never understanding."[6] When religion faces reality, the contrast creates powerful reversal:

> For the boys and girls who grew in spite of these things to be man and woman, to laugh and dance and sing and play and drink their wine and religion and success, to marry their playmates and bear children and then die of consumption and anemia and lynching.

Through biblical balance, "For My People" sets the White oppressor against the Black narrator. Social circumstance opposes racial and imaginative will, and disillusion opposes happiness. Blacks fashion a new world that encompasses many faces and people, "all the adams and eves of their countless generations." From the opening dedication (Stanza 1) to the final evocation (Stanza 10) the prophet-narrator speaks both as Christ and God. Ages ago, the Lord put His rainbow in the clouds. To the descendants of Noah it signified His promise that the world would never again end in flood. Human violence undermines biblical calm, as the first word repeats itself: "Let a new earth rise. Let another world be born. Let a bloody-peace be written in the sky. Let a second generation full of courage issue forth. . . ."

"We Have Been Believers," a visionary poem, juxtaposes Christianity with African conjure, and the Old Testament with the New, exemplified by St. John, St. Mark, and Revelation. The narrator ("we") represents the Black builders and singers in the past, for Walker seeks to interpret cultural signs. The theme is Black faith, first in Africa and then in America. As the verse shows movement from the past to the present, the ending combines Christianity and humanism. With extensive enjambment, the controlled rhapsody has a long first sentence, followed by indented ones that complete the meaning. The form literally typifies Black American struggle. The long line is jolted because an ending is illusory, and the reader renews his perusal just as the Black American continues the search for freedom. The narrator suggests the biblical scene in which death breaks the fifth seal (Revelation 6:11). There the prophet sees all the people who, slain in the service of God, wear garments as the narrator describes them.

The authenticating "we" is more focused than either Ellison's in *Invisible Man* or Baldwin's in *Notes of a Native Son*. Their speakers are often educated and upwardly mobile people who move between White and Black American worlds. Walker's, on the contrary, are frequently the secular and religious "folk" who share a communal quest. She blends historical sense with biblical implication: "Neither the slaver's whip nor the lyncher's rope nor the / bayonet could kill our black belief. In our hunger we / beheld the welcome table and in our nakedness the / glory of a long white robe." The narrator identifies Moloch, a god of cruel sacrifice, and all people who have died for no just cause. She prepares for the myth that dominates the last three parts of the poem, the miracle that Jesus performed on the eyes of a blind man. After He instructs him to wash them in the pool of Siloam, the man sees clearly (John 9:25). Another allusion suggests the miracle that Christ worked for the afflicted people near the Sea of Galilee. Walker's narrator knows the legend, but awaits the transformation (Mark 7:37). The waiting prepares for an irony phrased in alliteration: "Surely the priests and the preachers and the powers will hear . . . / . . . now that our hands are empty and our hearts too full to pray." This narrator says that such people will send a sign—the biblical image of relief and redemption—but she implies something different. Although her humanism embraces Christianity, she adds militancy and impatience. Her rhetoric illustrates liquid sound, alliteration, and assonance: "We have been believers believing in our burdens and our / demigods too long. Now the needy no longer weep / and pray; the long-suffering arise, and our fists bleed / against the bars with a strange insistency."

The impatience pervades "Delta," which has the unifying type of the Twenty-Third Psalm. Although the first part (ll. 1–35) presents the blood, corruption, and depression of the narrator's naturalistic world, the second (ll. 36–78) illustrates the restorative potential of nature. High mountain, river, orange, cotton, fern, grass, and onion share the promise. Dynamic fertility, the re-cleansed river (it flowed through swamps in the first part), can clear the Southern ground of sickness, rape, starvation, and ignorance. Water gives form to anger, yet thawing sets in. Coupled with liquidity, the loudness of thunder and cannon implies storm; the narrator compares the young girl to Spring. Lovingly the speaker envisions vineyards, pastures, orchards, cattle, cotton, tobacco, and cane, "making us men in the fields we have tended / standing defending the land we have rendered rich and abiding and heavy with plenty." Interpreting the meaning of earth can help to bridge the distance between past decay and present maturity when the narrator celebrates the promise:

> the long golden grain for bread
> and the ripe purple fruit for wine
> the hills beyond for peace
> and the grass beneath for rest

the music in the wind for us
and the circling lines in the sky
for dreams.

Elsewhere a gothic undercurrent and an allusion to Abel and Cain add complexity; so does an allusion to Christ and transubstantiation. Rhetorical power emerges because the harsh tone of the Old Testament threatens the merciful tone of the New one. Loosely plotted, the verse recounts the personal histories of the people in the valley. Still, the symbolical level dominates the literal one, and the poem portrays more deeply the human condition. The narrator profits from the gothicism which has influenced Ann Radcliffe, Charles Brockden Brown, and Edgar Allan Poe. Just as Walker's pictures create beauty for the African-American, they communicate a grace to all who appreciate symmetrical landscapes. The tension in her literary world comes from the romantic legacy of possibility set against denial: "High above us and round about us stand high mountains / rise the towering snow-capped mountains / while we are beaten and broken and bowed / here in this dark valley." Almost no rhyme scheme exists in the poem, but a predominance of three or four feet gives the impression of a very loose ballad. The fifth stanza of the second part has incremental repetition, as the undertone of Countee Cullen's poem "From the Dark Tower" heightens the deep despair, the paradox of desire and restraint: "We tend to crop and gather the harvest / but not for ourselves do we sweat and starve and spend . . . / here on this earth we dare not claim . . ." In the stanza before the final one the reader associates myth and history. While the narrator remembers the Blacks unrewarded in the Southern past, the imagery suggests Christ and transubstantiation. The speaker, however, alludes mainly to Abel slain by Cain (Genesis 4:10): "We with our blood have watered these fields / and they belong to us." Implicitly the promise of the Psalmist ("Yea though I walk through the valley of the shadow of death") has preceded.

In four quatrains, "Since 1619" strengthens Old Testament prefiguration. Aware of World War II, the narrator illuminates human blindness. She emphasizes the inevitability of death and the deterioration of world peace. With anaphora she repeats the Psalmist: "How many years . . . have I been singing Spirituals? / How long have I been praising God and shouting hallelujahs? / How long have I been hated and hating? / How long have I been living in hell for heaven?" She remembers the Valley of Dry Bones in which the Lord placed the prophet Ezekiel, whom He questioned if the bones could live. Whereas in the Bible salvation is external and divine, here the transformation comes from within. The poem contrasts moral renewal to the spiritual death during World War II and the pseudo-cleanliness of middle-class America. Written in seven stanzas, the verse has four lines in the first section and three in the second. Initially the poem portrays the ancient muse, the inspiration of all poetry, and later it illustrates poverty, fear, and sickness. Even the portrait of lynching cannot end the narrator's quest for cleanliness. Although Americans face death, they will continue to seek solace through intoxication and sex. The beginning of the poem foreshadows the end, but the directness in the second section supplants the general description in the first. The middle-class Americans in the first part have no bombing planes or air-raids to fear, yet they have masked violence and ethnocentric myth: ''viewing weekly 'Wild West Indian and Shooting Sam,' 'Mama Loves Papa,' and 'Gone By the Breeze!' '' Calories, eyemaline, henna rinse, and dental cream image a materialistic nation. With a deeper cleanliness, the speaker advises the reader within an ironic context: ''Pray for second sight and the inner ear. Pray for bulwark against poaching patterns of dislocated days; pray for buttressing iron against insidious termite and beetle and locust and flies and lice and moth and rust and mold.''

The religious types in the second and third sections of *For My People* rival neither those in the first section nor those in *Prophets for a New Day*. When Walker ignores biblical sources, often she vainly attempts to achieve cultural saturation.[7] Without biblical cadences her ballads frequently become average, if not monotonous. In ''Yalluh Hammer,'' a folk poem about the ''Bad Man,'' she manages sentimentality, impractical concern, and trickery, as a Black woman outsmarts the protagonist and steals his money.

But sometimes the less figurative sonnets are still boring.[8] ''Childhood'' lacks the condensation and focus to develop well the Petrarchan design. In the octave a young girl remembers workers who used to return home in the afternoons. Even during her maturity, the rags of poverty and the habitual grumbling color the Southern landscape still. Despite weaknesses, the poem suggests well a biblical analogue. As the apostle Paul writes ''When I was a child, I spake as a child: but when I became a man, I put away childish things'' (I Corinthians 13:11), Walker's sonnet coincidentally begins, ''When I was a child I knew red miners . . . / I also lived in a low cotton country . . . where sentiment and hatred still held sway / and only bitter land was washed away.'' The mature writer seeks now to restore and renew the earth.

In *Prophets* Walker illustrates some historical antitypes to the Old Testament. Her forms are the visionary poem, free verse sonnet, monody, pastoral, and gothic ballad in which she portrays freedom, speech, death, and rebirth. Her major images are fire, water, and wind. When she opposes marching to standing, the implied quest becomes metaphorical, for she recreates the human community in the spiritual wilderness. She looks beneath any typological concern of man's covenant with God, and even the pantheistic parallel of the Southerner's covenant with the land, to illuminate man's broken covenant with himself. The human gamut runs from death (''mourning bird'') to the potential of poetry (''humming bird''). Poetry recreates anthropocentric space. The speaker depicts the breadth through dramatic dialogue, sarcasm, and satire. Even the cold stone implies the potential for creative inspiration or Promethean fire. The narrator verbally paints urban corruption in the bitter cold and frozen water. Her portrait images not only the myth of fragmentation and dissolution, but the courage necessary to confront and transcend them. Her world is doubly Southern. Here the Old South still withstands Northern invasion, but the Black South endures both. One attains the mythical building beyond (sounds like

Thomas Wolfe), the human house, through fire. Form is imagined silence. Poetry, both catharsis and purgation, parallels speaking, crying, and weaving. The center includes geometric space and aesthetic beauty. To portray anthropocentric depth is to clarify the significance of human cleansing.

Although the sonnets and ballads in *For My People* are weak, the typological poems in *Prophets for a New Day* envision universal freedom. But neither Walker nor her reader can remain at visionary heights, for the real world includes the white hood and fiery cross. Even the latter image fails to save the poem "Now," in which the subject is civil rights. Here both images of place and taste imply filth as doors, dark alleys, balconies, and washrooms reinforce moral indignation. The Klan marks "kleagle with a klux / and a fiery burning cross." Yet awkward rhythms have preceded. In shifting from three feet to four, the speaker stumbles: "In the cleaning room and closets / with the washrooms marked 'For Colored Only.' " The ear of "Sit-Ins" catches more sharply the translation of the Bible into history. Written in twelve lines of free verse, the lyric depicts the students at North Carolina A & T University, who in 1960 sat down at the counter of a dime store and began the Civil Rights movement. The speaker recreates Southern history. In the shining picture, the reader sees the Angel Michael who drove Adam and Eve from Paradise, but the portrait becomes more secular: "With courage and faith, convictions and intelligence / The first to blaze a flaming patch for justice / And awaken consciences / Of these stony ones." The implement that in the Bible and Milton symbolized Paradise Lost becomes a metaphor for Paradise Regained. In viewpoint the narrator gives way to the demonstrators themselves: *"Come, Lord Jesus, Bold Young Galilean / Sit Beside This Counter / Lord With Me."*

As with most of Walker's antitypical poems, "Sit-Ins" hardly rivals "Ballad of the Free," one of her finest. The latter work portrays the heroic missions and tragic deaths of slave insurrectionists and excels through consistent rhythm as well as compression of image. At first the verse seems true to the title. Although the design of the typical ballad usually emphasizes a rhythmic contrast between two lines in succession, "Ballad of the Free," stresses a contrast between whole stanzas. Of the twelve sections which comprise the poem, each of the four quatrains follows a tercet which serves as the refrain. The narrator adds a striking twist to St. Matthew (19:30; 20:16), in which Peter asks Jesus what will happen to people who have forsaken everything to follow Him. Christ replies that the social status will be reversed. Although He speaks about the beginning of the apocalypse in which all persons are judged, Walker's narrator foresees the end of the apocalypse in which all are equal: "The serpent is loosed and the hour is come. . . ."

The refrain balances social history and biblical legend. The first stanza presents Nat Turner, the leader of the slave insurrection in South Hampton, Virginia, during 1831. After the first refrain, the reader recognizes Gabriel Prosser, whom a storm once forced to suspend a slave revolt in Richmond, Virginia. With a thousand other slaves, Prosser planned an uprising that collapsed in 1800. Betrayed by fellow bondsmen, he and fifteen others were hanged on October 7 in that year. After the first echo of the refrain, Denmark

Vesey, who enlisted thousands of Blacks for an elaborate slave plot in Charleston, S.C., and the vicinity, appears in the fifth stanza. Authorities arrested
131 Blacks and four Whites, and when the matter was settled, thirty-seven
people were hanged. Toussaint L'Ouverture, who at the turn of the eighteenth
and nineteenth centuries liberated Haitian slaves, follows the second echo of
the refrain. Shortly afterwards an evocation of John Brown intensifies the
balance between history and sound. With thirteen Whites and five Blacks,
Brown attacked Harper's Ferry on October 16, 1859, and by December 2 of
that year, he was also hanged. In the poem, as in the Southern past, the death
of the rebel is foreshadowed. Gifted with humane vision, he wants to change
an inegalitarian South. But the maintainers of the status quo will kill, so the
hero becomes the martyr.

In order to emphasize Turner as historical paradigm, the narrator ignores
the proper chronology of L'Ouverture, Prosser, Vesey, Turner, and Brown.
She gives little of the historical background but calls upon the names of legend.
What does she achieve, by naming her last hero, if not a symmetry of color?
The ballad that began with Black Nat Turner ends with White John Brown,
for if action alone determines a basis for fraternity, racial distinction is
insignificant.

For a central portrait of Turner, the verse moves backward and forward in
both typological and apocalyptic time. As with the narrator of Hughes's
"Negro Speaks of Rivers," the speaker can comprehend different decades.
Because she is outside of Time, L'Ouverture and Brown, who come from
different periods, appear to her with equal clarity. Until the eleventh stanza,
the biblical sureness of the refrain has balanced history. The note of prophecy
sounds in the slowness and firmness of racial progress: *"Wars and Rumors of
Wars have gone, / But Freedom's army marches on. / The heroes' list of dead
is long, / And Freedom still is for the strong."* The narrator recalls Christ
(Mark 13:7) who prophesies wars and rumors of war, but foretells salvation
for endurers. The final refrain interfuses with the fable and history: "The
serpent is loosed and the hour is come."

"At the Lincoln Monument in Washington, August 28, 1963," presents
analogues to Isaiah, Exodus, Genesis, and Deuteronomy. Written in two stanzas, the poem has forty-four lines. The speaker dramatizes chronicle through
biblical myth, racial phenomenology, and Judaeo-Christian consciousness. She
advances superbly with the participant to the interpreter, but even the latter
speaks from within an aesthetic mask. The poetic vision authenticates the
morality of her fable and the biblical analogue. The first stanza has twenty-
eight lines, and the second has sixteen. As the speaker recalls the march on
Washington, in which more than 250,000 people demonstrated for civil rights,
she attributes to Martin Luther King, Jr., the leader of the movement, the
same rhetorical art she now remembers him by. The analogue is Isaiah: "The
grass withereth, the flower fadeth: but the word of our God shall stand for
ever" (40:8). Two brothers, according to the fable, led the Israelites out of
Egypt.[9] Sentences of varied length complement the juxtaposition of cadences
which rise and fall. The narrator names neither King as "Moses" nor King's

youthful follower as "Aaron," yet she clarifies a richness of oration and implies the heroic spirit. King, before his death, said that he had been to the mountain top, and that he had seen the Promised Land. But the speaker literarily retraces the paradigm of the life; she distills the love of the listeners who saw him and were inspired: "There they stand . . . / The old man with a dream he has lived to see come true."

Although the first eleven lines of the poem are descriptive, the twelfth combines chronicle and prefiguration. The speaker projects the social present into the mythical past. Her words come from a civil rights song, "We Woke Up One Morning With Our Minds Set On Freedom." The social activist wants the immediate and complete liberation which the rhetorician (speaker and writer) translates into literary symbol: "We woke up one morning in Egypt / And the river ran red with blood . . . / And the houses of death were afraid."

She remembers, too, the story of Jacob, who returns home with his two wives, Leah and Rachel (Genesis 30:25–43). Laban, the father-in-law, gave him speckled cattle, but now the narrator understands that Jacob's "*house* (Africa-America) has grown into a nation / The slaves break forth from bondage" (emphasis mine). In Old Testament fashion, she cautions against fatigue in the pursuit of liberty. Through heightened style, she becomes a prophet whose medium is eternal language. She has mastered alliteration, assonance, and resonance.

> Write this word upon your hearts
> And mark this message on the doors of your houses
> See that you do not forget
> How this day the Lord has set our faces toward freedom
> Teach these words to your children
> And see that they do not forget them.

Walker's poetry alludes subtly to King but refers to Malcolm X directly. The verse dedicated to Malcolm portrays him as Christ. Nearly a Petrarchan sonnet, the poem is not written in the five-foot line, but has several lines of four or six feet. Neither of the last two lengths usually characterizes the form, and even a concession of off-rhyme does not make a Petrarchan scheme unfold. The comments sound repetitious because they are. As with the earlier sonnet "Childhood," "Malcolm" appears at first to deserve oblivion because here, too, Walker fails to condense and control metrics. Still, the quiet appeal is clear. The Christ story compels rereading, and one finds it a meaningful experience. When Malcolm is associated with a dying swan in the octave, the narrator alludes to the Ovidian legend of the beautiful bird which sings just before death.[10] Malcolm takes on Christ's stigmata: "Our blood and water pour from your flowing wounds."

Vivid and noble portraits of crucifixion, another type of martyrdom, give even more vitality to "For Andy Goodman, Michael Schwerner, and James Chaney" (hereafter "For Andy"), a poem about three civil rights workers murdered in Mississippi on June 21, 1964. The elegy complements seasonal and diurnal cycle through the reaffirmation of human growth and spiritual redemption. Despite the questionable value of martyrdom, sunrise balances sunset, and beautiful leaves partly compensate for human mutilation. In dramatic reversal, Walker's narrator uses the literary technique which distinguishes *Lycidas, Adonais*, and *When Lilacs Last in the Dooryard Bloom'd*.

The flower and the paradigmatic bird (lark, robin, mourning bird, bird of sorrow, bird of death) restore both an epic and elegaic mood. The reader half-hears the echo of the goddess Venus who mourns for Adonis; *mourning* and *morning*, excellent puns, signify the cycle and paradox of life.[11] The short rhythm, two feet, and the longer rhythm, three or four, provide the solemn folksiness of a very loose ballad or free verse. With interior rhyme, the musical balance communicates quiet pathos: "They have killed these three / They have killed them for me." The gentle suggestion of the trinity, the tragic flight of the bird, and the slow but cyclical turning from spring to spring intensify the narrator's sadness and grief.

Just as "For Andy" shows Walker's grace of style, the title poem of *Prophets* illustrates that the Bible prefigures the eloquence. As with the earlier poem "Delta," "Prophets" resists paraphrase because it abstractly portrays Black American history. The poem has three parts. The first shows that the Word which came to the biblical prophets endures, and the next presents the actual appearance of the ancient vision to new believers. In the third part, the reader moves to a final understanding about tragic death. While the poet marks the recurrence of sacred light, fire, gentleness, and artistic speech, she contrasts White and Black, dark and light, age and youth, life and death. Some allusions to Ezekiel and Amos now fuse with others from Ecclesiastes and Isaiah. Amos tells of a prophet-priest of sixth century B.C., a watchman over the Israelites during the exile in Babylon, by the river of Cheber (Ezek. 1:15–20). As a herdsman from the southern village of Tekoa, Judah, he went to Bethel in Samaria to preach a religion of social justice and righteousness. He attacked economic exploitation and privilege and criticized the priests who stressed ritual above justice. Because Amos is Walker's personal symbol of Martin Luther King, Jr., she provides more background about him than about others. The reader knows his name, character, and homeland.

But Walker socially and historically reinvigorates the scriptures. She is no eighteenth-century Jupiter Hammon who rewrites the Bible without any infusion of personal suffering. She feels strongly and personally that the demonstrators in the sixties antitypify the Scriptures: "So today in the pulpits and the jails, / A fearless shepherd speaks at last / To his suffering weary sheep." She implies perseverance even in the face of death, and her speaker blends the images of the New Testament with those from *Beowulf*. Her lines depict the beast:

> His mark is on the land
> His horns and his hands and his lips are gory
>   with our blood
> He is death and destruction and Trouble

> And he walks in our houses at noonday
> And devours our defenders at midnight.

The literary word images fear and sacrifice more than immediate redemption. What shadows the fate of the good? The beast

> has crushed them with a stone.
> He drinks our tears for water
> And he drinks our blood for wine;
> He eats our flesh like a ravenous lion
> And he drives us out of the city
> To be stabbed on a lonely hill.

The same scene relives the crucifixion.

Walker draws heavily upon the Bible for typological unity. Of the twenty-two poems in *Prophets*, seven of the last nine have biblical names for titles, including "Jeremiah," "Isaiah," "Amos-1963," "Amos (Postscript, 1968)," "Joel," "Hosea," and "Micah." A similar problem besets all, although to a different extent. The aesthetic response relies on historical sense more than on dramatized language, and passing time will weaken the emotional hold. In "Jeremiah," the narrator is conscious of both the fallen world and the apocalyptic one. She suggests Benjamin Mays, who has been a preacher and educator in Atlanta for over fifty years. Seeking to lift the "curse" from the land, Mays wants to redeem the corrupted city. The mythical denotation of the place—"Atalanta"—inspires the cultural imagination. Once a girl by that name lost a race to Hippomenes, her suitor, because she digressed from her course to pursue golden apples.[12] Yet Walker's poem does more than oppose Mays to urban materialism. Through his articulation (the spoken word), he signifies the artist and the writer. The narrator who recounts the tale is an artist, too, since Walker's speakers and heroes mirror each other. Although Jeremiah appears as a contemporary man, he exists in a half-way house between legend and reality. Despite limitations, the final six lines of the verse combine myth and anaphora, where the speaker compares the imaginative and historical worlds more closely than elsewhere. Once destroyed by fire, Atlanta suggests Babylon, capital first of Babylonia and then of Chaldea on the Euphrates River. As the scene of the biblical Exile, the city represents grandeur and wickedness. The book of Psalms portrays the despair of the Israelites who sat down and wept when they remembered Zion. With an undertone of an old folk ballad, Walker builds a literary vision. While anaphora strengthens solemnity, the voice subsumes both narrator and prophet:

> My God we are still here. We are still down here Lord,
> Working for a kingdom of Thy Love,
> We weep for this city and for this land
> We weep for Judah and beloved Jerusalem
> O Georgia! "Where shall you stand in the Judgment?"

Through the fire, the mark, and the word, "Isaiah" clarifies the typology which leads from "Lincoln Monument," midway through the volume, to "Elegy" at the end. Jeremiah expresses himself in the public forum as well as on television. He resembles Adam Clayton Powell, Jr., a major Civil Rights activist in Harlem during the depression. Powell persuaded many Harlem businesses, including Harlem Hospital, to hire Blacks. As Chairman of the Coordinating Committee on Employment, he led a demonstration which forced the World's Fair to adopt a similar policy in 1939. He desegregated many Congressional facilities, Washington restaurants, and theatres. He proposed first the withholding of federal funds from projects which showed racial discrimination; he introduced the first legislation to desegregate the armed forces; he established the right of Black journalists to sit in the press galleries of the United States House of Representatives and in the Senate. As Chairman of the House Committee on Education and Labor in 1960, he supported forty-eight pieces of legislation on social welfare and later earned a letter of gratitude from President Johnson.

In 1967, however, Powell's House colleagues raised charges of corruption and financial mismanagement against him. In January he was stripped of his chairmanship and barred from the House, pending an investigation. On March 1, 1967 Powell was denied a seat in the House by a vote of 307 to 116, despite the committee's recommendation that he only be censured, fined, and placed at the bottom of the seniority list. On April 11 a special election was held to fill Powell's seat. Powell, who was not campaigning and was on the island of Bimini and who could not even come to New York City because of a court judgment against him in a defamation case, received 74% of the Harlem vote cast.[13]

Even more clearly, the "Amos" poems reconfirm Walker's greater metaphor for Martin Luther King, Jr. The first of these two verses, twenty lines in length, portrays Amos as a contemporary shepherd who preaches in the depths of Alabama and elsewhere: "standing in the Shadow of our God / Tending his flocks over the hills of Albany / And the seething streets of Selma and of bitter Birmingham." As with the first "Amos" poem, the second "Amos (Postscript, 1968)" is written in free verse. With only ten lines, however, the latter is shorter. King, the prophet of justice, appears through the fluidity and the wholesomeness of the "O" sound: "From Montgomery to Memphis he marches / He stands on the threshold of tomorrow / He breaks the bars of iron and they remove the signs / He opens the gates of our prisons."

Many of the short poems that follow lack the high quality found in some of Walker's other typological lyrics. "Joel" uses the standard free verse, but the historical allusion is obscure. "Hosea" suffers from the same problem. The Bible presents the figure as having an unfaithful wife, but Walker's poem presents a Hosea who, marked for death, writes love letters to the world. Is the man Eldridge Cleaver? The letters and the theme of redemption clearly suggest him, but one can never be sure. The legend could better suit the man.

The last poem in *Prophets* appropriately benefits from some of Walker's favorite books such as Ecclesiastes, Isaiah, and St. John. "Elegy," a verse in two parts, honors the memory of Manford Kuhn, professor and friend. Summer and sunshine give way to winter snow and "frothy wood," since the green harvest must pass. But art forms ironically preserve themselves through fire, and engraving comes from corrosion. Eternity paradoxically depends upon decay. The first section concerns the cycle of nature which continually turns; the second, an elaborate conceit, depicts people as ephemeral artists. Reminiscent of Virgil's *Aeneid*, Shelley's "The Witch of Atlas," and Danner's short lyric, "The Slave and the Iron Lace," Walker's second section begins:

> Within our house of flesh we weave a web of time
> Both warp and woof within the shuttle's clutch
> In leisure and in haste no less a tapestry
> Rich pattern of our lives.
> The gold and scarlet intertwine
> Upon our frame of dust an intricate design. . . .

Here are her ablest statement and restatement of the iamb. The "I" sound supports assonance and rhyme, even though the poem is basically free. At first the idea of human transitoriness reinforces *Ecclesiastes* which powerfully presents the theme. In a second look, however, one traces the thought to Isaiah (40:7): "The grass withereth, the flower fadeth: because the spirit of the Lord bloweth upon it. . . ." But the speaker knows the ensuing verse equally well: "The grass withereth, the flower fadeth: but the *word* [emphasis mine] of our God shall stand for ever" (40:8). Poetry, an inspired creation in words, is divine as well. To the extent that Kuhn showed Christ-like love and instruction for his students, his spirit transcends mortality. For any who demonstrate similar qualities is the vision any less true and universal? To Nicodemus, the Pharisee whom Jesus told to be reborn (John 3:8), the final allusion belongs.

> We live again
> In children's faces, and the sturdy vine
> Of daily influences: the prime
> Of teacher, neighbor, student, and friend
> All merging on the elusive wind. (33–37)

Patient nobility becomes the poet who has recreated Martin Luther King, Jr., as Amos. She has kept the neatly turned phrase of Countee Cullen but replaced Tantalus and Sisyphus with Black students and sit-ins. For her literary fathers, she reaches back to the nineteenth-century prophets Blake, Byron, Shelley, and Tennyson. Her debt extends no less to Walt Whitman and to Langston Hughes, for her predecessor is any poet who foresees a new paradise and who portrays the coming. As with Hughes, Walker is a romantic. But Hughes had either to subordinate his perspective to history or to ignore history almost completely and to speak less about events than about personal and racial symbols. Walker, on the contrary, equally combines events and legends but reaffirms the faith of the spirituals. Although her plots sometimes concern murder, her narrators reveal an image of racial freedom and human peace. The best of her imagined South prefigures the future.

NOTES

1. See Paula Giddings, "Some Themes in the Poetry of Margaret Walker," *Black World* (December 1971), pp. 20–34. Although it fails to emphasize the importance of literary form, the essay gives a general impression of historical background and literary tradition.
2. See Margaret Walker and Nikki Giovanni, *A Poetic Equation: Conversations* (Washington, D.C.: Howard Univ. Press, 1974), p. 56. Through logic Walker has the better of the friendly argument.
3. Charles H. Rowell, "Poetry, History, and Humanism" (Interview), *Black World*, 25 (December 1975), 4–17.
4. Poems mentioned, other than those by Walker, are available in Dudley Randall, *The Black Poets* (New York: Bantam, 1971).
5. See Joseph Greenborg, *Language Typology* (The Hague: Mouton, 1974); Paul J. Korshin, "The Development of Abstracted Typology in England, 1650–1820," in *Literary Uses of Typology*, ed. Earl Miner (Princeton: Princeton Univ. Press, 1977); Mason I. Lawrance, "Introduction," *The Figures or Types of the Old Testament* (New York: Johnson, 1969); Roland Bartel, "The Bible in Negro Spirituals," in *Figures* (see above); Sacvan Bercovitch, "Typology in Early American Literature" in *Typology and American Literature* (Amherst: Univ. of Massachusetts Press, 1972); Emory Elliott, "From Father to Son," in *Literary Uses* (see above); Theodore Ziokowski, "Some Features of Religious Figuralism in Twentieth Century Literature," in *Literary Uses* (see above).
6. Primary texts used are Margaret Walker, *For My People* (New Haven: Yale Univ. Press, 1942) and *Prophets for a New Day* (Detroit: Broadside, 1970).
7. See Stephen Henderson, *Understanding the New Black Poetry* (New York: William Morrow, 1973), pp. 62–66.
8. Reviewers disagree about the form which Walker most ably succeeds in. See Elizabeth Drew, *Atlantic*, 170 (December 1942), 10; Arna Bontemps, *Christian Science Monitor* (November 14, 1942), p. 10; *New Republic* (November 23, 1942), p. 690; Louis Untermeyer, *Yale Review* (Winter 1943), p. 370. All discuss *For My People*. Drew praises the experimentation in rhythmical language. Bontemps says that the ballads and sonnets show a folk understanding, but comments less about their literary success. The reviewer in *New Republic*, on the contrary, finds the sonnets to be weak, but the ballads to be strong. Untermeyer praises Walker's success in winning the prize in the Yale series (a first for a Black), but discovers flaws both in the sonnets and ballads.
9. See Exodus, 4:14–17; 7:8–12; 32; 1–6; Numbers, 17:1–11; 20:12–29.
10. Ovid, *Metamorphoses* (Baltimore: Penguin Books, 1961), p. 322.
11. Ovid, p. 244.
12. Ovid, pp. 240–44. See the brilliant analysis in W.E.B. DuBois, *The Souls of Black Folk* (New York: New American Library, 1969), pp. 117–20.
13. Peter M. Bergman and Mort N. Bergman, *The Chronological History of the Negro in America* (New York: New American Library, 1969), pp. 354–55.